Genpei

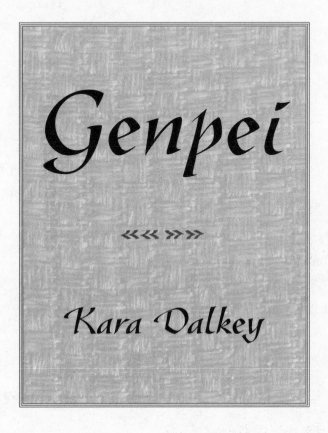

Genpei

Kara Dalkey

A Tom Doherty Associates Book

New York

This is a work of fiction. All the characters and events portrayed in this novel are either fictitious or are used fictitiously.

GENPEI

This book is printed on acid-free paper.

A Tor Book
Published by Tom Doherty Associates, LLC
175 Fifth Avenue
New York, NY 10010

www.tor.com

Tor® is a registered trademark of Tom Doherty Associates, LLC.

Library of Congress Cataloging-in-Publication Data
Dalkey, Kara.
    Genpei / Kara Dalkey—1st ed.
        p.   cm.
    "A Tom Doherty Associates book."
    ISBN 0–312–89071–0 (acid-free paper)
1. Japan—History—Genpei Wars, 1180–1185—Fiction.   I. Title.

    PS3554.A433 G4 2000
    813'.54—dc21   00-042585

Design by Jane Adele Regina

Map by Mark Stein Studios

Family tree art by Tim Hall

First Edition: January 2001

Printed in the United States of America

0 9 8 7 6 5 4 3 2 1

*For Lisa Anne
For the friendship and the music*

Japan
in the time of
the Genpei Wars

Oki

Tango

Izumo Hōki Inaba Tajima

Minasaka

Iwami Bingo Bitchu Bizen Harima

Tsushima Nagato Suo Aki Yashima

Iki Dan-No-Ura Sanuki

Chikuzen Buzen Awa

Hizen Chikugo Iyo Tosa

Higo Bungo Shikoku

Satsuma Hyūga Kyūshū

Ōsumi

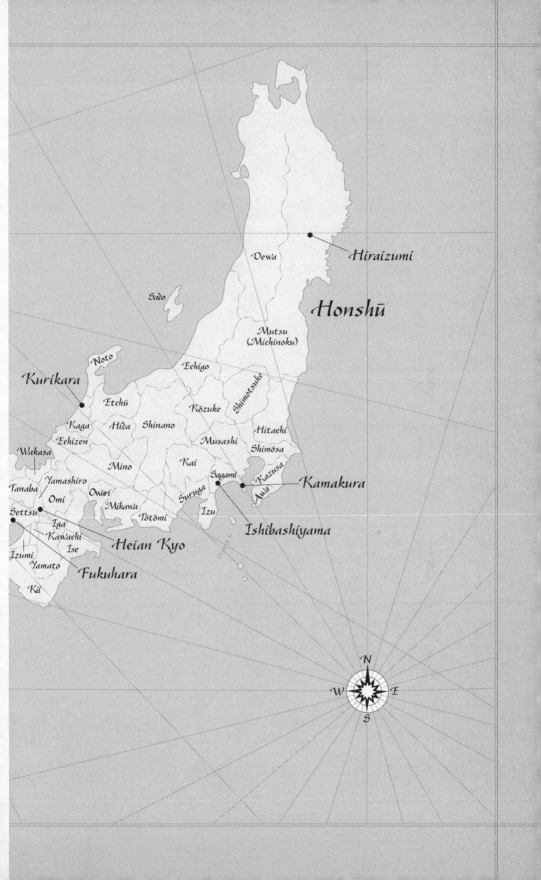

Author's Note

Genpei is a fantasy treatment of the great war, or series of wars, really, that ended the Heian period in Japanese history. The events referred to in the story took place roughly between 1153 and 1185 C.E. However, *Genpei* should in no way be taken as an accurate depiction of these events, not merely because of the fantasy elements. Although I tried to tie the narrative as closely to the incidents surrounding the fall of Heian Kyō as I could, I found this to be an impossible task. Many of the historical sources I drew from were written years, even centuries, after the events took place and they all contradicted each other as to what happened when, and who was present where. I've tried to make as coherent a narrative as I could, given the sources.

This book is written somewhat in the style of the war tales of the Heian and Kamakura periods, though I have made many stylistic concessions and simplifications for the sake of the Western reader. For example, there are far fewer characters than appear in the traditional war tale, far fewer allusions to famous ancient poems and heroes, and I spend far less time lovingly describing every bit of armor, weaponry, and clothing that each of the warriors wear. I hope the reader will see fit to forgive me for these omissions.

Nonetheless, there are some matters concerning Heian culture that the reader might wish to be aware of in order to forestall confusion. First and foremost, the Heian calendar was not in accord with the European calendar (which the Japanese would not even become aware of for another four hundred years after the events in the book). The beginning of their "First Month" corresponds roughly to somewhere in the first two weeks of February in our calendar, and their New Year was considered to be the first day of spring. Their hours of the day are the equivalent of two of our hours, and they did not measure days into anything like our weeks.

Heian people did not retain the same name throughout their lives—infants were given a child's name to be changed at the capping or trouser ceremony when a boy reached about seven or so. Noblemen were often referred to by their current government position, warriors often included their home province as part of their appellation, and if a man became a monk he took on another name as well. Noblewomen were often named for the residence they lived in, or their father's rank and position. And ladies of the highest noble families, who served or reigned in the palace, took the name of a gateway in the Imperial Compound. For the sake of the Western fantasy reader, I have greatly simplified this in *Genpei* so that names are more consistent for each character through the narrative.

Heian people were given responsibilities at a far younger age. Boys could become warriors as early as twelve years old. Boys and girls both might marry between the ages of thirteen and sixteen. And Emperors could rise to the throne as toddlers of three or four.

Regarding the structure of noble Heian families, a man of high rank was expected to have concubines in addition to a principal wife. The children of a noble household might be sent to be raised by another family, either to receive particular training in either martial or courtly arts, or for political reasons. In some houses, siblings rarely saw one another until they were adults.

Government during the Heian period was rigid in terms of protocol, but fluid in terms of who might hold actual power. The ruling Emperor did not always have complete command of the government—more often than not, in fact, he was merely a ceremonial figurehead. Power often shifted between the most noble families (the Fujiwara, for example), or other members of the imperial family. At times, a ruling emperor might abdicate the throne, leaving the onerous ceremonial duties to one of his offspring, and control the government from the sidelines as a highly respected Retired Emperor. And, of course, the capital could be controlled by those who had the greatest number of fighters at their ready command—an important factor as the warrior clans of the Minomoto and the Taira gained greater status at the end of the Heian period.

Genpei is heavily influenced by *The Tale of the Heike*, sometimes called the Japanese *Iliad*, as well as the *Hōgen Monogatari* and *Heiji Monogatari*. Further influences were *The Chronicles of Yoshitsune*, written three hundred years after the Genpei War; the *Hojoki*, a collection of diary poems written a few decades after the events; and the *Azuma Kagami*, a compilation of diary notations from the period assembled some one hundred years later.

Readers who wish to learn more about the unique and fascinating Heian culture might wish to look at *The World of the Shining Prince* by Ivan Morris, as well as literary works of the period such as *The Tale of Genji* by Murasaki Shikibu, *The Pillow Book of Sei Shōnagon*, *A Tale of Flowering Fortunes*, and, of course, the grand *Tale of the Heike* itself.

—Kara Dalkey

Imperial Family   Minomoto Clan Members   Taira Clan Members

Imperial Family

REIGNING EMPERORS
1107–1198

TOBA
(74th Emperor)
lived 1103–1156
reigned 1107–1123

Sutoku (Shin-In)
(75th Emp.)
lived 1119–1164
reigned 1123–1141

Konoe
(76th Emp.)
lived 1139–1155
reigned 1141–1155

Go-Shirakawa
(77th Emp.)
lived 1127–1192
reigned 1155–1158

Nijo
(78th Emp.)
lived 1143–1165
reigned 1158–1165

Rokujō
(79th Emp.)
lived 1164–1176
reigned 1165–1168

Mochihito
(attempts
rebellion
1180)

Takakura
(80th Emp.)
lived 1161–1181
reigned 1168–1180

Antoku
(81st Emp.)
lived 1178–1185
reigned 1180–1183

Go-Toba
(82nd Emp.)
lived 1180–1239
reigned 1184–1198

Minomoto Clan Members

Tameyoshi

Yoshitomo ═
- Yoshihira
- Yoritomo
- Noriyori
- Yoshitsune
- Gien

Yoshikata ═ Yoshinaka
Yoshinori
Tamenari
Tametomo
Yoshimori (later Yukiie)
Tameie

Taira Clan Members

Tadamori

Kiyomori ═
- Shigemori ═
  - Koremori
  - Sukemori
  - Kiyotsune
  - Arimori
  - Tadafusa
  - Munezane
- Motomori
- Munemori
- Tomomori
- Shigehira
- Tomonori
- Kiyofusa
- Kiyosada
- Kiyokuni
- Tokushi ═ Antoku
  (later Kenreimon)
- Six other daughters

Tsunemori ═
- Tsunemasa
- Tsunetoshi
- Atsumori

Norimori ═
- Michimori
- Noritsune
- Narimori
- Chukai
- Daughter

Yorimori
Tadanori

Prologue

THE BELL OF GION TEMPLE SINGS
ALL THINGS MUST FADE
AS SURELY AS THE BLOSSOMS OF THE SALA TREE.
THE PROUD LAST NO LONGER THAN A SPRING NIGHT'S DREAM,
THE MIGHTY VANISH, DUST UPON THE WIND.

So begins the great story of The Heike, beloved of the blind tale-singers who chant the tale as they strum upon their *biwa*. So sang the blind monk Hoichi, unknowing, to the ghosts of the Ise Taira, thereby losing his ears.

Great was the rising fortune of the Taira clan and great was its fall, like the tumbling of a boulder down a cliff face into the sea. And with the Taira fell the dream of the Heian Kingdom, the heavenly world of Those Who Live Above The Clouds, whose lives were filled with music and poetry, dancing and finely perfumed clothes, all elegantly suited to the seasons. This world of peace and beauty was overturned by rough men of war, whose arts were of the sword and bow, not brush and ink.

Much of the truth of the Genpei War has been lost with the passage of time. But the legends remain. What if the legends were all true? Who knows. Perhaps, somewhere, the Buddha created such a world where what follows was, indeed, how it happened. . . .

Scroll 1

≪≪ ≫≫

Beginnings

The White Fish

Who can say when the seeds of a war are sown? Sometimes the roots of conflict grow for generations before the clash of steel upon steel is heard. Sometimes a war may be only a continuation of past battles, as one prayer bead follows another on a silken string. Sometimes conflict becomes as inevitable as rain in autumn. Sometimes a change in circumstances will bring about conflict where none might have been thought possible before. The Genpei War may be said to have been all of these.

Let us begin, then, on a chill spring morning, in the fourteenth year of the reign of Emperor Sutoku, in the second year of the era called Hōen. Taira no Kiyomori, stocky and strong at nineteen years of age, stood at the prow of his boat, sailing the waters of the Seto Inland Sea. Some legends say that on this day he was on a pilgrimage to the shrines on the sacred island called Miyajima. Some say he and his men were patrolling the waters of Aki Province searching for pirates. Perhaps he was doing both.

For as long as could be remembered, the Taira had been remarkable sailors and warriors of the coastal waters. Under the leadership of Tadamori, Kiyomori's father, the Taira achieved more glory by doing battle with the pirates who had been harassing the merchants and fishermen along the coast of the Inland Sea. So successful were the Taira in this endeavor that rewards were showered upon them by Shirakawa and the Emperors that followed, Horikawa, Toba, and Sutoku. By the time Kiyomori was twelve, he held the post of Assistant Commander for the Military Guards. By the time he was eighteen, Kiyomori was elevated to Fourth Rank, and thereby officially made a nobleman of the realm.

On this spring morning, as Kiyomori and his men neared Miyajima, the air was still, and no wind stirred the boat's sails. His men had to row the becalmed craft across the smooth waters. There were no other boats to be seen, not even those of fishermen, who normally would be numerous. Kiyomori felt some concern and wondered if rumors of new pirates in the area had kept the fishermen away.

"What do you make of this?" Kiyomori asked one of his men, who wore the shaved head and plain robe of a Buddhist monk.

"My lord, I am as baffled as you," said the monk. "I cannot think of any sign in the Heavens or significance in the calendar that would be keeping the fishermen home."

As he gazed toward the horizon, Kiyomori saw something else that brought him unease. At first he thought it only a trick of his eyes—but a thick fog was rising from the waters, like steam from a hot bath on a winter's day. Denser and denser the fog became, swiftly obscuring their view, until Kiyomori and his men could scarcely see beyond the blades of their oars. Their ship seemed an island itself adrift in a world of gray.

"This becomes stranger every moment, neh?" Kiyomori commented to one of his men. "Normally a morning fog is melted away by the westering sun, not summoned by it." He sniffed the air, but there was no taint of ashes, so this was no smoke from a fire. The mist was rich with the brine scent of the sea.

"My lord, perhaps we should wait a while," suggested one of the rowers. "We cannot find our way in this fog, and we have no wish to run your boat aground. If this is any natural mist, it will lift in time, and we can proceed safely."

"If this is any natural mist," repeated Kiyomori, with a feeling in his bones that it was not. The Inland Sea was the realm of many mysterious things, including, it was said, the undersea palace of the Dragon King Ryujin. Kiyomori could not help but wonder if he or his family had done something to offend the *kami* of the sea. Or perhaps this fog was a whim of the gods he had merely blundered into, through no fault of his or his clan.

Kiyomori took up a handful of the rice cakes they carried for provender. He broke them apart and scattered the pieces onto the metal-gray waters, murmuring to the *kami* who reside there, "If I, or my own, have offended, forgive us. If not, and if this mysterious weather is the work of gods or demons who are bent on mischief, please aid us."

Huge fishes rose from the depths to suck the rice into their enormous gaping mouths, but Kiyomori could not tell what manner of fish they were. The boat rocked in the gentle swells of the sea, and the only sound was the lapping of the water at its flanks.

Suddenly, a great white bass leapt out of the water and landed on the deck of the boat. The big fish flopped about madly, and one of the rowers had to strike it on the head with an oar to subdue it. As the white bass lay still, gasping its last breaths, Kiyomori and the monk approached it.

"This is most remarkable," said Kiyomori.

"Surely it is a sign of the *kami's* favor," said the monk. "Though it violates the Ten Prohibitions, I believe we should eat this fish as soon as possible, and partake of the good fortune it will provide us."

"Yes," said Kiyomori, "I have heard of such events as this. Is it not said that, long ago, a white fish leapt into the boat of King Wu of Zhou?"

"My lord," said one of the rowers, "a sail."

Kiyomori peered through the mist. He saw what seemed to be a red sail, not too far away.

"Know you any fishermen in this region," Kiyomori asked, "who has such a sail on his boat?"

"No, my lord," said the rower. "And no merchant ship would be so foolish as to announce his presence so when there are pirates about."

"And might a pirate have such a sail?" Kiyomori asked.

"It would be a bold or mad pirate indeed, my lord, to have such an attention-catching sail when it is known the mighty Taira patrol these waters."

Kiyomori smiled. "Then let us row toward that sail," he told his men, "and see who this bold or foolish personage might be."

"My lord," cautioned one of the rowers, "there is danger that we might collide with the other boat, for we cannot see its speed or location clearly."

"Then you must row very carefully, neh? Begin. I will watch the sail and guide you."

So the rowers took up their oars once more and began to pull against the gray waters of the Inland Sea. Kiyomori told them when to steer to the right or left and when to feather their oars and drift. Closer and closer they came to the red sail. Then suddenly the mist between the two boats parted, as if blown aside by a *kami*'s breath.

What Kiyomori saw nearly took his own breath away. The red sail belonged to a little boat in the shape of a dragon whose scales were made of pearly iridescent shell. The silken sail was adorned with the crest of a coiled white serpent. Sitting in the boat were three beautiful ladies, dressed in the many-layered kimonos of the nobility of Heian Kyō, whose colors reflected the blues, greens, and grays of the sea. Kiyomori wondered how such ladies might have come to be here so far from land, although he was old enough to know that women often had fancies unfathomable to men. "Good morning, most noble ladies," he said, bowing to them.

"Hail, Assistant Commander Taira no Kiyomori," said one.

"Hail, Lord Governor to come," said another.

"Hail, Chancellor yet to be," said the third.

Kiyomori stepped back in astonishment, rocking his ship. "Surely you ladies are joking at my expense. Governor of a province someday, perhaps, should I prove myself worthy of it to the court. But Chancellor? Only those of the great Fujiwara clan, or of Imperial blood, ever rise so high. I am but of the lowly Taira. We are warriors, not governmental officials. Why do you mock me thus?"

The loveliest of the ladies smiled at him. "We do not mock you, Lord Kiyomori."

"Perhaps he truly does not know," whispered one of the other ladies.

"Does not know what?" demanded Kiyomori. "What do I not know?"

"That you are of Imperial blood," said the loveliest lady.

Kiyomori scowled. "You are repeating treasonous gossip. My father is Tadamori, Chief of the Taira clan. He is the only father I have known."

"Truly, it was he who raised you. But your mother—"

"Yes, she had been an Emperor's consort. She never let my father forget that."

"And she was with child when she was given to your father for services he had rendered to Emperor Shirakawa. That child was you."

"And it was that Emperor," said the lady to her left, "who gave you your name, in hopes that it would bring to you the *limitless prosperity* that your name implies."

Kiyomori felt a shiver run down his spine. Of course he had heard the whispered gossip. Naturally, as a boy, he had wanted to believe he was a secret prince of the Imperial line. But when he had traveled to Heian Kyō with his father and seen how the nobles sneered at him and Tadamori, claiming such provincial warriors were no better than servants, he realized the gossip was only meant to slander his father. "How can I possibly believe you?"

The beautiful woman blinked. "What may I do to make you believe?" She stroked the water with her hand and tiny winged women in pale gauze kimonos, their lower halves tucked into snail shells, rose fluttering into the air. They sang with sweet, piping voices for a moment, then plopped back beneath the surface.

Kiyomori gasped. "You, then . . . can it be that you are . . . Benzaiten, mistress of art and music and daughter of the Dragon King?"

Her smile grew wider. "At last you recognize me. I am pleased."

He bowed again, much lower this time. "How can I not know you, to whom my family prays so often for good fortune upon the sea? The white fish, then, came from you?"

"It is a gift to you from my father, Ryujin. Eat of it and good fortune shall be yours. So you understand, if we say you may one day become Chancellor, then it may indeed be so?"

"Of . . . of course, Great Lady." Kiyomori's mind reeled, trying to accept this new view of things. A vision of who he was, and what his future might be. "But why do you so favor me by telling me of my destiny? Why here and now?"

Benzaiten flirtatiously stroked the surface of the sea with her fingertips, letting her long sleeves float upon the water like seaweed. "Your prowess upon the sea is well-known, Lord Kiyomori, even to those in the court of the Dragon King. We have watched you from below, and we are impressed."

Kiyomori inclined his head to her. "I am pleased to have been noticed by one so illustrious as your father."

"And we have noted that your clan has . . . ambition."

"Naturally, as has every clan in the Empire, Great Lady. We all strive to climb as high as we can. That is the way of things. But the power of the Fujiwara clan is like a great wall against which other men only bloody themselves in striving for rank and position."

"Even such a wall as theirs may have cracks, Lord Kiyomori. The Fujiwara are like a wall of old stone, too long set in place without repair. They are masters of form and manners, but have forgotten the meaning of it. They sit in their precious capital and think it is the whole world, forgetting the countryside that surrounds them. And we fear they are forgetting the honor due to *us* as they chant sutras to their beloved *bosatsu* and Buddhas."

Benzaiten stirred the water more forcefully with her fingers. "My father has forseen dark days ahead. But he has grown fond of mortal humanity and wishes to ease its passage through the turbulent times to come. My father seeks the right man to captain the Empire, to steer it safely past the maelstroms of fate that await it. He believes you may well be that man, Lord Kiyomori."

Realizing that he was being offered a chance rarely given, and that his newfound heritage proved him worthy, Kiyomori felt a great pride and ambition fill him. "Then your father has chosen wisely, great Benzaiten. Tell me what I must do, how might I find this crack and achieve the fate you see for me."

"We will give you our aid, if you will promise, once power is yours, to build for me on the sacred island of Miyajima the greatest shrine the Empire has yet seen. Then you shall have my favor, and that of my father, the Dragon King. Do this, become our champion, and with your skill, courage, and wisdom we will see that your clan achieves great glory and that your name is remembered throughout the ages to come."

"Glory," Kiyomori whispered, as though speaking to a lover. "You will have your shrine on Miyajima, Great Lady. The grandest the Empire has ever seen. I swear this to you."

"Very good. And you shall take this color"—she gestured toward the red sail—"as the color of your clan's standard in battle, for battles there will be, Lord Kiyomori, great and terrible ones. But you will prevail, if you will but follow our advice."

Kiyomori gripped the railing of the boat so hard that it nearly splintered in his hands. "I will do as you ask, Great Lady. Everything."

"Your fervor impresses me, Kiyomori-san. You will receive more messages from us soon. I eagerly await the day I will see my shrine. Until that happy time, farewell." The red sail suddenly billowed with an unseen wind. The dragon boat with its three lady passengers sailed away into the mist and vanished.

Kiyomori turned to his men. "Have I just seen what I have seen and heard what I have heard?"

The men turned to him, wide-eyed. One of them said, "Indeed, my lord, that could only have been the *kami* Benzaiten herself! She is even lovelier than all the paintings I have ever seen of her. Our clan is truly fortunate, my lord, to receive her favor, as well as that of the great Dragon King."

The fog that was all around them melted away faster than the last snowfall of spring, revealing the wide-open sea once more. The sacred island of Miyajima could be seen on the southeastern horizon. A gentle breeze arose and billowed the sails of the ship. "Let us eat this gift, the white fish," said Kiyomori. "And dream on the great things to come. And then let us sail on to the shrines of Miyajima to honor the *kami* who have blessed us with this vision."

A Path of Dragon Lights

It was late afternoon when Kiyomori's boat at last came alongside the tiny dock at the sacred island of Miyajima. They had found no pirates that day. Perhaps it was just as well, for Kiyomori had been distracted by the prophecies of Benzaiten and the glory they promised, so much so that he could hardly think clearly.

Three Shintō priests in black caps and white robes were coming down the steep mountain path to the shore. They looked up in astonishment and concern when they saw a boat full of armored warriors tying up at their dock.

"Do not fear, Holy Ones!" shouted Kiyomori as he jumped into the shallow water and strode up the rocky shore. "I am Taira no Kiyomori, Assistant Commander of the Military Guards. I have this day received a vision of the *kami* Benzaiten, and I come to this, her sacred island, for offering and contemplation. She has directed me to one day build a great shrine for her here, and I wish to study the site on which I will build."

The priests' eyes opened wide, and they bowed low to him. "Then you are most welcome to Miyajima and our shrines, Kiyomori-san. Your fame is well-known even on these humble shores. We ask only that you disturb no rock nor living creature while you are here, and that you do not spend the night, for even we do not stay upon the island, but have our homes elsewhere. For by night, the island belongs to the *kami*, and no mortal may disturb it."

"It shall be so," said Kiyomori, inclining his head to them. "Wait here, on the boat, for me," he directed his men. "I must walk and think a while."

He saw the warriors mutter concerned words among themselves. It was getting late, and no sailor liked to navigate the Inland Sea by night, for the myriad tiny islands and rocks made the sailing treacherous. But Kiyomori knew his men well—their skill on the sea was matchless, and they would obey him bravely.

The three priests got into their little rowboat and rowed away with cries of farewell. Kiyomori first walked up the steep hill path to the shrines of the daughters of the Dragon King. His family had come to visit these shrines before, and he remembered being there as a child once. But the memory was faint, and now he saw the shrines with wiser eyes.

The thatch-and-stick structures blended so well with the bushes and trees surrounding them that Kiyomori at first overlooked them. The shrines were clearly well cared for, the dirt paths were swept and the thatch in good repair, but the structures were also clearly very old and primitive. Kiyomori did not perform the ritual washing of hands and mouth, or enter the shrines themselves. "No wonder Benzaiten has asked for a new shrine," he murmured to himself. "Surely she deserves finer than these."

Kiyomori descended the path again to the rocky shore and walked by the strand. Tame deer who nibbled grasses nearby bowed their heads to him as he passed. He walked for a long time, wondering what sort of shrine to build, which inlet or rocky outcropping might be pleasing to incorporate into the holy grounds, for the setting of a proper shrine should inspire a certain awe in the viewer to properly honor the *kami*. He could not keep his mind from drifting, however, to what it would be like to be Chancellor, what he would do with the power.

He walked until the sky above turned crimson, the color of Benzaiten's sail. The ripples of the sea reflected this, and it seemed as though a thousand red war banners waved just beneath the water's surface.

A few yards out, framing the setting sun, a *torii* of two upright logs stood out of the water, spanned by a length of twisted rope as thick as a man's waist. From the weathering on the wood and the rope, this, too, was clearly very old. Kiyomori imagined what he would put in its place: a grand *torii* of cypress wood, with two elegant curved crossbeams, all painted scarlet in the Chinese style. And the shrine itself would be here, on the shore, not hidden away on the mountain slope. And the shrine would also be of cypress, and would resemble the palace of the Dragon King himself. Or as close as could be known, for very few mortals who visited the palace of Ryujin ever returned.

As he turned to continue walking, he thought he saw a lumpy, shapeless mass lying on the shore just where the waves' edge touched the rocks. *Perhaps it is seaweed*, he thought, *or driftwood, or flotsam from some unfortunate ship*. But when he came closer, he saw it was none of those at all, but a woman lying there. Kiyomori ran and crouched beside her, uncertain as to whether it would be proper to touch her. She was wearing the elegant robes of those who serve at the Imperial Court, and her hair was glossy and fine. "Madam, are you all right? Can you hear me?"

Her eyes opened, and she smiled. Her teeth had been darkened with berry stain, in the high-court fashion, and her eyebrows had been shaved and her face powdered white. She sat up but did not hide her face behind her sleeves or act with the accustomed coy shyness expected of a lady. "Ah, Kiyomori-san, it is you. I have been awaiting you."

"You . . . you have? Who are you? How do you come to be here? Did you fall off a boat?"

She laughed. "Of course not. I have been sent here by my father, the Dragon King. You might call me Shishi, although perhaps that speaks too much of death. Call me Tokiko, then. You have met some of my half sisters already. One of them is Benzaiten, whom you met earlier today. As this is our sacred island, we hear your thoughts as you tread upon its stones. My father is pleased that you choose to be our ally. He has sent me to become your principal wife, so that I may assist and guide you."

Kiyomori gaped, for she was quite the most elegant girl he had ever seen. "Then your esteemed father gives me a far greater gift than I deserve." He took her by the elbows and helped her stand, for her kimonos were many-layered and heavy. He noticed with amazement that they were dry.

"Perhaps," said Tokiko. "But Father knows mortals are frail, and he wishes to be certain of your success." She took Kiyomori's arm boldly, as if they were already well acquainted. "He wishes me to remind you often that you must be ruthless in war, yet moderate in government."

Kiyomori frowned and smiled at the same time. "But what warrior does not know these things? They are basic as where to place an arrow on the bow before one shoots, or how to announce one's name before battle in order to find a worthy foe to fight."

"Nonetheless," said Tokiko, "my father has learned that mortals can become forgetful. Or be misled. I am sent to see that this does not happen."

Kiyomori laughed and shook his head. "Why your father sends a woman to advise a warrior bewilders me."

Tokiko released his arm and walked a few steps ahead of him. "Because a woman might not be overcome with zeal, as a man may be, and she may see things he may not. Besides, you will not always be only a warrior. If you are to be accepted as an equal at the Imperial Court, there is much you must learn."

Kiyomori remembered the slights and condescending remarks of the nobles of Heian Kyō. How they made him feel unworthy of their company. How clumsy and ignorant he felt in their presence. *And yet I am of royal blood—their equal if not their better by heritage. If I could but learn the arts and manners to prove it to them.* "There is something in what you say, Tokiko-san."

"Of course. I can teach you and your sons the courtly ways you must know."

"That will be . . . did you say sons?"

"Yes. I will bear you many. And they will become renowned for their courtliness and martial ability. And daughters whom you may place in advantageous marriages."

"Ah. Yes. That would be . . . most worthwhile, Tokiko-san." Kiyomori imagined the astonishment that would be on the courtiers' faces if he and his family entered the capital and behaved with the same graces, manners, and talents as they. "Again, I thank your father for this most undeserved gift."

Tokiko again walked a few steps on, then turned her head coyly back toward him. "There is . . . one request my father would make. A small thing."

Kiyomori walked toward her. "He may ask anything, my lady."

"Anything? Well, then. I trust you have heard of that which bears the name Kusanagi . . . Grass-cutter?"

Kiyomori stopped. "Kusanagi? What warrior cannot know the name of the Imperial Sword? It is only one of the three most sacred objects of the realm."

"Good. Then perhaps you know it was my father who made it."

"There are legends which say so, Tokiko-san."

"They are true. But the sword was swallowed by Orochi, one of the dragons of the sea. Perhaps you have heard that this dragon was slain by Susano-wo, the god of storms and earthquakes, and Susano-wo found the sword in the dragon's tail. Susano chose to give the sword to a mortal he favored, a certain Yamato Takeru, who gave it the name Kusanagi. But that was long, long ago. My father is patient and forgiving and has allowed the sword to stay in mortal hands for a time. But Ryujin sees darker days ahead for mortalkind, and fears the sword may be used for dire purposes. Therefore, my father wants Kusanagi returned to him."

Kiyomori stepped back. "Lady, do you know what you are saying? What your father asks? I cannot possibly steal the Sacred Sword—"

"Who said anything about stealing?" said Tokiko. "Those of Imperial blood may handle Kusanagi. My father has foreseen that one of Imperial blood will return the sword to him. Did we not tell you that you are an Emperor's son? When you are Chancellor, and grandfather to an Emperor, who is to say what you may do?"

"But I could not . . . did you say grandfather to an Emperor?"

"Oh, did my sister not tell you? One of the daughters I will bear you will marry a prince. She will bear a son. Thereby you may become grandfather to an Emperor."

"An Emperor of the Taira blood," Kiyomori whispered. "Surely there is no greater possible glory for my clan than this."

"Surely," said Tokiko, smiling.

"And I must only return the sword?"

"Only that."

"And that is but a small thing. For so many blessings."

"So it is."

Kiyomori rubbed his face. "So. Then. There can be no reason to refuse such an offer, neh?"

"Surely, none." Tokiko stretched out her hand to him.

Kiyomori stepped toward her, his footing on the wet stones uncertain. She caught his sleeve and led him into the deepening twilight.

It was full night when they reached the Taira ship. The slivered moon only dimly outlined its shape against the water.

"Lord Kiyomori, is that you?" called a man from the deck.

"It is I, with another. A lady who will travel with us."

"My lord . . . is that wise?"

"Did you bring more women for the rest of us?" grumbled another man.

Kiyomori said, "You will be respectful to this woman, for she is a daughter of the Dragon King and half sister to Benzaiten. And she is to be my wife."

After a pause, the first man said, "Then I humbly apologize, my lord and lady, for my ill-spoken words. Pray be welcome aboard. But I ask your permission, Lord Kiyomori, to let some of us gather wood on the island so that we may make torches to light our way. The night is dark, and there are many rocks nearby."

"No!" said Tokiko to Kiyomori. "This island is a sacred place. You must take nothing from it. I will provide the light your men need."

Kiyomori helped Tokiko onto the ship, though she seemed to be able to find her way in the dark. The warriors and sailors stepped back from her, respectful yet wary, as she stepped gracefully along the deck to the stern. There she took from her sleeve a small conch shell. She blew into it, producing notes as clear and sweet as those any flute would make.

Within moments, glimmering lights appeared just below the surface of the water, glowing pale green and blue. Kiyomori sucked in his breath. He had heard the sailors call these dragon lights when they appeared on warm summer evenings. Some said they were reflected glimmerings of the lights of Ryujin's palace beneath the sea. Fishermen said they were *kami* lights borne on the backs of the squid who swim there. But whatever the source, the lights that Tokiko had summoned now arranged themselves into a glowing, watery road that led from the dock of Miyajima clear across the Inland Sea.

"There," said Tokiko. "Now you may sail in safety along the path my father has lit for you."

The warriors and sailors whispered in awe and hurried to make the sails ready. Kiyomori bowed to her, and said, "Truly, if I ever had doubt of you, it has all vanished."

"That is good," said Tokiko. "Trust in what I say, keep your bargains, and your success will be assured."

The Jeweled Throne

At the time of Kiyomori's birth, there ruled a young Emperor of Nihon by the name of Toba. Toba's rule, it was said, conformed with the Original Vow of Abounding Mercy, and he had been a benevolent and wise Emperor. But he was also very shrewd, as well as ambitious.

How might an Emperor be ambitious, the humble listener might ask? Does he not reign supreme, descended as he is from the gods? So it is said. But matters were not so simple in those latter days of the Heian Kingdom as they had been in earlier, more elegant times.

As Kiyomori knew, it was the Fujiwara clan and their related and supporting families who truly pulled the strings of government in the capital of Heian Kyō. For centuries, they had been marrying their daughters into the Imperial family and thereby arranging for Fujiwara to be given the best promotions and governmental posts. By founding temples and shrines, both Buddhist and Shintō, and making large donations, the Fujiwara had the support of nearly all the monks and priests of any importance. And they became the arbiters of culture as well, encouraging the study of arts such as music and calligraphy, until the Fujiwara were seen as the pinnacle of all that was refined and noble. Under the nearly suffocating protection of the Fujiwara, the Emperor became little more than a figurehead, as subject to the Fujiwara whim as any servant.

Emperor Toba was a scholar of history and well aware that, in times past, the Emperor had held much more power. He resolved that he would be the one to return the reins of control to the Jeweled Throne. His scheme was simple.

It was not unknown in those times for an Emperor to retire from the throne while he still had years of healthy life left to him, assuming there was a male heir of reasonable age to take his place. It was expected that the Retired Emperor would then take the tonsure and robes of a Buddhist monk and spend his remaining years in contemplation and meditation, leaving behind the trials and cares of the material world.

So in his twentieth year, still young and hearty, Toba retired from the throne, leaving it to be inherited by his four-year-old son, Sutoku. At first this was shocking, and the Senior Council of Nobles scrambled to find precedent for such an act. Toba pointed out that he, himself, had risen to the throne at the age of four. Although the nobles claimed that his ascension at a young age had been necessary due to his father's death, at last the senior nobles were forced to concede that there was no reason to dispute it, and therefore had to permit Toba's retirement to take place.

Therefore, Toba became the Cloistered Zenjō Emperor Toba, also called Toba-In, and he shaved his head and put on the drab robes of a monk. He moved out of the Imperial palace into a mansion of his own. All the attention of the Fujiwara was then directed to the new child Emperor, Sutoku.

But Toba-In did not, in any way, give up interest in worldly matters. He surrounded himself with his most trusted advisors, some of whom were junior members of the Fujiwara clan itself who were also unhappy with Fujiwara control, and created a new government separate from the Imperial palace. Without the burdens of ceremonial duties, Toba-In could devote his attention fully to political matters. Toba-In refused to relinquish the right to give promotions to whomever he chose, and thereby slowly filled the government with those who obeyed him instead of the Fujiwara Regent of his son. Because the person and law of the Emperor, even a former Emperor, were sacred, there was nothing the Fujiwara could do to stop him.

But Toba-In made a mistake. Truly it is said in the sutras that the desires of this world are man's downfall, and here we see that it is so. For Toba-In had a mistress that he doted on, Bifikumon, and sixteen years after Toba-

In's retirement, she presented him with a son. So besotted with this new son was Toba-In that, even though there had been no fault in the reign of his first son, Sutoku, Toba-In arranged to have Sutoku forced into retirement himself at the age of twenty-two and the new son, who eventually was named Konoe, placed upon the Jeweled Throne at the age of three.

Again, the Senior Council of Nobles was shocked. Rumors spread that Toba-In had been unhappy with Sutoku, believing that the boy was not truly his child. Again the council was forced to search the annals of history for precedent. Toba-In made sure that precedent was found, amid the tales of the ancient kings of China. Again, there was nothing the council could do, and so Konoe, barely able to speak, was set upon the throne.

Sutoku, on the other hand, who became known as the New Retired Emperor, or the Shin-In, was still young, in the very prime of life. He found himself set adrift, dismissed and discarded by his father, whispered about by the people, no longer needed by his kingdom. The Shin-In felt no calling to holy orders, and he knew his rule had been moderate and fair. What was he to do? Remember him well, listener, for his decision forms a cornerstone of the Genpei War.

Tall Clogs

As for young Lord Kiyomori, all began to come to pass as Benzaiten had foreseen. His father Tadamori and he had served the Imperial Throne in rebuffing riots caused by the monks of the temples of Ninna-ji and Mount Hiei, and the government saw that they were well rewarded for this. At age twenty-five, two years after Konoe came to the throne, Kiyomori was made Chief of the Central Office, a governmental post, which required him to have residence in the capital city of Heian Kyō. Kiyomori began to build a mansion to the southeast of the capital. A few years before, a fine bridge, named Gojō, had been built to better serve the road south to Kiyomizu Temple. It was near this bridge that Kiyomori had grasses cut and hillocks leveled to have his great house built, which he named Rokuhara.

So proud Kiyomori became of his accomplishments and the good fortune of his clan, that he began to wear wooden clog shoes with taller supports than those worn by most others, and thus he earned the nickname Koheda. He would not allow any to speak ill of the Taira within his hearing, and any who did could soon expect a thrashing from Kiyomori or one of his retainers.

Tokiko, by that time, had borne him three sons, who would come to be called Shigemori, Motomori, and Munemori. As promised, she began to train them from a very early age in the ancient arts of poetry and flute playing, and how to properly dress and speak. She even taught Kiyomori, though he was a reluctant pupil at best. It was remarked upon by senior members of the Taira clan that Kiyomori seemed to pay too much attention and deference to his wife—an eccentric thing in a Taira. But Kiyomori told no one of Tokiko's true origins, and had sworn those of his men who had been at Miyajima to secrecy. Instead it was said she was a younger daughter of a once-noble but now much-fallen family, and this explanation satisfied most of the curious.

At the age of twenty-seven, Kiyomori was made Governor of Aki Province. Unlike most who received a provincial governor's post, however, Kiyomori was not merely content to stay in the capital and collect the income from taxes. He went to the maritime province itself and worked to improve the harbors and encouraged trade with foreign kingdoms, especially the mighty land of China to the east. This was thought eccentric as well until it was noted how much wealth this brought to Aki Province, which only increased the Taira fortunes further. It was clear that the Taira were able to improve shipping by keeping the pirates and brigands at bay. It was not understood how those merchants favored by the Taira always managed to have good winds and smooth waters whenever they passed through the Inland Sea.

Lord Kiyomori gave no more thought to the promise he had made to Tokiko, to return the sword Kusanagi to Ryujin. After all, there was nothing he could do about it until he was closer to those of the highest circles of government. Even though he was a lord of Fourth Rank, Kiyomori still was not permitted to sit in the Imperial Presence, or even to enter any building in the Imperial Compound without the express permission of some higher-ranked nobleman. So he contented himself with amassing wealth and leading the occasional attack upon pirates or rebellious monks in the name of the Emperor.

And before long, all in the land marveled at the increasing success of the Ise Taira, and how Lord Kiyomori's fortunes seemed to rise faster than the ascent of a startled bird.

A Flight of White Doves

The very year Kiyomori was made Governor of Aki Province, a son was born to the great general and head of the Minomoto clan, Yoshitomo. When the boy turned four, Yoshitomo brought this youngest son to the shrine of their clan *kami*. Like the Taira, the Minomoto were powerful warriors of the provinces, possessing many *shōen*. They, too, sought increased power in the capital, fighting brigands and insurgents for the Emperor and nobility, earning the nickname of "the teeth and claws of the Fujiwara." The Minomoto traced their lineage back to the Emperor Seiwa, who had ruled three centuries before, and therefore the main line of their clan was known as the Seiwa Genji. But unlike the Taira, who honored the goddess of fortune Benzaiten, the Minomoto worshiped the *kami* Hachiman, the god of war.

Yoshitomo brought his son to the Grand Shrine of Hachiman at Tsurugaoka, the Hill of Cranes, near the seaside village of Kamakura. At first the little boy was frightened by the great pillars hung with billowing ghost-white banners, the stone *koma-inu* lion-dogs who guarded the stairs leading up to the main shrine, and most especially by the fearsome image of Hachiman himself. Inside the shrine, the gilded wooden statue of the god scowled down from atop his great wooden warhorse, as if saying "prove yourself to me, unworthy one."

When he saw the *kami*'s image, the boy whined as if about to cry and pulled back on his father's sleeve, wanting to leave. But General Yoshitomo crouched beside the boy, and said, "Do not be afraid. Hachiman is our clan guardian and he watches over us. He was once a man, a great man . . . an Emperor known as Ōjin. He was the son of Empress Jingo, she who defeated the Koreans and brought back for us the sacred Jewel of the Sea. These are the same Sacred Jewel our Emperor now has in his care, and it is said the gem can control the tides and great armies of fishes.

"So great was Emperor Ōjin that he was made a *kami* when he died. Our clan banner is white because his sacred color is white. So you see, there is no reason to fear him. Rather honor him, and promise to him that you will become a great warrior to make him and me proud."

The boy listened with great seriousness to all his father told him, then turned to face the statue. He bowed to it, and said, "I promise. I will be a great warrior."

General Yoshitomo grinned and rubbed his son's head. "That is good. That is the way to be." Then Yoshitomo himself bowed and left offerings of rice, and he had the priests write prayer tags, asking Hachiman to bless his son and give him good fortune in battle.

As the general and his son were leaving the shrine, the little boy, filled with childhood spirit, ran ahead of his father down the the stone path. Just as he came to the high *torii* gate leading out of the shrine, a great flock of white doves burst out of the nearby gingko trees. The flock seemed endless, wings filling the sky like a rippling banner of white as they flew off toward the east, though a few flew to the north.

But as Yoshitomo caught up to his son, the direction of the doves' flight abruptly changed to the north, with some flying to the northwest. Father and son watched this display together with awe.

The shrine priests, resplendent in their long pure white garments and tall black hats, came running into the courtyard and stared up in amazement at the sky, pointing and exclaiming to one another. They shouted to Yoshitomo and his son to wait while they discussed the extraordinary event, for surely it could only be an omen of great import.

"Most significant is the direction in which the doves flew," the high priest explained. "For when your son was at the *torii*, the birds flew in the direction that indicates great power and leadership, the dragon strong upon the mountain, and this can only indicate good fortune. Yet some of the flock flew to the north, which is a more troubling direction.

"When you reached the *torii*, Lord Yoshitomo, the birds flight changed entirely to the north. This is the way of difficulty and cold spirits and darkness—the tiger lurking by the river. We interpret these signs thus: for the son, great power but there will be danger; for the father, success but at great cost."

General Yoshitomo nodded gravely. "I will take what you say to heart. I will send more offerings to this shrine regularly, so that Hachiman will see fit to guide my son and me. And I will keep my son near me, and teach him all that I know."

"May good fortune follow you both," said the priests, and they all bowed as one to Yoshitomo and his son.

The general took the hand of his son, who was to become known as Yoritomo, and led him out of the shrine. Though we will not speak of this boy again for some while, remember his name, too. Yoritomo. For he, too, will make a decision that will turn the tide of history.

Scroll 2

《《 》》

Hōgen and Heiji

Winter Smoke

The warmth radiating from the fire of the funeral pyre was strangely welcome to Lord Kiyomori. It was the only warmth in the air. A last gift from his father.

It was the First Month of the third year of the era Ninpei. Kiyomori's father, Tadamori, had died after a brief illness. Now Kiyomori would become Chief of the Taira clan at thirty-five years old. He held his robes tight around himself to ward off the biting winter cold.

Though he would greatly miss his father, Kiyomori dared not shed a tear or moan. He knew he was being watched closely by others of his clan, particularly his brothers Tadanori, Norimori, and Tsunemori. And his uncle, Tadamasa, who had never truly approved of Kiyomori, given the rumors that Kiyomori was not of Taira blood at all, but an Emperor's castaway bastard. He felt their chill, appraising gazes upon him even as he watched the fire burn. Kiyomori dared not show any sign of weakness. No one had yet challenged his right to become Chief of the Taira, and Kiyomori intended to keep it that way.

Kiyomori had even instructed his eldest son, Shigemori, to display no emotion. But as Kiyomori gazed down on his fifteen-year-old son's impassive face, he knew he need not have worried. Already many were remarking on how accomplished and poised the boy was. Although, to Kiyomori's dismay, Shigemori was more adept at reciting history and poetry and Buddhist sutras than he was at the arts of the sword and the horse.

The chanting of the Buddhist monks made the hair on the back of Kiyomori's neck stand on end. He watched the smoke rise into the dark winter sky, wishing he could call it back, wishing he could still consult his father's wisdom. Though by blood, he might be the son of an Emperor, Kiyomori still considered Tadamori his true father. Fondly he remembered Tadamori's squat, squint-eyed, ugly face as his father patiently taught him how to fire a bow and arrow from a rocking ship's deck, how to put on armor correctly, how to ride a horse, how to be a leader of men. The last would be most important in days to come.

How I wish you had lived long enough to see the fruition of the Dragon King's promise. To see your constant humiliation by the nobles at court avenged. You did not believe me when I told you of the prophecies of my destiny. Now I wonder if it will even come true. Can I become grandfather to an Emperor without your guidance?

As the chanting ended and the ashes were gathered for burial, Kiyomori turned away and walked back with Shigemori toward the ox-carriage where his wife Tokiko and his other children awaited him. Kiyomori's high clogs kept the snow from drifting over his swaddled feet, for now.

Rotting Fruit

Two years after Lord Kiyomori became leader of the Taira clan, in the autumn of the second year of the era Kyūju, a great calamity befell the country. The Emperor Konoe, beloved son of Cloistered Emperor Toba-In, fell ill, became blind, and then died at the age of seventeen.

Even for those times, it was a very young age at which to depart this world, and there were whispers that the death was unnatural. Rumors spread that Konoe was killed by a curse. It was said that the image of the Tengu Demon at the shrine on Mount Atago had had spikes driven into its eyes. Could that not be the cause of the poor Emperor's blindness? It was not unknown for those with wealth and thwarted ambitions to pay a monk or priest to beseech higher powers to bring misfortune upon another. But who would do such an evil deed? Perhaps it was to be expected that suspicion fell upon the displaced first son, the Shin-In.

In truth, the Shin-In had done no such thing. Now thirty-six years of age, the Shin-In had spent the years since his dethronement in quiet seclusion in the East Sanjō Palace, raising a family, dabbling in music, philosophy, and poetry, though excelling in none of them. After learning of Konoe's death, the Shin-In sat on the verandah of his small palace and watched the falling gold gingko leaves in the garden with the same melancholy as any other subject of the Emperor.

"Even the brightest ones fall," said an advisor, sitting beside him.

"Even they," the Shin-In agreed.

"Yet even cold winter brings hope of a following spring."

The Shin-In sighed. "And another winter to follow that spring. More sorrow to follow hope. What of it?"

"Your Retired Majesty does not understand. Misfortune to one may bring good fortune to another. It is unfortunate, is it not, that Konoe left no heir?"

The Shin-In turned and frowned at the advisor. He was a modest, shriveled little monk of the sort that always seemed to attach themselves to members of the Imperial Court, earning their keep by being clever or seeming wise, able to quote Buddhist scriptures at the appropriate times. The Shin-In had even forgotten this one's name. "Whatever might you be implying? I cannot become Emperor again. No man has ruled on the Jeweled Throne twice. There is no precedent for such a thing."

The little monk bowed. "Forgive me if I mispresent myself, Majesty. I meant no such thing. But . . . there is your son, Shigehito."

"Yes. But my father Toba-In has other sons whom he will surely prefer over any of my lineage. I wish I knew why he despises me so."

"There can be so many misunderstandings between offspring and parent, Majesty. Perhaps it is not that he hates you so, but that he loves his concubine the more, and therefore favors her children."

"Perhaps. There are those who say his concubine is the one spreading the rumors that it was I who cursed Konoe to death."

"Rumors build on rumors, Majesty. Who can say which are true? Of course, it does not help that Bifikumon'in is, herself, ambitious. Perhaps Your Majesty has heard that she wishes one of her daughters to be made Empress."

"To marry some cousin prince, you mean?"

"No, Majesty. To rule."

"What? There has been no woman on the Jeweled Throne for four centuries! That would be completely unacceptable to the council."

"Precisely, Majesty. Such meddling in political affairs is, of course, unattractive in a woman. Because of her outrageous suggestions, your father may have difficulty entirely having his way in determining the succession."

The Shin-In narrowed his eyes and studied the little monk. His face and shaved head reminded the Shin-In of the capering demons carved in the lintels and doorways of various temples. *Uncharitable of me*, thought the Shin-In. *It must be my mood.*

Any rise in the Shin-In's fortunes would lift those of his advisors, retainers, and servants, of course. It was natural that this advisor would try to encourage ambition in him. *But are there not times in history*, the Shin-In reminded himself, *when events hang in a scale so finely balanced that the slightest breath of wind might change who is up and who is down? It is true that at this time the succession is not clear, and if his concubine's reputation makes my father's choice unpopular . . .*

A breeze blew in from the garden, redolent with the odor of the fallen gingko fruit, which had begun to rot. The Shin-In wrinkled his nose and waved his fan energetically before his face. "I must find someone to clear away that stinking mess," he muttered.

"Majesty?" asked the monk, eagerly.

"I meant the gingko berries." The Shin-In gathered his robes of vermilion brocade silk around him and stood to go in search of more pleasant-smelling quarters.

"Ah. I had misunderstood."

The Shin-In paused. And then spoke softly, almost to himself, "Nevertheless, it might be helpful, to all concerned, if I could learn who would support my cause if matters with my father became . . . difficult. Though I have left the throne, it is still my duty to look after the peace and well-being of my people, neh? It would be remiss of me to allow discord to come to Heian Kyō. A list of loyal and valiant men would be valuable, in such circumstances, don't you think?"

The little monk smiled and bowed. "Most valuable, Majesty. I will see if such a list may be found."

"What temple are you from?"

"Enryakuji, Majesty."

"Ah, yes. Of course. You traditionally serve my family."

"We are blessed with that honor, Majesty."

"These . . . stories, that monks can, through prayer and ritual and . . . curses, change events. Are they true?"

"I am bound by vow to reveal no secrets, Majesty, not even to you. But let us say that we have been known to cause forces beyond the mortal realm to . . . listen."

"Ah. I am so poorly skilled at intrigue. I will need greater strength and knowledge to succeed in this endeavor."

"All my talents, Majesty," said the little monk, "are at your command."

A Turning Hand

It was intolerable that time should pass with the succession undecided, and therefore Retired Cloistered Emperor Toba-In was forced to quickly compromise with the Senior Council of Nobles. He also had to placate his first and principal wife, Taikenmon'in, who was still upset over his preference for his concubine Bifikumon'in. Therefore, Taikenmon'in's second son, twenty-eight-year-old Go-Shirakawa, was placed upon the Imperial Throne. Go-Shirakawa, like his brother the Shin-In, was not particularly accomplished or favored in comportment or intelligence, but he was the most acceptable choice to all.

In the winter of that year, at the age of fifty-three, Toba-In went on a pilgrimage to the shrines at Kumano to pray for the successful reign of his son Go-Shirakawa. As it was thought in those times that a journey of many hardships could cleanse a pilgrim of sins, Toba-In walked the long, difficult path called Nakahechi. The steep mountain path, which took fifteen hours to complete, wound through stands of cedar and camphor trees. It passed all three shrines: Nachi, with its great waterfall sacred to Izanami; Shingu; and the main shrine, Hongu.

Toba-In arrived at Hongu at dawn, walking up the one hundred stone steps just as sunlight was touching the banner in the courtyard. The banner depicted a three-legged crow, Yata-no-karasu, who was said to have guided the first Emperor, Jimmu Tenno, on his conquests of the eastern provinces. Toba-In bowed to the banner, honoring it, hoping for guidance himself.

Toba-In went before the primary building of the shrine, and made offerings and prayers to the Eldest *Kami*—Amataseru, Susano-wo, Izanami, and Izanagi, as well as to the Shōjō-Daibosatsu. It was then, to his amazement, that he saw a child's hand and arm emerge from the wall, palm up, and then the hand turned over. And then it turned over again. And then again. For some minutes this continued until the hand and arm vanished.

Toba-In was quite amazed, and he immediately called upon the monk who had accompanied him on his pilgrimage. "I have had a wondrous portent, Holy One, and I would know its meaning. Is there a medium nearby who could petition the *kami* of the shrine to advise me?"

The best medium of the Kumano shrines, a young maiden seven years of age, remarkable for her elegant and quiet demeanor, was brought before him. Toba-In commanded her to divine for him the meaning of his vision. She agreed and chanted many prayers and breathed incense in order to summon the *kami*, but even though hours passed, noontime came and went, the *kami* did not appear.

Then eighty wise old *yamabushi*, ascetics of the mountains, were brought to Toba-In, and together they chanted the Wondrous Hannya Sutra. The medium joined them in prayer, throwing herself upon the ground and begging the *kami* to possess her. At last, after many more hours, the medium sat up, a change having come over her features. Her face had the aspect of one who had lived centuries, not merely seven years. She turned toward Toba-In and held out her hand, holding it first palm up, then turning it palm down. "Is this what you are asking about?" she said in a voice not her own.

"It is!" said Toba-In. He slid forward onto his knees, his hands clasped. "Please tell me what it may mean."

"It means, o unfortunate one, that as the leaves fall from the trees in the autumn of next year, so must you fall. This year will be your last in this world. And with your departure, Nihon will lose its peace and harmony, turning over again and again like the turning of this hand."

Toba-In felt the blood run from his face. Tears began to form in his eyes. "My last year? I am . . . to die?"

The medium nodded solemnly. "Prepare."

"But . . . but surely there is something I can do, some offering I can make that will change things, that may prolong my life, neh?"

"Your fate is written in the Book of Heaven. The ink cannot be washed away. It is beyond anyone's power to change." Then the face of the medium once again became the face of a little girl, the presence of the god seemed to vanish, and she slumped onto the ground, exhausted. As she was carried from the Retired Emperor's presence, the other monks and all of Toba-In's attendants bowed to him, pressing their foreheads to the ground, to express their sorrow.

Toba-In continued his worship, making the offerings of *gohei*, knowing they would be his last. He prayed to the *kami* and the Buddha that he might be reborn in Paradise. He prayed that Go-Shirakawa might become a magnificent and worthy Emperor. When he had done all the prayers and rituals he could, Toba-In returned home to the capital.

And, indeed, it came to pass that late in the spring of the following year, the first year of the era Hōgen, Toba-In fell ill. Some in Heian Kyō said his illness was surely due to grief at the death of his son, Konoe. Some said it was divine retribution for the foolish actions of his wife. But those who had been with him at Kumano knew it was simply his fate, as written by the gods.

By summer, Toba-In's condition had worsened so much that his wife Taikenmon'in cut her hair and became a Buddhist nun in order to pray for him. But, of course, it was hopeless. At the beginning of autumn, as the medium had prophesied, Toba-In died, and the people of the capital said it was as though the sky had darkened, the sun and moon dimmed, and they wept as though a father or mother had perished.

Changing Palaces

Only days after Toba-In's death, General Minomoto Yoshitomo received a message he had been dreading. He was summoned to report to the Imperial Court. Given the recent events in Heian Kyo, it could mean only one thing. The rumored insurrection was imminent. There would be war.

Yoshitomo was now thirty-two years of age, and it had been six years since the omen of the doves appeared for him and his little son at the shrine of Hachimangu. Yoshitomo wondered if this would be the time when the truth of the omen would manifest itself, if now would be when he would achieve "success, but at great cost."

He dressed in his best robe of red-silk brocade, over which he put on a padded *waidate* that one would wear under armor. On his head, Yoshitomo placed the *eboshi* liner cap one would wear under a helmet. He hoped that this would show he was prepared for battle, though not yet armored for one. To wear armor or weapons into the Imperial presence was a crime so severe it brought a punishment of immediate execution.

Yoshitomo called for his horse, a fine black Eastern steed, and, accompanied by the messenger who had brought the summons, rode out of the gate of his modest mansion. The sky was gray, and a chill wind threatened snow to come. Yoshitomo turned his horse to ride down the broad, willow-lined Suzaku Avenue, which led to the Imperial Compound. But the messenger leaned over and grasped the bridle of Yoshitomo's horse.

"No, my lord. Not that way."

"Eh?"

Looking around him to see who might overhear, the messenger said softly, "The Jeweled Throne is seated elsewhere today."

"Is it? I had heard that the Shin-In had been changing palaces, but not His Majesty Go-Shirakawa."

"It is so, my lord."

"May I assume it is no ordinary directional taboo or astrological omen that has brought about this shift in residence?"

The messenger, watching the streets warily, tugged again on the bridle and led Yoshitomo eastward across the avenue. Yoshitomo noticed with some dismay that the merchants and tradesmen watched him warily from shuttered shops. He felt for them—if what he knew of troop movements in and near the city were true, it would go hard on the common folk once war began. There were many more armed men on horseback on the street, from many different warrior clans, and Yoshitomo tried to observe how many there were from each. Sadly, there were few Minomoto. He thought he saw one distant relative, who swiftly looked away when their gazes met.

"As you may have heard, my lord, the Shin-In left the East Sanjo Palace for the mansion of the Kamo Shrine Virgin, then went to the North Palace. The last word has it he is now lodged at Shirakawa Palace."

In fact, Yoshitomo's men had kept him informed of the strange movements of the former Emperor, but he did not necessarily wish a mere messenger to know this. "Indeed? The Shin-In would seem to have developed a restless nature."

"In my opinion, my lord, the Shin-In is trying to confound those who would spy on him. Or find the most defensible location."

"Very astute observation. You might make a general someday. But what of His Majesty? Why move out of the well-defended Imperial Compound?"

The messenger sighed. "Of course I am not privy to the thoughts of His Most Sacred Majesty. But I have heard others say that there are too many people and too many gates in the Compound for everyone to be watched. And perhaps it is hoped that the Shin-In is still fond of his former residence, the East Sanjō Palace, and will not attack it, for that is where the Emperor is lodged now, and where we are headed."

"Ah. I see."

After identifying themselves to the guards at the gate of the East Sanjō Palace, the messenger escorted Yoshitomo into the mansion compound. Servants came to see to their horses, and Yoshitomo was led to a verandah beside a garden of bare gingko trees. There he knelt on a cushion beside an ornate bamboo blind that was bound with gold-silk cord, and waited.

A servant arrived with warmed tea and some pickled vegetables for his refreshment. Knowing that much can be learned from observant servants, Yoshitomo asked him, "What do you make of all this?"

The servant, a thin, nervous young man, looked around startled, and asked, "Of all what, my lord?"

Yoshitomo idly waved his hand, "Of these changes. Do they worry you?"

"Worry, my lord? Why should anyone worry when seven thousand *kami* protect our land day and night? I hear there are sixty gods alone dedicated to protecting the Jeweled Throne. And surely the Three Treasures of Prayer, Law, and Buddha himself will protect us from any disaster."

"Yes, yes, of course." sighed Yoshitomo. "But surely a perceptive young man such as yourself might have heard or noticed some . . . things."

The servant looked around again and leaned as close as he dared. "Well, my lord, since you ask, and since I perceive you are a brave man not to be put off by fearsome tales, I will tell you this. Do you know the story of the Giant of Mount Higashi?"

Yoshitomo frowned. "Do you mean the statue of a warrior buried there when Emperor Kammu founded Heian Kyō?"

"The very same. You are a learned man, my lord. Well, I have heard it said that the mound where the statue is buried has begun to shake. It is said when that happens, danger is coming."

Yoshitomo could not keep from smiling. "The earth shakes rather often in this land, my good fellow."

"Oh, but, then, there was the comet in the east. And that always portends disaster."

"And strangely, there is always some misfortune that can be tied to a former omen. But, then, I am untutored in signs of the Heavens."

"Well, the bureaucrats of the Yin-Yang Office have been buzzing around the Emperor like bees of late, telling him of all sorts of these omens; that I know."

"I am sure that must be very reassuring to His Majesty."

"And," the servant went on, dropping into a whisper, "I have heard that the Shin-In is conspiring with . . . dark forces."

"Dark forces?"

"You know, demons, wizards, evil monks. They say that the Shin-In has conjured a fierce half-man, half-demon who has the strength of a giant. It is said he draws a bow as thick as a man's forearm and can fire an arrow that will pierce seven suits of armor, one after the other. This giant's name is . . . Tametomo."

Yoshitomo nearly spit out his tea. He coughed and wiped his mouth on his sleeve. "Indeed?"

"Ah, I see you have heard of this demon, too, my lord."

"Yes. I have." In fact, Tametomo was a much younger half brother to Yoshitomo. Yoshitomo had never met him—the boy Tametomo had been sent away from his mother's house at a young age because he was too wild and unruly to be controlled. There were many tales of what had become of Tametomo after that. Yoshitomo was not surprised that Tametomo had now earned the description of demon. But it saddened him to hear Tametomo had also joined the Shin-In's side. One sorrow on top of many others.

Yoshitomo heard voices and footsteps entering the room on the other side of the blinds.

The servant bowed, and said swiftly, "I must go now, my lord. I hope you have all that you require."

"As do I," murmured Yoshitomo, as the servant departed. A *shōji* farther down the verandah slid open and a man with shaved head and wearing black robes steeped out. The man knelt at the threshold and bowed toward whoever was in the room, then approached Yoshitomo. The noble monk had a high-bridged nose and eyes that conveyed intelligence, or shrewdness. He gave Yoshitomo the slight bow expectable from a lord of Second Rank.

"Ah, General Yoshitomo, I am glad you have arrived. His Majesty is most eager to hear your advice. I am Lesser Counselor Shinzei, and I will speak for you to His Majesty and convey his replies to you."

Yoshitomo bowed in return. "I thank you. I am honored to be of service to His Majesty."

"We are pleased to hear it, although there might be better circumstances, surely."

"You could say so, my lord."

"We understand that your father and your brothers have all joined with the Shin-In's cause. You alone, of all the Minomoto, have chosen to answer our summons and come to the rightful Emperor's aid."

Yoshitomo felt shame fill him, and he hung his head. "His Majesty is well informed."

"While pleased, we are also somewhat surprised. Perhaps you will forgive us if we ask . . . why?"

Yoshitomo replied, "I have been taught since childhood that the Minomoto do not serve two masters. And I have always believed that our true duty was to serve the Jeweled Throne. I cannot speak for my father and brothers, or why they have chosen to side with rebels."

"Perhaps," said Shinzei, "they felt that the Shin-In's dethronement in favor of Konoe was unfair. Or that the Shin-In's son, Shigehito, should have been chosen to succeed instead."

Yoshitomo wondered if he was being tested. "It is said that the gods do not permit anyone unworthy to sit upon the Jeweled Throne."

"A cautious answer. You understand, what we most require of you is your knowledge of Minomoto strategy. You will not see this as betrayal of your clan?"

Yoshitomo felt his cheek twitch. He hoped that Shinzei had not noticed. "In my opinion, it is the rest of my family who are betraying the clan."

"Well, then, we must admire you for your courage to stand alone. What do you advise, given what you know, in order to head off this rebellion and end it quickly?"

Yoshitomo worded his reply so as not to reveal any secrets of Minomoto strategy, for even in the face of betrayal a warrior does not tell his clan's secrets to outsiders. "My lord Shinzei, please tell His Most Sovereign Majesty that I have heard that one thousand warrior-monks from the temples at Nara are on their way to Heian Kyō. They will be arriving at Uji sometime tonight and will no doubt be joining the Shin-In's forces by tomorrow morning. This increase of forces will make matters difficult. Therefore, I advise an attack upon the Shirakawa Palace tonight, to surprise the Shin-In, before his reinforcements arrive."

"Yes, we see the wisdom of this. But how many men would you need in this attack? The Shirakawa Palace may be well defended."

With some pride, Yoshitomo replied, "I assure you I and my Seiwa Minomoto will be sufficient to finish this matter swiftly."

"Yes, yes, your valor and skill are not in question, good general. But we have received word that the Lord of Aki, Taira no Kiyomori, has arrived from Rokuhara with a force of his Ise Taira, wishing to participate in support of the Emperor. It is our thought that, with the Taira to reinforce you, a successful conclusion to the matter will be more certain, neh?"

Yoshitomo paused and rubbed his chin, feeling both reassured and dismayed. The addition of the Taira forces would be useful from a military standpoint, but to fight beside a rival clan would bring complications. Who would be superior in command? Would the presence of so many Minomoto on the rebel side cause the Taira to turn against *all* Minomoto? And if they fought with greater skill or luck, would their enhanced reputation make the Taira the preferred clan of the Imperial Court, with all the promotions and greater status that would lead to? "Well," Yoshitomo said at last, "it is good to hear there will be more men in His Majesty's forces. Perhaps it would be best to deploy the Taira to guard East Sanjō Palace and His Majesty's person. In that way, I and my men may fight with all assurance of His Majesty's safety."

The barest hint of a smile graced Shinzei's face. "We will consider your advice, good general. A moment, if you please." Shinzei inclined his head, then stood and walked back through the *shōji*, sliding it shut behind him.

Yoshitomo waited, listening intently to the murmurings within the Imperial Presence though he could only make out a word or two now and then. He had to will himself to patience. He glanced at the bare gingko trees and noted how skeletal they looked against the gray winter sky. A very light snow was beginning to fall.

The *shōji* slid open and Shinzei emerged again. He knelt before Yoshitomo, and said, "We have considered your advice, Yoshitomo-san, and for the most part we think it wise. We Who Dwell Above The Clouds are untutored in war, and so it is natural that matters of strategy fall to you. It is said that he who is first shall control, he who is last shall be controlled; therefore your plan to attack at once, tonight, is appropriate."

Yoshitomo acknowledged this with a grunt and nod of the head.

"However," Shinzei continued, "matters of diplomacy are our concern. His Majesty feels that any heartfelt show of support is of great worth in these troubled times, and therefore should be given the greatest respect. For that reason, His Majesty insists that Lord Kiyomori and the Ise Taira will join the Seiwa Minomoto in the attack upon Shirakawa Palace tonight. It is His Majesty's hope that this show of power will crush the rebellion all the more swiftly and show how foolish it is for any rebel to defy the Imperial will."

Yoshitomo nodded once. "It shall be as His Majesty commands, then."

The ghost of a smile appeared on Shinzei's face again. "His Majesty is aware that there is some . . . rivalry between the Taira and the Minomoto. I would suggest you forget your concerns. If your plan succeeds, as we have every expectation that it will, I can assure you that His Majesty will be generous in his gratitude and that promotions for you and yours are sure to follow. I suspect you will even receive the privilege of entry into the Imperial Presence."

Yoshitomo gazed toward the open *shōji*. "As you may know, my lord Shinzei, we warriors must expect to die in any given battle, for each man's luck gives out sometime or other. For all I know, this may be the last day of my life. What good is privilege to come, if I do not live to see it? Would it not be better to see a thing now and have it to remember as I leave this world?" With that, Yoshitomo abruptly stood and strode to the open *shōji*.

Shinzei sputtered behind him, "But, but, but . . . my good general, you cannot, you mustn't—" but he did not act fast enough to stop Yoshitomo.

Yoshitomo stepped across the threshold into the Great Meeting Room. Sudden, shocked silence fell among the black-robed nobles gathered there. Yoshitomo looked past them and saw the Imperial dais, ringed with gauze curtains, a golden guardian lion standing, one paw raised, at each corner. On the wall beside the dais hung the jade Sacred Jewel, the round Sacred Mirror, and the Sacred Sword, Kusanagi. Within the gauze curtains of the dais, Yoshitomo caught a glimpse of a man in vermilion robes wearing a tall black hat and an astonished expression.

Yoshitomo fell to his knees and did obeisance to the dais. "Forgive me, Most August Imperial Majesty," he said, pressing his face to the floorboards, "but I wished to see a bit of Heaven Upon the Earth before I see the Heaven after Life."

The silence went on a long moment more, and then he heard gentle laughter coming from the dais. Laughter caught, then, among the nobles as fire catches from house to house. Yoshitomo felt safe to sit up, his face only somewhat red from embarrassment.

"You are impetuous, Yoshitomo-san," said Emperor Go-Shirakawa. "Yet we hope that this bodes well for tonight's battle. Very well. Look your fill. And whether you live or die this day, keep it as a bright memory for the rest of your life."

"I will, Great Majesty," said Yoshitomo, bowing again. "I will."

The Whistling Arrow

At the Hour of the Tiger, the hour before dawn, two armies set out from East Sanjō for Shirakawa Palace; one under the command of Minomoto Yoshitomo, the other led by the Lord of Aki, Taira Kiyomori. Each were followed by nearly two hundred mounted warriors and their retainers.

Kiyomori breathed in the crisp winter air, felt it cold and sharp in his nostrils like the edge of a knife. The red light of the torches carried by his men glimmered off the snow and ice on the street. His blood quickened with the thought of battle. It had been some years since he had ridden at the head of an army. He had forgotten how keen it made the senses, much like the night he had visited his first woman, long ago. His hands gripped the reins of his horse tighter as the susurrus of the hooves on the paving stones soothed him like the waves on the shores of Ise.

Kiyomori had dressed with meticulous care in armor laced with red braid over a robe of oyster-colored silk, and his helmet bore the image of the butterfly, the Taira crest. He sat in a polished red-and-black lacquer saddle upon a spirited, well-groomed copper-bay horse. While a warrior's courage in fighting was, by nature, a necessity, it was no less required to be impressive in appearance. A warrior who was careless in dress might be careless in battle. And Kiyomori knew from his father's sad experience that one's looks played a major part in a man's reputation.

Even though he had been clan head now for three years, Kiyomori still had a need to prove himself. His disapproving uncle, Tadamasa, had now become his adversary, siding with the Shin-In. In a way, Kiyomori could not blame him. Gambling was a traditional vice of warriors, and to join an Imperial rebellion was the greatest gamble of all. *If the usuper wins, Tadamasa will have greater power than he has ever known and can supplant me easily. Probably have me and my family executed. If he loses, he loses his life, which he counts of little value without power.*

Beside Kiyomori rode his first son and heir, Shigemori, now eighteen years of age. The young man rode on a light bay horse and wore armor braided in water-plantain design with green cord over a red brocade robe. On his helmet were silver studs in the shape of stars, and he held a bow double-banded with rattan.

Shigemori's eyes were wide with excitement and, no doubt, a little fear. Kiyomori gazed at his son's eager face and felt both admiration and sorrow. Kiyomori still fondly remembered the boy's trouser ceremony, and the later cap ceremony at which Shigemori received his adult name—could they have been so long ago? Shigemori had learned well from Tokiko's instruction, and he was an accomplished flutist and poet, well-spoken and widely admired in noble circles. He had already achieved the appointment of Junior Vice Minister of Central Affairs. And now he was a strapping young warrior facing his first major battle with the eagerness of a bridegroom.

What a fine Taira he will be, Kiyomori thought. He silently sent a prayer to the clan *kami. Bring my son courage and glory this night. Let him kill many of the enemy. But if he should fall tonight, may he fall with honor and not bring shame upon our clan.*

"Father," said Shigemori, "I have heard it said among the other men that the Shin-In has a demon fighting for him, a creature named Tametomo who is taller than any normal man. His arms are longer and stronger, too, and he can shoot an arrow through anything!"

Kiyomori chuckled. "It is common, my son, for tall tales to be spread to the enemy to frighten them. I expect the warriors we will face will be no more supernatural than we are."

"But what if it is true?" Shigemori persisted. "Think what glory there might be in bringing down a giant or a demon, something greater than an ordinary man?"

"It is no easy thing to defeat even an ordinary man, and these Minomoto are well-trained Eastern warriors, my son. Do not discount them merely because they are flesh and blood and bone. Be mindful of their skill, and you are more likely to survive and win. Be content with human opponents. There should be glory enough for you in that."

Two riders, a man and a boy, from the group of warriors ahead slowed their horses to ride beside them. Kiyomori saw from the torchlight reflected off the man's helmet crest, a polished brass crescent, that it was General Minomoto Yoritomo himself. "Did I hear you speaking of Minomoto no Tametomo? I can tell you more about him, for he is my youngest brother. He is only eighteen or nineteen, your age I believe, young Taira. He was always a rough and unruly boy, but I doubt he has become a demon."

Shigemori ducked his head. "I was merely mentioning rumors I had heard, Lord General. I meant no offense to your family."

"A well-spoken boy," Yoshimoto said to Kiyomori.

"I am proud of him," said Kiyomori.

"This is my eldest," Yoshitomo said, indicating the boy riding a gray horse beside him. "He is Akugenda Yoshihira, and is just fifteen. This is his first battle."

The boy leaned forward over his saddle to peer around his father at Shigemori. "I'm going to take more heads than you," he taunted.

"We shall see about that," replied Shigemori.

The two generals laughed.

"A spirited lad," said Kiyomori. "But how will he feel if the heads he takes are those of his grandfather and his uncles?"

Yoshitomo's face hardened into a scowling mask. "A warrior does what he must. I believe you also have an uncle who serves the Shin-In, do you not?" He kicked his horse and pulled on the reins of his son's mount, and they cantered ahead to rejoin the men farther ahead.

"Father," asked Shigemori sofly, "should you have said such a thing? Is it wise to antagonize a man we must fight beside?"

"Though the battle may be paramount," said Kiyomori, "do not forget the war. Yoshitomo is our ally, but he is not our friend. If I unsettle him, perhaps he will not fight so well in the encounter to come."

Shigemori turned in his saddle wearing a bewildered glare. "Of what possible use is that to us?"

Kiyomori sighed. "Then we Taira will make better account of ourselves, by comparison, and receive more of the credit for the victory, and therefore more of the honors to follow. That is how things are done."

"Is it? It seems so . . . dishonorable."

"Do you think the Fujiwara achieved their power by following the Twelve Precepts to the letter? Your mother may have taught you philosophy, but I see she has taught you little of politics."

"I think I am glad of it."

"Oh, no, my son, politics is the most important study there is. You are my heir and will be Chief of the Taira yourself someday. You must remember this, and take heed."

"Yes, Father," Shigemori agreed, reluctantly.

*G*eneral Yoshitomo was seething from Kiyomori's rudeness when his son Akugenda Yoshihira distracted him with a question. "What is going to happen, Father? When does the battle begin?"

"Well, if this were an ordinary battle in the East, on an open field, my son, I could tell you easily. But this will be in a city, and, therefore, it is harder to predict. Normally, proper armies will settle beforehand on a time and place to fight. But this must be a surprise attack at night, and the rebels should not be expecting us. Then, to announce the beginning of battle one side or the other will fire the whistling arrows—it sends quite a thrill through your blood, I can assure you, when you hear hundreds of them humming through the air. But if we are fortunate, the enemy will not have time for whistling arrows, and we do not intend to announce ourselves.

"After that, both sides send flights of ordinary arrows into the enemy, to kill as many as possible before closing distance. It is to be hoped that tonight we will be the only side to fire our bows. Once the sides have ridden close to one another, some warriors may call out their name and where they come from in hopes of finding a warrior of equal quality with whom to fight. There are many Minomoto full of pride serving the Shin-In, and they may do this calling-out during the battle. Should someone challenge you in this way, remember how I have instructed you. Use your sword, but do not expect to kill a man from horseback. Your best chance is to knock your opponent off his horse and then stab him while he is on the ground."

"And then cut off his head?" asked Akugenda Yoshihira eagerly.

"Yes, my son. Then cut off his head," Yoshitomo patiently replied. He had often wondered why the omen at the Hachiman Shrine had been directed toward his youngest son and not this one, his eldest. Akugenda Yoshihira was so impetuous, Yoshitomo could easily imagine him as needing careful guidance to avoid recklessness and indulgence in darker passions. But the gods surely had their own plans for him. "Remember, however, if you should be mortally wounded, try to have one of our own take your head first, so that you will not dishonor us."

"I will remember," said Akugenda Yoshihira. "And . . . if it should be my uncle or grandfather that I defeat? What then?"

Yoshitomo sighed. "In that unlikely circumstance, you must do a clean cut and permit no suffering. Show no mercy beyond that, however, for they are rebels against the Imperial Throne."

"Is that what you will do, Father, if you meet them?"

Yoshitomo closed his eyes. "If I must, I will."

*T*he army of mounted warriors turned down Nijō Street, riding eastward toward the Shirakawa Palace. Lord Kiyomori suddenly stopped his horse.

"Father, what is it?" asked Shigemori.

"I have had a thought." Kiyomori picked one of his men to be a messenger and told him, "Ride forward to General Yoshitomo and tell him this. Before we left Sanjō Palace, one of the Yin-Yang Office prognosticators informed me that the *kami* Konjin sits in the east today, and it would be dangerous to shoot arrows into the morning sun. Therefore, to ensure victory, I should consider that direction taboo. Tell Yoshitomo I will be choosing a different direction by which to approach the enemy. Go."

The messenger bowed in his saddle and rode off to catch up to Yoshitomo's forces.

"Is this more . . . politics, Father?" asked Shigemori.

"Strategy," replied Kiyomori. "If we divide our attack, the Shin-In's men must divide their defense."

"But with our forces separated, there will be fewer to aid General Yoshitomo should he face strong opposition."

"Would there?" said Kiyomori with a slight smile. "Well, then there will be all the more glory for him should he be victorious. We are doing him a favor, neh?" He gestured to the riders behind to follow him, and Kiyomori turned his horse south. He led his warriors south for a block, then east very briefly, then rode across the bed of an ornamental stream before turning north again. All along their route, those merchants and administrators who had risen early to do their business saw the two hundred armored horsemen riding by and ran back to their homes. Commerce and government in Heian Kyō would be somewhat delayed that day.

The Taira rode northward along the east bank of the ornamental stream. A mist rose from the surface of the water, almost glowing in the predawn light. It wreathed the shaped pines and dead reeds that lined the stream bank. Though he would have expected the sky to be getting lighter, Kiyomori sensed an increasing darkness descending upon them as they came to where the stream ran under the Shirakawa Palace wall. A small iron-barred gate had been placed there, so no scouts could wriggle in and cause havoc from within.

Kiyomori led his men along the wall to the southeast gate of Shirakawa Palace. Dark figures lurked behind the tall wood lintel of the gate, lit from behind by lanterns and torches. The accoutrements of their helmets and armor made them appear more demonlike than human. It was impossible to tell of what clan they were or how many. Kiyomori sent a vanguard of fifty of his riders forward to within a few yards of the gate.

The first of these men called out, "You who watch the gate, identify yourselves! We are warriors who serve the Lord of Aki, Taira Kiyomori. We are residents of Ise and vassals of the Kammu Taira. We come in the name of the true and just Emperor, Go-Shirakawa. Be warned, we will deal harshly with any who support the usurper!"

Perhaps it was a trick of the light, but Kiyomori thought he saw a dark, unnatural smoke billow from the courtyard behind the wall. Lit from within and below by fire, the smoke had an orange-red glow not unlike the paintings of the fires of Hell. At first Kiyomori thought Yoshitomo might have set fire to the palace as part of his attack, but there was no sound of fighting, and the smoke did not smell of burning wood.

A shadowy figure emerged from the smoke to stand atop the palace wall, a figure taller than a normal human, with long arms and stooped posture. It spoke with a snarling voice that, indeed, sounded more demon than man. "So, it is Lord Kiyomori who leads you, eh? Hah. I have heard much of him. A proud pretender to honors he has not earned. A would-be noble who thinks wearing tall shoes will place his head Above The Clouds. One who hopes the tail of the Dragon King will sweep him into the arms of the Imperial Court.

"I am Chinzei Hachiro Tametomo of the Seiwa Genji, myself only nine generations from the Heavenly Throne. And you dare to call yourselves Kammu Taira," the creature at the gate continued to growl, "trying to make much of your Imperial descent. Hah. You Taira have degenerated much in the eleven generations since your ancestors dwelt in the Court of Abundant Pleasures. Begone, all of you. None of you, especially not that poser Kiyomori, is a worthy opponent for me."

Kiyomori felt his blood run cold with rage at the insults. Yet he also felt a shudder of fear. Whoever this was who barred the gate knew that

Kiyomori was guided by supernatural forces. How was that possible unless . . . the rumors were true and the Shin-In had supernatural help as well? Legends said there were ways a man might be changed into a demon. What if this youngest son of the Minomoto had, in fact, become an *oni*?

The Dragon King had offered Kiyomori his protection, but this battle was nowhere near the sea, Ryujin's domain. While Kiyomori had learned much of the arts of warfare, he knew nothing useful about what to do if faced with demons.

One of the vanguard nudged his horse slightly ahead of the others, and he called out to the gate, "I am Ito Kagetsuna of Furuichi. Perhaps you have heard of me. We once served under the same commander, years ago."

"Kagetsuna!" the demon replied. "Of course I have heard of you. You served my former lord well. Step aside! I've no quarrel with you."

"That cannot be, Hachiro-san. Your current lord has defied the Emperor. I am now Vice Commander in Chief of the Imperial forces, and, therefore, I now face you as your enemy. So though I have no particular claim to renown, other than having once captured one of the worst bandit lords of Ise, I challenge you. Let us see whether an arrow shot by a lowly fellow such as I is worthy of striking you." With that, he drew his bow to the full and let an arrow fly. But even in the uneven torchlight, it was clear that he missed.

The demon Tametomo called out from the gate, "Your words hit their mark better than your arrow, Kagetsuna. You have spoken so well that although you are an unworthy enemy, I shall give you an arrow in return. May it bring you honor in this life or be a remembrance in the next!"

Kiyomori and his men heard a whistling arrow fly through the air and a *shuk-shuk* as it struck a target. Kiyomori saw one of the men ahead of him fall from his horse.

"Roku!" Kagetsuna cried. "Roku my brother!"

Another warrior who had been behind Roku stared in horrified awe at the blood-smeared arrow stuck fast in the armor above his left arm. This warrior turned his horse and rode back to speak to Kiyomori.

"My lord, look at this!" He broke the arrow off and held it out to Kiyomori. "It is a blunt whistling arrow, yet it passed right through Roku's armor and body and landed on me! Roku was dead before he even left his saddle! What kind of archer can do this? Surely no ordinary man!"

Kiyomori stared at the arrow and heard the concerned mutterings of the men behind him.

Kagetsuna rode up, his face pale with terror. "It is true," he said softly. "Roku is dead, the arrow flew right through him as if he were no more than mist. There has not been such skill with a bow since Minomoto Yoshiie pierced three suits of armor with one arrow. Could it truly be such strength has come into the world again?"

Kiyomori sucked in his breath through his teeth, looking out at the dark gate and the huge figure slouching in its shadows. *I have a great destiny to fulfill,* he thought. *I have not yet built the new shrine at Miyajima. I have not yet returned Kusanagi to the Dragon King. I have a grandson not yet born who is to become a Taira Emperor. What if these things do not come to pass because I foolishly challenge a demon? I was chosen to lead the world out of the dark times. I must not let forces of evil keep me from my destiny.*

Lord Kiyomori turned to his men, and said, "No one has ordered us to attack and take this particular gate, only that we must enter the palace somewhere. This was merely the first gate that we came to. This palace has many other entrances. Why should we satisfy the demands of a braggart who was lucky with one arrow by attacking his gate? Let us ride to the east gate and try there."

Kagetsuna frowned. "That gate is still close by, my lord, and this demon archer could easily defend it as well. Let us go to the other side of the palace and try the north gate."

Kiyomori nodded to him. "Well said, Kagetsuna. Let us go there and hope for a more profitable battle."

As he turned his horse to lead his men northward, his son Shigemori rode up close to him, his face eloquent with disappointment and shame. "Father, it cannot be that you, Chief of the Taira, bound by Imperial command, are turning your face from the enemy?"

Kiyomori scowled at him. "Do not let the tales you have heard of reckless courage make you foolish, my son. In battle, strategy matters as much as bravado, and it is wise to seek the better advantage before you charge into the fray. Let Lord Yoshitomo deal with his wild brother. We will find a more suitable entrance elsewhere. Truly, you have much to learn about war."

"I have learned one does not run from a foe one has faced and challenged." Shigemori turned his horse, and shouted, "Those still with a stomach for glory, follow me!"

"Stop him!" Kiyomori cried to his men. "The demon will strike him down like a defenseless sparrow. This must not be!"

Though Shigemori plunged toward the gate, the other warriors pressed their mounts against Shigemori's horse, pushing and turning him toward the north. Soon there was little Shigemori could do but let his horse gallop northward with the rest of the Taira, to the other side of Shirakawa Palace.

Kiyomori took a last glance at the southeast gate. He heard the demon Tametomo laugh, and say, "Running away, Kiyomori-san? It will do you no good. A man's doom follows him like his shadow." Kiyomori did not reply, but whipped his horse with the reins to catch up to his men.

General Yoshitomo sat on his horse at the east gate of Shirakawa Palace, grumbling to himself. The pitiful excuse Kiyomori had given for splitting their forces still rankled him. Directional taboos might be all well and good for the nobility who could come and go at their leisure. For a warrior facing battle, it was foolish to the point of insult.

He heard shouts from the south and assumed Kiyomori had chosen to begin an attack there. *Very well*, thought Yoshitomo. *Let the o-so-brave Taira take the first blows. Once they are inside the palace, then I shall lead my men through this gate.* But soon there was silence broken only by the rumble of hoofbeats departing. *The Taira cannot be fleeing, can they?*

Something felt wrong to Yoshitomo. The atmosphere around him felt eerie and unsettled. The strange, glowing smoke within Shirakawa Palace cast a gloom that could not be natural. *Why has the sun not risen?* Yoshitomo wondered. *Surely it is near dawn, and yet it is still dark.*

"My lord, someone moves at the gate."

Yoshitomo narrowed his eyes and made out against the glowing smoke a tall, long-limbed man.

"So," growled a voice within the gate, "can this be my renowned elder brother who faces me now?"

Yoshitomo rode his horse forward, even within arrow distance. "Tametomo, is that you? In the name of Emperor, reject this rebellion. Come and join us, the side of the right. You sully your name by siding with rebels and usurpers."

Harsh laughter split the gloom. "What do I care which is the side of the right, my brother? The world of foolish mortals is not meant for one like me. I was born with a demon's nature and after being discarded from my home I found a wizard-monk who taught me to achieve full demonhood. What do I care which fool sits on the Jeweled Throne? The Shin-In appreciates the dark arts, as I do, and he has promised me a good fight, so here I am. And my changed appearance bothers our father and brothers so, it is most amusing to me."

Yoshitomo swallowed hard and tried to convince himself that his brother was merely boasting. "What can I offer you, Tametomo, to change your mind?"

"Nothing! Already the mighty Taira have fled rather than face me, and this is the greatest pleasure I have had in days. Why should you be any more courageous than they? Begone, elder brother, before I am tempted to hurt you. In the name of the blood we once shared, be off with you. Here is a memento to remember me by."

Yoshitomo heard the thrumming of a bowstring and the next moment his head was pulled sharply aside. An arrow protruded from the right flange of his helmet. Angrily, Yoshitomo turned his horse around and rode back to his men. The first he encountered, he ordered, "Take out that rude, boasting boy. Kill him and then we will storm the gate."

Seven men rode toward the gate, firing arrows from horseback, but none of them made it close to the palace wall. With a speed beyond mortal capability, Tametomo fired his bow and one by one each of the seven men fell from his horse, each transfixed by an arrow.

"It cannot be possible," Yoshitomo murmured.

"He truly is a demon," said Akugenda Yoshihira, his face pale.

"With even only one man of this strength," another man said, "how can we fight our way through the gate? Particularly if the cowardly Taira have fled and will not assist us."

Yoshitomo thought a moment as he attempted to control his horse, which had become skittish at the smell of blood. "We will not. There are other ways to fight. If you cannot get through to the enemy, you must make the enemy come out to you. We will set the palace on fire."

"But my lord, the Hōshōji Temple is just across the street, and it houses many treasures. There is a bit of wind, and the fire may travel. Is it worth the risk?"

Yoshitomo frowned. "True. It would be bad to antagonize the monks. I will place the final decision with the Imperial Court. Take a message to Lesser Counselor Shinzei and explain the situation. We will wait here for his answer."

The man bowed in his saddle and departed for the East Sanjō Palace. It was not long before he returned with the reply. "Lesser Counselor Shinzei says your plan has merit, and His Majesty gives his approval. If your efforts succeed and thereby allow the Emperor to retain the throne, he can rebuild whatever temples are burned. Do not fear. Only destroy the rebels as soon as possible."

"Very good," said Yoshitomo. "The wind is coming out of the west, so let us start the fire at the house to the west of Shirakawa Palace."

"My lord, that is Middle Counselor Fujiwara Ienari's house!" said the messenger. "He is a very powerful and influential man."

Yoshitomo smiled a grim smile. "As His Majesty has said, if we succeed, Go-Shirakawa will build him another house. Burn it."

Three of his men departed with torches and soon smoke was rising from the roof of Ienari's mansion. The powerful westerly winds carried sparks and embers from the burning wood across the road and the wall and the gate onto the roof of Shirakawa Palace.

The air filled with choking smoke and soon there came the screams of women and children. Servants and ladies fled the palace, whirling and scattering like autumn leaves upon a storm wind.

"Slow them down!" Yoshitomo commanded. "Some of them may be men trying to escape!"

But there were too many fleeing and too few horsemen to stop them. Yoshitomo and his men were able to ride into the palace, but the smoke, both natural and supernatural, confounded them, making it impossible to see clearly.

A shadow rode toward him, and Yoshitomo drew his sword. "Stop and declare yourself! In the name of the Emperor, I Minomoto Yoshitomo command it!"

The smoke cleared enough to show it was Taira Kiyomori riding in from the north. "Ho. Yoshitomo. It is good you announced yourself, or I might have killed you. Where is the Shin-In?"

"I do not know," Yoshitomo admitted. "In this smoke, and with so many fleeing . . ." he finished with a shrug.

"A brilliant plan," Kiyomori said sardonically. "Thanks to your fire, we have gained Shirakawa Palace, but lost the rebels. I presume there has been no sign of your unfortunate relatives either, then?"

"They will be easily found," Yoshitomo retorted. "After this morning, no one will support them. And at least I devised a plan. I heard you ran away from Tametomo at the southeast gate."

"I was merely looking for a better entry. There is no sense in getting one's men killed for nothing."

Their argument was broken by the sound of tolling bells. Shigemori came galloping up to them. "Father, Hōshōji Temple is burning! The scrolls! The sacred tapestries! So much will be lost!"

"Our good general Yoshitomo says that His Imperial Majesty permits it. That all will be rebuilt," said Kiyomori. "Apparently it was expected this might happen."

"Well," said Shigemori, his expression uncertain, "if it is an Imperial command, what can a man do? But so much holy work destroyed—it will bring bad fortune, I am sure."

"War is bad fortune enough, boy," growled Yoshitomo. "You need not look for further omens in its doings. I would have thought that you, a Taira, would know this." Yoshitomo did not wait for a reply but turned his horse and rode through the smoke to search for his own son and to salvage what victory he could.

Verandah Cushions

At the Hour of the Ox, early the following afternoon, Generals Yoshitomo and Kiyomori made their formal report at the Imperial palace. It was said they made a splendid entrance in their finest silk brocade robes. The day was bright with sunlight glittering off the snow and ice, and made the Imperial courtyard beyond the gate called Inpumon seem paved with silver. The atmosphere in the palace compound was one of great joy that the rebellion had been broken so swiftly.

Yet all was not joyful in the mind of Lord Kiyomori. He watched Yoshitomo carefully as they both dismounted their horses and proceeded on foot to the Great Hall of State. He watched for who among the nobles gathered seemed to be favoring Yoshitomo with bows, smiles, and nods, and whether more were favoring the Minomoto general than him. In the aftermath of a successful battle, it could be assured there would be promotions handed out and favor given. The Ise Taira commonly served the Imperial cause, so their participation in this battle might be considered merely a matter of course, while Yoshitomo was the only leader of the Kawachi Minomoto to remain loyal to the Emperor.

The court might choose to make an example of Yoshitomo, Kiyomori mused to himself, *and shower more honors upon him than upon the Taira. Surely the gods and the Dragon King will let nothing interfere with my prophesied destiny. But it is said the Minomoto are watched over by the mighty Hachiman. One cannot be too careful. Ah, well, I have a plan that may assist matters.*

Kiyomori and Yoshitomo were both guided to the verandah outside the Great Hall of State, and knelt there on cushions of gold thread and scarlet silk. From the whispers beyond the gold-leafed paper *shōji* beside him, Kiyomori knew the Emperor was already present within. He wondered that he and Yoshitomo were not ushered into the Imperial Presence itself. *After our great achievement are we still not worthy?* But he willed himself to patience. There were still some First Rank nobles who thought it improper for warriors to come near the Emperor under any circumstances. *Or perhaps that is an honor that will be bestowed upon us in time to come.*

The gold-paper *shōji* slid aside and Lesser Counselor Shinzei emerged to kneel before them. Shinzei bowed to them both, and Kiyomori thought he saw a knowing twinkle in the counselor's eye as he bowed in return. Shinzei and Kiyomori were well acquainted, having spent many evenings discussing history and politics at Rokuhara. With such a friend in high office, so close to the Emperor, Kiyomori felt reassured.

"His Imperial Majesty," Shinzei began, "would like to hear your stories about the attack on Shirakawa Palace and how events unfolded."

There was an awkward moment as it was unclear who should begin. But Shinzei nodded at Yoshitomo, indicating he should be first. Kiyomori could not help worrying as to whether there was meaning in this, or whether it would be to his advantage.

Yoshitomo spoke briefly, mentioning only that their forces divided to provide greater surprise and that the defense of the palace proved stronger than expected. If there had been disapproval of Kiyomori's actions, Yoshitomo did not voice them in any way. He finished with a description of how Shirakawa Palace had been set afire, in accordance with Imperial instructions, and how that led to the unfortunate burning of Hōshōji Temple.

Then Shinzei turned to Kiyomori, who chose to report much the same events as Yoshitomo, omitting how he fled from the demon at the southeast gate. Kiyomori went on to say he did not know of the order to burn the palace until after he and his men had already fought their way inside. Kiyomori finished by producing a scroll from his sleeve. "Here is a list, compiled by my men, of the rebels who died in the fire, and those who were captured."

Shinzei accepted the scroll, asking, "And the Shin-In? Is he among those listed here? The Emperor is most eager to know."

Kiyomori and Yoshitomo shared a brief glance before Kiyomori admitted, "No, my lord. The Former Emperor seems to have been spirited away. Very likely he has escaped to one of the nearby mountain monasteries, in which case it should be a simple matter to find him."

Shinzei made a noncommittal nod and excused himself to go into the Imperial Presence to make his report to His Majesty. Kiyomori knew the Emperor had already heard all they had said, but formalities needed to be followed. After Shinzei had slid the *shōji* shut behind him, Yoshitomo leaned over, and asked, "Are you going to tell him?"

"Tell him what?" Kiyomori replied, irritated.

"About how it was truly a demon we faced at Shirakawa Palace. About how those rumors that the Shin-In is involved with evil forces may be true."

Kiyomori replied cautiously. "In the dark, in the heat of battle, a man might imagine many things. Although he is a Retired Emperor and a rebel, the Shin-In is brother to he who currently sits upon the Jeweled Throne. To imply evil of any of the Imperial blood . . ."

"I understand," Yoshitomo said quickly. "I shall say nothing on the matter."

A minute later, Shinzei reemerged from the *shōji* and knelt before them again. "His Imperial Majesty has received your recountings with great plea-sure and commends you both on your great success. He asks now that you order your men to see that the houses of the captured and killed rebels are burned to the ground. As for your prisoners, those of lesser or no rank are to be executed as soon as possible. Any sons they may have still living shall be executed as well, in order to avoid any further rebellion in the name of vengeance. Now as to the higher-ranked rebels, and those still at large—"

Here Kiyomori put his plan into action. "Most Noble Lord, Great Hon-ored Majesty," said Kiyomori, pressing his forehead to the floorboards, "it is to my great sorrow that I admit that my own uncle, Tadamasa, took part in the rebellion. I regret that thereby he has brought shame upon on my clan and has stained our name. Therefore, I am in full agreement that he should be found as soon as possible and executed at once, as well as his sons. I shall behead them personally, for it is only proper that they meet death at the hands of a kinsman." Kiyomori sat up, looking straight ahead, careful not to glance at Yoshitomo.

Yoshitomo swallowed audibly. After a long moment, he said, "Most Noble Shinzei, Great Imperial Majesty, I also regret that my kinsmen have sided with the rebels, including my own elderly father, Minomoto Tame-yoshi." Yoshitomo flung himself forward to also press his forehead to the floorboards. "I, too, regret with deep shame that my kinsmen have sided with the rebels. I agree that Tameyoshi and my brothers should be brought to court to answer for their rebellion. Yet it would be the supreme unfilial crime for me to slay my father. I beg you, let there be mercy for him. He is old, and surely fate will carry him into the Other World soon enough. Let him live out his last years in far exile, if you must, but let him live."

Kiyomori smiled to himself, knowing this plea for mercy would not sit well with the Emperor.

Shinzei blinked at Yoshitomo. Then he said, "One moment, good gen-eral, if you please," and he hurried quickly back through the *shōji* to confer with the Emperor.

Yoshitomo remained in his prostrate position, and Kiyomori remained upright, but Kiyomori thought he heard the Minomoto general growl, "You bastard . . ."

Shinzei hurried out again to them, and said, "His Majesty replies that while it is indeed regrettable when a son must kill a father, this is not a situation in which it must be thought one of the Five Abominable Crimes. Your father has gone against Imperial authority and therefore must answer for it. Here, Lord Kiyomori has offered to execute his own uncle, Tadamasa, who has committed the same treason . . ."

An uncle who hated me, thought Kiyomori, with vengeful satisfaction.

". . . therefore how can you deny the same punishment for your father?"

It seemed Yoshitomo needed to collect himself before he replied. "There is, of course, much in what you say, Lord Shinzei," admitted Yoshitomo. "But there is a difference in the relation between a nephew and uncle, and that between a son and father. My father, I am told, has gone into hiding among the monks of Enryakuji on Mount Hiei. I expect, in time, he will be found or will give himself up. Let the time between now and then be put to thoughts of mercy, so that when he appears to answer to the court for his treason, there will be some kinder, more peaceful feelings held by all."

You are only piling mud higher on yourself, Kiyomori thought smugly. Trying to imply the threat that the warrior-monks of Mount Hiei will defend your father will not endear you to the court.

"I see," said Shinzei, perhaps a trace more coldly. "Would you be willing to go find your father at Mount Hiei and arrest him yourself?"

Lord Yoshitomo paused.

"Most Noble Shinzei and Honored Majesty," Kiyomori jumped in, "it is understandable that General Yoshitomo is disheartened by the thought of arresting and decapitating his own father. Therefore, let me and my men spare him these heartbreaking tasks. We will seek out where his father may have hidden and bring Minomoto Tameyoshi back to the capital to face justice. This is surely better than forcing a son to do such unfilial duty."

Again Lesser Counselor Shinzei excused himself to confer in the Imperial Presence a moment. This time Yoshitomo maintained an icy silence while he was gone.

Shinzei returned, and replied, "His Majesty says this offer is most generous of you, Lord Kiyomori, and therefore let it be done. But you need not depart immediately. You both are invited to stay and celebrate with us. Reward for the excellent service you have both given will be announced tonight. Therefore, stay and feast with us and let us rejoice in your victory."

So the generals stayed at the palace through the evening and into the starry night. They drank plum wine and sake, and feasted on pheasant, baked and pickled fish, sea-ear and scallops, rice with shredded daikon and *nori*, sweet red bean cakes and ginger ices. They were entertained by musicians playing *koto* and flute, and *shirabyoshi* dancers danced and sang for them. Many poems were composed that night to their valor, though they seemed more inspired by the rice wine than by art and skill.

The moon rose over the Imperial Gardens, reflecting off the artificial lake and the snow that mounded its banks. Drunken nobles and monks got up the courage to dance and sing, some more gracefully than others, beside the bronze brazier fires. Ladies laughed and flirted from behind their curtains of modesty. A feeling of peace and camaraderie amid people and furnishings of the finest quality pervaded the scene. Lord Kiyomori basked in it all in pleasant anticipation. *Someday*, he told himself, *someday I will be as often a visitor here as Shinzei or any Fujiwara. The Dragon King has promised it. Someday I will be promoted to First Rank and sit among the highest. Someday I will be allowed into the Imperial Presence, for surely a grandfather may speak to his grandson, neh? This splendid evening is but a foretaste of glory to come.*

Kiyomori wondered idly where the Sacred Regalia might be kept at the moment. He had heard that the Emperor had taken them to the East Sanjō Palace. *If the sword Kusanagi has not yet been returned to its traditional, well-guarded place, there might be an opportunity* . . . but Kiyomori quickly dismissed the thought. It would not do for him to be caught skulking around the palace. There would be time enough and better opportunity to get his hands on the sword in the future. *Besides, would it not be better to see that the Dragon King keeps his part of the bargain first? I will worry about returning Kusanagi later.*

Kiyomori saw his son Shigemori among the crowd of nobility, shyly exchanging poems with a pretty *shirabyoshi* dancer. *Now do you understand, my son, why I chose not to hurl myself into senseless death this morning? There is so much more to live for.*

Kiyomori then glanced over to where General Yoshitomo was sitting, somewhat apart from the others. Yoshitomo seemed to be distracted, his mind far from the gaiety, his laughter forced and hollow.

Good, thought Kiyomori, satisfied. *When this matter is done, he will slink home to the Kantō provinces and raise horses and speak sadly of his warrior days, never to bother with events in Heian Kyō again. With most of Yoshitomo's clan branded as traitors and little prospect of advancement for himself, the Taira need have no further fear of the once-great Minomoto.*

At midnight, the ministers came forth from the Imperial Presence to announce the promotions and rewards for the victorious warriors. Lord Kiyomori tried to hold his patience as the ministers unrolled their scrolls and droned on in praise of His Imperial Majesty's wisdom and gratitude. Finally, his name was announced.

"Lord Aki, Taira no Kiyomori, for his courage and martial skill in the service of the Emperor, shall be given, in addition to his current governorship of the province of Aki, governorship of the province of Harima, and all taxes it produces, as well."

Kiyomori sighed and bowed in acknowledgment. "I am thankful for this gift and pleased that I have the honor to be able to be of service to the Imperial house." It was not as much as he had hoped for. But it was a step, a small one, toward greater achievements. He allowed himself to be content with it. He listened acutely for what the Minomoto general would be given.

"Lord Shimotsuke, Minomoto no Yoshitomo, for his valiant efforts and great meritorious service to the Emperor, is awarded Acting Chief of the Left Horse Bureau."

Kiyomori covered his mouth to stifle a laugh. Acting Chief of the Left Horse Bureau meant essentially Master of the Imperial Stables. For a man who was also governor of a province, this was not much of an advancement. Some could even interpret it as a slight insult. True, it was a position within the Imperial palace itself, but it made one a master of horses, not men. Kiyomori noticed that one of the senior nobles on the Council was Middle Counselor Fujiwara Ienari, whose house had been burned in the taking of Shirakawa Palace. *I wonder if he had any influence in what reward the Minomoto general would or would not be given*, thought Kiyomori.

Yoshitomo got to his feet, unsteady and swaying from too much *sake*, and spoke as if stunned by surprise. "My lords, since this office has been held by an honored ancestor of mine, I am unashamed to accept it. However, it is . . . it would seem a small reward for such 'great meritorious service' as you have acknowledged that I have given to the Emperor. It is customary, I understand, to bestow at least half a province upon those who destroy enemies of the Jeweled Throne. And, as you may know, I alone of my clan chose to serve at the side of my Emperor, going against my own father and brothers, normally an unthinkable act, to obey the Imperial command. Yet . . . I am not even given the right of entry into the Emperor's presence, which was promised to me before battle began. This, when my service doubtless should qualify me for rewards greater than any other warrior has received this night!" Yoshitomo threw his arms out wide and looked around at the nobles seated near him for confirmation.

An embarrassed silence followed. And then a low, murmuring hubbub. Kiyomori leaned forward to try to catch what was being said. To his dismay, it seemed many of the black-robed First Rank nobles were agreeing with Yoshitomo's complaint. The senior ministers, who had read out the promotions, conferred with one another, and then announced they would withdraw to reconsider the matter.

As they hurried off to a chamber within the Great Hall of State, the speculation grew louder among the lords and ladies assembled as to what Yoshitomo's fate might be. Kiyomori rubbed his chin, unsettled. The Emperor might be offended by Yoshitomo's request for more, which could be useful to Kiyomori. But if the Emperor was swayed by Yoshitomo's argument—and Emperors were known to be occasionally capricious—Yoshitomo might earn a greater promotion than Kiyomori had. And that would be hard to bear. Kiyomori wondered if Yoshitomo was less drunk and more clever than he seemed.

At last, the senior ministers returned, and the nobles grew quiet in expectation of their new announcement. The Minister of the Right stepped forward wearing a pleased smile. "The Senior Council has discussed the matter of Lord Shimotsuke's claim and, with the permission of his Imperial Majesty, we have voted to change the appointment given to Minomoto Yoshitomo."

By all the bosatsu *in Paradise*, Kiyomori grumbled to himself. *Yoshitomo has won.*

"Lord Shimotsuke will no longer be awarded the post of Acting Chief of the Left Horse Bureau. His appointment has now been upgraded to . . . *Chief* of the Left Horse Bureau."

Kiyomori felt his jaw drop open. Polite, scattered applause spread among the stunned nobles. Such a small, token acknowledgment of Yoshitomo's request could not, again, quite be called insult, but it was clear the Minomoto general was not being taken seriously. Kiyomori looked at Yoshitomo and for a moment saw raw anger flash in the general's face. Then Yoshitomo bowed in acceptance and sat, clearly not daring to press his case further.

Kiyomori closed his eyes and sighed, silently thanking the Dragon King, all the *bosatsu*, his clan *kami*, the spirits of his ancestors, and whatever gods would listen. *All is unfolding as it should.*

Dragon Horses

Yoshitomo leaned against the doorway of the Stables of the Left, waiting for his groomsmen. The scent of cherry blossoms wafting from the Imperial Gardens brought him no pleasure. Their perfume seemed sickly-sweet to him, as though tainted with the smell of blood. From where he stood, he could look past the Bureau of Medicine and the Imperial Wine Office, and see workmen repairing the ornate, tiled roof of the Hall of Abundant Pleasures.

It had become the pet project of Lesser Counselor Shinzei to repair and rebuild those palace structures that had fallen into neglect in recent years. Shinzei was also encouraging the reintroduction of old pastimes to the nobility, such as poetry contests, great banquets, and sumo wrestling festivals. Praise for Shinzei was on every nobleman's lips, it seemed, as they claimed he was bringing back the gentility of ages past to Heian Kyō.

Yoshitomo was not impressed. In past times, clans such as the Minomoto were thought no more than country ruffians, and given no importance in government affairs. *Should such times return*, he thought, *there will be no hope for advancement for me or what is left of my family.*

He had already languished in the Imperial Stables of the Left for two years. Granted that Heian Kyō had been at peace; merchants no longer needed to bar their doors; and the sight of a horseman armed and armored on the streets had become rare. Granted that Yoshitomo knew much about horses, and therefore had made worthy contributions to the running of the Imperial stables. *Since when does it matter that a man has appropriate skills?* Yoshitomo thought glumly. *All that has ever mattered is having the right breeding and the favor of high-ranked nobles. And in these times, I have neither.*

Meanwhile, Yoshitomo had heard that Lord Kiyomori now lived at Rokuhara like a prince, entertaining the nobles and ladies of the highest ranks, receiving promotion after promotion. Kiyomori's eight-year-old daughter was betrothed to a Middle Counselor Fujiwara. It had been the talk of all Heian Kyō.

As he did almost every day since the end of the Hōgen Disturbance, Yoshitomo wondered what he had done to possibly offend the Emperor or the gods. How could he seem so unworthy of reward? Was it perhaps because, when his father had slipped back into the city, Yoshitomo had continued to plead for his old father's life, while Kiyomori had eagerly cut off his own uncle's and cousins' heads? Yoshitomo, pressed by Imperial order, had at last ordered a retainer to execute his father and brothers, being unable to bring himself to do the deed. *Did this make me seem cowardly or disobedient in the Emperor's eyes?*

Yoshitomo also suspected that the friendship between Shinzei and Kiyomori was no help to his own fortunes. *So long as Shinzei is in power, I will likely never see advancement again.*

His thoughts were distracted by the arrival of two grooms through the gate called Sohekimon, behind him. They were leading the two horses he was to inspect that morning. The grooms were having trouble controlling their charges, one a pale gray steed, the other a coppery bay, who strained at the ropes, rearing and trying to kick and bite. Yoshitomo smiled.

These horses were gifts sent to the Emperor from the eastern province of Sagami, a place Yoshitomo knew well. As they were Kantō horses, Yoshitomo had expected them to be fine, spirited beasts, and he was not proved wrong. Both steeds were large and well muscled. They tossed their heads and stamped their hooves as Yoshitomo approached. Their whinny was like the roar of wind in a cave. One could imagine that, if released, the horses would charge like whirlwinds, hooves striking like lightning, laying waste to all around them, possibly even each other. Yoshitomo sighed and nodded in approval.

He approached with respect and cautiously ran his hand down the muscled neck of the pale gray. The horse flared its nostrils and rolled its eyes, but it permitted the caress.

"What do you think, Yoshitomo-sama?" asked the groomsman. "Are these an appropriate gift for His Majesty?"

"Oh, yes. Indeed," Yoshitomo said. "In the East, boy, steeds such as these are called dragon horses. The best of the Kantō. His Majesty should be very pleased. I envy the warriors who will be permitted to ride them. Hachiman himself would be honored with such a mount."

The horse suddenly shied away from him with a high, piercing whinny, stamping its feet.

Yoshitomo spun around and saw behind him a pudgy, pale-faced man with slightly bulging eyes. The newcomer wore a tall hat and black-silk robes, and carried the many-fold fan of a very high-ranking noble.

"Y-yes!" said the startled nobleman. "Quite amazing. A very spirited beast."

Because it would be unwise in the extreme to offend one of such high rank, Yoshitomo held his anger in check and bowed. "Forgive me, my lord, but you should not have come so close. These horses are bred to be fierce. You might have gotten injured."

The nobleman grinned and waved his fan gracelessly. "Of course, certainly you are correct. Silly me, I always seem to be stepping into awkward situations. It is surely a gift of the gods that I ever survive them all. But . . . can it be? Could it truly be the great hero of the Hōgen standing right before me? Could this be the mighty general Minomoto no Yoshitomo himself?"

Yoshitomo, unused to high-court ways, was uncertain whether he was being mocked. "I am he, my lord."

The nobleman gasped in delight and bowed lower than he needed to. "Ah, what an honor this is, then! I have admired every tale of your exploits during the Recent Unpleasantness. The storming of Shirakawa Palace! Ah, what a triumph! What courage! And to fight against your own rebellious father and brothers—what loyalty!"

"You . . . honor me too much, my lord. I only did a warrior's duty."

"And what a sad, sad day when your father and brothers had to be executed. So many brave men dying. And the children, the blameless boys whose only crime was being born into the wrong family. I was told over seventy were executed that day."

"Yes," was all Yoshitomo could say.

"All your brothers and half brothers were then hunted down and executed, even the little ones, weren't they?"

Yoshitomo balled his fists. "Yes."

"I heard they died bravely, too." The nobleman sniffed and wiped an invisible tear from his eye with his sleeve. "None escaped, did they?"

"None." Yoshitomo managed to say. "Except . . . Tametomo."

"The one that has been called a demon?"

"Yes." Yoshitomo decided he did not like this man, who was clearly one of those nobles who felt that pity over the sorrows of others was an entertainment to be savored and wallowed in.

"What a time. I heard the rebels' heads were not even put properly on display on the tree by the prison, but they were thrown into a pond behind the Grain Storehouses to rot."

"Yes."

"You know, there has been no death penalty for three centuries, not since the reign of Emperor Saga. Then to have seventy in one day! No one dared speak of it two years ago, but now everyone is beginning to say this cannot bode well. Bad fortune must come of it, everyone says so."

Yoshitomo grunted.

"Oh, but here I am babbling at you of sorrows, when here you stand the saddest of all. You, the great general who saved the Emperor, are now a lowly judger of horseflesh in the stables. What an unfair fortune: how the gods must despair!"

Yoshitomo shifted from foot to foot, uncertain how he dared respond. Wrestling the nobleman to the ground and strangling him seemed an inappropriate choice, though it was tempting.

The nobleman tiptoed closer, so close that Yoshitomo was nearly overwhelmed by the man's perfume—a scent not unlike rotting plums mixed with cat-spray musk. "You know," the nobleman said in a conspiratorial hush, "there have been those of us who have noted your unfair treatment. Who say that you paid the higher price for your service to the Jeweled Throne and therefore are deserving of more honors. What did that upstart Kiyomori ever do that his band of brigand-bashers have not done before? Yet you, alone of your clan, stood for the rightful ruler. Such unswerving loyalty must surely be worth rewarding, neh?"

Yoshitomo paused. Was this man sent by Shinzei to test his loyalty? Had he grumbled too often to the wrong people? "What can I say, my lord?" he replied at last. "The Senior Council of Nobles saw fit to give me this post, in which I will serve to the best of my ability. A man may always hope for more, of course, but such dreams should properly be kept to oneself."

"Oh, not at all, not at all, my good general. Such dreams should be proclaimed to the world so that those in a position to make them come true will hear it. That has worked well for me, I have found. It may work for you, too. Fate is like the shifting sea, tides coming in and going out. A clam beneath the waves today may be high on the shore tomorrow. Be patient." He tapped Yoshitomo on the shoulder with his fan. "Remember there are those of us who would support you." With that, the odd nobleman turned and hurried away back toward the Hall of Abundant Pleasures.

Yoshitomo stared after him, not knowing what to think. Since the groomsmen of the Imperial stables were constant gossips, he turned to one of them. "Do you know that man?"

The groomsman stared at the bouncily retreating nobleman's back. "That is Fujiwara Nobuyori, my lord. My father says he's a good-for-nothing, boorish office seeker. Even Nobuyori's family doesn't like him. Er, please don't let anyone know I said that. But Nobuyori keeps getting titles that are not properly deserved. My father suspects that Nobuyori, because of his family's Third Rank position, can learn bad things about other people and uses it to gain favors. If this lowly one may offer advice, my lord, beware of him. As my father always says, 'To be noticed by the Fujiwara is both a blessing and a curse.' Besides, Nobuyori rather looks like a frog, doesn't he?"

"I will not repeat to anyone that you have implied any such thing," Yoshitomo said with a slight smile.

"Thank you, my lord," said the groomsman with a rushed, embarrassed bow. "I will go find a proper stall for this animal now, if I may."

"Do so." As the grooms led their snorting, stamping charges away, Yoshitomo turned and watched Nobuyori. The Fujiwara lord obsequiously greeted other nobles at the stairway leading up to the Hall of Abundant Pleasures. The ones he greeted averted their faces with the barest hint of acknowledging him and hurried away on their business.

Yoshitomo considered this, and thought, *He is repulsive. But if he is sincere, he is at least one high-ranked nobleman who acknowledges my plight, and might be willing to help change it. To a horsefly, even a frog's gaze is regard from On High. . . .*

Scrolls Thrown into the Sea

The summer air was heavy with an imminent storm. The Shin-In plucked at his light silk kimono, which was sticking to his skin. He walked aimlessly along a beach, on the northern shore of Shikoku, but even the breeze from the sea did not ease his discomfort. He felt much older than his thirty-nine years.

"How many days has it been?" the Shin-In asked the much put-upon servant who puffed along behind him.

"Days since what, Majesty? Days that you have been in exile or days since you sent the letter to Ninna-Ji?"

The Shin-In stopped and stared out across the gray, tossing water. "Either. I don't care."

"Two years, four months you have lived here in Sanuki Province, Majesty. Four months for the letter to Ninna-Ji."

The Shin-In slowly turned to face the servant. "I believe I asked for *days*."

"Y-your pardon, Majesty," said the servant, ducking his head. "Let me think . . ."

"Never mind," the Shin-In said with a sigh, and he continued walking. "Why didn't they simply execute me?" he muttered to himself.

"Because you are . . . were Emperor, Majesty! Such a thing would be unthinkable!"

The Shin-In closed his eyes. "Yes, I know. But it would have been kinder." At the end of the Hōgen Disturbance, the Shin-In had been found hiding at the Temple of Ninna-ji by Lord Kiyomori's men. He was brought back to the Imperial Compound to face justice and sentenced to far exile, to Sanuki Province on the Island of Shikoku, to the south and west of Heian Kyō.

Although Sanuki was no farther than some of the eastern provinces from the capital, it might have been the other side of the world as far as the Shin-In was concerned. He was permitted no visitors, other than the servants who brought his meals and the few ladies-in-waiting who attended him. He received no letters, not even from his wife and children, who had remained in Heian Kyō, forbidden to accompany him into exile. The warm, humid, windy shores of Sanuki were nothing like the cool, green hills of Heian Kyō. This new land was alien to him, friendless and inhospitable.

The Shin-In stopped walking again and stared out across the water, toward the north.

"Majesty?"

"It is too cloudy, of course. That is why I cannot see the coast of Honshū."

"Undoubtedly, Majesty."

"There is nothing in this day to bring me comfort. It is truly as though my life has ended. I feel suspended between two worlds, my past gone but no future existence beginning. I am a ghost."

"Please, Majesty, it saddens this lowly one to hear you speak so. Surely it cannot be so hopeless. You have spent your time here usefully, have you not?"

"I spend my time in dreams." In the two years that he had been in exile, the Shin-In often daydreamed of Heian Kyō, and the East Sanjō Palace, which he had nicknamed The Fairy Cave, after a Chinese legend. He missed the days he had spent languidly in the Dragon Pavilion and nights spent writing poems to the moon. He missed his family. But his homesick dreams would always be interrupted by the cries of unfamiliar birds, the moaning of the wind in the southern pines, and the pounding of the waves on the seashore, reminding the Shin-In that he was far, far away from anyone or anything that mattered.

"Why?" he whispered to the wind.

"Majesty?"

"Why was I even punished? I was merely being ambitious, as many men have been through the ages. Those who succeed are known as great and mighty and their names live on in legend. They become *kami* when they die."

"That is true, Majesty."

"My father was ambitious. *He* did not give up power when he left the throne. That is a usurpation of a sort, neh? And yet he was allowed to scheme and manipulate politics and live out his life with no interference. And he was mourned by all when he died. Yet I, merely because I had gathered some warriors to protect me in my endeavors, am sent into deepest exile, to a death that is not death."

"Though it is not my place to say so, Majesty, I beg you to try not to think on these things. You have already made good progress toward finding a better life to come. Surely the copy you have made of The Five Sutras Of The Greater Vehicle will be good karma for your next existence."

"Perhaps. If they find a worthy home." To ease his sorrow and homesickness, the Shin-In had copied in his own hand the lengthy Five Sutras Of The Greater Vehicle. The task had taken two years. To be of value, the sutras needed to be stored in a holy place. But there were no Buddhist temples in Sanuki Province. As the temple of Ninna-Ji had given him brief sanctuary after his defeat, the Shin-In had sent a letter to his half brother, who was abbot there. In the letter, he asked that his sutras be installed in a humble corner of the library of Ninna-Ji. It had been four months, and as yet the Shin-In had received no reply.

"Majesty, someone comes!"

The Shin-In turned around. A man was running along the shore after them, wearing the plain silk jacket and broad trousers of a clerical government functionary. The Shin-In waited for the man to catch up to them. He saw no weapons on the man, and was not sure if he felt relieved or disappointed. He sometimes dreamed that the Emperor would change his mind and send an executioner after all.

The man came up to them, gasping, and flung himself down onto the sand at the Shin-In's feet. "Former Majesty," the man said when he had caught his breath. "I bring you word from the capital, in regard to the letter you had sent to the Abbot of Ninna-ji."

The Shin-In's heart did not quite lift, but he felt some hope. "Tell me his reply, at once! Are my sutra scrolls to be accepted?"

The messenger swallowed hard before continuing. "Majesty, I must tell you, the abbot wished very much for it to be so. Often I was sent from the Chancellor's Office to the temple and back. The Chancellor even sent your appeal on to the Emperor."

"And?"

Softly, the messenger replied, "I regret that I must tell you that it is not to be, Majesty. Emperor Go-Shirakawa . . . still harbors great anger toward you. He . . . he has decreed that even your handwriting is not to be brought near the capital. It is exiled as well as you. Therefore, I have brought your letter back to you." The messenger held up the folded piece of paper, now much worn and a bit tattered.

The Shin-In took the letter. And then he crushed the paper in his hand as cold rage filled him. "Can he be so heartless, my half brother who sits upon the throne? Can he not see my sutras were an act of contrition, a striving for redemption? Hah?"

The messenger bowed his head and did not speak.

"Go."

The messenger swiftly departed.

The Shin-In closed his eyes and sucked the humid summer air between his teeth. He listened to the blood pounding in his ears and came to a decision.

"You," the Shin-In said to the servant. "Go to my residence at once and fetch the sutra scrolls. Bring them back to me here. Also bring one of my old vermilion robes but smear it with last night's ashes from the brazier in the great room. Also bring a scarf and a writing brush."

The servant had no choice but to obey. He ran to the Shin-In's forlorn house and found the long, black-lacquered box containing the sutras. One of the serving girls brought him the vermilion robe and, with great regret, he smeared the fine silk with the brazier ash. He also gathered the scarf and the writing brush and returned with them all to the beach as fast as he could.

By the time he returned, thunder was rolling across the sky, and the clouds had darkened to iron gray. Farther down the beach, an old fisherman was dragging his small boat onto the sand to wait out the oncoming storm.

"Here they are, Majesty. Now, if you please, Majesty, the weather is becoming dangerous. Will you not please take shelter?" But when he looked up into the Shin-In's eyes, he was astonished to see the change in the Former Emperor's face. The Shin-In's eyes were as hard and dark as chips of obsidian, and his brow was as threatening as the clouds above.

The Shin-In put on the ash-stained vermilion robe. Its wide sleeves flapped about him in the wind like great wings. "I have no thoughts of seeking shelter." He wrapped the scarf around his head. Then the servant watched in horror as the Shin-In knelt on the sand, bit his own tongue, and touched the writing brush to the blood beading on his lip. With this as ink, the Shin-In wrote something on the top of the scroll box. Then he stood, and said, "Come."

"M-Majesty?"

The Shin-In strode down the beach toward the fisherman, and the servant hurried to follow. "During the rebellion," the Shin-In called back over his shoulder, "I met a man, Minomoto Tametomo by name, who chose to become a demon. He told me the secret of how it is done. At the time, I thought he was mad. Now I see that he was very wise."

"Majesty, surely you cannot be considering such a thing!"

"They already think me a devil in Heian Kyō. Very well. A devil I shall become. The world of devils can have my sutras, and my soul as well."

The old fisherman looked up in astonishment as they approached him. "This is bad weather coming, my lord. Not good for a man to be out in."

"I am the Former Emperor, the Shin-In, and I want your boat."

"You . . . you can't go out on the water with this storm coming!"

"I command it!"

The old fisherman stared at the servant, who nodded regretfully. The fisherman bowed. "Very well, Majesty, the boat is yours. And may Ryujin and all his dragons be merciful to you."

"I shall require no mercy." To the servant the Shin-In said, "You will row." The Shin-In stepped into the little boat and sat down.

The fisherman and the servant pushed the boat out into the foaming water, and the servant rowed with all his might against the tide and the pounding waves. Once past the surf, the rowing became easier, but the little boat was tossed about by water and wind. The first hard rain began to fall, mingling with the tears streaming down the servant's cheeks.

At last, the Shin-In shouted against the wind, "Here! Stop here!"

The servant gratefully stopped rowing, and the Shin-In stood up in the boat. The servant was amazed that the Former Emperor was able to keep his footing.

The Shin-In held the box containing the sutras up over his head. Into the wind and the thunder, he roared, "I hereby give the power of these, The Five Sutras Of The Greater Vehicle, to the Three Evil Worlds of Hell! I, who am descended from the Great Goddess Amaterasu, have placed the power of my blood, my hand, and my vow upon these scrolls. In return, I ask to be made the Great Demon of Nihon, the Imperial Demon. Let my the rage of my spirit bring ruin and sorrow to the realm! Let it be witnessed by all the Buddhas of Heaven, the *kami* of the Earth, and the demons of Hell that I hereby lay bare the evil of my heart!"

He was answered by a blinding bolt of lightning, followed by a roar of thunder that sounded like the end of the world. The Shin-In threw the scroll box into the water, and the sea turned black. A dark whirlpool formed around the floating box, and the sutras were sucked down into the roiling water.

As the box vanished beneath the surface, a sudden calm passed over the water and the air. But it did not soothe the servant's terror. The calm was as frightening as the wind and thunder had been, the silence of deafness, the emptiness of death.

The Shin-In sat down again. "It is done. Now row us back to shore."

But the servant could not move, so shocked was he by the changes on the Shin-In's face. The Former Emperor's eyes and cheeks had become sunken and sallow. His hair stood out wildly from under his scarf. His nose and fingers had become long and crooked. Hate glowed from him, light from a very dark sun.

"I said ROW!"

The servant's arms jumped to the command, and he grabbed the oars. He pulled with all his might, rowing back toward the shore as if all the dragons of the sea were pursuing him.

Go Stones

*L*ord Kiyomori stared idly out at the side garden beyond the open *shōji*, waiting for his son Shigemori to make a move in their game of go. The leaves of the maples were just beginning to show hints of scarlet and gold, and the chrysanthemums were starting to blossom. It had been an audacious thing, planting chrysanthemums, the Imperial flower, in the gardens of Rokuhara. But Kiyomori had asked permission from the Office of the Imperial Household and it had been granted, just as so many other favors had been. In addition to being Governor of Aki and Harima, Kiyomori was now Deputy Governor-General of Daifazu, and there were intimations of more promotions and titles to come, just as Tokiko and the Dragon King had promised.

But like finding pulled threads in a costly gift kimono, all was not perfection this third year of the era of Hōgen. There were stirrings of trouble again in Heian Kyō.

"Father, I have moved."

He heard a clack on the *go* table, and Kiyomori turned his head. For a moment, he was unable to discern what move Shigemori had made. When at last he saw the new white stone, Kiyomori could not find the pattern in his son's moves. Perhaps there was none. The young man was not yet skilled in the game.

"Have you a move ready?" asked Shigemori, perhaps a bit bored.

"Give me time, my son. There is a time for swift action, and there is a time for studying the field."

Shigemori sighed. "About this matter of Go-Shirakawa retiring from the throne. What do you make of it?"

Kiyomori idly waved a hand. "It is no different from what his father tried to do before him. The Emperor is tired of ceremony and Fujiwara pressure. He wants to truly rule. An odd contradiction that he must leave the Jeweled Throne to do so, but that is the way of things these days."

"Yes, yes, of course. But why now?"

"Perhaps Heian Kyō has been at peace long enough. Perhaps Go-Shirakawa has enough faith in Taira strength to protect him. Perhaps we should take it as a compliment to our clan. Yet . . ."

Kiyomori sucked air through his teeth pensively.

"Yet?"

"Somehow I do not think Go-Shirakawa has the skill of his late father. I do not think he will be entirely . . . successful." Kiyomori leaned over the board and placed a black stone. Its position would not gain him much, but Shigemori's response might give a clue as to his son's thinking, if any.

"You are speaking of Fujiwara Nobuyori, who is making such a nuisance of himself these days, neh?" asked Shigemori as he swiftly placed a white stone that allowed him to take one of his father's black ones. "May I ask you something?"

"Of course, my son."

"If Nobuyori is truly the good-for-nothing people say he is, why was he given the post of Great Commander?"

Kiyomori sighed and set a black stone that had no purpose but to build his position on the board. "Nobuyori has campaigned for that position for a long time now. Perhaps the *In* felt that if he consented, Nobuyori would at last be content and cause no more trouble."

"Do you think that is what will happen?"

Kiyomori scratched his chin. "Men like Nobuyori . . . to them, ambition is like being drunk on *sake*. It makes them do things that to everyone else appear absurd. No, I do not think Nobuyori will be satisfied. He will find some other foolish consuming desire to strive for. What I do not understand is why our new young Emperor, Nijō, supports him so."

"Well, as to that . . ." Shigemori began.

"You have heard something?"

"Well, it is said that Nijō-sama has quite an eye for ladies."

Kiyomori chuckled. "That should not be surprising. With high rank comes desire, and being desired. All men know this." Kiyomori had certainly discovered it. Lady dancers and singers competed to perform at Rokuhara before the great Kiyomori. He often had his pick of the prettiest at the end of the night. Tokiko was not happy with the situation, but she bore it like a proper nobleman's wife: she ignored it.

Shigemori gave him an odd glance. "Ah. Well. It is said Nijō-sama has his eye on a certain lady, who is out of his reach."

Kiyomori looked up from the board, surprised. "Out of reach of an Emperor?"

"Yes, for she has already been an Empress. The Senior Grand Empress, in fact."

"Kin'yoshi's daughter, who was Emperor Konoe's consort?"

"The very same. Even though she is past her prime," said Shigemori. "Nineteen at least, possibly twenty."

"And you are but a strapping youth of twenty-two," Kiyomori gently reminded him.

"Well, it is different for a woman, neh?"

"She is still quite the beauty, I understand," said Kiyomori.

"So I have heard. Well, rumors say that Nobuyori has promised the Emperor that he will be a go-between for them, and that he will find a way to bring the Senior Empress back into the palace to become Nijō-sama's concubine. Nobuyori has helped him find other women, after all. I suppose such a service could make Nijō-sama grateful."

"Hm. Yes, I suppose. It is your turn to place a stone."

"Oh. Sorry." Shigemori chose a placement that did not seem well thought out. "With both Emperors favoring him, we will have Nobuyori causing us trouble for many years, I imagine. Always striving for greater glories he doesn't deserve. I know Middle Counselor Shinzei despises him. Odd, they are both Fujiwara, yet they are so different, those two. Unlike Nobuyori, Shinzei is a scholar and can accomplish things."

"But they are of different branches, my son. Shinzei is Southern Fujiwara, while Nobuyori is Northern. Is every Taira alike, or every Minomoto? You know better by now. You lived through the Hōgen."

"True."

"It is worth watching, this jostling amid the Fujiwara. It is as your mother once said, the old wall is developing cracks. If it crumbles, there may be great opportunity for us." Kiyomori put a stone at the edge of the board, taking two of Shigemori's.

Shigemori bit his thumbnail. "I see. Yes, one should watch more closely.

A thing I don't understand is why Shinzei became a monk all those years ago, when clearly he enjoys being involved with worldly matters. Now would be the perfect time for him to retire to a life of contemplation at Ninna-Ji, yet I hear Shinzei is moving to Sanjō Palace to join the Retired Cloistered Emperor's government." Shigemori placed a stone vaguely threatening to one of Kiyomori's positions.

"Well, as to that . . ." began Kiyomori.

"You have heard something?"

"During one visit to Rokuhara a while ago, Shinzei told me how he came to take his tonsure. One day, as he was looking at his reflection in a pond, to make sure his hair was correct before going into the palace, Shinzei saw a vision of his head stuck on the point of a sword. This distressed him, of course, so he went to the shrine at Kumano to reflect upon its meaning. There he met a physiognomist who reads men's fate in their faces. This fortune-teller confirmed Shinzei's vision of an early death by sword and suggested that if he were to become a monk quickly, perhaps such a fate might be averted." Kiyomori placed a stone in a position that might seem random, yet was part of a larger strategy.

"So Shinzei took on the monk's robes not to better his soul but merely to save himself from death?"

"What do a man's intentions matter," asked Kiyomori, "if he does the right thing? Your move."

"Oh." Shigemori placed another stone that seemed to have no purpose. "Anyway, with those two Fujiwara, Shinzei and Nobuyori, constantly trying to pull each other down, and the two Emperors, Go-Shirakawa and Nijō, getting in each other's way, nothing worthwhile will get done. What a trying and disappointing era this will be."

"Hmmm."

"You have heard the tales, have you not, that the Shin-In has somehow transformed himself into a demon? There are those who say his hatred can be felt for many *li* around Shikoku. Some say his curses upon the capital are stirring up trouble."

"It is possible, of course," said Kiyomori dismissively. "Yet it is also possible that Go-Shirakawa is . . . encouraging such stories."

"About his own brother, a former Emperor?"

"And a former rebel against the throne. So long as the Shin-In lives, there is a danger that some dissatisfied faction or other will try to support him, or one of his sons. Perhaps the rumors of the Shin-In's transformation are simply that—slander intended to make anyone who might take the Shin-In's side hesitate. Slander is a powerful weapon, my son, to be used carefully and guarded against with great vigilance."

Shigemori nodded thoughtfully. "So you have often said. It is sad. We sit like frogs in dry summer grasses, awaiting the day a bolt from Heaven will ignite a fire. Then we Taira must be called upon to put it out."

"That is why the Chinese character for *danger* also means *opportunity*, my son."

"But here we are, the most powerful clan in terms of military might, and yet we can do nothing to prevent trouble."

Kiyomori tapped a finger idly against his lips and regarded the board. "I would not say so. In the Hōgen, we stopped a rebellion before it spread. Many died, but it could have been much, much worse."

"But until a rebellion begins, we cannot know where to direct our power. One cannot put out a fire before it starts."

Kiyomori allowed himself a slight smile as a plan grew in his mind. "Not necessarily true, my son." He placed a black stone. "As we were just speaking of Kumano, I have intended for a long time to make a pilgrimage to the shrines there. When Toba-In did so, he found it most enlightening, as did Shinzei. Your mother has often encouraged me to give more observance to the gods. I expect I would learn something . . . worthwhile by making the effort. We could go together, you and I. Perhaps in a month or two."

"Father!" Shigemori sat up. "Is that not a most ill-considered move?"

"Hmm?"

"Look, I can place this stone here and take these three of yours. You must be more attentive and not leave your pieces open to capture so."

Kiyomori smiled. "Ah. But if I now place my stone *here*"—he set down a black stone with a loud *clack*—"I can take ten of yours. See?" With deft sweeps of his fingers, Kiyomori removed Shigemori's pieces from the table. "Now, you were saying?"

Shigemori drew his knees up under his chin. "Nothing, Father. It is clear there is much more for me to learn about this game."

"Ah."

Horse Bridles

Early one morning that same month, Minomoto Yoshitomo sat in a storeroom near the stables, going over the lists of broken saddles, torn bridles, lost stirrups, and the like, trying to make up the monthly request for new equipment. He grumbled to himself, knowing it would take weeks for the request to go through one bureaucratic office after another, needing seal after seal of approval, before replacements would actually be supplied. "In the Kantō," he muttered, "an Eastern lord need only demand of his retainers to make more, or commandeer supplies from those who owe him favors. None of these petitions, seals, and countersignings. It is a wonder the Imperial palace can muster mounted warriors at all."

Yoshitomo was suddenly distracted by the creak of sounding boards outside the doors and an unmistakable scent of fox musk and overripe plums. "My lord Nobuyori, please enter," Yoshitomo called out. "What may I do for you?"

Nobuyori slid the door aside and peered in. "Good morning, Yoshitomo-san. How did you know it was me?"

"A warrior must keep his senses well honed," said Yoshitomo, not wishing to say that the nobleman reeked.

"Yes, yes!" said Nobuyori. "I knew you were the man I should talk to." He slid the door shut behind him and clattered up to Yoshitomo.

Yoshitomo tried not to cough. "On what may I inform you, my lord?"

"On all matters martial, good general. Perhaps you have heard, have you not, that I have been appointed Great Commander?"

Yoshitomo bowed. "I have heard, my lord, and you have my congratulations." Privately, he wondered what sort of idiots they were in the Council to have made such an appointment, but the ways of nobility had always baffled him.

"But you have probably not heard of the great efforts made by that underhanded schemer, Middle Counselor Shinzei, to block that appointment?"

"No, my lord, I have not."

"The slanders he has spread as to why I was not worthy . . . has anyone ever heard of such a thing? It is as if he insults the wisdom of the Emperor."

Yoshitomo made commiserating noises.

"That is why I am here, General. It is becoming clear that Shinzei will stoop to anything to be rid of me. I believe even assassination would not be beyond him. Therefore, I wish to learn to defend myself. I wish to learn fighting and archery and horsemanship. To become a great warrior, like you. Then, perhaps, I need not fear Shinzei. Then, perhaps, I might do away with Shinzei myself before he can do anything to me. Hah!"

Yoshitomo gazed at the plump, clumsy nobleman who had probably never lifted anything heavier than a fan, and decided Nobuyori was either woefully ignorant or quite mad. However, Nobuyori was a politically very powerful madman, who at present looked with favor upon Yoshitomo—a fact not to be discarded lightly. "My lord," Yoshitomo said, "while it would be my honor to train you, I am not, in truth, the best man for such things.

You should inquire of my cousin, Minomoto Moronaka, who I believe is now Fushimi Middle Counselor. He is an excellent teacher, I hear, and as well versed in the fighting arts as I am if not more so."

"Ah. You are right, you are right," muttered Nobuyori. "It would look strange, my hanging about the Imperial stables, neh? Moronaka has a large residence nearby where I could hide and do these things without attracting notice. I knew it was a good choice to rely on your wisdom, Yoshitomo."

"I am glad I may be of service, my lord." *And glad I will not need to smell you day after day.*

Fingering a bridle of braided rope hanging on the wall, Nobuyori said idly, "I am thinking of having my son Nobuchika betrothed to one of Lord Kiyomori's daughters. That might give me and my family a tie to the Ise Taira in case . . . some unpleasantness should occur. What do you think?"

Yoshitomo swallowed hard, suppressing his dismay. "My lord, I must confess that I think it unwise. You know what good friends Kiyomori is with Middle Counselor Shinzei, whom we both have reason to be suspicious of. Such a marriage would be giving the Taira connections to your Emperor, which the Taira might then use to their advantage on behalf of the Retired Emperor Go-Shirakawa and Shinzei, perhaps shutting you out of your Emperor's favor. You know what scheming social climbers the Taira are. Besides, Kiyomori is so arrogant that he would probably turn your request away, claiming your son is unsuitable. Think how embarrassing that might be. Remember, even as high as they have risen, the Taira are only a provincial warrior clan, such as my own. You, however, are Fujiwara. Surely your son deserves a wife of better family."

Nobuyori turned, smiling. "Again, you speak much wisdom, Yoshitomo-san. I am glad I have consulted you." Coming closer, Nobuyori lowered his voice conspiratorially. "You understand, General, there may come a time soon when I will rely upon you for more than advice. I have already spoken with Great Counselor Fujiwara Tsunemune and Middle Commander Narachika, as well as Commissioner of Imperial Police Korekata. They have all pledged their support to me in case some discord should arise. May I have your pledge as well?"

Yoshitomo recognized it was one of those moments when one's life stands at a crossroads. The seconds slowed down, and his heartbeat sounded like thunder in his ears. He knew if he equivocated or hesitated longer, he might be trapped as Chief of the Left Horse Bureau for the rest of his life. Or worse, his post might be taken from him and his sons denied appointments so long as Nobuyori remained in power. But Nobuyori was allied with the present Emperor, was he not? And Yoshitomo always loyally served the Emperor.

Yoshitomo remembered the oracle at Hachimangu—success, but with great cost. Surely the cost had already been paid, with the death of his father and brothers and his toil in the stables. What was left but success to be achieved? If Yoshitomo served the Emperor and Nobuyori, well, might he not rise as high as Lord Kiyomori and the Ise Taira? Or higher?

Yoshitomo bowed low. "I will obey you wholeheartedly in whatever great undertaking you ask of me, my lord. I give you my pledge."

"Oh, good, good, good." Nobuyori clapped his hands like a delighted child. "I knew I could count on you. And in return, if there is anything you wish, you need only ask it of me."

Tentatively, Yoshitomo picked up the equipment list and held it out to Nobuyori. "My lord, the stables are badly in need of these items . . ."

Nobuyori snatched the paper out of his hands. "Done, done, and done! If great things are to be accomplished by Imperial horsemen, they must be well equipped, neh? I shall see to it at once." He turned to depart, then added, "We will speak again soon, good general, I am certain of it."

As the sliding door clacked shut, Yoshitomo took a deep breath. He paused to offer prayers to Hachiman . . . praying that he had made the right choice.

The Gift of a Sword

Two months passed and winter fell, a gentle blanket of cold settling over Heian Kyō. In the last month of the year, as he had intended, Lord Kiyomori left Rokuhara with his eldest son. Taking only a few servants, and wearing only the plain white robes of pilgrims, the head of the Taira clan and his heir departed for the journey to Kii Province and the Kumano Shrine.

Minomoto Yoshitomo knew matters had come to a head when he was awakened late in the night with a summons to report to Lord Nobuyori at the Imperial palace. Yoshitomo dressed and dutifully rode through the deserted, snow-dusted streets, both dreading and anticipating what he would hear. He bowed low as he entered Nobuyori's chambers in the Civil Affairs Ministry.

The room was outfitted with the finest painted-silk screens showing scenes from ancient mythical battles. Beautiful bronze lamps and braziers lit and warmed the room. Cushions were strewn everywhere, and Nobuyori was writing at a desk of carved teak with inlaid mother-of-pearl. Nobuyori wore heavy scarlet brocade robes that rivaled those of the Emperor himself in gaudiness. Yoshitomo could not reconcile his feelings of envy and disgust at the display of excessive wealth. "You sent for me, my lord?"

"Yes, yes, yes!" Nobuyori leapt to his feet and came over to Yoshitomo. Yoshitomo tried not to breathe deeply. "My good general, our hour has come at last!"

"My lord?"

"Surely you have heard that Kiyomori has departed to go on a months-long pilgrimage to Kumano?"

"I have heard rumors to that effect, my lord."

"Well, don't you see? Shinzei's watchdog has gone running off; his son, too, leaving the Taira leaderless. Now is our chance!"

"Chance, my lord?"

Nobuyori clicked his tongue. "You need not pretend to be the fool with me, General. We both know that Shinzei is an arrogant troublemaker who wishes to run the Empire. Even His Imperial Majesty thinks so, but has had no opportunity to do anything. The longer Shinzei stays in the world, the more calamities and confusions we will see."

Yoshitomo could only agree, though his reasons were personal.

"And what will become of you, good general?" Nobuyori went on. "So many of your clan have already met with disaster—would it not be a simple thing for the government of the Retired Emperor, with the help of the Taira, to wipe you all out completely? With Kiyomori so closely tied to the Retired Cloistered Emperor who is so closely tied to Shinzei, well, the wish of one becomes the duty of the other."

This, Yoshitomo had to concede, was a fear close to his heart.

"Do you not think," Nobuyori went on, "that now we are given this opportunity like a gift from Heaven, that we should not take it? What fools we would be to let Shinzei continue in his usurping of powers when it might lead to our own destruction. Surely, in the name of He Who Sits Upon The Jeweled Throne, we should strike while we can and restore peace to the Empire."

Yoshitomo clenched and unclenched his fists a moment. "I have long suspected," he said at last, "that Kiyomori would do away with me the first chance he saw. It is fitting, therefore, that, my chance coming first, I should do the same to him. Since you are now asking for the aid I have pledged, if the signs are propitious, I will with full heart put to the test the fortunes of the Minomoto."

"Excellent!" said Nobuyori. "I had expected such loyalty. Therefore, I have a gift for you." Nobuyori drew from beneath his writing table a magnificent *tachi* sword and gave it to Yoshitomo.

Yoshitomo bowed deeply. "I am honored by your gift, my lord, and I hope to use it well."

"I have another gift for you as well. Come." Nobuyori shouted to some servants, "Bring them out!" Then he led Yoshitomo outside. It was very dark and beginning to snow, so Nobuyori had to call for torches. When servants lit their torches and held them aloft, Yoshitomo gasped.

Standing before him were the two magnificent dragon horses, the gray and the bay. On their backs were wooden "mirror saddles" whose pommels and cantles were ornamented with highly polished gold.

"I remembered that you had admired these animals," said Nobuyori, "and I heard you had some hopes of riding them yourself. I made your wishes known to Emperor Nijō, and, because of your esteemed service, he wishes the horses to be yours."

"I . . . I am overwhelmed, my lord."

"I make note of what pleases people," said Nobuyori proudly, "and when they are my friends and serve me well, I see that they get what they most desire. I have found that such generous effort is never poorly spent."

Yoshitomo went up to the gray horse and ran his hand along its neck. "When a warrior goes into battle, nothing is so important as his horse. With steeds such as these, how could we not win against our enemies, no matter how strong they may be?"

"My thoughts exactly, good general."

Yoshitomo turned back to Nobuyori. "You should summon my distant cousins Suezane, Yorimasa, and Mitsumoto. They also have interest in our clan's survival, and I hear they, too, have been secretly planning for an event such as this. They may have wise strategies to offer."

"I will do so, good general. And I will send to your household fifty new suits of armor which I have had made for just such an occasion."

"My lord has great forethought."

"I have learned, my good general, that nothing is achieved without it. Go home and prepare your men. I will soon let you know the hour and manner of our attack upon that schemer Shinzei."

A White Rainbow

Five days later, in midmorning, Middle Counselor Shinzei stood in the garden of his mansion, admiring how the fresh-fallen snow lay upon the shaped pines and the bridge across the pond. A glint of light caught his eye, a reflection off the steaming water, and Shinzei looked up into the sky. There, behind a thin veil of clouds, he saw a white rainbow intersecting the sun. A chill filled his bones. It was an omen, but of what he could not be certain.

With so much uncertainty in the capital, and that idiot Nobuyori constantly scheming, Shinzei felt any omen should be paid attention to. After all, the vision he saw in a pool of standing water long ago had led to his avoiding death at the point of a sword. At least, so far. *And with Kiyomori's departure upon his pilgrimage . . .* The chief of the Taira clan had confided in Shinzei the reasons for his winter trip to Kumano. "If nothing occurs while I am gone," Kiyomori had said, "then it will reassure the people that peace remains with us, despite the changes in government. But it may cause Nobuyori to do something foolish, and thereby we can draw the poison from the wound before it spreads too far."

Shinzei had advised it was too risky, but who can tell a Taira anything, particularly the stubborn Kiyomori? So now the Taira were without their commander, and a white rainbow hung across the sun like a pale ghost, a finger of warning.

Shinzei's sons were attending an entertainment at the Retired Emperor's Sanjō Palace, so Shinzei knew he would have no trouble gaining admittance to Go-Shirakawa's presence. He could warn the *In*, and perhaps someone who had served in the Yin-Yang Office could give better counsel as to what the omen meant. Shinzei called for his oxcart to be brought to his mansion gate, and he went to the Sanjō Palace.

But when he arrived and stood in the courtyard of Sanjō Palace, Shinzei could hear the most heavenly music of *koto* and flute. Men were singing happy *saibara*, accompanied by the slap of the *gosechi* dancers' fans. Shinzei looked up and saw that the rainbow had vanished. *How dare I disturb such beauty and happiness with tales of a dire omen? One that is no longer even visible. It is possible I imagined it. We are given so few moments of peace and joy in this troubled world.* Shinzei left a message with a servant and departed.

But as he sat once more in the ox-carriage, heard the crack of the ox-driver's whip and the rumble of the wheels beneath him, Shinzei could not shake a sense of foreboding. As if the beautiful music he heard at Sanjō Palace was the last fragrance of cherry blossoms about to fall. Shinzei considered matters and realized he had no reason to remain in the capital at the moment. The plans for the New Year's festivities had been settled many days ago. It would cause no harm if he were to leave for a little while, and if the omen was important, it might save his life. Nara was only thirty *li* away, only a long day and a half's journey. *The monks of the temples there all support me, and I could return quickly, if need be. Lord Kiyomori thought it safe enough to depart on a pilgrimage. Why shouldn't I?*

When he returned home, Shinzei went to his wife and told her about the white rainbow. "It may be nothing, but as a precaution, I think I will take a short pilgrimage to the temples at Nara."

"That seems very wise," she said. "But please, if you think there is danger, take me with you."

Shinzei waggled his hand. "No, no, that should not be necessary. As I have said, it is probably nothing."

"But if it is *not* nothing, then these are the last hours I will see you, and these are the last words we will share. How could I bear knowing this?"

Shinzei sighed and at last told her the real reason. "You know how suspicious Nobuyori is of everything I do. How he believes I plot against him."

"But you *do* plot against him."

"Yes, but only in small matters."

"I doubt he believes your attempt to block his promotion was a small matter."

"*Nevertheless*, it might call his attention too much to my departure if you come with me. He might think I am trying to get you to a place of safety because I am planning some military action. Therefore, I will go alone. Be at peace, wife," he said, patting her arm. "It is very likely nothing, and soon we will be sipping the New Year's wine together with all contentment."

His wife had no choice but to relent. So the next morning, with only four retainers to accompany him, Shinzei departed for Nara. His last glimpse of his wife was of her standing on the mansion verandah, wiping away tears with her sleeve.

When evening fell, Shinzei stopped to spend the night at an estate called Daidoji. While chatting with his host, Shinzei happened to notice, through the open *shōji*, an odd configuration of stars. Jupiter and Venus were in conjunction. Shinzei was well taught in astrology and immediately knew the meaning of this new omen. "A loyal minister will sacrifice himself for his lord." Shinzei gulped down his rice and *sake* quickly to hide his sudden trembling, for he feared the loyal minister might well be himself.

The Well at Sanjō Palace

That night, at midnight, the Hour of the Rat, General Minomoto Yoshitomo and five hundred mounted men rode toward Sanjō Palace. He had the strange feeling he had slipped back in time, for here it was again winter, the streets of Heian Kyō dusted with snow, and here he was again about to make a surprise night attack upon a palace. It had worked to quell the Hōgen Rebellion, the reasoning went, and therefore it should work again. At least this time, he did not have the treacherous Kiyomori to deal with.

However, he did have the foolish Lord Nobuyori riding with him. Despite Yoshitomo's grave misgivings, Lord Nobuyori had insisted on accom-

panying the attack force himself. The corpulent Fujiwara apparently thought
his few months of *bugei* training with Yoshitomo's cousin had made him a
warrior. Yoshitomo had had no choice but to relent and hope the Fujiwara
lord would do nothing stupid.

When they reached Sanjō Palace, Yoshitomo chose to take no chances.
He split his force of five hundred horsemen, one hundred to each of the
five gates of the palace. He posted himself and Nobuyori with the hundred
at the main gate of the palace. An Imperial ox-carriage had been brought
along, and this was stationed just in front of the main gate as well.

The parts of the palace Yoshitomo could see were gaily lit with lanterns
in anticipation of the coming New Year's festivities. Yoshitomo allowed
himself a brief moment of pity for those within, for their holiday season was
about to be rudely shattered.

One of the palace guardsmen cautiously peered over the palace wall,
and called out, "Who is it who disturbs the peace of the Retired Cloistered
Emperor and the streets of the Imperial capital with such a show of arms?"

Nobuyori nudged his horse forward. "It is I, Fujiwara Nobuyori, Great
Commander and Colonel of the Gate Guards of the Right. While your lord,
the *In*, has favored me for many years, his chancellor Shinzei has slandered
against me and plotted against me, and intends to do me harm. In order to
prevent this, we have come."

The guardsman vanished behind the wall for some moments, then reap-
peared. "We have heard no such thing. Your fears are groundless. Go home
and leave us in peace."

"I do not care what you have or have not heard," Nobuyori shouted
back. "I have five hundred men surrounding Sanjō, led by the famed general
Minomoto Yoshitomo, who serves none but the true Emperor Nijō. We
wish no harm to the person of the Retired Cloistered Emperor Go-
Shirakawa himself. Bring him out so that we can ensure his safety."

"Bring him out? Why? What do you intend?" shouted the guard, nervously.

"The destruction of Shinzei and all who serve him!"

"Middle Counselor Shinzei is not here!"

"You might well be lying to save him. No matter. Bring out the *In*
before we begin our attack, or you will be responsible for the death of one
of Imperial blood."

There was the sound of hurried discussion behind the gate and shouting
within the palace. Presently, former Emperor Go-Shirakawa, now thirty-two
years old, and his sister, Jōsaimon'in, emerged from the front gate in dressing
robes.

"What is the meaning of this!" Go-Shirakawa exclaimed. "No one has threatened you, Nobuyori-san. You have been given all you asked for, including your title of Great Commander."

"I have not been given peace, Majesty. I spend sleepless nights wondering when your much-pampered minister Shinzei will succeed in some plot against me. Therefore, I strike first, in order to rid the capital of his menace before he can do any real harm."

"Have you not been told? Shinzei is not here!"

"Your Majesty is, perhaps, mistaken. My informants tell me Shinzei has not been seen at his residence tonight. Where would he be but Sanjō, which has been like a second home to him? I intend to root him out like the weasel he is. For your safety, I urge you and your sister to get into the carriage."

With an expression dark as storm clouds, the Retired Emperor said, "This is a great injustice and an offense to the gods. You will not succeed."

"I serve the true Emperor who sits upon the Jeweled Throne. I believe this puts the gods firmly on my side." Nobuyori turned his horse, and called out the order, "Set the fires!"

Go-Shirakawa turned and glared at Yoshitomo. *He thinks me a traitor, because it was he whom I fought for in the Hōgen. He who then rewarded me with a post in the Imperial stables. But I serve the throne, not the man who once sat upon it.* Yoshitomo kept his face impassive and gestured toward the ox-carriage.

As the first flaming arrows arced over the wall and onto the palace roof, Go-Shirakawa and his sister hastily bustled into the carriage. The carriage was shut and locked, and then immediately surrounded by Nobuyori, Yoshitomo, his Minomoto cousins, and fifty horsemen in order to prevent the possibility of rescue.

"Go!" Nobuyori ordered the ox-driver, and the carriage was drawn away from the palace. Yoshitomo could already feel heat against his back from the flames leaping on the palace rooftops. His ears were ringing with the screams of women and children, and he expected to see them fleeing from the palace gates at any moment.

But Nobuyori turned in his saddle and shouted out one final order. "Shoot them all, any who emerge from the buildings. Even women or children. They might be Shinzei in disguise or members of his family. No one must escape alive!"

Yoshitomo stared at Nobuyori aghast.

But Nobuyori merely smirked back at him. "A true warrior must be thorough, neh?"

As he followed the ox-carriage back to the Imperial Compound, Yoshitomo's stomach sickened as he heard behind him the many flights of arrows and the screams that followed. *It will bring peace*, he told himself. *It will return glory to my clan.* But he could not help feeling it would be a dishonorable peace and dishonorable glory.

At the Imperial Compound the carriage was led away to one of the outbuildings where the Retired Emperor would be imprisoned. Yoritomo then took fifty men and went out on another heart-rending mission.

They rode through the dark streets to Anegakoji Mansion, Shinzei's residence. The guards at the gate were wary, watching the glowing smoke rising from Sanjō. When Yoshimoto announced himself, the guards greeted him as a friend and ally.

"How good that you have come to protect us, Lord General!" said one guard. "Who is it who dares attack the Retired Emperor? Is it the Taira?"

Yoshitomo decided to be blunt. "We come seeking your master, Shinzei, who has been judged a traitor against the Emperor. Bring him forth and there will be no trouble."

"But . . . but he is not here!"

"By your refusal to cooperate," Yoshitomo said, "I must assume you are all traitors as well." Turning to the horsemen behind him, Yoshitomo ordered, "Release your arrows."

Again, an arc of flaming shafts flew overhead to lodge among roof-tiles and paper walls. The mansion caught fire swiftly and the screams of men, women, and children again pierced the air. Shinzei's wife and sons and grandsons were paying the price for Shinzei's petty scheming.

"Remember, none are to escape," Yoshitomo ordered his men. Then he turned away from the slaughter and destruction, and galloped back to the Imperial Compound to help defend against any counterattack that forces loyal to Go-Shirakawa might muster. All night long, Yoshitomo waited with the Imperial Guard at Suzaku Gate, watching. But no attack came. Yoshitomo was disappointed, hoping for some strenuous swordplay to distract him from his disquiet. He could not understand how a man might do the right thing, and yet also be committing evil. Yet he was also certain this was what he had done.

By dawn's light, the news came back to him of the horror that had been committed at Sanjō Palace. It was said the buildings were infernos to rival the flames of Hell. Almost all who had tried to escape the flames—courtiers, women, and children—were impaled with arrows or slashed with swords. The well of Sanjō had filled with the bodies of those trying to avoid both the flames and the weapons, who instead met with drowning, crushing, or suffocation. The heads of those few Taira who tried to defend Sanjō were taken and hung upon the Taiken Gate of the Imperial palace. The loss of life of Those Who Dwelled Above The Clouds was uncountable. Besides the *In* and his sister, only Go-Shirakawa's consorts and their ladies-in-waiting had managed to escape.

Yoshitomo sighed and sagged in his saddle, feeling the weight of a long night pressing upon him. *Success at great cost*, the oracle had said. But the cost had been far greater than Yoshitomo had ever imagined it would be.

Promotions in the Hall

The following evening, Yoshitomo knelt in the Great Hall of the Palace of Administration. The black-robed, tall-hatted nobles around him chattered pleasantly, as if the horror committed the night before was no more than a slight winter storm, a troubling nuisance but a trifling matter. Yoshitomo was at once honored to be in so exalted a company, yet a part of him was mildly disgusted. He was not sure why, at first. But as he observed the expectant gleams in their eyes and heard their false laughter, he understood. These men were not celebrating a victory well fought and well earned. They were simply giddy with greed, like thieves after a particularly profitable raid.

Yoshitomo wondered why the young Emperor Nijō himself was not present. *Perhaps he, too, is dismayed by these events, and wishes to distance himself from them. After all, his father is imprisoned in the Single-Copy Library. Surely that cannot be pleasing to him. It is most unfilial of him, really, even to permit it.* But Yoshitomo knew well enough from his own experience that events sometimes demanded one do unfilial things.

Yoshitomo glanced around at the huge scarlet pillars supporting the intricately carved and gilded roof beams. There was the faint odor of fresh paint and glue. Only recently had Middle Counselor Shinzei had this hall repaired and restored to its former glory of three centuries before. In the center of the room, dressed only in scorched underrobes and bound hand and foot, knelt five young men, Shinzei's sons, who had been captured running from the Anekagoji Mansion. Is it Nobuyori's cruelty, wondered Yoshitomo, or simply the jest of the gods that here within Shinzei's finest restoration, other creations of Shinzei's will be stripped of their offices and, possibly, their heads.

How true it is, thought Yoshitomo, *that at any time a man's luck may simply run out. Though I am promoted today, tomorrow my life might be in ruins.*

Yoshitomo looked down the long room at Nobuyori. The Great Commander sat on a dais scarcely lower than the Emperor's, squatting like a fat black toad. He seemed particularly giddy, which bothered Yoshitomo a great deal. *He, of all people, should understand and reflect the seriousness of what we have done.*

A scroll was delivered into Nobuyori's hands, and with an expression of great delight, the Great Commander rapped upon the edge of his dais with his baton of office. "If I may have your attention, gentlemen!" he announced. "The time you have surely all been waiting for has arrived."

The room quieted, though a low, expectant hubbub remained. Shinzei's sons looked up toward the dais, but there was no hope in their eyes.

Nobuyori cleared his throat and unrolled the scroll. "It is hereby declared to be the will of the Emperor and the Senior Council of State that the offspring of the renegade counselor Fujiwara Michinori, now known as Shinzei, will be dismissed from their offices, and all posts, income, and property taken from them and denied to their families in perpetuity. An investigation into their activities has been begun by the Council of Ministers, and should evidence of treason against the throne be found—"

Which is almost certain, thought Yoshitomo.

"—they will receive that justice due to traitors and rebels." Nobuyori looked up from the scroll. "I understand one son is still missing."

"My lord," said the Master of the Gate Guards of the Right, coming forward, "there is. He is a son-in-law of Taira Kiyomori and has gone to Rokuhara for sanctuary."

"Then send an Imperial order to Rokuhara summoning him," Nobuyori snapped. "If the Taira refuse, then we will know more about them, won't we?"

"Hai, my lord." The Master of the Gate Guards bowed.

"And take these away to the prison." Nobuyori waved his baton at the bound men.

"As you command, my lord." A member of the Gate Guards unbound Shinzei's sons' feet, and the men were led away. As they passed by him, Yoshitomo noted the expression on their faces. The look of men who were already dead.

"Now on to more pleasant things," said Nobuyori. "For myself, His Imperial Majesty has done me the honor to declare me both Minister of State and Great Commander."

This produced quite a stir in the hall, and Yoshitomo began hearing whisperings that this was not the doing of the Emperor at all, but Nobuyori himself. *What has happened to the Emperor?* Yoshitomo wondered.

His attention was jolted back to his surroundings when he heard his name announced. "—Minomoto Yoshitomo, for his great and meritorious service to the Emperor, shall be awarded the governorship of Harima."

Yoshitomo bowed while polite applause rippled around him. There was a certain sweet victory in receiving a post that had belonged to Kiyomori. But as he waited for more, Nobuyori went on to other names.

That is all? Is this my success at great cost? One governorship? But Yoshitomo again counseled himself to patience. *It is a step ahead, and there may well be more in future. Kiyomori is not yet returned, and there may be more chance to prove my worth in days to come.*

He felt a tugging at his sleeve and looked around. A servant had knelt beside him. "My lord Yoshitomo, a young man is outside, claiming to be your eldest son. He wishes to speak with you."

Yoshitomo smiled. *Ah, Akugenda. He must have heard there was fighting. He will be so upset that he missed it.* Yoshitomo rose to depart.

But Nobuyori again rapped the edge of his dais with his baton. "What is this? What is this? If it is an important message for my most trusted general, I believe we should all hear it."

"Fear not, it is no news of consequence, my lord," said Yoshitomo. "It would seem my oldest son Akugenda Yoshihira has ridden to the capital from Sagami, where he has been staying with his grandfather this past year. He asks to see me. Therefore, may I may be dismissed from this august gathering?"

"But this is wonderful news! Another brave Minomoto comes to the palace. I have heard rumors of your son's excellent valor. You need not depart. Your son is permitted to join us. Send him in."

"Ah. Thank you, Nobuyori-sama."

The messenger departed, and soon Akugenda Yoshihira entered, his hair still tangled from the wind and his garments still redolent with sweat of man and horse. Somewhat nervously, Yoshihira bowed to the hall and knelt by Yoshitomo. "Father, I have ridden all this way hearing there was a disturbance in the capital. If there is danger, if there is any way I may serve, I am here to fight by your side."

"Of course. But I regret to tell you—" Yoshitomo began but was over-ridden by Nobuyori.

"Well said, well said, young man!" exclaimed Nobuyori, clapping his hands. "What your brave father was about to say is that the disturbance is over. Nevertheless, there remains much to be done to right the wrongs that precipitated it. Your timing is excellent. We were just handing out promotions to the worthy who are assisting us in our cause. Your father is one such, and as you are his son, you will be another. What rank and office would you like? High or low, large or small province, it can be yours."

Akugenda Yoshihira blinked, bewildered. "Most high lord, you honor me too much. I have been taught that rewards must be earned, and I have not yet accomplished anything. It is too soon for me to accept a post. Let me prove myself first. I have heard that Lord Kiyomori is away on pilgrimage. Let me await him with a force of warriors at Abeno Plain. He is protected only by his servants, and he and his son may be easily captured and killed. When I bring their heads back to you, mighty lord, then may you give me provinces and higher rank."

This was heard by all the nobles in the hall, and they sighed and nodded with approval. Nobuyori himself wiped his face with a sleeve as if dabbing a tear from his eye. "Oh, well said, well said. Truly your son has a warrior's blood, my general."

Yoshitomo bowed in acknowledgment. "I am most proud of him, my lord."

"Do all your sons have such potential, General?"

"All of them, my lord." Yoshitomo was about to tell the story of his youngest, Yoritomo, who was now thirteen, and the strange oracle at Hachimangu. But then he stopped himself, concerned as to what Akugenda Yoshihira might think. Like any man of consequence, Yoshitomo had had, in addition to his principal wife, several concubines and lovers, all of whom had borne him children. Yoshitomo was well aware of the dangerous jealousies and rivalries that could erupt between brothers and half brothers. If he boasted of his youngest, it might seem a slight to his eldest, and Akugenda Yoshihira might never forgive his little brother Yoritomo. *We few Minomoto who are left must fight together to keep our clan alive. This is Akugenda's moment. Let him bask in it unchallenged.*

"However," Nobuyori's voice cut into Yoshitomo's thoughts, "your scheme of an attack at Abeno shows the inexperience and enthusiasm of youth. There is no need to go so far when the enemy is coming to you. Why wear out your horses? And you would only catch two Taira that way. Let Kiyomori and his son return to Rokuhara, where the rest of the Taira wait in their lair. Then we may surround them all and do whatever we wish. Trust me, we have had some recent success with such a plan."

A dark chuckle emerged from the assembled noblemen. One of them commented, "Here we are giving rank to men for having killed many people. We ought to give the well at Sanjō rank and promotion, too, for did it not kill many people?"

All the nobles present laughed aloud at this as though they thought it quite amusing. Or were pretending to. Yoshitomo was sickened, and ashamed for Nobuyori's offhand rebuke to his son, but he dared reveal nothing of these feelings. *By whatever karma I have made for myself, I am bound to this toad of a man.*

"Father", Akugenda Yoshihira said softly in his ear, "Lord Kiyomori is not such a fool as Go-Shirakawa, and Rokuhara is not a genteel palace but a compound brimming with armed men. If the Taira chief returns to Rokuhara and rallies his clan, the fight will be much more difficult. Why don't these men see that?"

Yoshitomo sighed. "These are Men Who Dwell Above The Clouds, my son. They do not see earthly matters that are beneath them."

"Perhaps I will go to Abeno anyway."

Yoshitomo caught his son's sleeve and tugged it hard. "Have you forgotten all I have taught you? A samurai obeys his lord."

"And if the lord is foolish and we die as a result?"

"Then we die as well as we can, and allow our deaths to shame him."

"It seems to me these men are not capable of shame."

Yoshitomo had no answer for that.

Shinzei's Head

Two days later, Yoshitomo had another displeasing duty. The day before, Shinzei had been reported found, buried alive. The Middle Counselor had apparently had news of Sanjō and had tried to commit suicide, in a method that would give him a lengthy time to chant sutras and pray before his body expired. But Nobuyori's men had found him first and ended what was left of Shinzei's life abruptly. Shinzei's head was being brought back to Heian Kyō to be paraded triumphantly down Suzaku Avenue, and Yoshitomo had to be witness to the procession.

"I tell you, I have never felt such joy," said Nobuyori, leaning out the window of his ox-carriage, "as the moment this morning when I identified the head as Shinzei's. Truly, this is an extraordinary day, neh?"

Yoshitomo also had to lean out the window of his own ox-carriage, parked beside Nobuyori's, in order to be heard above the throng gathered along the avenue and the banks of the Kamo River. He would have preferred to be astride a horse than closed up in a carriage like a woman, but Nobuyori had been giving him not-so-subtle hints that Yoshitomo should begin behaving more like a nobleman. "Indeed, my lord," Yoshitomo called back with less enthusiasm. "An auspicious day."

There was an excited hubbub to the south, and Nobuyori said, "Ah! Here it comes! Here comes the head of the Great Traitor!"

Yoshitomo reflected on this a moment. He had had personal reasons to distrust Shinzei, but he had no evidence that Shinzei had plotted against the Emperor, other than Nobuyori's word. And from close observation in recent days, Yoshitomo was beginning to wonder how well Nobuyori's word might be trusted. *The man seems mad at times, vengeful beyond reason one day, neglectful of important matters the next, as if possessed by a capricious spirit. There are those who say the demonic ghost of the Shin-In haunts Heian Kyō. Were I a superstitious man, I might believe them.*

Yoshitomo heard the clopping of many horses' hooves approaching, and he leaned farther out of his carriage to peer down the street. Row upon row of finely armored warriors were riding up on their prancing steeds. Yoshitomo recognized many of them, who were of Minomoto or related families. He was pleased they made an impressive sight. As the warriors rode past, they bowed to Nobuyori's carriage.

The crowd grew strangely silent, then. So much so that Yoshitomo could hear the winter breeze moaning through the bare branches of nearby willow trees. It was then that the head of Shinzei, impaled upon a sword, was going by, carried by the warrior who had found him.

The sky darkened perceptibly, as a cloud passed over the sun. The wind became colder. Perhaps it was merely the jouncing gait of the warrior's mount, but Yoshitomo saw the eyes in Shinzei's head open and the head nod, first to Nobuyori's carriage, then to Yoshitomo's, as if to say, "One day, you too."

Yoshitomo felt his skin creep and the hair on the back of his neck stand on end.

"Did you see that?" a commoner standing near Yoshitomo's carriage said. "He nodded at the Great Commander's carriage!"

"Ai," moaned another. "His ghost will seek vengeance upon his enemies. What unhappy times these are."

"Shinzei was not a rebel or a criminal. What could have led him to this horrid fate?"

"Surely he must have done terrible things in a previous life. That is the only thing that can explain it."

"Not necessarily. Perhaps it was because he insisted that the death penalty be carried out again after the Hōgen Disturbance. There were so many deaths. Perhaps this is divine punishment for that."

"Yes, perhaps that is it."

Perhaps, thought Yoshitomo, chilled to the bone. *But Shinzei was a powerful man. Powerful men play dangerous games. Play them long enough, and a man's luck eventually runs out. Any man's. Even Nobuyori's. Even mine.*

A Red Helmet Cord

A light snow was gently falling as Kiyomori and his son Shigemori finished their prayers at Kirime-no-ōji, one of the ninety-nine shrines along the Nakahechi pilgrimage road to Kumano. They turned away from the vermilion-painted shrine and passed between the stone lanterns flanking the path when they saw a horseman galloping toward them. Kiyomori, his son, and his retainers put their hands on their short swords as the horseman pulled his steed to an abrupt halt and flung himself onto the path before Kiyomori. "My lord," he said, his face pale with fear and woe, "I have ridden here straightway from Rokuhara. There is terrible news."

"Tell me. Be brief," said Kiyomori.

"The Sanjō Palace has been burned, with great loss of life, and the Retired Emperor captured and imprisoned in the Imperial Compound. Great Commander Nobuyori has made alliance with Minomoto Yoshitomo, and together they did this. Also Middle Counselor Shinzei's residence has been burned and all who were found there killed."

Kiyomori sucked in cold air through his teeth and stared off to the north. "I never believed he would be so bold. And so brutal." He looked back down at the messenger. "What of Rokuhara?"

"It still stood, when I left, my lord."

"Father," said Shigemori, "we must return to Heian Kyō at once!"

Kiyomori paused, staring through the falling snow toward the north. *How could I have been so blind? Everyone told me Nobuyori was an utter fool, who would blunder at anything he tried. Go-Shirakawa imprisoned and his palace burned? How could the Emperor allow this? It cannot be possible. There must be some mistake.*

"You are absolutely certain of this?" Kiyomori demanded of the messenger.

"I swear it upon the honor of my ancestors, my lord. I, myself, passed by the charred remains of Sanjō Palace on my way here. The smell alone was . . . please do not ask me to describe it, my lord."

Kiyomori curled his hands into fists. *I cannot have been outsmarted by Nobuyori. This must have been a Minomoto plot.* "You are certain he was accompanied by Minomoto Yoshitomo?"

"Yes, my lord. Most certain."

"Ah."

"Father—"

"Are you listening, my son? Did I not tell you years ago that Yoshitomo

94   Kara Dalkey

was not our friend?" *So, the Minomoto have somehow regained Imperial favor. And Yoshitomo has much reason to hate me. If, to oppose him, the Taira must act against the Imperial will, it will go hard on us. This cannot be happening. I have only just begun building the new shrine on Miyajima, and I have not yet returned the Sacred Sword to Ryujin. I do not yet have the grandson who will become Emperor.*

Kiyomori gazed down at a little moss-covered stone statue of Jizō, the *bosatsu* who protects the souls of all travelers who die along the pilgrims' road. Kiyomori wondered if he would be needing Jizō's protection soon.

"Father!"

"I am considering our position. Remember, we have no force of arms with us, not even a single suit of armor. If we return and are attacked along the road, we will be defenseless. And that is what the Minomoto will do, if they have any sense. Perhaps it would be safer to continue the pilgrimage. At the Kumano shrine, there may be warrior-monks to help us. And we can pray for divine assistance as well."

"If our purpose in the pilgrimage was to pray for peace," argued Shigemori, "how can we turn our backs when such peace is shattered? We must return!"

"My lord," said the messenger, "if I may have leave to speak, the Taira and Retired Emperor Go-Shirakawa have friends in this region, who remember your heroic part in the Hōgen Disturbance. Let me ride to them and explain the situation. Let me see if I and others can gather men and arms for you."

One of the scarlet cords on the messenger's helmet had worked free and now fluttered in the wind, a red banner. Kiyomori was reminded of Benzaiten's sail, and her promise. *She would not fail me*, he thought, *if I prove my courage.* It was a small sign, but it was all he needed. "Very well." He nodded to the messenger. "Go swiftly, and see what you can find."

"I shall be as the wind, my lord." The messenger bowed and got back on his horse. He rode off into the swirling snow.

"I, too! I, too!" said the retainers and servants, and they ran off to the nearest posting station to get horses.

Within hours, the great warrior and Governor of Chikugo, Iesada, who was a distant relation to Kiyomori, arrived at the shrine. Behind him marched men bearing fifty chests slung on long poles. These contained fifty suits of armor, fifty quivers of arrows, and swords. From within the bamboo poles used to carry the chests, the men brought out fifty bows. Iesada was greeted with a cheer, and Kiyomori's heart lifted.

The Abbot of Kumano Shrine himself sent more than twenty mounted men. Muneshige, the Acting Governor of Yuasa, rode up with more than thirty. All through that afternoon and night, more and more men came to the aid of the Taira. By midnight, the field beside Kirime-no-ōji held a force of over a hundred mounted warriors.

"Now, if we meet opposition on the road, we will have something to show them," said Kiyomori with satisfaction.

But one of the warriors called out, "My lord, a rider approaches from the north."

Their torchlight revealed, through the lightly falling snow, a rider galloping toward them. The warriors brought forth their bows and made arrows ready. But the rider called out, "I bring a message from Rokuhara. Is Lord Kiyomori here?"

As the man wore an armband with the Taira crest, Kiyomori was pointed out to him. The messenger rode up to Kiyomori, dismounted, and knelt before him. "My lord, I have ridden hard from Heian Kyō. One of Yoshitomo's sons has arrived in the capital, with plans to set a force at Abeno to ambush you if you should return. Rumors say he will assemble over three thousand warriors there."

Again, Kiyomori paused and stroked his chin in thought. "The Minomoto have many supporters in the Kantō, but that would seem an exaggerated number. Still, even a third of that, a mere thousand, would surely defeat our small band. What a waste that would be of the lives of those who showed their loyalty by coming to our aid. Perhaps we should not head straight for Heian Kyō, then, but ride to Shikoku and raise a larger army. Once we are ready, then we may enter the capital with greater assurance of success."

"Father," said Shigemori, anxiously, "that will take days. Who knows what might happen to Rokuhara or the Retired Emperor in that time. We have seen how fast Nobuyori moves, and how boldly. If we take so long, there may be nothing left to defend by the time we return. Besides, think of the glory to be attained if we defeat so great a force with our smaller one. And if we lose, there would be no shame in it. People will sing of our bravery."

"The boy is right," said Iesada. "Think of your family at Rokuhara, how frightened they must be. We should take our chances and hurry to Heian Kyō."

Kiyomori turned and stared at his son. *For a scholarly young man, he chooses the strangest moments to suddenly display the heart of a warrior. Usually to disapprove of my better sense and judgment. Did his mother make him so contrary? Ah, well. Perhaps I should be grateful to the gods that he has such moments at all. And Iesada, whose help we desperately need, agrees with him.*

"So be it," said Kiyomori. "Let us go directly then, and may our way be blessed by the Kumanobutsu." He and Shigemori put on suits of armor over their pilgrim robes and mounted horses that Iesada had brought for them.

With a cry of "Onward!" Kiyomori and his son led the small force of mounted men back through the snow, through the night, through the mountains that bordered Izumi and Kii Provinces. At dawn, at Mount Onino-nakayama, yet another single horseman came riding toward them at great speed, on a gray horse.

"Who might it be?"

"How fierce he looks!"

"He must be coming from the Minomoto at Abeno, to issue their challenge."

"Whatever message he carries," said Kiyomori, "we must hear it."

"Look," said Shigemori, "he, too, bears the butterfly crest on his arm! He comes from Rokuhara."

This messenger brought his horse alongside Kiyomori, and he bowed in his saddle. "My lord, I am glad I have found you."

Kiyomori's heart seemed to pause in his chest. "What news from Rokuhara?"

"Still standing, my lord, as of the middle of the night when I left. All of your family within are frightened but well, save one."

"Save one?"

"Your son-in-law, the Harima Middle Commander Narinori, who came to us for protection. Alas, he was summoned by Imperial command, so we had no choice but to put him out."

"What!" cried Shigemori. "How could we have done such a thing! One who has married into our clan comes to us for safety and we turn him over to the enemy? Who will ever trust us or join our cause if we treat people in this way?"

"They were afraid, my young lord," said the messenger, "because you and your father are not there to rally their spirits."

"We will be there soon enough," said Shigemori.

"Perhaps," said Kiyomori, firmly. He asked the messenger, "What of these rumors of a great Minomoto force waiting to ambush us at Abeno? How many are they, in truth, and how well prepared?"

The messenger blinked in surprise. "My lord, you have heard false news. There is an army at Abeno, but it is not Minomoto. Yoshitomo and his son, by order of the Great Commander Nobuyori, are keeping their forces in the capital. But at Abeno there are three hundred warriors led by Ito, who are waiting to see if you are returning so that they may join and fight with you."

A cheer rose up from Kiyomori's mounted warriors. "This is better news than I could have hoped for," Kiyomori said. "Not only is there no enemy, but there are allies awaiting us! We shall grow from one hundred to four hundred. Let us hurry onward!"

They rode ahead, racing with one another to see which horseman would be first, and the sound of their hoofbeats was the rumbling of thunder of an approaching storm.

The Single-Copy Library

Retired Emperor Go-Shirakawa and his sister Jōsaimon'in, sat dejectedly in the Single-Copy Library. Their afternoon meal lay uneaten beside them, like all the meals that had been delivered to them since their imprisonment. Very little light came in through the closed bamboo blinds. Now and then, a cold draft blew through the slats, bringing with it a few flakes of snow that swiftly melted in midair.

Jōsaimon'in pulled her kimonos tighter around her and gazed up at the scrolls and stacks of Michinoku paper on the shelves. "I had often wondered about this room," she mused softly, "when we lived here at the Imperial palace. I think I visited this room once or twice in my dreams. I wondered what books could be so unloved that they would have but one copy made of them, and then be stored away never to be read again."

"They are like us, neh?" said Go-Shirakawa. "Singular and unwanted, yet too valuable to destroy."

Jōsaimon'in stared down at the wood planks of the floor. "What will become of us?"

"Impossible to say for certain," said Go-Shirakawa. "I cannot imagine how my own son is permitting this to happen. He has no reason to hate me. He already has the throne. What possible threat could I be to him?"

"What if it is not Nijō's will at all," asked Jōsaimon'in, "and he has no say in what Nobuyori commands?"

"In that case I am forced to wonder what power Nobuyori has over my son. I wish I knew whether Kiyomori has returned to Heian Kyō yet. Surely the Taira will not allow this state of affairs to continue."

"I wish I had died at Sanjō"—Jōsaimon'in sighed—"rather than suffer this horrible waiting."

"Do not say such things, sister. Think of what terrible karma that would have brought upon the warriors responsible for your death. The shedding of Imperial blood is no trivial matter. Even Nobuyori will not risk his soul in that way. No doubt, if he remains in power, we will suffer the same fate as my brother, the Shin-In. We will be exiled to a far province where we may write our memoirs and sad poetry until our last days."

"That is merely a lingering death," said Jōsaimon'in. "To be haunting a place that is not home. Some say it drove the Shin-In to madness. I could well believe it would do the same to me."

There came a scratching at the wooden door.

Jōsaimon'in stood and backed away from the door. "What is it? A rat? A demon?"

"Your Majesty," came a muffled voice from the corridor outside.

"Who is it?" said Go-Shirakawa.

They heard the bolt barring the door being pulled aside and the door slid open just a little. A face wearing a cap of a Fourth Rank noble peered in and then bowed to the floor. "My ruler, my lady. I am Archivist Lesser Controller of the Right Nariyori. I have heard of your fate and found this time when your guards are absent to come speak to you. As I am an archivist, no one minds my being here. How may I serve you?"

"You are a *bosatsu* sent from Paradise, good Archivist Nariyori," said Go-Shirakawa. "Tell me all that is happening. Is there fighting in the streets?"

"Not as yet, Majesty, but there are rumors Kiyomori is returning to Heian Kyō with a mighty force."

"Ah. Excellent. And my son, the Emperor, where is he? What is he doing in all this?"

"Alas, it is a terrible, shameful matter, Majesty. Great Commander Nobuyori has tricked Nijō-sama with opium-laced wine and now keeps him confined in the Blackdoor Chamber of the Seiryōden. Nobuyori himself lives beyond the Comb Window in the Asagarei, where the Emperor should be living, wearing the red trousers and gold hatband of an Emperor himself."

"I should never have left the throne." Go-Shirakawa sighed. "And the Imperial Regalia, what of them? Where is the Sacred Mirror?"

"Where it always rests, Majesty. At Ise and in the Ummeiden."

"And the sword and the jewel?"

"In the Night Hall of the Seiryōden, Majesty."

"Where an Emperor sleeps."

"Yes."

"And where Nobuyori is sleeping now."

"Very likely, Majesty."

"Ah, well. At least he has not sold them."

"Majesty, how unthinkable!"

"Not for Nobuyori, I suspect. Is there rumor of what is to become of us?"

"Not that I have heard, Majesty. Perhaps things will change when Governor Kiyomori arrives."

"No doubt."

"Is there any other service I may do for you, Majesty? I regret that my power is small, but I will do what I can."

"For your loyalty, we thank you. Please return when there is more news. Your voice gives us hope."

The archivist pressed his forehead to the floor again. "As soon as I can, Majesty. Highness." The door slid shut, and his departing footsteps tapped away.

Go-Shirakawa smiled at his sister. "There can be no despair, while men such as he remain in the world."

The White Swan

As was customary before a great battle, Kiyomori and his men sought a place where they might petition the assistance and goodwill of the gods before proceeding into Heian Kyō. Therefore, they stopped at the ancient and venerable Otori Shrine. Snow had fallen the night before, and it was piled heavily on the shrine's elegantly sloping roofs and gables. Snow blanketed the iris gardens, renowned throughout the land for their summer beauty.

Kiyomori himself led the prayer, ringing the bell before the holy main shrine building, clapping twice and begging the aid of Yamato Takeru and Mioyanokami. Kiyomori thought it interesting that Mioyanokami was not only a god of *bugei*, the fighting arts, but also was a god of literature. *We may pray not only to prove ourselves well in battle but that perhaps someone will someday write favorably of our deeds.*

When he had finished, his son Shigemori said, "Father, should we not leave an offering here? Is it not said that the gods pay more attention when a sacrifice is made?"

"Very well, my son. I will let you select what our offering will be. Only do not take too long about it. We still have some distance to ride."

"Thank you, Father." Shigemori smiled and went back among his retainers to prepare his offering.

Kiyomori took a contemplative stroll through the grounds of the shrine. One of the priests had mentioned to him a legend in which the many varieties of trees on the shrine's grounds had sprung up overnight at the shrine's consecration. Kiyomori thought how his current army had grown, so swiftly, at his call for assistance. *May this be a sign of divine favor*, he thought, *for my force is yet small and we face great danger.*

Halfway around the shrine he turned and looked back at the main building. With the snow piled upon the eaves and clumped around the protruding crossed beams that rose into the sky, it looked as though a great white swan, its wings outstretched, had settled in this place to rest before flying on.

Another legend mentioned by the shrine priest went that Yamato Takeru, son of Emperor Keiko and a great warrior of ages past, had turned into a white swan upon his death and that this spot was his last landing place upon Earth before he rose into the Heavens. Kiyomori recalled that Yamato Takeru was the first mortal to wield the Sacred Sword Kusanagi, having been given it by Susano-wo. *And I might be the last mortal to touch the sword.* He bowed to the shrine, proud that he might be part of so ancient a story, yet feeling some fear as well. *What is my part in this legend? How will it end?*

He saw Shigemori with his retainers approaching the main shrine again, leading a dapple gray horse. Kiyomori returned to them, and said, "Did you not tell me that is your favorite steed, my son?"

"Yes, Father," Shigemori said, "this is Tobikage, and that is my best saddle on his back, the cedar one decorated with silver."

"This is a lavish gift to present to the shrine, is it not?"

"Father, I know you have faced many battles, but I have not. I feel what we face upon our return to the capital may be the most important battle of our lives. The most important of the Taira clan itself. If the gods judge us by our resolve, is it not wise to give the most precious thing, to show we are prepared to make the greatest sacrifice to win our goal?"

"Perhaps, my son, perhaps. Do as you think best." He watched Shigemori lead the horse to the priests' compound. Kiyomori idly wondered whether Shigemori truly intended the gift as a sign of resolve, or whether he wanted his prized horse to remain at a place where it would be fussed over and taken good care of rather than be harmed in battle.

Does it matter what a man's intentions are, Kiyomori reminded himself, *so long as he does the right thing?*

Kiyomori left an offering of his own—a poem written on stiff Michinoku paper and folded into the shape of a butterfly, the Taira crest. The poem was:

> The caterpillar
> Fully changed, prepares to fly home
> Protect it,
> Otori-no-kami.

Icy Streets

Very late that night, Kiyomori and his forces rode through the Rashō Mon, the southernmost gate into Heian Kyō. But no opposing force awaited them. As they rode down the broad Suzaku Ōji, the city appeared deserted. Only the pale glow of moonlight illuminated the fallen snow on the famous willows lining the avenue, and glittered on the ice lining the gutters. There was no sound other than the soft *clop* of their horses' hooves.

"This is very strange," Kiyomori murmured.

"Perhaps we are awaited at Rokuhara," said Shigemori.

They rode eastward through the city, Kiyomori gripping the reins of his horse tightly, expecting any moment that warriors would suddenly burst forth from the alleyways in ambush. But there came no attack.

When they reached the Rokuhara Mansion, the guards at the gate shouted joyfully upon seeing Kiyomori, Shigemori, and the new allied warriors they had brought back with them. Though it was late at night, all the household awoke and came to greet them and thank them for their return.

"What were you thinking?" Tokiko rebuked Kiyomori when he finally embraced her in their bedchamber. "How could you leave us so unprotected? With you and Shigemori gone, and Motomori so sickly now, Munemori would have had to become our general and he is still so young!"

"Wife, wife, I relied upon your wisdom and your magics to keep the capital at peace," Kiyomori said, nuzzling her graying hair.

"Did you? Did you think my skills at court etiquette would keep Nobuyori at bay? My father may be the Dragon King, but when I was permitted into the mortal realm to be your wife, I gave up most of my magics."

"I was jesting, wife. I thought Nobuyori was no more than a puffed-up nobleman, too impressed with himself to do anything requiring courage."

"He fooled all of us," agreed Tokiko. "But now you see why my father wishes the sword Kusanagi returned to him. Were such a man as Nobuyori to learn the power of the sword, and use it, such terrible things would happen. Terrible things."

"Peace, wife, peace. I will see to it. Have I not promised?"

"Will you see to it soon?"

"Is there not the matter of a Taira grandson who must first ascend the throne? Would it not be best attended to then?"

"I fear that may be too late. There are monks who now say that mankind is entering the Last Days of the Law."

"Monks are always saying such things in order to seem important."

"I beg you listen to me. If you care for your land and your beautiful city Heian Kyō, you must take heed."

Kiyomori sighed. "Very well, wife. I will think on what I may do."

For fifteen days and nights thereafter, the Taira at Rokuhara awaited an attack from the Imperial guards. Likewise, in the Imperial Compound, the forces of Nobuyori awaited an attack from the Taira. Spies shuttled back and forth in the night carrying news and rumors. Horsemen of both clans, Taira and Minamoto, rode up and down the streets in the daytime, waiting for a sign or signal that battle was to begin. Although the New Year was approaching, no one made plans for festivities or observances; there was only talk of war.

Kiyomori had to admit to himself that his bold strategy had not worked . . . or had worked all too well. Nobuyori had simply proved the bolder. The Great Commander still had an overwhelming force at the Imperial Compound, led by the formidable Minomoto Yoshitomo. And now Nobuyori had possession of Retired Emperor Go-Shirakawa as well the Emperor himself. "Why has he not yet attacked us?" Kiyomori would ask over and over as he walked the barricaded walls of Rokuhara. "Does he expect reinforcements? Does he plan to make a bargain with us?" No spy or warrior could give Kiyomori an answer. But Kiyomori did not allow the uneasy peace to make him idle. He used the time to conceive of a plan which, if it succeeded, might be the boldest move of all.

The Ladies in the Ox-Carriage

Young Emperor Nijō, seventeen years of age, awoke before dawn to the familiar sound of bustling servants. He let them ease him off of his sleeping dais and dress him in his vermilion robes and black hat. He waited patiently as they set out rice and vegetables for his breakfast, and listened as they cheerfully told him there was nothing of importance requiring his attention. With a sigh, Nijō prepared to spend the day much he had spent each day of the past several months, pretending he was drugged. The rice and vegetables were laced with opium, he knew from experience, and he was given only wine to drink.

Some days he was so discouraged, so disgusted with himself, that he needed not pretend. He would eat the food he was given and allow himself to drift in sad oblivion. Sequestered as he was in the Blackdoor Chamber, guarded by servants who only pretended to do his bidding, there was little else to do but watch, and listen, and wait.

On this particular day he chose again to forgo the food, stirring it with his chopsticks and spilling some to make it seem as though he had eaten. He let the wine spill down between the floorboards. The hunger and thirst he would feel through the day would be adequate punishment for what he had allowed himself to become.

Truly, it is as the Buddha says, Nijō thought. *A man's desires are his downfall. I was a fool to let Nobuyori know the wishes that were in my heart. He gave me my wish, but oh the price he has extracted in return. May all the gods and* bosatsu *forgive me. I did not think I would be giving up my kingdom for a woman.*

Emperor Nijō knew when the sun had risen, not by any light that penetrated his dim chamber, but by the changing of the guards outside his door. He wished again he had the strength to overcome them, to force them aside and see the sun's light for himself. To be able to stride into the Great Hall of State and stand before the assembled Senior Council of Nobles. To be able to point at Nobuyori, and declare, "He is a traitor to the state! Behead him!"

But Nijō had grown up a pampered prince, knowing nothing of the fighting arts. And the men outside his door were Minomoto, hardened warriors and loyal to Nobuyori. *The worst I could do is force them to harm or kill me. Someday, if this goes on, I may do just that. Though I am said to be descended from the gods, I am as powerless as a fish trapped in a fisherman's bucket.*

Nijō heard the guards talking outside his door, and he slumped onto the floor to place his ears closer to that wall. It was important to maintain appearances, for Nijō could never be certain when he was being observed and when he was not. In this manner, he had been able to learn some things about how matters stood. He learned of the death of Shinzei and the capture of the Middle Counselor's sons. He learned that Kiyomori of the Taira had left Heian Kyō. He heard how Nobuyori now fashioned himself as an Emperor, and how frightened and disgusted the nobles who served him were.

But all he learned this morning was that a "certain visitor" was to be expected and allowed to see Nijō, by permission of the Minister of the Right.

Then it cannot be anyone of consequence, thought Nijō.

Hours passed, and then at last there came the sound of hushed women's voices outside his door. For a moment, Nijō thought that Nobuyori had sent him more dancing girls to entertain him. Nijō felt quite uninterested in such delights.

And then the door slid aside and she entered. Nijō felt his breath catch in his throat. A stray beam of sunlight illuminated the wall behind her just before the *shōji* slid shut again. The Imperial Consort Yoshiko bowed low, and said, "My great lord, how fare you? I regret that only now have I again been permitted to be with you."

Nijō could hardly speak—as was often the case when he was in her presence, ever since he had met her. Yoshiko was no giggling dancing girl overawed to be in an Emperor's presence. For Yoshiko had been married to an Emperor before, Nijō's uncle. Her mature, beautiful face was composed with elegance, a mask of exquisite sorrow. *How well you mirror the feelings of my heart*, Nijō thought. In that moment, a small voice within noted that had he another kingdom, he might gladly exchange it for her as well.

Yoshiko glanced at the spilled food, then looked back at Nijō. "Have you eaten today, my liege?" she asked carefully.

"My only sustenance this day is the sight of you," Nijō answered. "And on that I might feed forever."

A very slight smile appeared on her lips, and she gracefully walked on her knees over beside him. Her hands caressed his arm and, he noted, transferred some rice cakes from her sleeve into his. "Then, I pray you, look long and feed well."

"I will. How have you been, my lady?"

"Sad for not being with you." Yoshiko placed her cheek against his. With her lips near his ear, she whispered, "Show no sign. But your father and aunt are held prisoner in the Single-Copy Library."

Nijō's hands gripped Yoshiko's arms tightly, and he shut his eyes. Nonetheless tears leaked onto his cheeks. "How can I bear this? How can I live with myself?" he moaned softly.

"You must. For the sake of your people. There is hope."

"What hope can there be?"

"Hold me close, for I have ached for the embrace of your arms, my lord."

Nijō gladly did so, pressing her as close to him as their many layers of garments would permit. He was momentarily lost in the perfume of her hair.

"The Lord of the Taira has returned to Rokuhara," she whispered into his neck.

"Ah!" he moaned. Then, understanding the game, he traced the curve of her jaw with his nose, and whispered, "So, there will be battle in the city again?"

"Perhaps." Yoshiko sighed. She began to loosen the layers of her kimonos around her neck and breasts.

Nijō eagerly slid his hand under her layers of soft, warm silk to caress the soft, warm skin beneath. "Will he attack the palace?" He breathed into her hair.

Yoshiko gently removed his hand and placed it against her cheek. "It would be thought unwise to move so quickly and boldly. Too much stands in the way."

"Then for what can I hope?" asked Nijō, gazing into her dark, gold-flecked eyes.

"Why, release, my lord, of course."

"And . . . how will this come about?"

"If you will let a lowly woman guide you, my liege, I have been informed of a plan that I think you will find most pleasing."

Indeed, for some hours after, Nijō allowed himself the first pleasure he had felt in a very long time.

And so it came to pass, on the evening of the Twenty-sixth Day of the Twelfth Month, an Imperial ladies' ox-carriage left the Imperial Compound via the Jōtōmon, the northeasternmost gate. It was accompanied by Korekata, the Commissioner of Police, who wore only informal dress and rode with a casual air.

The guards at the gate, unnerved by waiting for a Taira attack, regarded the carriage suspiciously. "What is this? Who are these people and where are they going at this hour?" the guards demanded.

"It is the Imperial Consort and her ladies-in-waiting," said Korekata. "She has learned that a cousin is deathly ill, and she wishes to see her. I am Commissioner of Police Korekata, and as the streets have been safe these many nights, I saw no problem with granting her request."

"If you will pardon us, Lord Commissioner, we will verify your word for ourselves." One of the guards lifted up the blind of the carriage window with the tip of his bow and, holding up his torch, looked into the carriage.

There he saw four stunningly beautiful noble ladies, their hair done up in elaborate pins and face powder elegantly applied, dressed in their finest silk brocade robes. The ladies demurely hid the lower half of their faces behind their sleeves.

"What is the meaning of this rude intrusion?" the Imperial Consort demanded. "My cousin is ill! She could be passing away this very moment. Let us continue our journey at once."

"Your pardon, ladies," said the guard, embarrassed, and he immediately lowered the blind. He waved Korekata and the ox-driver on.

The ox-driver whipped the animals until they trotted down the thoroughfare and turned a corner. Three ladies and the young Emperor Nijō lowered their sleeves from their faces with a relieved sigh.

"It worked," Nijō said, with amazement. His foot nudged the scabbard of the Sacred Sword Kusanagi, hidden on the floor of the carriage. The ladies sitting in the carriage across from him had stolen the sword from

Nobuyori's bedroom under their voluminous kimonos after getting the Great Commander quite drunk and distracted.

"People see what they expect to see, my lord," said Yoshiko. "And, you know, you do make a most beautiful woman. The way that guard gazed at you, I think he was falling in love."

Nijō made a face at her, and the other ladies giggled.

Two streets later, the carriage was stopped again. Nijō peered out through the curtains and saw three hundred mounted warriors. "What is this?"

"Fear not, my lord," said Yoshiko. "This is our escort."

Then Nijō saw the butterfly crest on the helmet of the foremost rider. "Ah. The Taira."

As one, the three hundred warriors silently dismounted from their horses. They knelt in the street and bowed low to the carriage. Nijō felt quite moved by this, and understood how his grandfather Toba could have come to trust the Taira so.

The warriors got back on their horses and surrounded the carriage, guarding it as one would the most precious jewel. Nijō ducked his head back into the carriage as it again moved forward.

"Did you see the tall one there?" asked Yoshiko. "That is Shigemori, Kiyomori's son. It is said he is the finest Taira there has ever been. Perhaps you should flirt with him."

"Hush," said Nijō, starting to blush, "or I shall be jealous."

Before long, the ox-carriage bump-bumped over the threshold beam of a manor gate. The carriage stopped, and the back door was flung open. Framed in the doorway was a powerful-looking, stocky, middle-aged man who Nijō realized could only be Lord Kiyomori himself.

"Welcome, Most Revered Majesty!" Kiyomori declared, bowing low. "Welcome to Rokuhara."

Green Robes

An hour later, Retired Emperor Go-Shirakawa and his sister were startled by the sliding aside of first the bolt and then the door itself of the Single-Copy Library. Kneeling in the doorway, smiling, were two men. One of them was the Archivist Lesser Counselor of the Right, Nariyori. In his arms was a lacquered wood chest.

He bowed, and said, "You have asked that I bring you news, my ruler, and the news I bring tonight is of the best and most amazing sort. The

world has been thrown into confusion, and the Emperor, your son, has fled
the palace to Rokuhara. I respectfully suggest that you flee somewhere as
well."

Go-Shirakawa smiled. "You are truly sent from the gods, good archivist.
But is escape possible?"

"This man," said Nariyori, indicating the fellow beside him, "is Taira
no Yasuyori. He is a warrior of much courage and has offered to stay here
in your place, acting as you do, so as to allay suspicion. I have brought in
this chest the green robes of a Sixth Rank courtier. No one would expect
to see a former Emperor in such a guise. And for you, my lady, I have
brought the poorer kimonos of a waiting woman. If you both do not mind
wearing such lowly apparel, we can ease your escape."

Go-Shirakawa smiled. "May the Amida bless you both. I will certainly
not mind stepping below the clouds for a time."

"Nor I," said Jōsaimon'in.

And so the Retired Emperor put on the green overrobes. His sister,
Jōsaimon'in, went with the archivist to mingle with the court servingwomen.

Go-Shirakawa slipped out of the library with the intention of making
his way to the palace stables. But to do so he had to cross nearly the entire
Imperial Compound, and just ahead of him was the Imperial residence itself.
Numerous black-robed men of First Rank were gathered just outside the
Kenshu Gate of the residence. Go-Shirakawa lowered his head and hurried
by them, meanwhile overhearing some of their conversation:

"—Dead drunk again. They have tried to rouse him, but it is no good."

"Well, I do not want to be the one to give him the news in the morning.
He will be furious!"

"What will it matter now? It is clear his power is gone. There is nothing
to be done about it. Let him rave all he likes."

Go-Shirakawa was nearly past them when one of the nobles called out,
"You, there. Green robes. Who are you, and what are you doing?" The
Retired Emperor recognized the voice as being that of Middle Counselor
Narichika.

Adopting a deferential stance and more quavering voice, which was not
difficult in his situation, Go-Shirakawa said, "Oh. Your pardon, most noble
lords. I am no one of importance. I have been working late in the Secretaries
Office, and I heard there was some commotion."

"This is no matter for you," said Narichika. "Go back to your offices."

"If I may, noble lords," Go-Shirakawa said, keeping his head low, "I
was on my way to deliver a request from a lady in the Empress's Household
to the Bureau of Medicine. She is having . . . woman's troubles. You understand."

Narichika waved his fan impatiently. "Go on, go on. But tell no one else of any commotion here tonight. Nothing of importance is happening, do you understand?"

"I understand perfectly, my lord. Nothing of importance."

Narichika came closer. "You look familiar. Have I seen you before?"

Go-Shirakawa tried to look even more humble than before. "Oh, quite possibly, most noble lord. I am on the palace grounds a great deal and often deliver papers requiring signature to the Central Affairs Ministry."

"That must be it, then. Be on your way."

Gladly, Go-Shirakawa bowed low and hurried off. The Bureau of Medicine was right beside the Imperial stables, and so his direction, he knew, should not give suspicion. *How true it is that men see only what they expect to,* he marveled. *Narichika has indeed seen me many times, back when I wore vermilion robes and sat upon the throne.*

Go-Shirakawa had no further interruptions before he reached the palace stables. There he found a horsegroom, and he said, "I wish to have a horse brought to me."

"Begging your pardon, my lord," said the stable hand, "but most of the horses have been taken by Lord Yoshitomo and his men for defense of the palace. And it may not be safe to leave the palace at this time."

Go-Shirakawa recognized the young man as one who had served as an Imperial page when Go-Shirakawa was Emperor. *Poor fellow, how you have come down in the world.* Moving more into the glare of the torchlight, Go-Shirakawa decided to reveal himself. "My good fellow, it would not be safe for me to stay."

The groom gasped and bowed low. "My . . . my liege, my former Majesty!"

"Shhh. Quietly. Will you get me a horse and help me escape?"

"Of course! I will bring you the best that is left." The groom quickly brought out a horse of fine breeding that was calmer than the preferred warhorse. "This is Kazan, who was left behind because of his age, but he will serve you well, Majesty. All we have left are saddles and tack needing repair."

"I will be content with the most serviceable of those. It will only aid my disguise."

So the horse was fitted with a cracked saddle whose silver embellishments were tarnished and a bridle missing its bright tassels. The groom insisted on accompanying Go-Shirakawa. "I may be branded a traitor if I stay and my service to you is discovered. I would much rather continue to serve you than that toad Nobuyori."

Go-Shirakawa was again grateful for the assistance, a feeling that was new to him in these strange days. The groom said, "Yoshitomo and his men are gathered at the southern gates awaiting a Taira attack. We will have an easier departure if we leave by a north gate."

Go-Shirakawa allowed the servant to guide him to the Jōsai Gate at the northwest corner of the Imperial Compound. To their astonishment, no guards were there. No horsemen or lancemen at all. "This is a sign of the gods," said Go-Shirakawa, "that I am permitted to escape." He dismounted his horse and made obeisance toward the Kitano Shrine, to the north, in acknowledgment of this gift. Then he remounted his horse and continued on.

A heavy snow began to fall as they made their way toward the Temple of Ninna-Ji, where one of Go-Shirakawa's brothers, Kakushō, an Imperial prince himself, was the abbot. The snow obscured the houses and the street, and the Retired Emperor felt isolated and alone. He made many vows to the gods and to himself: to not be so careless of government; to be more watchful of those striving for power beneath him; to never again believe that all was well; to trust no one who might be a threat to the country.

Alas, Nijō my son has proven himself too weak to govern. He let Nobuyori lead him as this servant leads my horse. I dare not permit him to rule—it would bring disaster. Yet, I cannot remove him from the throne just now. But if the gods permit, I will do all I can to keep my hold on power and see that the country is governed securely.

Go-Shirakawa wished he had another noble with him, one with whom he might discuss these things. But all he had were his horse, one servant, and the falling snow.

He composed a poem in his mind:

What sort of blossom grows from sorrow?
One knows when it bears fruit within oneself.

Kusanagi

There was no winter's isolation in the Rokuhara mansion that night. Instead, the compound bustled as if it were New Year, all the lamps and candles blazing, people bustling about trying to make proper accommodations for their new guest, the Emperor.

Lord Kiyomori played the proud host, ensuring that the kitchens were busy, for he'd heard that the Emperor had not been fed well for many days. One whole wing of the mansion was set aside for the Imperial entourage, and Kiyomori himself assigned which of his servants would wait upon the Emperor.

In a small, darkened side chamber in the South Wing, which had been given to the Imperial entourage, Kiyomori had just received the inventory of the Emperor's needs from one servant and sent another servant to arrange their acquisition, when he turned around—and stopped. There, lying humbly on a lacquered chest, was Kusanagi-no-Tsurugi, the Sacred Sword itself.

Kiyomori was profoundly aware that at this moment he was alone, and no servant was likely to enter again for some minutes, if not longer.

Kiyomori knelt before the sword and stared at it. There it was, Grass-cutter, Dragon-slayer, the very symbol of the Empire itself, divine seal of the right to rule, a sword out of legend. Unlike the slim, curved *tachi* blades Kiyomori and his sons wore into battle, Kusanagi was a wide, straight, doubled-edged sword, of the sort carried in the great Empire of Chang'an. It lay within a wooden scabbard, inlaid with gold and silver, wrapped in fish skin. Appropriate, Kiyomori thought, for a sword made by the Dragon King of the Sea.

Legend said the sword was as old as the Empire itself, and to Kiyomori's eyes it looked as ancient as the Earth. He could easily believe it had once lain in the tail of a seven-headed dragon. Kusanagi was said to be able to control all the winds of the Heavens if wielded correctly by the proper ruler of Nihon.

And yet I must someday, somehow, return it to the Dragon King, Kiyomori thought, sadly. It occurred to him that an opportunity such as this one might not occur again. *But what can I do? It is too large to hide beneath my clothing. Should I summon Tokiko and have her steal it? When its absence is noticed, should I claim that a Minomoto spy stole it?* That would give pretext to destroy that rival clan for good.

But should the ruse be discovered, Kiyomori and the Taira would be denounced as thieves, as evil as Nobuyori. What would become of the great Taira destiny then? Things were unsettled enough as it was, and the young Emperor needed the sword to show he was the rightful one to occupy the Jeweled Throne. *And we Taira need the trust of the young Emperor.*

Kiyomori wavered, knowing he might only have a little time in which to choose. *I cannot yet leave the capital with matters as they are. Even if I could steal the sword, when could I make my way to the sea to return it? Surely my theft would be discovered before I could grant Ryujin's request.*

And would theft not be a shameful way to treat Kusanagi? To simply throw it into the sea, as it was said the Shin-In had done with his sutra scrolls? Would it not be better to wait for a better time and return it to Ryujin with full ceremony? Perhaps my grandson could do it himself upon his coming-of-age day. Though a boy is often given a sword on that day, how more gracious

*that a young Emperor should give one to the Dragon King. Perhaps the grand
shrine at Miyajima will be finished by then.*

Kiyomori imagined what such a ceremony would be like, the young
boy in scarlet brocade robes bearing the chrysanthemum crest, standing
on a platform overlooking the sea. The boy would raise Kusanagi high—
and then, who knew? Benzaiten herself might return in her dragon-shell
boat to accept the sword on behalf of her father. Or a great dragon might
rise out of the waters and take the sword in its mouth. What a sight that
would be!

*The Dragon King has promised that I will have a grandson who shall be
Emperor. That promise is not yet fulfilled. Let him wait for his sword until
my grandson sits on the Jeweled Throne. Then he shall have the sword with
all proper ceremony. I must tell Tokiko that she is too impatient.*

Long moments passed, and still Kiyomori was alone with Kusanagi. He
longed to touch it. To draw the sword from its scabbard, to look at the
blade. It was said that a warrior could tell when a sword had taken blood.
Would the edge be notched from where it had bit into bone? Would the
metal be scratched from where it had slid against armor? The finest swords,
in well-trained hands, could fly silently through air, cut raindrops in two.
Was Kusanagi one of these?

I am of Imperial blood, Kiyomori reminded himself. *It would be no
offense to the gods if I held it.* Kiyomori slowly reached his right hand toward
Kusanagi.

The *shōji* behind him opened with a loud *clack.*

Kiyomori pulled his hand back. Not knowing which servant had entered, he said gruffly, "Has the wine been sent up from the kitchens to His
Majesty yet?"

An amused young man answered, "I have not seen the wine yet,
Kiyomori-san. And, to be truthful, I have had rather enough of wine for the
time being."

"Majesty!" Kiyomori pressed his forehead to the floor. "I . . . the servants had departed on other errands, and so I was watching over the Sacred
Sword for you."

"I can think of no better guardian, given that you have rescued me."

Kiyomori did not look up as he heard the susurrance of silk robes and
heard Emperor Nijō kneel beside him. "I wanted to personally offer my
gratitude to you for your assistance and your hospitality, and the protection
of your clan, Kiyomori-san."

"It is my great honor to do so, Majesty."

"It is quite a thing, neh? This Kusanagi."

"It is, Majesty. The symbol of Imperial power and your right to rule."

"Of late, I have been feeling . . . somewhat unworthy of it."

"Please do not say such a thing, Majesty. The very fact that it is here, safely, with you, must indicate that the gods hold you in their favor."

Emperor Nijō sighed. "I hope you are right, Kiyomori-san. I had not looked on it that way. We tried to get the Mirror and the Jewel, too, but Nobuyori's men prevented it."

"I have word, Majesty, that the other sacred accoutrements have also been moved to safe places."

"Ah. That is good. I have been so frightened. Both for myself and for the land. Will you pray with me, Kiyomori-san, for peace, even though I know there are battles yet to come?"

"It would be my privilege, Majesty."

Together they chanted to the Amida Buddha, and Kiyomori let pass his thoughts of stealing Kusanagi.

Sounding Boards

*T*he next morning Fujiwara Narichika entered the Asagarei. The "Great Commander" Nobuyori lay on the Imperial sleeping platform, like a pale, bloated dead horse, still drunk from carousing the night before. Narichika sighed. *Perhaps it is just as well that this petty tyrant's reign will end soon. Alas that my career and probably my life will end with it.*

There were no servants about, so Narichika himself shook Nobuyori's shoulder. "My lord, my lord! You must awaken!"

"Go away," grumbled Nobuyori. His clothing reeked of *sake* and plum wine.

"I will not go away and let you lie here to shame us all."

Nobuyori opened one bleary eye. "Narichika? How dare you—"

"I dare because the world turned upside down last night. I dare because there is no one else to tell you. The palace is deserted. The Emperor has flown the cage you made for him, and now he is gone."

Nobuyori opened the other eye. "Gone? What do you mean gone?"

"His Majesty was somehow spirited away in the night and now resides with the Taira at Rokuhara. An announcement was made before dawn that anyone who wishes to be thought a friend of the Jeweled Throne should appear at Rokuhara to pay their respects and pledge their loyalty. I have heard from my servants that nearly all the nobility of Heian Kyō now fills the streets around Rokuhara. One cannot move for the number of grand carriages and their escorts."

"Impossible!" Nobuyori narrowed his eyes and sat up. "Has no one told you that I despise jests of this nature?"

"It is not a jest, my lord!"

"And even if it were true, we still have Go-Shirakawa, neh? He's worth as much as his son."

"My lord, the Retired Emperor and his sister have fled as well. No one knows where." Narichika kept reviewing in his mind a certain conversation with a strange man in green robes the night before and wondering if he also ought to be ashamed of himself.

"This is a foolish trick to play on your liege lord, Narichika. I thought we Fujiwara were above such things."

"I say again, this is no trick! Look about the palace and see for yourself!"

"Very well. But if you are lying, your head may join Shinzei's on the prison gate."

"I assure you, my lord, it is true." *Though my head may eventually hang from the prison gate anyway.*

Nobuyori hastily threw on an overrobe and his short red pantaloons and strode across the Imperial Compound. Narichika followed him as the Great Commander berated the few servants and groundskeepers who remained in the Compound. They all corroborated what Narichika had said— all the people of quality had left. Nobuyori went to the Single-Copy Library and saw that the door stood wide open and the chamber within was empty. Nobuyori ran to the Blackdoor Chamber where the Emperor had been staying and saw it was deserted as well. He stared at the empty bed platform, the gauze curtains drifting in the morning breeze like ghosts. "Tell no one about this," he breathed to Narichika.

"My lord," said Narichika, "there is no one left in the palace to tell. Your guards and your general Yoshitomo know already."

"I . . . have . . . been . . . duped!" shouted Nobuyori, and as his anger grew he began to stomp and dance around as if to summon the wrath of the gods. But the only response he received was the groaning of the sounding boards beneath his feet.

Eight Dragons

Minomoto Yoshitomo was still reeling from the news of the disappearing Emperors. After another long night of waiting for a Taira attack that never came, Yoshitomo had allowed himself the luxury of returning to his residence to sleep. He had slept scarcely more than a couple of hours when a messenger from the Imperial Compound arrived at dawn to wake him with the news.

At midmorning, his son Akugenda Yoshihira came riding through their residence gate. The young man dismounted in the courtyard and rushed up to Yoshitomo. "Father, I was at the Kamo Shrine when I heard. Is it true? The Emperor and Retired Emperor have gone to Rokuhara?"

"His Majesty has, apparently. As for the *In*, no one seems to know where he has gone."

"What are we to do? Should we go to Rokuhara and pay our respects, as the other noblemen have?"

Yoshitomo scowled at his son. "The Minomoto do not serve two masters. I have pledged my service to Lord Nobuyori, and therefore tied the fate of our clan to his. Perhaps this was a mistake in judgment. But I will not go back on my word, for who would fight with us then, eh?"

"As you say, Father," Akugenda Yoshihira said, glancing about nervously. "But surely we cannot attack the Emperor?"

"We will do whatever the Great Commander bids us."

"And what are the Great Commander's orders?"

Yoshitomo sighed. "There have been none, yet. He is probably still asleep. Nonetheless, we can make preparations. Go among your men and all those you know, and make a list of those still loyal to Nobuyori, or at least still willing to fight with us. With that information, we will make what plans we can."

"At once, Father."

"Tell your brother Tomonaga to prepare for battle. I will see to young Yoritomo myself.

"Yes, Father."

Akugenda Yoshihira departed, and Yoshitomo fetched a large lacquered chest from his quarters and went to his son Yoritomo.

The boy was only thirteen, and as Yoshitomo entered Yoritomo's quarters, he felt his emotions roiling like storm clouds, fear overturning pride overturning hope. "My son, have you heard what has been happening?"

"I have, Father. The servants are all gabbling about it. Are we going to fight the Taira?" The boy seemed preternaturally calm that cold morning, as if only asking if they were going to visit a relative or going for a walk through the gardens.

"We are, my son. And as this will be your first battle, a battle that will be vital to the survival of our clan, I have brought you something." He set down the trunk before the boy. "I have been saving this for you, ever since the omen at Hachimangu. Do you remember that day?"

Yoritomo nodded. "*Hai*, the white doves."

Yoshitomo removed the chest lid. "This was the armor of your fabled ancestor, Yoshiiye. It is called Eight Dragons. You see the eight dragons there intertwined on the chest plate? Yoshiiye was also blessed by the favor of Hachiman, and therefore I thought it appropriate that this, his armor, should become yours."

The boy's eyes widened, but he said nothing.

Yoshitomo removed from the chest the first part of the armor, the archer's gloves.

The boy had already loosened his hair and tied it under an *eboshi* cap, and he was already wearing a narrow-sleeved kimono and wide breeches. His father began dressing him in the armor. First Yoshitomo placed the *yu gake* gloves on the boy's hands—the left one, for holding the bow, was stiff cloth lined with mail, the right one was of soft leather for drawing the bowstring.

Then Yoshitomo handed his son the under-armor tunic and matching *hakama* breeches. Yoshitomo helped him with the leggings and the lacings to anchor the *hakama*. Over these he tied the suneate shin guards, three iron splints laced together. On his son's feet Yoshitomo put shoes made of bear fur.

Then Yoritomo stood and allowed his father to tie onto him the padded *waidate* cuirass that would protect his right side while he was drawing a bow. Then came the armored sleeves, first left then right, and the tying of the tunic sleeves beneath them.

Yoshitomo now took the over-armor, *yoryoi*, from the box. Eight Dragons was unusual for the wide spacing between the metal plates, which were tied together with white Chinese brocade. It had metal fittings in the "round lion" design on the sleeve and skirt pieces, as well as the bronze decorations of eight dragons on the chest piece, which gave the armor its name.

Yoshitomo began with the cuirass and armored skirt, the *do*. Tied to it were the wide *sode* shoulder guards, which were the main shield to the body to deflect arrows.

At last, Yoshitomo turned his son around and straightened the *agemaki* knot at the back, which held the shoulder guards in place.

"Now you are properly dressed like a warrior," Yoshitomo said, proudly. "Here is the sword Higekiri, Beard-trimmer, which also was carried by your esteemed ancestor. Wear it well, my son, and use it honorably."

"I will, Father." The boy awkwardly tied the scabbard to his side.

Finally, Yoshitomo handed him the long rattan bow and a quiver of arrows whose fletching was gray spotted with black. "Now you are properly armed to defeat any enemy. Here is your helmet. Put it on just before you mount your horse."

As they were finishing, Akugenda Yoshihira came running in. "Father, there is more news."

Yoshitomo turned and noted his eldest son's face was pale. "What is it?"

"Three of your commanders, Yorimasa, Mitsuyasu, and Mitsumoto have gone to Rokuhara to join cause with the Taira. The word is that they did not wish to be traitors to the throne, so they would prefer to be traitor to you."

"So." Yoshitomo stared at the floor.

"Should we go strike them down, Father?" asked Yoritomo.

Yoshitomo took a deep breath. "If we take some of our forces away from defending the palace to fight a vendetta, we may lose the greater battle when it comes. If we were defeated, how much greater would be our trouble in reassembling another army to defeat the Taira. No, we must let them go. Now let us hurry to the palace and assemble what forces we have."

Yoshitomo watched the two young men hurry ahead of him to the courtyard. Though young Yoritomo nearly disappeared within his armor, being not quite sufficiently grown for it, he still seemed to wear it with ease. Eight Dragons swung to and fro around the boy as if eager to defend him and pull him into battle.

Chinese Leather

*L*ord Kiyomori, too, was dressing for battle. But at the Hour of the Dragon that morning, he received a summons to the wing of Rokuhara that was the Imperial residence. So when he arrived at the meeting of nobles to which he had been summoned, he was wearing only a deep blue kimono, his left and right gauntlets, and the *waidate* corselet on his right side tied with black cord.

Kiyomori entered cautiously and knelt with his back to the wall beside the *shōji*, hoping to be inconspicuous. If he was not noticed, perhaps he could leave quickly and get on with planning the defense of Rokuhara.

"Ah, Kiyomori-san, there you are," said the Middle Commander and Director of the Archives Bureau. "So glad you could join us. We were just discussing the finer points of your upcoming battle with Nobuyori's forces. We were thinking that although it is right and proper that the rebels be dealt with and punished forthwith, nonetheless we noted that the Imperial palace has recently been thoroughly repaired. His Majesty would be most distressed if the buildings were to be damaged by fire. It would be a great shame to the memory of Shinzei to have his work so soon destroyed. Therefore, it is the Imperial desire that there will be no burning of the Imperial palace during your battle."

This is what comes, thought Kiyomori, *of having Cloud Courtiers planning military matters*. As respectfully as he could, Kiyomori replied, "Because they are so clearly defying the Imperial will, it should be no problem to sweep up and punish the rebels, my lords. However, in any war, excesses happen. You may remember the burning of the Hōshōji in the Hōgen Disturbance. This will be a difficult order to obey. Nonetheless, I will try to devise some strategy by which harm to the Imperial palace will not occur."

"Very good, Lord Kiyomori. I knew we could count on you. Therefore, you may consider an attack upon the palace to be sanctioned by the Jeweled Throne, and a proclamation will be issued shortly to that effect."

"Thank you," said Kiyomori, bowing. "If that is all, my lords, I will take my leave and give orders at once."

"Of course, you may go," said the Director of the Archives Bureau dismissively.

Kiyomori bowed, sighed, and slipped back out through the *shōji*. As he walked back to his own quarters of the mansion he saw his son Shigemori coming toward him. Kiyomori was gratified to see that Shigemori was wearing the armor known as Karakawa, Chinese Leather. This armor had been passed down from great Taira warriors past, and was named for the strips of tiger skin that once braided its metal plates together. Now the armor was held by orange braids and decorated with bronze butterflies. It was said that Karakawa had a magical ability to repel all arrows and sword blows. While Kiyomori did not believe sorcery would be necessary to win this battle, anything that gave a warrior confidence was worthwhile.

At his side, Shigemori wore the ancient and venerable sword Kogarasu, Small Crow, the guardian sword of the Imperial household. Legend said that the sword had been given to the Emperor Kammu over 350 years before by a crow, which may have been a *tengu*, that claimed it had come from the Ise Shrine. It was a great honor to be permitted to wield it, and Kiyomori was proud that Shigemori was worthy of such an honor.

On Shigemori's head was a helmet crowned with a dragon, for Shigemori was, after all, a grandson of the Dragon King.

To Kiyomori's eyes, his son looked splendid. Kiyomori congratulated himself for the decision of making Shigemori the overall general for the day, ranking him even over Kiyomori's own brother. *A man with Shigemori's youthful fire and magnificent appearance will be the perfect inspiration for our men. How could I have ever doubted that Shigemori would become a fine warrior? He will surely only bring further glory to the Taira.*

"Father, the men are restive and wish to begin battle soon. We are not likely to see a greater force assembled on our behalf, so we should make use of them while we can. I have just had word that three of the Minomoto generals have left Nobuyori's cause to join our side."

"That is good. But there is a complication. His Majesty does not wish any part of the palace to be burned."

Shigemori seemed to take this with equanimity. "It had not been part of my plan to do so. But I will be sure to tell the others to set no fires."

"Good. My thought is, you should be able to lead the rebels out of the palace, encouraging them to attack you on the streets. That way little harm will come to the palace buildings, and the Genji may split their forces, making it easier to defeat them."

"A good plan," said Shigemori.

"His Majesty has given his sanction, and the Emperor will issue his proclamation soon."

Shigemori's face beamed. "Excellent. I shall lead the men out at once. Are you sure you will not come with us, Father?"

"No, someone must stay and see that Rokuhara is well guarded. The Emperor must be protected, for if he is taken again our cause is lost."

Shigemori bowed to him and departed swiftly.

Before putting on the rest of his armor, Kiyomori went to a guard tower in the northwest corner of the compound wall. There he saw Shigemori at the gate, astride a spirited cream-colored horse, amassing and encouraging the warriors as scarlet banners unfurled. At Shigemori's final command, the warriors roared, drums rumbled, and gongs sounded. Shigemori led the mounted warriors, three thousand strong, northward up the thoroughfares toward the Imperial Compound.

Kiyomori felt his breath catch in his throat and water well up in his eyes. *Never have I seen so impressive a sight. I may never see its like again.*

Taiken Gate

General Yoshitomo sat astride his dragon horse in the courtyard beside the Seiryōden. With him were his sons and those men who still supported Nobuyori—only about eight hundred horsemen in all. The morning was bright and chill, and Yoshitomo had to squint from the reflections of sunlight off the snow. His gray horse stamped impatiently, and vapor steamed from its nostrils, giving it even more the appearance of a dragon.

Lord Nobuyori, dressed and fully armored at last, sat on the threshold beam of the Shishinden tablet bay. He was twenty-seven, in the prime of his life, looking for once like the Great Commander of his title. He wore a red brocade robe over which he wore armor whose cords shaded from pale to deep purple. He wore a silver-star helmet, and at his side hung a sword in a golden scabbard. His fine black horse, formerly belonging to the Retired Emperor, stood beside a nearby mandarin orange tree.

The morning felt brittle, thin ice on an early-spring lake, and Yoshitomo waited for the first crack.

Then they heard it—softly at first, the *clop* of many, many hooves on the street pavement approaching the Compound, accompanied by the jingle and rattle of armor and harness. The tips of scarlet banners could be seen waving beyond the wall. Yoshihira felt it in his bones, the force assembling beyond the wall was massive, greater than he had ever faced in his life. For a moment, there was silence.

Then a great war cry roared across the wall from the street beyond, a thundering waterfall of noise that rolled over the horsemen in the Imperial courtyard. Three times the sound came pouring over the wall, filling their ears, upsetting the horses. Yoshitomo's steed shied and nearly reared up, but he managed to retain control.

"We must answer them!" Yoshitomo shouted to his men, and they responded with three war cries of their own, but although the shouts were vigorous and heartfelt, they were nothing to match those of the Rokuhara forces.

Lord Nobuyori seemed to be turning green with fear and had difficulty standing. He wobbled down the steps, and a servant led his horse up to him. Nobuyori put one foot in the stirrup, but could not get himself onto the saddle. The servant finally had to give Nobuyori a shove from behind, but this only pushed Nobuyori completely over the horse's back and onto the ground on the other side.

Yoshitomo's men were too sickened to laugh. Nobuyori stood, dirt on his face and blood streaming from his nose. He glared at the warriors and then at his assistant, and then finally managed to hoist himself onto the horse.

In disgust at Nobuyori's cowardice and incompetence Yoshitomo turned and rode to southeastern Ikunō Gate, taking his sons Akugenda Yoshihira and Yoritomo with him, along with two hundred horsemen. Lord Nobuyori, still somewhat shaky in his saddle, rode to the eastern Taiken Gate followed by three hundred horsemen. Another force of three hundred horsemen went to defend the northeastern Yōmei Gate.

At the calling of the Hour of the Serpent, the three east gates were flung open.

Yoshitomo faced his opponents, a thousand strong, through the gateway, but neither side moved. He heard a shout from his left and looked to see Lord Nobuyori riding away from the Taiken Gate toward the center of the palace, pursued by a young horseman in orange-corded armor decked with butterflies.

"Ai!" cried Akugenda Yoshihira to his father. "That is Shigemori, Kiyomori's son. And Nobuyori does nothing to resist him! What good is a commander who runs from battle?"

They watched in mortification as Shigemori, with a force of five hundred horsemen, chased Nobuyori as far as the sandalwood tree in the center of the courtyard.

"Already the coward Nobuyori has lost Taiken Gate," growled Yoshitomo. "Take a few men, Akugenda Yoshihira. Show what true warriors can do and drive the lordling from Rokuhara out."

"Gladly, Father." Akugenda Yoshihira selected seventeen of his best horsemen and rode off to face the enemy.

Yoshitomo turned to the young Yoritomo, who sat very calm on his small horse. "Watch, my son, and learn."

Yoritomo nodded, his face shadowed by his helmet.

As Akugenda Yoshihira and his seventeen approached the Taira forces, he announced, "You see before you Akugenda Yoshihira, resident of Kamakura, son and heir of Harima Governor Yoshitomo of the Minomoto clan! I am eighteen years, fought in battle since fifteen, and have never been defeated. I believe the warrior I see before me, wearing orange-corded armor is none other than Major of the Gate Guards of the Left Shigemori, Kiyomori's son and heir. There is your worthy target, men. Seize and kill him!"

The seventeen riders charged as a single line abreast into the five hundred horsemen of the Taira, harrying them with such fury that Shigemori's forces beat a hasty retreat through the Taiken Gate and out onto Ōmiya Avenue.

"Hah!" cried Yoshitomo on seeing his son's success. "That is how it should be done!" Seeing Nobuyori hiding behind the sandalwood tree, Yoshitomo shook his fist at him. Though he was too distant to be heard, Yoshitomo yelled at the craven lord, "You see, you coward? That is how it should be done!" To another horseman beside him, Yoshitomo said, "Ride to my son and tell him to press his advantage. He must keep up the attack."

The horseman rode off with the message. However, Akugenda Yoshihira pulled back from the Taiken Gate and began to regroup his seventeen riders in the courtyard.

Suddenly fresh troops of the Taira, led again by Shigemori, poured in through the Taiken Gate.

Akugenda Yoshihira cried, "They may be fresh troops, but it is the same general. Same orders, men, aim for no one but him."

Again the seventeen horsemen charged into the Taira forces, beating fiercely with their swords. Immediately Shigemori's men had to surround their general to protect him from the attackers. Akugenda Yoshihira fitted an arrow to his bow and fired several bolts at Shigemori, but they bounced and broke off the Taira armor. "He is wearing the armor called Chinese Leather," cursed Akugenda Yoshihira. "Clear a way, men. I will fire at his horse."

At this, the Taira warriors again retreated hastily through the Taiken Gate. This time Akugenda Yoshihira and his brave seventeen charged after them out onto the avenue.

Yoshitomo grunted with satisfaction. "Well, that is a relief." Noting that the enemy forces outside the gate he guarded seemed to be preparing an attack of their own, Yoshitomo turned to his two hundred men, and said, "Come, it is time we set our own example." He raised his sword and, with a shout, charged through Ikunō Gate. His force of two hundred plowed into a mass of about one thousand, in the midst of thick clouds of dust. Yoshitomo could spare little attention for his young son, but he did note that the boy was keeping his head down to protect his face and neck from arrows and that the *sode* of the armor Eight Dragons swirled furiously about him, protecting him as though it were a thing alive.

The Taira forces must have been surprised by the ferocity of the Min-omoto attack, for they pulled back quickly, split into three groups, and galloped away down the avenue back to Rokuhara.

"Hah!" cried Yoshitomo, shaking his sword in triumph. "These men have lost their stomach for real fighting."

"Father," said Yoritomo, tugging at his sleeve and pointing back toward the Taiken Gate. Three hundred warriors were coming out, their horses at a walk, taking down their white banners. These riders followed after the retreating forces toward Rokuhara.

"Traitors!" growled Yoshitomo. He did a quick mental calculation and realized the defending forces were now down to a mere five hundred or so, his two hundred and Nobuyori's three hundred. "We must attempt an attack on Rokuhara while we can, before we lose any more men. Send word to that idiot Nobuyori that we must make our move now, gods curse that bungling demon of a man."

Rokuhara

Lord Kiyomori, dressed in full armor but for his helmet, sat in the Northern Office of Rokuhara, surrounded by his most trusted warrior-advisors. Before them was a hastily drawn plan of the compound, with pieces of red and white paper placed on it. The markers were used to show the likely places the Minomoto would attempt an attack and where the best defense might be set.

He had already directed that nearby Gojō Bridge be torn up and made into two shield walls on the east side of the river. Messengers reported that the tactic was successful at holding the Minomoto forces off for the time being.

The paneled door flew open and Shigemori rushed in, helmetless, his orange-corded armor spattered with blood. "Father," he said breathlessly, "I have returned."

"Are you wounded, my son?" asked Kiyomori.

Shigemori shook his head. "This blood is not mine. My horse was shot out from under me and I fell onto a pile of cut wood that was floating in the Horikawa River. Akugenda Yoshihira himself would have taken me there, but for my retainers Yosozaemon and Kondo, who put me on a horse and took the blows meant for me. They are dead, and Yoshihira has their heads."

Kiyomori put his hand on Shigemori's shoulder. "They did their duty admirably, then. It is the greatest honor to die in place of one's lord. Do not feel sorrow for them; instead be proud. Now tell me, how is our plan working?"

Shigemori took a deep breath. "So far as I could see, it is working well. We have drawn all of the rebel forces out of the Imperial Compound, and they are headed this way."

"Good. Go and assemble a new force, then, that they may be brought deeper into our trap."

General Minomoto Yoshitomo led his forces at a brisk walk down the avenue toward Rokuhara. The craven Nobuyori rode beside him, huddled fearfully in his saddle. *How different he is now from just a few weeks ago, when he burned Sanjō Palace,* thought Yoshitomo. *Then he was puffed up with arrogance. Now he is a sodden rag with the shape of a man.* Again Yoshitomo prayed that Nobuyori would do nothing shameful.

Along the way, Yoshitomo noted that every street corner in the southeast quarter of the city had a guard posted, and barriers were being put up. Looking up the street, he saw more troops of warriors, as well as noblemen's carriages, hurrying to Rokuhara to obey the Imperial summons. When Yoshitomo and his horsemen reached the place where Gojō Bridge had been, instead they found two fence shields, one on each side of the river. Behind each fence was a line of archers, bows and arrows at the ready.

"This . . . this . . . this is impossible!" Lord Nobuyori exclaimed. Suddenly he whipped his horse with his reins, bolted from the Minomoto forces, and galloped away west down Yamamomo Street, fleeing for his life.

Yoshitomo stared after him, aghast and sick to his stomach.

"Father," said young Yoritomo, "shouldn't we chase him?"

Yoshitomo spit on the pavement where Nobuyori had ridden. "Let him go. If he were with us, he would only get in the way. We are better off without such leaders."

"Father, here comes Akugenda Yoshihira."

Yoshitomo's eldest son came riding up to them. "Curse it, I had Taira Shigemori nearly in my hands, but he escaped."

"You will have another chance, my son. Who comes here?"

A force of three hundred men came riding up within a few yards of them and stopped there. Yoshitomo recognized them as the force that had deserted the Imperial Compound, led by his cousin Minomoto Yorimasa. Yoshitomo hissed softly.

"That traitor," said Akugenda Yoshihira. "He seems to be trying to decide which force is the stronger and therefore the one he should join. I will show him that is not how a Minomoto behaves." Akugenda Yoshihira drew his sword, took his seventeen horsemen, and charged Yorimasa's forces. So fierce was their charge that Yorimasa and his men took flight down a side street, Akugenda Yoshihira in pursuit.

General Yoshitomo, while proud of his son's spirit, was concerned that Akugenda Yoshihira was wasting his energy on one who was not the main enemy. To Yoritomo, he said, "We had better go after your brother and remind him of what we are here to do."

Yorimasa's forces had galloped across the Kamo River, apparently making the choice to join with the Rokuhara warriors. Yoshitomo and his two hundred horsemen caught up to his son and joined in the pursuit, smashing the two fence shields and charging across the river up to the wall of Rokuhara compound. Yoshitomo and his men fought like demons, firing arrows over the wall onto the roofs of Rokuhara like the dragons of storm clouds delivering unrelenting rain.

Lord Kiyomori heard the clatter of arrows striking the paneled doors behind him, and he whipped around. "What is this? Have our warriors become so lax that the enemy can get this near? Things are either disorganized or dire. I'd better go lead the forces myself." He put on his helmet and his sword, slung a quiver of eighteen arrows onto his back, and strode out to the verandah, calling for his horse.

His mount, a large, well-muscled black stallion with a black saddle, was brought to him, and he mounted from the verandah. Thirty of his foot soldiers carrying *naginata* surrounded him and thirty horsemen, including two of his sons, Shigemori and Munemori, rode by his side to protect Lord Kiyomori from becoming the target of enemy arrows.

As they rode out, they encountered Minomoto Yorimasa and his warriors. "Ah, fresh troops!" cried Shigemori. "Drive Yoshitomo and his men away from the walls. We will circle around from another way and surprise him."

Yorimasa nodded his assent and led his men ahead of the Taira horsemen, charging into General Yoshitomo's warriors, forcing them back across the river to the western bank.

From that side of the river, Yoshitomo cried, "It shames me to have to ask, Yorimasa, why you have chosen to serve the Ise Taira. You disgrace the martial fame of our house by your betrayal."

"How is it betrayal," Yorimasa answered back, "to answer the call of the Emperor of Ten Virtues, particularly when it may save our house and our martial fame? The fact that you chose to serve the most spineless villain our land has ever seen has brought the greater shame to our clan."

General Yoshitomo did not reply, for he felt in his heart the truth of Yorimasa's words. Instead he turned to his men and his sons, and said, "There shall be no more retreat from here. This is where we prove our skill and our courage. If they attack again, fight with all your will and take as many of them as you can."

"Father," said Akugenda Yoshihira, pointing westward. A force of five hundred horsemen, led by Shigemori, was coming down toward them from the right. Another force could be seen slipping past them beyond the houses to the left. "We are being surrounded. They plan to catch us in a trap."

The Taira hooted at them from the opposite bank and the walls of Rokuhara. "Now you see our lovely plan? Now you see why we pulled back from the palace? Come and attack us now, if you dare!"

"*So ka,*" Yoshitomo said, a coldness filling his heart, "here is where we die. Let us fight bravely and well to the last, then, and shame those who would dishonor us."

One of his retainers, Kamata, leapt off his horse and grabbed on to the bit and reins of Yoshitomo's mount. "My lord, hear me, I beg you. The warrior skills of your clan are legendary to all, even to the great *kami*. This is not the place to die and lose all, trampled beneath the hooves of the Taira. Do not lose sight of what chance there may yet be for victory. If you flee now, and return to the Eastern Provinces, there will be many more men to serve you. Then you may return and achieve the victory that now eludes you. There will be no future praises for a general who has thrown away his life. But much would be said of a man who outwitted his enemies and overcame them."

"You suggest I should flee, like that coward Nobuyori?" asked Yoshitomo, astounded. "Should I let tale-singers link my name in infamy with his? Never. Let go of my horse." Yoshitomo put his heels to the steed's flanks and tried to charge across the river.

But Kamata held fast. Other retainers joined him, grabbing Yoshitomo's saddle and bridle. "No, my lord!" they cried. "We cannot let you. It would be disloyal. Go!" They pushed and shoved and slapped his horse until it took off, surrounded by his sons, to the west. Taira warriors chased them, sending flights of arrows against their backs, until Yoshitomo and his men scattered like geese before a storm, heedless in their escape.

Snow on a Stone

Snow drifted down gently as the evening darkened outside the temple of Ninna-ji, high in the hills north of Heian Kyō. Good news drifted in gently, too, as messengers arrived every hour from the capital. Thus Retired Emperor Go-Shirakawa learned that his sister Jōsaimon'in had made it safely to the monastery of Kuramadera. Thus he learned that the Minomoto rebels were fleeing and that the Taira were victorious.

Go-Shirakawa sat with the abbot, his brother Kakushō, and they sipped at cups of warmed sake as they watched the snow.

"This is so much more pleasant," said Kakushō, "than the last time Ninna-Ji hosted a former Emperor during a rebellion. The last time, it was our brother who is now called the Shin-In, and it was he who was the rebel. I could not turn him away, but I could not, in good conscience, show him much courtesy either. I suspect his brief stay with us was not a happy one."

"I do not think he is happy anywhere," said Go-Shirakawa. "Certainly not in exile on Sanuki."

"Some of the monks here," Kakushō said, "have claimed they have seen his spirit scowling in at them through the *shōji.*"

"But our brother is not yet dead," said Go-Shirakawa. "How is it possible that his ghost wanders?"

"It is said," replied Kakushō, "that the truly evil can send their spirits anywhere they choose, no matter where their physical body may reside. And I have heard that the Shin-In has transformed himself into a most fearsome demon, by dedicating sacred sutras to the forces of Hell. I have occasionally worried as to what such a demon, of Imperial blood, descended from Amaterasu herself, might be capable of."

"Even on holy ground such as this?" asked Go-Shirakawa.

Kakushō tilted his head. "Even here. But perhaps the monks are only imagining things and these stories are of little consequence."

Another messenger was escorted into the room, snow still clinging to his *sode* and helmet. He knelt and bowed low. "Former Majesty, Holy One,

I bring you good news. The Taira have chased the Minomoto forces into the mountains to the east, where the snow is storming far worse than here. The rebels can surely not escape for long in such weather."

Go-Shirakawa nodded and smiled at the messenger. "This is good news indeed. I thank you."

Kakushō said to the monks beside the messenger, "Take him to the kitchens and give him food and drink like the others."

When the messenger had departed, Kakushō added, "I suspect not all of the rebel forces will have fled westward. Before long, we will be seeing some of those unfortunates here, begging for sanctuary. If they do, I will have them brought to you, so that you may have the amusement of dealing with their punishment yourself."

"That is generous of you."

"Anything for so esteemed a guest as you. Who knows, perhaps we will be graced with the presence of the mighty Yoshitomo himself."

Go-Shirakawa paused a moment before saying, "I doubt it. I have met the Minomoto general. He has too much fire in him, I think, to hide away in a shrine and wear monk's robes. I expect he will eventually head back to the Kantō to try to raise more men to his banner."

They drank their rice wine in companionable silence for a while before Kakushō said, "This victory is welcome for another reason. There are some monks here and at other temples, monks skilled in observing the heavens, who claim that we are entering the *mappo*, the Age of the End of the Law. It is to be marked by great calamities, the high falling low, and so forth. The fact that the Imperial will prevailed may be a sign that the astrologers' calculations may not be entirely accurate."

"One could hope so," said Go-Shirakawa. One of the large bamboo blinds beside them was still rolled up so that they might look out on one of the temple gardens. The coals in the little braziers between the two men had given enough warmth for them to be comfortable. But the breeze seemed to have changed direction, and now Go-Shirakawa felt a discernible chill.

Out in the center of the garden there was a large, round white stone, almost a boulder. As snow fell upon it, the shape and shadows created the illusion of a skull staring back at Go-Shirakawa. His skin went cold, and he pulled his heavy brocade robes tighter around himself. Go-Shirakawa turned his gaze away and stared down at the sake cup in his hand. *Have I drunk so much to be seeing things?* He blinked and looked back at the garden. The wind had changed the shape of the snow on the stone.

Now he saw a face with sunken cheeked and hateful eyes, a mask of pure malice. He recognized it as his brother, the Shin-In. And then another gust of wind blew the snow away, and the rock was again merely a rock.

When Go-Shirakawa looked down at his hand again, it was shaking. *Surely it is just the story Kakushō told that influenced my mind. That and the drink, that is all.*

"Are you all right, brother?" asked Kakushō. "You are trembling. Shall I have the blinds lowered to keep out the drafts?"

"Though it is early, perhaps it is time for me to get some rest. It has been a worrisome day."

An inner door of the room slid open and an acolyte of the temple knelt and bowed at the entrance. "Holy One, Majesty, a visitor has arrived with his attendant, seeking sanctuary."

"Aha! Just as I predicted," said the abbot with a wry smile, "our first guest. You cannot go to bed just yet, brother, without seeing the fish who has washed up on our shore."

"You are right, Kakushō. I would be sorry to have missed it. I can stay up a while longer." To the acolyte, Go-Shirakawa said, "You may send our visitor in."

But before the acolyte could respond, a fat, bedraggled nobleman wearing only his white under-kimono stumbled in past him, followed by a frightened looking attendant also only in his underrobe.

"*You,*" said Go-Shirakawa, recognizing the once-arrogant Lord Nobuyori.

"My . . . my former Sovereign!" said Nobuyori, falling to his knees before them. His hair was thoroughly unkempt, and there were three lines, dark blue bruises, across his pudgy left cheek. "How, er . . . fortunate I am to find you here! Good abbot, I am blessed that you allow me in your presence."

Both men set down their sake cups solemnly. "What makes you believe that you are welcome here?" asked Kakushō.

"Well, surely, as a holy man, you must understand that I have been a victim of Fate, neh? I only did what I have done because of that horrible false monk Shinzei. Surely you can understand that, neh? And my former Sovereign, surely you can be forgiving. Is that not one of the Ten Virtues? You once looked upon me with favor. It was your influence that allowed me to become Great Commander, after all."

"And I have since," said Go-Shirakawa, "come to regret it."

"But . . . but I treated you well while you resided in the Single-Copy Library, did I not?" protested Nobuyori. "All your needs were met, you were well looked after?"

"You . . . burned . . . down . . . my . . . *palace!*" Go-Shirakawa growled. "You murdered my friends and my servants and their children!"

"B-but that was necessary, neh? To get at Shinzei. Forgive me, O-Dai-In, but I cannot be blamed if you chose to listen to the counsel of a syco-phantic schemer—"

"I have heard enough!" Go-Shirakawa roared. "Secure this man in a cell and send word to Rokuhara that we have him."

"Mercy, my lords, mercy!" cried Nobuyori. "Look at me! All my friends have deserted me. When I met General Yoshitomo as he fled into the mountains and asked for his help, he called me a great coward! He whipped me!" Nobuyori pointed at the bruises on his cheek.

"And then he deserted us, and we had to wander these hills alone. We met with robber monks in the woods, and they stole our clothing and goods and horses. We have nearly frozen ourselves walking here. Have I not suffered as much as any man ought? If you send me to Rokuhara, the Taira will execute me!"

"*Hai,*" said Go-Shirakawa. "They will."

Kakushō called for armed monks to come take Nobuyori and his attendant and lock them up in a rice-storage shed for the night.

Go-Shirakawa added, "And send a messenger to Rokuhara immediately, informing them of the once-high leaf, fallen in winter, that has blown through our door. Have them send someone to take these two away in the morning."

The monks bowed and the former Great Commander Nobuyori was dragged away whimpering and weeping into his sleeves.

When they had gone, Kakushō again picked up his sake cup, saying, "Sometimes, even when the night appears dark, the All-Seeing Buddha will send a gift."

"Indeed," said Go-Shirakawa.

Winter Rain

The morning was gray with brooding clouds, and a chill winter rain fell fitfully from the sky. Taira no Shigemori sat on a leather stool on the riverbank outside the Rokuhara compound, the *tachi* sword Kogarasu lying across his knees. He stared down at the shivering, once-grand Nobuyori, who knelt before him. Never had Shigemori had so satisfying a task as bringing the former Great Commander from the Temple of Ninna-ji to his sentence of execution at Rokuhara.

When the messenger had come from Ninna-ji the night before, Shigemori had begged his father for the honor of bringing Nobuyori to justice. To his surprise, Lord Kiyomori had readily agreed, also permitting him the honor of executing Nobuyori.

Early that morning, Shigemori had taken a hundred horsemen and ridden to Ninna-ji to retrieve the prisoner. Nobuyori and his aide had not fared well from spending the night in a rice shed. Their skin was clammy and cold, and they shook dreadfully, as if struck with palsy. There had been argument among the Taira escort as to whether Nobuyori should be given extra clothing to ward off the cold winter rain. Shigemori finally had ordered him to be dressed in a peasant's straw raincoat. "I want him to live to watch the sword that will cut off his head," Shigemori had said. But Nobuyori couldn't stay in his saddle at all well, particularly with his hands tied. By the time Shigemori had led his men back to Rokuhara, Nobuyori's face was a mess of muddy bruises and bloody scrapes.

"So," said Shigemori, "what have you to say for yourself?"

Nobuyori held his hands, palms up, before him. "You s-seem a wise young man. What s-sensible person would have acted as I d-did, in such total disrespect of the Emperor? S-surely you can see that none of this could have been my fault. It was all the work of a demon, I swear."

"A demon," repeated Shigemori, dubiously.

Nobuyori clasped his chubby hands together and stared at the ground. "Yes, a demon. In dreams, I saw him. The Shin-In. He told me he would help me get everything I desired. He told me the desires of other men in the palace, so that I could gain their goodwill. The Shin-In told me I would become known as a hero for this, that I would make Nihon strong again. I was not aware that I was committing crimes. How can you blame me? Please, speak with your father for me. Send me into exile, if you must, but s-spare my life!"

Shigemori stood, frowning. "You are the most despicable man I have ever seen. I think the only demons riding you were named Greed and Ambition. The nobles who have come to Rokuhara have told us of your excesses and your evil. His Majesty the Emperor himself has told us how you imprisoned him and tried to set yourself up in his place. After all you have done, there is no saving you now."

Nobuyori bent down, his forehead to the ground, his body shaking with his sobbing.

Shigemori drew Kogarasu from the scabbard and, with a swift stroke, beheaded Nobuyori.

A Vision of Hachiman

Young Minomoto Yoritomo crawled on his hands and knees through the snow up the mountainside. His gloves and shin guards were soaked, and he couldn't feel his hands or lower legs anymore. He could barely see more than an arm's length ahead of him, so thick was the blowing snow. He could barely hear his breathing for the howling of the wind. *Hachiman, do not let me die here, he prayed. I have only lived thirteen years, and I have not yet brought you glory.*

When the Minomoto had fled east from the capital, General Yoshitomo had decided the road would be unsafe, and so they escaped through the wilderness, up the very side of mountains where no paths led. But the mountain *kami*, it would seem, were not pleased, and sent heavy snowstorms to plague the fleeing warriors. First they had had to abandon their armor, for the wind in the wide *sode* would have blown them off the mountainside and the *yoryoi* would have hindered their movement. Then they had to abandon their horses, for the beasts could not climb the icy rocks and steep hillsides.

It brought tears to Yoritomo's eyes to remember dropping Eight Dragons into the snow. *What unworthy bandit will find it? Surely my ancestor Yoshiie must be dismayed. What will protect me now?* All Yoritomo had with him now of his warrior's kit was the sword, Higekiri.

But because he was young and small, Yoritomo had not been able to keep up with his father or brothers, and in the heavy storm he had soon lost sight of them. He had no idea where they might be or where he was. Yoritomo had never felt so tired, so hungry or so cold in his life.

With a groan, Yoritomo collapsed facefirst into a snowbank, cursing his weakness. Surely the Taira and their supporters could not be far behind. *I must keep going.* As he turned his head, he saw a glimmering light on the snow around him.

Yoritomo pushed himself up onto his knees. The falling snow was now swirling in a circular pattern, as if a great mirror were appearing before him. *Have I gone mad?* thought the boy. *Or is this what one sees when it is time to die?* Out of the bright spot of light rode a warrior on a great white horse.

"Father?" Yoritomo whimpered, ashamed of the childishness in his voice.

The man on the horse rode closer, and Yoritomo recognized him from another place, a temple he had visited long ago.

"Hachiman . . ." Yoritomo breathed.

The apparition inclined its head.

Yoritomo bowed three times, and then asked, "Great Hachiman, help me. Where is my father?"

In a hollow voice like wind in a cave, impressive as the battle cry of a great army, Hachiman replied, "Think no more on your father, Yoritomo. Your fates are now forever parted. I come to fulfill a promise I made long ago."

Yoritomo hung his head and murmured a portion of the Sutra of Filial Piety. When he finished, he asked, "Am I to die now?"

"You have much more yet to accomplish in this world. It is not yet your time to leave it. Take hold of my stirrup."

As if in a dream, Yoritomo did so. Hachiman turned his horse and rode into the storm, up the mountainside. Yoritomo stumbled along beside him as best he could.

"Great Hachiman, if I will not see my father again, what of my brothers?"

"Those who live will be scattered like seeds of autumn."

Yoritomo did not want to ask which ones would live. "Where are we going?"

Hachiman did not answer.

The boy did not know how long he walked beside Hachiman's horse. They traveled through pine forest and over bare, ice-covered slopes of rock and gravel. The snow in the air around them was so dense that it was like walking through a cloud. The light that emanated from the *kami* illuminated strange shapes, and at times Yoritomo imagined he saw great dragons peering out of the mist at him.

At last, the *kami* stopped his horse. "Here."

"Where are we, Lord Hachiman?" Yoritomo asked through lips so cold he could not feel them.

But the horse and the rider simply faded away, and Yoritomo fell to his hands and knees again with a hopeless cry.

A strong gust of wind cleared the air before him, and Yoritomo saw a small stick-and-thatch hut nestled into the mountainside. An old monk was emerging from it, coming toward him, robes held tightly against the cold.

"Who is there?" called the monk. "Who cried out?"

"Me, it was me!" said Yoritomo trying to stand. "Help me please!"

The old monk came up to him and took his arm. "What is this? What is a boy like you doing out in this weather, up here on the mountain? You look half-frozen to death! Come in! Come in at once and sit by my fire."

Yoritomo let the old monk lead him into the hut, hoping his shameful tears would not freeze upon his face.

New Year's Day

*I*t was a solemn, yet contented New Year's Day at Rokuhara. The traditional decorative balls made from silk ribbons and iris blossoms hung
from the roof beams to keep demons at bay. Although there would be no
procession to the Imperial palace for feasting and celebration this year, the
Taira had reason enough to celebrate on their own. Lord Kiyomori gazed
proudly at his family, seated on straw mats and silken cushions as they ate
the holiday rice gruel mixed with the Seven Lucky Herbs.

The ladies, daughters, wives, and concubines of Kiyomori and his
sons did not need their curtains of modesty, for everyone was family here.
They and their serving maids reclined on the floor, their bright colorful
kimonos and long, flowing black hair adding to the festive appearance of
the great hall.

"Let us have a round of toasts," Kiyomori said, raising his cup of New
Year's plum wine. "I will begin. To His Imperial Majesty. May the monks
cleanse his palace of Nobuyori's taint quickly so that His Majesty may return
to it soon."

"To His Imperial Majesty," everyone echoed, bowing before they drank.

Shigemori, as the eldest son, was next. "To His Retired Majesty Go-
Shirakawa, who ordered exile instead of execution for the unfortunates who
fell under Nobuyori's sway, and thus avoided the excesses of the Hōgen."

"To the *In*!" everyone replied. Kiyomori noted that although Shigemori
had become more of a warrior in the past year, still he was a Buddhist
scholar and nobleman. Thoughts of peace and just dealings were never far
from the young man's mind. Though the fact that Go-Shirakawa had declined Kiyomori's offer to stay at Rokuhara until his new palace was built
was a matter of concern among the Taira. *Perhaps Shigemori is being shrewd
in case the In has spies among us.*

It was now Motomori's turn. "To our father, Lord Kiyomori, who is
now Daijin and an exalted member of the First Rank."

This was met with a resounding cheer, which Kiyomori acknowledged
with a smile and a bow. He flicked rice grains off the sleeves of his new
black robes, his swelling pride distracted when Motomori fell into a fit of
coughing. The people around Motomori pounded his back and rubbed his
arms until his fit passed, but Kiyomori watched him with concern. *Motomori
is a fine second son and will make a good warrior when his illness lifts. If it
ever does.*

The next toast fell to Munemori. "Um. Well. To us!" Munemori said at last. "We three brothers are all now governors of provinces, with riches and higher rank to come. Let us drink to the good fortune of the Taira!"

It was somewhat tactless of Munemori to boast so, but everyone echoed "To us!" and drank nonetheless. Kiyomori reflected that it was just as well that Munemori was the third son. Munemori showed no particular talent at anything, scholarship or swordsmanship, and therefore it was good that not much authority would ever be expected of him.

There were more toasts after that and a round of poetry competition where nothing of much value was created. As the night wore on, Kiyomori learned from one of his servants that a particular *gosechi* dancer Kiyomori had admired would be waiting for him in a guest chamber. Kiyomori excused himself from the festivities and began to leave the hall.

He nearly tripped when the hem of his trousers was caught in a gripping hand. "A word with you, husband," said Tokiko, who had been seated near the sliding door.

Kiyomori swallowed his impatience and sat with her. He noticed again that she was aging; there were strands of silver now among her raven tresses, and her face was not so fine as it once had been. It had been a while since he had slept beside her. "What would you, wife? I am quite tired and wish to rest."

"Is that it?" she said, tilting her head. "Or does a sweetness beyond dreams await? No matter. The warning I must give is not of a domestic sort."

"We must not speak of the sword here!"

"Not that either, though I am heartened that you still remember your promise. It is this matter of the palace going unoccupied through the New Year."

"What is that to us?"

Tokiko stared at him as if he had gone mad. "It may be everything, husband. No one is protecting the Imperial palace at a time when demons and evil spirits run free. No one is giving His Majesty the Medicinal Offerings to keep him in good health. His Majesty is not performing the Worship Rite prayers before the Sacred Mirror, to keep the country in harmony."

"There are practical reasons for all of this."

"Yes, so it is said. But now is not a time for complacency. The Minomoto general and his sons are still at large. It benefits the wise man to be cautious and remain vigilant."

Kiyomori sighed. "All is being done that need be done. What matter that we pause to take a little pleasure in life?"

Tokiko turned her face away. "My father thought you a man of great foresight. I regret that his choice of heroes may have been mistaken."

Kiyomori felt himself flush with anger. "If you are so disappointed in me, why do you stay? Why don't you return to the sea and your father's kingdom?"

Tokiko gazed back at him, her eyes cold. "I cannot. I swore an oath to save you sorry mortals from your doom—though I am beginning to think my efforts are in vain."

"Perhaps your father should have sent a man to become a hero among us, then, instead of a woman who can only fight with her tongue."

"My father has no sons," Tokiko hissed. "Only daughters. Perhaps my father hoped my loins might produce the hero you want."

Kiyomori gazed back over his shoulder at his sons. "Shigemori?"

"Perhaps. Perhaps our grandson yet to be. Who can say? But hear me, husband. Now is not a time to rest from care. The battle is over, but the war is not. I beg you once more, be vigilant!"

His patience at an end, Kiyomori stood. "Believe me, I do not forget your words of warning. They follow me day and night. But your habit of seeing every flaw in a silver mirror is tiresome, woman. We have won. The Emperor is safe. The Taira are ascendant. Your father and all the *kami* look after us. We need no longer start at the chirp of every cricket or imagine that the rain on the roof is a rain of arrows. Be at peace, wife, and give me peace as well."

Kiyomori strode away, not looking back at Tokiko. He hoped the dancer could keep his evening from being completely spoiled.

A Ghostly Procession

Taira no Munemori, Lord Kiyomori's third son, also slipped away from the celebration early, in order to have a tryst with a completely unsuitable woman. For once, Munemori was glad that he was the unimportant son. All attention was paid to the shining Shigemori, somewhat less to the dutiful if sickly Motomori. No one cared at all when Munemori excused himself and hurried out to where the ox-carriages were kept.

Munemori chose to take no escort, only the ox-driver of the carriage. The house he was visiting was in the deteriorating northwest quarter of the city, the lady of a family that had fallen into poverty and deep disfavor. The fewer witnesses there were to this ill-considered visit, the fewer tongues there would be to wag to his wife and parents.

Munemori settled onto the seat of the carriage and heard the whip crack ahead of him. The carriage lurched forward and bumped over the threshold gate beam. As it rumbled down the street, Munemori drifted into reveries about the poor creature he would be seeing soon. He tried to form a poem in his mind, but he was never good at poetry, he had always found the art rather silly and worthless, in fact. Fortunately, his lady of the tall weed house would not care about such things. She would be flattered enough that a Taira was paying call on her. Munemori knew her hopes of advancement through him were in vain, but there was no need to discourage her just yet. Not when she was so giving of herself for the sake of those hopes.

A strong, cold wind was blowing from the north, making the eaves of the houses they passed creak and moan. Now and then, Munemori would peer out through the carriage window curtain. There was no moon in the clear, dark sky, but the stars were very bright. The streets were deserted, few wishing to venture out on a night when demons might be abroad, few wishing to leave the New Year's celebrations in their warm homes.

After some time and travel, the carriage suddenly stopped.

It did not seem to Munemori that they had gone far enough to be at his destination. "What is it? Why have we stopped?" he called up to the ox-driver.

The response was only a strangled cry of fear.

"What is wrong? Is it bandits?" For a moment, Munemori regretted not having brought a few horsemen along, but whom could he have trusted? Any bandits foolish or desperate enough to attack a Taira carriage would surely know there would be swift retribution.

"N-no, my lord," the ox-driver said at last. "We are at Suzaku Avenue, and the oxen will not continue."

"Well, whip them, man."

"My lord, if you could see what they and I see, you would not wish to continue either."

With a grunt of impatience, Munemori opened the back door of the carriage and stepped out. He was prepared to grab the whip and apply it to the back of the driver himself if need be. Munemori walked around beside the oxen, the high stone wall of the Imperial Compound to his right. Munemori looked down Suzaku Avenue, and his breath caught in his throat.

A ghostly procession was coming up the avenue. It consisted of a tall, ornate palanquin borne by five men in front and six in back, all dressed in warrior's armor. The procession approached at a stately pace, the pale men marching with gaze straight forward, never wavering.

Munemori would have liked to run, but his feet seemed frozen in place by fear. As the procession came closer, Munemori could see the dark lines that crossed every one of the ghostly warriors' necks.

"I know those men," Munemori said softly. "That is my great-uncle, Tadamasa, in the front, with his sons. Behind is Minomoto Tameyoshi and his sons. These men were all executed at the end of the Hōgen." Behind him, he could hear the ox-driver muttering rapid prayers to the Amida Buddha.

The gate to the Imperial Compound was just ahead and to their right. Munemori watched as the palanquin proceeded right up to the gate itself, stopping right in front of them.

"Surely they cannot enter," murmured the ox-driver. "The Imperial palace is a holy place, guarded by Fudō-Myō with sword and rope."

But Munemori knew, for he had overheard his mother, that the palace was poorly guarded this New Year's night.

The curtain of the palanquin was pulled aside, revealing a darkness seen only by the denizens of Hell. Within it was a creature that might once have been a man, but the hair was wild and unkempt beneath a stained silk scarf, and his fingernails were long and clawlike. His eyes were deep-sunken, and a pale light glimmered in them: his skin was sallow and his chin pointed. This creature smiled and nodded at Munemori, one nobleman graciously greeting another.

Munemori did not know what compelled him, but he fell to his knees on the cold wet paving stones and walked upon his knees up to the palanquin. There he bowed low to the creature as if it were the Emperor himself. "Wh-who, what are you? What do you want of me?"

A long, thin arm snaked down from the palanquin, and cold fingers wrapped around his head. "Ahhhh. Taira Munemori. Wise of you to give obeisance to your former sovereign. I sense you are somewhat empty of spirit. Good. There is room for me here."

Munemori felt a chill of fear in his bones, as if they had become icicles. "You are the Sh-Shin-In?" Everyone in Heian Kyō had heard tales of the Emperor who had become a demon.

"I am. Be on your way. We will meet again." The icy hand withdrew from his head. The curtain of the palanquin was drawn closed once more.

Munemori looked up as the procession moved forward again, passing right through the thick wooden gates of the Suzakumon and into the Imperial Compound itself. He jumped to his feet and ran back to the carriage.

"The ghosts have entered the palace! W-we must warn someone!" said the ox-driver.

"No!" said Munemori. "Who would believe us? And there would be questions as to why I was here and where I was going. No, we will continue on as if nothing has happened. It is merely a vision from the New Year's wine, nothing more."

Munemori got back in the carriage, reassured as the whip cracked again and the carriage rumbled forward. There were cold, wet stains on his long robe where he had knelt on it. He suspected the silk might be torn. Munemori knew the lady of the tall weed house would pay little attention to such things. But he doubted even she could lift the dread that had settled on his soul.

Bathwater

General Minomoto Yoshitomo gazed at the gate of the Osada country mansion, his soul as numb as his feet. He had come many *li*, fighting through bands of rogue monks, and pushing through blinding snowstorms in the mountains. In Ōmi Province, he and his sons had been forced to remove and leave behind all the Minomoto heirloom armor in the snow, and then had to abandon their horses.

In Mino Province, they had been set upon while taking refuge at an inn. One of his retainers disguised himself as the General and then killed himself so that Yoshitomo might get away. Yoshitomo had had to kill his second son, Tomonaga, who had been wounded in the leg so badly that he could not continue the journey.

Yoshitomo's other sons, Yoshihira and Yoritomo, had fallen behind in the blizzards. For all Yoshitomo knew, he was the only member of his immediate family still alive.

Only he and his retainer Kamata had continued on together, hiding in a boat that took them downriver to Owari Province and the town of Utsumi, where the Osada family, hereditary retainers of the Minomoto for generations, lived. One of the Osada family was Kamata's father-in-law, so the two of them felt certain that, at last, here they would find help.

Guards came out of the gate of the Osada mansion and confronted them. "Who are you? Are you ruffians? Vagabonds? What do you want?"

Wearily, Kamata replied, "Do you not know a great man when you see him? This is the Lord Director of the Stables of the Left, briefly Lord Governor of Harima, Minomoto Yoshitomo."

The guards gasped, for that name was known everywhere in the land.

"And I am Kamata Hyoe, son-in-law of Osada Shoji Tadamune, who, I believe, is one of the family you serve."

"Ah! Please, forgive our not knowing you both! Come in, come in at once, and we will announce you have arrived."

The two of them were guided into an outer chamber of the mansion, where they were seated before a hearthfire and warm braziers. They were given warm cloaks and dry stockings for their feet. Ladies of the household brought them cups of warm broth and cooked rice. Throughout the household they could hear servants whispering to each other in awe, "The great general is here! Yoshitomo is here!"

At last, Osada Tadamune himself came in to greet them, smiling nervously at his unexpected guests. "My lord, my son, what a great honor and joy it is to see you. Please forgive our unprepared state, but we had no idea you were coming this way."

"This is all very well," said Yoshitomo, unable to enjoy the hospitality. "But I do not need fussing. I need men and arms and horses, and I need them quickly."

Tadamune's smile fell a little. "Well, but that will take time to assemble, my lord. And it is clear you are both exhausted and in great need of rest before you face whatever trials are to come. Kamata, it has been so long since you have graced our house with your presence. I have already sent word out that there is to be a welcoming party in your honor, and all the family who are here are assembling to see you. Surely you must stay for at least a while."

Yoshitomo saw the happiness and hope on Kamata's face. After suffering so much hardship together, he could not deny his faithful companion a little familial pleasure. "Very well," Yoshitomo grumbled. "We will stay through the night."

"Thank you, my lord," said Kamata softly, bowing very low.

"But I expect, Tadamune," Yoshitomo went on, "that you will also send word to all the able-bodied men of your house that they must bring arms and horses by morning to serve at my command."

"Of course, my lord, rest assured it shall be done. Now, if you will excuse me, I will see that suitable quarters are prepared, and that a hot bath is drawn for you. For there is nothing that so restores a man's health and wits as a soothing soak in hot water." Tadamune bowed and departed.

Yoshitomo allowed his mind to drift through the hours of the late afternoon, answering solicitous questions from the Osadas with only grunts. When Kamata was at last summoned to go join his family reunion, Yoshitomo waved him away with no happy words.

He tried to focus his thoughts on the days ahead, how many men he needed, where he could find more, what households in the Kantō could be counted on to support the Minomoto now. It all had seemed so clear when Nobuyori was in power—how persuasive that despicable man was! But now that the Emperor had made cause with the Taira, now the Minomoto were the rebels against the throne, and that was a difficult position to take, given that Nijō-sama had done no wrong.

Yoshitomo thought about Rokuhara, and how the compound might be breached with even a small force, although fires would have to be set right away. Even the thought of Kiyomori and the Taira burning in flames gave him no pleasure. It was only the cold prospect of a task that needed to be done.

Success at great cost, the priests at Hachimangu had said. What greater cost could a man pay, than the death of all his sons? Yoshitomo thought briefly of his youngest boys, children of his concubine Tokiwa. *By now, no doubt, the Taira will have found and killed them. And what of Tokiwa, beautiful Tokiwa herself?* Yoshitomo dared not think about her, for it might bring a pain too difficult to bear.

"My lord?" said a servant from a doorway. "Your bath is prepared. If you will please do me the honor of following me."

Yoshitomo rose and followed the servant to a room in which a large, round tub was set into a raised wooden floor. Wisps of steam rose from the hot water, dancing like ghosts at a festival. Yoshitomo disrobed and eased himself into the water, his muscles and skin at last convincing him that rest and a bath were a very good idea. He closed his eyes and breathed in the soothing steam and tried to empty his mind as monks were said to do through chanting of the sutras. He wondered if, after his battles were done, he would ever retire to take the tonsure, sit in a lonely mountainside temple, and copy sutras until his spirit passed to the other world. Somehow he could not imagine such a future for himself. More likely a Taira arrow would take him when he again attacked Rokuhara.

He heard noises and opened his eyes. Servants were entering the room bearing towels, averting their faces. "Be quick about your task and then leave me in peace," Yoshitomo grumbled at them.

"We will, my lord," they said. They drew knives from under the towels and leapt onto the platform. Before Yoshitomo could pull himself from the water, the knives plunged into his chest with a cold shock.

Betrayed . . . was all he had time to think as his blood mingled with the bathwater, running out as his luck surely had.

Matters of Disgrace

Seven days later, Kiyomori watched from the wall of the Imperial Compound as the Osadas, Tadmune and his son, hurried away in their carriage in shame.

They had brought the heads of Minomoto Yoshitomo and his retainer Kamata to the capital, proud of themselves. The Emperor had dutifully given them minor governorships in reward, but there was underlying loathing for the Osadas. A sworn hereditary retainer who betrays and kills his master, as well as killing a son-in-law of the family, cannot expect respect.

When the Osadas expressed displeasure with their appointments and demanded greater reward, the court saw fit instead to summarily strip them of the posts they had been given and throw them out. As the carriage proceeded down Suzaku Avenue, rocks and vegetables rained down from the palace walls onto the carriage roof, and jeers and insults were shouted after them.

Kiyomori looked to his right, where the Imperial prison stood. On a great tree beside the prison hung the heads of Yoshitomo and other rebels. Already a crowd had gathered by the tree, paying respects and staring up at Yoshitomo's head, as if waiting for it to speak, or give an omen as Shinzei's head was said to have done.

It was a bad sign. If the cause of the Minomoto gained too much sympathy, it could only cause more problems for the Taira. Already, Kiyomori had sent his warriors out in search of all of Yoshitomo's male children. One should not leave heirs to seek revenge in future years. Kiyomori had learned that Yoshitomo's favorite concubine, Tokiwa, had fled the city with three children, all boys. Rather than chase her down, Kiyomori had cleverly arrested the woman's aged mother and let it be known throughout the capital that the old woman would be tortured and killed unless Tokiwa presented herself and her children to the Taira.

Although this was only practical, there were whispers spreading that Kiyomori was a disrespectful brute. Kiyomori had had to send several bands of his red-jacketed boys after such whisperers to see that they did not speak such hateful slander again.

At last, at midday, Kiyomori left the wall and called for his own carriage. As he was riding back to Rokuhara, the carriage stopped, and there was a rapping on the roof. Kiyomori peered out through the curtain, wondering who would dare to stop a Taira carriage. He was pleased to see it was his son Shigemori, on a horse.

"Father, I am sorry to interrupt your journey, but I bring you excellent news!"

Kiyomori smiled. "News that could not wait until I had returned?"

"I did not know you were already on your way. But listen, we have captured Yoshitomo's eldest son, Akugenda Yoshihira."

"This is good news indeed." To have captured the Ason, the heir of the Minomoto clan, meant fewer worries of a Minomoto uprising in the Eastern Provinces. "Was he found on the Tōkkaidō?"

"No, Father. He has been in the capital quite a while, apparently. He was in disguise and attempting to spy on Rokuhara when we found him."

"What have you done with him?"

Shigemori's face became more solemn. "Because the Council has put a sentence of death upon him, we have taken Akugenda Yoshihira out to the riverbed. But when I heard you would be coming home today, I held off the execution. Would you like to interrogate him before we carry out the sentence?"

Kiyomori paused, and then said, "Yes. It would be proper to let him speak his final words to me. He fought bravely and well, I am told, for his misguided father."

Kiyomori's carriage followed Shigemori back to Rokuhara. He noted there seemed to be quite a crowd assembled nearby. When they passed into the main courtyard, Shigemori dismounted and gave his horse's reins to a servant. Kiyomori got out of the carriage and followed Shigemori to the bank of the Kamo River on the north side of the Rokuhara compound.

Akugenda Yoshihira was kneeling on the rocky bank, surrounded by Taira retainers. To Kiyomori, the Minomoto Ason looked very young and thin and pale. He remembered the brash young boy who had ridden with Yoshitomo at the Hōgen, the boy who spoke so excitedly about taking heads. *And now it is his own head that will be taken.* Kiyomori felt both pity and admiration for the young man whose life was soon to be cut short.

Across the river, Kiyomori saw what the crowd was about. Many of Heian Kyō's citizens were watching with anticipation. *Are they here to see a traitor executed, or are they here to honor the son of a mighty general of a formidable family?*

"So. Akugenda Yoshihira," Kiyomori said to him, and honored him with a slight bow.

"So. Taira Kiyomori," said Yoshihira, defiance in his eyes. "The great schemer. You who made my father kill my grandfather after the Hōgen. I regret only that I do not face you with a sword in my hands."

Kiyomori nodded, expecting no less. "You were the finest of your father's generals, I have heard. Yet my son tells me you were easily caught just outside Rokuhara. What has brought you to this?"

"Only that my fortune had reached its end, o Lord of the Taira. After we Minomoto had fled, I had become lost in the snowstorms on the mountains. As I did not know my father's fate, I returned to Heian Kyō. I could have simply killed myself, but instead I hoped to fight to the death and take a few Taira with me. So I disguised myself and tried to get close to Rokuhara, but your watch was too strict, and I had become weak from exhaustion and lack of food. Only my desire to kill some of you has kept me alive. But I'm ill, and that made it easy for your lackeys to capture me. Had it not been for that, no one could have taken me."

"No one could accuse you of being without courage, Akugenda Yoshihira," said Shigemori.

Kiyomori wondered if his son Shigemori felt akin to Yoshihira, both being the heirs of great warrior clans. Certainly Kiyomori had felt that way at times toward Yoshitomo, though he never allowed such feeling to change his strategy.

Akugenda Yoshihira blinked up at the bright sun in the sky, then gazed across the river at the spectators gathered there. "In times past, warriors put their enemies to death in the dark of night, so as not to shame them. Yet here I am, defeated and, in the full light of day, shamed. Therefore, let us finish quickly and let my last words be these. May curses fall upon those pale-faced court toadies who told me not to attack you at Abeno. Had I been permitted to carry out my plan, Lord Kiyomori, you and your son would have been long dead.

"And let my curse fall upon you and your clan, Kiyomori-san. Now you see how the once mighty can fall, overnight. After I die, I shall become a demon like my uncle Tametomo, or the Shin-In. I will become a demon who can throw thunderbolts so that I might strike down each and every one of you. You shall be first, Lord Kiyomori, or"—he looked at Shige-mori—"perhaps you. Enough. I will not babble just to live longer. Cut off my head, quickly!"

He leaned forward, stretching out his neck.

Shigemori drew Kogarasu from its sheath, and with a swift stroke it was done.

There were audible gasps from the spectators across the river, and Ki-yomori could hear sutras being chanted for the brave Yoshihira.

As they were leaving the riverbank, Shigemori said, "It is a curious thing, Yoshihira's final speech."

"Curious? How?" asked Kiyomori.

"The curse he laid upon us."

"By now you should know that is nothing unusual, my son. Warriors often curse their enemies at their deaths. It is the last weapon they have."

"But he mentioned the Shin-In. Nobuyori, before his death, also spoke of the Shin-In. He said he had seen the former Emperor in dreams."

"What of that? What criminal would not prefer that his misdeeds be blamed upon demons? And blaming an Emperor who has turned himself into a demon is all that more impressive, neh? As for Akugenda Yoshihira, he was probably only hoping to frighten us, to seem brave at the last. Do I believe he will turn into a demon as well? Hah. All this talk of demons. Superstitious nonsense. It means nothing."

After a long pause Shigemori said, "My mother claims to be a daughter of the Dragon King of the Sea. Is this superstitious nonsense as well?"

Kiyomori looked away and did not reply.

Changing Winds

Tokiko watched the sun rising over the hills to the east from the verandah of her quarters at Rokuhara. Already the *kami* known as the Lady of Mount Sano was weaving her tapestry of spring. The willows in the mansion gardens were bringing forth yellow-green leaves, and the scent of new-opened cherry blossoms drifted on the air. Spring was traditionally a time of joy, for many. But spring was a young woman's season, and Tokiko was no longer young.

She shifted within her voluminous brocade kimonos, feeling the looseness of her hips and the slight ache in her back, testimony to the fact that she had borne Kiyomori ten children. Tokiko reflected again on the odd bargain she had made with her father, the Dragon King. "Live as a mortal," he had asked her, "marry a mortal and give him sons and daughters, and we may yet save mankind from its folly."

Tokiko had spent little time in the mortal realm before, and the stories that the drowned sailors and noblemen had brought to her father's undersea palace had made her curious. So she had agreed. But there was much the sailors had not said, of sorrow and loss. For the sailors had not been women.

A servant brought Tokiko morning green tea, and a bowl of onion broth with shredded daikon and some grains of rice. Tokiko could not miss the look of embarrassment and pity on the serving woman's face, and Tokiko dismissed her quickly. Tokiko had no wish to be consoled into shame.

The former mistress of the late general Yoshitomo, Tokiwa by name—and how Tokiko hated that similarity—had finally surrendered herself to the Taira in hopes of sparing her mother from torture and her sons from death. Surrendered herself in more ways than one. Kiyomori had gone to "interview" the woman and had stayed the entire night. Tokiko had heard the servants whispering as to Tokiwa's beauty, how she had sweetly pleaded for the life of her three little boys, one of whom was still a suckling babe. The servants spoke of how Kiyomori was enraptured and promised the woman her sons would be saved. How it was natural that the man who was conqueror was entitled to the former possessions of the conquered.

Tokiko was coldly enraged by what she had heard and therefore had not slept the entire night. Though she had never loved Kiyomori as the poems describe mortals who love, she had developed a strange fondness for him, a steadfast concern for his fate. Tokiko faced the spring dawn with aching eyes and heavy heart. Her mind kept saying over and over, *The fool. The fool!*

Kiyomori had had mistresses before, of course. Many of them. Tokiko had learned that older wives must accept these things. But this woman, this Tokiwa, was different.

Tokiko remembered how her father, the Dragon King, had searched the mortal world of Nihon for a man with the cunning and strength and sheer pigheadedness to achieve what needed to be done. Every dragon that swam among the coastal rocks, every turtle and koi in ornamental ponds, every snake and worm slithering in rain puddles had been put to the task. And the answer had been sailing over their heads all along. It could be Taira Kiyomori and none other. And now all of Tokiko's guidance and teaching, which had led the Great Kiyomori to the brink of being the powerful leader the kingdom needed, was to be rendered useless. By a woman. The irony was cold as a sword thrust through her gut.

What more could I have done to prevent this? thought Tokiko. Even the hissing of the wind in the willow boughs seemed to chide her for her carelessness.

"He must be ruthless," Ryujin had counseled Tokiko. "You must see that Kiyomori follows the straight path, for only in that way will he gain command of the sword Kusanagi and be able to return it to us." And so Tokiko had counseled Kiyomori, earning her many dark names among the Taira, although some respected her for her will of steel. It was a given, among the samurai, that the sons of your foe must not be spared, no matter how young. They must not be allowed to rise to wreak vengeance when they are older.

But the boy Yoritomo had been found and taken to the Imperial Prison with all courtesy and kindness. He had not been brought to Rokuhara to be at the mercy of the Taira, Tokiko noted. Many nobles were already pleading with Kiyomori that Yoritomo be spared. Yoritomo was fourteen, and had fought beside his father! Surely an adolescent whose heirloom sword had tasted blood would dream of nothing but vengeance for his clan. And now the seductive concubine Tokiwa whored with Kiyomori in order to save three more of Yoshitomo's sons. If Tokiwa were to succeed in softening Kiyomori's heart . . . Tokiko had thrown the bones and observed the stars. She had spoken to the fish in the lotus pond. If Kiyomori changed, it would bring disaster.

Tokiko had sent word to every servant that Kiyomori was to be requested to speak with her as soon as he would. But already the sun's disc hovered above Otowoyama, and Kiyomori had not presented himself at her *shōji*. It was possible, Tokiko reflected, that he might not return to her at all.

The destruction of the mortal realm would not extend to her, of course. When the time came, Tokiko would return to her father's undersea palace, to be young again and still immortal. It made the aging of her earthly body easier to bear. But she had become fond of the beauty of Heian Kyō, the earnest striving of the mortal people against the most horrible tragedies of fate. Their poetic dreams, their enchanting gardens, their singing and dancing, had charmed Tokiko into caring about their future. She now understood why her father wished to save them. She could not abandon them just yet.

Tokiko raised the bowl and sipped the onion broth. But it had turned cold and was no longer pleasing to the throat. Tokiko set the bowl aside and waited.

The Wandering Monk

Yoritomo sat calmly on the floor of his prison cell, sketching with charcoal on rice paper the design for a memorial stupa for his father. He expected he did not have long to live.

He had done all he could to escape the Taira. He could not remain with the mountain monk for long without being discovered, so he had to wander from village to village, heading eastward, hoping to reach the Kantō. In one village, a family had taken him in, and fed and housed him for a time. Rumor soon arrived that the Taira were coming in search of him, and Yoritomo had exchanged his fine clothing for a plain cotton jacket and straw sandals. But Yoritomo would not give up the sword, Hagekiri, and that proved to be his undoing. As he had run up the road to evade the searchers, his sword caught in the bushes and the Taira had easily found him.

Yoritomo did not try to deny who he was to his captors, for that seemed dishonorable. He allowed himself to be brought back to Heian Kyō to await his fate. Hachiman had guided him this far. If it was Hachiman's will that he die beneath an Imperial sword in the capital city, then it would be so. Yoritomo chose to face it bravely and peacefully, so as not to bring shame to the Minomoto clan.

But all of the samurai and noblemen who had brought Yoritomo to his cell had been very kind, even deferential. They spoke highly of his father, praising his courage and his honor, and recounting with remorse the terrible manner of Yoshitomo's death.

Yoritomo sensed there was growing dislike among the nobles for the Taira. Perhaps it was the way the Taira swiftly punished any percieved slight, sending gangs of young men to cudgel anyone thought to have uttered slander against the clan, or starting brawls in the street if the carriage of a lesser family would not give way. Perhaps the nobles believed the coarse Taira were rising higher in rank than their blood deserved. Perhaps many among the nobility believed Kiyomori had arranged Yoshitomo's betrayal and murder.

Were I older, thought Yoritomo, *I would make use of this somehow.* He did not know how many of his brothers and half brothers still survived. He had heard that Akugenda Yoshihira had been executed and had died well. For all Yoritomo knew, he himself might now be Ason, heir to the chieftainship of the clan when he came of age. But given that he expected to die soon, Yoritomo thought little of it.

A guard came to the cell door, morning sunlight glinting off his helmet. "Ho, there, young lord. I hope you have slept well. We bring you tea and rice cakes from the Imperial kitchens themselves." The door opened, and a servant placed a tray within just beside the door. The servant bowed and left silently.

"And you have a visitor come to speak with you," the guard went on.

Another, thought Yoritomo with a patient sigh. Many nobles, lords and ladies both, had come into the prison to see him and say words of encouragement. He wondered if they merely wanted to touch someone who had been close to the greatness of the Minomoto. Or if they merely wished to gaze with pity upon the doomed little warrior before Yoritomo's short life was snuffed out. "Who is it?"

"A monk, my young lord."

Yoritomo wondered if it might be the same monk who had housed him on the mountain. "From what temple?"

"Er, Hiei-zan, I believe."

Yoritomo could sense from the guard's hesitation that he was lying. No monk kept his temple secret, just as no warrior would hide the badge of his clan. But what did it matter? "Very well. I will speak with him."

The guard left, closing the door after him. Soon a conical straw hat appeared at the barred window, hiding the face beneath. "Minomoto Yoritomo?"

"I am he, Holy One."

The door opened, and the monk entered. He still held his head low to shadow his features, and he walked with stooped shoulders. But Yoritomo could tell by the way the gray robe hung on the monk's shoulders that he was well muscled and strong. *A warrior-monk, perhaps*, thought Yoritomo. *If he wishes to learn fighting secrets from me, I must disappoint him.*

"You are a fine-looking lad," said the monk.

The accent and timbre of his voice was not of the East, or even much of the capital, although this monk had clearly tried to learn cultured ways.

"Thank you, Holy One. Have you come to pray with me?"

"Perhaps. But I have first come to take your measure. Are you prepared to meet the fate you have earned?"

"I am prepared," said Yoritomo, bowing his head.

"What is that you are drawing?"

"A stupa for my father, to honor his memory. When I am executed, I will give this to the Taira and ask them to see that it is built."

"A stupa. A most peaceable last request. Are you not thinking on vengeance for your clan?"

"Why should it be my place to think on vengeance?" said Yoritomo. "I am only fourteen. I am a captive of the Taira. I surely will be executed soon. What better way to spend my time than this?"

"And what if . . . you are not to be executed?"

Yoritomo blinked. "Holy One, that would surely be a gift from Hachiman and the Buddha. And I do not think it will happen. But if they did, then they must send me into far exile, which would be like this, neh?" Yoritomo gestured at the cell around him. "What vengeance could I plan from a faraway island? Exiles do not receive letters or visitors."

"So if you were sent into exile, what would you do?"

"I would become a monk like you, Holy One. I would study the sutras and see that a stupa for my father is built."

"You would not plot and plan?"

"That would only bring greater danger to whoever of my family still lives. And the Taira serve the Emperor. It would be great treason to fight against the Imperial will. My father did so because of oaths he made to Nobuyori. I have made no such oaths."

The monk nodded. "You speak wisely and well, young Yoritomo. Perhaps I will visit the Taira and plead for your life to be spared. I have been known to have access to even the Great Kiyomori's ear."

"That would be kind of you, of course, Holy One. But my life is in the hands of Hachiman and the Buddha. And Lord Kiyomori is a brute, everyone knows it. My father said that Kiyomori was to blame for the great killings of the Hōgen. How can I expect mercy from the Taira?"

The monk blustered, "W-well, sometimes people can surprise you, boy. And not everything you hear is true. Be patient and we will see what can be done. Good day to you." The monk inclined his head and was out the door before Yoritomo could say good-bye.

A strange one, thought Yoritomo, and then the truth hit him. *A Taira spy! Trying to find out if I am plotting. Oh, and I said hateful things about Lord Kiyomori. I am doomed for certain.* He went back to work on his sketch with greater speed, wondering if he had lifetime left to finish it.

Black Robes

*K*iyomori stormed out of the prison, tearing off the straw hat and flinging it at a servant. *Of course I am a brute, boy*, he thought darkly. *Is that not how one achieves respect and gains power? What sort of Minomoto are you if your father did not teach you this?* He passed under the Traitor's Tree, still bedecked with rotting heads, and strode toward the gate called Kōgamon, where his ox-carriage awaited him.

Still weary from his long, lingering night with the beautiful Tokiwa, for which the price had been sparing her sons, Kiyomori had felt compelled to visit this other captured son of Yoshitomo. Tokiwa had not pleaded for Yoritomo's life, as she was not his mother. But many others in the palace had, even among the retainers of the Taira. Much sympathy was gathering for the Minomoto and the way Yoshitomo had been ignominiously murdered. Kiyomori wondered at the change in mood at the palace—as though something was clouding the eyes of Those Who Live Above The Clouds. Politically, Kiyomori was sensing that, for the moment, wisdom lay in mercy, not in ruthlessness, no matter what his wife counseled.

At the carriage, Kiyomori removed the gray robes of his monk's disguise and handed them to a servant, exchanging them for the black robes of First Rank. As the servant helped Kiyomori put on the black robes, he said, "My lord, your wife has instructed us to tell you she wishes urgently to speak with you whenever you are available."

"I know," Kiyomori growled. "You are the tenth person to tell me so today." Holding the robes around him tightly, he stepped through the back door of the ox-carriage and slammed it shut behind him. He sat down on the cushioned bench and sighed heavily.

It had been a simple thing to promise clemency for Tokiwa's children. The oldest boy was scarcely seven years, and the youngest, Ushiwaka, had been out of the womb only a few months. Such children would surely not remember their father and, if brought up in exile away from their family, would feel little call to avenge their kin. But Yoritomo was another matter.

Still, the boy had seemed peaceable enough, wanting only to become a monk if sent into exile. It would be a risk, to be sure. The sympathy for the Minomoto could turn into military support, eventually. But that would be years away. There would be time for the Taira to consolidate their power. But if the boy were executed, the outcry would be immediate, and the Emperor might be prevailed upon to look on the Taira with less favor.

Imperial politics is like walking through a forest choked with under-growth, thought Kiyomori. *There is no clear path, and any direction might lead to danger.*

The right shoulder of his new black robe slid down onto his arm, and Kiyomori impatiently tugged it back into place. Somehow the overrobe was not fitting right, and Kiyomori wondered if he might find a tailor he could trust to make it more suitable. A poem arose in his mind:

New black robes
Do not bring stillness
Even the dark waters at Miyajima
Toss to and fro
Unceasingly

He decided it was a poor effort and mentally set it aside to work on later.

As the carriage lurched forward, Kiyomori's thoughts drifted to hours before when Yoshitomo's concubine Tokiwa had relinquished herself to him.

It had been an unusual tryst for Kiyomori. The singers and dancing girls he usually took as his night's entertainment were so eager to please him, to be able to boast to each other for the rest of their lives of how they had dallied with the Great Kiyomori. Or there were the unwilling ones, with whom Kiyomori employed his rank or veiled threats in order to pressure them into letting him have his way. Their poignant tears and weak protests brought a pleasure of a different sort.

But Tokiwa had offered herself, clear-eyed and unafraid, in exchange for the life of her sons. She had told him how she had hidden in the Temple of Kwannon while the Taira were searching for her, and received a vision from the Goddess of Mercy. Kwannon had told her how to save her children, even though it meant some loss of honor. For Tokiwa, therefore, their lovemaking was an act of piety, a religious offering, a gift to the gods. Her serene detachment as Kiyomori had taken his pleasure had been quite unlike anything he had ever experienced.

The bump-bump of the carriage wheels going over the threshold beam of the gate to Rokuhara jolted him from his thoughts. As Kiyomori dismounted from the carriage into the courtyard of his mansion, he decided he must at last take on the dreaded task of speaking to his wife.

He made his way to her quarters and sat on the verandah outside her receiving chamber. The blind had been lowered to shade the room from the midday sun, so he could not see inside. He heard the rustle of kimonos approaching the blind and a young woman's voice say, "Pardon me, but who is there?"

"It is Kiyomori. I have come to speak with my wife."

"Ah! Kiyomori-sama. Please forgive this lowly one for not knowing it was you. We see so little of you. I will tell her at once you are here. She is most anxious to speak with you. Wait but a moment, if you please." Her footsteps hurried away from the blind.

Kiyomori sighed and gazed out at the garden, which Tokiko herself had designed, as it was the view she would look upon most often. The ornamental stream that wound around the entire estate of Rokuhara seemed even more serpentine here. The willows drooped over it sadly, and the cherry blossoms drifted down from the trees to float away on the water. It was a perfect expression of *aware*, the sublime sorrow at the impermanence of things. Kiyomori wondered how much more impermanent the things of the world must be to a woman who was immortal. For a moment, he felt just the slightest sympathy for her.

But remembering that she was immortal reminded him that she was also the daughter of the Dragon King. And it had seemed to Kiyomori that, of late, Tokiko had come more and more to resemble the minions of her father's kingdom. Her voice hissed, her gaze burned . . . what man would not seek pleasures elsewhere with such a wife as this?

Presently, he heard the slither of heavy brocade silk kimonos, which called to his mind the sliding of reptilian scales over stone. "The sunlight is bright, husband. Why do you not come inside?"

"I am admiring your garden," Kiyomori said.

"The garden is not at its best. It is more green when the rains come in summer. It has not seen rain for some time."

"Then I must imagine what beauty it will attain when the rains fall. Who knows? Sweet moisture may fall this very evening if the dragon who lives above the clouds is willing."

There was a pause on the other side of the bamboo blind. "And if the dragon feels too cold to receive rain?"

"Then the dragon should let a distant ray of the sun bathe her in his warmth until she is willing enough."

"Tcha. What nonsense is this? You come speaking like an admiring courtier."

"Is it not pleasanter for me to greet you in this way?" protested Kiyomori. "We never had a proper courtship, you and I. Why could we not begin now?"

"You sly dog. An old wife such as I is more likely to find such a capricious change of behavior . . . suspicious."

"Suspicious? What is there for you to suspect me of?"

There was another pause before she replied. "Do you think I am a fool?

Even curtains of modesty have gaps through which one can see, and they are no barrier to hearing at all."

"And what have you been hearing?"

"That a certain Taira of high rank has become besotted with his new black robes and makes choices that look foolish to those of sober mien."

"Tell me who this Taira is, and I shall correct him." Kiyomori thought he heard a soft snarl of frustration from the other side of the blind.

"Enough. You know all too well. I have heard that the late Minomoto general's son Yoritomo has been captured."

"So he has, and he is being well looked after."

"And yet he still lives?"

Kiyomori sighed. "He is just a boy."

"He is fourteen, and fought beside his father against you. He would have killed any of our sons, had he the opportunity. And he may grow to have the opportunity again. Have I not told you that one must be ruthless in war?"

"The war has ended, Tokiko, and there has been enough killing. Already I am called a butcher for having killed my uncle in the Hōgen and forcing Yoshitomo to kill his father. I am told by his keepers that this boy has a peaceful nature, and speaks only of someday building a stupa to honor his fallen father. You are a woman. It is unseemly for you to speak of killing children."

A low hiss came from the other side of the blind. "You would choose the life of one boy over the fate of so many. What can possibly have blinded you so? Or who?"

"It is not blindness to be aware of politics, woman. The feeling at court is that I should be merciful."

"The Imperial Court has been tainted since the rise of Nobuyori. The ministers who served him still advise there. Why should your thoughts be in accord with theirs?"

"What does it *matter* whether my thoughts are in accord?" Kiyomori shouted. Then he lowered his voice, knowing servants would be listening. "The Taira Emperor is not yet on the throne. I still serve at the whim of Emperor Nijō and those ministers you fear. If I am to achieve what your father has demanded of me, I dare not risk the court's displeasure now."

There was a long pause before Tokiko spoke again. "My poor father, how he failed to consider the greed of men. You think more on the Taira Emperor to be than the Last Days of the Law to come. And on a certain concubine of Yoshitomo, with whom you spent the night. Did she pay you well for the life of her sons?"

Kiyomori stood. "I will hear no more of this."

A hand snaked out from under the blinds and caught hold of his *hakama* trousers. "Listen, and listen well, husband," Tokiko hissed. "Your insult to me is only a small thing. The insult you do the Empire is far greater. This old dragon does not fear these fallen times. But even a man who walks on tall clogs can be tripped up by the smallest stones. The children of Yoshitomo must die."

Kiyomori tugged his *hakama* out of her grasp, hearing the cloth tear against her fingernails. "Enough, woman. I will hear no more such ugliness from you." He strode away along the verandah. A chilly wind had come up that tugged at his black robes, threatening to blow them off his back. Kiyomori held the edges of the robes tightly around him, holding them on by sheer strength as he walked back to his quarters.

The Widening Rift

Summer came to Heian Kyō, and with it the warmth of peace. Merchants felt free to display their wares on the street, and warriors sent their weapons to be repaired and horses to play in pastures.

Retired Emperor Go-Shirakawa sat on a canopied platform in a garden of his mother's mansion, having tea with his sister Jōsaimon'in. The platform was situated in the midst of a lotus pond on which the sacred white flowers floated in full bloom. The air was heavy with the scent of tachibana blossoms.

"Oh, what *is* the matter, brother?" asked Jōsaimon'in. "Here it is the sweetest of days, and you sit brooding as though the clouds of winter still hung over us."

"No day is unclouded for the one that rules the land," said Go-Shirakawa. He watched as a frog on a lotus pad snatched a fly out of the air with its tongue.

Jōsaimon'in studied him a moment. "Brother, is it not time for that rule to fall to another? Your son Nijō is now free of Nobuyori."

"But not of his ministers."

"Then you should visit the Imperial palace more often."

"I do not like what I see at the palace." In truth, Go-Shirakawa was appalled by his son's behavior. For young Nijō now filled his days with nightly drunken celebrations, and his rumored voraciousness for women had only increased. *It is as if the boy learned nothing of the consequences of Nobuyori's acts. As if somehow Nobuyori's influence remains. The boy has no understanding of the solemnity of his office. Surely our* kami *ancestors must look down upon him with shame.* Worse still, Nijō would not give up the woman who had been his uncle's Empress. For Nijō to disobey Go-Shirakawa, his father, with this flouting of tradition was a filial insult of the gravest sort.

"I am sure your wise influence would be most helpful."

"My son does not wish my wise influence. I am told he even sends away all priests and monks who call upon the palace. No. I cannot let power fall solely into Nijō's hands. He might prove worse than Nobuyori ever was."

"You are simply upset," chided Jōsaimon'in, "that he gathers more nobles to his side than you do. The great families have begun to whisper that we are unlucky, after what happened to Shinzei. And they say it is easier to be in the right if a minister serves the ruling Emperor than the retired one."

"Or easier to manipulate a younger Emperor than an older one."

Jōsaimon'in sighed and laid her hand on Go-Shirakawa's sleeve. "You take too much care upon yourself. Why not truly retire? Take the vows of a monk and let the heaviness of worldly life go. You bring danger to your family if you continue to involve yourself in politics this way. This mansion may not be as grand as Sanjō was, but with luck it will not be burned to the ground."

Go-Shirakawa felt the muscles in his jaw tighten. He threw a rice cake at the frog in the pond, but it hopped away with ease. "I cannot," he growled at last. "I will not live to see Nihon brought to ruin. Not even if it means becoming the enemy of my son."

A Dream of Bows and Arrows

Young Minomoto Yoritomo gazed out at the waters of the Inlet of Ise, waiting for the boat that would carry him into exile. He was amazed still to be alive.

But word had come, shortly after the visit of the strange monk, that Yoritomo, along with his much younger half brothers, would not be executed. It had taken several months for the Taira and the Imperial Council to decide where the sons of Yoshitomo would be sent. But the answer, when finally arrived at, astonished even Yoritomo.

The younger boys were being sent to monasteries—Ushiwaka, the very youngest, would be at a temple not far outside of the capital itself. And Yoritomo was being sent . . . east, to Izu! Close to the Kantō, to the homeland of the Minomoto clan. *Surely*, Yoritomo thought, *this can only be another sign of Hachiman's favor. With family nearby to look after me, it is unlikely that the Taira will change their mind and execute me later. And there will be support for the building of the stupa to my father.* Yoritomo was thinking that if he ever had the influence, he would build more shrines to Hachiman.

A sailboat came into view, heading up the inlet to where Yoritomo and his guards stood. The guards went down to the beach to help guide the boat in, leaving Yoritomo momentarily alone.

Alone except for Moriyasu, the one servant Yoritomo was permitted to take into exile with him. Moriyasu had served the Minomoto faithfully for many years, and Yoritomo was heartened when he heard that Moriyasu had been chosen as his companion.

"My young lord," Moriyasu said, "it is true what they say about you. You have the courage of a hawk."

"Why say you this?"

"Because other men who are exiled to far provinces are known to weep into their sleeves until their garments are soaked. They fall to their knees on the sand and try to grasp the earth so that no one can move them. They wail to the skies their poems of woe so loud that the hearts of all around them might break. But you stand with calm visage, with no tear in your eye. You do not sigh or sulk or gnash your teeth. Instead you gaze upon the sea as if it were merely another foe to conquer."

"Oh," said Yoritomo who, by now, was becoming used to fuss being made over him. "Well, I do not love Heian Kyō, as others do. I do not think I will miss it. Too many people. I'd rather be riding a horse in the Kantō."

"I dare say someday you will, my young lord. Someday you will do that and more. If I may, I would like to describe to you a dream I had last night."

"A dream?"

"It was a very brief dream, but it felt very real. I dreamed I saw you as a grown man, receiving bows and arrows from an impressive general who sat on a white horse. A radiant glow surrounded this warrior, and he nodded to you with great respect."

"Ah. That sounds like Hachiman."

"It could well have been, my young lord. Surely this is a sign of great favor. It must be that you will become a renowned general as your father was."

Yoritomo looked swiftly around, but fortunately no one else was nearby. "Moriyasu, you must watch what you say! Some might think your dream is traitorous talk, and I might yet lose my head."

The servant bowed low. "Forgive me, my young lord. I had no wish to put you in danger. I only told you my dream so that you might have hope at this sad time."

"This is not a sad time for me, Moriyasu. I still live, to honor my father.

I may yet have sons someday to bring honor to my clan as well. Hachiman has turned the hearts of the Taira to spare my life. This is still such a wonder to me that I have barely even begun to think of what to hope for."

The boat was pulled in close to the beach, and the guards shouted for Yoritomo to approach and get in. Murmuring a prayer to his clan *kami*, Yoritomo stepped into the roiling water of the sea and climbed aboard the boat.

Island of Sutras

A year passed, and an uneasy peace settled onto the capital. Go-Shirakawa continued to try to retain influence among the court nobles. The Minomoto, what few remained, retreated to their eastern landholdings and did nothing to bring the wrath of the Emperor down upon them. The major temples, Hiei-zan and Ninna-ji, waited to see which sect the young Emperor would favor, should he ever decide to receive holy men into his presence again.

As for the Taira, Kiyomori used his newfound wealth and influence to build great works in his home provinces along the Inland Sea. The construction of the new shrine on Miyajima was well under way, though it would take some time to complete. He built harbors and waterways in Aki and Settsu. But he paid special attention to the harbor at Fukuhara.

Fukuhara was a small village on the coast of the Inland Sea, down the River Toba from Heian Kyō. It was the closest part of the sea one could reach from the capital, and Kiyomori found himself at Fukuhara often, sometimes residing there for weeks at a time. He had not forgotten the Taira origins as masters of the waters.

That autumn, in Leaf Month, of the first year of the era Ōhō, Kiyomori sat on the verandah of his house in Fukuhara. A strong wind brought the scent of the ocean. The house sat on a hillside, and he had a good view of the sea. He could see the artificial island that his men were constructing not far offshore. They had been building it for six months, and Kiyomori could see the stones rising well above the surface of the water, even though the swells were high and topped with white foam. Dark clouds were gathering on the horizon.

If the barrier island succeeded as Kiyomori hoped, it could turn Fukuhara into a usable port where ships could safely harbor. *Had I been given the fortune to become Emperor*, Kiyomori mused, *and therefore have the power to choose a capital city, I would choose it to be here. What lord could truly call himself Emperor if he does not have control of the sea? Those of*

Chang'an have mighty trading vessels and have commerce with many lands.
Why should we not do the same? Too long, our nobles have hid themselves
among the pleasant hills of Nara and Heian Kyō, paying little attention to
anything else. There are many islands to the south peopled only by savages,
legends say. Why should we not conquer them? When there is a Taira Em-
peror, I will counsel him on these things.

A servant came, and said, "My lord, your engineer general has come to
speak with you."

Kiyomori nodded and waved his hand to indicate the man should be
brought to him.

The engineer general came out onto the verandah. He was a short,
stocky, bearded man whose clothing still smelled of salt brine. The man
knelt and bowed. "Kiyomori-sama."

"What have you to report?"

"The construction of your island goes well, but we are concerned. You
see the dark clouds to the south. We have word from sailors arriving from
Harima that a great storm is coming. It may be a *taifun*. We are already
spreading word among the villagers to shore up their houses."

"Then you have done all that can be done," said Kiyomori. "My island
is built of stones. What can even a *taifun* do against that?"

"The material is stone, my lord, but many of the supports are wood.
And I have seen the damage the winds and tides of such a storm can do."

Kiyomori sighed. "Then you must have men upon the island to guard
it and hold the pylons in place."

The engineer general was silent a moment and regarded Kiyomori with
sad eyes. "My lord, if I may say so, in all respect, to ask such a thing is to
condemn those to their deaths."

Kiyomori narrowed his eyes. "Is it no longer an honor for a warrior to
die at the behest of his lord?"

"Against other warriors, in the thick of battle, my lord, your men would
gladly fight and die. But you are asking them to fight the gods, against whom
no man can expect victory."

"Is it not a greater honor to be asked to contend against the *kami?* Men
survive storms all the time. You exaggerate the danger. Go now and see
that it is done."

The engineer general opened his mouth to speak, but then did not.
Instead, he stood and bowed silently and went away.

That night, a dreadful storm did arrive at Fukuhara. Kiyomori huddled
under a pile of brocade robes in the centermost room of his house, while
the wind howled through the eaves. Rain spattered hard against the blinds
and the *shōji*-like arrows. The clatter of the roof tiles resembled the hoofbeats of warhorses and the moaning of the wind was the wailing of warriors

in their first charge upon the enemy. Thunder resounded like the rumbling of great *taiko* drums, and the house creaked and shifted around Kiyomori as if it were about to rise off its foundations and fly away. At the height of the storm, Kiyomori imagined he heard voices chanting his name in the wind, and he wondered if the spirits of the dead Minomoto had come seeking vengeance at last.

But the storm subsided, and, in time, Kiyomori slept. He was shaken awake by a servant late in the morning.

"My lord, my lord, please waken. It is already the Hour of the Snake."

Kiyomori threw off the robes he had slept under and hurried out to the verandah. Under a lightly clouded sky, he saw that many of the houses on the hillside below had sustained damage, but were still standing. But when he looked out to sea, his island was gone.

"Send for my engineer general. At once!"

"As you wish, my lord."

It was some hours later, at the Hour of the Monkey, when the engineer general finally arrived. He was accompanied by two sailors who wore bandages on their arms and faces, as well as a very old Shintō priest in white robe and hat.

"Where have you been?" Kiyomori demanded.

"There were villagers trapped beneath fallen beams, my lord. It took some time to rescue them."

"What about my island?" Kiyomori shouted. "What happened to my island?"

"I fear it was destroyed in the storm, my lord, as you can see."

"That should have been impossible! How could it happen?"

The engineer general scowled and indicated the two sailors. "My lord, these men can give better account than I."

The sailors knelt and bowed low, almost pressing their foreheads to the polished floorboards. "Most noble lord," one of them began, "there were seven of us on sentry upon the island, as you had ordered, when the storm came up."

"The waves grew higher and higher, my lord, and the wind grew stronger," said the other man. "Nonetheless, we all held tightly on to ropes we had tied on to the pylons to keep them in place."

"We held on, my lord," continued the first sailor, "even though the rope dug into our hands and the waves battered us from every side."

Kiyomori grew impatient. "Enough of your boasting. Tell me what happened to the island."

The two sailors glanced at each other before the second one went on. "My lord, at the height of the storm, a mighty wave rose over us. The lightning . . . it showed us that the wave held . . ."

"Dragons, my lord," said the first. "Dragons of the sea."

"These dragons fell upon the island, tearing at it with their claws. We were all washed into the water. We heard our fellows screaming as they drowned. But we, this man and I, we were carried to shore. On the backs of a dragon. We fell asleep from exhaustion on the sand. When we awoke, the storm was gone, and so was the island."

"We believe, my lord," the first one added, "that we were spared to tell you of this event."

"Tcha!" said Kiyomori derisively, knocking his teacup over with a sweep of his hand. "Dragons, indeed." But within he felt a shiver of concern. "No matter. The island must be rebuilt. You will begin at once."

"Kiyomori-sama," said the engineer general, "perhaps you should hear the words of this worthy one"—he indicated the priest—"before you decide what to do."

The old Shintō priest in the white robe bowed low, and said, "Noble warrior-lord, we have had indications at the shrine that Ryujin-wo, the Dragon King of the Sea, is displeased with you. We believe this destruction of your island is a message, a warning to you. Perhaps you know, or do not know, what you have done to gain his displeasure, but at the shrine we are certain that you must, somehow, appease him, or your island will never stand."

Kiyomori knew what the Dragon King wanted. *It is not fair. He promised me a Taira Emperor of my blood, and now he wants the sword before the deal is fulfilled. Or perhaps he disapproves of how I treat his daughter, my wife. But I will not be frightened into compliance. Even the Dragon King must keep his bargains.* "I fear I do not know how I may have offended Ryujin so," Kiyomori temporized. "Have you any suggestions, Holy One, as to what might be done to appease him?"

"Ryujin is one of the old *kami*," said the priest. "The dragons are not of the line of Izanami and Izanagi, and therefore they are not soothed by mere offerings of rice and incense. They prefer the old ways, as performed by our ancestors long ago."

"And what ways are these?" asked Kiyomori.

"Dragons are sated by blood, my lord. It has been customary, in times past, to offer precious life to a dragon who is causing trouble."

"A human sacrifice," Kiyomori said softly.

The engineer general and sailors stared at him aghast.

"Just so, my lord," said the priest.

"Yes," Kiyomori went on, "in the old tales, that is what dragons are given. Usually a young, unmarried woman, isn't it? One of particular beauty?"

"So the tales say, my lord," said the priest. There was something too eager in his eyes.

Kiyomori tapped the lip of his teacup. "But we are dealing here with the Dragon King. Surely a mere girl would be an unworthy offering to the mighty Ryujin. No, we should offer him something far more sacred. A priest, perhaps. One who has seen many years, and is very wise."

Alarm sprang into the eyes of the old priest. "S-surely you cannot mean me, my lord?"

"Whyever not? You know the severity of the problem. Your soul, when freed, may speak well on my behalf in Ryujin's kingdom. Who better?"

The old priest bowed. "My lord, if you will, allow me to return to my shrine and we will consider the matter more carefully."

"Do that," said Kiyomori. "But remember, the humble sacrifice of your own life would be recounted in legend down through the ages, should you offer yourself."

"I . . . I will remember, my lord." The priest hurried away, his clogs clattering on the verandah boards.

The engineer general and the sailors sighed audibly with relief.

"Bloodthirsty old fool," grumbled Kiyomori. "As if there were not better uses for pretty girls than killing them. He has been at his shrine too long, and his genitals are shriveled and forgotten."

"My lord," said one of the sailors, "if I may, I have a suggestion. It is said among men of the sea that the Dragon King respects the ways of the Buddha, though he does not follow them. If you were to inscribe each stone of the island with a word or phrase from the sacred sutras, thus making the island a holy work, he might be less inclined to destroy it."

And that, thought Kiyomori, *would be a way to stop Ryujin without appeasing him. A way to show him I am not intimidated by his power. Besides, I am thought enough of a brute already. I'll not sacrifice a life to him just so it can be used against me later.* "This is an excellent notion, good fellow. I thank you. Go to the nearest temple and arrange it, and I will award you a captaincy and your own boat to command."

A smile split the sailor's face, and he bowed low. "Most excellent lord, it shall be done."

The Death of the Shin-In

Two years later, in the third year of the era called Eiryaku, the demon who had been Emperor Sutoku, and then known as Retired Emperor Shin-In, finally passed away in Sanuki Province. He was not mourned. Those few present at his final rites said that his corpse had a most fearsome appearance, no longer human at all. His body was burned on a funeral pyre, in accordance with custom. But as the black smoke rose skyward on that windless day, instead of drifting up to Heaven, the column bent and pointed northeast, toward Heian Kyō, at times pointing like a cursing finger, or reaching like a grasping claw.

His remains were buried at Shiramine, and by Imperial order no marking stone was laid to mark the place. But the residents nearby had no trouble knowing where the Shin-In's ashes lay, for the earth above it remained bare: nothing would grow there.

Three nights after the Shin-In was buried, Taira Munemori, Lord Kiyomori's third son, was returning to Rokuhara. He had been out again to visit the lady of the tall weed house. But she had left him a surprise. She had not been home, and her one elderly maidservant claimed that the lady had realized Munemori would do no good for her. So the lady had gone away to become a nun, to forget Munemori and the sorrows of the world. The maidservant would not say which temple she had gone to.

Thus Mumemori rode home in his ox-carriage, lonesome and unsatisfied. He had always expected to be the one to break things off. He had already composed the farewell poems. For her to leave him first! How unfair! A sole tear formed in his eye and dropped heavily onto his sleeve.

The ox-carriage stopped abruptly, and Munemori peered out the side window. The walls of Rokuhara were beside them, but they had not yet gone over the threshold beam and entered. "What is it?" he called up to the ox-driver.

"M-my lord. It is the ghosts again."

Munemori felt a sudden chill. "It is only an illusion. Drive on."

"My lord, the palanquin stops. The one within . . . he beckons for you."

Masking his fear with anger, Munemori stormed out of the back door of the carriage. He walked forward beside the oxen and stopped. It was, indeed, the same ghostly procession, with the executed Taira generals before the palanquin, the dead Minomoto behind. Only now, on a horse of deepest black, the ghost of the great Yoshitomo himself had joined the parade at the rear.

The palanquin's curtain was open, and the space within was filled with a sickly green light. The Shin-In sat there, as before, but looking more wicked and powerful in aspect. His hands were now claws, and his face was so shriveled and sunken it could not have ever belonged to a living man. He held out a long arm and beckoned again to Munemori.

Unable to stop himself, Munemori staggered up to the palanquin and knelt in the mud before it. "M-most High Retired Majesty," stammered

Munemori, "what do you want of me now?" He tried to remember a sutra to chant, but could not bring a single holy phrase to mind.

"Several of my companions here," rasped the Shin-In, in a voice like slithering serpents, "wished to return to the place they had been killed, for such is the nature of spirits, neh? As for myself, I ask only for your hospitality. His Imperial Majesty speaks highly of his stay here at Rokuhara. I came to see if he was correct in his assessment."

"You—you can't stay here!" Munemori blurted out. "This is the home of the Great Kiyomori of the Taira."

"Ah, yes, the Great Kiyomori," said the Shin-In, leaning out of the palanquin so that his horrible face hovered over Munemori. "The one responsible for my downfall and who brought several of these brave gentlemen to their deaths."

"But I heard *you* had died," whimpered Munemori. "Why have you not gone on to another life or to . . ."

". . . to Hell?" the Shin-In suggested with a terrifying grin.

"To the court of Emma-O, I was going to say, Majesty. Where your life would be judged fairly."

"Because your beloved noblemen so desperately wished me gone, I have chosen to stay. They thought my vengeance would be finished with my death, but they were wrong. My hate extends beyond life, beyond death. And no mere daughter of a Dragon King can spare the Taira from my hate. No mere magical sword can spare the Empire from its destruction. And I have many friends now"—he gestured toward the dead warriors—"who have reason to hate the Taira as well."

"Please, o Great Retired Emperor," begged Munemori, "spare my clan. We have only done what any aspiring family would do, and we have always loyally served the Jeweled Throne."

"You did not loyally serve *me*. Spare you? I think not."

The ghost of the Shin-In sat back in the palanquin, and the curtain slid shut. The dead warrior bearers, with dignified mien, carried it through the high stone wall, not bothering with the gate. The procession vanished into the mansion itself.

"No, no," sobbed Munemori. "This cannot be."

The ox-driver came up beside him. "My lord, you will tell Lord Kiyomori of this, then, yes? Shall we wake him?"

Munemori shook his head. "Not . . . not now. I must think on when would be a good time. Not now. Not now."

Burial Tablets

A light, early-autumn rain was falling, dampening the sleeves of the monks as they marched by in slow procession across the slope of Mount Funaoka. Retired Emperor Go-Shirakawa, seated upon the platform for the Imperial family, thought it entirely appropriate weather. He only wished the patter of the raindrops on the oiled-silk canopy overhead would drown out the weeping of the women around him.

"He was so young," sighed Jōsiamon'in, dabbing at her eyes with her sleeves.

"People die at any age," Go-Shirakawa grumbled.

"Not when they seem so hearty," Jōsaimon'in said.

"He was so handsome, so charming," a lady-in-waiting sobbed somewhere behind them.

Yes, thought Go-Shirakawa, *willing to entertain ladies of all sorts, Nijō was.* Yet a long illness and death had claimed the young Emperor of twenty-three.

Jōsaimon'in leaned closer and said, "Begging your pardon brother, but you should allow yourself to make your grief more public. He was your son, after all."

"We were estranged. That is no secret."

"But people are beginning to talk."

Go-Shirakawa allowed his head to droop. *True. And now I understand why Taira Kiyomori has the rabid reaction to gossip that he does.* People were whispering that Go-Shirakawa had a hand in his own son's death. *I may be a political creature, but even I would do nothing so sinful. Very likely Nijō drank too much, spent too long in the rain, and caught a fever. Or perhaps his beloved former Empress-Aunt passed along to Nijō the same thing that killed her first Emperor, Konoe, who, I recall, also died young. But it would be disrespectful to speak of such earthy matters regarding the Emperor, neh? Therefore, someone must be at fault. And I am not popular with those lords who once served Nobuyori.*

"That is better," said Jōsaimon'in.

"You know I had nothing to do with this," Go-Shirakawa growled, loud enough so that others nearby might hear.

"Of course, of course," his sister said quickly, fluttering her fan in embarrassment.

"It was the Shin-In," he heard a lady behind him whisper. "I saw the Shin-in's ghost when I was staying at the palace one night. I am sure his curse felled our Nijō."

It was all Go-Shirakawa could do not to roll his eyes and sigh in disgust. Rumors of sightings of the Shin-In had abounded in the capital during the year since his death. *Unhappy people often seek supernatural causes for their misfortunes. But if those causes loom too large, they can become reason for unrest and riot.* "How strange," murmured Go-Shirakawa, "that so many have seen my poor dead brother, and yet he has not graced me with a visit." Still, he remembered his vision at Ninna-Ji, and it worried him.

Jōsaimon'in shot him a scandalized glare but said nothing.

"His poor little son," wept another lady. "So young to be placed upon the Jeweled Throne. He will never know his father."

That was another thing that severely annoyed Go-Shirakawa. As soon as Nijō had realized that his illness might be fatal, he had his two-year-old son declared Crown Prince. As soon as the decree was passed, Nijō had abdicated, leaving a toddler who could barely walk and speak sitting upon the throne.

He did it to thwart me, Go-Shirakawa thought. *To prevent me from choosing the successor. Another sign that he cared little for this country.* The Great Council had been upset, of course, there never having been an Emperor younger than three, but as they were Nijō's sycophants, they did nothing but waggle their tongues and shake their heads and let the child have the Jeweled Throne, giving him the name Rokujō.

Jōsaimon'in tugged on his sleeve urgently. "Brother, look!"

"The monks are fighting!" cried another lady.

Peering past the curtains of state, Go-Shirakawa saw there was, indeed, some disturbance among the monks at Nijō's grave. He could see monks from the Kōfukuji Temple attacking something with swords and *naginatas*. They sang their temple songs as they hacked at something on the ground.

"Oh, no!" the ladies-in-waiting all cried. "There will be battle here! Over the Emperor's grave! How horrible!"

Go-Shirakawa stood, enraged by the disrespect to his son's grave and fearful that the monks might start a riot. "Go," he said to the ladies and his sister. "Leave now, quickly, all of you. There is no telling what might happen."

The ladies shrieked and hurried off of the platform, running to their carriages. Go-Shirakawa strode out to where his Captain of the Guard of the Right stood as if paralyzed by astonishment.

Go-Shirakawa grabbed the man's arm and shook him. "What is happening?"

"A most bizarre thing, Majesty. The monks of Enryakuji placed their tablet second, out of order."

It was customary, at an Imperial funeral, for each of the major temples near Heian Kyō and Nara to place burial tablets inscribed with prayers for the fallen Emperor upon his grave. But there was a prescribed order in which each temple would place its tablet and do observance, based on age and importance to the throne. First should have been Tōdaiji, as it was founded by Emperor Shomu four centuries before. Next should have been the Kōfukuji. Third should have come the Enryakuji temple of Mount Hiei.

"Why?"

"Who can say, Majesty? You know how presumptuous Mount Hiei has become lately. Anyway, the Kōfukuji monks were upset with this and have been chopping up the Hiei tablet."

"You and your men will go to them and, in my name on behalf of the Imperial family, order them to stop. This is a sacred and solemn occasion, and it is unseemly for them to disturb it so."

The Guard captain swallowed hard and bowed. "As you wish, Majesty." Gathering some of his men, the captain went to the procession of monks.

To Go-Shirakawa's relief, the orders had some effect. The Kōfukuji monks stopped their attack on the stone tablet, although it was already in so many pieces, it hardly mattered. The Hiei and Kōfukuji monks were guided away from the gravesite, and the rest of the temples continued to place their tablets in the proper order. But Go-Shirakawa noted the hard looks on the faces of the Mount Hiei monks both toward the Kōfukuji and toward him, as they passed by. Their thunderous expressions were more frightening than words or blows would have been.

This does not bode well, Go-Shirakawa thought.

A Chill in Sunlight

*T*wo days after the Imperial funeral, at midday, Taira Munemori returned to Rokuhara and leapt from the carriage as soon as it rumbled over the threshold beam. He ran across the great courtyard, which was filling with samurai unhurriedly putting on their armor. Munemori stopped to ask one or another of them where his father might be found. At last he was directed to a side garden, where Kiyomori stood conversing with a retainer. "Father, have you heard?" Munemori gasped.

Kiyomori looked at him with impatience. "That the monks of Enryakuji are marching on the capital. Of course I have heard. Hours ago."

"Ah. That would explain the arming of the warriors, then," Munemori said apologetically. "You are going to do battle with the monks?"

"We have received no summons from the Emperor," Kiyomori replied.

"So, for now, the Taira do nothing. But we should be prepared. We have heard they may attempt to attack Rokuhara, but I doubt even Enryakuji would be so foolish."

Munemori glanced around to reassure himself that the walls of Rokuhara were tall and in good order. "The Imperial Constables have been sent to stop them. Perhaps that will be all that is necessary."

Kiyomori made a noise short of spitting. "A few hundred noblemen's sons against thousands of armed monks? Well. I wish them good fortune."

"Begging your pardon, Lord Kiyomori," said the retainer, a man Munemori did not know, "but rumor on the street is that the *In*, Go-Shirakawa, has stirred up the monks against the Taira."

"No, no, no, that cannot be—" Munemori began.

"That would be extremely foolish, if so," said Kiyomori, rubbing his chin. "The Taira have given only good service to the *In*. He is a poor strategist indeed if he thinks such an attack would serve his interests."

"Father, I know it cannot be true—"

"But where is your armor, Munemori? Where are your men? Wait, who rides here?"

A pony came around the corner, bearing a ten-year-old boy. Munemori recognized his youngest brother, Kyokuni. The boy expertly brought the pony to a halt and he slid off its back. Running up to them, Kiyokuni cried, "Father! Brother! I bring an urgent message!"

Kiyomori beamed at the boy and grasped his shoulders. "Kiyokuni! What a fine young man you are becoming! Tell us your news."

"I am sent to tell you that Shigemori went to ToSanjō Palace because His Retired Majesty wishes to come to Rokuhara for protection. Shigemori is arranging the escort now, and they should be here within one hour. He asks you if you would be so kind as to make quarters ready."

Kiyomori looked at Munemori.

"That was what I was about to tell you," Munemori said. "Shigemori and I were summoned to ToSanjō. That is why I am sure the *In* is not behind this attack. He would not request our protection if he meant to destroy us."

"I have lived long enough to know that the intentions of Emperors and would-be Emperors is often difficult to fathom. But I will trust you are right. Kiyokuni, return to your brother and tell him the *In* is welcome to reside at Rokuhara as long as he wishes. We will make quarters ready at once."

The boy bowed. "I will tell him. Thank you, Father. Good day, Munemori." Kiyokuni then ran off in search of his pony.

"A stalwart boy," said the retainer. "You must be proud of him, my lord."

"Indeed," said Kiyomori. "He reminds me of my eldest, Shigemori. I have every hope that Kiyokuni will grow to be as fine a man."

Munemori seethed in silence. It was always Shigemori. The first son could do no wrong, while he, Munemori, was ignored, given little encouragement, set aside as superfluous. Even this youngest of Kiyomori's sons, Kiyokuni, was given more admiration than Munemori had ever received. *It is unjust*, he thought.

Kiyomori dismissed the retainer, and said, "Munemori, come with me. Let us go prepare the Southwest Wing, where His Late Majesty Nijō stayed when he was with us."

"Southwest Wing?" Munemori's stomach went cold with panic as he remembered the sight of the Shin-in's ghostly palanquin entering that wing of Rokuhara.

But Kiyomori had already run up the nearest steps into the mansion proper. Munemori caught up to him as he was striding down the long wooden main corridor.

"Southwest Wing? Err, Father, as to that . . ."

"Well?"

"Are you sure that is an appropriate quarter for His Retired Majesty?"

"How do you mean? If it was good enough for Nijō—

"Nijō is dead, Father."

Kiyomori stopped and scowled at Munemori. "What are you implying?"

"N-nothing, Father, only that . . . there might be . . . unfortunate associations."

Kiyomori growled and continued on his way. "The Retired Emperor will be expecting to be put up in the same quarters. He would be insulted with anything else. The Southwest Wing is the best appointed and the best defensible, should an attack come. Besides, it would disrupt the entire household to have to move some of our family from another wing. I doubt we could manage it within an hour."

When they reached the Southwest Wing, Kiyomori began to order servants to prepare the rooms. The servants obeyed, but with nervous glances and worried sighs.

"What is the matter with them?" Kiyomori asked Munemori.

"Well, you know how foolish servants are," said Munemori. "They think that this wing is, well . . . haunted."

"Haunted?"

Munemori conjured up a false laugh. "Ha-ha. Yes. Isn't that silly? Haunted."

Kiyomori fixed him with an iron glare. "Rokuhara is *not* haunted."

"Oh, of course, of course not. But . . . the servants have reported a certain coldness in the rooms, and things vanishing or moving about with no one touching them. With the servants so jittery, are you certain you want the *In* staying here?" *Especially since there is already an* In *staying here,* Munemori added to himself.

Kiyomori whirled about and strode through the rooms, now and then pausing to sniff the air. "There is a faint, lingering odor of rot and ashes," he said at last. "The wood floors seem not to have been polished recently, and a few of the *shōji* panels are stained or torn. The servants must be using their story of ghosts to excuse their laziness and unfinished work." Kiyomori turned to the nearest cowering menial. "See that these things are taken care of at once!"

The menial bowed very low and hurried off.

Munemori became acutely aware that although he stood in a shaft of sunlight coming through the open bamboo blinds, a strange chill settled upon him. "Father, do you not feel anything is . . . amiss?"

Kiyomori seemed to shiver slightly. But he said, "Nonsense. These rooms have always been drafty. We need more braziers brought in. You will see to it. As you did not come prepared for battle, I will leave the task of preparing this wing for our visitor to you." Kiyomori left without another word.

"Very well," Munemori grumbled to himself. "But if anything goes wrong, I will know I tried. I know whose fault it will be." Then he allowed himself a heavy sigh. He also knew who would be blamed. Glad that it was still daylight, Munemori began an inspection of the rooms.

A Scent of Ashes

Retired Emperor Go-Shirakawa sat on the floor of the receiving room in the guest wing of Rokuhara, feeling less than comfortable. The place smelled musty, the rooms had only been hurriedly cleaned, and worst yet, his moving-in was hovered over by the bumbling Munemori. Go-Shirakawa could not imagine how the Lord of the Taira could have such disparate sons as Shigemori and Munemori. He had tried several times to dismiss Munemori from the proceedings, but the young man would not be dissuaded and constantly tried anxiously to offer advice as to where things should be placed and where Go-Shirakawa should sleep.

"If His Retired Majesty wishes," Munemori burbled, "I could send for a priest to chant sutras, which you might find soothing at this troubled time."

"Thank you but no," Go-Shirakawa said through gritted teeth. "I have had quite enough of monks this day, and we do not wish to bring in any Enryakuji spies, do we?"

"Oh, of course not. His Majesty is wise to think of such things. I only thought—"

"Tax your brain no further, good Munemori. You have done quite enough for us."

"But if there is anything more Your Majesty wishes—"

"I will send a servant with a request should I have one. Now surely you should join your father's forces and help see to Rokuhara's defense, neh?"

"Oh, I am sure my father and brothers have such matters well in hand," said Munemori. "I was expressly ordered to see to your comfort."

Or were you ordered to bedevil me to ensure I did not stay long? thought Go-Shirakawa. *Such a thing would not be beyond the crafty Kiyomori.* He gazed fixedly at Munemori. "My comfort now requires that I be left alone to confer with my counselors. Should I require anything further, I will let you know."

"But if Your Majesty could suggest to me some possible future need so that I might—"

"Begone!" cried Go-Shirakawa, finally losing all patience.

Munemori's mouth set into a tight, thin line, and he bowed deeply. Then he scurried away like a mouse escaping a burning granary.

How like him to force me into rudeness, thought the *In*.

Middle Counselor Narichika entered then, and knelt before him. Narichika amazed Go-Shirakawa. He was one of the few noblemen to have survived both the Hōgen and the Heiji. Even though he had served the monstrous Nobuyori, Narichika maintained ties with the Taira, having once been Shigemori's tutor and Narichika's youngest sister was now married to Shigemori. And now Narichika had offered his services to the Retired Emperor. Though he did not know if Narichika could be trusted, Go-Shirakawa was impressed by the man's ability to swim through the political cross-currents, and therefore found Narichika's advice advice invaluable.

"Majesty," said Narichika, "there is word on the movement of the monks of Mount Hiei."

"Yes? Are they headed this way?"

"Apparently not, Majesty. Nor did they stop at the Imperial Compound, as we had expected."

"They are not at ToSanjō Palace, are they?"

"They came nowhere near there, Majesty."

"Hmm. After the look the monks gave me when I ordered a halt to their altercation, I was certain I would be the target of their wrath. Where have they gone, then?"

"They were seen marching east, Majesty, straight through the capital. It is now thought their target is Kiyomizudera."

"Ah. That temple is affiliated with Kōfukuji, is it not?"

"So it is, Majesty."

"So they merely wish to make protest for the destruction of their tablet at the funeral. They will probably march around the temple, singing their songs and shaking their sacred palanquins and be done with it. Am I a fool for having overreacted and fled here?"

Narichika shook his head. "One can never predict what angry monks will do, Majesty. And the monks of Mount Hiei are formidable in their wrath. You were merely being prudent, Majesty. Such acts are never foolish."

"You put things in good perspective, as always, Narichika. Hmm. Do you feel a chill?"

"Now that you mention it, Majesty, it does feel a bit cold."

"Light that brazier for me, will you?"

As the evening wore on, messengers came to Rokuhara to report the continuing events. The Hiei monks did go to the ancient and revered temple of Kiyomizudera. But instead of marching and singing, they burned all its buildings to the ground before returning up the mountain to Enryakuji.

Go-Shirakawa could smell the ashes and smoke from the burning temple on the drafts that blew in under the bamboo blinds and through the *shōji*. He was relieved to hear that the monks were leaving Heian Kyō, but he was reluctant to lie down to sleep. He felt antsy and on edge, fearful that he had made some dreadful mistake by coming to Rokuhara. *Am I afraid that the Taira will keep me here, holding me prisoner as Nobuyori did in the Single-Copy Library? Do I fear that the Regent's faction will accuse me of inciting the monks to terrify the Emperor? Or do I simply fear that Munemori will return to annoy me through the night?*

So Go-Shirakawa sat up, hour after hour, staring at the little bronze brazier on which he had set some incense burning to banish the unpleasant smells. His nose and forehead hurt, and his eyes watered. He tried to remember one of the sutras, but the words kept slipping out of his mind.

At last, after a Taira watchman had called the Hour of The Ox, Go-Shirakawa wavered, drifting in and out of a strange half sleep. At some point he became aware of someone else sitting in the room.

"Who is there?" he murmured. "Is that you, Narichika?" The shadows cast by the hastily assembled screens and tables were confusing and unfamiliar. He could not make out a person's shape anywhere in the room.

"Good evening, brother." The low voice was just above a whisper.

"Brother? Who is there?" Surely he would have been informed if the Abbot of Ninna-ji had arrived. What other brother could it be?

"I have come to warn you."

"Warn me?"

"Beware, brother. You are in grave danger. The Taira mean to destroy you."

"Destroy me?"

"They wish to destroy the entire Imperial house and set Kiyomori up as Emperor."

"That . . . that cannot be."

"Oh, but it can. Kiyomori is of Imperial blood and is aware of it. Be watchful, brother."

"Lineage is not enough," Go-Shirakawa argued, wondering if he was making sense.

"Kiyomori is using magic. He has the aid of supernatural powers. He wants the Imperial Regalia, the mirror, the gem, and the sword, Kusanagi. With them he will wreak tyrannical terror over Nihon. Do not let him do this. Trust no Taira. Beware."

"But who are you? How do you know this?"

It suddenly seemed that Go-Shirakawa was alone, no one else in the room, nothing in the air but the scent of ashes.

The following morning, Go-Shirakawa quietly conferred with Middle Counselor Narichika.

"Yes, Majesty, I also had a strange dream. Someone claiming to be Akugenda Yoshihira, the brave young Minomoto leader who was executed near here, whispered in my ear. He told me to beware the Taira," said Narichika. "I was shown visions of a future world, where Heian Kyō is fallen into ruins, where the Empire is ruled from some other city, and the men in power are not courtiers and scholars but rough warriors. The land is split with constant civil war and those of the best families, even the Emperor himself, are mere puppets of the generals."

"We often rehearse our worst fears in dreams," Go-Shirakawa said. "Perhaps your vision was only this."

"No, Majesty," said Narichika. "I think perhaps this was a true vision of what will come if the Taira continue to rise in power."

Someone else in the room said, "It is said Heaven speaks through men, as it has no voice of its own."

"Who is that?" Go-Shirakawa demanded. "Who is there?" A small, elderly monk in gray robes shuffled out from behind a screen and knelt, bowing, before them. Go-Shirakawa vaguely remembered him. "Saikō, isn't it?"

"You have it exactly, Majesty. I arrived during the night while you were sleeping and did not wish you disturbed on my account." The old monk's eyes were very bright, as if he had taken opium. "This is a most interesting place, I found. Very . . . inspiring."

Go-Shirakawa could not recall how long ago Saikō had attached himself to the Retired Emperor's court. Go-Shirakawa did remember that his brother, the Shin-In, had had a monk advisor very similar to Saikō when he was Retired Emperor as well. *Why do I know this?* Go-Shirakawa wondered.

"Someone could have informed me of your arrival," said Narichika. The Middle Counselor did not entirely trust Saikō, Go-Shirakawa knew. Many of the nobility who were hangers-on at ToSanjō did not.

"Perhaps it was merely an oversight that you were not told," said Saikō. "Then again, the Taira do not seem entirely comfortable with your presence here, and they may have thought the courtesy unnecessary."

"What are you saying?" asked Go-Shirakawa, narrowing his eyes at the monk.

"There is a rumor, you understand, that you deliberately stirred up the monks in hopes that they might march against the Taira."

"That is foolishness!" said Go-Shirakawa. "Why would I be here if I had wanted such a thing? The Taira have served me well. Even my latest concubine is a Taira girl."

The old monk waggled his hand from side to side. "Forgive me, Majesty. I said it was only rumor. But perhaps all this talk, and your dreams, are to a purpose, Majesty. Perhaps the gods and *bosatsu* are sending you a message in the only way they can. Perhaps the Taira have become too arrogant for the gods, and they wish to see the Taira punished."

"Hush! Talk no more of this. We are their guests, and the walls have ears." But Go-Shirakawa made arrangements to return to his own residence that same day, in order to stay among the Taira as short a time as possible. But as he rode back to ToSanjō Palace, drowsing with the rocking of the ox-carriage, he pondered Saikō's words and found them strangely sensible.

Dried Iris Balls

After the hasty departure of Go-Shirakawa and his entourage, Tokiko convinced two of her handmaidens to escort her through the Southwest Wing of Rokuhara.

Poor Munemori, she thought as she fingered a slightly torn paper panel on the *shōji* leading into the guest wing. *No one would believe him, so at last he came to me. If I had known sooner, I might have done . . . something. Now Go-Shirakawa has departed without saying what frightened him away.* The Retired Emperor had claimed pressing business, but pressing business tended to come to the court, not the other way around. Something had driven him out of Rokuhara.

The air was heavy with sandalwood incense, masking other smells. The smoke from Kiyomizudera was still in the air as well. But there was something else, underneath. Tokiko moved from room to room with as much calm dignity as she could. But the servants could sense her unease. Tokiko examined the hastily repaired sliding doors, the frayed reed mats. There was a tiny piece of paper in one corner. It was part of someone's writing exercise, perhaps a sutra, but it had been torn to bits. The scrap held only two characters—"no peace." Tokiko placed the paper in her sleeve and walked on.

She tried to calm her anger . . . and fear. An evil presence had been here. In her own home. Gone now, but who knew how much damage it had done while it was here. Or whether it would return. Munemori had claimed it was the Shin-In. If that were true, then her husband Kiyomori faced a greater and more uncertain threat than she had expected. Her father had warned her there would be opposition, but Tokiko expected it would come from mortal warriors and nobles. Naturally the *kami* chose sides, giving aid here and there to mortals, just as Ryujin had done for the Taira. All the *kami* observe certain limits, so as to avoid returning the world to utter chaos, but a rogue demon, beholden to no one but himself, of Imperial blood and therefore descended from the most ancient of *kami*, might not recognize any limits at all.

Tokiko had been sent up into the mortal realm only to teach and advise. She had little magic of her own. What could she do to battle a great demon?

There would be no point in trying to discuss it with Kiyomori. He would only think she was being alarmist and too strident for a woman. He was spending more and more time away from Rokuhara, either at the Imperial palace or at his harbor by the sea. He hardly spoke with her at all these days. Tokiko knew she would have to act without consulting him.

Finally, she turned to the nearest servant. "Do we still have the decorations from New Years? The iris balls in particular?"

"I think we may, my lady, though they will not be in the best repair. The revelers that night . . ." The servant fluttered her hands to indicate that some of the decorations might have been trod upon by drunken guests.

"No matter."

"And they are doubtless dry and shriveled, my lady. I fear they will look shabby. A dreary sight for future guests."

"It is my hope we will have no future guests for a while. Of any sort," said Tokiko. "Put them up where they will be least conspicuous. Then summon two monks from Ninna-ji to purify these rooms. Discreetly, you understand. My lord Kiyomori has many matters on his mind, and I do not wish him unduly distracted."

"Of course, my lady. As you wish."

Tokiko acknowledged the servant's bow, then hurried off to the garden. She needed to speak to the turtles in the pond to send a message to her father, the Dragon King.

The Taira Ascendant

Retired Emperor Go-Shirakawa did not act upon his fears immediately. As he had heard the wise Minomoto general Yoshitomo once say, "To know a horse, you must give him free rein. Note his behavior when there is neither heel to the flank nor tug on the bit. Then you may truly judge his spirit."

So it had been with Nobuyori. His evil did not become fully apparent until great power was given him. So it might be, thought Go-Shirakawa, with Kiyomori.

Therefore, Go-Shirakawa waited some three years, slowly building up a second government in Heian Kyō consisting of those nobles who preferred the leadership of a mature Retired Emperor to that of a child and his Fujiwara Regent. With exquisite patience, through gifts, bribes, and promises of advancement, Go-Shirakawa saw to it that no important appointments or decisions were made by the Senior Counsel of Nobles without first consulting him.

Thus, when the time seemed auspicious, in the third year of the era Nin'an, Go-Shirakawa and his own carefully appointed Counselors removed the young Emperor Rokujō, at the ripe age of five, from the throne. It was said to be the first time in the Empire's history that an Emperor retired before his coming-of-age ceremony.

In Rokujō's place, Go-Shirakawa named his own son, Crown Prince Takakura, who was seven. Determined to keep Takakura from going the way of the unfortunate and sinful Nijō, Go-Shirakawa removed the meddlesome Fujiwara nobles from their posts in the palace and named a Taira, Tokitada, to be Regent. And for good measure, he betrothed Emperor Takakura to Kiyomori's fifteen-year-old daughter.

As a last slap in the face to the Fujiwara, Go-Shirakawa elevated Kiyomori himself to Chancellor, the most powerful post in Heian Kyō, short of the Emperor and Retired Emperor themselves.

All in the Taira clan were ecstatic, of course, with this elevation in status.

They strutted about the capital in their new black robes with overweening pride. It was said at Rokuhara and all over Heian Kyō, "If one is not a Taira, one is simply not a human being."

This done, Go-Shirakawa settled back at ToSanjō Palace and waited to see how events would play themselves out.

Itsukushima

Chancellor Kiyomori stood near the prow of his boat as it sped across the Seto Inland Sea. Sunlight sparkled on the water, and the great square sail behind him billowed on the wind. It was hereabouts, he reflected, that he had met the dragon boat bearing Benzaiten and her sisters so long ago. There was no dragon boat now, but off in the distance, he could see the green island of Miyajima. And at its base, where the hillside met the sea, a glimmer of red and gold where the Shrine of Itsukushima, now finished after ten years of labor and Taira treasure, stood awaiting his arrival and final approval.

The entourage attending him was not as splendid as Kiyomori had hoped for this grand occasion. Retired Emperor Go-Shirakawa had refused to allow his son, little Emperor Takakura, to accompany Kiyomori. "It would be terrible if His Young Majesty were lost at sea," Go-Shirakawa had said. True enough, but Kiyomori understood the message that, despite all the honors showered upon the Taira, Kiyomori was still not entirely trusted.

A shame indeed, for there had been the possibility that with the Emperor would come the Imperial Regalia, including the sword Kusanagi. Kiyomori might finally have been able to appease the Dragon King, and have their bargain settled and done with. Then again, Kiyomori thought, it might be a disguised blessing. For Ryujin had fulfilled all parts of his bargain but one.

To Kiyomori's utter bafflement, his wife Tokiko had also declined to accompany him to Miyajima. At first he thought it was grief for their second son, Motomori, who had finally succumbed to his illness and died six months ago. "Don't you want to pray for his soul, wife? Don't you want to see the temple I built for your sister?"

Tokiko had shrugged and said, "I can pray for Motomori here, and the temple was Benzaiten's request, not mine. I am too old for a journey at sea. Go and enjoy your new shrine."

Kiyomori accepted that perhaps it was best she stay home. Tokiko would doubtless have been poor company.

His eldest son, Shigemori, also remained behind. Shigemori reminded Kiyomori of what had happened the last time they had gone off on a pilgrimage together. "One of us should stay behind, to rally the Taira warriors should it be necessary."

Kiyomori could not argue with such logic. And so he set off for Miyajima with only Munemori and other lesser sons, and those nobles who wished to ingratiate themselves with the Taira, as his entourage. Nonetheless, as the boat sped across the waters toward Miyajima, Kiyomori felt a great surge of pride and accomplishment, that the great shrine he had imagined and designed ten years before had finally become a reality.

As the boat came to the island, instead of the tiny dock that had been there years before, there was now a long pier that easily allowed Kiyomori's boat and the five other ships behind it to tie up with ease and safety. As Kiyomori and his sons disembarked, they were met by dozens of shrine priests dressed in white robes and black hats, blowing on horns and banging on little gongs. With deep, sweeping bows, the priests guided Kiyomori's entourage on an inspection tour of the shrine.

Despite his other disappointments, the new Itsukushima Shrine was as lavish and beautiful as Kiyomori had imagined it. The main shrine and treasure-house had elegant swooping roofs of tile. The long corridors between them were hung with the finest cast-iron lanterns. A tall red-and-gold pagoda stood upon a nearby hillside. Large platforms on which sacred dances and dramas would be performed jutted out onto the sea. A great *torii* stood out in the waters beyond the platforms, framing the distant hills of Aki Province across the Inland Sea.

Everyone, including Kiyomori, exclaimed delightedly over the beautiful tapestries, brocade hangings, painted screens, and carved images. When the tour was finished, some of the shrine maidens did a sacred dance on the raised platforms, while others served the visitors a meal of fish and pickled vegetables. Many of the noblemen had brought their own casks of sake, and, to the consternation of the priests, soon the drink was flowing liberally as well.

Now that there was so much more to watch over and protect, the shrine priests were no longer required to leave the island at sunset. It was expected that noble pilgrims would also wish to spend more than one day at the shrine, and so visitors' lodging had been built as well to accommodate them. Chancellor Kiyomori and his entourage were the first such visitors not to follow the ancient custom, and they remained through the day.

As the sun was setting, Chancellor Kiyomori distanced himself from his celebrating sons and nobles, choosing to walk down the painted-wood colonnades alone. He watched as the shrine priests diligently lit every iron lantern until the shrine glowed with light. The lights reflected off the water of the sea that surrounded much of the shrine, as if in imitation of the dragon lights that Kiyomori remembered from long ago.

Truly, he thought, *this place must rival the palace of Ryujin, the Dragon King, himself for splendor. He and Benzaiten cannot possibly think me remiss any longer.*

The evening dwindled to twilight, and the priests diplomatically herded the tipsy noblemen to their visitors' quarters. Some of the nobles, including Munemori, took some no-longer-to-be-shrine-maidens in with them. Kiyomori stood apart from them, and when he was approached by a priest asking whether he would like to be shown to his rooms, Kiyomori declined, saying he would like to walk and meditate a while longer.

Now that the main part of the shrine was deserted, Kiyomori strolled out to the edge of the farthest platform that stood out on the Inland Sea waters. The Evening Star was framed between the uprights of the great *torii*, and the clouds above the western horizon still glowed with the last remnants of sunset. Leaning on the railing of the platform, Kiyomori addressed the waters lapping against the pier posts below. "Well, Lady Benzaiten. Are you pleased with my gift?"

Dragon lights, pale blue, green, and yellow, appeared in the waters, sparkling and glimmering. They filled the small bay of Itsukushima. Something moved in the waters below, and a giant clamshell rose above the water. Benzaiten herself knelt in the shell as if she were a pearl, her shimmering green kimonos spread out around her. Indeed, her unimaginably beautiful face glowed in the remaining twilight with an iridescent sheen. "Greetings, Chancellor Kiyomori. Yes, I am very pleased with your shrine. I will see that it lasts through the centuries as testimony to your good faith."

Kiyomori bowed to her. "I am most gratified. May I assume, then, that all is settled between the Taira and your family?"

Benzaiten looked away. "Alas, as you know, there is another matter. If you will but remain here, my father would speak with you."

Kiyomori gripped the railing but fought to show no other signs of fear. "Of course. Let your father come. I have nothing to . . . I will gladly speak with him."

Benzaiten inclined her head, and her clamshell slowly sank again beneath the surface of the water.

Kiyomori waited as the sky darkened and a chill wind blew across the sea from the west. The water before him began to roil and billow as something enormous and serpentine moved beneath the surface. Suddenly a dark form breached the waters with a gust of water like a whale spouting. A great reptilian head rose on an enormous column of scaled neck. Its eyes glowed golden as if there were fires within, and seaweed hung from the long whiskers on its jaw. Seawater ran out of its enormous, gaping maw, through its serrated teeth, dripping past its scythe-like fangs. It stared down at Kiyomori and snorted a blast of briny mist through its cavernous nostrils. In a voice

that boomed and hissed like the surf in a storm, Ryujin said, "So. At last
we meet, Kiyomori-san."

Kiyomori held fast to the railing. He understood why Ryujin had chosen
his most fearsome guise in which to appear. *He wishes to frighten me into*
submission. But if I am to bargain with a god, I must not show fear. "It is
an honor to be in your presence, Ryujin-sama," Kiyomori said, bowing.

"This is no time for pleasantries," hissed the Dragon King. "What of
the sword? What of Kusanagi?"

"You shall have it, of course," Kiyomori said. "In time."

The dark shape rolled in the waters, churning up green phosphores-
cence. "Time for mortals grows short. I must have it returned."

"It will be," said Kiyomori, "when my grandson is Emperor."

The water was churned faster. "No. Soon. You do not know the danger
you face. Already forces of evil strive to destroy your kingdom. The demons
have a new soverign, over whom I have no power. If he gains control of
the sword, he will cause utter disaster. You must bring me Kusanagi."

Firmly, Kiyomori said, "When my grandson is Emperor, according to
your daughter's promise. Then you may have Kusanagi."

"You fool! Is your ambition greater than your wish for survival? It will
be years before your daughter, the Empress, will bear a son. By that time,
it may be too late!"

"It is too risky to release the sword now," Kiyomori argued. "Takakura
is but a child. He needs all the symbols and trappings of legitimate rule.
Already, we in Heian Kyō are beset by alarms and false rumors of conflict.
If the sword should go missing now, it might plunge the country into war.
You cannot have Kusanagi until I decide the time is appropriate."

The dragon lights went out. A gust of the Dragon King's breath reeking
of brine and seaweed smote Kiyomori in the face, and fish, "You dare to
tell me what I can have and when, I who am older than your precious clan,
your precious Heian Kyō? You dare to try to bargain with a *kami*? You
who have insulted my daughter? Did you learn nothing of my wrath when
I destroyed your paltry little island at Fukuhara?"

Kiyomori felt anger, then. The same anger he had felt when his father
was insulted by the lofty lords of Heian Kyō. The same anger he felt whenever he heard of slander against the Taira. And, unwise as it might have
been, he felt that anger reach his mouth and speak. "You chose me as your
hero to save this world, and this is how you treat me? You disregard my
judgment, even though I know the mortal realm and you do not? If you are
so powerful, what need do you have of a magic sword? If such a sword
matters so much to you, why can't you make another? If you are such a
mighty *kami*, why do you have to bully puny mortals into doing your work
for you?"

The Dragon King raised back his head and roared. His serpentine tail rose out of the water and struck it with a mighty slap that boomed like thunder and nearly drenched Kiyomori. "Foolish mortal! You have no idea what disasters await you. Perhaps it is true what is said . . . that the arrogance of the Taira is such, they strive to be greater than gods. So be it. Since you will not bring me Kusanagi, I withdraw my aid and protection. Let us see how long the Taira, and their sad mortal realm, will last through their own efforts."

For a moment the sea boiled as if a volcano were rising from beneath its surface. The Dragon King's great head sank back down into the water, glaring at Kiyomori as it went. And then all was dark and silent once more.

Kiyomori leaned against the railing, trying to control the pounding of his heart and the rapidity of his breathing. *I am Chancellor Kiyomori, chief of the mighty Taira clan. I have no reason to fear.*

Running footsteps rumbled behind him, and Kiyomori turned to see several priests approaching.

"Lord Chancellor, are you all right? We heard noises like thunder. You are wet. What has happened?"

Kiyomori made placating gestures. "It is nothing. Some errant waves boomed against the pier beneath me, and one sent water splashing up. That is all."

The priests sighed and laughed with relief, though one or two seemed uncertain about Kiyomori's response. He knew they would not dare question him, however.

"If you please, Holy Ones," Kiyomori went on, "I should like to go to my lodgings now, and put on robes that stink a little less of the sea."

The Reproachful Carp

That night, Tokiko was writing an advice-full letter by lamplight to her daughter Kenreimon'in, the Empress. Her brush jerked as she was startled by the sound of violent splashing out in her garden pond. For a moment she hoped it was merely a duck taking flight. But as the splashing continued, she knew it could be only bad news.

Tokiko called for a servant bearing a lantern on a stick and together they went out to the pond. Tokiko knelt by the water's edge, and a great golden carp swam over to her. "You were slow this time," said the fish.

"I do not want to hear what you have to say," responded Tokiko. "But I am here. What is the news from my father?"

"He says it is all over. Your husband remains obstinate. Ryujin says it is time for you to return home, under the sea. There is no more for you to do here. You must leave the mortals to their fate."

Tokiko sighed. She turned and looked back at Rokuhara, where she had borne and raised so many children. How the years had flown by since Kiyomori had brought her to Heian Kyō. It had been twelve years since the Hōgen Disturbance, nine years since the Heiji. And she had managed to live through it all, teaching her children to become wise and accomplished, all but Motomori, of course, who now resided in the Pure Land. She thought about Shigemori, of whom she was so proud, and poor, untalented Munemori who needed so much guidance. And her daughter Kenreimon'in who needed guidance as well, not just for herself but for the entire land of Nihon.

Ryujin's palace under the sea was beautiful, but so full of gloom, Tokiko remembered. It was so lonely, empty at times, visited only by the dead. To return now would mean not seeing the sun again for who knew how long. It would mean not knowing what would happen to her children. It meant never seeing her youngest grow to maturity. It meant never seeing a future grandchild seated on the Jeweled Throne. It meant never seeing some grandchildren at all.

"Tell my father . . . I cannot return. Not just yet."

"He will not be happy with you," chided the carp.

"Tell him I might yet be able to look after his interests. That we should not give up hope just yet. There might yet be a Taira who can do what my father requires. I cannot give up on these people," said Tokiko, feeling a hot tear roll down her cheek. "I cannot."

"You are a foolish female," said the carp. "Still, I do not think your father can force you. Do what you will. You understand, however, that you may be placing yourself in danger?"

"That is the risk in becoming a mortal," said Tokiko. "I accepted that risk long ago."

"Have it your way, then," said the carp, "but don't expect any help from home." With a flash of his golden scales in the lamplight, the fish turned and swam away into the depths of the pond.

Tokiko sighed.

"My lady, did you learn what you . . . hoped?" asked the servant uncomfortably. She wouldn't have been able to hear the carp, so to her it only seemed like Tokiko was talking to herself. But the servants had long ago learned of Tokiko's eccentricities and resigned themselves to thinking she was either mad or a sorceress. In either case, they were careful not to insult or upset her.

"Not what I hoped," replied Tokiko. "But I must carry on. It is chilly out here, neh? Let us return to the house."

"Yes, my lady."

A Wooden Sword

For others besides the Taira, the nine long years since the end of the Heiji had brought great changes as well. At the mountain monastery of Kuramadera, where the Kamo river begins its flow through the forested hills down to Heian Kyō, eight-year-old Ushiwaka, son of general Minomoto Yoshitomo and the unfortunate Tokiwa, half brother to Minomoto Yoritomo, was serving in exile as a page for the monk Tōkōbō.

As he had on every evening he could remember, Ushiwaka brought in the wood for the cooking fires, and buckets of water from the Kamo River. He swept the corridors and scrubbed the flagstones of the garden pathways. As the temple bell boomed and the monks began their evening meditations, Ushiwaka slipped into his room and pulled his hand-carved wooden sword from its hiding place between the paper walls. Making as little noise as possible, he sped down the garden paths and out into the forest.

Ushiwaka's mind was not on his work or the philosophy and sutras the monks were trying to teach him. His thoughts were on vengeance.

Though he had been only a month old when the great Lord Kiyomori of the Taira spared his life, and had been told nothing by the monks of Mount Kurama of his past, Ushiwaka had slowly learned who he was. Even here, in the mountains, stories came up from Heian Kyō with the pilgrims and the rice merchants and the noble visitors. Even the monks loved to hear the latest gossip from them.

Ushiwaka would spend hours hidden behind the bamboo blinds, listening to the wagging tongues of the people from the capital. He heard noble pilgrims ask the monks about him, whether he knew he was a Minomoto, that his father had been a great general, that his father had been murdered by treachery. They asked if Ushiwaka knew his life had been bought by his mother's dishonored bed. Well, he knew now.

Ushiwaka walked and walked until he came to a small clearing in the mountain forest, surrounded by pines and sugi trees. There he planted his feet and began his sword exercises. A few months before, Ushiwaka had begged the guardsman of a noble lady to show him some sword-fighting moves. The guardsman had been quite bemused by the serious little boy and therefore showed Ushiwaka techniques more advanced than might have been taught to a child his age. Moves that might not have been wise to teach at all to a boy with Ushiwaka's past. But Ushiwaka had memorized everything he was taught and now practiced diligently every night.

"*Hai! Hai!*" Ushiwaka swept the sword before him in the Circling Monkey move, imagining each stroke connecting with Lord Kiyomori's legs, arms, neck. He imagined flesh parting, blood flowing, Kiyomori's body collapsing to the ground. He imagined himself placing Kiyomori's head on a lance and riding triumphantly through Heian Kyō, receiving the cheers of the people. Ushiwaka thrust again with his little wooden sword, but he stepped forward onto a rock, lost his footing, and fell over.

"Ha, ha-ha!" He heard cawing laughter behind him. "You must watch your step, young man, if you are to defeat your enemies."

Ushiwaka jumped to his feet and spun around, pointing his sword at the trees. "Who are you? I'm not afraid of you!" But, in fact, Ushiwaka was afraid, for he feared at any time the Ise Taira might change their minds about their leniency and send someone to kill him.

"Peace, young fellow." A figure glided out of the trees and alighted in the clearing before him. It was a strange-looking creature—a man with a long nose in black robes that billowed behind him like wings. He wore a little boxlike hat on his upper forehead in the manner of the *ubasoku* mountain wizards, and carried a ringed staff in his hands.

Ushiwaka gasped. "A *tengu*!" He did not know whether to stay or run; the shape-changing demons of the mountains could be helpful to mortals, but also could play nasty, mischievous tricks.

The *tengu* inclined his head. "You are a perceptive boy. I am Sōjō-bō, prince of the *tengu* of Mount Kurama. We have been watching you. We are curious as to why a little lad like you is disturbing our forest with his toy sword and his silly cries and stumbling footsteps."

Ushiwaka reddened, but he lifted his chin, and said, "I want to be a great warrior, like my father."

"That is admirable."

Ushiwaka knew it would be unwise to say, but he could not help himself. "And I want to kill Lord Kiyomori of the Taira!"

"Ah," said Sōjō-bō. "A worthy goal indeed."

Ushiwaka could not tell if the *tengu* was mocking him. "Lord Kiyomori is responsible for my father's death. And . . . and . . . he dishonored my mother." Ushiwaka was too young to know what sort of dishonor his mother suffered, but it seemed to be a very bad thing and deserving of vengeance.

"Lord Kiyomori has a great deal to answer for," the *tengu* agreed. "We have been watching events in Heian Kyō, and we do not like what we see. The Taira have become pompous tyrants, and we *tengu* have no patience for such. The Great Kiyomori has even angered King Ryujin of the Sea. A poor choice indeed to stave off the dark times to come. But Lord Kiyomori made a fatal mistake, didn't he?"

"Mistake?" asked Ushiwaka.

"Yes. He let you live. You and your brothers."

"I have brothers?"

"Yes, at least two or three, I think."

"Where are they? Please tell me!"

"They are in exile, as you are, in faraway places, and now is not the time for you to find them, little Minomoto. They would be in danger if they came to Lord Kiyomori's attention, just as you would, wouldn't they?"

Ushiwaka swallowed his hopes hard. "Yes. Of course. But I want to see them someday."

"And so you will. Someday. But I wonder if you will be worthy when you meet them. One of them, after all, has received the blessing of Hachiman, the god of war, and he is destined for greatness. Another of them is already learning sacred magic. But what will you have to show for yourself, hmm? I wonder . . ." The *tengu* stared up at the trees and tapped his chin thoughtfully.

Ushiwaka fidgeted with his wooden sword. He knew the stories that told how the *tengu* were masters of all the fighting arts, especially swordsmanship. He had heard how great heroes of the past had been taught by *tengu* sensei. It was also said that one should beware the gifts conferred by demons, for they exact a high price. Those heroes taught by *tengu* were never again the same as ordinary men, isolated and sometimes feared and hated for their differences. But Ushiwaka knew he was already unlike other boys and that his fate would take an extraordinary path. "Will you . . . would you . . . teach me, Sōjōbō-sama? Teach me to fight with the sword and become a great warrior, worthy of my brothers?"

A slow smile spread beneath the *tengu*'s long nose. "Well, now, there is an interesting notion. One which, I am sure, my fellow *tengu* will think foolish and perhaps a waste of our time. But . . . why not? Perhaps, if you are dedicated and follow our lessons well, then at least you will not fall on your face when you meet your brothers, neh?"

Ushiwaka got to his knees and pressed his forehead to the ground in gratitude. "Thank you, Sōjōbō-sama! I want to learn everything! I will do anything you wish!"

"Anything I wish? No, no, no, little Minomoto, we *tengu* are not tyrants. We make no demands. Only learn, and then do with your skill what you think best."

"Will I get to kill Lord Kiyomori?"

"Well, now, as to that I cannot say. But we will teach you all the skills you might need so that, should you have a chance . . . well, you may do what is necessary."

Ushiwaka got back to his feet, and asked, "When can we begin, Sōjōbō-sama?"

The *tengu* raised his hands toward the trees. "Now."

There arose a great fluttering in the pine branches, and many winged creatures descended. Some were no larger than ravens; others were of raven shape at the size of a man, with both wings and muscled arms. They stared at Ushiwaka with glittering eyes and laughed with clattering beaks.

"These are my Leaflet Tengu," said Sōjō-bō. "They will begin your training. If you do well with them, then I will take up your training myself later. So. Begin." Sōjō-bō clapped his hands, and the smaller tengu flew at Ushiwaka's face.

He swung his wooden sword wildly at them but missed, and he stumbled around the clearing like a drunken nobleman. One little *tengu* got close enough to scratch his face with its talons.

"Your stance is too narrow!" shrieked one of the *tengu*. "Keep your feet even with your shoulders!"

"Bend your knees more," cried another, flying at his face. Ushiwaka missed that one, too, but he was able to duck out of the way. "Remember to breathe!"

Ushiwaka felt angry but exhilarated. The *tengu* worked him hard for an hour, and he was very tired by the end but felt he was learning so much that his skill had improved already. He knew he was on the way to becoming a great warrior.

When the *tengu* were done, they flew up into the night sky, becoming shadows against the stars. They called down to him, "Come back tomorrow night, little mortal, so we can laugh at you some more."

Ushiwaka bowed to them, and then happily walked the moonlit path back to the monastery, his soul seared with joyous fire.

He had hoped to return to his room unseen. But as he neared the pages' dormitory, Ushiwaka had to pass the open *shōji* of the abbot's quarters. He could see the gray-robed abbot, Tōkōbō, seated cross-legged on his floor mats, moonlight glinting off his shaved head. He was quietly copying a sutra by lamplight. Ushiwaka tried to tiptoe past, hoping not to be noticed, but it was not to be.

"Ushiwaka?" said Tōkōbō without looking up from his brush and paper.

"*Hai*, Holy One," Ushiwaka replied, dropping into a low bow, holding his wooden sword behind his back.

"Come here."

Ushiwaka stepped onto the verandah beside the abbot's room but did not enter. "I am here, Holy One. What do you wish?"

"Where have you been?" Tōkōbō asked in the tone adults use when they know very well where a child has been.

"In the forest, Holy One. I have been . . . meditating."

"Hmm. It is a curious meditation that leaves one's face so flushed and scratched."

"I ran home, Holy One. And . . . I ran into some pine branches along the way."

"Hmm. It must be the weight of that pointed stick you carry that makes such a run so wearying, neh?"

Ushiwaka glanced guiltily at the sword behind his back. "It must be so, Holy One."

The abbot set down his brush and at last looked up at him. "I am worried for you, Ushiwaka."

"Please, do not even think of me, Holy One. I am well. All is well."

"How can I not worry? I had hoped, perhaps foolishly, that you would never learn of your lineage. But it seems I could not prevent it. What I have long feared may be coming to pass."

"What have you feared, Holy One?"

"That you would neglect your religious studies, and lose yourself in dreams of vengeance."

"But, Holy One—"

Tōkōbō held up his hand for silence. "Your life was spared because Lord Kiyomori hoped the circle of vendetta could be broken by mercy. There is no sense in men killing one another over past injustices, for such killing never stops. Your father died in war, Ushiwaka, and in war men do dreadful things. There is no sense in laying blame upon the Taira for doing that which war demands. Trust that the evil men do shall be visited upon them in lives to come. You must forget your past and focus on your future."

Ushiwaka wondered if the abbot somehow knew that Ushiwaka had met the *tengu*. Tōkōbō sometimes surprised Ushiwaka with his understanding of things, but Ushiwaka did not know if this was because the abbot had mystical powers, as some of the monks claimed, or was just old and wise. But Ushiwaka could hear no words of mercy or forgetting. The certainty of his destiny was singing too loud in his blood.

Tōkōbō looked back at the sutra on his writing table. "You know that we have entered *mappo*, do you not?" He went on.

"So it is said, Holy One." In fact, Ushiwaka had tired of hearing the monks drone endlessly on the subject of *mappo*, the Buddhist Age of the End of the Law. Every little mishap, misfortune, or rumor of new Taira evil was attributed to the inevitable decline of the world.

"Then you know there can only be days of darkness and despair ahead. And you are no longer too young to know that, if not careful, you will find yourself at the heart of it."

But that is where I want to be, thought Ushiwaka.

"You would be better served," the abbot said, "to study the sutras, and prepare for the World to Come than to poke about in the woods with a toy sword."

"But Holy One," Ushiwaka protested, "if things are going to become bad, shouldn't we try to change it or stop it? Does *mappo* have to come? The Buddha would not lead us into bad times, would he, if we show ourselves worthy and brave?"

"Ah." A sad smile curled the edge of Tōkōbō's mouth. "That is the illusion of *jiriki*, that one can make the world better if one only strives hard enough. An ant may move a stone, my son, but it cannot move the man who treads upon it. Ants may build small mountains, but nonetheless the rain will wash them away. This world brings only sorrow, and to strive against it is only to waste one's spirit in useless endeavor. You have a great spirit, Ushiwaka. Learn the sutras and use them as a guide to act wisely. Live in peace, though the world falls around you, and await the better world to come."

"I . . . I will think on all you say, Holy One. Do you need me for anything else? May I go?"

Tōkōbō sighed and then nodded. "You may."

Ushiwaka hurried back toward his room. But he could feel the sad gaze of the abbot upon his back as he left.

A Mist in the Forest

That same year, Ushiwaka's half brother, Minomoto Yoritomo, turned twenty-two years of age at the monastery to which he had been exiled, in the province of Izu. Yoritomo had proven to be a calm, studious young man through the eight years of his exile, giving no one any cause for concern. He spent the majority of his days studying the Buddhist scriptures and designing a great stupa to be dedicated to the memory of his fallen father. Although some of the monks thought Yoritomo too aloof, this was seen by others as a sign that Yoritomo truly intended to retreat from the world, someday to take vows and have nothing more to do with the troubles in Heian Kyō.

Now and then, letters would arrive from the hereditary vassals of the Minomoto living in the Kantō. They would inquire as to his health and, subtly or directly, remind Yoritomo that he was the Ason. The Minomoto had not chosen a new clan chief since the death of Yoshitomo, fearing the

Taira might make the one chosen a target for their suspicion and vengeance. But should the time come when the Minomoto felt strong enough, Yoritomo would be expected to assume the clan leadership.

Disturbing letters came from Yorimasa, a Minomoto spy in Rokuhara, describing the latest depredations of the overweening Taira—how they were demanding all the best Imperial posts, how they stifled all opposition with violence, how no man's daughter was safe if a Taira desired her.

All these messages Yoritomo read and put away without reply and he never spoke of them with anyone.

Very early in the morning on the day after he turned twenty-two, Yoritomo took a walk along a forested mountain ridge above the monastery. It was one of his favorite walks, giving him a view of both Sagami Bay to the east and the perfection that was Mount Fuji to the north. As he was walking, meditating upon the Sutra of Filial Piety, he noticed a mist rising out of a murky forest pond. The mist drifted over to the path before him and took on a more discernible shape—the shape of a man with sunken cheeks and hollowed eyes and a scarf wrapped about his head. The apparition had no feet.

Yoritomo stopped and gestured in mudras of warding—left hand held up in the Fudō-In with smallest and index fingers extended as horns, right hand in the Gōma-In pointing toward the ground to signify the Buddha's subjugation of the demons. He began to chant the first lines of the Lotus Sutra.

"That is not necessary!" said the apparition, writhing as if in pain. "I do not come to harm you, o Beloved of Hachiman."

"What are you?" demanded Yoritomo.

"I come as a friend! A counselor. A very distant relative, in fact."

"Who are you?" Yoritomo asked. "You are like no Minomoto I have heard of."

"I was once Emperor of all this land. But I was rudely supplanted. Now, in afterlife, I have chosen to serve those who have been unjustly wronged by ambitious noblemen."

"The Shin-In!" Yoritomo said, and again he did the mudras of warding, for he had heard of the Emperor who had turned himself into a demon.

"Please, cease!" cried the Shin-In, turning his face away. "I have come to give you aid."

"I have no need of your aid. People say you were the one who set Nobuyori to evil and led my father to destruction."

"No, it was not me. Should I be blamed if Nobuyori's ambitions overwhelmed all common sense? Your father served bravely and blamelessly, and for his loyalty suffered at the hands of the Taira."

Yoritomo found he could not argue.

"But I wonder," the apparition went on, "why you while away your time here, when Hachiman himself has said you have a great destiny."

Yoritomo stared at the ground and did not answer.

"The unwise Kiyomori," the Shin-In continued, "has let some of your brothers live as well. One or two of them are not as reluctant as you to do their filial duty. If you remain this detached, someday it will be one of them who receives the glories of the Minomoto yet to come, and you will be a forgotten notation in the scrolls of history."

Yoritomo sighed deeply. "The luck of the Seiwa Minomoto has run out. All those who hope to conquer the fortunate Taira hope in vain. Why should I lead the sad remnants of my clan to utter destruction? During the Heiji, my father was prevented from attacking Rokuhara so that the skills and knowlege of the bow and arrow, which is the glory of our clan, should not be lost. But my father died anyway, through treachery. Now you suggest that I risk the future of my clan again, when there is even less hope. You ask too much."

The apparition gasped. "Are you suggesting that your clan *kami*, Hachiman, *lied* to you?"

Yoritomo swallowed hard and again could not speak.

"O Unfaithful Genji," the Shin-In chided him, "what a terrible thing to reject the protection of a *kami*. I know of another to whom such behavior will prove disastrous. Such bad fortune it brings. Do you truly wish to endanger yourself and your clan by denying your destiny?"

"I am therefore caught between two impossible choices," said Yoritomo.

"Nonsense," said the Shin-In. "The wise man does not try to walk upstream. The superior man guides the stream flow to where he wills, and then rides it."

Yoritomo balled his fists. "I will think on all you have said. Now begone."

"Do not dismiss me so hastily, Ason of the Minomoto. I can give you much assistance." The apparition gestured, and twelve sticks of peeled and twisted hemp appeared at Yoritomo's feet. "Should you wish to summon me, burn one of these in the dark of night, and I will come to you."

Hesitantly, Yoritomo picked up the sticks and put them into his sleeve. "I pray these will not ever be necessary."

"Oh, they will," said the Shin-In. "Trust me, they will."

The apparition smiled a terrible, wicked smile, then vanished.

Yoritomo hurried back to the monastery and the cleansing sound of the chanting monks and the booming of the temple bells.

Water Writing

Weeks passed after Kiyomori returned to Rokuhara from Itsukushima. His return trip by sea had been smooth and untroubled, and there had been no calamities at home. Tokiko chose to ignore him and demanded no conferences, which Kiyomori viewed as a blessing. Nothing untoward occurred as spring turned to summer and summer faded toward autumn. Kiyomori began to wonder whether the Dragon King had relented and continued to extend his protection. Or, perhaps, whether his protection had never been necessary at all.

But on the Twentieth Day of Poem-Composing Month, as the Lord Chancellor was taking off his black robes and preparing for sleep, a wave of dizziness overcame him. He grasped at a screen to balance himself and knocked it over, narrowly missing a brazier that would have set it ablaze. His strength flowed out of him until, unable to stand, Kiyomori crumpled to the floor. The very air around him seemed to grow warmer and warmer as if aflame with invisible fire. Yet he trembled and shuddered as if in the chill of a winter storm.

Kiyomori had never been seriously ill in all his fifty years, and he was terrified. *Is this Ryujin's vengeance? Or can the spirits who bring disease strike me now because I lack a kami's protection?* He called for his servants. "Send word to the Buddhist temples," he ordered them. "Bring priests and monks to pray for me, for I do not know if I will last the night!"

Frightened, the servants ran off to do his bidding, and within the hour they returned with monks from all the nearby temples. The monks tried to reassure Kiyomori. "We have seen this ailment often this season. Many who have it recover within a few days, though for a man of your age it may take longer." Nonetheless, at his urging, they sat in the next room rocking and chanting from the sutras, as Kiyomori lay on his sleeping platform and suffered miserably.

Lord Kiyomori had never felt so weak, so frightened. For a warrior, used to leading battles and defeating all enemies, it was humiliating. To have achieved the rank of Chancellor, to be so close to having a Taira Emperor on the throne, and still to be struck down was infuriating. Truly Fate was no respecter of privilege. As he shivered and burned beneath his bedclothes, Kiyomori began to envy the monks who chanted in the next room. They lived their simple lives with no expectations, no hunger for advancement, no dreams of glory. Therefore, they could suffer no humiliation, no defeat.

Kiyomori began to see there was a kind of power in this, to be beyond hurt and despair.

As the hours passed, Kiyomori drifted in and out of fever dreams. He no longer knew whether he remained in the mortal realm or whether he had already fallen into one of the 168 Hells. He did not know whether Lord Emma-O, judge of the dead, had already sentenced him to torment. *If the teachings of the temples are true*, Kiyomori thought during one of his lucid moments, *then I am surely deserving of punishment. All the men I have killed, the scheming I have done. Would Lord Emma-O care that I have done these things for the sake of my sons and my clan?*

Certain that his luck had run out and his days were ending, Kiyomori wept in self-pity and despair.

Now and then, faces appeared, hovering above him. Sometimes it was Shigemori, or Munemori, or other sons, concern in their eyes. Sometimes it was even Tokiko. They asked how he fared and what they might bring him. More terrifying were the faces of Minomoto warriors whom he had beheaded. These asked him whether he was ready to join them in the realms of the dead.

Kiyomori did not know what time of day it was when he awoke suddenly to the boom of thunder. He was alone in his chamber, and there was no sound of chanting priests nearby. Kiyomori tried to move or call out, but he could not. The paper paneling of the nearest *shōji* was lit with a pale light, but he did not know if it was morning sun or evening moon or ghostly light of another sort.

Rain began to patter against the *shōji*. As the water dripped down the paper panels, some dirt or stain traveled with it, creating a mark like a slow brushstroke. As Kiyomori watched in horror, the dripping water beads wrote characters, words, on the *shōji*, to make this message:

Proud Taira
Like the Minomoto, you have thrown away
Your precious armor.
You leave yourself
Defenseless!

Lightning flashed beyond the *shōji* and thunder rolled through the room as if the world were being torn apart. Kiyomori remembered the words of Yoshihira before he was executed—that he would return as a thunder demon to strike the Taira down. Kiyomori shut his eyes in terror and felt the room spin about him. *Is this the beginning of my end?* He wondered. *Am I to be sucked down into the netherworld now, as a ship is pulled into the maelstroms of the sea, never to be seen again?* Darkness overtook him, and he faded into unconciousness.

Kiyomori was amazed, therefore, when he awoke again. He still lay upon his sleeping pallet, drenched in sweat. The air was heavy with incense and the sound of monks chanting sutras rolled over him soothingly. He glanced over at the *shōji*, but saw no words there, merely damp paper.

I have been spared, Kiyomori mused in wonder. *How can this be?* Slowly he sat upright. The room spun a little, but he did not fall. He noticed he was hungry. There was a bowl of rice beside him, and he ate some, chewing thoughtfully. *Perhaps it is the praying of the monks that has saved me. Perhaps, just as the sutras carved on my island off Fukuhara spared the stones from Ryujin's wrath, the spoken words of the sutras have protected me from vengeful spirits. Perhaps, if I cannot have the protection of the Dragon King, I must seek the protection of the Buddha.*

Kiyomori summoned the monks to him. They were quite surprised and pleased to see him sitting up, awake and aware. "I believe I owe my returned health to your prayers," he told them. "I will see that bountiful gifts of rice and silk and horses are sent to your temples. You have all been an inspiration to me. I now find that I wish to take the tonsure and become a monk. Please send for your wisest teacher to instruct me."

The monks were gratified, but not altogether surprised, for it was not unknown for a man who had faced death suddenly to seek the divine. So notice was sent that a teacher was sought by the great Chancellor and because of Kiyomori's high rank, the Tendai abbot, Major Archbishop Meiun himself, came down from Mount Hiei to see to Kiyomori's religious instruction. Kiyomori's head was shaved and he was given the plain robes of a monk to wear, and he was given the monk name of Jokai. It was announced that Kiyomori had "left the world" and therefore the leadership of the Taira clan was officially given to his son Shigemori, although how much actual power Shigemori would be allowed to wield was uncertain.

Ryujin would not dare to harm me now, Kiyomori thought as he wrote out another sutra and studied another law of the Blessed Amida. *No one in the capital will dare speak slander of a holy man. Ha! If all it takes to gain respect and heavenly protection is to lose one's hair and fancy robes, then it is a small price to pay.*

Mirror Image

"Kiyomori has become a monk?" laughed Retired Emperor Go-Shirakawa when his advisor Saikō gave him the news. "Dare I believe this? Does anyone believe he is serious?"

The wizened Saikō shrugged. "A frightened man will often do strange things, Majesty. There are those who say Lord Kiyomori was much unsettled by his illness."

Go-Shirakawa rubbed his chin. "No. No I cannot see Kiyomori unsettled by a mere disease. No, there is some scheming in this, I am sure. I am not certain that I believe he was even sick. Kiyomori knows that his reputation has suffered as he has become more arrogant. Perhaps all of this, his convalescence and his conversion, was a ploy to gain sympathy."

"Majesty," interjected Narichika, his other closest advisor, "it can be dangerous to see plots where none exist. It can make a man look foolish and fearful."

Go-Shirakawa scowled at him. "It is more foolish to assume all is well when there is treachery afoot. I have known Kiyomori most of my life. He has never been seriously ill. He has never been religious. He gives lip service to his clan *kami* and builds a great shrine at Itsukushima to impress everyone with his wealth. He is not a man to suddenly choose to become a monk, unless there is some advantage in it."

Narichika looked as though he were swallowing his tongue to remain silent. At last he said, "Your Majesty knows best, of course."

"Yes, I do," growled Go-Shirakawa. "It was perhaps foolish of me to allow the Taira so much power, but having done so I must now watch them with the utmost caution. Ever since that night I stayed at Rokuhara, I have become convinced that Kiyomori will turn out to be another Nobuyori, who will use his authority only to sate his greedy desires. Therefore, is it not best to be suspicious?"

"Naturally, Majesty", said Saikō, darting a knowing glance at Narichika. "This is surely the wisest course."

Desperately, Narichika tried again. "Majesty, already the Senior Council of Nobles is having difficulty accomplishing anything. The Taira do not cooperate with the Fujiwara, and those nobles loyal to you do not cooperate with either clan. Everyone is vying for the best posts for themselves and their supporters. Nothing practical is getting done! There are rumors that the Minomoto are trying to organize themselves in the East, and who can say with whom they will ally themselves when they are ready?"

"So you see!" said Go-Shirakawa. "Times are treacherous indeed. I must do all I can to maintain order, and keep the Taira from bringing us to ruin." He turned to Saikō. "So, Kiyomori thinks to make himself more respectable by taking the tonsure, does he? Then I shall do the same. Send word to the Tendai Abbot Meiun to come to ToSanjō Palace to instruct me as well. Kiyomori must not be allowed to become more respectable than I."

Saikō bowed low, "It shall be as you wish, Majesty. I will send word at once." The little monk stood and quickly left, favoring Narichika with one last smug smile.

Go-Shirakawa picked up a round bronze mirror that had been left lying about by one of the ladies-in-waiting. He held it before his face, and asked, "Do you think a shaved head will suit me, Narichika?"

Sadly, Narichika replied, "It will no doubt suit you as well as it suits Lord Kiyomori, Majesty, for I expect you will be as devout as he."

Go-Shirakawa set down the mirror. "Don't be tiresome, Narichika. I was merely wondering if it would set off my features. My ladies tell my my graying hair makes me look older and wiser. I would hate to lose the gravity of a mature appearance if the tonsure robs me of my years."

"I am sure that your people will judge your wisdom, Majesty, by what you have accomplished for Nihon, not your appearance," Narichika said, standing and bowing. He excused himself from the former Imperial Presence and walked out to a long corridor-bridge that connected the Receiving Chambers of ToSanjō Palace with the guest quarters where he was staying.

As he walked, Narichika gazed out at the gardens between the buildings, watching the gingko and maple leaves drift to the ground. The visions of a ruined Heian Kyō had not left him ever since the night he spent at Rokuhara. At first, he had been willing to believe that Go-Shirakawa's premonitions matched his own, that the Taira would be the ones to bring the land to its doom. Now he was no longer certain. Now he suspected it no longer mattered which way the winds blew, which tree gave up its leaves first. Winter would come, and there would be no stopping it.

Scroll 3

≪≪ ≫≫

Genpei

Arrows Shot into Palanquins

*S*higemori's horse stamped beneath him, uneasy at the growing roar beyond the palace wall. A scent of late-spring wisteria from the Imperial gardens drifted on the air. "It is curious," Shigemori commented to the Taira warrior beside him, "how a man's fate goes in circles, neh? Here it is sixteen years later and again I am at the Taikenmon."

"Indeed, my lord," replied the horseman, "but this time we face the enemy from the other side. This time it is we Taira who are within the Imperial palace, awaiting a rebellious foe. To my mind, this is a change for the better."

Shigemori wondered. It had been nine years since his father, Kiyomori, had taken Buddhist vows and become a novice monk. And yet his father had since shown little interest in studying the laws and sutras, instead continuing to concentrate on governmental power. Kiyomori had, in fact, become even less tolerant of any who might challenge Taira supremacy, and showed his displeasure in ways that far outstripped the insult. Just a few months before, Shigemori had found himself having to apologize to the entourage of the Royal Regent because a band of young Taira warriors refused to give way to them on the street. After Shigemori's apology, however, Kiyomori had sent a group of thugs to beat up the outriders of the Regent's entourage, with the message "All must give way before the Taira."

The reputation and honor of the Taira were slipping in the minds of the people; noble, merchant, and peasant alike. Everyone grumbled about Kiyomori's high-handed ways. Shigemori did what he could to present a good example of fairness and courtliness as his mother had taught him. It had gained Shigemori much favor in the Imperial Court, but alas it had made the excesses of his father and fellow Taira only stand out the more in comparison.

Shigemori turned in his saddle to regard his men, the leather lacings of his laminate armor creaking. There were only two hundred warriors at this gate, but they were seasoned Taira horsemen for the most part, with a smattering of Fujiwara and Oe scions eager for a taste of battle and glory. Peace had not sat well on the youth of Heian Kyō. Shigemori was concerned. Glory would not be easily won in this situation.

"This business of fighting monks," commented the horseman beside him, as if he had read Shigemori's mind, "makes me uneasy.

Is it not said that to kill a monk increases one's bad karma tenfold? And that a man will never see the Pure Land if he takes the life of a holy man?"

"So it is said," agreed Shigemori. "But these monks are bringing the battle to us. Despite their peaceful vows, they have marched down from Mount Hiei, bringing bow and *naginata* to harass the Emperor. For a monk to break his vows and kill must surely bring him misfortune a thousandfold greater. Our duty is clear."

"I understand, my lord. But I have heard the monks have reason for complaint."

That was another thing that needled Shigemori. It should not have become an Imperial matter. Former Emperor Go-Shirakawa had given a joint governorship to the sons of his strange monk advisor Saikō. Those sons had misused, damaged, and destroyed property of the temples in their province, temples related to Enryakuji on Mount Hiei. *These Hiei monks should be bringing their complaint to ToSanjō Palace, to the attention of Go-Shirakawa. After all, the Emperor Takakura himself is still only a boy of fourteen.*

The sound from the approaching army of monks swelled louder, and now Shigemori could discern distinct temple songs and chanting of the Thousand-Armed Sutra. It was frustrating not to be able to see the movement of the enemy because of the high palace wall. Shigemori called up to the nearest sentry standing atop the wall. "You, can you see them? How near are they?"

The sentry turned and shouted back, "Lord General, the monks are passing to the north of us on Ichijō Avenue."

"Hmm." Shigemori turned to the warrior beside him. "Who is guarding the northern gates of the palace?"

"Minomoto Yorimasa, my lord. With only three hundred men for all three gates."

"Ah. Perhaps the monks have heard that quarter was lightly defended." It had been the honorable thing for Takakura to do, to invite what pitiful remnants of the Minomoto that remained in Heian Kyō to participate in the defense of the Emperor. Still, Shigemori was nagged by the worry that the Minomoto might make a strong show of *bugei*. Esteem for the Taira had fallen so low, that the Minomoto could easily gain favor. And Shigemori knew, no matter how strong the Taira were upon the sea, for knowledge of the horse and bow no clan could surpass the Minomoto.

"Should we send Yorimasa assistance, my lord?"

Shigemori considered this a moment. "No. Yorimasa would be offended. He would think we Taira were insulting his courage and skill. Let us send one observer to see how matters go. If the observer returns with news that the monks have overpowered Yorimasa's forces, then we will go and give aid."

A rider was dispatched to the north side of the Imperial Compound. Shigemori and his men heard the singing of the monks become softer in the distance, then silent. Long minutes passed, filled only with the snorting of horses and the clacking of armor. Then they heard a distant cheer and the singing of the monks began again, approaching them this time.

"My lord!" called the sentry from the wall. "They are coming this way!"

The rider sent to observe at the northern gates returned, cantering his horse up to Shigemori. He was badly trying to conceal a bemused grin.

"What is it?" demanded Shigemori.

"That Yorimasa is a clever fellow," replied the rider, "you must give him that. He told the monks that no one would respect their petition if they simply overpowered his small force. He said their demands would be taken all the more seriously if they were victorious over a much larger force."

"Such as ours?"

"Indeed. And they believed him. So the monks are headed here to challenge us."

Shigemori sighed. "Clever indeed. The Amida protect me from such men." He shouted up at the sentry, "What weapons have they?"

"Rude spears and *naginata*, my lord. Swords, of course, and some shovels and farming tools. No shields. I expect they plan to hide behind their holy palanquins."

"Good," Shigemori murmured. "No bows. With luck we need not even open the gates to give battle." He called out loudly to his men, "Dismount! We will not need our horses. To the wall, everyone! Shoulder to shoulder, as many as can fit. We will give the monks a rain of arrows in answer to the thunder of their voices!" Shigemori himself dismounted and scaled one of the wooden ladders up to the top of the high stone wall.

From there, Shigemori could see the tide of monks flowing onto Omiya Avenue, bearing their painted and gilded palanquins like flotsam on a river after a flood. Sunlight winked off the blades of *naginata*, and the shaved heads of the swelling throng of chanting, singing monks. They assembled on the street, facing the Taikenmon, so many in number that they spilled onto side streets. From his perch on the wall, Shigemori could not see a single paving stone, so thick was the crowd below.

Shigemori unslung his bow from his back and pulled a blunt humming arrow from his quiver. He sent word down through the ranks that his men should do the same. "But do not fire until I give the word." The rippling movement of bows along the wall reminded Shigemori of a war banner waving in a brisk breeze.

Shigemori waited until the monks below had finished their temple song. Then he called out, "Who is it who comes to disturb the Imperial harmony so?"

A cacophony of voices replied:

"We bring a grievance to His Majesty!"

"We seek justice!"

"Shame upon the council and His Majesty!"

"The *bosatsu* are angry!"

Shigemori shouted back, "Return to your temples! This is unseemly behavior for holy men! You should be praying for peace, not bringing war!" But he knew he could not be heard over their clamor.

With a sigh, Shigemori raised his arm to signal to the archers along the wall. When he had their attention, he dropped his arm in a chopping motion. *"Hajime!"*

A wave of blunt humming arrows arced into the mass of men, like a curl of surf pounding onto a shore. The eerie drone of the arrows blended into the cries of wounded monks, for though blunt, the arrows could still do great damage when striking flesh. Still, though many monks went down, they did not disperse. A few light spears and arrows rose out of the crowd of monks to clatter against the stone wall or lodge harmlessly in the armor of the Taira archers.

"Battle arrows!" Shigemori called out to his men. Many scores of arms reached back to their quivers to pull out the sharp, steel-headed arrows. He hoped the monks below would see this and decide to leave. But either their anger or their fervor or a wish not to seem cowards held them there, pressed against the palace wall, chanting tirades at the Emperor.

Shigemori again raised his arm, gazing down at the monks with a mixture of admiration and regret. . . .

*H*oly One, I bring news, as you asked," said the boy with bowl-cut hair as he knelt before the ancient advisor-monk Saikō.

"Tell us your news," said Saiko in contented anticipation.

"The Enryakuji monks have reached the Imperial palace, and they intend to give battle," said the messenger.

"Very good. You have done well," said Saikō, giving the boy a tiny satchel containing a few flakes of gold. "Go and observe more so that we may learn how the battle progresses."

"*Hai*, Holy One." The boy bowed and ran out the *shōji* and down the hill from the little hunting lodge.

Saikō stood, not minding the ache of his bones as much as usual, and went to join Middle Counselor Narichika, who was standing on the veranda. From there, one had a good view of Heian Kyō in the valley below. But although the capital was just a few *li* away, the only visible indication of battle was a haze of dust hanging over the northern section of the city.

"It has begun," Saikō said.

"I still do not understand," Narichika grumbled. "Why did you have to bring the Enryakuji monks into this? They are untrustworthy and unpredictable."

"A still pond has no power to offer. Swirling, chaotic waters, however, can be channeled in useful directions."

"I hope your channel is deep and sure," said Narichika. "I fear a flood might burst its banks."

Saikō smiled. Narichika had never been comfortable around him, which suited Saikō quite well. "Do not fear, Middle Counselor. Our cause is guided by greater powers."

"So it must be. I still do not know how you managed to divert the monks' anger against the Emperor instead of the *In*. It was your son who did the damage in Kaga Province and Go-Shirakawa who appointed him."

Saikō merely blinked, and said, "Surely the *bosatsu* smile upon me. But I do not understand your dissatisfaction, Middle Counselor. Did you not come to me when you were being passed over for promotion to Major Captain because the post was to be given instead to the hapless Taira Munemori? Did I not arrange for a hundred monks at Yawata to chant the Great Wisdom Sutra for seven days on your behalf?"

"And on the third day," Narichika argued, "three white doves appeared at the shrine and pecked each other to death. It was such a disturbing omen from Hachiman that the monks had to stop."

Saikō idly waved a hand. "Who can say what the omen meant? Perhaps it means there will be trouble within the Minomoto clan. Perhaps it merely indicated that war is to come, which we know already and are preparing for. And did I not also arrange for an ascetic at the Kamo Shrine to perform the Dagini ritual for a hundred days on your behalf?"

"He performed it in a hollow cryptomeria tree. Which was struck by lightning. The other priests found him and beat him and drove him out of the shrine."

"Well, these things happen," said Saikō.

"I begin to fear, Holy One," said Narichika, his voice tightly controlled, "that the gods do not look with favor upon our endeavor. All I hoped to do, to bring down the Taira before the visions that I saw at Rokuhara come to pass, now begins to seem a hopeless dream."

"Do not lose heart, Middle Counselor," Saikō said soothingly. "Believe me, all is progressing as it should."

"For all our sakes," said Narichika, glaring at him with anger and fear, "I hope you are right." Narichika glanced once more at the city, then stalked away to another wing of the villa.

Saikō retired to a small, dark antechamber and took a stick of incense from his sleeve. He lit it in the coals of a small bronze brazier and let the aromatic stick smolder. A compact cloud of smoke gathered above the brazier. Saikō chanted a few words and a face appeared in the smoke: hollow-cheeked, sunken-eyed. Saikō bowed. "Dark Majesty, it has begun."

*S*higemori dropped his arm again, barking *"Hajime!"* once more. Hundreds of battle arrows were loosed in a deadly rain from atop the palace wall. Shigemori's men were excellent archers, although at this range it hardly mattered. The monks were packed in so tightly that every arrow found a target. A forest of arrows sprouted in an instant from eyes, throats, shoulders, arms, chests. Blood spouted and flowed onto the paving stones. The chanting was replaced with screams of agony and horror. Many monks slumped to the ground, dead or wounded, their companions trying to aid them or give them merciful killing blows.

Shigemori took no satisfaction from this. It was like hunting wildfowl that had already been penned in a crate. He raised his arm again, and again his men took arrows from their quivers and nocked them.

This time the monks took notice and ran, screaming, into the side streets. Many were trampled in the widespread panic. Some tried to carry their wounded fellows with them, but many monks were left behind to die.

"Open the gates!" Shigemori commanded. "Bring in the wounded and the dead. The Imperial healers will see to those who can be helped and perhaps the Guard will wish to question them."

After a halfhearted cheer of victory, the archers left the wall and went to the Taikenmon. Shigemori gazed over the bodies in the street. Many of them appeared to be scholar-monks, pale of skin, unmuscled, and thin. He felt sick at the waste of wisdom and knowledge.

Shigemori noted that even the sacred shrine palanquins had been left behind, so desperate had the flight of monks been. And then he noted something very disturbing. There were a few arrows sticking out of the palanquins. To attack a sacred palanquin was worse than insult to the shrine to which it belonged. It was as though one had attacked the *kami* or *bosatsu* itself. His men were expert marksmen, and at this close range there was no excuse. Fortunately, every warrior of importance always marked his arrows with his name and a particular pattern of fletching—it made for more truth in claiming the honor of one's kills. In this situation, it would make finding the perpetrators of this shame all the easier.

Another man had noticed the violated palanquins and came running up to Shigemori. "My lord, Mount Hiei will be enraged. What shall we do?"

Shigemori replied, "We are not savages. No matter the cost, we must do what is right and follow form and custom. Therefore, when those arrows are removed, see that they are brought to me. Whoever fired them into the palanquins must be punished."

"It will be done, my lord."

Clouded Waters

How could he have allowed such a thing!" Kiyomori roared. "Four Taira imprisoned, not to mention a Fujiwara and an Oe, all because their arrows found an unsuitable target. Is Shigemori trying to bring shame upon our clan?"

"He is trying to do the honorable thing," said Tokiko calmly, as she gathered azaleas at the ornamental pond's edge, "as he has been taught. Surely this can only be seen as a noble act."

"I would wish Shigemori would act more the warrior than the nobleman. Heian Kyō has enough effetes in black robes. What are you gathering flowers for? Don't you have maidservants to do that?"

"They are for the Buddha's birthday observance," said Tokiko, "and it is an act of worship to gather them oneself. Have you forgotten?" There was a trace of irony in her voice.

Irritated, Kiyomori stood. "I have more important things to do. I don't know why I talk to you anymore. You have renounced the world of your father and become a novice nun and yet you still chide me. Will you never give me peace, woman?" He strode off through the garden, peach blossoms drifting in his wake.

Tokiko raised the azaleas to her nose and inhaled their scent as she watched him go. It had been ironic . . . soon after Kiyomori took his vows it was expected that Tokiko would do likewise. A woman who remained "in the world" after her husband retires to monkhood was considered immoral. Therefore, Tokiko was obliged to learn the laws and the sutras, have her hair cut to shoulder length, and wear the plain robes of a novice nun. Tokiko knew Kiyomori had not intended to punish her this way—it simply hadn't occurred to him that she was affected by his actions.

At first, Tokiko had feared that her father the Dragon King would be outraged, but if he was, she did not know it. The pond denizens that she had used so often for sending and receiving messages no longer came to her call. The waters were clouded, muddied, and offered no clear reflection.

Instead, Tokiko had come more and more to rely upon her knowledge of the mortal world, the gossip her handmaidens brought her, what little news of the political arena her sons would share with her. When she went to the temples to give offerings and prayer, she would surreptitiously try to listen to the monks and learn their concerns. It was not so difficult for a well-connected woman to get a picture of the world around her, even from behind *kichō* curtains. What was difficult was doing anything with the knowledge.

The attack by the monks upon the palace seemed a spiritual dagger aimed at the Imperial family itself. One of whom, the Empress, was her daughter. Tokiko could work very little magic, but she hoped she could still pull the right political strings.

Before long, a maidservant came running up to her and knelt and bowed in the wet grass. Tokiko recognized her as one of her daughter's handmaidens. "My lady, I have just come from the palace," she gasped.

"What news?"

"The Council agrees with your concerns for the safety of the Imperial family, and they will be moved to other residences within the city."

"Blessed Amida be thanked," Tokiko murmured, and then was surprised at the ease with which the prayer fell from her lips. "What of the regalia?"

"My lady, the sword, the mirror, and the jewel will also be moved to remain with the Emperor's person at all times."

Tokiko paused. If only there were some way she could become caretaker, for however short a time, for the sword . . . she might find a way to return it to the sea. But she could think of no way it would be permitted. She would be able to visit her daughter, Tokuko, of course. Although her daughter now had a name suiting an Empress, Kenreimon'in, for great ladies of the court traditionally took the name of a gate in the Imperial Compound. Tokiko had wondered if there was something symbolically obscene in the practice of naming a woman after an opening, but she never voiced this to anyone.

Tokiko had told her daughter some things about Kusanagi, but she had never intended her to play a part in Ryujin's demands. *By paying call on her I could be close to the regalia. But what then? What could an old woman like me do?*

To the servant, Tokiko said, "Send word when it is known where the Empress Kenreimon'in will be living."

"We will, my lady."

As the girl bowed and departed, Tokiko sighed. *It is like moving a large pile of rocks by removing only the lowermost stones*, she thought. *Pick the right one, and the pile tumbles where you will. Pick the wrong one and you are crushed beneath an avalanche. The trick is picking the right stone.*

Summer Wind

*E*mpress Kenreimon'in awoke suddenly. She had been having disturbing dreams, threads of which still clung to her mind like frayed strands of silk cling to the hand on a dry day.

Takakura slumbered on, snoring contentedly beside her beneath the bedclothes. She envied the young man his ability to sleep. Kenreimon'in was now all of twenty-two and she was beginning to wonder if she suffered the old woman's disease of insomnia. She certainly had not slept well since having to leave the palace after the monks' attack, fourteen days ago. Certainly she was not comfortable here in her husband's grandmother's mansion. All her servants thought of it as a holiday to change residence, but growing up in the Taira household, Kenreimon'in knew it meant "we are in danger."

She slipped off the sleeping platform and put on an overrobe. The air was warm and still, so not much clothing was needed or desired. Pushing back her long hair with her hands, Kenreimon wandered out into an adjoining room where some of her handmaidens slept, hoping a short walk might help.

They had left the *shōji* open out onto the garden, so moonlight spilled into the room. Kenreimon'in gazed over the sleeping forms, sensing that she was looking for something. Or something was looking with her eyes. Something left from her dreams.

Her gaze fell on the wooden stand on which was hung the Sacred Sword Kusanagi. Drawn to it, Kenreimon'in went to the stand, stepping over two handmaidens as she did so, and knelt before the sword. The sheath glimmered in the moonlight.

"It's something, isn't it, Majesty?" whispered one of the handmaidens, who had woken up at Kenreimon'in's passing.

"Yes," Kenreimon'in said softly.

"You know, they say whoever wields it can command the winds."

Kenreimon'in nodded. Something within her knew that very well.

"They say it can be wielded only by one of Imperial blood."

Kenreimon'in knew that, too. "My father, everyone says, is the son of an Emperor."

"Well then, Majesty, you can swing it."

"Me? A woman?"

"Why not?" giggled the maid. "We handle men's swords all the time."

Kenreimon'in smiled. She lifted the sword off the stand and held it in two hands. It was heavy. "Do you think I should?"

"I think His Majesty would forgive you. And we won't tell the priests."

Kenreimon'in tugged on the hilt and slowly drew the sword from the scabbard. She was disappointed in what she saw. The blade was tarnished, and the edge was chipped. It looked very old and worn and used. "Why hasn't someone cared for this?"

The handmaiden shrugged. "Kusanagi is so sacred, I suppose no one dares, Majesty."

Kenreimon'in held it up to catch the moonlight. She did not know if she imagined it, but the blade appeared to glow. "Command the winds, you say?"

"So the tales go, Majesty. Why not try it and see? We could use a breeze to ease this heat and let us sleep."

Filled with a mischevious spirit she had not felt in years, Kenreimon'in said, "Let's find out." She carried the sword out onto the verandah and held it up to the sky. "O Great *Kami*, I who am descended from Amaterasu request that you send a wind to ease our discomfort." Kenreimon'in swung the sword from right to left, from southwest to northeast. A shimmer of light ran up the sword blade, but that was all.

Kenreimon'in dropped the point of the sword and it stuck in the wood planking of the verandah with a *thunk*. Her arms were heavy and tired, and she felt a strange combination of satisfaction, disquiet, and fear. "What have I done?"

Her hair blew around her face as a strong wind came up suddenly from the southeast.

"Majesty! You have done it!" whispered the handmaiden in delight.

Fear became Kenreimon'in's overriding emotion. "I think . . . I should not have done this." She hurried back inside and placed Kusanagi into its sheath once more. She hung the sword back on the stand, and said to the servant, "Tell no one about this." Then Kenreimon'in went back to the Imperial sleeping dais and crawled beneath the bedclothes. And trembled.

The Dancer's Fire

That same night, that same hour, the monk Saikō was standing on a
street corner in the southeast section of Heian Kyō, an area where
artists and entertainers commonly lodged. He, too, felt the warm, early summer wind come up from the southeast and he smiled. *The Shin-In said weak
is the mind of woman. It appears he was right.*

Saikō walked into a modest tavern nearby, bowed to the tavern keeper
and went up the wooden stairs to the lodgings in the second story.

There he was greeted by three young women and a young man, all
smiling and eager to see him. They had clearly spent the last hour straightening up, but their room was still bestrewn with dancing kimonos, fans,
long silk scarves, and other bits of costume of their art. The girls were clearly
from lower-class households, as there wasn't a single *kichō* in the room, and
they greeted him without covering their faces.

"It is an honor that you come to us, Holy One," said one of the dancers,
a pretty but very thin girl.

"It is fortunate that I have found you," said Saikō, bowing to them all.
"His Retired Majesty is very selective about the dancers he wishes for his
Festival of the Weaver party. Though it is still two months away, the *In*
asked me to begin the search, for that is how particular he is. And so I have
wandered up and down the streets of Heian Kyō, asking who is best, who
is best? You would be surprised how often I heard your names." *Which is
to say, not at all.*

The dancers bobbed and bowed and smiled.

Saikō clapped his hands. "Let us have some refreshment, and then let
me watch you dance." He sent down to the tavern below for pitchers of
sake, plates of rice and pickled vegetables. Tavern girls brought these up,
along with three braziers over which they cooked fish for Saikō and the
dancers. As the food was laid out and prepared, the monk was careful to
sit near the door.

The expense was nothing to Saikō, for, being the chief advisor of the
Retired Emperor, he was a wealthy man. The dancers, however, feasted as
if they had been transported to Paradise. It was likely they had never seen
such a meal.

After much sake and plum wine had been drunk, mostly by the dancers,
Saikō clapped his hands again, and declared, "Enough feasting! Now let me
see the marvelous dancing for which you are renowned."

"Tanoshiko!" the three other dancers said to the thin girl. "You are the best of us! You must dance first."

The girl smiled shyly and stood, wavering a bit. Apparently the sake had had a strong effect on her small body. The other dancers moved aside to give her room, as she put on a silk brocade dancing jacket that was a little too large for her, the bottom of the wide sleeves brushing the floor. It had clearly been made for someone else and seen years of wear since.

The young man picked up a small drum and began to beat out a slow, measured rhythym. Tanoshiko held out her arms, bowed her head, and began to move in stately, sweeping patterns across the floor. Despite her inebriation, she managed to bob in time to the drum and snap her fan at the appropriate moments. Saikō could see that, had she been blessed with the right family and upbringing, the girl could have had promise. *Alas, she will have to hope for better in a future life*, Saikō thought.

After she executed one slightly wobbly spin, Saikō interrupted her, and said, "That was marvelous, that move! Let me see it again!"

Blushing, Tanoshiko again performed the spin, not recovering her balance very well.

"Oh, how splendid! I know his Retired Majesty loves dancing such as this! Come closer and let me watch it again."

With only a little sigh of tried patience, Tanoshiko walked over to where Saikō sat next to the cooking braziers and again performed the open-armed spin. Her sleeves drifted over the top of the braziers and one of them caught on the grate. She did not notice, and her movement pulled the brazier over, spilling hot coals on the hem of her dancing jacket and the frayed straw mats on the floor. They caught fire at once. Tanoshiko looked down and screamed. One of the other dancers flung the dregs of the plum wine on the flames, which only made matters worse.

Saikō jumped up, kicking over another brazier. "Oh, dear! Oh, dear! I shall go get help at once!" He hurried out the door and down the steps, ignoring the shouted questions of the tavern keeper. Out on the street, Saikō slowed his step and walked as if nothing was the matter. He found a shadowed doorway upwind of the fire and waited a bit, watching the tavern. Soon flames roared out of the windows of the upper story and he could hear the desperate, dying screams of the dancers. The flames leapt to the thatch roof and quickly engulfed it. There had been several months without rain, and the dry straw was perfect tinder for the fire.

People rushed past Saikō, carrying buckets of water, but as he was an old monk they paid him little heed. He nodded and blessed them as they passed, knowing they were too late to help.

The wind from the southeast was quite strong now, and the sparks and embers from the tavern roof were flung onto neighboring buildings. Their wood roofs also exploded into flame until the entire neighborhood became a conflagration. Would-be firefighters staggered screaming in the streets, their clothing burning against their skin. People fleeing the buildings trampled one another in their haste to get to safety, and panicked horses and oxen ran down still more. Women with wide sleeves afire unintentionally set more fires on carts, carriages, store banners, and other refugees as they dashed hither and thither, shrieking in confusion, fear, and pain.

As the fire intensified, the smoke became so thick that even those who escaped the flames themselves lay choking and gasping in the streets like beached fish. Buildings exploded with the great heat, and their thatch-and-wood roofs were blown into the air as enormous fiery pinwheels, to land on other buildings and start more fires afresh.

Saikō smiled. Only several blocks to the northwest, directly downwind, lay the Imperial palace itself. And it was clear now that no bucket brigades, no high stone wall, no prayers or archers or chanting priests would keep this horror from engulfing the Imperial Compound. The Emperor and Empress were not there at the moment, but it didn't matter—their deaths were not the aim. To diminish all courage and hope of the people of Heian Kyō, however, was, and it appeared that was being accomplished nicely.

Saikō hurried westward, allowing the crush and flow of frightened refugees to carry him along. His mind was awash with wonder at how a little evil could lead to such a great one. It had the power to change the world. He looked forward to making his midnight report. The Shin-In would be pleased.

The Bronze Mirror

As twilight fell the next evening, Ushiwaka, now fifteen years old, slipped away from Kurama monastery and headed back into the forest where he had been training for seven years with the *tengu*. He had not had the chance to meet with Sōjō-bō and the Leaflet Tengu for several weeks. But now, with the monks occupied with the refugees from the fire in Heian Kyō, Ushiwaka saw his chance.

But when he reached the clearing where he had been training for so many years, no *tengu* greeted him. Ushiwaka looked around, and called out for them, but no one answered. Finally, in the dim light, he saw on the ground one black feather pointing to a path that led farther up the mountain. Ushiwaka followed the path and found that it led to a cave he had never seen before. He entered into a large chamber and there, beside a glowing fire in a bronze brazier, stood Sōjō-bō in half-bird, half-human form.

"Ah, there you are, Ushiwaka. I see you got my little message."

Ushiwaka bowed. "Sōjōbō-sensei. I was surprised no one had met me at the training place. I thought perhaps you had lost faith in me. I am very sorry I have not attended lately."

"Oh, we understand. Life is getting . . . interesting for you at the temple these days?"

Ushiwaka sat on a rock and sighed. "Abbot Tōkōbō is determined to make me take the vows. He has not said so outright, but I believe that if I continue to refuse, he will turn me over to the Taira. If they learn that I have violated the terms of my exile, they will very likely execute me."

"Ah. You fear the Taira. Is that why you have been spending many evenings hurrying down into the capital to the Temple of Kwannon? I understand to get to it, you must go right by Rokuhara, hmm? Or do you enjoy tempting fate?"

"My mother often worships at that temple, and she has claimed that it was Kwannon's intercession that turned Lord Kiyomori's heart and saved our lives. Though, I admit, I have been looking over Rokuhara as I pass."

"Looking for a way a resourceful swordsman might enter unseen, eh?"

"You could say so."

Sōjō-bō chuckled. "You are a good student of *tengu-do.*"

"But I do not know if the great fire has done my work for me and burned Rokuhara to the ground."

"My spies have flown over the city," said Sōjō-bō, "and they tell me Rokuhara still stands, more's the pity."

"It is strange, but I am glad of it," said Ushiwaka. "It means I have not been robbed of my dream."

"The Imperial palace, however," Sōjō-bō went on, "has been quite badly damaged. Many venerable buildings destroyed."

"How can that be?" asked Ushiwaka. "Who can harm the Emperor, who is descended from gods? Who can harm his palace, which is warded day and night from demons and evil spirits?"

Sōjō-bō chuckled. "You believe so much of what you are told."

"Sōjō-bō-sensei, what caused the fire? Was it the wrath of the gods, or a curse of the Hiei monks, or the work of demons?"

The *tengu* shrugged his great black wings. "The signs are unclear. Even our wisest *tengu* wizard was baffled. He said that, as far as he could determine, one of the Imperial family used the Sacred Sword Kusanagi to summon a great wind. The fire itself could have started any number of ordinary ways."

"Why would the Emperor want to burn down his own palace and half the city with it?"

"How would I know?" squawked Sōjō-bō. "We *tengu* don't know everything. We merely act like we do."

"It has been fortunate for me that you know everything about sword fighting."

"Yes, that is a thing we know. And you have been an excellent student. So good, in fact, that I have the pleasure of telling you that your studies are ended."

"Ended?" Ushiwaka stood up, his joy mingled with regret.

"Just so. You have learned all we have to teach you, and much faster than we expected, to be honest. The time is coming soon, it is clear, for you to make your way in the world."

"It is true that I cannot stay at Kuramadera much longer," agreed Ushiwaka. "But I don't know how I can escape without being caught. The monks are watchful."

"Leave that to us. We *tengu* have some skill in these things. Now, I have a parting gift for you."

"A gift? Oh, no, *sensei*, it is I who should be giving a gift to you, after all you have taught me. If I had known—"

"Hush. Your gift to me will be the good use of our teachings. *My* gift to you has been acquired with no little trouble, so you would do well to pay attention. Take note of that Chinese mirror hanging on the wall."

Ushiwaka looked and saw a great round mirror of polished bronze, as tall as he was, leaning against the far wall of the cavern.

"Pick up the sakaki twig and the cryptomeria branch lying near it, and perform the Spirit Summoning rite I taught you."

Assuming this was some sort of final test, Ushiwaka picked up the branches, one in each hand. He drew a circle in the dirt of the cave floor and began his dance. He stepped precisely in the pattern he had been taught, feet never leaving the circle, but Ushiwaka knew he would always be a better swordsman than sorcerer. He chanted the right words at the right time, if not with such fluency as he might wish. When he finished, the mirror began to glow with a golden light.

Within the light, Ushiwaka saw a man in nobleman's robes and black hat, seated on a lotus. Ushiwaka wondered what *bosatsu* this might be, and then he saw the sword across the man's lap and the helmet off to his side. White banners fluttered behind him. *Is it Hachiman I have summoned, then?* But the face of the man was not like the images of Hachiman that Ushiwaka had seen.

The man smiled. "Ho. Ushiwaka. I was told you would be calling for me."

"Great lord," said Ushiwaka, "I have summoned you at my teacher's instructions, yet I do not know who you are."

A momentary sadness crossed the man's face. "The *tengu* wished to surprise you, did they? Well, it is reasonable that you do not recognize me. I am Minomoto Yoshitomo, your father."

"Father?" Ushiwaka fell to his knees. Tears began to well up in his eyes.

Yoshitomo inclined his head. "By virtue of my service to Hachiman and the prayers others have said for me, I found myself escorted to the Pure Land upon my death. The poor *tengu* who found me and asked me to speak with you nearly had his feet burned off, so holy is the ground of the land in which I now dwell."

"I am so very glad to learn this." Ushiwaka sighed. He turned to the master *tengu*, and said, "Sōjōbō-sensei, this is the most wondrous gift you could have given me."

The *tengu* bowed.

"It is a gift to me as well," said Yoshitomo from the mirror. "The few times I saw you, Ushiwaka, you were no more than a squalling babe in your mother's arms. Now here you are, nearly a man. The *tengu* say they have taught you swordsmanship."

"They have, Father, and I have mastered it well!" said Ushiwaka, jumping to his feet. "Want to see?" Feeling childish but unable to stop himself, Ushiwaka used the sakaki branch in place of a sword to demonstrate three of the most difficult thrust-and-parry patterns.

When he had finished, Yoshitomo smiled and nodded at him. "Ah. Very good. Very good indeed. The Minomoto blood truly runs within you." Then he frowned, and added, "But I see a darkness clouding your future. Hachiman has pledged his protection to your older brother, not to you. I am concerned as to what path you may choose."

Ushiwaka knelt before the mirror. "My path is this: I want to avenge you, Father. I want to kill Lord Kiyomori and all the Taira. I will do it in your name and the name of all the Minomoto who have been wronged. I pledge my life to this!" He pressed his forehead to the cold stone floor of the cavern, then sat up again.

A tear fell from Yoshitomo's eye and crept down his cheek. "More important than vengeance, Ushiwaka, is to earn a good name for yourself with proper and courageous acts. Bring honor to the Minomoto. I am proud that you are my son." With this, the vision in the mirror vanished.

"Father! Come back!" Ushiwaka leapt up and embraced the mirror. He pressed his face hard against it, as if it were a doorway he could pass through. But the bronze was cold and unyielding against his cheek.

"You mustn't be greedy," said Sōjō-bō behind him. "The souls of those who have gone beyond can spend very little time with their mortal kin. It is part of your father's reward, after all, that he is now distanced from all worldly cares."

Ushiwaka sighed and let go of the mirror. "You are right, of course. Thank you, *sensei*. Thank you, again, for this gift. It is precious beyond price."

"I know," said Sōjō-bō offhandedly. "Now, it is time for you to go back to the monastery. We *tengu* will begin arrangements to help you leave Kuramadera soon. Your unfortunate bewildered abbot will have much to do to take care of the refugees from the fire, and therefore he will not be so watchful of you for a while. Consider carefully where you wish to go next, for your choice will have great importance."

"Thank you, *sensei*. I will."

"Here is a scroll containing the most important of my teachings." The *tengu* placed a tube of lacquered bamboo into Ushiwaka's hands.

Ushiwaka bowed deeply. "I will treasure it."

"Good. Now begone. Use our teaching well, and may good fortune follow you."

Ushiwaka backed out of the cave, bowing. Outside, from the pine boughs, the little Leaflet Tengu cried, "Ushiwaka! Ushiwaka! *Sayonara! Sayonara!*"

Ushiwaka smiled sadly and waved to them, then ran back down the forest path to Kuramadera. Just outside the temple compound, he paused beside a torch set on a high pole. Unable to contain his curiosity, he took the *tengu* scroll out of the tube, unrolled it a little way, and read what was written there:

"Herein is contained the Tengu-sho, including
knowledge of the Ninefold Sword and Flying Dragons..."

Ushiwaka unrolled the scroll still further and saw listed many of the sword techniques he had been taught, such as Reciprocal Mist and Sword of Nothingness, Garden Lantern and the Circling Monkey, Dance of the Tengu and Thunderbolt. He unrolled it a little more and a separate slip of rice paper drifted out. Ushiwaka picked this up and read it:

1. NEVER SUFFER THE COMPANY OF FOOLS
2. FOLLOW YOUR HEART
3. THERE IS ALWAYS A WAY AROUND TROUBLE
4. STOP READING THIS AND GET ON WITH YOUR LIFE.

Ushiwaka laughed, rerolled the scroll, and put it back in its tube, and then he got on with his life.

Abbot Meiun

Seven days after the fire, Go-Shirakawa awaited the arrival of the monk Saikō for a private audience at ToSanjō Palace. The heat of summer was upon the city, and the Retired Emperor fanned himself furiously to move air against his perspiring face. Yet every flick of the fan brought the scent of ashes to his nose. It reminded him of the funeral of his son, the former Emperor Rokujo who had died of illness this last year, at the young age of twelve. *First Nijō, now Rokujō. What karma did I bring to this life to watch my sons rise to glory and wither to death so soon?*

Go-Shirakawa was also reminded of the evil premonitions he had dreamed at Rokuhara. *Could the Taira have set this conflagration?* he wondered. *What possible good would it do them? Would Kiyomori do a thing so monstrous? Yet I note that Rokuhara is still standing, as is his new house, Nishihachijō. That, in itself, may be telling.*

A servant at the threshhold to the meeting chamber announced, "Your advisor Saikō is here, Majesty."

"Send him in."

The small, old monk entered and knelt on a cushion at a slightly closer than proper distance. He bowed but did not press his forehead to the floor as a proper subject might. Go-Shirakawa wondered if the faint smile upon Saikō's face was a sign of inner peace or of insufferable smugness. It was unsettling.

"Former Majesty, I thank you for allowing me this time with you. I trust you will find it worth your while."

"Your advice has usually been perceptive, Saikō. What would you tell me?"

"You have asked your advisors for information on who may have set this deadly fire, Majesty."

"Yes?"

Saikō leaned closer. "My informants tell me that it may have been the work of monks of Enryakuji, under the orders of Archbishop Meiun himself."

Go-Shirakawa sat back, alarmed. "Abbot Meiun? But he is a most mild and learned old man. It was he who took my vows and taught my son Takakura the Lotus Sutra."

"Indeed, Majesty, but his monks were dealt a crushing blow when they tried to reprimand your son at the palace gates. Many were slaughtered. On top of that, great sacrilege was done to their palanquins by arrows from the palace defenders. Is it not natural that Enryakuji may have wished vengeance?"

"Ah. Now that you explain it that way, I can see the truth of it. And here I was thinking the Taira might be responsible."

"Well," Saikō said offhandedly, "Meiun was the one to give Kiyomori his vows. And the Taira often ask Meiun for spiritual guidance."

"Ah," Go-Shirakawa said again. "So there may indeed be a connection there?"

Saikō tilted one shoulder and glanced away. "It is only speculation, of course."

"This could be terribly dangerous," said Go-Shirakawa. "I knew the monks could be destructive, but before they have limited their burning to each other's temples. An alliance between the Taira and such ruinous power . . . it must not be allowed."

Go-Shirakawa pondered the situation. Over the past seven years, his control over the government had only gotten stronger. His son, Emperor Takakura, did nothing without the Retired Emperor's advice. The Senior Council of Nobles, as well, consulted him before any major decision. *And surely they will not disapprove of my punishing those who dared to attack the Imperial Compound.* The time was right for a bold move, to remind the Taira they were not the only power in Heian Kyō.

"Saikō, assemble my advisors. I will demand of the Senior Council that Abbot Meiun be stripped of his position, placed under house arrest, and subjected to water privation until his place of banishment is decided. Let him become an example, so that the Taira will not be tempted to again misuse the holy temsples so."

Saikō smiled and bowed again. "It will be done, Majesty. You are surely wise in all things." He stood and shuffled out through the *shōji.*

Am I wise? wondered Go-Shirakawa. *Am I too late to prevent the destruction I have foreseen?* He called out to his advisor, "Saikō!"

The old monk peered around the doorframe. "Majesty?"

"How are Narichika's . . . preparations going?"

"They go well, Majesty."

"Ask him to . . . expedite his work, if you will. We may need him to be in readiness soon."

"I will do so, Majesty." Saikō's head disappeared again, and his footsteps could be heard hurrying down the hallway.

Shishinotani

Two weeks later, Lord Kiyomori sat in his new house, Nishihachijō, late at night. It was fortunate that he and his family had had this other house to move to after the great fire. Even though the clan *kami* had spared Rokuhara from the flames, the great Taira mansion was unlivable for the time being, as it was coated with ash and reeked of smoke. But the fire reminded Kiyomori of the dangers of living in the crowded capital, and now he mulled over drawings his housebuilders had made—plans for a larger, grander mansion farther outside Heian Kyō.

When Rokuhara had been built, there were few houses on the east side of the Kamo River. Now there were many. And where there were many houses, there was greater chance of fire, more places for spies and assassins to hide, less room for Taira warriors to maneuver.

Add to that, Heian Kyō had become a less attractive place to live. When Kiyomori had been young, the capital was a city of beauty and elegance beyond imagining—to visit it was as if one had been transported to the island of the Spring Blossom Fairies. It had been exciting to be at the heart of all things, where every decision that mattered was made, where everyone who mattered dwelt.

Now thieves lurked in the alleyways, and no one was safe, not even the Taira. Shopkeepers shuttered their markets early, even in summer, and regarded every stranger with suspicion. The streets were jammed by large cohorts of warriors escorting some nobleman, and there were often small battles over who would let the other pass. Parties at noblemen's mansions were now heavily guarded, and the entertainments within now seemed furtive, having lost their innocent pleasure.

The Taira were blamed for this change, of course. People were whispering that the many bands of thieves were led by Taira warriors. The Taira were even being blamed for the great fire itself. Kiyomori would have liked to slit the throats of those who spread such vile talk, but slander was like a serpent—slippery, poisonous, and difficult to kill. *It is pure envy, nothing more*, thought Kiyomori. *If it had been the Minomoto in power instead of my clan, they would have been the villains instead. Why is it so difficult for others simply to accept that the gods and the bosatsu favor the Taira?*

Kiyomori had been hoping to have Archbishop Meiun help bless the new residence. But Go-Shirakawa had suddenly decided to exile Abbot Meiun, on the advice of his strange monk-counselor, Saikō. Publicly, the

Retired Emperor blamed Meiun for the Enryakuji monks' attack on the Imperial palace. Kiyomori had tried to intercede on Meiun's behalf, but had found the Retired Emperor surprisingly unwilling to meet with him or hear his plea.

The wind moaned in the gardens outside, blowing through trees singed bare by the conflagration. It was a sorrowful sound, as if the wind mourned what had become of summer, what had become of Heian Kyō. Kiyomori sighed, then laughed ruefully at himself. It was one thing to sigh over fallen orange blossoms, for beautiful as they were, there are always more next year. But what sighs were heartfelt enough, deep enough, for the withering of Heian Kyō, of which there was not likely ever to be another?

I must be feeling my age, Kiyomori thought. *Is it possible I will next be taking these gray robes seriously and thinking of retiring from the world? Not likely. My clan still has need of me, and I will soon have a grandson who will be an emperor. Who could leave the world with such matters to attend to?*

A servant startled him by coughing discreetly behind the *shōji*. "Yes, what is it?" demanded Kiyomori.

"My lord, a visitor has come to our gates and sends you a message."

"At this hour? What is the message? Who sends it?"

"He is called Tada no Kurando Yukitsuna, and he says he has something very important to tell you."

Kiyomori felt a prickle up his spine. The name was of one of the Settsu Minamoto, one of Narichika's cronies, and Narichika was a close advisor to Go-Shirakawa. "I may have heard of this man, but he is not an expected visitor to this house. Only dark messages are delivered in the dark of night. Do not answer him immediately. Have one of my guardsmen find out what he has to say."

"My lord, he will not give his message to any intermediary. He says it is too important, and he must tell it to you personally."

"I do not like the sound of this," Kiyomori grumbled. "Do not send him in. I will come out to speak to him myself."

Kiyomori wrapped his robes tighter around him and strode out to the open raised corridor that connected the main buildings of Nishihachijō. He had Yukitsuna brought into the garden beside the railing of the passageway. Kiyomori glared down at the frightened-looking nobleman. "It is late. We do not receive visitors at this hour. What is your business?"

"I come when it is dark, Lord Kiyomori," Yukitsuna said in a loud whisper, "because there are too many eyes to see in daytime. Perhaps you have heard that His Retired Majesty Go-Shirakawa-In is mustering warriors and stockpiling weapons."

Kiyomori waved his hand dismissively. "I hear such rumors every day. They are saying the Retired Emperor intends to send men to attack Mount Hiei. He will be a fool if he does."

Yukitsuna shuffled closer. "This is not the truth of it, for I am one of those who was chosen to gather weaponry. The armed men are to attack the Taira, not the monks."

Kiyomori swallowed hard and gripped the railing. "If this is more slander—"

"My lord, it is not. I have taken orders from Narichika himself. He is the instigator. We have met over the past five years at the villa at Shishin-otani, in the hills near Miidera Temple. It began, at first, as just a place where some discontented men met to complain about the Taira, to drink and tell jokes and do foolish, disparaging dances. A monk named Saikō said the worst things against you. But the talk became more and more serious, and now an actual plot is under way. I felt I should tell you, my lord, before matters became too serious."

"Does the Retired Emperor know of this plot?" Kiyomori growled.

"How could he not, my lord? Go-Shirakawa attended some of our meetings, and Narichika says he takes his orders directly from the Retired Emperor himself. Often through the advisor, Saikō."

Kiyomori felt rage building within him. *Go-Shirakawa-In was a guest in my house. Twice I fought for him. How many Taira have died for him? And now he plots against me!* "Tell me everyone who is involved!"

Yukitsuna listed names, many North Guardsmen, dissatisfied monks and priests, and even two Taira noblemen whom Kiyomori had slighted for promotion.

"This shall not continue," Kiyomori growled. He bellowed into the night, "Send for my sons! Send for my samurai! Have any who are loyal to the Taira come with armor and swords and horses! At once!" He heard running feet as his guardsmen hurried off to do his bidding.

"I . . . had better be going, my lord," said Yukitsuna, bowing low. "Certain persons will be suspicious if I am gone too long." He picked up the hems of his kimonos and ran away to the gate, as though ghosts were chasing him.

Over the following hour, warriors by the hundreds began to arrive at Nishihachijō, answering Kiyomori's call. A rider was sent to the Office of the Imperial Police with a message for Go-Shirakawa. It stated Lord Kiyomori had learned of a plot against his house by some of Go-Shirakawa's associates, intended to make certain arrests, and requested that the Retired Emperor kindly not interfere. The Retired Emperor's reply relayed back to Kiyomori was so vague as to be proof to him that Go-Shirakawa had indeed been part of the conspiracy.

Kiyomori noted with satisfaction that the main courtyard of Nishihach-ijō had become filled with torch-bearing, armored men. *How dare Go-Shirakawa challenge the might of the Taira? It must be he has gone insane. Let him now learn the magnitude of his madness.* "Here are the men I want arrested!" Kiyomori announced to the assembled warriors in the main court-yard, and he read off the list of names provided by Yukitsune. After each name, he sent a group of warriors off to make the capture.

But for the last man on the list, middle Counselor Narichika, the pri-mary conspirator, Kiyomori used a different tactic. He merely sent one mes-senger to the Middle Counselor's home, requesting that Narichika come to advise Kiyomori on an urgent matter.

The ruse worked. An hour later, as the sun had begun to rise, Nari-chika's finest oxcart rolled up to the gate of Nishihachijo and the counselor stepped out, dressed in his most elegant casual robes.

"Look at him," said Kiyomori to his son Munemori, as they peered out through the bamboo blinds. "The counselor comes as if attending a morning social gathering. As if he expects to have music and dances and plum wine with his breakfast. Well, we shall give him a surprise, but not nearly such a pleasant one."

Narichika looked around in concern as he walked in the gate and saw the courtyard filled with warriors. Kiyomori's samurai grabbed Narichika's arms and dragged him up onto the nearest verandah.

"Wha-wha-what is going on?" stammered Narichika. "There must be some mistake."

Kiyomori came out from behind the blinds and stepped out onto the verandah. "There is no mistake, Major Counselor."

"Lord Kiyomori! This is a rough way to treat your invited guest!"

"But it is the normal way we treat conspirators."

"Conspirators? Nonsense! I demand to speak to Lord Shigemori!"

And you are hoping that my son, having married your youngest sister, will be more lenient? We will see about that. Kiyomori smiled with false politeness. "My eldest son has not yet arrived, Counselor. I'm afraid you will have to wait."

"My lord, should we tie him up?" one of the warriors asked.

"That should not be necessary," said Kiyomori, dryly. "Place the traitor in a suitable waiting room, if you will."

The warriors hustled Narichika off to shut him up in a tiny sto-rage room.

Other warriors arrived. "My lord, we have captured the monk called Saikō."

"Excellent." Kiyomori stood and went out onto the wide verandah fac-ing the main courtyard. "Bring him to me."

The samurai brought forward an ugly little bald man in dark robes with his hands and feet tightly tied. They dropped him on his knees directly in front of Kiyomori.

"So," said Kiyomori, "you are the man who has brought a blameless abbot to ruin and would have done the same to me. Now see what has become of you." He kicked the monk in the face with his clog-shod foot. "Is this how you best serve your master, the Retired Emperor? You who were of inconsequential birth, and given rank beyond your deserving? You who allowed your sons to deface holy property, and your slanders to cause an innocent abbot to be defrocked and exiled? And you start a conspiracy against my clan! Confess everything!"

Although his nose and cheek bled, Saikō sat up with an impudent smile on his face. "Inconsequential birth? Do I hear a fish calling a turtle wet? Oh, yes, I participated in such a conspiracy. But who is the true upstart here? Your father was a wart that attached itself to the Courtier's Court, and all resented his presence there. I remember when you first came to Heian Kyō, so proud on your high clogs, because you had beaten a bunch of pirates. Everyone thought it outrageous that someone of your blood should get even a Fourth Rank Assistant Commandership. Whereas I am of decent samurai family. When someone like *you* achieves the office of Chancellor . . . is it not good service to the throne to see such a wrong righted?"

Kiyomori balled his fists so tight his hands ached. "Take him away and torture him," he said at last. "Record every word of his confession and bring it to me. Then take him to a main thoroughfare and behead him. As an example."

"Oh, yes, kill me if you dare," said Saikō. "But know this—though you destroy this mortal form, you have not seen the last of my handiwork. I am servant to a master greater than you, greater than Go-Shirakawa. My soul is destined for a high seat in the Realm of Demons, and from there I will serve my master's will with more power than ever before. Hear me, o Lord of the Taira: you are doomed, as is your puny mortal realm. What chance you had to prevent this is lost. Now there is nothing you can do." The little monk laughed as he was carried away.

"What sort of monster can such a man be?" Kiyomori said to Munemori, who had come up behind him. "Who is this master he speaks of?"

Munemori cleared his throat. "Um, Father, you know the rumors that say the ghost of the Shin-In, the vengeful former Emperor, has been seen in the city. . . ."

Kiyomori turned to scowl at his son. "I tire of hearing of ghosts and demons as excuses for behavior. I have come to believe that some men are a manner of demon all their own."

"Father?" Munemori asked more softly, "Mother has told me . . . that perhaps our family is . . . no longer favored by the *kami*. I mean, there was the fire. And now this—"

"Foolish nonsense!" said Kiyomori. "We survived the fire. And we have been told of the conspiracy before it did us harm. Our luck has not yet run out, my son, never fear. Your mother suffers an old woman's worries. Do not listen to her."

Munemori went away, but to Kiyomori's eyes, he did not seem mollified. *He has always been more cowardly and superstitious*, thought Kiyomori. *But, then, he is a younger son. Perhaps someday I can arrange for him to have a distant governorship and send him somewhere where he won't be any trouble.*

At midmorning, Saikō's confession was brought to Kiyomori, along with word that the monk had been executed. Kiyomori took the sheets of paper and went to the storage room where Narichika was being held. Kiyomori could hear the nobleman murmuring anxiously to himself within. Kiyomori slid the *shōji* door aside with a loud bang.

The sweat-dripping Narichika visibly jumped. "Oh. It is you, Lord Kiyomori. I thought it was samurai come to—"

"*Why?*" Kiyomori demanded. "I spared your life after the Heiji Disturbance, after my son begged me to, because you had been his favorite tutor. In a normal man, gratitude incurs obligation. Yet you have plotted against my house. What grievance have you against us that has brought you to this? I want to hear your story from your own mouth."

"No, no," insisted Narichika. "As I have said, there is some mistake. Someone has told you lies."

Kiyomori flung the paper with Saikō's confession onto the floor before the cringing nobleman. "We have interrogated the Retired Emperor's closest advisor, and he names you as the primary conspirator! What can you say to that?" Kiyomori slammed the door shut again and strode away. The first two warriors he saw, Kiyomori ordered, "Take Narichika and make him howl until he tells you all he knows."

The samurai looked at each other distressed and confused. "But . . . but Lord Shigemori will be most unhappy if we—"

"Who is it who gives orders in this house? Am I not still head of the Taira? Am I not Chancellor? Do as I say!"

The warriors bowed nervously and hurried off to Narichika's cell. Kiyomori was soon gratified to hear, in the distance, the Counselor screaming like a wounded horse.

Shigemori did not arrive at Nishihachijō until evening. And when he did, he was dressed in court robes rather than armor, and had brought no warriors with him. But he had brought his fourteen-year-old son and heir, Koremori.

"What is the meaning of this?" Kiyomori demanded. "Where are your men? Haven't you heard we are facing a crisis?"

"A crisis?" asked Shigemori mildly. "That is an odd term to use for a private matter, Father."

"A private matter!"

"There has been no summons or announcement from the Imperial palace, or the Great Council, or ToSanjō Palace. Therefore, this must be a private matter. I have come to see about the welfare of Counselor Narichika, who I hear has been mistreated here. As you may recall, my wife is his younger sister, and this boy is his nephew. After I have seen Narichika, we will talk." Shigemori turned away, taking the boy with him, and began to make motions of searching the house.

Seething, Kiyomori instructed one of his men to show Shigemori where Narichika was being held. "When he is through, bring my son to speak to me in the great room."

Kiyomori put on a corselet and forearm guards over his monk's robes. *How dare my son speak to me in such a manner? What has come over him? Has he forgotten who he is? Perhaps if I arm myself, it will bring home to him the seriousness of the matter.*

But when Shigemori and Koremori were guided into the great room where Kiyomori sat awaiting them, their reactions were not what he expected. Shigemori regarded him with barely hidden dismay and disgust, and Koremori openly glared at him with hurt reproach.

"So you see," Kiyomori said. "Narichika still lives."

"Barely. He says your men have mistreated him."

"I wanted to hear why he conspired against us." To Koremori, Kiyomori said, "Whatever you may think of your uncle, you must understand. Narichika is our enemy."

Shigemori patted his son on the shoulder. "Go wait for me in the carriage." The boy went swiftly and silently.

"So. You would turn my own grandson against me as well?"

Shigemori did not answer, but went to another part of the room and sat down.

"Do you think Narichika, or any of them, would have spared you," Kiyomori went on, "just because you are his brother-in-law? Would they have spared Koremori, if the conspiracy had gone forward?"

"A conspiracy," said Shigemori softly, "whose only proof is the word of one frightened man. Plus the confession of one foul-mouthed old monk, and Narichika, both of whom you tortured."

"And at least the monk is dead now, thanks to me."

"Yes," said Shigemori. "I have heard."

"But no Taira are dead, and you do not thank me for *that*."

"I do not know if any would have been."

"Narichika was amassing weapons!"

"The monks of Enryakuji have threatened to attack. Of course Narichika would be prudent in the defense of his lord, the Retired Emperor. This is no cause for you to jump at shadows."

"What? What is this, do you now reproach me for acting too precipitously?" Kiyomori laughed, though he felt no humor. "I remember you in your first battle, when you were only a little older than your son, in the Hōgen. How spirited you were! You reproached me then, because I hesitated to fling myself into battle at your side against that monster Tametomo. Do you remember, hah?"

"I was but a child then."

"You were a *warrior* then. And how glorious you looked at the Heiji, when you wished me to join you in battle against Yoshitomo and Nobuyori. When you were wearing Chinese Leather and were taking your first command. How you shone! I thought then that you were the best of us. That you would be the finest Taira who ever lived. I remember thinking it a shame that it would be some future, unknown grandson who would become Emperor, when it should have been you."

"You must not say such things!" said Shigemori. "Father, if any of those weapons Narichika is supposedly stockpiling had been used against any of Taira blood, I would be there beside you in full armor, my sword drawn, my bow ready. But you are passing verdict and sentence before any crime has been committed!"

"These men were slandering our house!"

"And that is a crime worthy of death, is it? First you send out gangs of boys to beat up anyone who even makes a joke about us, and now your answer is to lop off heads?"

"If necessary, yes! I cannot believe that you care so little for the reputation of our house."

Shigemori looked away. "I cannot believe that you think such behavior will enhance the reputation of our house."

"We are respected."

"And feared and hated. There are times . . . there are times, father, that I am ashamed to call myself a Taira."

"Do not say such things!" Kiyomori bellowed. He jumped up and ran at Shigemori, intending to strike him. But he stopped himself in time and simply stood over Shigemori, glaring down at him. "What has become of you?" Kiyomori said at last. "Once you were the finest of our warriors. Once you had courage and spine. But now, you prefer the robes of courtiers and scholars, and you ape their cowardly, effete ways." Kiyomori lifted one of Shigemori's silk brocade sleeves and tossed it aside derisively.

"And what of you, Father? Look at yourself. You have taken the robes of a monk, the vows of a monk, including those to kill no living thing. Yet here you are with armor over your simple novice robe."

"It is good enough wear for the monks of Enryakuji," Kiyomori retorted.

"And everyone knows what ruffians and bumpkins they are," said Shigemori. "Oh, you should have seen them at the Taikenmon, Father. How they shouted and shook their *naginata*. But when the first arrows fell, they ran like dogs with their tails between their legs. Such brave warriors you choose to emulate, Father."

"You will not speak to me like this," said Kiyomori, keeping his voice low and deadly. He turned his back and walked across the room.

"Yes, I wear the robes of a scholar now," said Shigemori. "I abide by the Five Commandments, I try to uphold the Five Constant Virtues, and I have watched and learned from what I have seen in life. I remember after the Hōgen how so many were put to death, and how that led to the vendettas of the Heiji. And yet here you are planning on even more executions, on less cause. How can this do anything but make matters worse? Already you are sowing the seeds of future insurrection. These are the Latter Days of the Law, and so many mistakes have already been made. We have lost the wise Shinzei and others because men wielded death too quickly.

"I have come to realize that, for there to be peace in Heian Kyō, men must think beyond the concerns of their families and their clan. They must not dwell upon every petty or imagined slight, nor satisfy every ambition and desire. They must think on what is best for the realm, what is best for civilized life."

"A man who forgets his family and house," growled Kiyomori, "is nothing and no one."

"But a man must also remember," said Shigemori, "that one clan is but one part of Nihon, as one flower is but one part of a garden. As it is said in Shotoku Taishi's Seventeen Article Constitution, 'All men are possessed of minds, and all see things in their own way.' I beg you to think carefully on what you plan to do. If you will not open your mind to mercy, then consider politics. Narichika is respected by many in power. If you must punish him further, then exile him. To kill him will only bring more danger to you and our house and to the realm."

Kiyomori rubbed his chin, his anger cooling though not abating. He turned his back on Shigemori and pretended to examine a brocade screen. "I shall think on this. Meanwhile, as long as you are here and so full of advice, there is another thing you ought to know. I am considering arresting the Retired Emperor and confining him here or at the Toba Northern Mansion." Kiyomori heard a choking gasp behind him, much like a sob. Kiyomori turned to see Shigemori pressing his face into his sleeve. "What is the matter with you?"

"By all the *kami*, Father, don't you see? You speak of the past battles we have faced together, and yet you yourself have forgotten them. To arrest the *In . . .* this is how Nobuyori behaved! Nobuyori, the monster whom we all despised. There is but one head that, Amida forgive me, I am still proud, *proud* to have removed with my own sword, and that is Nobuyori's. Yet here you are, ready to behave just like him, ready to disobey the greatest of the Four Obligations, our debt to a soverign."

"Our sovereign Emperor is your brother-in-law, Takakura."

"Who is Go-Shirakawa's son. And it is Go-Shirakawa who has overseen the advancement of our house, the blessings of rank and offices that have been showered upon us. If he has grievance with us, perhaps we should hear it."

"What if I have grievance with him? What then?" Kiyomori turned away again, disgusted.

"Have you not often said that it does not matter what a man's intentions are, only that he do the right thing? Doesn't it equally not matter what your reasons are, if you do the wrong thing? Father, please! Do not ask me to choose whether to fight at your side or at the side of my sovereign, for either choice is a grievous sin. It would be better if you were to cut off my head now, to spare my soul, rather than ask that of me. It is a choice I cannot make."

Kiyomori looked back at his son, who had hung his head as if expecting a sword blow across the neck. *He is a wise scholar*, Kiyomori thought with grudging admiration, *but he truly has no stomach for politics. He is too good a man.* "No, no," Kiyomori said, walking over and placing a hand on Shigemori's shoulder. "It will not come to that. Don't you see? I want to protect Go-Shirakawa. I merely wish to see to it that His Retired Majesty receives no more bad advice from scoundrels."

"If you were to consult with him more," said Shigemori, "seek his advice before acting, show your loyalty, treat his people—*all* people—with respect, punish wrongdoers only so far as they truly deserve, then what cause would he have to listen to scoundrels? I believe that you can win back Go-Shirakawa's goodwill, and that the good fortune of the Taira need not end."

"It will not end, my son. I have pledged my life to that. Now go and see to that strapping young boy of yours. I am sure he is wondering what has become of you."

"Yes, yes, I should be going. But Father . . . please think on everything I have said." Shigemori stood, bowed, and hurried out to his carriage.

Kiyomori followed him out to the verandah and watched him go. Shigemori paused to say something to the guards at the gate, and they looked nervously back and forth between him and Kiyomori. After Shigemori got in his carriage and it drove away, Kiyomori called over one of the guards. "What did my son tell you?"

"My lord, Lord Shigemori requested that, if you ordered us to march on the Retired Majesty's mansion and arrest the *In*, that we should first go to Lord Shigemori's house and cut off his head."

"Ah. I see." Kiyomori wondered if it was his son's fine sensibilities that caused him to issue such an order, or if this was a clever form of blackmail. *Perhaps he is more of a political creature than I thought.*

*S*higemori stared at the swaying roof of the carriage as it moved, but he was not studying the woven bamboo.

"Father," said Koremori beside him, "what is the matter? You look upset."

Shigemori reached over and squeezed Koremori's forearm hard. "I pray you never see me become what I have just seen in my own father."

"What's wrong with Grandpapa? Why did he do that to Uncle Narichika?"

"I do not know. Men who seek only power often fear everyone is trying to take that power from them. I had hoped, Koremori, that you would grow up in a Heian Kyō like that of centuries past, a peaceful and gracious one. But it appears that is not to be."

"What are you going to do? Will we have to fight?"

"I do not know. But somehow, withought committing the sin of filial disrespect, I must let Kiyomori know that he cannot continue to issue sweeping, fatal orders without consulting others. A man in his position cannot think only of the Taira. Somehow . . ."

*H*ours passed as evening became full nightfall. Kiyomori sat in a darkened meeting chamber with only one lamp for illumination, drinking many cups of sake and pondering his argument with Shigemori. *I no longer understand him,* Kiyomori thought over and over. *We raised him well. When he was young, he knew the importance of his family and blood. Now his studies have addled his mind so, he wants me to think of everyone when I make a decision. As if all of humanity were one family, one clan. What nonsense. It is Tokiko's fault. She wanted him to be a scholar not a warrior. She said the Dragon King wanted heroes to save us poor mortals from ourselves. What sort of hero is it who defends his clan with scrolls and pithy sayings and hides behind the Five Virtues as if they were a shield?*

A warrior, still in full armor, coughed discreetly from the *shōji*.

"What is it?" Kiyomori demanded gruffly.

"My Lord, some of us were wondering what is to be done with Middle Counselor Narichika."

"Huh. Since my son has spoken so eloquently on the Middle Counselor's behalf," grumbled Kiyomori, "we will not execute him. Give Narichika more comfortable quarters but keep him watched closely. With Imperial permission, I will have him exiled."

The samurai bowed and ran off to do Kiyomori's bidding. Kiyomori could not help but notice that the man seemed to be smiling with relief. *Weak. My forces have become weak under my son's influence. What will become of the Taira when Shigemori takes full power?*

He heard a commotion outside and walked out to the open corridor. By the light of the flickering torches in the courtyard, he saw the guards at the gate gathering up their helmets and bows and sending for their horses. Like the recent conflagration, some spark of urgency passed from man to man among those warriors gathered in the courtyard, and they, too, began silently to don their helmets and quivers and run to their horses, some in such hurry that they rode out the gate more out of the saddle than on it.

"What is the matter?" Kiyomori shouted. "What is happening? Where are you all going?"

But the warriors did not answer him, did not speak at all, only casting nervous glances in his direction as they hurried past.

"Stop! I command you!"

But no man stopped.

Finally, Kiyomori jumped off the raised corridor and grabbed the arm of a very young warrior, pulling him to the ground. "Tell me what is happening, or I will take your head off myself!"

The young man's eyes rolled back in his head. "M-my lord, I know not how, but we are summoned to Lord Shigemori's Hojijō Mansion."

"Why?"

"My lord, I do not know. I only know that it is an emergency. He is calling for us. Please let me go."

Kiyomori released him, and the young samurai hurried after the others out the gate and down the street. At his departure, Kiyomori was left alone, abandoned, in the courtyard, all his warriors gone.

*I*t is done," Tokiko said, her eyes closed. "They are coming."

Shigemori took a deep breath, inhaling the smoke of the burning sakaki leaves on the brazier before him, and then released it. He shuddered, and said, "I had intended never to use my scholar's knowledge for sorcery."

"Do not berate yourself, my son," said Tokiko. "It was wise that you chose to do this. It is a small thing which does no harm, yet may bring great benefit." She released his hands and sat back on her heels.

"I feel . . . unclean."

"Some scholars feel unclean when they pick up a sword," said Tokiko, "and yet a sword is merely a tool. You swung a sword before you ever learned the sutras."

"But I have never before used the sutras as a sword. It is said that is how the Shin-In became a demon—by a perverted use of holy words."

"But your intent is not evil, as the Shin-In's was."

"If my father is right and what a man thinks does not matter, what then?"

Tokiko sighed. "That is all very well in war and politics. But prayer and sorcery are different. In these intent is what truly matters."

Koremori ran into the room. "Father, the warriors have started to arrive! What shall I tell them?"

Shigemori slowly stood. "I will talk to them myself. It is only right. I expect they will be quite surprised."

An hour later, the warriors drifted back through the gates of Nishi-hachijō, confused and sheepish. They said to Kiyomori, "Lord Shigemori said he was testing a new way to summon forces should an emergency happen. He only wanted to see if we would come, and how quickly, when he summoned us, that is all."

But Kiyomori learned the lesson Shigemori had intended. *He has powers I knew nothing of. The Taira warriors will obey his call, and swiftly. If I choose to try to take Go-Shirakawa, I might find myself with no warrior at my side, and all the Taira allied with the Retired Emperor against me.*

Kiyomori put aside any more thought of imprisoning Go-Shirakawa and went to bed feeling very old and alone. *It would seem*, he thought, *my son has learned how to move* go *stones very well.*

Gojō Bridge

Ushiwaka walked through the burned and ruined streets of Heian Kyō, idly playing a flute. He wore a woman's cloak draped over his head, in the manner of the *chujo* boys who served at the temple of Kiyomizudera. He draped it lower, however, to hide more of his face. The only thing that might distinguish Ushiwaka from the temple boys was the long sword in a gold-trimmed scabbard he wore at his side. Given the thievery and thuggery that nowadays plagued the capital, Ushiwaka had a ready answer if anyone asked about the sword.

But he almost did not need his disguise, this time, for most of the people were busy repairing or rebuilding their houses. Those who had completely lost homes wandered the streets so devastated that they took little notice of him. Now and then, someone might shout, "Hey, boy! Do you know any carpentry? Know how to thatch a roof? We will pay you well." Ushiwaka would play his flute louder and pretend he did not hear.

As always, his route took him past the Taira mansion of Rokuhara. Above the walls, he could see workmen sweeping the ashes off of the roof tiles. Guards were stationed at the gates, so Ushiwaka did not stare long. He had heard that even though Rokuhara was spared by the fire, Lord Kiyomori had moved elsewhere and might even build a new clan head-quarters far outside the capital. Ushiwaka cursed his luck, fearing that all his reconnaissance of Rokuhara over the past weeks had been for nothing.

It was a warm summer evening, and to Ushiwaka's dismay, Gojō Bridge was crowded with people. Apparently many had come seeking the cooler air above the Kamo River in which to gather and gossip with their neighbors. He would have to pass close to some of them and who knew if any of them had been to Kuramadera and might recognize him? Ushiwaka ducked his head lower, but it did not help. As he approached the bridge, the comments began.

"Who is this boy?"

"Why won't he show his face?"

"Perhaps he is very ugly."

"No, the monks only choose pretty ones to serve them."

"Perhaps he was burned by the fire.

"Perhaps he is diseased."

"Then we should avoid him."

"Perhaps he is scarred from fighting."

"No, a warrior would be proud to show his scars."

"Perhaps he is visiting a girl he shouldn't be seeing and doesn't want word to get back to his family."

"Or he is going to gamble and drink or some other disreputable pastime."

So the whispers went. Ushiwaka kept his eyes straight forward, his gaze on the planks of the bridge, and did not acknowledge them.

Suddenly someone stepped away from the crowd at the bridge rail and stood right in front of him, blocking his way. Ushiwaka glanced up, and up, and up at a very tall, rough-looking man. He wore black armor over the black robes of a monk, but he was unshaved and the long hair on his head flowed freely. He wore on his back both a *tsurugi* sword and a *naginata* pike, and at his side hung a *wakizashi* short sword.

"You should watch where you are going, boy," rumbled the man-mountain. "You might step into something unpleasant. In fact, you just have."

Ushiwaka heard the others on the bridge start to sidle away.

"There is going to be trouble," they whispered.

"Perhaps we should stay and watch."

"Perhaps we should flee. I have heard of this character, the big man. He is a bad one. Let's go."

Ushiwaka sighed. He did not wish a confrontation, not now. He began to play his flute again and tried simply to walk around the man.

But the unkempt ruffian stepped in his way again. "You are a rude fellow! Do you think yourself above all others? You are certainly not above me. No one is. Ha-ha, ha-ha!"

Ushiwaka steamed inside, but still he said nothing.

"Have I frightened you into silence, boy? Understandable. Let me begin the conversation then. I am Saitō Musashibō Benkei, and I am the toughest, strongest, cruelest bandit in all Japan. I have made an oath to all the *bosatsu* of Heaven and all the demons of Hell that before my death I will steal a thousand swords. I have already taken ninety-nine, and as I notice that you wear a lovely katana at your side, I have decided yours will be the lucky number one hundred. Hand it over to me, and you may go on to your prayers in peace."

Ushiwaka put his hand on his scabbard and stepped back.

"Oh, ho," said Benkei. "Reluctant to part with it, are you? I understand. It looks very valuable. Perhaps it is an heirloom, yes? Perhaps your elders will be furious if you lose it. But allow me to point out to you that I am very big, while you are very small. And thin. And young. And I will be furious with you if you do not hand it over. Think about this a moment as you decide."

Ushiwaka took another step back and tucked his flute into the belt of his robe. He grasped the hilt of the sword and withdrew it just a little from the scabbard.

"Oh, no, no," said Benkei, "You do not need to show me, I am sure it has a good blade. Now please to hand it over before someone gets hurt."

Ushiwaka sighed again, decided there was nothing for it, and drew the sword out all the way and held it before him. He heard the running footsteps of the last stragglers on the bridge fleeing behind him.

"Perhaps it is the dimming of the daylight that has dimmed your wits, boy," growled Benkei as he drew the huge *tsurugi* blade from off his back. "I was a monk at Enryakuji on Mount Hiei, and I have been trained by some of the best warrior-monks who live. Though I once took vows to kill no living thing, those vows were broken long ago. Therefore, it is with regret that I tell you to prepare for death. It is good that you were on your way to prayer, for I am sure that will bring you better karma in your next existence." Benkei brought the sword down in a mighty swing, but Ushiwaka had already stepped well out of the way.

"You are quick," said Benkei. "Let us see if you can do that again." He swung the sword once, twice, at the level of Ushiwaka's neck.

But Ushiwaka ducked easily both times. On Benkei's third swing, Ushiwaka beat at Benkei's blade with his sword. He knocked the *tsurugi* out of the giant's hands and sent it spinning, to fall with a splash into the Kamo River.

"Oh ho," said Benkei, some surprise in his voice, "so you have some fire in you after all. Well, let us see what you can do with this!" He pulled the *naginata* off his back and thrust with it at Ushiwaka's chest.

Ushiwaka deftly stepped aside and with one swing of his sword cut the haft of the *naginata* in two.

Benkei stared down at the much shorter length of wood in his hands. "So. You are clever as well. And your sword is sharp. But I doubt it is sharp enough for this." He dropped the wood and pulled from within his robe an iron rod, which he swung at Ushiwaka.

Ushiwaka jumped high into the air, tucking his legs up underneath him as the rod passed harmlessly below him. He laughed softly at the perplexed astonishment on Benkei's face.

"So! You laugh at me. I will teach you no one mocks Benkei!" The big man swung again and again with the iron rod.

Ushiwaka began to enjoy himself, for this was very much like the training the Leaflet Tengu had given him. He jumped onto the railing of the bridge to avoid one blow, over Benkei's head to evade the next. He slid between Benkei's legs for another, and finally twisted Benkei around so that Ushiwaka was able to pin Benkei's arm behind him and pluck the iron rod from his hand. The iron rod quickly joined the *tsurugi* at the bottom of the Kamo River.

For good measure, Ushiwaka struck Benkei on the temple with the hilt of his sword, and Benkei fell to his knees on the planks of Gojō Bridge.

Red in the face and gasping for breath, Benkei said, "What are you? No one before has bested Benkei. It is as though you know my every trick. I will tell you a secret. My father was a *tengu*, and I have had some training in the fighting skills of the demons. Yet you, a stripling of a lad, have overcome me. How can this be?"

Ushiwaka smiled and finally spoke. "You need feel no shame, Benkei-san. You fought very well. I, too, have been trained by *tengu* these past seven years. Sōjō-bō, prince of the Mount Kurama *tengu*, taught me himself and has given me his scroll of knowledge. So I did know all your tricks. I'm just younger and faster, that's all."

"Ah." Benkei sighed with awe as he looked up at Ushiwaka. "Sōjō-bō himself taught you? Even among the *tengu* he is known as the best fighter. It is no wonder, then, that you have defeated me. You must have been a great personage in a former life to have come to his attention so young in this one."

"As to that, I cannot say," said Ushiwaka. Softly he added, "But I told him I wish to defeat the oppressive Taira and kill Lord Kiyomori, and Sōjō-bō was kind enough to teach me all he knew so that I might accomplish this."

Benkei pressed his forehead to the boards of the Gojō Bridge. "Then your destiny must be mighty indeed. Please, young master, accept the service of this unworthy one. I came to Heian Kyō seeking my destiny, but now my oath to steal a thousand swords sounds petty compared to your lofty goals. Take me as your retainer, I beg you. I swear to serve you faithfully until death, young master, if you will have me."

Ushiwaka felt a surge of joy. All his boyhood he had been alone, without friends or companions he could trust. He had often longed for someone with whom to share the heavy burden of his fate. Benkei had been trained by *tengu* as Ushiwaka had been. Benkei would understand him and had the strength and courage to walk with him on his difficult path. "Please rise, good Benkei-san. I can think of no better companion I could have at my side. I gladly accept your service. Come, let us meet our destiny together."

Gray Robes

Tokiko paused, her writing brush held in midair as she became aware that someone was staring in through the *shōji* at her. A drop of black ink fell upon her gray-silk kimono. She turned her head and saw it was Kiyomori, kneeling on the verandah just outside. He held a fan in his right hand, but though there was perspiration on his face, he did not use it. He looked sad and old, and she could not help but pity him.

"Well, it would seem my astrologers are right again," said Tokiko. "This is a time of communication with those from my past." She put the brush down and blotted at her sleeve.

Kiyomori stared down at his hands. "I . . . regret that I have not spoken with you in so long, wife."

Tokiko frowned. *He is so humbled. This is not like him.* "Are you going to come in, or are you going to wait until the moon rises so you may admire it?"

Kiyomori sighed and entered, but no farther than just within the threshold. He clearly did not want to be there at all.

"What is the matter? What brings you to your son's house in such a melancholy state?"

Kiyomori waved his fan in a vague gesture that told her nothing.

"Have the blossom fairies stolen your voice?"

Kiyomori began to say something, then stopped. In that moment, Tokiko saw he was suppressing great anger. At last, he stated, "Today I banished Narichika to the province of Bizen."

"Well," said Tokiko, "that was merciful of you. Shigemori will be reassured, though I cannot say he will be pleased."

"Hm. So. How are you, Tokiko, old dragon?"

"Me?" She paused in surprise. "I am Nii no Ama, now, you must remember. Nun of Second Rank. And I am finding the process of growing old to be . . . interesting."

"Interesting, is it, o Nun of Second Rank? I must say, I find your appearance improved now that you do not wear white face paint or stain your teeth. You look healthier. Like someone's grandmother."

"Like an Emperor's grandmother, perhaps?"

"Perhaps." The ghost of a familiar twinkle appeared in his eyes, and Tokiko felt relief that his charming old self had not entirely faded.

"Who knows?" asked Tokiko playfully. "When I have returned to my father's kingdom and become young again, perhaps I will miss these aches in my joints."

The anger returned to his face, like a cloud crossing the sun. "Return? You are not planning to desert us soon, are you?"

"Soon? By the Amida, no! It will be many years, I am sure. Why? You cannot possibly be implying that you will miss me."

Kiyomori looked away, gazing past the *shōji*. When he spoke again, it was to murmur, "You are copying sutras."

Tokiko blinked at the change of subject. "Yes, it is a thing required of nuns. At first it was tedious, but now I find it soothing. I do not know why I comply . . . I do not even know if I have a mortal soul like yours. I suppose it can do no harm. I tell myself I do it for our children."

"Our children . . ." Kiyomori echoed still not looking at her.

"We have been blessed, neh? Shigemori has become quite a man."

The fan snapped in two in Kiyomori's hand. "*Hai*," he growled. "Quite a man."

So that is it. "You are upset with him."

Kiyomori turned a gaze upon her so full of hate that she hardly recognized him. "What have you done to him, witch?"

Tokiko paused. "I have done nothing but advise him."

"You have transformed him! You have taught him sorcery! Turned him against me!"

"I have done no such thing!"

"I received word last night that Shigemori sent out a secret request to be caretaker of the Imperial Sacred Regalia while the Imperial palace is being repaired."

Ah, I had forgotten, Tokiko thought, *that Kiyomori still has spies in high places, and that he is not entirely a fool.* "Shigemori had every right to make such a request. He is effectively head of the Taira clan and brother-in-law to the Emperor."

Kiyomori leapt upon her, pushing her shoulders down to the floor. "Do you think me an idiot?" he shouted in her face. "Shigemori wants control of Kusanagi!"

"Shhh! I pray you, keep your voice down, husband! Servants will hear."

"Let them hear! Let them learn of my family's duplicity! The Dragon King has made another deal, hasn't he? Only this time with my son!"

Tokiko tried to control her breathing. "It is true that I have spoken to my father again. He says his oracles still tell him the sword must and shall be delivered to him by one of Taira blood. We have given up hope that you would ever return the sword. So why not Shigemori?"

Kiyomori slapped her, hard, with the back of his hand. "Treacherous woman! How will our grandson, the Emperor-to-be, rule with no Imperial sword?"

Tokiko sucked at blood from her split lip. "Listen to me. We have learned that a copy of Kusanagi was made long ago and is being held safe at Ise Shrine. No one need know when the real Kusanagi is gone."

"A copy!" Kiyomori roared. "How nice! A copy! If my grandson should need the magic of Kusanagi to make men bow and the winds howl, he will have to be content with a *copy*!"

Servants came in and fluttered their hands at Kiyomori. "Please, my lord, desist! Look at what you are doing. You mustn't treat a nun this way." And behind them she heard the murmurs, "So it is true, Kiyomori has gone mad!"

"These things should no longer be your concern," Tokiko told Kiyomori. "You now wear gray robes, as I do. You took the same vows I took. You have declared your intent to retire from worldly matters, and now you should do so!"

"A wife does not speak to her husband like this."

"I am an old nun, and I say what I choose!"

"You have always said what you choose," said Kiyomori, getting up off her. "You have never needed gray robes for that. I must go speak with Shigemori."

"Leave him be!"

"Silence, wife. I am done with you."

As he strode off, the servants helped Tokiko to sit up and dabbed at her lip with silk kerchiefs. Tokiko waved them away, saying, "Go after him! Detain him somehow! Warn Shigemori he is here!" The servants hurried out to do her bidding.

As his father had gone to speak with his mother, Munemori took advantage of the opportunity to talk privately with Shigemori. "This is good, is it not?" he said, "We so rarely chat brother to brother anymore."

Shigemori fidgeted impatiently with a writing brush. He had clearly been doing administrative work, and Munemori had been an unwelcome interruption. "It is true, we have become distant. But the demands of duty often interfere with familial pleasures."

"Demands of duty!" cried Munemori, laughing. "Why should duty demand anything of us? We are Taira, brother. The most powerful clan in Nihon and perhaps the world. We may do whatever we choose!"

"Possibly so," murmured Shigemori.

"I am Major Captain now, and I have underlings begging to do my duties for me," said Munemori. "Who am I to deny them? Yet look at you, you are still acting as though you are a Sixth Rank Administrator, not the Palace Minister. People laugh at you, you know, behind your back. They say 'there goes Taira Shigemori, who still writes his own requisition forms.' "

Shigemori sighed. "An administrator who loses sight of the daily workings of his office soon loses all control of it as well. As you say, brother, we Taira may choose our pastimes. I've chosen mine."

"Suit yourself. Listen, I've heard that you've asked the Emperor to allow you to be caretaker of the Imperial Regalia—"

Shigemori glanced worriedly from side to side. "Where have you heard this?"

"Father knows, of course. Father knows everything. But if Takakura agrees, why not let me take that burden, at least, from you? You needn't tell anyone."

Munemori saw immediately the distrust in Shigemori's eyes. "If His Majesty agrees," Shigemori said, "I would not ever be so dishonest as to let him think I am performing a duty I am not. I could not honorably do what you ask, brother."

You don't think I'm worthy, do you? Munemori thought. *You think of me only as the worthless younger brother who can't do anything. You are the precious eldest son, and only you deserve praise and glory, is that it?* "How dare you speak of honor," Munemori said softly, "when you used sorcery on our father."

Shigemori shut his eyes and opened them. "I did not enchant Kiyomori. I merely wanted to see if our warriors would respond to an urgent call. These are perilous times, and we need whatever advantage we can hold."

"You don't trust Father, do you? You don't trust me, you don't trust him, you don't trust *anyone* but yourself!"

"That is not so."

"Oh, that is right. You trust Mother. You moved her here so that she would share all the secrets of the Dragon King with you."

"I moved her here in filial devotion. A son has the duty to look after an aging mother."

"I offered to let her move into my mansion, but she chose you. The shining Shigemori. Father laughs at me, Mother ignores me, you don't trust me. What is there in the world for poor Munemori?"

"Do not talk like that. There is much you could accomplish if you would only try."

"Is there? When I am doomed before I begin by people's opinions of me? I offered my services to Go-Shirakawa, but he turns away my requests for audience as though I were nobody. At court, the Fujiwara keep me away from anything important. How can a man accomplish anything in such a situation? It could all be overcome, of course, if only Father would help, but he still treats me like a child!"

"You should not concern yourself so much with our father's opinion," said Shigemori, softly. "He is . . . changed, of late. Or, rather, he has not changed, and that is not seemly in one who has taken religious vows. I fear he may not be fully master of his own mind and heart."

A servant appeared at the *shōji.* "My lord, your father, Ki—." He was roughly shoved aside, and Kiyomori stepped in.

"Father!" Munemori stood and bowed. "We were just talking about you."

Kiyomori ignored him. To Shigemori he said, "So, what your servants say is true. You think I am mad."

"That is not so," said Shigemori. "But I am concerned for your health, Father."

"More than you are concerned for the health of the Taira?"

"I don't understand."

Kiyomori leaned close to Shigemori. "Are you really going to throw Kusanagi into the sea?"

"What?" cried Munemori, but no one took note of him.

Shigemori wiped his brow, and said softly, "If it will ensure peace in our land, then yes, I would do such a thing."

"*Peace.*" Kiyomori spit out the word as if it were a fly that had gotten into his mouth. "You would choose peace over the fortunes of your clan. I tell you that if there is peace but the Taira are weak, then it is a worthless peace. If there is war, but Taira are the victors, then it is a good war."

Shigemori said, "We will never agree on this matter."

Kiyomori paused, glaring at him. At last, he said, "Then you are no true Taira, and I regret that you are my son."

Munemori gasped.

Shigemori sucked in his breath as if he had been cut by a knife. Standing, he went to the nearest *shōji* and called for a servant. "My father is not feeling himself. He must return to Nishihachijō at once." To Munemori, he said "Please arrange escort for our father and see that he does no further harm to himself or others."

Munemori saw opportunity in the midst of turmoil. "Father, let me take you home. Clearly, Shigemori no longer cares for your concerns. I will gladly listen with open ears—"

"What good can you do me, you worthless, whining, chattering monkey?" Kiyomori roared at him. "I should never have had sons!" He stormed out of the room and could be heard ranting as he departed down the corridor.

Shigemori gave Munemori an awkward little bow. "Please excuse me." And he hurried out of the room after their father.

So, thought Munemori, nearly shaking with roiling emotions. *That is it. Munemori is worthless, and there is nothing to be done. Well, we will see about that.* He called for his carriage, but instead of telling the ox-driver to return him to his own mansion, or Nishihachijō, Munemori asked to be driven to Rokuhara.

Night had fallen by the time the carriage bumped over the gate lintel at Rokuhara. Munemori was greeted by only a pair of elderly servants as he exited the carriage.

"My lord, if only you had sent word that you were coming. There are very few of us in residence right now, and we fear that our service to you will not be of appropriate quality."

Indeed, Rokuhara seemed to be largely dark and deserted. "That is fine," said Munemori sharply. "This suits my needs quite well. Bring me a lantern and a brazier with hot coals and then begone."

The servants did as they were bid, and soon Munemori was walking down a long empty corridor into the Southwest Wing of Rokuhara, the wing that was haunted.

Munemori's hand shook, and the lantern swayed, casting shadows that seemed to leap out of the corners at him as he walked. He started so that it was all he could do not to spill the coals out of the little brazier. His feet kicked up ashes and dust from the recent fire, and he could not see his feet, as though he were, himself, a ghost. In the dark, the rooms seemed like a labyrinth, and he felt lost, even though he had been born and raised in Rokuhara.

After Munemori had told his mother about the Shin-In's visit to Rokuhara, she had brought in monks to purify that wing of the mansion. But she had confided in Munemori that even the monks had been disturbed by what they felt in those rooms, and therefore they had worked hurriedly and left the task unfinished. Not every room had been cleansed. With cold irony, Munemori thought, *Their mistake is now my advantage.* He made his way to the one room his mother told him he must, at all costs, avoid.

It was a tiny storage room, and the walls were water-stained and smelled of rot. Munemori set the lantern in one corner and the brazier before him. The room felt cold even though it was the height of summer.

He placed on the coals a lock of his hair, a sakaki twig, and a torn piece of paper from a document he had stolen from the Imperial archives.

As the items burned, Munemori shut his eyes, and intoned, "Once you greeted me as an equal. Let me greet you again, that I may be of service to you." He waited for long seconds, but nothing seemed to happen. He opened his eyes and stared at the brazier but saw nothing in the smoke. With a sigh, he prepared to give it up and go. He looked up—

And the Shin-In was sitting across from him, sunken-cheeked and hollow-eyed. "I have been waiting for you," the Shin-In said.

"W-waiting?" Munemori asked, suddenly certain this had been a bad idea.

"I knew we would meet again, eventually. And here we are."

"Yes," said Munemori. There was a long, awkward pause.

"Well? What would you?"

All the grand speeches Munemori had rehearsed flew out of his head in a second. Instead, Munemori pressed his forehead to the dirty floor, and wailed, "No one respects me! Everyone tells me I'm worthless! Even though I'm a Taira! I don't want to be worthless! I want to be somebody! I would do anything to be somebody."

"There, there," the Shin-In said in a consoling tone. "I know exactly how you feel. Rejected and abandoned. But you have made the right decision. I am the right person to help you. Perhaps the only one who can. Together we will see that great things become of you."

"Truly?" sniffed Munemori, sitting up. "Such as what?"

"Well, what would you? How about Lord of the Taira? Chief of the clan? How does that sound? Serve me, and that title shall be yours."

"C-could you do that? Could I be Ason, chosen even over Shigemori?"

"Tcha, Shigemori will not be an issue."

Munemori began to feel much better. "Kiyomori will not object?"

"He will not be an issue either. It will happen that you will be the perfect choice. The only choice."

A choking laugh escaped from Munemori's throat. "That will surprise all of them, won't it? Me, worthless Munemori, Chief of the Taira!"

"All will be surprised, yes."

"Chief of the Taira! That is even better than Emperor!"

The ghost's mouth quirked. "A matter of opinion, but I am glad you think so."

"Good! Then let it be done."

"There is, you understand, a price."

"A price? What would you? Should I have a stupa built for you, or a temple dedicated to you, or arrange to have a hundred monks chant your name for a hundred days?"

"Nothing so grand. I follow the old ways. A sacrifice is a sacrifice."

Munemori felt a chill. "Someone must . . . die? Who?"

"No one important."

"Oh." Munemori sighed with relief. If it was just some servant, well, they die all the time, do they not? "I . . . I won't have to . . ."

"Fear not, you will wield no sword and let no blood."

"But I will . . . cause it to happen?"

"Indirectly. You won't even know until it is done."

"Ah. What could be better then? I agree to your price. It is a bargain."

Faster than an arrow from a bow, the arm of the Shin-In shot out and his clawlike hand grasped Munemori's head in a fierce, cold grip. Munemori sat bolt upright as though a shaft of frozen lightning had been driven down his spine. "Welcome to my service, Taira Munemori," said the Shin-In.

A Visitor from Shijō

Ushiwaka was tending to the gardens of Kuramadera when Abbot To-kobo came by, escorting a visiting monk. Ushiwaka had heard that the visitor was named Shōmon, also known as the Holy Man of Shijō, and was a personage highly regarded in religious matters. They were near enough that Ushiwaka could easily overhear their conversation.

"Yes, Kuramadera has a marvelous setting," said Shōmon. "Such views! Just as it was described to me. I should like to see more. If you could have one of your acolytes show me around the mountain paths, I would appreciate it greatly."

"I can easily arrange a guide for you," said Abbot Tōkōbō.

"How about him?" said Shomon, pointing at Ushiwaka.

"Oh, you wouldn't want that one," said the abbot. "He is obstinate and stubborn."

"Stubborn? I find that an entertaining quality in an acolyte. It brings forth spirited arguments."

Tōkōbō lowered his voice, but Ushiwaka could still hear him. "That is one of the sons of the famous general Yoshitomo. He should have taken the tonsure long ago, but he takes little interest in his studies. He would rather practice the sword than the holy teachings. Just the other day a ruffian warrior-monk from Enryakuji appeared demanding to be allowed to be that one's servant. I expect he is actually teaching the boy *bugei*. It is intolerable. If we cannot force the tonsure on him soon, we will have to return him to the capital."

Ushiwaka knew what that meant. He hoped the *tengu* would come up with a plan for his escape soon.

"How fascinating," said Shōmon. "Why not let me talk with the boy as he guides me. Perhaps I can be . . . persuasive, where others have not been."

"If you wish," grumbled Abbot Tōkōbō. "But I doubt even you can get through to him." He turned and glared at Ushiwaka. "You! Ushiwaka! Come here!"

Ushiwaka sighed, dreading that he was going to be lectured at for the next several hours. But he dared not upset the abbot any further. He put down his rake and went over to them. "What may this lowly one do for you?" Ushiwaka asked with a polite bow.

"You will guide Shōmon-san through our mountain paths, and you will listen to him, for he has some things to say to you."

"As you wish."

When Tōkōbō had left them alone, Shōmon favored Ushiwaka with a small, knowing smile. "I am pleased you have agreed to speak with me. I think you will find it worth your while."

"Will I?" asked Ushiwaka, not very hopeful.

"Judge for yourself when I have finished. Come, let us walk."

When they were far enough from the monastery buildings that no ears could hear, Shōmon said, "So, you are a son of the great Minomoto general, Yoshitomo, neh?"

This was more worrisome than a religious lecture would have been, and Ushiwaka feared he was in the presence of a Taira spy. "So they tell me," he answered cautiously.

"And you study the arts of the sword."

"Well, I enjoy the exercise. That is all."

Shōmon smiled again. "Sōjō-bō is a good teacher, isn't he?"

Now Ushiwaka was truly frightened. If the Taira had learned of his dealings with the *tengu* . . .

"Fear not," Shōmon added. "Sōjō-bō sends his regards and begs you remember the third item of advice on his note included with the scroll."

"The third . . . Ah, I remember it. *There is always a way around trouble.* Sōjō-jō sent you to help me!"

Shōmon nodded. "He did."

"But . . . how is it such a holy man as you knows a *tengu*?"

"Oh, any monk who wanders in the mountains eventually meets a *tengu*. Whether he knows it or not. Now here is what you must know. There is a branch of the Fujiwara who have holdings in the province of Ōshū. They are the descendants of the hereditary retainers of your esteemed ancestor Yoshiie. Hidehira is the clan head now, and he has a force of 180,000 warriors. The Fujiwara, however, are not known for their skill in strategy. Therefore, he would like his forces to be commanded by a Minomoto general. He feels it would do much for the morale of his men. You understand, the long-noble Fujiwara have no love of the upstart Taira."

"Yes, I imagine not. So, when do I leave for Ōshū? Tonight?"

"You are a brash boy. No, there are enemy spies all along the way, in every mountain temple, at every inn and post station. We must make careful preparations."

"I now have a retainer who is a great warrior-monk. His name is Benkei. Between the two of us, I am sure we can fight off all trouble."

"Hm . . . Benkei. I have heard of that one. A bandit who has sworn to steal a thousand swords, isn't he?"

"He has renounced that oath in favor of helping me defeat the Taira."

"Then you have already done the world a great service, Ushiwaka. But why take risks when Hidehira needs you well and whole, and you need his men to succeed? You must travel in disguise."

Ushiwaka was not convinced. "It seems . . . dishonorable. But, if you think that is wise."

"Were you not taught by the *tengu* that deceit is sometimes necessary for victory? Do you not sometimes feint with the sword so that you may strike your opponent from a better angle? So. Here is what we will do. When we return to the monastery, tell Tōkōbō that you have found my arguments convincing and that you wish to study with me longer. We will spend another day together, and then I will take you to Juzenji Shrine, where you will meet up with a certain gold merchant who often travels the road between Heian Kyō and Ōshū. As part of his entourage, you are more likely to travel safely and without incident."

"Very well," said Ushiwaka. "It shall be as you say. I am very grateful for your help."

"Nihon will be grateful to you, young Minomoto, if you can rid it of this infestation of Taira."

"I will do my utmost to accomplish it, Shōmon-san."

Prayer Tags

*K*enreimon'in sat fanning herself in the tiny room. The wood-and-ivory prayer tags on her sleeve clattered with the movement of her arm. Ever since the fire, she had sequestered herself in Imperial abstinence, alone but for the servants who brought her meals. The official story was that she was praying for the *kami* to bless her with a child. The truth was that she could not bear the guilt of having caused so many deaths, and she prayed for redemption and forgiveness.

She had commanded that monks chant over the Imperial Regalia to purify them, without explaining why, and asked that arrows be shot and iris balls hung to drive away evil spirits. She did not know if this had been wise—it felt rather like trying to gather up rice that had already been spilled into dirt.

The *shōji* beside her slid open and her chief maidservant knelt there, holding a tray. "Majesty, it is time for your midday repast. May I enter?"

Kenreimon'in waved the fan to indicate she should. The maidservant came in and set the tray on the sole low table in the tiny room, then bowed, pressing her forehead to the floor.

"Majesty, may I be so bold as to speak with you?"

Kenreimon'in sighed. "If you wish."

The servant shut the *shōji* and then sat beside her. "Majesty, you have been observing seclusion and abstinence for a month now, and people are beginning to wonder."

"I . . . regret that I must do this," said Kenreimon'in. "But I dare not show my face for fear that I will burst into unstoppable tears and thus cause more questions."

"I understand, but truly you blame yourself too much. How could you have known that a simple cooling breeze could be so . . . well, it was not your fault."

"I am not sure I believe that."

"Your husband, His Majesty, misses you. He is baffled and says he will gladly help you with the getting of a child, if that is your wish."

A cough escaped from Kenreimon'in's throat that was both a laugh and a sob. She pressed her sleeve to her face, and when she could speak again said, "Poor Takakura. How could I ever tell him what I have done?"

"There, there, you do not have to if you do not wish to. There is a little news concerning the sword."

"News?"

"It seems your brother Shigemori has made a request to be keeper of the Sacred Regalia until you can move back into the Imperial palace."

"Shigemori?" Kenreimon'in was instantly comforted by the name. She had always admired her elder brother, and he had always been kind and helpful to her. "Yes. Yes, that would be good. Shigemori would take good care of them. You may let it be known that I approve of his request."

The maidservant smiled sadly and lowered her head. "Alas, Majesty, it is not to be. Your father-in-law, Go-Shirakawa, would never let the sword, the jewel, and the mirror fall into Taira control. Begging your pardon, but he is deathly afraid of what Lord Kiyomori might do."

"But Shigemori is wise. He would not let my father do anything foolish or rash."

The maidservant tilted one shoulder. "It is the *In* who has made the decision, not I. Ah, speaking of brothers, here is a letter from another of your brothers, Munemori." She drew from her sleeve a folded piece of Michinoku paper that was sealed with the butterfly crest. She placed this before Kenreimon'in, bowing as she did so.

"Oh, what does he want now?" moaned Kenreimon'in. Munemori mostly had ignored her when they were children. Since she had become Empress, however, he often pestered her to whisper good things about him into the Emperor's ear.

"As to that, I cannot say. Majesty, won't you please consider ending your seclusion? We are all concerned about you and your beautiful, smiling face would cheer this dreary mansion so. Surely all the *kami* and *bosatsu* have heard your prayers by now, and the Amida knows there was no evil in your heart. You can always request one of the temples to devote prayers for you. Please consider this."

"I will. I thank you for your kindness. I will. But please leave me for now."

The maidservant bowed again. "As you wish, Majesty. I look forward to seeing you laughing in the gardens once again." She shuffled out and closed the *shōji* quietly behind her.

Kenreimon picked at the tray of pickled vegetables and rice, but as usual she did not feel hungry. Feeling too distracted to return to prayers, she picked up the letter from Munemori and unfolded the paper. Perhaps there would be something pathetically amusing in Munemori's words.

Greetings to Her Most High Sacred Majesty.

Dear Sister,
I hope you are well. I understand your wish to have a child. I know
how eager Father and Mother are to see you bear "the Taira Emperor" as they put it, but aren't you overdoing it a little? Seclusion
is not the way children are born. I expect mother has explained this
to you.

But I have excellent news! I have recently learned that I will soon
receive a most unexpected and amazing promotion. I cannot divulge
exactly what it is yet, but I am sure that you will be very proud of
me. So thrilled was I by this news that I went home and made
amends to my wife, as you so often wisely counseled me to do, and,
well, let us say that we may ourselves soon be expecting a child.

Good health to His Majesty, good fortune to you. Long live the
Taira!

I would end this with a poem but I find such playing with words
to be foolish and wasteful. I have never understood what people
see in such an art.

                                                    Munemori

Kenreimon laughed despite herself. *Of course Mumemori does not like
poetry. He is so bad at it.* She set down the letter with a sigh and gazed out
at the hibiscus blossoms in the garden. *So, even the useless Munemori receives amazing good fortune. How is it that even as so many suffer, the Taira
continue to rise and prosper? It is unseemly, somehow.* While many extolled
the luck of the Taira as evidence of the gods' blessing, Kenreimon'in was
beginning to view it as a curse.

A Straw Raincoat

Two days after his meeting with Shōmon, Ushiwaka stood on a path
near Juzenji Shrine at dawn with his retainer Benkei. Ushiwaka had
dressed in many layers of white and pale yellow silk, and wore a corselet
named Shikitae beneath his clothing, yet he still shivered. He played softly
on his bamboo flute, blending the notes with the birdcalls of morning.
   "That seems a sad tune, master," rumbled Benkei beside him.

Ushiwaka stopped. "Yes. I am sad to be leaving Kuramadera. It's the only home I've really known. I will miss Abbot Tōkōbō. He meant well for me and looked after me. I simply cannot choose his life."

"Hunh. Just as well. You're too young to become a monk. You'd miss too much. Wine. Women. Poetry parties. Women. The joy of battle. Women."

"Pardon me for noticing, Benkei, but are you sure you have mentioned women enough?"

"Thank you for pointing that out, master. Women. There, I think that is sufficient."

Ushiwaka idly rubbed his flute, saying, "I hardly know anything about women. My mind has been on swordsmanship and revenge. Though, of late, I had been . . . noticing some of the women from the city."

"Well, I am sure once we are on the road, you will be able to do more than notice girls. There are entertainers at every inn and post station these days. Ho, I think I hear our escort approaching."

There was, indeed, the sound of jingling and hoof footfalls in the forest, and presently a train of horses and oxen came down the path. They were led by a man on horseback who appeared to be in his forties, though his face had been weathered by days riding in the sun so it was hard to tell. He wore riding trousers of bear fur and an over-jacket embroidered with flowers and herbs. He stopped his horse just in front of Ushiwaka.

"Good morning, young fellow," said the merchant. When he smiled he revealed that one of his front teeth was capped with gold. "I am Kichiji, dealer in gold, silver, and fine wares of all sorts. You must be the precious property of the Minomoto that I am to deliver to Ōshū Province."

Ushiwaka bowed. "Yes, I am Ushiwaka, and this is my retainer, Benkei."

"Ushiwaka? That is a child's name," said the merchant, frowning. "Yet you look to be fifteen or so."

Embarrassed, Ushiwaka stared at his feet. "I . . . have not been given opportunity to take a man's name. I have not even had a proper trouser ceremony. Everyone expected that I would take tonsure and vows and be given a new name then."

Kichiji sighed, and said, "Then we have rescued you in time. You may choose your own name now."

"Yes, I expect so. Well, good merchant, if you will show me which horse I am to use, we may hurry on our way. I fear the monks may find me gone soon and come to look for me."

"Horse? Ha!" Kichiji turned to the other bearers and riders behind him and they laughed with him. The merchant hopped off his horse. "I was told that you were to be traveling in disguise."

Ushiwaka looked down at himself, confused. "I am not dressed like a temple acolyte."

"No, you are dressed like a young lord expecting to come into his inheritance. Just what your enemies will be looking for. And your face is visible, so your monk friends can easily recognize you. I can see Shōmon did not advise you very well."

"Well, what do you suggest?" asked Ushiwaka.

"I have just the thing." Kichiji walked back to one of the oxen and took from its back what appeared to be a bundle of straw. He came back and draped over Ushiwaka's shoulders a large, heavy, smelly straw raincoat of the sort peasants wear. On Ushiwaka's head, he plopped a conical straw hat and tugged it low over Ushiwaka's face. "There!" said Kichiji, "that is more what I had in mind."

Benkei began to laugh. "Oh, ho! He is right, master! I never would recognize you in such a guise. You look more like a walking hay bale, a tottering granary than . . . than . . ." He withered under Ushiwaka's glare. "Than the fine and noble warrior lord that you truly are, master."

"But those swords," said Kichiji, "do not suit a peasant at all. You will have to give them to me for safekeeping."

"No!" Ushiwaka said, hand on the hilt of his *wakizashi*.

"Kindly take my advice, good merchant," said Benkei, "and let his young lordship keep the swords."

"Oh, very well." Kichiji sighed. "We'll just say you're my sword-bearer. Now come along. If we are to have people on our heels searching for you, we had better move quickly." The merchant remounted his horse. To Benkei, he said, "I trust we can rely upon your help if trouble arises?"

Benkei bowed. "I am honored to serve any who give assistance to my lord and master."

"Good. I can always use another treasure-guard. You two may walk behind my horse there. That's good. Come along. Hei-yup!" He nudged his horse forward, and the caravan began its journey once more.

Ushiwaka trudged behind the merchant's horse, fury and shame warring with gratitude and relief.

"Adventure, hey my lord?" said Benkei happily. "We're on our way to adventure at last."

"Hmpf," said Ushiwaka, trying to get comfortable under the itchy, heavy straw raincoat. It was not an auspicious beginning to any adventure he wanted to be part of.

Fukuhara

*L*ord Kiyomori sat on a cushion on the verandah of his villa at Fukuhara, savoring the scent of the sea air. It was clean, pure, unlike the ashen stink of Heian Kyō. A man might calm himself and gather his wits in such an atmosphere. From where he sat, he could see the restored artificial island and the harborworks, evidence that he had made his mark on the world, that he was still a power to be reckoned with.

Kiyomori had left the capital the day after his argument with Shigemori. He feared what his son might use his newfound power to do. *Will he throw in his lot with Go-Shirakawa? Would he have had me arrested and held prisoner in my own house?* Kiyomori now believed Shigemori capable of such a thing, and so he had fled. *What a wretched thing it is to be afraid of one's own son. I will show him I have power yet. That I was the one who taught him the game of* go.

From Fukuhara, Kiyomori could summon distant relatives and retainers who remained loyal to him from the provinces of Aki and Ise, across the Inland Sea. Already Kiyomori had sent word by messengers to those men he knew still to be loyal to be prepared for battle. *If Shigemori should send troops against me, he will not find me a cowering old man. He will find me at the head of many hundreds of warriors who still remember how to fight.*

A servant knelt nearby and bowed, informing Kiyomori that Kaneyasu, one of his most trusted Ise generals, had arrived.

"Excellent."

Kaneyasu, a warrior of notable courage who had not been tainted by the capital's effete ways, came to the verandah, bowed, and sat beside Kiyomori. "My lord. All is well with you?"

"It may be, if your news is good."

"There are no untoward movements of men in the capital. Shigemori is performing only his usual duties and activities. The Retired Emperor is being circumspect, although he is still angry with the Enryakuji monks and it is not known what action he may take with regard to them. Middle Counselor Narichika has reached the Island of Kojima safely to begin his exile."

"And what of Narichika's sons?"

"They have all been found and will be exiled to Kikaigashima as you have ordered."

"Very good. Treat them with courtesy and kindness so as not to disturb Shigemori's sensibilities."

"As you wish, my lord."

"As to Narichika . . ."

"Yes?"

"I fear my son has been bewitched by his long association with the wicked Middle Counselor. Yet Shigemori gives me no assurance that Narichika will not continue to conspire against me. It seems I can do nothing concerning the Retired Emperor. But as to Narichika . . . Let it not be tomorrow, or next month . . . but see that he dies within the year."

Kaneyasu bowed again. "It shall be as you command, my lord."

Aohaka Station

*U*shiwaka trudged behind Kichiji's horse, glad he had spent those many evenings hiking from Kuramadera to Heian Kyō. His legs could bear the distance. Still, he had never undertaken a journey this long, and with the heat of summer, by the second day he was wilting under the straw raincoat. Kichiji finally took pity on him and let Ushiwaka ride one of the packhorses.

"Do not be ashamed, master," said Benkei to cheer him up. "At least you are stronger than those Fujiwara lords who faint if they have to walk from their front door to the gate."

"I suppose that is so," grumbled Ushiwaka, whose thighs had begun to hurt after a few hours. He was not used to riding horses, and he realized that, to be a proper leader of warriors, he would have to have a great deal more practice at it. At the moment, however, Ushiwaka would have given much to be a weak-legged Fujiwara lord, able to call upon a palanquin or ox-carriage in which to travel.

The caravan had proceeded down the west shore of Lake Biwa, emerging at last onto the great highway of the Tōkaidō, perilously close to Heian Kyō, but fortunately no one stopped them. The guards at Ōsaka Barrier watched them suspiciously as they passed through, but no one suspected that a scion of the great Minomoto house would be traveling in a smelly, soggy straw raincoat, carrying swords for a gold merchant. For good measure, Kichiji called Ushiwaka some choice insults and cuffed him a couple of times on the shoulder. Surely no Minomoto lordling would allow himself to be treated that way. Ushiwaka bore it well, but he had to restrain Benkei from knocking Kichiji off his horse when they were out of sight of the barrier.

The few rogues on the highway who eyed the rich caravan with gleams of greed in their eyes quickly lost interest when they locked gazes with the fierce-looking Benkei.

The caravan went over the mountains to the east of the capital, past the Ōtsu Shore at the southernmost tip of Lake Biwa. By the evening of the second day, they reached the post station at Kagami. The following day they passed through Ono-no-suribari, Bamba, and Samegai, and finally stopped for the night at Aohaka post station.

As Kichiji was a wealthy merchant, and well-known along the Tōkaidō, he was able to secure lodgings at the most reputable inn at Aohaka. The caravanners were welcomed, and the mistress of the inn, who was well acquainted with Kichigi, brought forth her most beautiful and skilled girls to entertain them.

When Ushiwaka removed his conical hat and raincoat, the mistress of the inn looked at him and turned pale a moment, then studied his face. "Are you certain, Kichiji, that you have never brought this fellow with you before?"

"Quite certain," the gold merchant replied. "He's a new servant I'm trying out. Although with his sloppy service so far, I'm not sure I'll be keeping him."

"He's such a lovely young man," said the mistress of the inn. "Still, I cannot help thinking he looks familiar. Like someone I had met before . . . someone who met an unfortunate fate here. It was so long ago, but perhaps he is a relation."

"I do not think that is possible," said Ushiwaka with a polite bow, wondering whom the mistress might mean.

The caravanners were well fed with plentiful rice and plum wine, and the girls did their best to be entertaining. Thus Ushiwaka and Benkei spent a most enlightening evening, and the girls were quite enchanted with the handsome young sword-bearer who was so accomplished with the flute. They giggled when Ushiwaka mentioned his name, however, and allowed as to how, after that night, surely he deserved a man's name.

Although the night's entertainments had been rather tiring, still Ushiwaka found himself woken up, in a dark inn side room, at the Hour of the Tiger, just before dawn. He had the sense that there was someone else in the room. Slowly, he reached for his long sword.

"Peace, brother," said a gentle voice softly. "You need not fear me."

Ushiwaka sat up and saw a pale young man dressed in ragged finery and the breastplate and greaves of a noble warrior. The young man's head was not quite attached to his shoulders. "Who are you?"

"I am your half brother Tomonaga. We fled here, Yoshitomo and my brothers, after the failure of the Heiji, fifteen years ago. Alas, I was wounded in the leg by an arrow. By the time we reached this place, my leg was so swollen that I could not continue. So I asked our father to cut off my head, so that I might not be captured by the Taira. Father had to flee, and so he could not bury me. I am afraid the mistress of the inn received a most unpleasant surprise and unhappy burden when I was found the next morning."

"Yes. That must be why the mistress thought I looked familiar. But why are you still here? Why have you not passed on to the Pure Land, as our father has?"

"I do not know. I think I have been waiting for something. Waiting for some proof that our father and clan will be avenged. Perhaps I was waiting for you."

"I have sworn that I will avenge the Minomoto," said Ushiwaka. "I have studied swordsmanship with the *tengu* for seven years for this."

"I am pleased to hear it," said the ghost of Tomonaga. "But we spirits are given some small ability to see into the future, and I have appeared before you to give you two warnings."

"What are they?"

"The first: you must use caution when dealing with our brother, Yoritomo. He is the chosen of Hachiman. You must remember this."

"So I have been told," said Ushiwaka. "It is my sole intention to be of service to him." This was not quite the truth, for Ushiwaka dreamed of being a great general of the Minomoto someday, but he was aware that an elder brother was to be respected.

"That is good. But be warned. There are supernatural forces that are allied against humankind and who use the greed of men to bend their will. Yoritomo may be listening to the advice of untrustworthy . . . persons. Be careful."

"I will. What is the second warning?"

The ghost of Tomonaga raised his head and stared toward the *shōji*. "There are bandits in the garden of the inn. They have come to steal the caravan's gold. I understand you are traveling in secret. You may need to reveal yourself in order to drive them away."

Ushiwaka leapt to his feet, drawing his katana from its scabbard. "Kichiji has only been kind to me. I will not let him be robbed, let people say what they will."

The ghost of Tomonaga bowed, head floating eerily above the body. "You are truly our father's son. Go quickly."

Crying aloud, "Ai-yi-yi-yi!" Ushiwaka kicked open the *shōji* and jumped out onto the verandah. Three bandits, in the midst of climbing over the railing, looked up astonished. With three deft slashes, Ushiwaka separated their heads from their necks. Two bandits behind them cried out in fear and turned to run. But Ushiwaka was faster, and he leapt onto the railing and from there onto the bandits' backs. He made quick work of them as well.

By this time, Ushiwaka's cry had awakened others, and Benkei came storming out of his room like a demon. Though there might have been fifty more bandits in the garden, Benkei and Ushiwaka charged into the thick of them and soon there were many fewer than fifty. Those bandits not felled by their slashing swords went screaming into the night, not to be seen again.

"Surely," the girls whispered to one another, "this is no ordinary sword-bearer. The mistress said he looked like a Minomoto who had died here long ago. Do you think . . . ?" Though they carefully inquired of Ushiwaka when the battle was over, he told them nothing but pleasant lies.

The following morning Kichiji and his caravanners prepared to move on, as if nothing untoward had happened. Ushiwaka and Benkei spent a long time on farewells, and many of the girls were openly weeping into their sleeves. Benkei, in particular, had to disentangle one ardent young woman from his arm with sweet words and promises that he would one day return.

Ushiwaka had found out by careful questioning of the mistress of the inn where his elder brother had been buried, and he left prayers upon the grave as they passed it. Toward the end of the day, they came to Atsuta Shrine, at which relatives of Yoshitomo served. Ushiwaka left the caravan, promising to catch up to them in a day, and, risking discovery asked the high priest of the shrine to conduct a capping ceremony for him.

The priests of the shrine were most pleased to do so, and Ushiwaka was received with great honor. Ushiwaka purified himself to appear before the shrine gods, a cap of black silk was found for him, and he was asked to choose his adult name. As it was customary for a son to take part of the name of his father as his own, and as his father was Yoshitomo, Ushiwaka became Yoshitsune. And with that name he left the shrine as a grown man.

A Messenger from Kuramadera

Late at night, two weeks after arriving at Fukuhara, Lord Kiyomori sat in his favorite chamber on the east side of the mansion, the one that best caught the breeze from the sea. Not feeling tired, he spent the hours idly looking over letters he had received from supporters in Ise and Aki. He could hear the distant surf booming against the shore, regular as breathing, as if the ocean were one great living thing. He thought again how natural it was that the Dragon King had chosen the Taira to be his champions, an alliance of he who rules the sea below with those who dominate the sea above. He wondered, however, if it were deliberate on Ryujin's part that his demands for the alliance might well cause the Taira's downfall. *And*

Shigemori willingly participates in this, Kiyomori thought. *Is he blind, or simply the most disloyal man who ever lived?*

Kiyomori was no longer so upset about Shigemori, and instead of dwelling on him as a betraying son now considered him part of the puzzle, merely another obstacle to advancing the Taira fortunes. The days spent in Fukuhara had soothed his spirit. There, Kiyomori could play the great lord, receiving visitor after visitor as if he were Emperor of his own small kingdom.

One such visitor had proclaimed that, given the shrines and stoneworks Kiyomori had built, surely he was the reincarnation of legendary Buddhist archbishop Jie, of Chang'an. *Me, a former archbishop*. Kiyomori chuckled to himself. *If true, the ways of the Amida are stranger than I had thought.*

The pounding of the surf became overridden by another rumbling sound . . . the thunder of hoofbeats. A horse was being ridden into his courtyard, and Kiyomori heard excited voices. He waited with concern. *What man rides so hard at night except one who is desperate?*

Shortly, a servant appeared at the *shōji*. "My lord, a monk has arrived from Kuramadera with, he says, urgent news for you."

Kiyomori frowned. Messages delivered late at night were generally bad news, he had learned. He could not remember any concerns he had with that northern temple, but given how Go-Shirakawa was offending temples left and right, he could not afford to turn the messenger away. "Very well, I will hear him."

The servant departed, and a young monk appeared in the doorway, his head newly shaved. The monk knelt and bowed. "Kiyomori-sama, Abbot Tōkōbō has sent me to speak to you. I have sailed down the River Kamo and ridden from Daimotsu without rest, so that you may have this news at once."

The young monk seemed afraid, and Kiyomori felt a prickle like spiders crawling up his back. *Very bad news, then*. "Abbot Tōkōbō is very thoughtful," he said to the monk.

"The abbot wished me to say that it may be a small thing. Nothing at all, really. Only, he felt you should know."

Kiyomori had developed a healthy suspicion of seemingly small matters. "By all means, then, tell me of this oh-so-important nothing."

"Fifteen years ago, Kiyomori-sama, Kuramadera had the honor to receive a certain personage into its care."

Kiyomori scowled. So many "personages" had fled to the various temples surrounding Heian Kyo over the past decades. How should he remember them all? "Remind me. Of whom do we speak?"

"Of a boy called Ushiwaka, who, you may recall, is the son of the late Minomoto general Yoshitomo."

"Ah. What of him?"

"He has disappeared from the temple, my lord."

Kiyomori paused before asking, "And Abbot Tōkōbō feels that this news concerns me?"

"My lord, for the past several years, Ushiwaka has paid little heed to his religious studies, refused to take the vows and tonsure and, it is rumored, he spent his nights studying swordsmanship. He has learned of his parentage, and some say he has vowed to kill you."

Kiyomori felt the spiders scuttle down his back again, bearing icicles this time. "How old is Ushiwaka now?"

"Fifteen or so, my lord."

Kiyomori rubbed his chin. "Perhaps this Ushiwaka fell in with bad company or thieves and lies dead somewhere."

"That is, of course, an unfortunate possibility," said the young monk, "but Ushiwaka was last seen in the company of a *yamabushi* named Shōmon. We have since learned that Shōmon has some sympathies with the Minomoto. It is feared that this holy man may have somehow helped Ushiwaka travel toward the East."

To the East, the base of Minomoto power and support. I had thought the Minomoto weakened beyond hope. But the Taira have many enemies, and if those foes find a Minomoto heir to rally around, if Go-Shirakawa decides to use the Minomoto once more as a check on Taira power . . . Kiyomori tried to hold his growing fear and rage in control. He could not let the visitor see he might be upset by the news of one delinquent boy. "I see. I trust all efforts are being made to find him?"

"Messengers were sent to post stations and barrier gates as soon as Abbot Tōkōbō suspected he was gone for good. But no one has reported seeing a youth of Ushiwaka's description."

"Then the boy may not have yet gotten far. I thank you for bringing this news. Please feel free to take lodging here tonight. When you return to Kuramadera, let Tōkōbō know that this Ushiwaka is to be brought to Rokuhara as soon as he is found. We cannot let the mercy of the Taira be flouted in this manner. If the boy will not observe the strictures of his exile, then he must be punished."

"Yes, of course, my lord. Er, Kiyomori-sama . . . ?"

"Yes?"

"Do you know of *tengu*?"

"What, those fairy stories about bird-men? What of them?"

The young monk paused and then shook his head. "Never mind, my lord. Forget I spoke of them. It is late, and I am weary."

"Huh. Then you had better go and rest." Kiyomori called for a servant to escort the young monk to guest quarters and gave orders for preparations to return himself to the capital within a day. He gave orders to another servant to ride to Heian Kyō and alert his spies in the capital to watch for Ushiwaka. He managed to maintain his calm until they had all left.

Then he grabbed the letters before him and tore them all savagely into little pieces.

Hiraizumi

For over twenty days, Yoshitsune, the former Ushiwaka, traveled, going ever eastward through Shinano Province, and Suruga. He had hoped to visit his brother, Yoritomo, who was also in exile at a monastery in Izu. But Yoshitsune was told that his brother was well guarded, so Yoshitsune had to content himself with sending a brief message:

> This fledgling white dove
> at last flies, hoping to catch
> butterflies in his beak
>
> He hopes that he may be
> a good omen to you.

They traveled through Ashigara Pass, through the provinces of Musashi and Shimotsuke. Kichiji did his trading as though it were his usual business, while Yoshitsune offered prayers at any temple they stopped near and tried to gather word on what supporters there might yet be for the Minomoto clan. What he learned was heartening, although he needed to use great caution.

Farther north and eastward the caravan traveled, through the Shirakawa Barrier, past Asaka Marsh and Mount Atsukashi until they finally reached Kurihara Temple in the far reaches of Ōshū Province.

Many tales are told of Yoshitsune on this journey, of women he wooed and left, of bandits he fought, of narrow escapes from suspicious Taira retainers and jealous husbands. He would not have had time for them all to be true, and surely had he made such an impression along the way, word of who he was and where he was going would easily have gotten back to Heian Kyō. But he was a young man on the first grand journey of his life, so let us assume that a few such tales are true and he arrived at Kurihara Temple a more seasoned young man than the one who had left Kuramadera.

Yoshitsune was warmly received at Kurihara Temple and made a guest of the abbot, while Kichiji went on ahead to Hiraizumi to announce their arrival.

When Kichiji returned the next day, he was accompanied by 350 mounted warriors to escort Yoshitsune into Hiraizumi.

Yoshitsune was astonished when he saw the escort. "Do I need an army, Kichiji, for my protection even in this far province?"

Kichiji laughed, "No, my young lordling. These are the household warriors of Fujiwara Hidehira, who sent them, as well as two of his sons, as a sign of his regard for your family. Hidehira would have come himself, but he suffers a slight cold. He has had an auspicious dream about you, however, and anticipates your arrival with great joy."

Benkei clapped a meaty hand on Yoshitsune's shoulder. "Three hundred and fifty warriors, hmm? Not a mighty force, but it is a start, neh?"

"It is a start," Yoshitsune murmured as he stared out from the temple verandah at the assembled warriors. They raised their armored fists in salute, and cried, "Hail to the son of Yoshitomo! Hail to the great Minomoto!" Yoshitsune felt a warmth fill him, an expanding joy. This was where he was meant to be, a leader of warriors. He could not stop grinning as he was led to a fine, spirited black warhorse and helped into the saddle.

"So," Yoshitsune said to Kichiji, "I assume I will not be needing the straw raincoat today?"

"You will not," said Kichiji. "And the swords you bear will be your own. Please forgive any insult this humble servant has given you, for I am proud to have been able to escort you."

"All is forgiven, good Kichiji."

"Then shall we ride on to Hiraizumi, my lord?"

"Let us ride!"

A cheer roared out of the throats of the assembled warriors, and Yoshitsune happily let the horse have its head, riding to the front. He led the warriors, galloping, up the road to Hiraizumi.

Yoshitsune was astonished as they entered the city gates, and slowed his horse to a walk. Hiraizumi was nearly the equal of Heian Kyō in size and beauty. Gold and silver and jewels of all sorts decorated the buildings, and an enormous temple called Chusonji dominated the city. Though it was still late summer in the capital, autumn was just beginning to arrive in this far northern province, and the tips of the gingko trees had begun to turn gold to match the gold on the building roof tiles.

Crowds lined the streets in curiosity, waving and cheering at Yoshitsune as he passed. Yoshitsune felt like a prince arriving in some glorious fairy country to reclaim a throne that had always been his. He rode proudly up to the gates of the mansion of Fujiwara Hidehira, which was of course the largest, most elegant mansion in the city.

Hidehira himself was waiting on the steps of the mansion as Yoshitsune and his escort rode into the Fujiwara compound. "Welcome! Welcome, son of Yoshitomo, to my house! It is a great honor to me that you have traveled all this way to be my guest. Your arrival brings a new era to the Two Provinces, and now we may act according to our hearts."

Yoshitsune dismounted and bowed. "It is my great honor, Hidehira-sama, to be welcomed into your esteemed house. Without your assistance, I would not have a hope of reclaiming the glory of the Minomoto. But with your help, we may again prove ourselves."

"And help you shall have. These 350 are yours to command, and I will add more to their number. Thousands, if you wish it."

Yoshitsune bowed again. "You are more than generous, Hidehira-sama. I shall try to prove worthy of your gift."

"Speaking of gifts," Hidehira said, "we must not overlook the good Kichiji, who has risked his fortune and his life to see you safely here." He called to some servants who brought forth chest after chest of goods to set before the amazed gold merchant. "In these chests you will find a hundred tanned deerskin hides, a hundred eagle feathers, a hundred bolts of Oshu's finest silk, a hundred pairs of bear-pelt boots, and a hundred bottles of plum wine. You will also be given three of our best horses and, as you are a gold merchant by trade, a box of pure gold dust. I hope you will consider these offerings sufficient recompense for your brave and noble efforts."

Kichiji stared at the chests, openmouthed. "This . . . this . . . is more than sufficient, Hidehira-sama."

Yoshitsune walked up to the gold merchant and grasped his arm. "It is no less than you deserve, good Kichiji-san. I would give you gifts myself, had I any to give. Wait, here, I have these swords which I have already borne in your name—"

"No, no, good young lordling, keep those I beg you," said Kichiji. "It was my honor to guide you here. As for your gift to me, well, remember this gold merchant kindly when you are lord of Heian Kyō in place of that tyrant Kiyomori. That will be a suitable time for gifts."

"Those sound like words of parting," said Hidehira. "It is hardly time for that yet. Come in and be feasted. There will be time for parting later."

The Dharma Lamp

Lord Kiyomori plucked a fallen red maple leaf from his charcoal gray sleeve. He paced the verandah of Nishihachijō in Heian Kyō, gazing to the north and east, awaiting news. *Demons take Go-Shirakawa for his meddling,* he thought.

Kiyomori had returned to the capital in late summer only to learn that

the Retired Emperor had been again offending temples. Kiyomori was unable to learn whether it was deliberate or inadvertent on the *In*'s part, but
it hardly mattered. Ever since the funeral of Emperor Nijō, the Buddhist
temples had been spoiling for a fight, and leapt on any pretext to take
offense.

This time it was the *In*'s consecration, as he went from novice to full
monkhood. Go-Shirakawa had originally chosen the temple of Miidera for
the Dharma-Transmitting Water ceremony, but this set off such political
contention that the *In* was forced to change his plans. Instead he had gone
to Tennoji, the oldest Buddhist temple in Nihon, to have the five flasks of
wisdom-water drawn from the Kamei Well.

But, as it turned out, this solved nothing. For the worker- and warrior-
monks of Enryakuji had been considering revolt against the very scholar-
monks they served. And because the warrior-monks were not equally invited
and represented at the *In*'s consecration ceremony, the temple complex atop
Mount Hiei erupted into war.

Kiyomori was awaiting news of the battle, as several hundred Taira
warriors had been sent to aid the scholar-monks. But from the verandah he
could see smoke to the northeast blending in with the autumnal haze, and
he feared things were not going well.

A messenger arrived, but he had not come from Mount Hiei. He was
one of Kiyomori's city spies, delivering his seven-day report.

"What is it?" Kiyomori demanded of him.

"There is no further word of the Minomoto boy, Kiyomori-sama, not
in Heian Kyō."

"Hmm. And elsewhere?"

"Rumors come in from everywhere, my lord, but few are to be believed.
Far to the north, they tell of a young warrior who has entered Fujiwara
Hidehira's service. But there is so much said of that one's fighting prowess
that he cannot be the same boy. No one raised in a monastery could be
such a swordsman without your knowing of it."

"Ah. It has been over two months," Kiyomori mused, "and there is no
confirmed sighting of Ushiwaka. Perhaps we can put this matter to rest and
have you put to better tasks."

"My lord, if I may be so bold, I have learned where the boy's mother,
Tokiwa, now resides. Your wife, the Nii no Ama, has a suggestion. Just as
you had captured Tokiwa's mother to ensure Tokiwa's surrender, perhaps
you should capture Tokiwa and threaten to torture her in order to ensure
the son's surrender."

Cold dragon bitch, thought Kiyomori. *Does she seek a wife's vengeance
after so many years? Or does she just want to rub my face in the fact that she
was right—the boy should have been killed long ago.* "No!" Kiyomori

shouted. Then he added, "As my son Shigemori so often reminds me, what I do affects the reputation of the Taira. Anything so brutal would be used as further proof that I am a tyrant. No, I will assume Ushiwaka has run into bad fortune and should no longer be considered a threat. Regarding my son, Shigemori . . ."

"I am sorry, my lord. He still will accept no messages from you and will send no additional men for your effort on Mount Hiei."

"Hmm." Shigemori had been aloof to Kiyomori ever since the news had arrived in Heian Kyō of the exiled Narachika's death. It seemed the former middle counselor had somehow managed to fall off a high cliff onto a field of sharpened bamboo. Shigemori had seemed curiously unwilling to accept Kiyomori's explanation that it must have been an accident. "Ah, well, if my son insists upon remaining estranged from me, then—"

There came the clatter of hooves in the main courtyard. "The scouts from Mount Hiei have returned!" came a cry from the gate of Nishihachijō.

"Go," Kiyomori said to the spy, who bowed and left silently.

Kiyomori went out to the courtyard, where two men in dirtied, blood-stained armor knelt at the bottom of the steps. He noted the despair in their faces. "Well?"

"Kiyomori-sama, we were too late. Your men did all they could, but General Munemori seemed . . . unprepared for the opposition we faced."

"I should not have sent Munemori," Kiyomori grumbled to himself. "He has no skill in warcraft, but I thought this would be a simple mission. And Munemori claimed he needed a victory to bring honor to his name."

"General Munemori should not be blamed, Kiyomori-sama," said the other scout. "The warrior-monks had gathered every brigand, thief, criminal, and ruffian they could find to fight with them. The scholar-monks were overwhelmed before we even reached Enryakuji."

"He did have some difficulty deciding where to lead his forces," the other scout conceded. "But once the sanctuaries were destroyed by fire, General Munemori fought most assiduously to drive the ruffians off the mountain."

After a moment, Kiyomori decided. "Bring me a horse. I will go see this and speak with Munemori myself." Putting on only a cuirass and a helmet, Kiyomori gathered a hundred warriors of his household and rode out of the capital.

It took the rest of the day to travel the road that wound up the flanks of Mount Hiei. The bodies of monks, scholars and warriors both, lined the sides of the road as a testament to the fierce battle that had been waged there. As the sun touched the top of the western hills, Kiyomori and his men reached the smoldering ruins of what once had been the greatest temple complex in the land.

The gates of Enryakuji were battered and broken open. Perhaps more disturbing than the bodies were the shattered remnants of sacred statuary, bits of Buddhas, *bosatsu*, and guardian demons scattered heedlessly in the trampled ground. Sanctuaries that had housed the sacred writings of centuries were no more than piles of charred wood and ash. The treasure-houses had gaping holes in their roofs and walls.

Kiyomori looked about at the destruction with dismay. Although he was not a strongly religious man, despite his studies and novice vows, there was something deeply disturbing about the loss of so ancient and grand an edifice. That the *kami* and *bosatsu* would allow such a thing to happen did not bode well.

Three Taira horsemen in armor emerged from the ruins and came riding up to him. The middle one removed his helmet and mask. It was Munemori. "Father, you should not have come."

"I had to see this for myself. What are the current conditions?"

"Muneshige and his men have driven the ruffians off the mountain and it is doubtful the worker-monks will return. Though the worker-monks were victorious in killing many of the scholar-monks, they will taste no fruit of that victory."

"What madness caused such a rebellion, Munemori?"

Munemori shifted uncomfortably in his saddle. "Only the greed of men who had forgotten their place in the world, Father, and strove for greater rewards than they deserved."

Kiyomori narrowed his eyes at Munemori, for such words had at times been used against the Taira. "My observers tell me you hesitated before choosing to attack."

"Forgive me, Father, but they were not in the midst of things, and, therefore, they could not know the terrible confusion that reigned here. Some of the worker-monks fought on behalf of the scholars, and I dared not press an attack until I was certain who was the enemy."

Kiyomori nodded, but this was only confirmation to him that Munemori was still lacking in martial talent. *I shall not give him such leadership again.*

A heartrending cry erupted from a nearby ruined building. "Ai! Ai! Oh, woe! Most grievous woe."

Kiyomori put his hand on his sword hilt as an ancient monk, clearly one of the scholars, hobbled out from between two broken pillars. Tears streamed down his seamed face, and his eyes rolled in grief and fear. Kiyomori rode up to him. "Peace, Holy One. I, Jokai, also known as Taira no Kiyomori, offer apologies that my men did not reach you in time to spare your temple buildings. But they can be rebuilt, and Enryakuji can be made great again. Lend your thoughts to hope, not despair."

But the old monk did not seem to hear him. "The lamp! The dharma lamp!"

"What of it?"

"It has blown out!"

Kiyomori felt a chill in his soul, though he could not think why. "Then have it relit."

The old monk shook his head. "It was first lit three centuries ago by the founder of the temple. It cannot be relit until a man of equal holiness comes again, which I fear we will not see. It is surely a sign of the *mappo*, the End of the Law. There is nothing to be done."

Munemori rode up beside Kiyomori. "What is the old man raving about?"

"Shhh."

"There will be no more protection from the demons," wailed the old man. "Without Enryakuji in the northeast, there will be nothing to protect Heian Kyō from the evil winds."

"Peace, fellow," Kiyomori repeated. "Enryakuji will be rebuilt."

"That will take a great deal of time, Father," said Munemori. "The monks are scattered in the four directions, and His Majesty may be reluctant to spend so much at this time."

Kiyomori scowled at his son. *Does Munemori want Enryakuji to stay in ruins? Or is he simply bad at diplomacy as well?*

Munemori seemed ill at ease beneath Kiyomori's gaze. "I . . . I only meant that it is an unkindness to reassure this holy one with misleading blandishments. Mount Hiei will see difficult times ahead before things are better, that is all."

Kiyomori turned again to speak to the ancient monk, but the old man was lost in his sorrows, sitting on the broken temple steps, rocking back and forth.

"There is nothing more for us to do here," said Kiyomori to his men. "Let us return to Nishihachijō." With a parting glare at Munemori, Kiyomori led his warriors out past the ruined lintels of the temple gate, feeling a cold wind at his back.

The Comet

You see, it has grown larger and brighter, Majesty."

"Yes. Quite discernibly." Retired Emperor Go-Shirakawa stood on the verandah on the eastern wing of ToSanjō Palace, staring up at the comet in the winter sky. He pulled his gray brocade robes tighter around him to ward off the night chill.

The New Year's festivities marking the arrival of the second year of the era of Jishō had been less than pleasant—his guests had worn a veneer of civility over their tension and distrust. Particularly the Taira. *How like Kiyomori and his kin to blame me for all that has gone wrong. Has Narichika not paid for the Shishinotani plot? As if I did not know that Kiyomori arranged his death. And now the Taira think I caused the destruction on Mount Hiei.*

In truth, Go-Shirakawa had done nothing to incite the monks to riot and destroy Enryakuji. But the Retired Emperor had had to admit to himself that he was not entirely displeased at the outcome. There would be no more armies of warrior-monks disrupting the city and harassing the Imperial palace. The ruins on Mount Hiei were a symbol of shame to the monks of other temples, too; therefore, they also had been quiescent the past several months. For this reason, Go-Shirakawa delayed giving any decision on Kiyomori's petition to have Enryakuji rebuilt. Why disturb such peace, no matter what calamity had brought it?

And so the Retired Emperor and Lord Kiyomori had sat declaring toasts to each other over cups of the New Year's rice wine, with smiles like those upon painted masks.

Until the old man from the Imperial Yin-Yang Office had arrived, requesting that Go-Shirakawa view the comet with him. The Retired Emperor had been pleased for the distraction and readily agreed.

"The comet has revealed itself as the sort called Chi Yu's Banner, or Red Spirit," said the man beside Go-Shirakawa. He was an elderly member of the Northern branch of the Oe family, who held the post in charge of Celestial Portents in the Imperial Yin-Yang Office. "You will note, Majesty, that the tail has taken on a distinct reddish hue."

"Yes," said Go-Shirakawa. "The Taira are boasting that this is yet another good omen for them, since red is the color of their banner. Lord Kiyomori claims this shows the Taira remain ascendant in the eyes of Heaven."

A hint of an embarrassed frown crossed the elderly Oe's brow. "I regret to say Lord Kiyomori is in error, Majesty. A comet is always an inauspicious sign. That is why His Majesty, Emperor Takakura, requested that I come speak to you."

Go-Shirakawa closed his eyes. "My son is concerned for his wife, the Empress Kenreimon'in, and her illness. I understand that your office is performing rituals on her behalf?"

"Everything we can, my lord. As is every temple surrounding the capital. The palace is overflowing with doctors."

Go-Shirakawa gripped the railing of the verandah. *Surely the Amida would not be so unkind*, he thought, *to allow Kenreimon'in to pass from this world so soon.* Though she was Kiyomori's daughter, Go-Shirakawa felt no ill will toward her. Quite the contrary, for Kenreimon'in had spent some years in Go-Shirakawa's household as a child, learning the ways of the Imperial Court. She was like a daughter to him.

The elderly Oe's gaze was averted, darting from one thing to another. Clearly there was something more he wished to say.

"What is it?" asked Go-Shirakawa. "Feel free to speak your concern to me."

"I . . . I am not so worried for the Empress as some might be, Majesty, for illnesses come and go, and ladies are prone to many complaints of the body. The portent of the comet disturbs me not because it may bring misfortune, but because some will see the comet as a sign justifying the evil already present in their thoughts."

Go-Shirakawa narrowed his eyes. "I am not sure I am understanding you."

"Majesty, it is no secret that many wish the Taira ill will. Some of these may use this opportunity to bring a rebellion. Such an uprising might, unfortunately, be blamed upon yourself, Majesty. We at the palace feel it would be dreadful if such rumors were to spread, staining the reputation of the Imperial House. We all know how tirelessly you have worked for peace in Heian Kyō."

Is the old goat chiding me, warning me, or is he simply an imbecile? wondered Go-Shirakawa. "Yes, certainly, this is a matter for concern. I thank you for alerting me to this possibility.

The man from the Yin-Yang Office bowed low. "Then I have done all I was sent to do. May you have an auspicious New Year, Majesty."

Minomoto Yoshitsune gazed out at the winter moon and the comet that hung beside it. He was still entwined in his lover's arms, a lady-in-waiting of Fujiwara Hidehira's household, with whom he had left the New Year festivities early.

"What are you staring at?" whispered the girl. "I think I am becoming jealous that you would rather look at the moon than at me."

"Not at all," said Yoshitsune. "I was comparing the moon's face to yours and noting that her visage cannot possibly match your beauty. How pockmarked and gray the moon is, while your cheeks are smooth and white as pearls."

"Silly flatterer. Do you see the comet as well?"

"Yes, of course, but I did not wish to bring up a bad omen at such a time as this. Clearly it indicates the coming downfall of the Taira."

"And you will be the one to bring that downfall," said the girl, wriggling eagerly beneath him. "Everyone says so. Hidehira is amazed with how well you are training his men. We ladies constantly overhear him boasting about you. You are the greatest swordsman in the land, and you will be the greatest hero Nihon has ever seen."

Yoshitsune blushed, but he had to concede that, in his own opinion, Hidehira was probably right.

*M*inomoto Yoritomo also observed the comet that night, from the verandah of his house in Izu, escaping for a moment the family New Year's party. As the years had passed, the monks of the temple had come to trust and admire Yoritomo, and so they had allowed Yoritomo to move into his father-in-law's house when he married, and no longer watched his every movement. Yoritomo was well aware he was still not a free man, but it hardly seemed to matter. He had lived a quiet life, a sober life, and he was in a way grateful to the Amida that he had been exiled here, away from the decadent influences of the capital.

"Yori-chan," said his wife chidingly as she appeared at the *shōji* doorway behind him, "aren't you returning to the festivities? Father says he wishes to have a poetry contest."

Yoritomo frowned. "Why? That is a Heike thing, a Fujiwara thing. We are in the provinces, and there is nothing to be ashamed of in that. Why should we ape the ways of those who think themselves Above The Clouds? I would no more do so than stain my teeth or paint my face white."

His wife sighed. "You are upset by the comet, aren't you?"

"I merely needed to take some fresh air. The smoke from the lamps was distressing me." But, in truth, she was right.

"Father says the comet indicates there are dire events ahead. He has heard the Empress is ill."

"These are events that will occur in the capital, far from us. Not our concern."

He felt his wife's gaze on his back for long moments. Then she said, "Return to us soon."

"I will."

He heard the rustle of her kimonos as his wife departed for the common room.

Yoritomo looked back at the comet. In fact, he feared it did portend matters that would be his concern. Yoritomo had been receiving more letters from the Minomoto spy who served in Rokuhara, informing him of how Lord Kiyomori appeared to be going mad, of how the Taira were bullying the citizenry on the streets, of how they allowed Enryakuji to be destroyed. "Someone must save us from this terrible tyranny. Who but the Minomoto could accomplish such a thing? Who but the son of Yoshitomo could lead such a righteous war and avenge his father?"

The comet hung in the sky, wavering like a red banner in the wind, the banner of an enemy summoning him to war.

News of Infants

*T*wo months passed, and the snow and ice of winter melted, turning the Imperial gardens into mud. It was Kenreimon'in's least favorite time of year, for though the air beckoned warmth to come, still the trees bore no leaves, and no flowers bloomed. The ailment that had plagued her during the winter had passed but a new illness had taken its place, and she had been unable to eat.

Do the gods punish me for wielding Kusanagi? she had wondered.

But after her woman's blood did not come, she began to wonder, remembering stories her mother had told. Kenreimon'in sent for the Minister of the Imperial Bureau of Medicine, and he in turn sent for an elderly nun.

Now this old woman poked and prodded at very private places on the Empress's person, mumbling the Lotus Sutra. Kenreimon'in gazed out at the bleak gardens, trying to think on other things. She concentrated on not crying out or wincing when tender spots were touched.

"For how long has your Majesty missed your bleeding?"

"Ten days, I think."

"And how long have you been ill?"

"Um, fourteen days, I think."

"And how old are you?"

"Twenty-three."

"So you were born in a year of the Serpent?"

"Yes."

"And your husband, His Majesty?"

"Born in a year of the Rooster."

"Mmm." At last the old woman sat back, a satisfied smile on her face. "May I be permitted to make the announcement, Majesty?"

"Announcement?"

"That you are with child."

"Ah. Yes. Of course. You may do so." Kenreimon'in smiled, but she was aware there was pain in her expression.

"Fear not, Majesty. All will be well." The old nun bowed low and, more swiftly than one might expect for her age, passed through the vermilion gauze curtains and hurried to the *shōji*. Kneeling at the doorway, she intoned, "I have blissful news. Her Majesty is with child!"

As swift as the fire that had burned the capital, word spread out from that doorway. Kenreimon could hear clearly through the wood-and-paper walls the word being passed from servant to servant and noble to noble. It always surprised her that such private things could be of such public interest. But she was Empress, and very little of her life was private.

Kenreimon gazed down at her belly, which was long from showing signs of the resident within. "So, you will be the Taira Emperor who was foretold," she murmured. "Stay warm and safe, little one, for I do not know what sort of world will greet you when you at last arrive."

Munemori had been at the palace on other business when the word reached him. He called for an ox-carriage and left immediately for Nishihachijō, pleased that he would be the one to deliver the news to Kiyomori.

The ox-carriage bounced and jostled Munemori, but he did not mind. He had told the driver to go as fast as he could, and he could hear the driver haranguing the traffic ahead. "Make way! Make way for the important Taira personage! All must allow my master to pass!"

Munemori meanwhile daydreamed of the future, and what this news might mean. Surely this was the beginning of his good fortune, for surely the new little Emperor would come to see his uncle Munemori's worth and promote him to high positions. *Perhaps that is how I will become Chief of the Taira*, Munemori thought. *Perhaps I will even someday achieve my father's post of Chancellor.*

Visits to the palace might become frequent, for Munemori's own wife had a child on the way, due in only a couple of months. *If it is a son, he and the Crown Prince will be playmates, and I will be invited to dine with Takakura as we watch the boys at play. If a girl, perhaps someday she may be consort to the little Emperor, for it is not unknown for cousins to marry. And then I, myself, might have a grandson who is Emperor.*

Munemori arrived at Nishihachijō drunk on visions of future glory, and demanded to be taken to his father Kiyomori at once.

His father looked up in surprise and annoyance when Munemori walked in. Munemori noted the gray of Kiyomori's hair and the sagging of his frame. *He is getting so old*, thought Munemori. *No wonder he is not long to be Chief of the Taira.*

"Munemori. What is the meaning of this? Have you lost all sense of manners and filial deference?"

"Rejoice, Father, for I bring you good news. Your daughter, my sister, the Empress is with child."

For once, his father's reaction was not disappointing. Kiyomori's eyes widened, and he smiled. "With child? With child? At last! How wondrous!" He jumped to his feet and did a little dance of joy. Kiyomori grabbed every servant and relation who happened by, and said, "Have you heard my son's news? The Taira Emperor is coming! My daughter is with child!"

Soon the whole mansion was bubbling and burbling with the happy news, and Munemori stood in the midst of it, steeping in the joy and good-will like a ball of spring tea leaves. Kiyomori invited him to stay through the evening, and they drank plum wine and sake together, toasting every member of Emperor Takakura's family, even Go-Shirakawa.

Other Taira arrived, including Munemori's younger brothers Shigehira and Tomomori, as well as his mother, Nii no Ama, to join in the celebration. Smugly, Munemori noted that his elder brother, the shining Shigemori, did not make an appearance.

It was well after sundown when a servant arrived from Munemori's household. "My lord, you must come home at once."

"What? Go away. I will come home when I am ready."

"My lord, I regret that I must be so bold, but you must come."

"My wife sent you, didn't she?"

"It . . . is a matter concerning her, my lord, yes."

It was then that Munemori noted the paleness of the servant's face and the redness in the eyes. "Is she ill? What is it?"

"These are matters not to be spoken of before others. Please, my lord. Come home and see."

Nii no Ama overheard the servant, and she looked over and said, "Do not be a boor, Munemori. Go home and see to your wife."

So Munemori again got into the ox-carriage, in a far worse mood, and endured another jostling journey. This time his thoughts were more grim. "If this is merely another whim of hers, I will strike her. If she is ill, I will chide her for being careless." He heard the wheels and ox hooves squelching in the spring mud and thought it a most dismal sound.

When at last the carriage bumped over the threshold beam of his mansion's gate, Munemori peered out the carriage window. The buildings were dark, as lamps of the mansion had been left unlit, and he could hear weeping from within. A cold fear began to fill him. Munemori jumped out of the carriage and rushed into the mansion, despite the servants trying to catch his sleeve to slow his progress.

Munemori ran to the sleeping quarters and there he saw the body, wrapped in white silk, stained with blood at the edges. The body was sur-rounded by weeping maidservants and chanting monks, who looked up at Munemori's arrival.

He fell to his knees. "Wha—what happened?"

"The child . . ." one of the women gasped through her tears, "it came too early. We tried to help her, but the blood . . . there was too much blood."

"Ah." Munemori felt tears welling in his eyes. He could hardly speak for his throat closed tight. "And the baby? What of the baby?"

The woman only shook her head.

"Noooo!" Munemori screamed, and he fought his way through the seated people to where the body lay. He grabbed his dead wife's shoulders through the silk and shook her. "How could you do this to me? How could you do this? We might have been grandparents to an Emperor!" He fell forward onto the body and wept upon her cold breast.

The servants surrounded him and tugged gently on his sleeves and shoulders. "My lord, this is unseemly. My lord, come away and let the monks see to her. My lord, there is nothing more you can do. My lord, you are not to blame." Munemori let himself be led away to a dark room, where he wept into his sleeves for a long time. The servants brought him tea, and hot cloths blessed by the monks with which to wash his hands, for he had touched the dead. Munemori demanded that the servants leave him alone, and they did so.

When his thoughts again gathered themselves, Munemori wondered at what one of the servants had said, that he was not to blame. "But am I?" he murmured to himself. He became aware of the scent of ashes in the air. Munemori looked up and saw the ghostly form of the Shin-In sitting across the room from him.

"Munemori-san," said the ghost with a regal nod. "Why do you weep?"

"Is this it?" Munemori demanded. "Is this the sacrifice that you told me would be nothing?"

"At the time the bargain was made," intoned the Imperial demon-spirit, "your wife meant nothing to you."

"I was becoming fond of her again!"

"How was I to know your heart would change?"

"And the child . . . Why did you have to take the child?"

The shade shrugged. "What does it matter? You can always have another."

Munemori sputtered and grabbed one of the blessed towels, which he threw at the Shin-in. But the ghost merely leaned aside, and the cloth splatted harmlessly against the wall.

"If you wish to break our bargain," the Shin-In continued, "I am sure I can find another candidate to lead the Taira into glory. You have other brothers, I have noted."

"No!" growled Munemori, clenching his fists. "I have paid the price, so now you must give me what I have paid for!"

"That is all I have ever intended," said the Shin-In. "And, I assure you, my side of the bargain shall be kept."

"It had better be," said Munemori.

"Oh. One more thing," said the Shin-In. "When it comes time for your sister, the Empress, to do her lying-in, you will see to it that she is taken to Rokuhara. I am sure you remember which wing of Rokuhara it is that I intend?"

"The guest wing," Munemori said bleakly, "where you have haunted."

"Where I still haunt, from time to time," said the Shin-In, "to keep an eye on things. Since Kiyomori and Tokiko moved out, the servants have been criminally lax about maintaining the wardings. And now that Enryakuji is in ruins, my kind can travel about the capital with much greater ease. Thanks to you."

"So pleased to be of service," hissed Munemori. "*Why?*"

"Why?"

"Why do you wish the Imperial birth to be at Rokuhara?"

"Should I not be present for the birth of my relation? Anyone of importance makes a point of attending a royal birth. Am I not important?"

"In what manner will you be . . . present?"

For a moment, the Shin-In's eyes grew cold. "It is not wise for a servant to question his master. All will become clear in time." Then his expression lightened. "But calm yourself, Munemori-san, and be of good cheer. After all, you will soon have a nephew who will be an Emperor." With a knowing smile, the Shin-In vanished.

Munemori flung himself to the floor, moaning and tearing his silk robes into rags.

Preparations

Lord Kiyomori strode happily through the corridors of Rokuhara, overseeing the preparation of the guest wing to receive the Imperial lying-in. The lesser Taira who had been residing there were moved out, the floors completely repaired and repolished, and new screens of brocade silk with gold thread moved in, along with low tables of ebony and teak, and lacquer chests with jade inlays. An army of servants would have to be hired to tend to the monks, priests, and nobles who would also be in attendance at the birth. Arrangements had to be made with rice farmers in Taira-governed provinces to ensure enough provisions would be available. Taira sailors were commissioned to bring precious oranges from the south and ample fish from the sea. The expense was enormous, but Kiyomori was a very wealthy man.

And besides, it was for the Taira Emperor. He would spare no cost to see that everything was perfect.

Kiyomori's robes stuck to him in the summer heat, yet he felt no discomfort, as he directed the hanging of lanterns and tapestries, and the replanting of gardens so that they would be at their best in early winter when the Empress and her newborn might see them. The planning had occupied his mind for months, yet no one in his family or the government complained of his obsession. In fact, they seemed to encourage him. Kiyomori was beginning to suspect the nobles of the council were pleased to have him out of their hair for a while.

It had been Munemori's suggestion that the lying-in be at Rokuhara. "What better way to show the world it is a Taira Emperor than to have the birth at the seat of the Taira clan itself?" he had said. "Kenreimon'in is your daughter, no one could possibly argue the propriety. And that way you may ensure the safety of the child, for there are still those in the palace who harbor animosity toward our clan."

Kiyomori could not fault his son's logic and had readily agreed. *For once, Munemori is the one speaking sense,* Kiyomori thought. *Ever since the death of his wife and child, he has sobered into a thoughtful, serious young man. Perhaps he will amount to something after all.*

Shigemori and Nii no Ama had protested, of course. Shigemori had suggested his own mansion, or even Go-Shirakawa's palace, but Kiyomori would not hear of it. Nii no Ama had said dire things about how Rokuhara had been haunted. But Kiyomori assumed she wanted control of the child for the Dragon King's sake, and Kiyomori did not even reply to her messages. Curiously, Go-Shirakawa had remained silent on the matter. He would have had the right to complain, given that he was father to the Emperor and would be grandfather to the child. But the Retired Emperor had demurred, saying he would agree to whatever the Imperial couple wished.

Kenreimon'in herself had sealed the decision, stating in a letter to Shigemori that she looked forward to returning to Rokuhara. "I have such fond memories of playing there as a child that surely the familiar surroundings will comfort me as I bring a child of my own into the world."

Kiyomori surveyed the great room in the guest wing with some satisfaction. *Soon any Emperor would be proud to say he had resided here,* he thought. Glancing up, Kiyomori noticed some dried flowers and tattered silk ribbons stuck onto the crossbeams. "What are those?" he shouted to a nearby elderly maidservant.

She bowed low and said, "My lord, Nii no Ama had us put those up there after the . . . unpleasantness some years ago. They are to protect this room against evil spirits. She was most emphatic that they should not be removed."

Kiyomori frowned. "We will have monks from every temple and priests from every shrine attending this birth. Do you think they cannot protect Her Majesty from demons and spirits? Remove those ratty ornaments at once! They are out of season, and therefore inappropriate and may bring bad luck themselves."

"As my lord wishes," said the old woman, fear and uncertainty in her eyes.

The Lying-In

Kenreimon'in leaned upon the arms of her maidservants as they led her out to the awaiting carriage. Her belly felt so heavy and full she could scarcely breathe. She could not see her feet to know whether she would be treading on the early-winter ice. She was afraid.

Kenreimon remembered hearing how her sister-in-law, Munemori's wife, had died. It was not unusual, even in the capital of Heian Kyō, for women to die in childbirth, often after much pain. Despite the reassurances of her servants and the Office of the Imperial Household, Kenreimon found herself often fingering her prayer beads and murmuring sutras for a safe delivery.

Her feet slipped out from under her, and Kenreimon'in cried out. It was only the many hands of the servants surrounding her that kept her from falling. As it was, she nearly embarassed herself by letting water. She wanted to cry but put on a brave face for the sake of her ladies. She must set a good example of how an Empress behaves.

I have borne up well these past few months, Kenreimon'in reminded herself. *I even politely tolerated the monks who came to do spells to turn the child into a boy in case the gods had chosen otherwise. I can surely bear a few indignities a while longer.*

At last, Kenreimon'in arrived at the covered ox-carriage. The street was thick with Taira warriors in full armor on horseback, waiting to escort her to Rokuhara. The warriors bowed low from their saddles to her. She recognized one of them as her brother Shigehira, just a couple of years older than she. He smiled at her from beneath his snow-dusted helmet, and his smile gave her courage.

The back door of the ox-carriage was opened. The maid servants took Kenreimon'in's arms and helped her up the tiny steps and through the narrow doorway.

"How are you, my daughter?" The voice was familiar, and came from a woman draped in a gray kimono and hood.

"Mother!" Kenreimon'in said with joy. Though her mother, Nii no Ama, had sent her many letters of encouragement, Kenreimon had not seen her in a long time. "You are coming with me to Rokuhara?"

"I will stay with you until the child is born, and even after."

Kenreimon'in smiled and ascended the little ladder up to the carriage. With the help of many hands, she squeezed through the narrow doorway and fell heavily onto the bench seat beside her mother. As she arranged her many layers of kimonos, five of the other ladies-in-waiting climbed in as well and jammed themselves onto the bench opposite her. One last lady appeared at the doorway carrying a long, narrow object wrapped in brocade white silk. Kenreimon'in knew what it was at once.

"Stop!" Kenreimon'in cried. "Do not bring that in here!"

"But Majesty," protested the baffled lady-in-waiting, "this is part of the Imperial Regalia!"

"I know that it is Kusanagi, and I will not allow it near me. It is . . . a powerful thing, and its magic might bring harm to the baby. Or it will surely bring bad fortune. Send it with His Majesty's carriage."

"But Majesty," the lady continued, "the Emperor directed that this should be sent with you, since the Imperial Divination Office has determined that your child will be a boy. He felt it would bring good fortune to the new Crown Prince to have the symbol of Imperial power nearby."

"I will not have it with me," Kenreimon'in said firmly.

"But Majesty—"

"Did you not hear her?" said one of the ladies seated inside. "She is the Empress. Do you disobey her orders?"

The lady-in-waiting bowed. "I am most humbly sorry for my disagreeable nature. I will, of course, comply." She hurried away with the wrapped sword, and the door to the ox-carriage was slammed shut.

Kenreimon'in sighed and turned to her mother. But Nii no Ama was staring at her in distress. "Mother? What is wrong?" Then she remembered there was some connection between Kusanagi and her mother's father, the Dragon King of the Sea. But Kenreimon dared not tell her mother, particularly in front of the court ladies, why she did not wish to be near Kusanagi again. "Did I not do the right thing?"

Nii no Ama glanced warily at the other ladies. She was also, apparently, keeping secrets. She took Kenreimon'in's hand and held it. "You did what you felt was best for your child. That is all a mother can do." She smiled, but her smile was tight and sad.

Two Brothers

M unemori looked up from his teacup as Shigemori barged past the servants and into the room. "Brother, this is exceedingly rude of you."

"Rude of me? It is you who insult our sister and the Emperor by not attending the lying-in!"

Munemori glanced away. "I have sent my apologies and my reasons."

"Yes, yes, you mourn for your lost wife and child. We are sorry for your grief, Munemori, but locking yourself away at this time does no honor to you or her. Meanwhile, you embarrass our family."

"You once told me there is no shame in a nobleman shedding tears."

"A nobleman knows what times are appropriate for displaying his sensitivity. What has come over you, Munemori? Once you were an affable, if foolish, fellow. Once you at least tried to please others around you. You have turned sullen and cold. Surely this cannot be due entirely to grief. If you would only be more open with those of us in your family, we might lighten your burden for you."

"Father finds the changes in me to be admirable."

"Father is—" and the Shigemori shut his mouth and turned away.

"You were about to say Father is mad, weren't you?"

"I was only going to say he tires easily these days and does not always say what he means."

"Well, it appears you take after our father in at least one way, after all. Some of us had been worried you were someone else's get."

Shigemori whirled around and glared at him with narrowed eyes. "These are not the words of a man in grief. Why do you not come to Rokuhara?"

"I have said."

"Then why did you insist on where the lying-in should be if you knew you would not attend? What does it matter to you?"

"Better Rokuhara than To-Sanjō and the aegis of Go-Shirakawa."

Shigemori sighed loudly. "Whatever you may think of him, Go-Shirakawa-In is a man of peace. He would have treated our sister and her child well."

"He also is the enemy of our father, had you forgotten?"

Shigemori shook his head like a horse clearing away flies. "There is no cause for them to be enemies. If only Kiyomori would treat the *In* with trust and respect—"

"He would be trampled over, and our family's fortunes would lie in the dust. If only you would trust our father more, your sight might be more clear on these matters."

"I see that there is no talking sense to you. I beg you to reconsider and come to Rokuhara. For our sister's sake, if no one else. She is fond of you, and it would cheer her to know you are there."

"Please give my regrets to the Empress, but I have made my decision."

"As you wish." Shigemori spun on his heel and departed.

Munemori sighed and went to the verandah where he stared out at the winter garden. He regarded the bare, dead trees, his bare, dead heart. And he shed one genuine tear, for his sister's sake.

The Thousand-Armed Sutra

*K*enreimon'in awoke with a scream. Immediately she was grasped by servants and ladies, who began to raise her up. It felt like the lower half of her body was burning.

"What is it, Majesty? Is it the baby? Is the baby coming?"

Kenreimon'in grabbed a fistfull of silk and hair, she didn't know whose. "My mother . . . where is my mother?" she demanded.

"I am here," said Nii no Ama, her face appearing like a beneficent moon among the concerned women around her. "What is it? Is it time?"

"Mother, I have had a horrible dream! Some man . . . some terrifying man was trying to . . . to enter me. He . . . he's trying to take the baby, Mother!"

The ladies-in-waiting wailed and fluttered. "How awful! What a terrible experience! But it is normal for pregnant women to have nightmares, neh? Surely this is nothing."

But Nii no Ama loosened Kenreimon'in's kimono and rubbed her arms with warm cloths damp with water in which chrysanthemum petals had been steeped. "Tell me more of your dream, if you can."

Kenreimon'in could hardly speak, still gasping in pain and fear. "He was ugly, and grinning, and said something, but I forget what. I don't know now . . . if he was going to kill the baby or possess it! Oh, Mother, it hurts!" Kenreimon'in wished desperately, irrationally, for a knife to slice open her belly, to get the painful thing out.

Nii no Ama said to one of the ladies, "Go and bring us an exorcist. *Now!*"

· · ·

*G*o-Shirakawa sat in an antechamber with Taira Kiyomori, but not companionably close. *Here we are*, he thought, *two old monks about to become grandfathers again, and yet we barely trust one another enough to converse politely.*

The birth was not going well. Despite the presence of all of the abbots from the major temples, each performing his special ritual—the abbot from the Ninna-ji doing the Peacock Sutra ritual, the Tendai abbot executing the Seven Healing Buddha's rite, the Miidera abbot enacting the Kōngo Dōji—there was a spiritual disturbance with the Empress. Despite the Five Great Bodhisattvas ritual and the Five Great Mystic Kings ritual, some evil force was trying to have its way. Rokuhara vibrated with the sounds of bells and holy chanting. Smoke from incense and burning offerings filled the corridors. And still a *yamabushi* with his assistant mediums had to be called for to attend the Empress. Go-Shirakawa could hear the young mediums wailing and thrashing within the chamber. With so much being done on her behalf, how could the Empress be experiencing discomfort?

Go-Shirakawa looked again at Kiyomori. The grizzled old Taira was pale and seemed to be trembling. He often sighed and wiped sweat from his brow. Already there were whispers that the difficult birth was the vengeance of the spirits of the Minomoto warriors who had fallen at Taira hands. *This must be nearly intolerable for him to hear,* thought Go-Shirakawa. *The Buddha taught that compassion is one of the greatest of virtues. Surely, at this time of mutual concern, I can show compassion even to my greatest adversary.*

The Retired Emperor got up and sat next to Kiyomori. "It is difficult, this waiting, neh?"

"Do you know," Kiyomori said softly, "I have never felt such fear, even during the worst of my battles."

"That is because in this battle we are only the standard-bearers. Your daughter's fate must be left to the skills of the holy men."

"Are we not holy men?" asked Kiyomori with a wry, sad smile.

Go-Shirakawa could not think of a reply.

The *yamabushi* emerged from the birthing chamber, also pale and trembling.

"What news?" asked Go-Shirakawa and Kiyomori together.

The *yamabushi* shook his head. "I fear I am at a loss, Majesty, Lord Kiyomori. It is a very strong spirit that we fight, stronger than any I have encountered. He taunts us from the mouths of the mediums and says he will kill the Empress if we do not let him have his way. If only I could learn the spirit's name or the identity he had in life, that might give me the leverage I need. But he is clever and evades my questions. Please excuse me. I must get some air to clear my head a moment so that I may continue the struggle." The *yamabushi* bowed low and shuffled away. He left behind him the scent of ashes hanging in the air.

The scent triggered a memory for Go-Shirakawa, a memory of the last time he had stayed at Rokuhara. He remembered a dream in which a spirit spoke to him, the spirit of his dead brother Sutoku, the Shin-In. Go-Shirakawa stood and faced the doorway to the birthing chamber. "Oh, no," he whispered. "No, brother, you shall not have your way. You may have been falsely removed from the throne, but you shall not regain it in this fashion. I swear by the vows I have newly taken to the Amida, I will defeat you."

Go-Shirakawa turned and shouted after the *yamabushi*, "It is the Shin-In! It is Sutoku!" But the *yamabushi* could apparently not hear him over the din of the mediums and the chanting monks. Go-Shirakawa went to Kiyomori and, grasping his arm, hauled the bewildered Taira to his feet. "You are right, my friend, we are indeed holy men! Let us now put that to good use." Clapping his hands, Go-Shirakawa began to chant loudly the Thousand-Armed Sutra. He began to stomp his feet in time with the chanting and clapping, and, nodding to Kiyomori to do the same, the Retired Emperor began to march around the building.

He stopped at the group of monks from Ninna-ji and, without pausing the chanting in the slightest, he commanded them with his eyes to join in. As he was the Retired Emperor, the monks had little choice but to obey.

Go-Shirakawa continued on to the monks from what was left of Enryakuji, and those from Kiyomizudera, and those from Miidera, Izu, and Nara, and commanded them also to join in. Soon hundreds of voices were chanting as one the Thousand-Armed Sutra. The monks followed Go-Shirakawa marching in circuit around the building, hundreds of hands clapping, hundreds of handbells chiming. Even the Shinto priests joined in, shaking their sacred sakaki branches in time with the chanting. The very floorboards of the building shook with the stamping feet, the walls vibrated with the pulsing drone of so many voices speaking as one.

As the fourth circuit was completed, there came screams from within the birthing chamber. This sound was soon followed by the tiny wail of a newborn baby. The *shōji* was flung open and Kiyomori's fifth son, Shigehira, who was Assistant Minister of the Empress's Household, knelt there, his face flushed with joy. "The Empress has delivered safely," he announced, "and it is a boy!"

A mighty shout of joy erupted from all the throats that had been chanting, rattling the very roof tiles. Tears streamed from Lord Kiyomori's eyes, and many wondered at the sight of Go-Shirakawa and Kiyomori grinning and dancing with each other as if they were old friends.

Shigemori, dressed in his finest robes, fired off arrows made from mugwort boughs from a bow made of mulberry wood into the four directions as well as to Heaven and Earth, to drive off any lingering evil spirits. Go-Shirakawa and Kiyomori together followed Shigemori into the birthing chamber to watch him place ninety-nine gold coins on a pillow for the new prince. Shigemori intoned to the baby, "Heaven is your father and Earth is your mother, and the spirit of the Sun-Goddess Amaterasu is your own."

There was much singing and dancing and drinking in celebration throughout the day. The Seven Yin-Yang Masters arrived to perform the purification rituals, although one had such trouble making his way through the crowd that his sandal and hat were knocked off. The customary rice steamer was rolled from the ridgepole of the building—it should have been rolled to the north, for the birth of a boy, but it instead was dropped to the south. But these small, inauspicious portents were overlooked in the general gaiety of the occasion.

When Retired Emperor Go-Shirakawa at last prepared to depart, Lord Kiyomori intercepted him. "Whatever disagreements we may have had, Majesty," Kiyomori said, "it is impossible to express my gratitude for the use of your holy power in saving my daughter and grandson."

"You forget we have done this together," said Go-Shirakawa. "Would that we could always share skills so well in the cause of peace."

A cloud seemed to cross Kiyomori's eyes. "Of course, of course," he said. "But, nonetheless, I am having sent to your home a thousand taels of gold dust, as a small token."

Gasps went up among those around them who heard. It was an unseemly large sum, and of greater value than the many horses that Go-Shirakawa had given the Empress as a birthing gift. To outshine the Retired Emperor in such a manner was, in the very least, rude. Go-Shirakawa chose to overlook it. "This is . . . more than generous, Kiyomori-san."

"It is my hope," said Kiyomori bowing, "that it will bring you to remember this day fondly in times to come."

Or to be lenient with you should there be future transgressions? wondered Go-Shirakawa. *Truly, no matter how many vows you have taken, Kiyomori-san, the scheming old warrior in you never vanishes.*

The news of the Imperial birth spread throughout the capital, and for just a moment of time the sorrows of past years were erased from people's thoughts. They danced and sang openly in the streets with great, uncaring joy.

Munemori's Visitor

Munemori received with equanimity the news of the Imperial birth. He was pleased to hear, at least, that his sister was in good health and spirits. *But how well will she be*, he wondered, *when, in time to come, the boy's demonic nature begins to show itself?*

Unable to sleep, Munemori sequestered himself again, with only one brazier for warmth and only a pot of green tea for sustenance. He began to contemplate ending his life.

What use is there for me now? True, I have been promised chieftanship of the Taira, but what good would it be when serving under a demon Emperor? I would have to watch the destruction of Heian Kyō and preside over the fall of my family and clan. I have no wish to see such things.

The Shin-In surely has no more use for me. But how might I accomplish my own destruction? I do not have the courage for the cuts to the belly that have become popular among noble warriors these days. I am no warrior, despite what Father hopes. I could use the knife to the neck and let my blood in woman's fashion, but that would be dishonorable. Poisons are unreliable. I do not think I could starve myself—

His thoughts were disrupted by a strong scent of ashes in the air. Munemori looked up and saw the shade of the Shin-In floating above him. "Well. Congratulations," Munemori said, sardonically. "What will be your first task as Emperor, biting my sister's breast?"

The Shin-In scowled thunderously at him. "Do not take that tone with me. We have failed."

"Failed?" Munemori felt an unexpected surge of happiness within him. "How can that be?"

"The Empress refused to have Kusanagi near her. And my meddling brother—never mind. They will feel my vengeance. All of them. We must consider what to do next."

"We?" Munemori's heart sank once more.

Nii no Ama, formerly Tokiko, wife of Lord Kiyomori, lay on her side gazing fondly at the new little Crown Prince in his mother's arms. She remembered holding her own little infants, a blissful smile on her face, just as Kenreimon'in was wearing now, all her pain forgotten. It was one of the wonders of this strange mortal world, this giving birth. The fear and the pain, the joy and the love.

It brought an all-the-more-poignant stab to the heart to think it would all come to an end. They had averted disaster this time, but there would not always be a divinely inspired Retired Emperor to save the day.

If only Kenreimon'in had allowed Kusanagi to come with her, Nii no Ama thought sadly. *Somehow Shigemori and I would have slipped away with the sword, perhaps replacing it with the copy Shigemori says lies at Ise. We could have returned the sword to my father the Dragon King, and humanity might yet have a chance. I would do such a thing no matter the risk, even if I had to pay for such theft with my own life.*

But now it is clear that the Demon Realm has designs upon the Imperial Throne itself. If they should gain control of the regalia, especially Kusanagi . . . Nii no Ama shuddered, startling Kenreimon'in.

"Mother? Are you all right?"

"Merely a chill, my daughter."

The newborn Crown Prince began to cry, a thin, pitiful wail.

Yes, cry, my grandson, thought Nii no Ama, *for you will rule over the most terrible days this land has seen.*

Shigemori's Dream

*H*e had walked a long way, along a beach that he had never seen before. The ocean was a deep green, and the sand felt spongelike beneath his feet. Deer nibbled at the grasses at the inland edge of the strand. One of them, a white deer, looked up at him, then bounded away. Shigemori walked and walked, aware that he was in a world not his own.

After some while, he rounded a sharp cliff spur and beheld an enormous *torii* standing out in the water. The *torii* was taller than any he had ever seen. Its uprights and crossbeams were larger than any natural tree. "To what shrine or god does this *torii* belong?" he asked himself.

"It is for the Kasuga *kami*," a voice rumbled out of the ocean.

Shigemori wondered at this, for the god of the Kasuga Shrine was one of the most venerated of the ancient *kami*. The *kami* was originally known as Ama no Koyane, and had been the priestly god whose prayers helped bring Amaterasu out of her cave. *What should such a venerable one have to say to me?* thought Shigemori.

As if out of mist, a crowd of people appeared upon the beach, walking toward him. Shigemori was not afraid of them until one of them held up in both hands the severed head of an elderly monk.

Shigemori asked, "Whose head is that? Why do you show it to me?"

"It is the head of the one who calls himself Jōkai, the Taira Chancellor-

Novice. The Kasuga god brings justice to him to pay for the many great sins he has committed."

"My father," Shigemori breathed, now recognizing the face. Jōkai was the monk-name Kiyomori had taken, though he never used it. *The Kasuga god had once said, through an oracle, that it would accept nothing from a man with an impure heart. Has my father, because he ignores his holy vows, so offended the Kasuga god that it now demands justice?*

Shigemori awoke suddenly, his heart pounding. He sat up, and thought he saw, out of the corner of his eye, the pale ghost of Akugenda Yoshihira, the late general Minomoto Yoshitomo's eldest son, standing beside him. Shigemori turned his head, and the apparition was gone.

The sun was rising and a sweet breeze of spring was wafting through the blinds. Six months had passed since the birth of the Crown Prince, and the happiness the event had brought had faded like New Year's irises. Again Lord Kiyomori was behaving with suspicion regarding Go-Shirakawa. Shigemori suspected that his father was jealous of Go-Shirakawa's impressive display of holy magic at the Imperial birth. Despite Kiyomori's attempt to have the Taira dominate the event by having the lying-in at Rokuhara, the Retired Emperor had outshone the Taira lord, and Kiyomori would likely never forgive that.

Shigemori sighed in regret for his father's pigheadedness. The feel of the ominous dream stayed with Shigemori while he rose and dressed, as dew will cling to sleeves when one has walked through tall grasses. "It is time, then," Shigemori said to himself. "The luck of the Taira has run out."

He was startled by an urgent rapping at the *shōji*. "Who is it?"

"My lord, your father's advisor, Kaneyasu, is here. He seems quite distressed."

Fearing the worst, Shigemori arranged his robes around him. "Send Kaneyasu in."

The old general entered, his tanned and weathered face a mask of concern. Kaneyasu's gray hair was unknotted, and his robes hung wrong on his thin frame as though he had hastily dressed.

"Your face does not bode good news, good Kaneyasu," said Shigemori. "Do you bring word of my father?"

Kaneyasu bowed and sat down. "Not news as such, Lord Shigemori. But . . . something has occurred, and I do not know whom to tell of it. You are his son, and acting chief of the Taira, and therefore, perhaps, I thought it best to bring it to you. Although, it may be nothing, and I am disturbed by only a mist on the mountains."

"Please feel free to unburden yourself to me. Any matter of concern to the Taira and Lord Kiyomori I will hear with greatest interest."

Kaneyasu sighed and stared at the floor. "You may think it foolish, my Lord. But . . . I have had an extraordinary dream."

Shigemori's skin prickled. "Does it concern a long beach and a great *torii* and the voice of the Kasuga god?"

Kaneyasu looked up, his face pale. "So it does, my lord."

"I have, just this morning, had this same dream."

"Then it must be more than a mere dream, my lord. It is a message from the divine."

"I fear so. Have you told my father?"

"I have not. I am afraid of what his reaction might be."

"I understand. I would tell him myself, but it would be pointless. My father no longer fully trusts me, though he has no cause for such suspicion."

Kaneyasu rubbed his gray-stubbled chin. "There is a thing I wish to confess to you, Lord Shigemori."

"What is it?"

"It was my men, under my orders, who saw to the death of your brother-in-law Narichika. I was commanded by your father to see that it was done."

Shigemori looked away. "I had suspected it. My father was upset that I overstepped his authority in pleading for Narichika's life. I suppose I am as guilty of Narichika's death as you are, Kaneyasu."

"But your father is most guilty of all," said Kaneyasu. "Even if Narichika had been involved in a rebellion, exile should have been enough punishment. He did not deserve to die in such a dishonorable fashion."

Shigemori nodded. "It is no wonder the Kasuga god demands justice. So much unnececessary death has been dealt at my father's urging."

"There was one thing in the dream, my lord . . . I wonder if you heard it, too?"

"What thing is this?"

Kaneyasu took a deep breath. "The Kasuga god said that now the Dragon King's promise has been fulfilled. But because Lord Kiyomori has broken his promise to the Dragon King, and has broken his vows to the Amida, the *kami* are lifting their protection from the land and allowing the demons to have their way. Do you know what this might mean, my lord?"

Shigemori found himself in the uncomfortable position of having to lie. "No, I awoke before I heard any such thing. I cannot imagine what that part of your dream might mean, although it does not bode well."

With another sigh, Kaneyasu slowly stood. "I agree, it portends bad times to come. I fear I must leave now, Lord Shigemori, before Kiyomori learns of my whereabouts."

"I understand. I thank you for having the courage to come here and speak with me. If there is ever anything you require of me, you need only let me know. Your loyal service to my family has always been . . . admirable."

Kaneyasu paused and tilted his head. "Except for Narichika?"

"As I have said, I hold you blameless for that. To have disobeyed my father would have required your own death."

"A true warrior does not shirk death in the face of doing what is right. I do not hold myself blameless. Good day, Lord Shigemori." The old man bowed and departed.

What can I do? thought Shigemori, his pulse beginning to pound harder with fear. *Has my caution in dealing with the matter of Kusanagi doomed the world? Surely it cannot be so. Perhaps Kaneyasu misunderstood his dream, and yet it is so full of truth. I must learn if there is anything I can yet do. I will go to consult the famous oracles at the Shrine of Kumano, and see what they can tell me.*

Shigemori called for his servants and told them to make preparations for a pilgrimage. But by midmorning, another visitor was announced to him.

"My Lord, your brother Munemori has come. He says he wishes to relate to you a dream."

Shigemori went cold inside. *How many others have the gods informed of my father's shameful behavior?* "Yes, of course I will see him. Let him enter at once."

Munemori entered the meeting room with dignified calm and even managed to bow and sit with a manner of grace. *How he has changed,* Shigemori thought in wonder. *Perhaps bearing up under the burden of his grief has made him a more sober and thoughtful gentleman.*

"Brother, your visit delights me," Shigemori said. "I am glad to see you have chosen to leave your seclusion and be part of the world once more."

"While it is true that the time for personal grief has passed," said Munemori, "I fear a time for greater grief may be upon us. I have had a most terrible dream, brother."

"Ah. Did it involve a beach, a *torii*, and the voice of the Kasuga god?"

Munemori's brows rose, but his eyes held no surprise. "Why, so it did. Have you had the same dream?"

"I did and so did one other, who, I am sure, would prefer to be unnamed. How did your dream . . . end?"

Munemori glanced away. "With the showing of our father's head and warnings of dire events to come."

"Ah." Shigemori's heart sank. "It would seem the good fortune of our clan has run out at last."

"Perhaps not," said Munemori, hastily. "I woke in the middle of the night from my dream and immediately consulted . . . a spiritual person as to what it might mean, what I might do. And I received an answer."

"Yes?"

Munemori leaned closer. "Are you certain there are no servants listening?"

"One can never be certain, brother. But speak softly, and I am sure no one else will hear."

"Very well. Um, I am aware of our family's . . . duties concerning the Imperial Sacred Sword."

"You are?"

"Mother has been worried of late. What if something should happen to you? Naturally it was best that I also be informed."

"Ah. Yes. Of course." Shigemori was certain he was missing something in Munemori's meaning, but he could not comprehend what. "Did the . . . spiritual person you consulted refer to the sword?"

"Indeed," said Munemori. "It is important that Kusanagi be given to the proper hands."

"I know that. I have been awaiting the proper time—"

"The time must be soon, brother," Munemori said.

Shigemori looked away, chagrined. "Yes, yes. I understand. But I will be leaving very soon on a pilgrimage to Kumano to learn more of this dream. As soon as I return—"

"A pilgrimage!" said Munemori. "But that is perfect!"

"Yes, I thought it would be appropriate but—"

"You misunderstand. It is better that you be far from matters, and therefore be thought blameless."

Shigemori paused. "You are correct. I do not understand."

Munemori looked humbly down at his hands. "I am offering to take your burden from you, brother."

"Burden?"

Munemori sniffed and dabbed at one eye with his sleeve. "Though I may have returned to the world, I have found I take no joy in it. My grief has drained me of all interest in continuing my existence."

"Do not speak so, brother. It saddens me to hear you say such things."

"It is true. Therefore, I am willing to take the risk, to save our clan. To save the world. I will steal Kusanagi. If I am caught, I will blame no one but myself. I will accept my execution gladly, and join my beloved wife and child in Paradise."

Shigemori reached over and touched his weeping brother's sleeve. "This is a most courageous offer. But I cannot ask such sacrifice of you, Munemori."

"You must!" Munemori said, gripping Shigemori's arm so hard it almost hurt. "Our clan relies upon you, brother. Without your leadership, we are lost. You are the most respected of the Taira. If you are dishonored, so are we all. While I, I am of no account. No one expects anything of me. If I am to fall, people will merely shrug and say, 'It is no matter. He was no one of importance.' "

Shigemori had to admit Munemori was right. "You speak no less than truth, Munemori-san, much as it pains me to say so. Already you are proving that you are worthy of much more in people's estimation."

Munemori waved his hand. "That is of no consequence. I no longer care what others think of me. Only . . . please allow me to do the world this one service. If I succeed, only the gods will know, but my soul will be at peace, and I will feel like my insignificant life has had some worth."

Shigemori was touched by his brother's plea. *To deny him this chance to prove himself would be heartless of me. And he is right, the matter of Kusanagi must be dealt with soon.* "Is there anything you require of me?"

Munemori's tears dried almost instantly. "A small thing, only. You are Palace Minister, and therefore permitted to go wherever you wish in the Imperial Compound. Assign to me some of your duties while you are gone to Kumano. Give me a writ with your permission and seal. That way I may have access to . . . whatever I may need."

"I understand. Yes, that makes sense. You are wise, Munemori. I regret having underestimated you in times past."

A slight smile appeared on Munemori's lips. "It is my hope, dear brother, that my deeds may elicit from you even more such regret in time to come."

The Whirlwind

And so, as Shigemori made preparations for his pilgrimage, Munemori gradually began to take over some of Shigemori's duties at the Imperial palace. Every morning, Munemori would arrive just before dawn, dressed entirely correctly in First Rank black robes and silk hat. Munemori would proceed to Shigemori's office in the Palace Ministry Building and look over the plans for further repairs on the older palace buildings. He approved only those which Shigemori had already authorized. Then Munemori would hear the recommendations from the household ministries on preparations for the upcoming Iris and Weaver Festivals. Again, he would approve only those preparations Shigemori had instructed him to.

At midmorning, Munemori would conduct an inspection of the chamberlains to ensure they were in proper dress and deportment. Munemori would visit each of the Household Ministries offices to learn what resources they needed and authorize purchasing of rice and silk for them. At midday, Munemori would take a modest meal with others of middle rank of the

Taira clan who served at the palace. In the afternoon, Munemori would speak with the various ministers of the palace guards and police. There were many different, often competing, martial offices in the Imperial Compound, and Munemori would have to play peacemaker and ombudsman, ensuring that the Guards of the Left were no more favored than the Guards of the Right, and the Guards of the Inner Ward had their requirements met as often as the Guards of the Outer Walls.

In late afternoon, Munemori would pay a call upon his sister the Empress, to see if there was anything she or the Crown Prince needed.

In all these things, Munemori performed exactly according to Shigemori's instructions, in a calm and dignified manner. In this way, although the Fujiwara and other non-Taira nobles of the palace did not initially trust Munemori, soon they took no notice of him whatsoever. As the days passed, Munemori was able to walk anywhere within the Imperial Compound without incurring challenge or suspicion.

Fourteen days went by and then, on the Twelfth Day of the Fifth Month, Rice-Sprouting Month, in the third year of the era Jishō, Munemori received word that Shigemori was departing at last for Kumano. Munemori arrived at the Imperial palace at the usual hour, only this time he brought with him a large, long chest of lacquered wood. Within it lay several silk brocade winter kimonos, and the copy of Kusanagi that had been hanging in the shrine at Ise. Shigemori had apparently spared no expense to purchase the silence of the priests at Ise, and Munemori doubted that even the shrine attendants who had delivered it to Munemori's mansion had known what they were bringing him.

At his midmorning inspection of the chamberlains, Munemori arranged the meeting for a room next to the Fan Window Chamber where the Imperial Regalia were currently being kept. At the end of the inspection, Munemori opened the lacquered box, saying, "My brother, Lord Shigemori, offers these as a gift for your servants in hopes for their prayers for his safe journey—What is this? Why, these are for the wrong season! There must have been some mistake. Please forgive me, my lords. I must have been given the wrong box. I will see that the matter is corrected immediately."

The chamberlains politely bowed, saying they took no offense, and they were certain the generous Shigemori had made a simple mistake, and they certainly would include him in their prayers.

Munemori thanked and dismissed them. In the moment he was alone, Munemori slid open the *shōji* to the Fan Window Room and carried the box in.

Two young women, only sixteen or seventeen, lay on the floor, scribbling poetry. Beside them, on the wall, hung Kusanagi and the jade jewel. The mirror, of course, would be in the Imperial Shrine. It was a sign of the decadence of the times, the ghost of the Shin-in had told Munemori, that the Imperial Regalia were no longer guarded by warriors but often only by little maidservants. Fortunately for Munemori.

The girls' long raven hair spilled down their backs like the flow of ink from a brush, and Munemori realized it had been a long time since he had enjoyed the company of a woman. One of them looked up at him and coyly hid her face behind her wide sleeve, smiling.

> "Oh, look, a great Taira
> Comes blundering amid the
> ripe cherry blossoms . . .
> Have you lost your way, my Lord?"

Munemori recovered himself. "Didn't you hear the chamberlains calling for you? They have something important to announce to all the household servants. You had better go at once."

The girls gasped and sat up, straightening their kimonos, dithering because it was improper to be seen standing up, improper to be seen by a strange man at all, improper to leave the regalia unattended.

"I will remain with the regalia, ladies," Munemori said, "until you can send someone to watch in your place."

The girls bowed low to him. "Thank you, you are most kind and generous—"

"Go, go, do not make the chamberlains upset with your tardiness."

The girls lifted the hems of their long kimonos and hastened out through the *shōji*, closing it behind them.

As soon as the *shōji* was shut, Munemori pulled the copy of Kusanagi from the lacquered chest and went to the wall. He took Kusanagi from its scabbard, feeling the faintest hum and vibration when he grasped its hilt. Swiftly, he placed the copy into the scabbard and placed Kusanagi in the chest, tossing the kimonos over it. He put the lid firmly back on the chest and sat down to wait.

It was some minutes before the girls noisily returned, arguing with each other as they opened the *shōji*.

"You should not have been so rude!"

"I was not the one who called the Head Chamberlain a—Oh, your pardon, my lord Taira. It appears there has been a mistake. The chamberlains did not call for us at all."

"You are certain?" said Munemori, using his most officious frown.

"Well, that is, the ones we spoke to knew of no such thing."

Munemori sighed, rustling the paper in his hand. "It is no wonder Shigemori despairs of his chamberlains. They change their minds more often than the spring wind changes direction. This is a very charming poem, by the way. You are referring to the Regent, are you not, in this one about the 'old, bent, and withered root?' "

One of the maidservant's clapped her hands to her mouth, her eyes wide. "You have been reading our poetry?"

"I have a great appreciation for poetry. You show quite a bit of skill in . . . depicting the foibles of those around you. And am I incorrect in assuming that this one is something of a love poem to the Emperor himself?"

"Oh, please, my lord!" cried the maidservants, hurrying in and shutting the *shōji* behind them. "Please tell no one of what you have read there. These are foolish things. Mere practice poems. We would not dare think them worthy of eyes other than our own. Please tell no one about them!"

Munemori attempted his warmest smile. "I am certain I will have no cause for that." He put the paper back on the floor and stood. "Now I will leave before I cause any question to your reputations. However, if either of you would like some . . . instruction regarding the art of poetry, I would be happy to be of help. I am a widower now, and my nights are long and lonely. Having a young person to . . . instruct in such arts would be . . . beneficial to both, don't you think?"

The girls blushed and giggled nervously behind their sleeves. Munemori picked up the chest, favored them with a slight bow, and departed, knowing that the regalia, and any possible tampering with the sword, would now be the last thing on the maidservants' minds.

At midday, Munemori pretended to a slight ailment of the stomach and after accepting some herbal tea from the Imperial Bureau of Medicine, he made apologies to the Ministries of the Guards and left the palace. He did not go home.

Instead, Munemori's ox-carriage made its way, by back streets, to the house where he used to visit the lady of the tall weeds. He had sent a servant the day before with rice and gold to buy the house from the woman's aging mother "as a gift of apology for any harm I may have caused your daughter." Therefore, as he had hoped, the dilapidated house was empty when he arrived. The tall weeds that grew in the former gardens had grown taller and thicker still and hid him from view of the street as he entered the gate.

Little clouds of dust swirled around his clogs as Munemori strode into the main chamber of the house, carrying the lacquered chest. The air was still and heavy with early-summer humidity. Golden dust motes danced on the sunbeams that slanted in through the broken bamboo shutters and slashed paper walls.

Munemori set the chest down in the center of the room and knelt before it. Though he had often been afraid of the demon Emperor Shin-In, and what the creature had asked him to do, this moment was nearly payment enough for all he had been through. Never before had he had such power within his grasp. *Blessed Amida, thank you for allowing me to live to see this day*, Munemori thought as he lifted off the lid.

His hands fished in among the kimonos and grasped the hilt of Kusanagi. Munemori raised the ancient sword out of the box and reverently carried it out to the verandah of the house. Taking a moment to find solid footing on the broken and rotting boards, Munemori lifted the sword, higher and higher, until it pointed at the zenith of the sky.

"By the blood of my Imperial ancestors," Munemori intoned, "I command you, Kusanagi. In the name of my father's father, who was Emperor, I command you. In the name of my mother's father, who made you, I command you. Bring me winds. Bring me the most terrible storm winds this land has ever seen."

Munemori gasped with shock as a lightning bolt traveled up his arms, into the sword, and out into the sky. Clouds began to gather overhead, rushing in from every direction. They billowed like rippling silk, flowing like seafoam at the shore. The sky above darkened deeper and deeper gray, and then turned a sickly yellow-green. The daylight faded into the darkness of an early night.

And the winds began, lifting the edges of Munemori's robes, flapping his wide sleeves like the wings of frightened birds. The tall weeds around him sighed and chattered as their stalks were bent this way and that. The roof tiles over his head rattled ominously.

Then Munemori heard the roar. It was the sound of thousands of horsemen galloping across the Kantō Plain, a continuous thunder as if the very gods had become *taiko* drummers, or chanting monks, their rhythym faster than the mortal ear could catch. As the wind became stronger, tearing at his tall cap, whipping his robe around him, Munemori heard the howling, a wailing and shrieking like the voices of vengeful ghosts, riding above the thunder. For one moment he thought he heard his dead wife screaming his name.

Staring up the blade of the sword, Munemori saw the black clouds begin to swirl in a circle, tighter and tighter, and then a protrusion, like the arm of a black-scaled dragon, began to descend directly toward him.

"Noooo!" Munemori screamed, although he could barely hear himself above the wind, "That way!" He pointed Kusanagi toward the east, toward the Imperial palace. "Go that way!"

Slowly, slowly, the descending funnel twisted and turned, moving toward the east. As Munemori watched, the tip of the funnel reached toward the ground and touched down only a block of houses away.

Munemori could barely stand; the winds buffeted him and pushed him.

He had to duck his head as broken boards flew off the roof and walls and struck him. The floorboards of the verandah beneath him shuddered and bounced, nearly tossing him off his feet. The noise became so tremendous he feared he would go deaf.

Kusanagi became increasingly difficult to hold. The sword pulled up and forward, as if it wished to leap out of his hands and into the swirling darkness. Munemori cried out with the effort of gripping the hilt. His arms ached with the strain. Munemori knew he was not a particularly strong man. He did not know how long he could hold on.

Long, long moments passed as the screams of the living joined the unearthly screams of ghosts in the wind. Munemori could see entire thatched roofs rising into the air, whirling like autumn leaves. Whole bits of houses were plucked up as easily as a child picks flowers.

The moment came when Munemori knew he could hold on no longer. As the floorboards buckled beneath him, Munemori cried, "Stop! I command you, Kusanagi! Stop the wind! By the blood of Ryujin and all the Emperors, by Amaterasu, *Stop!*" With all the strength he had left, he forced the point of the sword down.

The winds subsided and the dragon's-arm funnel rose back into the sky. The clouds began to disperse. Rocks and boards and bits of thatch rained down. The point of Kusanagi fell and lodged itself in the wood at Munemori's feet.

Munemori's arms felt like twisted bars of metal. He could not bend them, or even barely move them. He managed to free one hand from its paralyzed grip on the hilt. Munemori turned and walked slowly back into the house, dragging Kusanagi behind him. The main room was now missing half of its roof, and two walls had gaping holes in them. Munemori shuffled over to the lacquered chest, flung Kusanagi into it, and replaced the lid. Then he lay down beside the chest and let exhaustion overtake him.

The Lock of Hair

Two days after the cyclone, Lord Kiyomori sat in the central room of his mansion of Nishihachijō, fuming. Though night had fallen, the temperature and his temper had not eased. The hot, humid air his fan delivered to his face could not soothe the discomfort of the summer's heat no matter how fast he fluttered it. "Our fault?" he growled at the red-jacketed youths kneeling before him.

"I fear so, my lord," said the taller of the young men. "It has been difficult for us to keep up with the rumormongers. And the people are getting bolder, my lord." He indicated the younger boy beside him, who had a broken nose and a black eye. "They are no longer afraid to fight back."

Kiyomori flung down his fan in disgust. "How can they say such things? First the comet and now the winds are blamed upon the Taira!"

"There is worse, my lord," said the younger boy. "Some are claiming they are only saying what the Yin-Yang Office has officially stated. That the whirlwind was an omen—"

"Yes, of course! Everything is a portent for the downfall of the Taira! Have we not brought peace to Heian Kyō? Have we not given the country an Empress and future Emperor? What ingratitude!"

"Yes, my lord. Indeed, my lord," agreed the cowering boys.

"I will wager Go-Shirakawa is behind these rumors. He does all he can to harm my reputation. He has always resented my rise to power. How it must disturb him so that there will be a Taira Emperor on the throne. I'll wager he would not be spreading these rumors if Shigemori were still in the capital. But with his beloved Taira ally gone, Go-Shirakawa feels free to say whatever he wants against the rest of us."

"Yes, my lord," the boys mumbled.

"But Shigemori felt no need to stay to protect his fellow Taira. No, now he has become a holy man. He had to go to Kumano because he has had a *dream*," Kiyomori sneered. Word had reached Kiyomori of his son's dream. Servants talk, and a servant felt the Great Lord of the Taira should know what his son had prophesied for him. *Or is it Shigemori's hope?* Kiyomori wondered. *Does my son spread rumors of doom to cover whatever he is plotting to do? An excuse to have me exiled, or have an accident happen, as I arranged for the death of Narichika? No one would think the worse of the wise Shigemori. Even the Dragon King protects him now.*

Kiyomori noticed the boys kneeling before him turning pale and he realized he had said more than he should before servants. "Are you still here? Begone. You must continue to stop these rumors. Put anyone who is spreading them in fear of losing his life. Go!"

"*Hai*, my lord," the youths said, and hurried out of the room.

Kiyomori sighed. *Blessed Amida, I am getting too old to carry the burden of my clan's fortune alone.* He stood and went to the *shōji* that opened onto the north garden and slid the door aside. Given his thoughts and the heat of the still air, he knew he would sleep little that night. Kiyomori walked out onto the verandah, hoping for a cooling breeze. But he stopped.

An old man was kneeling on the verandah, his hair and skin white as stone in the moonlight. Indeed, he was so still for a moment, Kiyomori wondered if he were a statue dressed in robes, left as a prank, or a surprise gift. The old man wore the box hat on the forehead that indicated a Shinto priest, and he held the ringed wand in his hand of a *yamabushi*, a wandering wizard.

The old man suddenly turned, startling Kiyomori. "Ah! Lord Chancellor," the old one said, "it is an honor to meet you at last."

"Who are you?" asked Kiyomori, recovering himself. "What are you doing here?"

"Forgive me, my lord," the old man said, bowing stiffly. His eyes were unnaturally pale and reflected the moonlight as if they were lit from within. "I am no one important. Only, I came in hopes of doing you a small service. You may call me Mukō. I have been waiting quite a while to speak with you. Perhaps your servants forgot to announce me to you."

"I see." Kiyomori was not surprised. Matters had been so disrupted since the whirlwind that his servants had been overlooking things. "What small service do you speak of?"

"As you may note from my garments, my lord, I have studied the Mysteries. I once served in the Imperial Bureau of Divinations. Here . . . here are my . . . credentials." The old man reached a clawlike hand into his sleeve and pulled out a rolled-up piece of paper. The old man placed the paper on the floor before Kiyomori.

Kiyomori picked it up, untied the black-silk ribbon, and read it. It was a formal declaration of office, indeed for the Bureau of Divinations. But the ink was smeared here and there. "This chop," Kiyomori said, "it is that of Emperor Sutoku. The one called the Shin-In."

"Yes," said Mukō. "The document is old, I fear. I received the post forty years ago. Incredible how the time passes, neh? But I left the post a few years later and since that time I have been wandering from temple to temple and visiting the remote places of this land, learning whatever I can."

"So what has brought you here?"

"Oh, I remember the great days when the Taira first began their rise to power. What a warrior you were then, my lord. Er, which is not to say you are no less impressive now, my lord. But I have heard men are saying unkind things about your clan, about you. I am concerned for you."

Kiyomori sighed with impatience. "I thank you, old man, but—"

"I have even heard strange things concerning your son Shigemori, whom many favor."

Kiyomori crouched before the old man. "What have you heard?"

"On my travels, I happened to pass through the shrine at Ise. A priest I befriended there told me of a strange request made by your son, a request for the copy of Kusanagi that hung at Ise to be delivered secretly to him here in Heian Kyō."

Kiyomori felt his heart turn to cold iron. "And was that done?"

"I believe it was, my lord."

Kiyomori sucked in air through his teeth, and he rubbed his stubbled chin. "That can only mean Shigemori intends something with the Imperial Sword."

"While it is not for me to suggest anything, my lord, is it not true that Kusanagi commands the winds?"

Kiyomori stared at the old man. "The whirlwind?"

"It is not for me to say, my lord. But, of course, Shigemori had left the city by that time, I understand."

"So he knew he would be safe."

"That is only conjecture, of course."

"But why would Shigemori call down destruction upon the city?"

"I do not say he did, my lord. But I notice his mansion and that of the Retired Emperor were spared."

"Is it to bring blame down upon me? Or is it to distract attention from what else he may do?" A terrifying thought occured to Kiyomori. *What if he has taken Kusanagi and intends to throw it into the sea at Kumano, denying it to my grandson, perhaps blaming the loss of the sword on me?*

"That is not for me to say, my lord."

"Shigemori must be stopped. I thank you, good Mukō, for this information."

Mukō held up one hand. "I believe I said I came here to offer you a small service."

Kiyomori scowled. "And what is this small service you offer?"

"As you see, I am a man of rite and ritual. I have learned many ways of making a thing so, or not so."

"You mean you do magic?"

"If you would call it such. I merely believe I am persuading the *kami* to see things my way. You fear your son may attempt to do . . . something foolish. If you like, I can arrange that such a thing will not happen."

Kiyomori paused. He was reluctant to have anything more to do with supernatural forces. But if his enemies would use the winds and the Heavens to call for the Taira's demise, why should he not employ greater powers as well? Something about the old man suggested otherworldliness, that he had seen and done things out of the ordinary. His very name meant *Beyond*. *What could it hurt to let the old man do a ritual on my behalf?* "Very well, you have my permission. Go and do this ritual."

The old man blinked slowly. "I would already have done so, my lord. Only, there is something I need from you."

"What is it? A payment of rice or gold?"

"Not even that, my lord. But if this rite is to concern your son, Shigemori, I need something personal of his. It need only be a small thing, but it must be something he had worn or kept close to him for a long while. This will ensure the ritual will focus upon him alone."

For a moment, Kiyomori wondered if the old man might not be a skilled beggar, hoping for a robe or writing brush that he might sell, proclaiming that it belonged to the great Shigemori. But Mukō did not seem that sort of creature.

Kiyomori wondered what he might have of Shigemori's. After all, his son had never lived at Nishihachijō, and rarely visited. All he had of his son's possessions were keepsakes from childhood that his wife had kept out of fondness—

"The only such thing I can think of still in my possession," said Kiyomori, "is a lock of hair taken from Shigemori just before his trouser ceremony, when he was but a boy. I doubt that would be helpful to you, for it has not been on his person for a long time."

"On the contrary," said Mukō, "that would be perfect, for it is a part of the man himself. You could give me nothing better."

So Kiyomori sent for a servant to bring him a particular small cedar box from his wife's old quarters. When the box arrived, Kiyomori withdrew from it a folded piece of heavy rice paper flecked with gold. Within the fold of paper lay a thick lock of fine black hair. As he gazed upon it, Kiyomori remembered the day, long ago, when the little Shigemori had stood at the entrance to the family shrine, his young face so eager and happy. Kiyomori felt tears fill his eyes, and he cursed his old age that had made him so sentimental.

He flung the folded paper with the lock of hair down at Mukō's knees. "There. Take it. I hope it is useful to you. It means nothing to me anymore. I ask only that you stop Shigemori from committing his foolishness."

"Fear not, my lord. He will be stopped," Mukō acknowledged, with a bow. The old man put the folded paper in his sleeve and departed.

Kiyomori watched him go. The otherworldly old man moved in slow jerks and limps as if he were a *bunraku* puppet and not an inhabitant in his own flesh. On an impulse, Kiyomori called for servants and asked that the old man be followed and watched. "These are dangerous times, and I do not wish him to be harmed on the dark streets. See where he goes and make sure that he is safe."

The servants hurried off to comply and Kiyomori stood to walk to his bedchamber feeling a strange and terrible calm.

Under the Tachibana Trees

Kenreimon'in and her mother, Nii no Ama, sat under the tachibana trees in a side garden of the Inner Ward of the Imperial Compound. The barest hint of a summer breeze brought the scent of oranges wafting down from the tiny flowers overhead. An ornamental stream wound around the mossy knoll on which the ladies sat, sunlight sparking on its surface.

"This is like reading a beautiful poem, written by a friend who has died," Kenreimon'in murmured. "Pleasant, but I can take no joy in it."

"I understand," said Nii no Ama.

A peal of laughter arose from another knoll across the stream, where the maidservants were fussing over and playing with the little Crown Prince. "Have you decided what he will be named yet?" asked Nii no Ama.

"The Council of Ministers are saying that when the boy becomes Emperor, he should have the name Antoku."

Nii no Ama nodded. "And do they know when that will be?"

"How can anyone say?" replied Kenreimon'in, looking down at the withering grass beside her. "Are you so eager to be an Emperor's grandmother that you wish it to be soon?"

"Oh, no, no," replied Nii no Ama, gently grasping her arm. "I do not ask from ambition or vanity. I am worried, my daughter. I do not know . . . how much time we have left."

"You speak of the whirlwind," Kenreimon said, still not looking up. She plucked at the drying tips of the grass beside her.

"Yes. The fish in my pond still insist it was Kusanagi."

Kenreimon'in grasped a handful of grass in her fist, viciously pulled it up, and threw it on the ground. "I thought the fish were no longer speaking to you."

"After the whirlwind, I visited the pond at Rokuhara. Oh, they spoke to me then. Ryujin is very concerned."

Kenreimon'in stared down at the hem of her outmost kimono and rubbed at a grass stain. "It cannot have been Kusanagi, Mother. The sword has never left the palace. I checked on it myself, after I received your troubling letter. Someone is always watching the regalia. Naturally, I could not inquire too much, lest I raise suspicions. But I have heard of no tampering with the sword." Kenreimon'in noticed one of the young ladies-in-waiting looking back at her with a worried expression. *I should not speak so loud,* Kenreimon'in chided herself. *An Empress should never raise her voice. Particularly on this matter.*

"Nothing else . . . untoward happened in the palace that day?" asked Nii no Ama.

"There were bad omens, if that is what you mean," said Kenreimon'in. "The birds and animals were noted to be particularly quiet. Munemori delivered a box of kimonos that turned out to be for the wrong season. Then he, himself, became sick and went home, an hour or so before the whirlwind came. The Crown Prince fussed more than usual. His Majesty noticed that—"

"What was that about Munemori again?"

"That he became sick and left early, you mean? It was a stomach ailment, I believe. No one else in the palace caught it, that I know of."

Nii no Ama seemed particularly thoughtful, her face shadowed by her gray silk cowl. "There has been some reconciliation between Shigemori and Munemori. They have been corresponding more of late. I am pleased to see my sons amicable toward each other again, but there is something . . . secretive about their new friendship. Something Shigemori is not telling me."

"Before the whirlwind, Munemori occasionally used to have tea with me. Should he do so again, should I ask him about it?"

"Do not press him on it. But if he should reveal a thing or two . . ."

"I will let you know."

"Thank you."

Louder laughter from the knoll opposite made Kenreimon'in look over at the maidservants. One was holding up the Crown Prince and swinging him around, swooping him here and there as if he were a chubby little bird.

"Be careful!" Kenreimon'in called out. "Do not drop him in the stream! He might drown."

Nii no Ama glanced sharply up at her.

"What is it, Mother?"

"Merely . . . a dream. I was reminded of a dream."

"A dream?"

Nii no Ama shook her head. "One should not speak of bad dreams." Slowly she stood, grimacing from the aches in her joints. "I believe . . . I will go play with my grandchild. While I still can."

Kenreimon'in watched her mother walk carefully across the ornamental stream over the perfectly placed stepping-stones. She wished she could tell her mother about the time she had touched Kusanagi. But guilt always seemed to stop her mouth and catch her voice in her throat. *Did my sin bring the whirlwind? How will I live with myself if that is so?* She looked down at her hands in her lap. They were stained with the green blood of the grass she had pulled.

The Empress sighed.

Wet Robes

Walking the many *li* in their white pilgrims' robes, Shigemori, his sons, and their entourage were most of the way to the Kumano Shrine when the messenger reached them with news of the whirlwind. "It was a wondrous and most terrible sight, my lord," the messenger said. "Five city blocks were damaged. No one had ever seen anything like it. Surely it is an omen of great import."

Shigemori felt his stomach grow cold. *Kusanagi commands the winds they say. But surely Munemori would not . . . did not . . .*

Koremori, now a young man himself of sixteen, interrupted his thoughts. "Should we return to Heian Kyō, Father?"

Shigemori paused and then asked the messenger, "Were any of my family . . . harmed?"

"No, my lord, no Taira holdings were touched. This has caused some people to wonder, as you might understand."

"And the Imperial palace? There was nothing untoward there?"

"Spared also, blessed be the Amida, although the whirlwind was moving in that direction. Only the homes and shops of merchants and a few lesser noblemen's mansions were destroyed."

"Ah, no one of account, then," said Koremori.

"Say no such thing, my son," Shigemori chided him. "A person of lesser rank is by no account a lesser person. Anyone's fortunes may change, as our own family has seen." Turning back to the messenger, Shigemori asked, "And what of the Retired Emperor and his household?"

"Also spared, my lord."

Shigemori sighed. He stared up at the sky as if answers might be written in the clouds. "Well, there is little my returning to the city would accomplish, then. It would be better to continue on and ask the *kami* at the shrine the meaning of this extraordinary event." He paid the messenger, and the procession continued onward to Kumano.

But when Shigemori and his sons reached the cedar-shaded main shrine of Kumano, he was faced with disappointment. His request for a medium to interpret his dream was denied.

"We are most sorry to disappoint you, noble lord," said the priests, "but we have no one suitable here right now. Our best mediums were sent to the capital to serve at the Imperial birth seven months ago, where they quite wore themselves out. Our last one nearly tore all her hair out foretelling the coming of the whirlwind, and she is now recovering. We have not yet found any worthy replacements among our shrine maidens."

Shigemori took this as a sign that no further interpretation of his dream was needed. He had been told all the *kami* would permit him to know. Shigemori ensconced himself within the Hongū Shōjōden Hall all day and all night, kneeling in prayer. To the *kami* Kongō Dōji, he prayed, "I find I have not the skill or the courage to bring peace and prosperity to my people. Though I try to correct my father, as unfilial as that may seem, I am powerless to change him. Let it be, then, O Kongō Dōji, that if we Taira are still worthy in the sight of the gods, then may you or some other great power change Kiyomori's heart and make him a man of wisdom and peace.

"But if we are not worthy, then please remove whatever divine protection I may have, so that my life may be taken from me. I have no wish to see my sons' and relatives' fortunes decline, to watch a world grow in misery. If the whirlwind was only a foretaste of disasters to come, then spare me from them. Let my spirit journey on to a better life and leave this world of woes behind."

A voice emanated from behind the curtain that hid the *kami's* image. "Blameless Shigemori, you have been heard. But your fate already has been sealed. Be at peace. The winds of Fortune blow beyond you now."

It was later said by the *chujo* boys of the temple that Lord Shigemori glowed with an eerie light when he finally left the chamber of prayer in the dark hours before dawn.

As Shigemori walked back toward the rooms in which he and his sons were lodged, a summer thunderstorm announced its arrival with a great flash of lightning and a mighty rumble of thunder. It was so bright, Shigemori had to shield his eyes a moment. Then came a strong gust of wind, which tugged hard at his hair. He gasped, and fat drops of rain lodged in his throat. Shigemori choked and coughed, but though he cleared the water from his throat, he had difficulty breathing, as if he had been poisoned. The lightning flashed again and in its afterimage, Shigemori saw the face of Akugenda Yoshihira, the executed son of Yoshitomo, who had claimed he would become a thunder demon, smiling in satisfaction. Shigemori understood. *The kami have chosen to allow you your vengeance.* He bowed to where the lightning had been and continued on.

Shigemori did not run to the shelter of the overhanging eaves as the rain came down in a torrent. Instead, he walked calmly the long path to his rooms, as if the night were fine weather. He allowed the wind to batter at him, allowed the rain to drench his clothing. After all, his fate was now sealed, his life now in the hands of the gods.

The Empty Vessel

"Dead?" asked Kiyomori, unbelieving.

"Yes, Great Lord," said the servant, his forehead pressed to the tatami mat. "We followed the *yamabushi* Mukō, as you directed. For three days we watched him in his wretched hovel, performing foul-smelling rituals. Then he fell over and did not rise again. We sent for a physician, who said, from the condition of the body, that Mukō had been dead not one hour but one week."

"That is impossible."

"Of course. Stranger still, according to papers hidden in the hems of the old man's robes, his name had been Sewa and he had been troubled by visits from the spirit of the Shin-In."

Kiyomori remembered the official document "Mukō" had shown him, signed with the chop of the Shin-In. "Blessed Amida," whispered Kiyomori. "What have I done?"

The Hidden Chest

All the *shōji* were open to the gardens outside, but no breeze came in to ease Munemori on a hot summer night. He tossed and turned on his sleeping mat. Beneath him, underneath the floorboards, was a possible cure for the weather. But Munemori had sworn to himself never to touch Kusanagi again.

Since the whirlwind, Munemori had again sequestered himself in his home, pleading an intermittent illness that kept him from his brother's duties at the palace. Munemori had no intention of giving the sword to his brother Shigemori. He had told Shigemori that he had been prevented from taking the sword, first by his illness, then by the tumult caused by the whirlwind.

But Munemori could not risk returning Kusanagi to the Imperial palace. Not yet. And choosing never to wield it again himself, there was little to do but keep the sword hidden. Munemori had considered over and over what further lies he would tell Shigemori, but he had thought of none yet that would be convincing. And his mother, demons take her, was sending letters of subtle inquiry. She was suspicious, and Munemori knew he had not the skill to dissemble to her.

As for the Shin-In, though Munemori had expected the demon ghost to appear every night since the whirlwind, he had had no such visitation. Munemori had expected to be punished for his failure to send the whirlwind into the palace. Munemori had hoped the Shin-In would choose to kill him and free his soul from this troubled, confusing world. But no such mercy had arrived.

As these thoughts bedeviled him, Munemori became aware of someone in the room. *Ah*, he thought. *My time has come.*

Munemori sat up, and, indeed, it was the Shin-In, floating at the foot of his sleeping mat. "Good evening, Majesty," Munemori said. "I am ready." He inclined his head as if expecting a sword blade to fall across his neck.

"Ready for what? Oh. You truly do conceive some strange notions. I have come to bring you news."

"News?" Munemori did not wish to hear any news from the Shin-In.

"You are on your way to becoming head of the Taira, as you requested of me."

"How is that so?"

"Your much envied brother, Shigemori, is dying."

Munemori had thought he could not possibly feel worse than he had already. The ache in his stomach told him he was wrong. "Dying?" he asked weakly. "How soon?"

"A few months yet. Akugenda Yoshihira and I intend for Shigemori to suffer. And thereby your father Kiyomori also. As well as most of the Taira who love and respect Shigemori. It will be a glorious period of sorrow, neh?"

Munemori fell back on the sleeping mat and stared up at the ceiling. "Why don't you just slay us all and be done with it?"

The Shin-In's hollow-cheeked face drifted over to hover above Munemori's. "Vengeance, done properly, is like a fine geisha. One must spend a long time savoring the many entertainments she has to offer. It would be an insult to thrust the sword blade quickly, once, twice, and be done. Vengeance is no common street whore. Attention must be paid to detail or else one invites embarrassment at the least, disaster at the worst. You, once an appreciator of women, should understand this."

"Very well, I understand," Munemori nearly shouted. "What do you want of me?"

"Of you? For now, nothing, since you have chosen to be good for nothing. Be at ease. Watch the dance of Fate and Fortune. The time will come for you to take your place again upon the sacred platform. I will have further instructions for you then."

"What should I do with the sword?"

"It is best where it is, where no one can find it."

"I won't wield it again for you."

"I know. No matter. A master of vengeance never uses the same blow twice. One must keep the opponent guessing and off guard. I have other tricks in mind to play upon the good people of Heian Kyō. The greatest favor you did us was to help us destroy Enryakuji. Without the monastery to guard the northeast mountain passes—"

"Please! I beg you, go away!" Munemori wrapped his head in the bed-clothes to shut out the sound of the Shin-In's voice.

"Very well. I will overlook your rudeness and go. I have said enough. For now."

Munemori waited long moments before he pulled the cloth down from his face. The Shin-In had gone.

Offers of Assistance

Summer faded into autumn, and Taira Shigemori faded with the seasons. He could eat less and less and became thinner and thinner. Yet, through it all, Shigemori remained very calm and peaceful. He shaved his head, took Buddhist vows and changed his name to Jōren. He spent his days lying alone in a room, studying the sutras.

On one such day, a messenger came from Nishihachijō. "Lord Shige-mori, I am sent by your father Kiyomori," said the messenger, distress and pity obvious on his face. "He begs you to reconsider your refusal to accept any medical help."

Shigemori managed to smile, and he spoke barely above a whisper. "My father is . . . kind. But as I have said many times, the gods have decided. This is how it shall be. Who am I to defy the will of the Buddha and the Kasuga *kami?*"

"Begging your pardon, noble lord," said the messenger, bowing, "but your father has found a physician from the great kingdom of Chang'an who has been traveling in our land. Kiyomori is most impressed with the wisdom of this man, and he asks that you permit him to see you, so as not to insult such a distinguished visitor."

Shigemori sighed. "Please tell my father I am grateful for his efforts. But I am a Minister of State. For me to accept treatment from a foreign doctor, when I have already turned down the help of the good physicians of Nihon, would be an insult to my countrymen. Please help my father to understand. My life is in the hands of Heaven."

The messenger let his head droop sadly. "Lord Kiyomori expected this might be your answer. He wishes you to know his prayers are with you. As you do not require his help, he will be leaving for Fukuhara. As he might not be with you at the end, he wishes to know if there is anything you would ask of him upon your . . . departure."

"Nothing that he surely does not know already. I wish my son, Koremori, to be Ason of the Taira, although he is yet too young for any responsibilities. I remind my father to be respectful in his dealings with the Retired Emperor. I ask my father to give up his meddlings in matters of the world and accept the freedom from care that his gray robes permit him. Tell him these things, if you please." Shigemori ended with a rasping cough.

"As you wish, Lord Shigemori," said the messenger. "Shall I leave you now so that you may recover in peace?"

Still coughing, Shigemori nodded and waved him away.

Shigemori's cough eased a short while after the messenger left and he sipped at some cold green tea. There was a scratching at the *shōji* beside him. "Who is it?" Shigemori whispered.

The *shōji* slid aside to reveal Nii no Ama kneeling there in her gray robes and cowl.

"Mother."

"My son. I heard you coughing and came to see if there is anything I can do for you."

Shigemori shook his head.

Nii no Ama came in, walking on her knees, until she was beside him. "I was told you turned down your father's offer of a physician."

"I did."

Nii no Ama looked down and gently caressed his sleeve where it lay on the floor between them. "I have a last offer of my own to make. You know my father, the Dragon King, accepts the souls of admirable noblemen into his palace under the sea."

"You told me so when I was a boy."

"As you are my son, his grandson, that offer is certainly yours to take. You would be welcome to sit among the great heroes at Ryujin's hall and live in the elegance of days long past forever."

Shigemori smiled at her and shook his head.

"Why not?" asked Nii no Ama as tears welled in her eyes.

"Because I do not wish to live as noblemen do for eternity. I have experienced that life and found it . . . unsatsifying. I wish to travel to the Pure Land and sit upon the lotus at the hand of the Amida Buddha."

"But you do not know for certain that is where you will go."

"Then I will await another turn at the Wheel, for a chance to prove myself worthy in another life. I do not fear leaving this world, Mother. I look forward to this journey. To the fact that I will see amazing things and know amazing truths no matter what happens."

A sob escaped Nii no Ama's lips, and she covered her mouth with her sleeve.

"Please do not weep, Mother. I see now that I was not meant for this world. I did my best to behave honorably to all men, to live with dignity and compassion, and pursue wisdom. But I was born to a family that honors war and ambition. I had no place here. I am pleased to leave it behind. I worry most for Koremori and my other children. You will see that they are treated well?"

Nii no Ama nodded.

"And will you see that my father does not behave irresponsibly once I am gone?"

"You know I have no control over him. I never did."

"Ah, well. I expect that Munemori will become Chief of the Taira until Koremori is of age. Though so much may change. Will you tell Munemori that . . . I was pleased by his efforts, and I regret that we cannot grow old together as brothers?"

"I will tell him. I was pleased to see you two reconciled. I had the impression there was some project that had brought you together, though I could not discern what it was."

Shigemori shook his head. "We had hoped to present you with a pleasant surprise. But, now, it appears that is not to be. Fate was not with us. There is no point in explaining further. It would only dishearten you."

Nii no Ama looked down. A single tear dropped from her cheek onto the gray silk of his sleeve, making a spot dark as an ink blot. She said, "It is not right, that you should leave before your parents. It is unnatural. I should never have been here to endure this."

"Is it not better, Mother, that you see me this way, rather than see my head on a pike or the prisoner's tree, the victim of a terrible war? My death is but the passing of a breeze compared to some I have . . . foreseen. Forgive me, I should not speak of such things."

"I understand," said Nii no Ama. "I have had such dreams myself."

"Well, then. I need not tell you to take care. Ahead truly lies the *mappo*. The End of the Law."

"I know."

It was clear his mother was going to lose control of her emotions at any moment. Shigemori put his hand on her shoulder. "Mother, is it not time for the midday prayers? There are many who are in need of them, are there not?"

"Yes, yes you are right, my son." Nii no Ama took up his hand and briefly pressed it against her aging cheek. Then she stood and walked swiftly to the *shōji*, sliding it shut behind her.

Shigemori sighed deeply and lay down on the floor. *Dear gods, if you*

would take this burden of life from me, I pray you do it soon. Do not force
me to watch my family suffer on my behalf.

And so it came to pass that, on the First Day of the Eighth Month, in
answer to his prayers, Shigemori's spirit left this world.

The Roaring Sea

The sky was a gray wall in the distance where an offshore storm lashed
the sea. The rocks on the shore were rimed with white ice from frozen
salt spray. The waves broke in gray curls like dragons' talons upon the stony
beach of Fukuhara, where Kiyomori stood. The foamy tops of the waves
were carved by the wind into white dragons' heads that gaped, mouths full
of fangs, at Kiyomori.

"So!" Kiyomori shouted at the surf. "You think to bring me down by
allowing the gods to take my son? You think I will destroy myself from
guilt because I was tricked by the Shin-In?

You think, perhaps, I will bring you Kusanagi out of shame? Think
again, Ryujin-sama! As ever, I defy you! I defy all the gods and all the
demons who beset me! I am Kiyomori, Lord of the Taira! My grandson
will be Emperor, and the sword will give him right to rule, and there is
nothing you can do about that!"

A large wave rose out of the sea and rolled toward Kiyomori. But it
broke upon the stones a few yards from where Kiyomori stood, merely
splashing him with briny water. The foam surged beneath the uprights of
his high clogs, but did not submerge his feet. "Hah!" cried Kiyomori, and
he shook his fist at the ocean.

Another wave rose, higher this time, black as lava stone, and it rushed
toward him. It broke at his feet, knocking Kiyomori down, soaking him to
the skin instantly with cold, cold water. Kiyomori felt the weight of it atop
him as if a dragon had landed and sat itself upon his chest. He could not
move. His mouth filled with salt water, and he wondered for a moment if
he would drown. Then the wave receded, leaving him sprawled out on his
back on the beach. Kiyomori spit the water out. Behind him, he heard voices
approaching.

"My lord! My lord!"

"There he is! He has fallen down."

Two servants grabbed his upper arms and shoulders and hauled Kiyomori to his feet.

"Dear me, he is soaked through!"

"My lord, why are you out here? A storm is coming, and it is dreadfully chill. I pray you, come inside with us at once!"

Kiyomori wanted to shout at them, to fight them off, but his teeth chattered so that he could not speak. His muscles cramped, so intensely did he shiver in the cold. He could do nothing but allow his servants to pull him back up the hillside to his mansion.

I will not be this helpless, thought Kiyomori, enraged. *Though I am old, I am still a warrior of the Taira. So long as there is breath in me, no one shall bring me down. No one! Not until I see my grandson seated upon the Jeweled Throne.*

A Servant's Request

Munemori stood and walked slowly toward the *shōji*, the letter from his father still in his hand. Sorrow and loss had emptied Munemori of his will, leaving him as hollow as a clay statue. He felt as though someone else moved his mouth, his hands, his feet, while he, himself, moved in some featureless land of fog and mist. He slid the *shōji* open and stopped, startled. Three of his eldest servants knelt there, two men and a woman who had been with him ever since he had left Rokuhara as a youth. The eyes in their wrinkled faces were wide with concern.

"What is it?" Munemori asked.

The three pressed their foreheads to the floorboards. "My lord," said one, whose name was Gamanshō, "we could not help but overhear your conversation with the messenger."

"We could not help but hear," said the old woman, whose name was Ogiko, "that you are considering turning down the Taira chieftanship. That you are thinking of becoming a monk."

"This is so," said Munemori. "What of it?"

The three bowed low again. "Please, my lord, hear us."

"We understand," said Ogiko, "that you have been visited with great sorrows. First your wife and child, and now your brother."

"Surely no one has cause to mourn more than you," added Gamanshō. "But there are other things to be considered in this matter."

"What other things?" asked Munemori, becoming impatient.

"Think how disheartening it would be for your clan, my lord," said Ogiko, "if you were to abandon them at this hour. Your younger brother Tomomori is far less ready to accept leadership than you are. How could you force this responsibility on his shoulders when it is rightfully yours?"

"Tomomori is thirty-three, he is certainly mature enough," sighed Munemori.

"Then, if you will," pleaded Ogiko, "think of *us*."

"We may be only lowly servants, my lord," said Gamanshō, "but we have tended you and your family for many years, our loyalty unswerving. If you were to take the robes of a monk, giving up all your worldly possessions, what would become of us? We are too old to be welcomed into a new household. Very likely we would have to end our lives rather than face the poverty and misery to come."

"But if you accept the position of Chief of the Taira," said Ogiko, "we could continue to spend our last years in service to you, in a household we have come to love."

Munemori felt his mood turning sour. He could hear the hopeful ambition in her voice, and it sickened him. If he chose to become a monk, he could very easily find another Taira household for them—the Taira valued loyalty and rewarded it. But the elderly servants wished to spend their last years serving the Lord of the Taira. It was ambition, not fear, that drove them to this request.

But Munemori had no will to argue anymore. It hardly mattered. "Very well. You may send someone to catch up to the messenger, and tell him I will accept the chieftanship."

Their faces beamed with joy. The old servants stood and bowed. "A most wise decision, my lord, very wise. We knew we could rely upon your kind heart." They hurried off to spread the good news throughout the household.

Munemori stepped out into the corridor, the south side of which was open to a garden. The last leaves on the maple trees were falling, tossed about by the wind. On the ground they lay blood-red against a white dusting of snow.

In his mind, Munemori composed the poem:

How the leaves dance!
Do they not see?
It is the cold wind of winter
That blows them so and brings the snow
That soon will bury them.

The Earthquake

Three months later, on the Seventh Day of the Eleventh Month of the third year in the era of Jishō, the Empress Kenreimon'in was taking a late-night walk through the inner compound of the Imperial palace. She could not sleep. She had slept only fitfully since the death of her brother Shigemori. Her many layers of winter-weight kimonos hissed and whispered around her like the wind through winter snow as she walked. Her mind seized upon thoughts just as the Crown Prince would seize upon a favorite toy and not let it go. *Is it my fault?* she wondered, as always. *Did Shigemori die because I wielded Kusanagi?*

She did not care where her feet led her. She paid no attention to the grumbled whispers of the two ladies-in-waiting who followed her. Kenreimon'in walked down every corridor of the Inner Ward searching for a peace she could not find.

As she padded down an interior corridor of the Dairi Compound, she heard a low, distant rumble. "Thunder?" she murmured. "In winter?"

Then it hit. The floor seemed to leap up beneath her, tossing her back into the arms of her ladies-in-waiting. The boards at her feet shuddered, and the walls beside them swayed. Ahead down the corridor, *shōji* opened and shut like the jaws of snapping turtles. The roof beams overhead groaned, and dust rained down upon them.

"*Jishin!* Earthquake!" cried the ladies-in-waiting. "We must get outside!"

But the rolling ground beneath them would not let the Empress and her ladies keep their balance. They fell to the floor, and she fell atop them in a mass of silk. Desperately Kenreimon'in clung to the ladies in a huddle against one of the stouter walls. She could hear frightened screams from every direction.

My child. Is my son safe? I must find him. She prayed to the Amida to spare the Crown Prince, to spare her, or to make her death swift if that was to be her fate.

At last, the rolling stopped. The walls shuddered, then remained at rest. A momentary silence descended on the palace.

"There will be more," one of the ladies-in-waiting said. "It is the baby serpents after the mother serpent, as they say."

"Then we should do our best to get out while we can," said the other lady. "Majesty, are you all right? Can you stand up?"

With effort, Kenreimon'in managed to disentangle her sleeves from those of her ladies pull herself upright. "I seem to be unhurt. Where was the Crown Prince nursing tonight?"

The two ladies stood and shook out their robes. "He was in the Nishi Ga'in, Majesty."

"I must find him." Disoriented and vaguely ill, Kenreimon reached over and opened the *shōji* nearest her. She stumbled into that room and saw two young girls pulling on their underrobes. They had been nearly naked. The room was a mess—kimonos all over, chests overturned. And then Kenreimon'in saw the rack on which Kusanagi was usually kept. It was lying on the floor and the sword was not on it.

"What has happened here?" she asked in horrified wonder.

The girls looked as though they were about to cry. They flung themselves to the floor at her feet. "Majesty! Please forgive us!"

"What have I to forgive? What have you done?"

"Someone . . . we, we had a visitor. We were discussing poetry."

By the way the girl said "visitor," Kenreimon could assume she meant a lover. "Here? While you are supposed to be guarding the Imperial Regalia?"

"It's all right, Majesty, he's—" And the other girl slapped her hand across the first girl's mouth and shook her head.

Kenreimon'in sighed. This would have to be dealt with later. "Put the sword back on the rack and then get outside for your safety."

"Yes, Majesty!" The girls searched through the sea of silk.

"I've found it!" cried one.

"No, I have it," said the other.

They both stood up, holding identical swords.

"There are *two* of them," said one in awed wonder.

"What miracle is this?" Kenreimon'in felt faint and leaned against the wall.

"Majesty, are you all right?" asked one of her ladies-in-waiting.

"But which one is the real Kusanagi?" said one of the girls holding a sword.

Kenreimon'in knew she could tell. If she dared touch the hilts of both of them, she would know which one was real. Perhaps they were both real, and the gods were playing a terrible trick on her. But she had sinned enough. She dared not touch either sword. "Choose one," Kenreimon'in said, irritably, "and put it in the sheath on the rack. We will sort it out later." Kenreimon'in staggered toward the raised blinds at the far side of the room. She had to get outside, get air, get away from the thing that seemed to be the bane of her life.

At the verandah, she nearly bumped into someone climbing over the railing to get in, and she staggered back. In the moonlight, she recognized him. "Munemori?"

"Sis—Majesty! Are you all right?"

"Yes, I appear to be. Are you?"

"Yes. I leapt outside as soon as I felt the first shake."

"Why are you at the palace so late?"

"Business to attend to. Please, let me help you to the ground. You must get to safety in case there are aftershocks." Munemori helped her get over the railing of the verandah and eased her down onto the snowy courtyard below.

Kenreimon'in turned to thank him and saw Munemori disappear into the room she had just come out of. She heard the girls squeal his name and ask him what to do about the swords. *And what have you to do with Kusanagi, brother?*

Servants grasped her shoulders and guided Kenreimon'in to the safety of the central courtyard. There, a whining Crown Prince was placed in her arms, and they spent a long, cold night huddled together, to await the next aftershock.

Many Thousand Warriors

Munemori shifted uncomfortably on the cold saddle beneath him. His horse stamped and tossed its head, its breath steaming in the chill winter air. Munemori was grateful for the padded jacket beneath his armor, but it still did not keep him warm enough, and he had grown unused to the weight and balance of the laced metal plates on his chest and arms. *We have had so many years of peace*, Munemori thought. *Why this, why now? Shigemori why did you have to die so soon?*

He could hear the laughter and wry comments of the thieves and prostitutes who inhabited the enormous southern gate to Heian Kyō, the Rashō Mon, behind him. His two lieutenants turned around to scowl at them. "Should we deal with the ruffians, Lord Munemori?"

"Their laughter will cease soon enough," said Munemori. He could hear the low rumble already, a sound not unlike the earthquake of seven days before. *And no doubt its source is as destructive in its power*, thought Munemori, feeling a small shiver of fear.

The rumble became louder and then the first of the horsemen rounded the curve in the Tōkkaidō. At their head rode Lord Kiyomori himself, sunlight glinting off the bronze butterfly on his helmet. The horsemen behind him all bore the red banner of the Taira, snapping in the chill breeze. Though the warriors approached at a sedate, slow pace, the inexorable numbers of them—Munemori estimated there must be thousands—was enough to drive dread into the heart of anyone watching. Indeed, Munemori heard the thieves and prostitutes gasp and scatter to whatever places they considered safe. *It is no use*, Munemori thought. *In these times, there will be nowhere that is safe.*

As he came to a few yards from Munemori, Lord Kiyomori raised his arm in signal for his horsemen to halt. In silence and perfect order, the Taira warriors did so.

Taking a deep breath of chill air, Munemori nudged his horse forward until he came alongside Kiyomori. "Father."

"Did you bring your forces?" Kiyomori growled without preamble. His mustache and skin were gray, and the creases in his skin made the old Taira appear to have been chiseled out of stone, his eyes cold and dark as flecks of obsidian.

"They await on the other side of the gate, Father."

"Good. Let us proceed, then."

Munemori turned his horse to ride alongside Kiyomori. Softly, he asked, "Father, your messenger did not tell me, what enemy do we face with such a massive force?"

"All of them. All enemies of the Taira." Kiyomori raised his arm and flicked his hand forward.

The army of warriors started forward again and proceeded toward the gate. Munemori urged his horse on to keep ahead of them. "Father, who has threatened us?"

"Who has not threatened us? Surely here in the capital you have heard it. The earthquake is our fault, it presages our doom. Likewise the whirlwind and the fire. All the gods, they say, are speaking against us. It is time, is it not, to show that we Taira do not care what the gods say. We will not let even the gods gossip against us. If it is turmoil the gods foresee, then it is turmoil they will have. And we, the Taira, shall be the victors."

Munemori swallowed hard. Shigemori had often hinted that he believed their father was mad. Munemori had not been certain, but had not particularly cared one way or the other. Now he realized his carelessness might have been foolish.

His two lieutenants turned their horses and rode ahead of them through the gate. The hoofbeats of the mighty force echoed with surprising softness off the wood beams of the Rashō Mon, sounding more like the burbling of a brook, the way a great flood can sound if one stands only at its edge.

Munemori's forces, scarcely a couple of hundred mounted warriors, awaited a couple of blocks ahead down Suzaku Avenue. The shopkeepers and common folk who had been eyeing them with curiosity now suddenly caught sight of the approaching army. Their eyes went wide, and they scattered back to their shops and homes, closing shutters and doors as soon as they could.

Kiyomori halted his warriors again as they came up to Munemori's forces. "Munemori, you will take your men and half of mine to Rokuhara, where you will set up a base of defenses. I will take the rest with me to Nishihachijō, where I will locate our headquarters. Once you have established your preparations, you will come to me again, for I have a particular task for you to perform."

"What task might that be, Father?"

But Kiyomori shook his head. "Let us say only that it is time to settle some affairs with certain persons." Kiyomori then turned in his saddle and began to shout orders to divide the forces.

Munemori realized in that moment that he had become more afraid of his father than he was of the ghost of the Shin-In.

The Insult

"This is outrageous," Go-Shirakawa said softly.

"Yet it was so, Majesty" said the Dharma Seal Jōken, shivering in his gray monk's robes, trying to warm his hands over a brazier. "Lord Kiyomori left me sitting in the snowy courtyard all day. He only deigned to speak to me just as I had risen to leave at sunset."

Go-Shirakawa motioned for a servant to bring more robes to drape over the shoulders and head of the esteemed Jōken, who was a son of Shinzei and deemed a wise and fair man by all. To have been treated so by the Lord of the Taira was a slap in the face not only to Go-Shirakawa but to civilized behavior in general.

"Did Lord Kiyomori tell you anything as to why he arrived yesterday with so many forces at his command?"

Jōken managed to nod. "At first, he said he thought the grievances he has against you were so obvious not to require mentioning. But since I remained to have audience with him, Lord Kiyomori deigned to correct our ignorance.

"His first complaint was that you held no official observance of sorrow for the death of his son, Shigemori."

Go-Shirakawa sat back with a frown. "Had I done so, Kiyomori would surely have complained that I was abrogating the right of his clan to arrange mourning as they chose. This is hardly a worthy complaint at all."

"He further went on to say," Jōken continued, "that you observed all the usual festivals and even held entertainments not long after Shigemori's funeral, with no thought of respect for Kiyomori's grief or the loss of such a fine and able counselor as Shigemori."

"Shigemori was a man who appreciated the fine things of life. He told me himself before he died that he did not wish the capital to become solemn after his death, claiming that would only hasten the dark times to come. This only proves that Kiyomori no longer knew his eldest son very well. Or it is mere pretext."

"Anyway," said Jōken, "that was the first thing. Next, Kiyomori said that the governorship of Echigo Province was supposed to be passed from father to son and kept with Shigemori's family. Yet, as soon as he died, that post was taken back to be given to another, not of his family."

"Shigemori's eldest is not yet old enough for such a post, and Echigo is an important province. I do not even remember ever making such an agreement. Go on."

"The third thing was that you, Majesty, ignored a recommendation Kiyomori made on behalf of Middle Captain Motomichi for a counselor post. He thought this a petty insult."

"Motomichi is Kiyomori's son-in-law, a toady to the Taira, and not worthy of the post. Surely he knows this and is using it for pretext."

"And of course," Jōken said finally, "he brought up the matter of Shishinotani again."

Go-Shirakawa leaned forward. "Did he know you were involved in that?"

Jōken sipped at a cup of green tea. "I am not sure, Majesty. But I did my best to absolve you of any involvement and reminded Kiyomori of the many blessings you have showered upon his house. He did not seem moved."

"Naturally, he would not be." Go-Shirakawa rubbed his chin and sighed deeply. "How I wish these were the old days. When one clan of warriors became too strong there was always another to call upon, to keep matters in balance. No longer."

"Majesty," said Dharma Seal Jōken, "the Minomoto are not yet vanished from this Earth, much as the Taira would have it so. I have heard of two of the great Yoshitomo's sons who are gaining influence in the eastern provinces. One, a younger son, has been building quite a reputation as a swordsman and leader."

"But the eldest and Ason," argued Go-Shirakawa, "Yoritomo, sits meekly in a monastery and refuses all calls to lead."

"Yoritomo has grown into an honorable man, Majesty, who obeys the

Imperial law, and thus obeys the terms of his exile. But if he were to understand that it is the Imperial family in danger, if he were handed an Imperial edict ordering him to act, I have no doubt Yoritomo would prove himself equally honorable in taking up arms against that threat. The Taira still have little influence in the eastern provinces, and it would not be difficult to amass a Minomoto force there."

Go-Shirakawa studied the weave pattern of the tatami mat beneath him. "Were I to send such a request myself, it would bring an immediate attack by the Taira upon my house. I do not wish another Sanjō."

"I understand, Majesty."

"Nonetheless, Kiyomori's threat cannot go unanswered. Or he will become a greater tyrant than Nobuyori ever was. I will think on all you have said, Jōken. I will think on it."

"May the Amida inspire you, Majesty, for the sake of us all."

Distressing News

Kenreimon'in felt the blood draining from her face. "Father has done what?" It was only the second day after Lord Kiyomori had returned to Heian Kyō, and already Kenreimon'in could see the world overturning.

Her mother, Nii no Ama, sighed and shook her head. "His Taira warriors have taken control of the city. No one dares make a move lest it bring instant destruction down upon them. Kiyomori has demanded that the Regent be dismissed, as well as the Chancellor. He demands that your brother-in-law, Motomichi, become Regent and Minister of State as well. The Senior Council of Nobles is quivering with fear over what Kiyomori's men might do if he is disobeyed, so I am certain they will comply. There is no one, no clan, they can call upon to oppose him. Many nobles who expect to be dismissed are fleeing to the outer provinces. Some, I fear, will not choose to remain in this world rather than face whatever wrath your father will bring down on them." Nii no Ama paused to clear her throat and made a noise that might have been a laugh. "I confess, I did not think the old goat still had it in him to be so bold. Were he not bringing about the destruction of the world, I might admire him."

Kenreimon stared down at her hands in shock. "I heard the weeping from the ladies-in-waiting, but they would not tell me why they were leaving the palace. It has been so empty here these last hours. Why? Why is my father doing this?"

"The charitable side of me," said Nii no Ama, "would claim that Lord

Kiyomori values the fortunes of his clan above all other things. He would do anything, even destroy the world we know, in order to prevent any loss in Taira power."

"And the uncharitable side?"

"Would say it is mere pride that drives him on. He has always been a proud one, your father, back when he was a strutting youth in his high clogs and high-handed ways. He has not changed. Only become more of what he is."

"Can not your father, the Dragon King, do anything?"

"Even the messengers in the pond laugh at me for asking. 'You have made your choice,' my father tells me, 'and now you must live with it.' "

Kenreimon'in sighed. "What am I to do? I briefly saw my husband today, and for the first time in my life I saw Takakura afraid, truly afraid."

"You have little to fear," said Nii no Ama. "You are Kiyomori's daughter, and mother of his grandson who will be Emperor. Your position is the most secure in all the world."

"But for my son to become Emperor, my husband must no longer be on the throne. What will become of Takakura?"

Nii no Ama stared down at the polished cedar floor. "As to that, I cannot say."

A Plain Ox-Carriage

Retired Emperor Go-Shirakawa awoke to the sounds of screams and running feet. Half out of a dream, he sat up on his sleeping platform, expecting the scent of fire on the air.

The *shōji* slid open with a loud clack and servants came rushing in. "Majesty! Are you awake?"

"I am. What hour is it?"

"The Hour of The Monkey, nearly dawn. There are warriors surrounding Hōjūji Mansion! They demand you come out at once!"

Hōjūji, thought Go-Shirakawa, *not Sanjō. This is not the past.* And yet, as he wrapped a hunting robe around himself, he could not help thinking some demon had transported him back to the most horrible moment in his life. He went out to the corridor and saw women, noble ladies and servants both, running past without even covering their faces, so fearful were they that fire might explode around them at any moment. As swiftly as his old body could manage, Go-Shirakawa ran out to the main gate and onto the street.

He half expected to meet the ghosts of Nobuyori and General Yoshitomo there, staring down at him from their dragon horses. Instead he saw an uncomfortable-looking Taira Munemori, who was clearly not fully in control of the steed beneath him.

"Munemori-san! What is this?"

Not meeting the Retired Emperor's gaze directly, Munemori gestured toward a plain ox-carriage that was being drawn up toward the gate. "Majesty, I must ask that you get in the carriage, quickly."

"What karma is this, that I must repeat my past horrors?" asked Go-Shirakawa. *Was there a spy in the room when the Dharma Seal Jōken gave me his advice? But I have sent no edict to the Minomoto yet. The Taira have no proof that I intend to act against them.*

But Kiyomori was far crueler than the idiot Nobuyori had ever been. This was likely no quick exile to the Single-Copy Library. To enter the carriage might well mean a short journey to Rokuhara and a swift journey to death. "What is it your father intends, Munemori? What wrong have I done that it comes to this? If it is only that I have guided my Imperial son in the running of government, that is because Takakura is still young. If this is what disturbs your father, then I will no longer do so."

Munemori replied, "I do not know, Majesty. My father has only instructed me to say that he fears there will be unrest and he wishes to remove you to the Toba Mansion for your safety."

The mansion that once belonged to the late Retired Emperor Toba, Go-Shirakawa's father, was on the far edge of the city and had been long abandoned. "Am I to be exiled then?"

"I do not know, Majesty."

"Will I be allowed my guards and my servants?"

"No, Majesty. Please hurry into the carriage."

"Munemori-san, what can I expect if I am unguarded? Surely you cannot permit a former Emperor to be treated in this fashion. Come with me and bring your men and serve as my guard. You Taira have always served me and my family honorably. There can be no shame in you performing such a service now."

Munemori looked around himself anxiously. "I . . . I cannot, Majesty. I do not know what my father would do. Please, get in the carriage. We do not want another Sanjō."

Go-Shirakawa's heart sank, realizing that Munemori did not have the strength of spirit of his late brother Shigemori. *There will be nothing to stop Kiyomori now. These may well be my last hours.* Sadly, he climbed into the back of the carriage. Only his former nurse, now a Buddhist nun, was allowed to ride with him. His only armed escort were some lower-grade North Guardsmen from the palace. None of the Taira nobility rode alongside the carriage. His only consolation was that no fire was set to the Hōjūji

Mansion as the carriage set out, and no screams of the dying accompanied
his departure.

As dawn broke, pouring light over Suzaku Avenue, the people of the
city came out to watch Go-Shirakawa's carriage pass. Many of them were
openly weeping, for word had traveled fast as to what had occurred, and
they, too, feared the worst for the Retired Emperor's fate.

So it has come to this, Go-Shirakawa could not stop thinking, as he
pressed his sleeves to his face. *So it has come to this.*

Before the Vermilion Curtain

Munemori knelt on a silk cushion before the vermilion-gauze curtain
that was all that stood between him and the august presence of
Emperor Takakura. No longer did Munemori have to sit on the verandah
outside and have his words transported by minister to the Sovereign of the
Jeweled Throne. It had been only a month since Kiyomori had reentered
Heian Kyō with his warriors. But so terrifying was his swift action in firing
the ministers that no blood was shed, other than by suicide. The Taira were
now indisputably the supreme power in the capital and could do as they
wished. And because so many ministers had recently been sent packing,
there was no one available to do the traditional speaking for and to the
Emperor. Therefore, by right of power and position, as well as practicality,
Munemori could sit in the same room as the holy descendant of Amaterasu
as if he were any other lord. It felt, somehow, obscene.

It was no easier task now that Munemori had, in essence, arrested the
Emperor's father and locked him up in a distant mansion with only two
servants. "Majesty," Munemori began, "my sister, the Empress, tells me you
do not eat and that you spend all your time in prayer."

"She is correct," said Takakura. Munemori was reminded of how young
he was, only in his late teens, and yet his expression, what Munemori could
see of it through the vermilion gauze, was solemn and sad.

"She has said," Munemori went on, "that you are considering retiring
from the throne and becoming a monk."

"I am," said Takakura.

"I bring you word from Lord Kiyomori that he has no wish for you to
do so. In fact, your father was . . . is being protected only so that he cannot
be used by forces who mean ill. My father wishes that you now rule in your
own right, create your own government as you see fit, since you will soon
be of age. So confident is my father in your abilities that he has left for
Fukuhara, pleased to leave the capital in your able hands."

"I cannot possibly rule," said Takakura. "Until my father the Retired Emperor cedes responsibility to me. Were it not for the letters I receive from my father begging me to remain upon the throne, for his protection, I would have stepped down the moment you had taken him into your custody."

"Such an act would be quite unnecessary, Majesty" said Munemori, "and quite distressing to your people."

"Little Antoku would then become Emperor," Takakura said. "Is that not what Lord Kiyomori wants?"

Munemori laughed, an embarrassed bark. "Antoku has only been in this world for one year, Majesty. There is plenty of time until he will be ready to ascend the Jeweled Throne."

"I truly do not understand why you are talking to me at all, Munemori-san," said Takakura. "So far as you Taira seem to be concerned, I am no one of importance."

Munemori bowed low to hide the shame on his face. "That is surely not so, Majesty."

"You are officially Palace Minister now, are you not?"

"I am honored to have that position."

"Then I expect you will run the palace as you choose. For matters of government, I suggest you speak with my Regent, as Kiyomori-sama seems determined that I must still have one. Now if you will excuse me, I wish to return to my prayers."

Munemori opened his mouth to protest, but realized he was being summarily dismissed. It would have been beyond rudeness to remain. Munemori stood and bowed his way out of the Imperial chamber.

He returned home. At nightfall, he burned the special incense upon a brazier and waited. It was not long before the Shin-In appeared.

"Why have you summoned me?"

"Because I am at a loss for what I am to do now."

The ghost sucked in air through his teeth, making his cheeks even more hollow. "You are Palace Minister. You are Chief of the Taira clan—"

"No, my father is. I have only the title. Kiyomori is the one whom the Taira warriors obey."

"Is that your complaint? That you still haven't power enough?"

"No, not at all. It is only that . . . I do not understand your plans for the future."

"Who are you that you should know my plans?"

"I have been your loyal servant these several years."

"Hmmm."

"I could be of more help to you, if I knew what you intended. But there is still much I do not understand. For example, Takakura is devastated over my father's treatment of his father. Takakura wants to leave the throne. The palace is nearly deserted, and I am sure the wardings have not been maintained. If you truly wished to rule Heian Kyō, would this not be a fine opportunity to possess Takakura himself?"

"There truly is much you do not know. Takakura has the protection of Amaterasu herself, and I am not so powerful as the First Kami. I could have possessed your sister's child until the moment your brother made the incantation giving Antoku's spirit to Amaterasu. If only my meddling brother hadn't interfered. No, were things so simple, Munemori-san, I would have done them long ago."

"So what is your intent, Majesty?"

"I intend to ride the *mappo* like a wild horse. As I am still denied rule, I will destroy that which I cannot have. I have done well so far, with the fire, the whirlwind, and the earthquake. But it is not enough. I will see to it that Heian Kyō itself ceases to be a place of any importance."

"I suppose you will want more of my help in this endeavor."

"Perhaps. Eventually. But it is Kiyomori-san himself who is helping the most at the moment."

"I had noticed," said Munemori.

Snow on Mount Fuji

Minomoto Yoritomo sat in the uppermost garden on the grounds of the monastery of Hirugashima, admiring the distant snow on Mount Fuji. It was only a week until the New Year, the beginning of the fourth year of the era of Jishō, and the air was bright with sunlight, but cold. Beside him sat a monk named Mongaku, who had been recently exiled from the capital himself.

"What perfection," murmured Yoritomo, nodding toward the cone-shaped mountain.

"Yes," agreed Mongaku. "How different from matters of this world."

"But that is why you became a monk, is it not?" asked Yoritomo. "To remove yourself from worldly matters?"

"Not entirely, I confess," said Mongaku. "Or not as it turned out. Did I tell you of the time I—"

"Got thrown out of one of Go-Shirakawa's music parties because you were demanding temple donations from him? Yes, you had mentioned it."

"Ah. Did I tell you I spent twenty-one days beneath the waterfall at Kumano chanting invocations to the Mystic King Fudō?"

"And how you were rescued by his messengers. And of the time you lay on a sun-baked hillside for three days, letting flies and mosquitoes bite to see if you could withstand suffering. Yes, Mongaku, your austerities are legendary, there is no doubt of it." Yoritomo had spent nearly eighteen years in exile now, and although his mild behavior had earned him the respect of his captors, he was still allowed few visitors. Mongaku was one of the few, and Yoritomo enjoyed discussing philosophy and history with the lively and strange little monk.

"Ah. I should save some of my stories, so I will not bore you with repetition, then."

"You are never boring, Mongaku."

"That is reassuring, in any case. The New Year approaches. Do you and your wife's family have any plans for the occasion?"

"A quiet observance, I think, will be all. What good is it to plan a celebration when I can invite so few to attend?"

"True." Mongaku sighed. "What good is it to plan a celebration when there is so little to celebrate these days? I do not know what will become of our poor country."

"It is said these are the Latter Days of the Law," Yoritomo murmured. "I suppose we cannot expect much." He looked around and noticed that the monks who normally observed him seemed to have wandered off. They often did when Mongaku came to visit. It seemed they had heard his stories too often themselves.

Mongaku apparently noticed the absence of the watchers, too. He narrowed his eyes at Yoritomo, and said in a low growl, "It is one thing to not expect much. But to ignore calamity, that is entirely another!"

"Ignore calamity? What are you talking about?"

"Have you not been hearing the news from the capital?"

"I believe my guardians tried to shield me from it, when they can."

"You have not heard of the fire and the whirlwind and the earthquake?"

"Ah. Yes, I had heard of those. Sure signs of the *mappo*."

"Surely signs that the gods are not pleased with things, neh?"

"So they say," Yoritomo replied cautiously. He feared where Mongaku's words were leading.

Mongaku leaned closer, and said in a harsh whisper, "Have you not heard that Taira Shigemori has died?"

"Yes, there was some word of that, but what is that to me?"

"It should be everything! The wisest man in the capital is gone, and now there is no check upon his father. Have you not heard that Kiyomori has locked up the Retired Emperor in the Toba Mansion and will not say when he will free him?"

Yoritomo blinked, startled. "I had not heard this."

"Just as that fool Nobuyori did, he locked up the Retired Emperor. Rumor has it Kiyomori might even kill Go-Shirakawa."

"He would not dare!"

"What would he *not* dare? Kiyomori is supreme, now. They say he is going to make Takakura abdicate soon and put his own puling infant grandson upon the Jeweled Throne. No doubt, Kiyomori will then make himself Regent, and the Taira hold upon the land will be complete. No other family will have the highest posts. No one will dare speak against the Taira, or deny them anything they demand. Their tyranny will be total."

Yoritomo felt his jaw clench. "That would be . . . regrettable."

"Regrettable! Is that all you can say? You, whose clan was nearly exterminated by the Taira? I realize it is improper to speak for any other man, but it surprises me your blood is not boiling!"

Yoritomo looked around again, hoping no one was in listening distance. "Given my situation, good Mongaku, I have felt it important for the sake of my clan not to cause trouble."

"How much worse could it be? With Taira Kiyomori in complete control, he may have his men seek out what is left of your clan and wipe you out entirely. What is there to stop him? Your time may be running out. If the Minomoto at least attempt to fight back, there will be honor and glory to your name. If you continue to do nothing, you and all your family has known and accomplished will vanish like books burned in a fire."

Yoritomo noticed some movement in the woods nearby, and he feared his guardians might be returning. "I am one who upholds the law, Mongaku. It would stain my reputation and that of my clan were I to turn renegade now."

Softly, Mongaku said, "I have had word from the Dharma Seal Jōken, who now is one of the few to tend the Retired Emperor in his exile. Jōken says Go-Shirakawa was contemplating sending an Imperial edict to you before he was arrested. Would such a thing not change your mind?"

Yoritomo swallowed hard. "If I were commanded by Imperial edict, how could I not obey? But until I see such a thing, I will obey the strictures of my exile." The guardian monks had moved out of the trees and were now approaching through the garden. Yoritomo stood, and said, "I thank you, good Mongaku, for your history lesson today. You have such interesting views on matters of the past. I must go to prayers now. But, as always, I will think on what you have said."

"Do so," said Mongaku. "Think upon it. There are many who would thank and bless you if you do. We will speak again." Mongaku stood and bowed and walked away.

Yoritomo took a last glance at Fuji-san as a cloud passed across the sun, causing a shadow to flow over the perfect mountain. A cold wind rose, and Yoritomo had to pull his robes closer around him. He nodded to his guardians and began to walk back to the monastery buildings, putting his hands into his sleeves for warmth. His left hand fell upon a folded piece of paper. He did not pull it out, for he knew what it was—he read it almost every night. It was a message from someone claiming to be his brother. "This fledgling white dove . . ."

A New Emperor

So. He has done it at last," muttered Retired Emperor Go-Shirakawa over his cold, meager bowl of rice.

"He has," said Dharma Seal Jōken, sadly. "Your son must abdicate the throne and now a one-year-old shall sit upon it, wearing the vermilion robes."

"A one-year-old Taira," growled Go-Shirakawa. "That is all that matters." In the distance, he could hear the fulling mallets of weavers and the boom of the bell of a nearby temple. Looking out on the winter garden, he saw the snow was unswept from the path, untouched by even the footprints of birds. "While I matter not at all, it would appear."

"That is not so, Majesty, or he would not keep you here."

"Keep me alive, you mean. Alas, while my son was Emperor, I had some modicum of protection but now . . . I fear these days may be my last."

"I would not worry so, Your Majesty. Had Kiyomori wanted you dead, he would have done so shortly after your arrest."

"He's just biding his time. Remember Narichika? Kiyomori wanted him dead, but waited months before he had the execution carried out. What think you? Is there a fall off a cliff onto sharpened stakes in my future, too?"

"Surely not, Majesty. You are of an entirely more elevated rank. Kiyomori might defy the law of the land, but surely he would not defy the law of the gods."

"You do not know Kiyomori-san as I do. I would not put it past him to defy anything. Even his son, Shigemori, thought he was mad. Do you know, there are rumors Kiyomori hired a wizard to kill Shigemori?"

Dharma Seal Jōken sat back in astonishment. "I can scarcely believe such a thing."

"Oh, I would believe it. I would."

Jōken paused before saying, "I have heard Kiyomori is extending to himself and his wife the Equality of Three Empresses."

"Hah. I am not surprised. It merely means Kiyomori can now come and go as he pleases in the Imperial palace. He can use any palace servant or bureaucrat, high or low, as if they were a Taira household servant. It's as much as if Kiyomori had appointed himself *Emperor*." Go-Shirakawa flung down his rice bowl bitterly and cradled his head in his hands.

"Majesty, Majesty, take heart. Calm yourself, for I have other news as well."

"What other news can matter?"

"Only this. I have a source who has spoken with Minomoto Yoritomo at Izu. The Ason of the Minomoto is reported to have said that if an Imperial edict was sent him, he would obey it."

Go-Shirakawa snorted a laugh. "What a shame I did not issue one while I could."

"Majesty, you still have breath within you, and there are those here who will serve you unwaveringly. Whether your days are long or short, only the Amida and the *bosatsu* can know, but do not spend them in despair. Is it not more honorable to spend one's last hours fighting to save the land one loves? Your chance to change the course of things, however, may be fleeting."

Go-Shirakawa rubbed his stubbled chin thoughtfully. "But you feel there is a chance, nonetheless."

"There is, Majesty. The people on the streets mutter that it is unseemly that Kiyomori, who has reputedly renounced the world with his monk's vows, now drains wealth from the Imperial palace into Rokujō and Nishi-hachijō. They resent the red-jacketed thugs whom the Taira send after any speaking ill of Kiyomori. The noble families resent being shut out of all promotions and fear losing their livelihoods. The support for opposition is there, Majesty, if you will only use it."

Go-Shirakawa sat up straight. A cold wind blew in from the garden, ruffling the hems and sleeves of his robes. But he did not feel the chill, for a fire of determination spread through him of a sort he had not felt in a very long time.

Three Goddesses

Newly Retired Emperor Takakura stood on the great platform of the Shrine of Itsukushima, looking out upon the Inland Sea. The sun was setting, framed within the great *torii* standing out in the water. The early-spring breeze brought the scent of new-growing things from Aki Province across the sea. But Takakura did not feel the optimism of spring, despite being only seventeen. He felt the desperation of a man who did not know how much time he had left in the world.

He had come to Itsukushima, the great shrine Kiyomori had built, on the advice of Kenreimon'in and her mother Nii no Ama. When word arrived at the palace that Takakura was to abdicate, Takakura had accepted the news calmly. He knew it was inevitable.

But Kenreimon'in became beside herself with worry. She told Takakura to go on a pilgrimage to Itsukushima and seek the protection of the Dragon King of the Sea.

And so, Takakura let it be known that he would undertake pilgrimage to the great shrine of the Taira, to show he bore them no ill will. For eight days he sailed downriver and by sea to the great shrine. There he was received with great celebrations and ceremonies. He had made a show of admiring the pagoda, the rich votive hangings, the bronze and gold fixtures. Sutras were dedicated for the occasion, and shrine maidens danced to the honor of the Imperial family and to Benzaiten and her sisters.

At last, Takakura had managed to convince the shrine priests that he wanted some time alone to commune with the *kami* of the sea. The entire east wing of the shrine, where the walkway jutted out over the water, was cleared of attendants, shrine maidens, priests, nobles, and servants, so that Takakura could have solitude.

Takakura took some sacred rice cakes from a box and crumbled them over the water. "Lord Ryujin-wo, Great Kami, Dragon King of the Sea, hear me. I, who am descended from Amaterasu, beg that you hear my plea. I have come—" But he stopped speaking in astonishment as three women rose from the sea until they hovered over it, their toes just above the waves. Their long black hair hung down their backs, just touching the water. Their kimonos were the same gray as the sea beneath them, the same gray as is worn for a funeral.

"Hail, former Emperor of Nihon," said the one on the left.

"Hail, Retired Sovereign," said the one on the right.

"Hail," said the one in the middle.

Takakura bowed to them. "Greetings to you, goddesses of the sea. Am I correct in assuming that you"—he nodded to the one in the middle,— "are Benzaiten herself?"

"I am," said the goddess. "We are honored, former Emperor, that you bring your petitions all this way to us. We are not often so noticed by those so exalted as you. Tell us what you wish of us, and we will answer."

"I have come at the behest of your sister, Nii no Ama."

The three ladies laughed. "Yes, we have heard she is a nun now. How strange. And only of Second Rank."

"Please, hear me," Takakura persisted. He knelt on the wet boards of the pier and grasped the railing uprights as if they were the bars of a cage.

"You have come to ask for the Dragon King's protection," said Benzaiten. "That is a bold request, even from a former Emperor."

Takakura took from his sleeve a small knife and swiftly, before he could change his mind, he sliced a cut across the palm of his left hand. He let the blood flow freely down to join the seawater below. "By the blood of the Imperial line, I beg you, hear my plea! I will spill all I have, if I must."

Benzaiten reached up her hand and clasped Takakura's palm. "There is no need, Majesty. We are pleased to listen to your request."

"We merely wished to know the strength of your resolve," said one of her sisters.

Takakura felt as if ice was pressed into his left hand. He looked at it as Benzaiten took her hand away. His cut had completely healed. "Then I ask you this, honorable Benzaiten. I wish protection, but not for myself. I ask on behalf of my father, Go-Shirakawa. He has the courage and wisdom to rule this land well, I know he does. But he has always been opposed by Kiyomori. I am told by your sister Nii no Ama that the Dragon King withdrew his protection from Kiyomori. So I now ask that that same protection be given to my father, so that he may prevail over Kiyomori. For myself I ask nothing. I will be content enough if my father may be saved."

"Such filial piety is impressive," said Benzaiten. "I have conveyed your words to my father Ryujin, he has listened through my ears, and he says he agrees to your request. Go-Shirakawa will be spared and supported by the *kami* of the sea."

"Thank you!" Takakura breathed. "Thank you! If there is anything else I may do to seal this pact of protection, you and your father need only ask it."

Benzaiten said, "Alas the thing you might have done to bring peace to your land, you can no longer do. Had you come to us while you still held the Jeweled Throne, and commanded the Sacred Regalia, there was a way. But now . . . it cannot be asked of you. Now only your son can perform that task."

"Then I hope he will prove brave of heart enough to accomplish it."

Benzaiten opened her mouth to speak again, but her eyes suddenly went wide and she and her sisters vanished into sea mist. Takakura heard footsteps behind him and he turned.

An old warrior, one of Kiyomori's cronies, had come up behind him, concern on his creased face. "Majesty, are you all right?"

"I thought I had instructed the priests that I should be left alone."

"So you had, Majesty. But even in solitude, you must have guards who watch you from afar. I thought I saw you injure yourself, so I came to see that all was well."

"All is well, I assure you." Takakura stood up.

"You have been weeping, Majesty."

"Who would not weep, in my situation?"

"Ah. And did the gods hear you?"

"They did," Takakura said.

"I see," said the old warrior. "And were your prayers answered?"

Takakura wondered how much the old Taira retainer had heard. But it hardly mattered, Takakura thought. Bravely he answered, "They were."

"Then will you return to the main compound, Majesty, and let your former subjects rejoice with you? I am told the sea can be untrustworthy, and dash you with its waves when it pleases."

Takakura managed a smile. "The sea can dampen my sleeves all it likes, so long as it bears another boat to safety." He turned and walked back to the main shrine building, aware of the old warrior's gaze on his back.

A Distressing Revelation

Kiyomori sat on the verandah of his mansion at Fukuhara, watching the spring sunlight dancing on the water of the sea. *I hope the spirit of Shigemori is watching from the Pure Land or wherever he has gone,* Kiyomori thought. *I know he does not approve, but surely he must see the importance of what I have done since he left. All is proceeding as it should.*

His thoughts were broken by a discreet cough to his right. Kneeling by the *shōji* was old Kaneyasu, Kiyomori's general and advisor. "Kaneyasu! Come out and speak with me. You know I never turn away your company or counsel."

The old warrior walked out, bowed, and knelt beside Kiyomori. "My lord. It is good to see you in pleasant humor."

"Who would not be in my place? I trust young Retired Emperor Takakura is comfortable in his guest quarters, after his long journey from Itsukushima?"

"He is, my lord, though I suspect he fears his rooms may at any time become a prison."

Kiyomori waved a hand dismissively. "There should be no need for that. You should have heard him, Kaneyasu, when I gave him audience to do me homage. How prettily he begged that I spare the life of his father. How he offered to shower promotions on my family! I tell you, it is good we removed Takakura from the throne. The young man has no spine."

Kaneyasu cleared his throat and pinched his nose. "Er, my lord, there is a matter I wished to bring up with you."

"Speak freely, old friend. I am in expansive mood today. I tell you, this surety of power is more intoxicating than plum wine or the perfume of a young woman's hair."

"Er, yes. Surely. But, my lord, while at Itsukushima, a curious thing happened. I was standing guard for Takakura as he went to do solitary prayers by the water. I saw him take a knife from his sleeve, and, fearing he might do himself harm, I went toward him. I heard him begging of Benzaiten and the Dragon King to protect his father, and he shed blood from his hand into the sea. By the time I reached him, however, his hand was healed, and he told me that his prayers had been answered. He seemed content, after that. I thought I should tell you."

Kiyomori scowled and felt his stomach grow cold. "Tricked," he growled. "All this time I thought the boy harmless, and he has gone behind my back to make alliance with my enemy!"

"My lord, perhaps this is not a time for overreaction—"

"Silence." Kiyomori thought a moment, staring out at the sea, its surface now glittering like a thousand knife blades poised to stab at him. "I cannot do away with Go-Shirakawa. By holding him hostage, I hold his followers in check. Too many would rise up at his death to avenge him. But for Takakura . . . let it not be now, let it not be soon—"

"My lord," Kaneyasu exclaimed in horror, "Think on what you are saying! Narichika was one thing, but a member of the Imperial family? Do not ask this of me!"

"I am not asking, Kaneyasu. I am ordering it."

The old warrior hung his head and stared at the floorboards. "As I am your sworn retainer, naturally I must obey. Perhaps the gods will forgive my soul for this. But they will never forgive you for making such an order. You doom yourself, my lord."

"I am already doomed, Kaneyasu. Nearly every night the ghosts of the Minomoto whisper vengeance in my dreams. I already know my soul will find the Hell of Eternal Smoke and Fire upon my death. What better purpose, then, can there be for the last days of my life but to commit those sins that will permit the Taira to stay in power forever? Is that not the task of a warrior, to do those horrible things that allow his lord and family to prosper? What does it matter that I become a demon, if my evil is put to the service of the Taira? Let all blame fall upon me, for I am already damned. Let all glory fall upon the Taira who live after me and who will sing my praises in time to come."

Kaneyasu sighed. "I can see there is no dissuading you. I shall do as you command."

"Good. Nothing obvious like cliffs and stakes this time, however. More subtlety is called for. Poison, I think. I will return to Heian Kyō with Takakura, to let him believe he has my confidence and goodwill. I'll show him I can be as good a liar as he is. And show his father there is a price for challenging Taira power, eh, Kaneyasu?"

"All shall be as you command, my lord," Kaneyasu said softly. He bowed low, got up, and departed.

"Indeed," Kiyomori agreed, glaring out at the sea. "All will be as I command."

The Accession Audience

Kenreimon'in took one measured step after another down the center of the great chamber of the Shishinden. She was grateful the many layers of stiff red-and-gold brocade kimonos hid her trembling. It was all she could do to control little Antoku, who staggered ahead of her in baby steps. His attention was so distracted by the many Taira nobles and ladies who sat to each side of the chamber that she had to hold his wide sleeves to keep him from running over to look at them.

Kenreimon'in could see her mother and father sitting near the Imperial dais at the far end of the hall. Kiyomori's old face was wreathed in smiles, and he seemed to glow. She had not seen him so happy since the birth of Antoku. But she could not share his joy. *You are doubtless annoyed, Father, that this ceremony must take place in this austere building that looks like a simple Shinto shrine, rather than in the Great Hall of State. Alas that, between all the calamities and uncertainties of these times, the Great Hall of State has still not been repaired from the fire over two years before. The fire whose spread was my fault. Perhaps the gods intended it this way to remind me of that sin.*

Her mother, Nii no Ama, was also smiling, but her smile was bathed in sadness. *Sometimes I wish I knew what future you have foreseen for us,* Kenreimon'in thought, *but more often I am glad I do not.*

Kenreimon'in managed to guide Antoku to the Imperial dais, where he became fascinated with the bronze guardian lions that stood at each corner. Kenreimon'in had to pick him up by the waist and set him upon the Imperial Chair.

Antoku wailed and flailed with his little arms and legs, but his voluminous vermilion robes prevented him from doing harm. The Minister of the Right, imperious in his black robes, placed the tall, black-silk cap on the toddler's head. By waggling the ebony baton of state in front of the boy's eyes, the minister managed to get Antoku to grasp the baton in his own tiny hands. Cheers erupted from the assembled nobles. Speeches were made, sutras were chanted, but Kenreimon'in stood in a daze, not listening to any of it.

She had gotten a letter from her husband, New Retired Emperor Takakura, when he was staying at Fukuhara. It had read:

> I suppose now that I can no longer come to the palace when I choose, that we will see little of each other in days to come. It must seem strange to you that I spend so much care on my father and so little on you and Antoku. But I know Kiyomori will look after you and our son.
>
> Nonetheless, I want you to know that my journey was successful, and I believe I have secured protection for my father. As for me, I care little as to what happens. I feel as if my life is already over. And from the whisperings I am hearing here at Fukuhara . . . Think no more upon me. Consider yourself a widow. Raise Antoku to be a fine Emperor. May Fortune treat you well. But, then, you are a Taira. I am sure it will.

Kenreimon'in stared at the painted panels behind the Imperial Chair. They depicted meritorious Chinese sages from times past. *Please inspire my son with wisdom*, she begged them silently. *He will be so in need of it. Please inspire my father with sense, so that he will do no worse than he has already done.*

An Imperial Edict

Four months after Monkagu's previous visit, Yoritomo was surprised to have the monk escorted into his presence in the garden at his father-in-law's home. It was a fine, late-spring day, and the flanks of Mount Fuji glimmered blue-green in the distance. Birds sang in the cherry trees, and the fragrant plumes of white wisteria blossoms swayed gently in the breeze.

Yoritomo welcomed Mongaku warmly, but noticed that the wizened little monk seemed anxious. "Please sit down, Mongaku. You must have had a trying journey here. Have you had more troubling news from the capital?"

"Yes and no, my lord," said Mongaku seating himself upon a cushioned bench. "I come bearing an urgent message for you. May we speak freely here?"

Yoritomo paused. "The only person of note who may hear us is my father-in-law, who is in that room beside the garden. Whatever may be said to me may be said to him as well, for we are of one mind about most matters."

"As you say, then. I have spoken with a monk named Yukiie who has spoken with the Dharma Seal Jōken, who serves the Retired Emperor Go-Shirakawa. He has passed along to me this message to deliver to you." Mongaku reached into his voluminous sleeve and pulled out a folded piece of paper. On the top fold of the paper was an insignia bearing the image of the Kikumon, the chrysanthemum sigil of the Imperial family.

Yoritomo felt the blood leave his face. "Ah, good Mongaku. I fear I know what this message contains."

"It is an edict," said Mongaku, "drafted by the former Governor of Izu, Minomoto Nakatsuna, and ratified by His Retired Majesty Go-Shirakawa on behalf of his second son, Prince Mochihito."

Yoritomo took it in a shaking hand. "They are calling upon the Minomoto to rise and overthrow the Taira."

"That is the sum of the edict, my lord, but you will want to read it for yourself. Yukiie has already moved on to deliver the same edict to other relatives of yours throughout the Kantō. You were first to receive it, however, because you are the Ason of the Minomoto; therefore, it is expected . . . well, it is hoped that you will be the leader of this uprising."

Yoritomo stared at the edict, still not opening it. "Can this be true?"

Mongaku said, "My lord, I am certain it is. This is the sign you have been awaiting, neh? Here, I have brought something else for you, for luck." He tugged at a string around his neck and pulled a bag out of his robe. Mongaku fished in the bag with his fingers and pulled out a piece of human jawbone. This he placed reverently in front of Yoritomo.

"I have been in the capital, in secret, hoping for news, my lord. While there, I spent some time idling around the palace prisons, as many beggars do. While seated on the ground, I found this in the dirt beneath the Tree of Severed Heads. That is where your father's head had been displayed and where they had buried it. The other beggars told me that trophy seekers had gone and dug up your father's skull, and they showed me the place where the dirt was disturbed. I ran my fingers through the dust and I found this. Since then, I have carried it with me and prayed over it at every temple and shrine I have stopped at. Now it is only fitting you should have it."

Yoritomo picked up the bone fragment and felt a tear well up in his eye. "Ah. Poor Yoshitomo. I can still remember him, Mongaku. A man of great strength and wisdom. A general without equal. A warrior of incomparable virtue. How poorly Fate treated him, when the world should have been grateful for his efforts against the Taira. If this is truly a relic of my father, then you have brought me a gift beyond price."

Mongaku bowed. "I am pleased to have done so. Now you must excuse me as well, my noble lord, for I should follow after Yukiie and make sure he doesn't get into trouble. May all the gods and Buddhas give you courage and ensure your success." Mongaku also swiftly departed.

Carefully, Yoritomo picked up the bone fragment and the edict and hurried to the *shōji*. When he slid it open, he discovered his father-in-law sitting just beyond it, wide-eyed. "You have heard?" Yoritomo asked.

"I heard everything, my son. What an extraordinary day this is!"

"I . . . I cannot read it myself. I feel unworthy. Here. Hold this for me a moment." Yoritomo handed the edict to Tokimasa and went to perform a ritual cleansing of the hands and mouth. He put on the white robe and black cap of a pilgrim and, returning to his father-in-law, bowed three times in obeisance to the Imperial edict. "There. Now I am ready. If you please, Tokimasa, do me the honor of reading the edict to me."

With great formality, Tokimasa unfolded the paper and began to read in a sonorous voice: "It is ordered that the Minomoto and their troops . . . proceed immediately against the Chancellor-Novice Taira no Kiyomori and all those who support him."

Yoritomo let the words wash over him as he rocked back and forth, murmuring the Lotus Sutra.

"They have incited rebellion . . . caused the people to suffer . . . confined the ex-sovereign . . . seized lands, usurped offices . . . therefore I, Prince Mo-chihito, second son of Go-Shirakawa-In . . . proclaim war . . ."

When Tokimasa finished reading, he folded up the edict again and was silent some moments.

Yoritomo finished his prayer and looked up. "There can be no doubt, then. It is time. But surely this is the very day you have dreaded since I came into your care so long ago. Your people have long served the Taira, and it was by Taira order that you became my warden. What will you do, Tokimasa?"

"It is true that the Hōjō were loyal vassals of the Taira at one time. But that is because we believed they served the best interests of the Emperor. Now it is clear the Taira no longer do so, for here the Imperial family demands the Taira be suppressed. Therefore, I gladly make my forces yours, Yoritomo, and you are no longer a prisoner here, but free to go where you will."

"You do not know how much this pleases me, Tokimasa. I had dreaded the possibility that I might become your enemy."

"I feel surprisingly pleased as well, Yoritomo, as if a weight has been taken from my shoulders. I will go spread word among the men in my service that they should prepare to fight on your behalf and at your orders. How extraordinary. Surely we must have known one another in a previous life to have so important a connection in this one." Shaking his head, Tokimasa stood and went out.

Yoritomo went to his writing room and, opening a chest of small drawers, found a brocade silk bag. Into this he put the bone fragment and the edict, and then he hung the bag from his neck, vowing to himself to wear it always. Also in the drawer was a long wooden box that Yoritomo had not looked at in several years, though he had often thought about it.

The box contained sticks of incense that had been given him by a spirit. A spirit who had claimed to be a former Emperor. A spirit who claimed to be doing the will of Hachiman, and who had prophesied that this day would come to pass. *I have spent my life in religious studies and quiet contemplation*, Yoritomo thought. *I have not dealt with matters of war since I was a boy. Surely there is no harm in asking the messenger of Hachiman for guidance.*

He pulled out two sticks of the incense and, lighting a small bronze brazier, set the incense upon it.

As soon as heavily scented smoke began to curl upward from the brazier, a ghostly face appeared in the vapors—the face of the Shin-In. The spirit smiled, and said, "Ah, so, it is time."

A Serious Matter

Munemori was also savoring the breezes of spring, early in the Fifth Month. The iris and azaleas were in bright blue and purple bloom in his garden, and the yellow globe flowers drooped over the ornamental stream.

His mood was almost optimistic. Things had been calm in the capital, since Takakura had gone on his pilgrimage. Kiyomori was happy now that his grandson was on the throne. Not much was being expected of Munemori, and he found he liked it that way. *The trouble with having become an important person is that people expect you to make important decisions, and then blame you terribly if things go wrong*, he thought. *I wish I had known when I was younger how much better my life was when I was taken for a fool.*

Munemori paused to admire one particularly lovely iris when the gate burst open and Koremori, Shigemori's eldest son, now all of seventeen, rushed in. "Have you heard the news, Uncle?"

"News?" Munemori said, his heart sinking.

"Somehow the Retired Emperor Go-Shirakawa has sent out an edict, demanding the Minomoto rise up against the Taira. It is circulating through-out the Eight Eastern Provinces, and there are rumors that already armies are amassing to march against us."

Munemori let the iris fall from his hand. "This . . . this cannot be true. He would not dare."

"I have word from too many sources that it is true. Apparently Go-Shirakawa has decided to take the chance. You are Chief of the Taira. Give me my orders, and I will take all the warriors we have and ride east."

"Um . . . er, you know, I cannot truly do anything without Kiyomori's approval. It would be wrong of me to act on my own without his advice. Someone must go to Fukuhara and inform him. That is the task I give you. Ride to Kiyomori and tell him the situation." *That way I do not have to face my father's wrath*, thought Munemori.

"But Uncle," Koremori protested, "the longer we delay, the more time we give the enemy to organize against us!"

"Have you forgotten? The Minomoto are scattered like grains of rice upon a beach. It will take them months to have any sort of army ready, and when they do it will still be no match for the Taira. Now get along with you and inform Kiyomori of the situation. Speak with me again when you know his mind on the matter."

Koremori scowled, but he bowed obediently and departed.

Munemori sighed and headed for the darkest, smallest room of his man-sion. Though he had not used it in a while, it still stank of ashes and incense. Closing all the blinds and shōji, Munemori lit the incense and waited. And waited.

"Where are you?" he growled into the empty air.

The incense blazed into flame and vanished. The ghostly, hollow-cheeked face of the Shin-In appeared in the air. "Do not summon me as though I were a child!"

"S-sorry," said Munemori, "but matters are urgent."

"I do not care!" shouted the spirit. "I am done with you, you weak, miserable excuse for a man. I have found a better servant to work my will. You are on your own, great Chief of the Taira. Do all you can against the forces I shall bring to bear against the Taira, I dare you!" Laughing, the face of the Shin-In faded, leaving Munemori to sit, stunned, in the darkness.

Old Stories

Nii no Ama did not let the rumors of rebellion distract her. She spent the days of late spring on a much more important mission: being the doting grandmother of little Emperor Antoku. She taught him to say *Obaa-san* and gladly welcomed his smiles and chubby-armed hugs.

Now, with the Freedoms of Three Empresses, Nii no Ama could go where she pleased in the Imperial Compound. And she pleased, whenever possible, to be with the little Emperor. Whenever she could, she would lead Antoku to the shrine in the center of the Daidari and say, "There is where the Mirror of Amaterasu is kept. Amaterasu is your great-grandmother many times over. That mirror is what beckoned her out of her cave when she hid from the world."

Then Nii no Ama would take Antoku to wherever the other regalia were being kept, for often they were moved around the palace in these late days. The Imperial Compound was no longer so safe a place as it once had been.

Nii no Ama would point at the curved jade jewel, and say, "That is the Sacred Jewel. It is said that it commands all the fishes and the creatures of the sea. Long ago, a wise Emperor used its power to feed his hungry people."

Lastly, she would point at the Sacred Sword. "That is Kusanagi, the Grass-Cutter. I have a long story to tell you about that one, and it is an important story, so listen well." Nii no Ama would look around to see that no ladies-in-waiting were too close by. Then she went on, "Kusanagi was made by my father, your great-grandfather, the Dragon King Ryujin. It is said that someday, in order to save the world, someone of the Imperial family must return the sword to the sea. . . ."

Antoku would listen, eyes very wide, bobbing his head as if he understood perfectly.

Prince Mochihito's Head

Kiyomori sat sweating from the summer heat in the stifling, covered ox-carriage. The sun was setting, but it was the sort of summer evening when the air would not cool for some time. Kiyomori did not care, the heat warmed his old bones, and he reminded himself that given where his soul was bound, he had best become used to it. He proudly listened to the excitement of the crowds surrounding the carriage and lining Suzaku Avenue, awaiting the victory parade.

Kiyomori had reason to be proud. As soon as he had received word of the rebellion, Kiyomori had returned to Heian Kyō and sent forces after the traitorous prince. Kiyomori bribed the monks who were rebuilding Enryakuji so that they did not join the rebellion. Mochihito's seven-year-old son was captured, and Mochihito's mansion razed to the ground. The prince had fled to the temples at Nara and taken refuge there. But Taira forces had followed, fought the prince's forces at Uji Bridge, and killed Mochihito, all in less than a month. Another great success and proof, to Kiyomori, that the Taira fortunes had not fallen.

"Do you think it will nod," asked Munemori, the only other occupant of the carriage with him, "as Shinzei's head is said to have done?"

"You are in morose humor today," said Kiyomori. "Are you not proud that we have yet again prevailed against rebellion? Besides, Shinzei was a good man who was wronged. Mochihito was a rebel and a traitor."

"He was a prince, a member of the Imperial family," said Munemori. "Is it not . . . unseemly to display his head on a pike this way?"

Kiyomori turned and looked at Munemori. How pale and drawn Munemori had become over the years, Kiyomori noticed. His cheeks more hollow and his eyes more sunken as if life had been drained from him. "What is the matter with you?" Kiyomori asked. "You are not going to begin chiding me like your brother Shigemori did, are you?"

"No, Father," Munemori replied. "I could never be like Shigemori."

"Good," Kiyomori grunted. "Shigemori was a fine gentleman, but he was born in the wrong age, to the wrong family. He would have made a fine Fujiwara, but he was no Taira."

Munemori was silent a moment. Then he said, "I have heard that the Retired Emperor Takakura has taken ill."

"Has he?" asked Kiyomori, unable to suppress a slight smile.

"They say he is unable to keep down his food."

"Well, in these latter days, what can one expect? You see how weak the Imperial line has become? Take a young Emperor from his throne, and he wilts like a chrysanthemum that is removed from sunlight."

"Then we must see that Antoku remains upon the Jeweled Throne into old age," said Munemori.

"Indeed, we must," agreed Kiyomori. "You must make that your foremost concern, Munemori. The day will soon come when I am no longer in this world to guide you."

Munemori was again silent.

Cheers erupted from the crowd around the carriage and Kiyomori pushed aside the curtains bearing the butterfly crest that covered the rectangular window. Suzaku Avenue was now filled, gutter to gutter, with mounted Taira warriors, their armor shining, their banners fluttering, their horses stepping proudly. At the front rode Koremori, bearing the pike on which rode Mochihito's head. Kiyomori watched the procession go by, daring Mochihito to nod at him, but the head did not.

"Hah!" cried Kiyomori, "I will see you in one of the One Hundred Hells, Mochihito!"

"Father," Munemori said, reaching for Kiyomori's sleeve.

"What?"

"N-never mind."

"You were going to say that I am behaving in an unseemly manner."

"No, nothing of the kind."

"Something is the matter with you. You have not been this weak-willed in years. Are you ill?"

"No, Father. It is merely . . . I had received some . . . disappointing news some time back. I have not yet quite recovered. A personal matter. Nothing to concern yourself with."

"Ah. A woman, then."

"No. A . . . spiritual matter."

"Ah. Speaking of spiritual matters, I want you to order Taira troops to ride down to Miidera Temple at Nara. The monks there are clearly traitors as well, for they harbored the rebel prince. Raze the temple and then burn it. Let Miidera be an example that treason will not be tolerated, even among the holy."

Munemori was silent.

"Well?" Kiyomori roared.

"It shall be as you say, Father."

A City Floats Downriver

"What, today?" cried Kenreimon'in, as the servants rushed about, packing up her things. It was early morning, and she had hardly finished dressing. Her long black hair was still unkempt from sleeping and not yet fastened with pins and combs.

"It is so, Majesty," said Munemori apologetically. "Father has given the order to speed up the transfer of the capital. I think he wants to keep everyone on edge, to forestall objections, by doing the unexpected."

"Or Shigemori had been right."

"You had best not say such things, sister. I cannot vouch for Father's mood anymore. There is no saying whom he will strike down, whom he will think to be a threat."

That made Kenreimon'in pause. Kiyomori had ignored her in her childhood, played the proud father when she married a prince, and doted upon her after she became pregnant with the future Taira Emperor. But she had heard many stories of how Kiyomori threw away people who were no longer of use to him. Many a dancing girl had had her life ruined and been forced to become a nun when Kiyomori lost interest. She had heard the dark rumors that Kiyomori had had Shigemori cursed to die, though Kenreimon'in chose not to believe them. And there was Takakura's mysterious illness. *Indeed, what might Kiyomori do to a daughter who is no longer dutiful?*

She allowed the servants to sweep her along through the palace corridors, out to where a carriage awaited by the gate.

"Wait, where is Antoku?"

"The Imperial Palanquin has been brought for him," said Munemori, who had followed along behind her. "You are to ride in separate conveyances."

"But why?"

"I do not know. I no longer question Father's orders."

"Antoku should not travel alone!"

"The wife of the Taira Major Counselor will be with him."

"I do not understand!"

"I am afraid it is not Father's way to explain things."

"What of my husband? I have heard he is too ill to travel."

"Nonetheless, Takakura will be going in your procession as well as his father, Retired Emperor Go-Shirakawa. Now please get in the carriage."

Kenreimon'in did so, followed by several of her ladies. Kenreimon'in leaned out the carriage window. "Munemori, this Fukuhara ... what is it like?"

"It is ... by the sea, Majesty. By the sea." Munemori bowed and hurried off to perform some other duty.

The carriage lurched forward, and Kenreimon'in fell against one of her ladies-in-waiting. Normally this would bring laughter, but this morning everyone merely thought it bad fortune.

"I have heard of this Fukuhara, Majesty," said one of the ladies. "A gentleman who visited me often told me of it. A dreary place, he said, where the wind never ceases and the ocean waves roar in your dreams. The cries of the seabirds are like tormented souls, and there are few flowers and no pleasant streams. It is only hills and sea, that is all."

"Why?" whispered Kenreimon'in. "Why would my father wish us to move to such a place? Why do we have to abandon Heian Kyō to make Fukuhara the capital?"

The ladies did not answer, only staring down at their laps in uncomfortable silence.

As soon as the carriage rolled out of the Imperial Compound gate of Suzakumon, the carriage was surrounded by Taira warriors on horseback. Kenreimon'in glanced out, but saw no friendly, familiar faces this time. Hemmed in by horseflesh, she felt as though her carriage had become a rolling prison cell.

Sometime later, the carriage slowed as the road went uphill. Kenreimon'in peered out through the bamboo blind that covered the window. She could see down a slope to the Kamo River in the valley below, and the morning sun illuminated an astonishing sight. Many of the great mansions of Heian Kyō had been made into gigantic rafts and were floating down the Kamo River. From the road, Kenreimon'in could hear the bellowing of oxen as they strained to haul wheeled pallets on which lay roof beams and carved pillars and *shōji* and even garden gates down to the water's edge. The streets of Heian Kyō were torn up from their transport.

"What is this?" Kenreimon'in exclaimed softly. "Why are they tearing down the whole city?"

"I have heard, Majesty," said the lady-in-waiting who knew about Fukuhara, "that there are no building materials to speak of in the new capital. I have heard that noblemen have had to take over the homes of peasants in order to find places to live. Therefore, those who can are bringing their houses with them."

"They drift down the river like leaves borne on the winds of fate." Kenreimon'in sighed. She let the blind fall shut again. She leaned against the wall of the wobbling carriage and closed her eyes. "This is a dream. This is all some terrible dream."

"It is karma," muttered one of the other ladies. "I have an uncle who was a monk at Miidera. He barely escaped with his life when your father ordered the temples burned. All those ancient images and books lost. No wonder the gods permit this to happen."

All the women in the carriage stared at the complainer in shock. Her eyes suddenly widened and she held her sleeves up to cover her face. "Your pardon, Majesty. I meant no disrespect. Please forgive me." The women now turned their heads to stare expectantly at the Empress.

Kenreimon'in knew she had the right to have the woman dismissed from palace service, or worse, for speaking so against a member of the Imperial family. Kiyomori would have insisted on a harsh punishment for speaking against the Taira. *But I am not my father, and in these dark times there is a place for mercy.* "We are all very tired," suggested Kenreimon'in, "for being rushed so suddenly, so early, into this journey. It is surely understandable that careless things may be said. And forgiven."

The air was filled with many sighs of relief as the ox-carriage rolled on to Fukuhara.

The Prison Palace

Retired Emperor Go-Shirakawa had not had a pleasant journey to Fukuhara. His ox-carriage had been poorly furnished with cushions, and his old joints complained with every jolt of the road. His only company were an elderly nun and the Dharma Seal Jōken. Go-Shirakawa had also seen the tearing-down of mansions out of his carriage window, and the great rafts floating down the Rivers Kamo and Yodo. He, too, knew that the once-great capital of Heian Kyō was undergoing irreparable ruin.

It all seemed of a piece to Go-Shirakawa. His son Mochihito had been executed. His son Takakura was dying. This in addition to the many other sons, daughters, wives, and concubines he had lost through his long life. *All my efforts against the Taira have been in vain*, he thought, as his carriage bumped toward the new capital. *Surely the gods mean to destroy the world. My sins in a former life must have been many and terrible that I am forced to remain alive to witness the end of things.*

It took two days to travel the forty *li* to Fukuhara. When the Imperial procession stopped for the evening, at a post station at Daimotsu, Go-Shirakawa was kept separate from the others. He only got a glimpse of the pallet on which his ailing son Takakura had been carried, as he was escorted into the inn. But Go-Shirakawa was hustled into a dark, heavily guarded room, not allowed to speak with anyone. He spent the night listening to voices, those of his son, his grandson the Emperor, Kenreimon'in, and others he remembered from the palace, as they were lodged in rooms nearby. He could hear them speaking of him and inquiring how he was. *It is as though I am already dead,* he thought, *and haunting the lives of others.*

The next day, he arrived in Fukuhara at sundown, although the overcast from the sea obscured the sunset. As soon as Go-Shirakawa stepped from the carriage, his face was swept by the cold wind from the ocean. He could hear the distant roar of the surf, behind the confused babbling of transplanted nobility.

"This way, Majesty," said the fully armored Taira warrior standing before him. Go-Shirakawa turned to follow his gesture and found himself standing before a rough wooden gate that clearly led to a small house of poor quality.

"Welcome to your new home, Majesty," said the Taira with a cruel smile. "It has been prepared for your arrival. We call it the Prison Palace."

Go-Shirakawa sighed and allowed himself to be escorted through the weedy garden into the rough-hewn, rustic house. He noted the one gate was the only entrance. The nun and Dharma Seal Jōken were charged with bringing in what few belongings Go-Shirakawa had been permitted to take with him. The house had only three small wings, and Go-Shirakawa was taken to the one farthest from the gate and shut in.

Go-Shirakawa sat on the floor in the middle of the darkening room, listening to the sea wind rattle the *shōji* and roof tiles. He wondered if there was any object in the room with which he could kill himself. *Why does Kiyomori keep me alive? Would it shame him if I took my own life? Probably not. The man has no shame, no honor. There are those who would rise in indignation at my death to fight the Taira. But what if they fared no better than Mochihito? Would my soul rest knowing I had asked so many to ride to their doom?*

He heard a fluttering among the roof beams and he looked up. In the dim light, he saw a dark pair of wings. *Ah, a bird or a bat. Trapped here as I am.*

The creature flew down to alight on the floor in front of him. It was a black bird, slightly larger than a crow. Curiously, it had a little boxlike hat strapped to its head. Curiouser still, it bowed low to Go-Shirakawa, and said, "Greetings, Majesty. Be of good cheer, for I have been sent to bring you good news."

"A *tengu*!" Go-Shirakawa said, and to his own surprise he smiled. "I have heard of such creatures but never seen one."

The bird tilted its head. "Oh, you have probably seen more of us than you know, Majesty. I am a Leaflet Tengu. I have the honor to have been sent by our prince, Sōjō-bō, as his messenger."

"But you spoke of good news. I thought such a thing was no longer possible in these dark days."

"It is rare, to be sure, Majesty. But my news is this. Your son was successful in speaking with the Dragon King of the Sea, Ryujin. Therefore, Ryujin has extended his protection over you, and here, so close to his domain, no harm will come to you."

Go-Shirakawa raised his eyebrows. "To have the protection of one of the Great *Kami* is no small thing."

"Indeed," agreed the *tengu*, "for, you know, it was Ryujin who was responsible for the success of the Taira, which he sorely regrets, I can tell you."

"Yes, I see. But why have you come to tell me this, little *tengu*, rather than a serpent in a pond or a dragon out of the sky?"

"Because now the interests of the *tengu* and those of Ryujin are joined. We *tengu* have long been suspicious of the Taira and their tyrannical ways. So we have made alliance with the dragons of the sea and air."

Go-Shirakawa sighed. "You offer me much hope, little *tengu*. Yet I do not know if I dare grasp that hope after so much disappointment."

"Then hear this. The rebellion you incited is not extinguished. Though it cost you one son, there are still many sparks from that fire that the Taira did not put out. The Minomoto are rising to answer your edict. One of them, in fact, has been trained from childhood by our prince and is now a swordsman without compare. The other, the Minomoto Ason, has the protection and guidance of Hachiman . . . as well as one other great spirit whom we hope will not cause too much trouble."

"With so much power arrayed against the Taira," Go-Shirakawa breathed, "is it possible they will be defeated at last?"

"Let us say the chances are better than they have been in a long while. Therefore, do not despair, Majesty. Stay hopeful. Stay alert. Stay alive. Let what forces we can amass fight for you. There are better days to come." The little *tengu* bowed again and flew up into the rafters and out through a hole in the roof.

"Good-bye," whispered Go-Shirakawa. Feeling weary, he curled up on the floor, tucking one arm under his head. Now the wind and the distant booming of the sea were no longer disturbing to his spirits. Now they lulled him, like a nursemaid's song, to sleep.

The New Capital

This is madness," thought Munemori, as he rode down the main street, if it could be called such, of Fukuhara. Drizzling rain pattered against his wide brocade sleeves. The mud sucked at his horse's hooves and passing oxcarts splashed dirty water onto his hunting jacket and breeches. No one bothered to dress formally in Fukuhara; there was no point. Finery did not remain fine in this place for long.

It had been a week since the arrival of the Imperial family in the new capital, and it had rained nearly every day. Munemori glanced up at the overhanging clouds and thought he saw a gray dragon's head leering down at him. He shook his head, and the illusion was gone.

"Munemori-san," said someone riding up beside him. It was a young man, a Fifth Rank bureaucrat who was still trying to balance a high silk hat on his head despite the winds from the sea. "They are asking for you at the meeting of City Planning Ministers."

Munemori let out an explosive sigh. "What am I to do? I am the Palace Minister, not a geomancer. When they have the proper Nine Zones mapped out, then I will help lay out the Palace Compound. But the last I had heard they had only measured five." Munemori saw a poor family being rousted out of a thatched house that was being commandeered for a nobleman's household. The poor man and wife, their possessions in baskets on their backs, glared at Munemori as Taira warriors hurried them down the road. Munemori turned his face away.

"That is so, my lord. There is so little level ground in this place that zones have proven nearly impossible to measure."

"Hmmm." Munemori's horse stopped and nearly reared up as a pile of enormous house beams rolled into the street just ahead. "What is this?" Munemori cried. "Why is this here?"

The workers apologized with many humble bows as they hurried to get the beams rolled out of Taira Munemori's way. Munemori watched as they returned the beams to a pile of waterlogged lumber, muddy tiles, and soggy *shōji* beside the road.

The young bureaucrat clicked his tongue and shook his head. "It is the rains, my lord. These hillsides are so unsteady, once they are cleared of trees and brush so that construction may begin, the mud slides down to erase all the work of leveling. No one can put up the houses they rafted all the way here from Heian Kyō because there is no safe place to put them."

"Madness," Munemori muttered again.

"My lord," the young bureaucrat said hesitantly, "the city planners are beginning to think, well, that some other site should be considered for the new capital."

"Hah. What does my father say to that?"

"They have not yet brought it up to him."

"Of course not."

"They were hoping they could ask you to do it."

Munemori whirled around in his saddle. "Me?"

"You are his son and Chief of the Taira, my lord. If Kiyomori-sama was to listen to anyone, we assumed it would be you."

"By now you should be aware that Kiyomori listens to no one but himself. I told him not to bribe my uncle Yorimori with Senior Second rank so that we could commandeer his mansion for the temporary palace. I told him not to use provincial taxes to pay for the new palace. I told him people would talk. Did he listen? No! And now there is more grumbling against the Taira. I told him we should not cancel the Great Purification Ritual. But he did. And now it is claimed the Taira wish to remain impure so that we may commit more sins. And the council thinks he will listen to me?"

The young bureaucrat coughed lightly with embarrassment. "Will you at least consider bringing the matter before him, my lord?"

Munemori sighed again. "I will consider it." *But do no more than that.* "Now begone. I have work to do." He nudged his horse forward.

The bureaucrat rode off to be a nuisance to someone else, and Munemori urged his horse up the steep hillside track that led to the construction site of the new palace. To his surprised disappointment, when he arrived, he saw that no progress had been made from days before. Wooden lintels and beams still lay at the edges of the muddy clearing, and piles of floorboards were still heaped amid puddles.

The foreman of construction noticed Munemori arrive, grimaced fearfully, and came running over. "Good day to you, Munemori-sama," he said, bowing many times.

"It is not a good day," growled Munemori. "Why is the building no further along than this? Are you all a bunch of layabouts? My father will be most displeased."

"Forgive us, Munemori-sama!" said the foreman, bowing many times again. "We have tried. Every day we have the posts planted and the string laid out to precise measure. The boards are cut and carefully stacked ready to be assembled. We leave at the end of each day ready to raise up the first wing. And then the next morning, we return to find the posts pulled out, the string entangled in the trees, the board piles pushed over, the roof beams rolled into the woods, and the roof tiles scattered everywhere. Each day we must start all over again!"

"Have you not requested guards to watch over the materials?"

"We have, my lord. For the past three nights, Imperial archers have kept watch." The foreman crept closer to Munemori's stirrup and ducked his head. "And my lord, each morning the archers report that they hear the laughter of *tengu* in the trees. The archers fire whistling arrows into the woods and give chase to any creatures that they see. But by the time they return," he gestured out at the mess, "it is the same. All is undone."

"*Tengu,*" Munemori said, sneering.

"So the archers claim, my lord."

"It is more likely the natives who were thrown out of their homes getting their revenge," grumbled Munemori. "I shall have the guard doubled on this site. See that there is progress from now on, or I will have the lot of you fired and punished for your failure."

"Yes, Great Lord. It shall be so, Great Lord." The foreman backed away, bowing as though his spine were a reed in a storm wind.

Munemori turned his horse and headed back toward the rude, rustic hovel he had been given as his lodging. The rain was soaking through his thick silk hunting jacket, chilling his skin.

Smoke in Moonlight

Two months later, on a clear, moonlit autumn night, Minomoto Yoritomo stood on the verandah of his residence in Izu, watching anxiously to the west. He thought he heard, carried on the wind, the sound of a whistling arrow, signifying an attack. Yoritomo sighed. *Now it begins.*

The movement of the capital had not changed Yoritomo's plans, nor had the defeat of Prince Mochihito at Uji Bridge. In fact, he paid these things little heed. The Shin-In had advised him that the signs were clear—the time had come to reunite the Minomoto. The Taira would be defeated.

Yoritomo had spent the last two months slowly gathering those forces still loyal to the Minomoto and learning through espionage which forces were not.

Yoritomo was determined not to repeat the bad fortune of his father, attacking with too small an army. He did not wish to risk the total annihilation of his clan. Yoritomo had no illusions about the power of the Taira. If he was to have any hope of success against them, he would have to amass a great and powerful force.

The key to having such a force lay in the Kantō, the Five Provinces that lay to the north and east of Heian Kyō. It was there that the remnants of the Minomoto survived, along with the families of their hereditary retainers. Yoritomo knew that if he could conquer and unify those five provinces, the Taira could not possibly stand up to him.

But that lay in the future. Tonight was the first foray, an attack against the Governor of Izu Province, Izumi Hangan Kanetaka, a member of the Taira clan. Yoritomo had carefully arranged for maps to be made of the governor's mansion, and although he had originally planned an attack by day, the delay of arrival of some of his warriors moved the battle to nightfall. Yoritomo had told his trusted warriors to burn the Kanetaka mansion, so that the column of smoke would inform Yoritomo that they had been victorious.

But the hour grew later and later, and there was no fire. Yoritomo became more anxious and asked a servant to climb a nearby tree. "Do you see any smoke?" he called up to him.

"I am sorry, my lord, I do not."

Yoritomo paced the verandah, as the hours of night turned toward the hours of dawn. The pale light that heralds the coming of the sun began to glow in the eastern sky.

Yoritomo vowed that the next battle he would face in person. *The chosen of Hachiman should not hide in his residence*. No more playing general at a distance, sending others to do his bidding, no matter how trusted. *A commander belongs with his warriors*. Even though Yoritomo had not worn armor or ridden into battle since he was a boy of thirteen, surely his very presence would help spur his men's courage. As well as give him a better view of how the battle was going.

"My lord, I see it! A column of smoke!"

Yoritomo stared intently toward the moonlit hills where the Yamaki Mansion lay. And then he saw it, too, a thin wisp of rising gray that grew thicker and darker. He almost imagined he could see the golden light from the flames as they consumed the governor's house.

A messenger on horseback galloped into the courtyard. "My Lord, lord Hōjō and Moritsuna are returning with Kanetaka's head. They should be here by sunrise."

Yoritomo sighed with relief. "Good. Our first victory. By the sword of Hachiman, may it not be our last."

On the Shore

Nii no Ama strolled along the rocky beach, letting the incessant ocean wind whip her gray nun's robes about her. In the scent of the salt sea air, in the roar of the waves, in the sighing of the sand, she could feel her father's presence. She could see the white dragons' heads in the seafoam atop the curling breakers, though others could not. They always seemed to be laughing at her, crying, "Come home, Tokiko! Come home!"

But now was not the time. She had an Imperial grandson to look after.

Two months she had lived in Fukuhara now, watching the pitiful efforts of the Heian Kyō nobility trying to make a home here. But it seemed her father was doing all he could, with the waves and the weather, to make the port inhospitable. There had never been a more miserable autumn for Those Who Live Above The Clouds. Illness and melancholy were rampant. Every poem written sang of homesickness. Ryujin was proving that even the highest of rank, no matter what they called themselves, lived *beneath* the clouds.

Every day Nii no Ama came down to the shore, to pray to her father to be merciful. She knew he was listening. She knew he would not acquiesce. She knew what he wanted.

She had thought about snatching Kusanagi herself, now that they were so close to the sea, but she did not know precisely where the sword was being kept. And she had heard that Munemori had ordered the regalia to be held under very heavy guard, ever since the earthquake. The one time she had mentioned Kusanagi to him, shortly after their arrival in Fukuhara, he had become anxious and suspicious and had quickly changed the subject.

As for her husband, Kiyomori had not wished to be in her presence at all since the move, except for occasions of state, of which there had been few. For nearly all purposes, Kiyomori had become Regent, Chancellor, and Emperor all in one. No one dared contradict him. No one dared disobey him. No one dared speak against him. Only the *tengu* in the hills laughed at him, in the night.

Nii no Ama had heard them in the treetops, near the temporary palace, jeering the Taira archers sent to hunt them. She did not know what it meant, but she feared it did not bode well. Usually the *tengu* involved themselves little in human affairs, except to play tricks and taunt the holy. That they should be so bold was disturbing.

A wave broke particularly close and flowed up the sand to Nii no Ama's feet. The cold water swirled around her sandals and sucked at her legs as it withdrew. It felt like cold fingers grasping at her ankles, and she staggered a couple of steps closer to the sea.

"No, Father, no," she protested, almost laughing. "I am not ready to come home. Not yet, not yet." She saw a large swell starting to rise out on the water. She turned and ran up the beach. Despite her aged legs, she managed to just outrun the rushing seafoam as it broke upon the shore.

Ishibashiyama

Minomoto Yoritomo was beginning to regret his decision to lead an army himself. The miserable autumn rain spattered against his armor, soaking the cords that held the metal plates together, making it twice as heavy. His scalp itched beneath his helmet, where he had tied an ivory image of Kwannon, the goddess of mercy, into his topknot. He wondered at the wisdom of his gesture of faith, for Kwannon was choosing not to be merciful at this moment.

Yoritomo had led three hundred mounted warriors here to Mount Ishibashi in response to the news that the local Taira were sending horsemen eastward toward Izu. They had had to leave suddenly, in the middle of the night, in order to gain the advantage of surprise. He had arrayed his forces just south of the great road, Tōkkaidō, along which the Taira would have to ride. If his men, few as they were, could draw the Taira off the road, into the rugged terrain of the Hakone Mountains, there was a chance of taking them by ambush and thus achieving victory over a much larger force.

But he hadn't expected the rain. The clouds completely obscured the moon, which should have lit their way. It had been difficult to keep torches alight. Even whenever faint flames could be coaxed from them, it was hard for Yoritomo to see his surroundings. The raindrops glittered in the firelight like curtains of topaz gems, demurely hiding the hills around them. Once off the Tōkkaidō, it became very difficult to find the way, and nearly impossible to determine the best position for observing the approach of the Taira forces. At last, the rain had softened to a drizzle as dawn approached, and Yoritomo was able to align his forces along the ridge of Ishibashiyama, facing west, to await the arrival of the enemy.

It was shortly after dawn when one of his outriders returned, urging a laboring horse up the ridge toward them. "My lord, they are coming!" the outrider cried, his face pale.

"How many are they?" asked Yoritomo.

"I cannot count so high, my lord. They are thousands, while we are but a few hundred."

"What of Lord Miura's men, who were to reinforce us?"

"They have not yet arrived, my lord."

Yoritomo swallowed his fear. He took heart that the men he had brought with him had sworn fealty with great intensity. They would be loyal. They would not falter.

As the sky began to lighten, Yoritomo could see horsemen appearing at the top of the ridge opposite them, warriors bearing the red banners of the Taira. But these warriors did not shout out announcements of name and region, sought no challenges to other worthy warriors. They did not loose a flight of whistling arrows, or declare a charge with drums and gongs. They did not even stop to form a line. Instead, they began pouring down the hillside, pressing the attack without formal preamble. Indeed, there appeared to be thousands of them, their torches and red banners held aloft. It seemed as though a flood of fire was racing toward the Minomoto. As the Taira thundered up the ridge toward them, one of Yoritomo's aides asked, "My lord, what shall we do?"

It was only the second battle of his rebellion. For the sake of his reputation, Yoritomo did not dare flee. But he did not know how victory could be achieved in this situation. He felt the acute absence of experience, the many years spent as a scholar instead of a warrior. He wondered if bearing the blood of Yoshiie and Yoshitomo was enough. *Has Hachiman led me into this as a test?* He glanced around at his men, who were staring back at him expectantly.

"It is time for the battle to begin," he said to them, calmly. "Forward!"

With a mighty shout, the Minomoto line surged ahead, flowing down the hillside to meet the approaching tide of Taira. As Yoritomo watched from the height of the ridge, his men hit the Taira line with all their strength. The rain began to fall again, and raindrops spattered off the halberds and helmets, *sode* and sword blades. Soon red drops flew and fell as heavily as the rain, running in rivulets down the hillside. Yoritomo watched in horror as his men were reduced from three hundred to one hundred, to fifty, to ten.

His aides beside him said, "My lord, we must flee."

Yoritomo remembered Rokuhara, the moment that his father had to be prevented from charging the Taira stronghold back in the Heiji Uprising. He marveled that his fate might so resemble that of Yoshitomo, but did not wish the failure of his father. He pulled out his own bow and began to fire arrow after arrow into the approaching mass of warriors. He scarcely paused to take note whether many of his arrows hit their mark. It did not matter, for the Taira kept coming, closer and closer.

"My lord!" The aide grabbed Yoritomo's horse's bridle and turned the horse roughly. At last, seeing no other course, Yoritomo threw down his bow and rode east, deeper into the Hakone Mountains. The Taira pursued, firing arrows and throwing stones as they jeered him.

Praying desperately to Kwannon and Hachiman in his shame, Yoritomo wondered if, like his father, he now faced a flight into death and ignominy.

Rolling Skulls

That very night, in the middle of the Eighth Month, in the fourth year of the era Jishō, Taira Kiyomori awoke to a hollow rattling and clacking from the garden beside his sleeping chamber. he could no longer hear the sea. Kiyomori sat up and slid open the *shōji*, allowing the damp night air to blow in.

In the moonlight, in the garden, over a bed of fallen leaves and pine needles, hundreds of skulls were rolling around and around, like balls chased by children. As he watched, the skulls began to organize their movement, rolling closer and closer together, then beginning to pile up upon each other. Now and then, Kiyomori could see a ghostly face superimposed upon the skulls—and he recognized them. One was the Minomoto general Yoritomo, another his son Akugenda Yoshihira. Narichika was among them, as well.

"Hah!" said Kiyomori. "Come to torment me again, have you? It will do you no good. I am not afraid."

The pile of skulls grew and grew until it became an enormous skull-made-out-of-skulls, three times the height of a man. The holes that would be eye sockets in this giant skull glowed with a red light.

"Very impressive," growled Kiyomori. "Is that all you can do?"

A ghostly face appeared over the giant skull—a face with hollow cheeks and sunken eyes.

"Ah," said Kiyomori. "The Shin-In. We meet at last."

"Beware, Kiyomori-san," intoned the Shin-In, in a voice like wind from a cave. "These skulls are the power I bring to bear against you. They and their living descendants will see that the Taira are brought to ruin."

"You do not frighten me," said Kiyomori. "Your own brother was able to sing you out of Rokuhara. All your threats and scheming have so far done nothing to diminish the Taira. You ghosts and demons can do nothing unless the will of man allows it to be so."

"Indeed," agreed the Shin-In. "Unless the will of man allows it to be so. Which is why, with your daughter's help, I burned the Imperial palace. Which is why, with Munemori's help, I destroyed Enryakuji, and summoned the whirlwind. Which is why, with your help, I killed Shigemori and destroyed Heian Kyō."

"Lies," hissed Kiyomori.

"And which is why, with Yoritomo's help, I will destroy the Taira."

"Never," whispered Kiyomori. "Through my sins, I have become as great a demon as you. I have defied the Dragon King. I have broken my vows and defied the Amida Buddha. I have defied all the *kami*. It is no great matter for me to defy *you*." He sat and glared at the giant skull long into the night, until the apparition vanished.

A Messenger from the East

*B*ecause the new capital had been moved, it was not only farther from trouble, but it was farther for news from the Eastern Provinces to travel. It was not until seven days later, on the First Day of the Ninth Month that word came to Fukuhara of Yoritomo's rebellion.

Munemori sighed with exasperation when a servant informed him that an urgent message awaited him in the courtyard. Munemori was at his father's Fukuhara mansion, where Lord Kiyomori was hosting a celebration of the completion of the New Imperial Palace. It was the first pleasant event to have occurred in that desolate place, and Munemori was irritated to be drawn away from the *gosechi* dancers and *koto* musicians.

"Could this message not be given to another?"

"That would not be appropriate, Lord Munemori."

"Not even to my father?"

The servant paled and shook his head. "You are Chief of the Taira, Munemori-sama. It is best you hear this first."

With great reluctance, Munemori stood and followed the servant out to the courtyard. A cold drizzle was falling on the huddled, miserable messenger and the dead horse he stood beside. "The horse was ridden to death, my lord," the servant whispered in Munemori's ear, "so desperate was the messenger to reach Fukuhara."

"Then I suppose I had better hear him," muttered Munemori, wishing this were a burden someone could take from him. He invited the messenger onto the verandah, under the sheltering eaves, and said, "I am listening. What is your message?"

The messenger bowed many times, perhaps more to warm himself than out of excess politeness. He reeked of sweat, his own and his horse's, and his clothes and hair were askew from many hours of riding. He said through chattering teeth, "My lord, Minomoto Yoritomo has raised a force of warriors in the province of Izu. He has already defeated and beheaded Governor Kanetaka."

The rain seemed to fall a bit harder, and Munemori felt a distinct chill even through his heavy autumn silks. "Where were our partisans? Were there no retainers of the Taira to deal with this upstart?"

"My lord, there were. The lords of Sagami gathered their men, numbering in the thousands, and met Yoritomo at Ishibashiyama. He only had a few hundred men, and the lords of Sagami destroyed most of Yoritomo's force, causing him to flee for his life."

"Then what is the urgency of this message, man, if the matter is dealt with? Why do you bother us at all?"

The messenger sighed and took a deep breath. "My lord, news of the battle has spread like a flood across the Kantō. Although Yoritomo lost, his men fought so valiantly for him that anyone of Minomoto blood, or whose family ever served that clan, are now clamoring to join with him. Horsemen from every province are arriving in Izu seeking to bring down the Taira and raise the Minomoto to their former glory."

Munemori's stomach went cold. *So. That is it. The Shin-In has joined with the Minomoto.* "Give this messenger a warm meal, dry clothing, and a new horse," he ordered the servant. Munemori returned to the festivities and wondered how best to get his father's attention for a private conference.

Kiyomori sat on a raised platform, tapping his thigh with his fan in time to the drums and flute. He smiled occasionally at one of the pretty dancers. Munemori thought he would not like to be the girl who was awarded such a smile. Then Kiyomori turned his head and caught sight of Munemori.

"My son! What has taken you from our celebrations?" Kiyomori shouted over the music.

"Father, there is news."

"News!" Kiyomori shouted so loud that the musicians tootled and twanged to a stop and the dancers ceased their arm-waving. Kiyomori's watering eyes and uncertain balance betrayed how much sake he had been drinking. "Then tell us all this news, that we may share in what so interests the Chief of The Taira."

All the assembled nobles and ladies and dancers and musicians turned to stare at Munemori.

Feeling trapped, Munemori paused before announcing, "There has been an uprising in the East."

Kiyomori stood. "An uprising? Led by whom?"

"Minomoto no Yoritomo. Yoshitomo's son. He raised a force and killed the Governor of Izu."

A shocked murmuring flowed among the nobles.

"One of the sons I pardoned into exile, neh?" Kiyomori staggered off the dais into the center of the room. "So Tokiko was right. How it galls me to admit that. I should have killed them all. All the little boys."

Munemori went on, "Our retainers in Sagami, however, have also raised a force and defeated Yoritomo."

Kiyomori barked a laugh and stretched out his arms. "There, you see. The *kami* have not deserted the Taira. We defeated Narichika, we defeated Prince Mochihito, and now we have defeated Yoshitomo's son."

These words were met with a cheer, especially from the young noblemen. "Lord Kiyomori!" cried Koremori among them, "let us send out a great army to smash the Minomoto, and show them what fools they are for even thinking of rising against us!" This brought forth another cheer.

Of course, thought Munemori sourly, *these young men are eager for any excuse to leave dreary Fukuhara. Even if it means getting themselves killed. All for glory and making a name for oneself. How glad I am that I was never such a young fool as that.*

"Excellent!" said Kiyomori. "I am glad to see not all Taira have lost their warrior spirit. So, Munemori"—Kiyomori wobbled over and clapped a hand on Munemori's shoulder—"are you ready to put on armor again, my son, and lead the Taira into battle?"

"Er." Munemori paused, and said softly, "Father, I am not so young a man as I once was, and I have duties here in Fukuhara. Let one of the younger men have a chance at making a name for himself. Koremori seems eager. I respectfully suggest that you make him the general for this punitive expedition."

Kiyomori took a step back, his contempt unmistakable. "Yes, of course. I remember Enryakuji. Perhaps another would be better." Kiyomori turned to address the young noblemen. "Koremori-san, we have decided it should be you to lead the Taira forces to the Kantō!"

With great joy shining in his face, Koremori said, "Thank you, Grandfather! You honor me!" The other young men eagerly congratulated Koremori and begged to be allowed to follow him to the eastern provinces.

Munemori hurriedly left the room in shame.

Hachiman's Gift

For days, Minomoto no Yoritomo had hidden in the Hakone Mountains after his defeat at Ishibashiyama. With only a few men to serve him, he had lodged in caves and crevasses, drinking from rocky streams and eating what game they could catch. He had prayed to Kwannon and Hachiman for guidance and aid. He dared not, however, summon the Shin-In for fear of what his men would think.

At last a messenger found them with word that Yoritomo should return to his father-in-law's house. He did not know if it was a trap or whether he might be ambushed and killed there, but Yoritomo could not face himself, hiding forever like a frightened rabbit.

So on the Seventh Night of the Ninth Month, Yoritomo and his few trusted men rode out after dark and followed the Tōkkaidō back to Izu.

When Yoritomo arrived in the middle of the night, the guards of Hōjō Tokimasa's mansion eagerly opened the gate for him. Keeping his head low and his hand on his sword scabbard, Yoritomo rode in, expecting a blow or a piercing by arrows at any moment.

Instead, the *shōji* of the house, glowing golden from the lamplight within, slid open with a loud *clack*, and Hōjō Tokimasa himself came out.

"Welcome back! Welcome back, my son! We have long been awaiting your return."

Yoritomo wearily slid out of his saddle. "I regret I must return in shame. I fear I acquitted myself badly in battle. I was a fool not to have chosen a better general."

Yoritomo's wife came out then and silently rushed up to him, pressing her face against his shoulder. Yoritomo held her for long moments. "I wish I had more to bring back for you than this sorry sight."

"Do not say such a thing," whispered his wife as she caressed his face. "A miracle has happened. You must come see."

"A . . . miracle?"

Hōjō Tokimasa smiled at him. "A wondrous thing, my son. It is how we knew you must return. Come with us."

Yoritomo allowed himself to be led through the west wing of the mansion out to the verandah that overlooked the central courtyard. It was filled with people, who all stood as Yoritomo emerged onto the verandah. As one, they all bowed to him.

Yoritomo did not know what to say. He looked over the assembled crowd in astonished silence.

Then, one by one, they approached the verandah. First came his aged former wet nurse, leading an adolescent boy by the hand.

"This is my son, Kirenawa. It would honor us if you would let him serve with you."

Others came forward. "Here is my son. Take my son to serve you."

Generals in full armor came forward. "I have three hundred men." "I have five hundred men." "I have a thousand men. Let us serve you."

Tears of gratitude welled in Yoritomo's eyes, and it was all he could do to keep them from rolling down his cheeks.

Last came a powerfully built, gray-haired warrior. "I am Taira Hirotsune. I have twenty thousand men. Let us serve you."

"But . . . you are a Taira," said Yoritomo in wonder.

"I have no regard for Kiyomori, or his foolish son Munemori," said Hirotsune. "Kiyomori has shamed our clan's name with his excesses. I would gladly see his head on a pike."

Or see him defeated so that you may take his place, thought Yoritomo. Nonetheless, Yoritomo raised his arms, and said, "I thank you all, and I will welcome all who wish into my service. Hachiman has surely blessed me with a gift this day: the gift of hope. Together let us defeat the forces of the tyrant Kiyomori, and bring glory once again to the Minomoto."

The cheer that resounded in the courtyard warmed his heart.

A Post Station Bell

It was a glorious autumn day, with a stiff breeze blowing from the sea. Kiyomori stood at the top of the stairs leading into the New Imperial palace and gazed down over the main road that passed through Fukuhara. The road was filled with warrior horsemen, all bearing the red banner of the Taira.

Kiyomori had taken sixteen days to gather the forces to send to the East. The Kantō was the birthplace of many a legendary warrior, and the skills of the Minomoto were not to be lightly regarded. Kiyomori wanted a force that could not only capture Yoritomo, but also be able to go on to punish any Kantō lords who chose to continue to fight for the Minomoto.

He wanted the Minomoto themselves obliterated. Therefore, he had waited until the Eighteenth Day of the Ninth Month, by which time thirty thousand horsemen had been raised, to send the Taira punitive force eastward to the Kantō.

Kiyomori's mood lifted as he watched his grandson, Koremori, go riding by with the first contingent of warriors, over a thousand in the first vanguard alone, bound for the Kantō. Koremori, the Ason—heir of Shigemori and destined to be clan leader one day—was seventeen and already a handsome and accomplished young man. He was attired splendidly in a suit of green-laced armor over a red brocade *hitatare*. Koremori's helmet, adorned with a bronze butterfly, glittered in the sunlight. The Taira heirloom sword Ko-garasu, sparkled in its scabbard at his side. Koremori rode in a gold-edged saddle on a copper-colored horse dappled with white. Kiyomori saw much of what had been best of Shigemori in him.

Stay a warrior, Koremori, Kiyomori thought as he watched the men ride past. *Do not soften as your father did.*

Behind Koremori, a riderless horse bore a Chinese chest containing the heirloom suit of armor Chinese Leather. Kiyomori did not approve of armor being used as a talisman rather than being worn, but it was an honored tradition in some houses, so he could not chastise Koremori for it.

Koremori had expressed some dissatisfaction, the night before, with his parting gift. It had been traditional for a commander in chief serving the Emperor to be presented with a special Sword of Commission, and to be feted with a great ceremony and an enormous banquet which all of the nobility would attend. But the new palace in Fukuhara was not large enough to accommodate such a gathering. And it did not have the same structures or design, so that the ministers in the Imperial Affairs Office would have had to create a new ceremony, the rituals of which they were unable to decide upon. Therefore, harking back to a two-centuries old precedent, the Ministers of State performed no ceremony, held no banquet, and merely presented Koremori with . . . a bell, the sort of bell used to requisition men and horses at post stations. Koremori had put it in a leather bag and given it to a servant to carry. "New traditions for a new era," Kiyomori had told him, but Koremori had not been mollified.

Behind the horse bearing the armor rode Munemori. Kiyomori narrowed his eyes, knowing he must swallow his disgust and disapproval. Munemori was only intending to go as far as Rokuhara in Heian Kyō and play commander from there. Such a thing went against every philosophy Kiyomori possessed, and yet it had been the best decision. After Enryakuji, Kiyomori knew truly it was the safest thing to keep Munemori as far away from any battle as possible.

Kiyomori watched the magnificent column of mounted warriors ride

away to the north and east, down the dusty main street of Fukuhara. Kiyomori recalled the day long ago when he watched Shigemori ride from
Rokuhara to the palace at the head of such a force. What a glorious day
that had been. This parade of Taira might was no less impressive, and Kiyomori had no doubts that they would return victorious, but the glory and
spirit were gone. It was no longer a matter of proving Taira worth and
achieving power, but of retaining it. Kiyomori often imagined himself now
as a pillar to a great house, holding up an increasingly heavy roof. *I cannot
live forever. Surely my time to leave this world will be sooner, not later. But
Munemori cannot lead and Koremori, though he is Ason, is still very young.
If I break, will the house fall? When I die, what then?*

The Grand Procession

To Koremori, the ride eastward was a gift from the gods. After they
passed through the ruined glory that was once Heian Kyō, more and
more warriors rode up to join the column of the Taira. By the thousands
they came, swelling the ranks some said to seventy thousand, until even
from the top of a high hill Koremori could not see the rearmost riders of
his army. With their fluttering banners and shining halberds and helmets, it
was the grandest parade Koremori had ever seen. His heart swelled with
pride and he wished his father, Shigemori, had lived to see this day. Koremori could well understand the feeling that had prompted a great-uncle
once to say, "If one is not a Taira, one is not a human being."

Given the success of the Taira over recent rebellions, others felt safe
joining their expedition. Courtesans and camp followers by the hundreds
rode along in their merry carts, singing and flirting with the warriors. Traveling merchants, bringing fruit and rice cakes, found ready customers among
the travelers. Ironmongers and tailors rode along to ensure every warrior
was arrayed at his finest. And every warrior of any note had at least two
servants to look after his horse and weapons. It was a grand procession, as
if an entire city flowed down the Great Eastern Sea Road, as Heian Kyō
had flowed down the Kamo River months before.

At night, whether atop mountain passes or on wide grassy plains, the
campfires of the army dotted the landscape as far as the eye could see. There
was music and laughter everywhere as courtesans poured the plum wine and
plucked upon the *biwa*. Poems were composed to the glory of the Taira, or
to the future misfortune of the Minomoto. The autumn nights were clear
and the stars seemed to shine on every Taira aspiration.

But as the days passed and the warriors pressed eastward, the horses began to tire. The autumn wind blew more chill from the north, knifing through every slit in one's armor. After passing the Kiyomi Barrier, Koremori found that information about the loyalty of the local landowners, or how many troops Yoritomo might have, became more unreliable. Some would say, "Yoritomo? Oh, you need not fear him, my lord. He has but a few hundred loyal followers, no more. Once he sees your mighty forces he will run like he did at Ishibashiyama."

Others, however, said, "You must take care, my lord. There are many who hate the Taira, and they are all joining up with Yoritomo. He has become very strong, and is able to intimidate even those who would oppose him into sending him men. They say he has nearly two hundred thousand under his command. Be wary, my lord."

Koremori sought advice from the warriors among his army who had lived in the Kantō, asking them what sort of fighters the famed Eastern horsemen were in truth.

Those who knew the Kantō shook their heads, and said, "There are no finer warriors than those who ride the plains of the five eastern provinces. Here, you think these arrows are long? An average fighter of the Kantō can draw a shaft at least fifteen fists long. The bows they use require six strong men to string them. Their best archers can fire an arrow through four suits of armor. Think what that would do to a man, eh?

"And an Eastern warrior has none of the fine sentiments of your Fukuhara nobleman. A Kantō fighter will ride over the bodies of his father and brothers to continue the battle. He will not think of food or water, heat or cold, life or death. They fight more fiercely than any bear or enraged bull. If those who say Yoritomo has two hundred thousand such men speak the truth, then I regret to say, my lord, that we will not be returning from this battle alive."

Naturally, this was most unsettling to the young Koremori, and he asked his tactician, Tadakiyo, for advice.

"My lord," Tadakiyo said, "we have come a long way in a short time. We should not advance farther than the Fuji River. Particularly if Yoritomo's force is as great as they say, we should not face it in our present condition. I expect we will be reinforced with men from Izu and Suruga, and we should wait for them to arrive."

As Koremori had little experience in the art of war, he readily accepted Tadakiyo's advice. On the Sixteenth Day of the Tenth Month, he encamped his forces to the west of Fuji River, with Mount Fuji towering to the north and east.

But word of the possible size of the opposing army had spread, as well as the rumors of the Kantō warriors' prowess in battle. And as rumor will, tales grew and became exaggerated. Men saw ghosts and baleful demons in the mists that rose off the river marshes just north of the encampment.

"This is no good," the Kantō-bred warriors said. "If we wait here, the Minomoto will have time to sneak around Mount Fuji and attack us from behind, unexpected. That is what we would do."

"But that is ignoble," Koremori protested.

The Eastern warriors faced him with hard, narrowed eyes. "Kantō horsemen," they said, "do not fight for sport. They fight to win."

No longer was laughter heard in the camp, and the drinking and enjoyment of the entertainment ladies took on a more furtive, desperate nature. The Taira warriors spoke little and watched over their shoulders often. And they waited.

Administrative Matters

In the days soon after his return to Izu, Yoritomo had found himself busily administering the lands his forces had already taken. He had heard a saying once that to be thought a ruler one must behave as one, and this he began to do. Throughout the Ninth Month, Yoritomo dispatched many of his new volunteers to put down the ambitious rival Minomoto landowners. In mid-month, he sent a force to subdue the acting governor of Suruga Province, and the Minomoto were victorious.

Yoritomo gave the landholdings of the vanquished to those who were loyal to his side, or to favored shrines and temples. He searched for new headquarters and at last settled on the town of Kamakura, on the seacoast of a peninsula of Sagami Province, well located between the Eastern Provinces and western, Taira-controlled Nihon. There, Yoritomo commandeered a local official's dwelling for his own residence and brought his wife and children to join him.

But by early in the Tenth Month, Yoritomo received word of the enormous Taira force that had been dispatched from Fukuhara. Yoritomo summoned together as many of the newly mustered men as he could, for he did not wish a repeat of his earlier disaster. This new army, whom some numbered as many as two hundred thousand, rode west with Yoritomo at its head.

Even as he traveled up the valley of the Haya River, over Ashigara Pass and down the valley of the Kisegawa, administrative matters followed Yoritomo. There was the petition from the monks of Izu Temple requesting that the warriors stop plundering the temple's lands. Yoritomo, knowing it was wise to have monks on one's side, immediately issued an edict forbidding his men to cross those lands.

There was the matter of a monk spy who tried to slip away by boat. There was the matter of the prisoners taken in the battle with the Suruga governor, and rewards to be given to the fighters who had captured them. There was the matter of coming to agreement with the allied lords as to what should be the day of battle with the Taira. The Twenty-fourth Day of the Tenth Month was selected.

Yoritomo and his vast army reached Kajima, on the eastern bank of the Fuji River, on the Twentieth Day. Across the river, he could see the fires of Koremori's forces, but Yoritomo had gotten conflicting assessments of how many men the Taira had, or how well prepared they were.

"My lord, there are but a couple of thousand of them, and they spend their days in games of chance, indulging in women and drink. You know how those effete capital lordlings are. They will be no match for us."

Or, "My lord, we must exercise caution. There are over a hundred thousand Taira, and daily more march into their camp to serve them. Do not be deceived if they seem idle, for the Taira are ruthless when it comes to holding power. Remember Ishibashiyama and take care."

Therefore, on the night of the twenty-third, Yoritomo chose one man, Takeda Nobuyoshi, to sneak across the river into the marsh north of the Taira camp, then to report back on the size and condition of Koremori's army. The man willingly bowed and left on his mission, and Yoritomo wondered for a moment if Nobuyoshi had any chance of returning alive. If he did not, then Yoritomo would send another man, and another until one survived to bring back the needed information.

Yoritomo retired to his tent, put on a formal white robe, and offered prayers to Hachiman.

Marsh Wind

Left Minor Captain and Commander in Chief Taira Koremori paced in front of his tent. Beside him, on a folding chair of sticks and cloth, sat his advisor Tadakiyo, who was admiring the waning autumn moon. Word had come to the Taira camp that the Minomoto forces had arrived at Fuji River and that they were, indeed, as large as had been feared. Reinforcements from the Oba and Hateyama families would not be coming, as they were on the other side of the Minomoto line. And Koremori had heard of the defeat of the Suruga governor, meaning no more men could be expected from that quarter.

The cold, damp marsh air, smelling faintly of rotting things, hung heavily over the camp. "When will they attack, do you think?" Koremori asked Tadakiyo.

"It could be any time, my lord, unless they are waiting for more men, as we are."

"With two hundred thousand, how many more do they need? Particularly if these Eastern warriors are as powerful as they say."

Tadakiyo sighed. "As many as to be certain of victory, my lord. Yoritomo must win this time if he is to gain the respect of the Eastern overlords."

"I do not like your pessimism, Tadakiyo."

"Your grandfather himself asked me to advise you, my lord. I do not think he would wish me to lie to you."

"I cannot think," said Koremori, "that the gods would have let me come so far, so grandly, on my first command, only to have me lose to a provincial upstart rebel."

"It is better for a warrior to rely upon his own strength and courage than to rely upon the whims of the gods, my lord. The *kami* have reasons we cannot know. The *bosatsu* will save those they can, but each man earns his own karma. Do your best, forget the rest."

Koremori looked down at his hands in the moonlight. They were trembling. He felt profoundly untested and unready. He swallowed hard and stared eastward across the Fuji River, and wondered how many more days he had left to live.

A Flight of Waterfowl

Takeda Nobuyoshi crawled up the western bank of the Fuji River, muddy, sopping wet, and chilled to the bone. He tried to ignore his discomforts and concentrate upon his mission. After all, if one was supposed to be willing to give his life for his lord, what was a little cold and wet?

Nobuyoshi slithered through the moss and the reeds, trying to keep sufficient distance between himself and the Taira sentries. But even in the bright moonlight, the tall marsh grasses made it difficult for him to see where he was. It was hard to distinguish the noises of the camp from the croak of frogs and the *ank-ank* of waterbirds in the marsh. The muck seemed to tug at his shoes and his sleeves, slowing his movement.

Nobuyoshi saw glittering light ahead of him—moonlight reflecting off water. Perhaps, he thought, he could swim through the flooded grasses and make better progress. More eagerly than he should have, Nobuyoshi plunged into the water, making a big splash.

A deafening cacophony erupted around him. Thousands of beating wings, sounding like the pounding of drums or the thunder of hooves. An enormous flock of geese and ducks rose into the sky, screaming and squawking and chucking as if shouting war cries. Great clouds of the birds flew up out of the marsh to the heavens, blocking out the moon and all the stars.

Nobuyoshi rolled onto his back in the water, cursing himself over and over. *Fool, fool, what a fool I am! Now it is done. I have revealed myself, and soon the Taira will come looking for me. With luck, I might kill one before I am slain, but I will have failed on my lord's mission. What have I ever done in this life or past ones to earn such a fortune?* Nobuyoshi pulled out his dagger, huddled in the long grasses, and waited for the Taira sentries to find him.

A Flight of Taira

*K*oremori fairly jumped into the air when he heard the noise. "What is that?"

Tadakiyo leapt from his chair. "It sounds like thousands of marching feet! It is coming from the marsh, behind us!"

Koremori ran to the other side of the tent. Birds were rising in great numbers from the marsh, squawking in fright.

"The Minomoto! They are attacking!"

"Just as our warriors feared they might," said Tadakiyo. "They have come around behind us while we waited. We are only fortunate that the birds have given us warning."

"We must rally the men quickly!"

"No, my lord, it would be useless to fight. If there are two hundred thousand ahead of us and now many thousands behind us, we cannot hope to win. We must retreat and return to the capital at once!"

Koremori was all too willing to take this advice. He called for his horse, shouting, "Retreat! To the Owari River, to the capital!"

Word and panic spread like brush fire through the Taira camp. Voices echoed the cry "Retreat! Retreat!" Men ran to their horses, without saddle or bridle, leaving their bows, armor, and other belongings behind them. Men leapt onto the backs of tethered horses, only to ride round and round in circles until the ropes were cut. Courtesans and camp followers screamed and ran from the tents, only to be kicked and trampled under the hooves of the fleeing horsemen. Their retainers and groomsmen had no choice but to run on foot after them, some leaving their shoes behind. Each man had no thought but to save himself, and the Eastern Sea Road was soon clogged with fleeing Taira.

An Empty Field

The following morning at the Hour of the Hare, just after dawn, Yoritomo sat on his horse on the eastern bank of the Fuji River. The spy had not returned, so Yoritomo assumed Nobuyoshi had been caught and killed. Such is the way of war.

Behind him, two hundred thousand horsemen waited restively for the order to attack. Yoritomo scented the wind and decided there was no point in waiting further. He raised his sword into the air. "Let it begin!" he cried.

With a mighty shout, the army surged forward across the broad but shallow river, thundered up the eastern bank, and charged into the open fields to meet the Taira camp. But the horses had galloped no farther than a few yards when the warriors pulled their steeds to an abrupt halt and called for their commander.

Yoritomo rode across the river to join them and learn what had halted the attack. The sight that filled his eyes astonished him. The camp lay in complete disarray. Arrows littered the ground, boxes of armor and clothing lay burst open. Tents had been demolished and strewn across the grass. The only inhabitants of the camp were clusters of disheveled women, weeping, bruised, and bleeding. They stared up at him with wide, fearful eyes. Then Nobuyoshi emerged from a group of such ladies and sheepishly came forward, bowing to Yoritomo.

"My lord, it is my fault that you have no foe to fight today. I disturbed the waterbirds, and the Taira thought I was your army. I would have come back to tell you, but I was so astonished I did not think I would be believed. And these ladies needed someone to help bandage their wounds. I know something of the healing arts."

A miracle, Yoritomo thought in wonder. *Hachiman has sent me another miracle.*

Laughter erupted among the Minomoto warriors. "The Taira run from ducks and cranes! What cowards they are!"

Yoritomo dismounted, removing his helmet, and performed a ritual washing of his hands and mouth. "We owe this victory to the Great Bosatsu Hachiman. There can be no other explanation for this gift from the gods."

"My lord," said one of his men, "Let us chase the Taira back to Heian

Kyō and finish them!" A few warriors, not waiting for commands, took off down the Eastern Sea Road to give chase.

Yoritomo was about to give assent that the whole force should go when Taira Hirotsune rode up.

"My lord, it is tempting, I know, to consider riding after your foe. But they have had some hours' start, and to follow them to Heian Kyō or Fukuhara would take us well out of Eastern territory. This would mean all of the warriors who support you would be gone from the Kantō and those who envy your position, such as Fujiwara Hideyoshi, might decide to take advantage of your absence. Would it not be better to make sure your control of the Kantō is complete before marching on the capital? The gods have, indeed, blessed us this day. Let us not waste their gift chasing foxes through the marsh grass. Let shame be the Taira punishment for now."

Yoritomo regarded Hirotsune a moment. *And thereby let the warriors of your clan be spared?* he wondered. But Yoritomo remembered the fate of his father Yoshitomo during the Heiji, how he was drawn out of the Imperial palace to chase fleeing Taira, only to be caught in a trap.

Yoritomo nodded. "Very well. We will return to the Kise River and decide there what is to be done next. Gather what weapons and armor were left here. Nobuyoshi?"

The spy replied, "*Hai*, my lord?"

"Though you may not have intended it, you have done us a great service. Therefore, I will delegate more men to you and you will have the post of Shuko here in Suruga Province. I will rely upon you to ensure that the Taira do not return this far again."

Nobuyoshi smiled and bowed. "My lord, I will gladly do so. Even if I must surround all of Suruga Province with geese and ducks."

Whispered Names

A *late autumn wind* whipped sleet against the *shōji* of the Fukuhara palace. "I am most sorry, Majesty," said the wizened physician to Kenreimon'in, who knelt in the hallway outside of the sickroom, "but it would do you no good to see him. He drifts in and out of dreams and whispers . . . names."

"I know the names he whispers," the Empress said as calmly as she could, hiding the sorrow inside. Monks in a nearby room were chanting in a mournful drone, a reminder that death was not far.

In the year before he was forced to retire, the young Emperor Takakura had had mistresses. What Emperor did not? Two he had been quite fond of, Aoi and Kogo. Aoi had been a girl of lower class, only a servant. But she died after the Emperor had sent her away for fear of gossip. Kenreimon'in herself had presented the Emperor with her beautiful young serving maid Kogo to ease his grief. Her gift apparently had been successful, for Takakura had soon become enthralled with Kogō as well.

But then Kiyomori had found out. Kenreimon'in still burned with shame, remembering how her father had forced Kogō out of the palace to become a nun, fearing that Kogō would interfere with his daughter's happy marriage. While she was fond of her husband, Kenreimon'in had no illusions that hers had been anything but a political marriage.

"Kiyomori has much to answer for," whispered Kenreimon'in.

"I beg your pardon, Majesty?" said the physician.

"Nothing, good doctor. Has the nature of my husband's illness ever been determined?"

The physician tilted his head. "Who can say about such things, Majesty? An evil spirit perhaps, some improperly prepared food, or . . ."

"Or?"

He lowered his voice. "There are some vicious gossips who claim it is poison."

"Poison?" Kenreimon'in exclaimed softly. "Who would possibly dare to do such a thing?"

"Who indeed?" replied the physician. He suddenly seemed to think better of speaking more and abruptly bowed and walked away.

Kenreimon'in covered her face with her sleeves. *They think my father is responsible. It might even be true. What karma caused me to be born into such a wicked world, to such a wicked father?* Tears fell at last, and Kenreimon'in could not stop them.

Brothers Meet

Minomoto Yoshitsune and his towering retainer Benkei paced on the flagstones in front of a residence in the Suruga provincial capital of Numazu.

"You are certain he will see us?" Benkei rumbled, scratching his curly black beard.

"Of course he will," said Yoshitsune, with more certainty than he felt. "He is my brother."

"Those aides didn't seem too convinced when you told them who you were."

"I'm sure the Lord of Kamakura has been getting a lot of visitors or one sort or another lately, people claiming all sorts of things. They can't be too careful."

"But Yoritomo has never met you."

"He may have seen me once."

"When you were a baby."

"Hmm." Yoshitsune brushed some dust off the sleeve of his red brocade *hitatare*. His armor, tied with lilac-colored cords, a gift from his former host Fujiwara Hidehira.

Word had finally arrived in the far north of Yoritomo's rebellion a month after it had begun, but Yoshitsune had departed almost as soon as the messenger had finished speaking. Hidehira had only been able to send three hundred men with Yoshitsune, so precipitous was Yoshitsune's departure. Yoshitsune rode hard the many miles from Hiraizumi to Suruga, stopping only to ask where his brother Yoritomo might be found. Compared to this, waiting on the flagstones was nothing.

Finally, a frowning aide-de-camp appeared on the verandah of the residence. "My lord says he will have audience with you."

"Aha! You see?" Yoshitsune said to Benkei. "I was right."

"You win the wager, young master," said Benkei. "And I am glad of it. My feet were getting sore."

They followed the aide into the cool interior of the house and then out to a broad courtyard. The last leaves on the gingko trees were drifting down, shimmering like gold coins. Several men in partial armor sat on padded straw mats in the courtyard. One of them stood as Yoshitsune and Benkei walked up. "You are the one who says he is my brother?"

He was a tall, broad man, Yoshitsune noticed, and past thirty years old. His face had been reddened by recent sun, but he was not weathered and brown as was the nature of a Kantō warrior. Yoritomo had more the face of a scholar. Only the fact that his teeth were unstained and he wore no white face powder showed that he was not a courtier. Yoritomo's expression was welcoming, but his eyes remained wary, the eyes of a man who never revealed himself fully to anyone.

Yoshitsune removed his helmet and bowed. "Yoritomo-sama, I am, indeed, that one whom you may have known as Ushiwaka. My mother was Tokiwa, a favored concubine of our father, General Yoshitomo. I was exiled to Kuramadera as a child, but three years ago I escaped and fled to Hiraizumi. The lord there, Fujiwara Hidehira, treated me well and taught me the skills of horsemanship and the bow. No less a personage than a prince of the *tengu* taught me the ways of the sword."

"A *tengu*?" asked Yoritomo, blinking in surprise.

"The very same, brother. Sōjō-bō by name. Before I was fifteen I had mastered *tengu-do*, and I must say I have only improved in skill since then.

I single-handedly defeated an attack of bandits at a post station, and have won numerous duels with other warriors."

The amused murmuring of the other warriors in the courtyard alerted Yoshitomo that he might be perceived as boasting too much, so he changed the subject. "Now I bring three hundred men under my command to serve you, if you are willing to have them. Here is my heirloom sword, which should prove that I am a Minomoto. Now what do you say? Shall we catch butterflies together, as happy brothers do?"

The other gentlemen in the courtyard laughed, and Yoritomo smiled. "Indeed, you must be the one who wrote me this poem." He reached into his sleeve and pulled out a folded piece of paper. Yoshitsune recognized it as the note he had sent Yoritomo as he was passing though Izu years before. "I have carried it with me ever since I received it," said Yoshitomo. "Come, sit with me and let us talk about days gone by."

Yoshitsune accepted the seat of honor to Yoritomo's left, and Benkei knelt behind Yoshitsune. Yoshitsune listened with rapt attention as Yoritomo told him tales of their father's courage in the Hōgen and Heiji and how their father had been cruelly ambushed by traitors. Yoritomo told him of his other brothers, Tokiwa's other sons, now named Noriyori and Gien, who had also spent their childhood in exile. These brothers also had offered their services to the Minomoto cause. Yoritomo said he intended to build a great monument to Yoshitomo someday. Both brothers talked sadly of their days in exile, and of those who had treated them with kindness.

Yoshitsune also was able to tell Yoritomo what he knew of the loyalty of the lords of the far provinces of Oshū and Dewa, and whether they might be sending more men to assist them in the rebellion.

Afternoon passed into evening into night with the brothers deep in conversation. Food and drink were brought to them and neither noticed when the chill of the late-autumn night settled around them. At last, when the watchman cried the Hour of the Rat, Yoshitsune stood to take his leave.

Yoritomo grasped his arm. "Brother, I cannot tell you how pleased I am to have you and your men join our forces. Surely it is a good omen, as it was for our esteemed ancestor Yoshiie when his brother joined him at the Battle of Kuriya River. There are so few of my allies I can completely trust. It will be good having you with me."

"I am honored to have the chance to serve you at last," said Yoshitsune, feeling a tear escape from one eye. "Together, I am certain we will vanquish our foe."

"As am I."

Yoshitsune and Benkei bowed and were escorted out of the residence. Both were feeling the effects of the plum wine and sake. "There, you see?" said Yoshitsune. "My brother knew me. All is well."

"So it would seem. But he looked a bit startled when you told him about the *tengu*, master. It is not wise to imply you are a better fighter than the commander in chief."

"Well, perhaps that was an indiscretion. But he's my brother! And I'm going to fight for him. He ought to know what my skills are."

"Yes, but are you sure you should have boasted about your defeating those bandits at the post station?"

"How is my brother going to trust me as a warrior if I don't tell him of my victories? You worry like a nobleman, Benkei."

"Sorry, young master. It is my duty to look out for you. Here is the street. Look out for that pothole, master."

"Whoops! Ah. Thank you for catching me, good Benkei. It would be shameful to come all this way and be felled by a broken ankle."

"Indeed it would, young master. Your horse is over here."

"No, he is over here."

"No, master, this way."

"No, I am certain it is this way ... If he's over there why can't I see him?"

"Because he is a black horse, master. There, did you hear him snort just now?"

"Oh, very well." Yoshitsune allowed Benkei to guide him to their horses, happy in the thought that now all was very well indeed.

Advice in the Dead of Night

As Yoritomo watched his brother leave, his smile faded from his face. *How young he is*, Yoritomo thought. *He looks scarcely out of childhood to me. And what vigor he has! He had ridden for days, and yet seemed as energetic as a puppy. Yoritomo could not help feeling a pang of envy. Ah, to be young in these times. How easily a young man can ignore the certainty of death and fling his heart into war. Here I am, an aging man, and yet called upon to do battle. I have little time left to establish a reputation as a warrior general, and yet I must to gain the respect of my clan. All those years wasted in Izu. During my exile I studied to be a scholar, while my brother secretly studied the arts of war. How much more prescient he was than I. It will be the young men, such as Yoshitsune, who will gain the glory from this rebellion.*

"Are you well, my lord?" asked one of the other Minomoto warriors present. "You have been silent for a time, and you seem to be frowning at some faraway vision."

"I am well," replied Yoritomo immediately. Now was not a time to show any sign of weakness. There were many Minomoto who would cheerfully usurp his place as Ason. "Merely in need of a night's sleep. There will be much to do in the morning."

"Of course, my lord," said the warrior, bowing. "We will leave you to your rest."

Yoritomo's guests all stood and bowed and politely departed, though he could feel their last gaze on him as they left, watching him, judging him. Yoritomo decided there was one last task he ought to do before going to sleep.

He found a room that was separate from the other wings of the mansion, and there lit a stick of incense and placed it on a brazier. And waited.

Soon, Yoritomo felt a chill deeper than the autumn night. A voice at his ear said, "At last you call upon me. I have been waiting."

"I regret that I could not before now," said Yoritomo. "I must apologize. All has proceded as you said it would."

"Did I not long ago tell you that you were the chosen of Hachiman?" said the Shin-In. "That he, and I, would not let you fail?"

"So you did, and I should have believed you."

"You have passed the tests set for you admirably, and now you see that you will be rewarded."

"Yes. And now one of my long-lost brothers has joined my forces as well. I should be filled with joy at his arrival, and yet I am not. I do not understand this."

"Ah. That one. That is the one I warned you to beware of long ago."

Yoritomo glanced over his shoulder at the glimmering, sunken-eyed shade of the Shin-In. "Ah, it was he? Well, Yoshitsune does seem to think much of himself. He said he has been trained by *tengu*."

The Shin-In nodded gravely. "Beware of one who has received the teaching of *tengu*. Such men become as untrustworthy as their teachers. He will serve you well, but he may be a threat to you when all is done. Never let him think he is your better. Never let him forget that you are the chosen of Hachiman, not him. Do not let him gain too much fame or reward, or you will have cause to regret it."

"I will remember," said Yoritomo.

A Trod-Upon Sword

Munemori cringed inside as he watched Kiyomori pace slowly back and forth. Young Koremori knelt in the middle of the room, his forehead pressed to the cold floorboards. Koremori's advisor, Tadakiyo sat beside Munemori, trembling and pale.

"You ran," Kiyomori said softly.

"My lord—" Koremori began.

"You ran from a flock of waterbirds," Kiyomori continued.

"My lord," interjected Tadakiyo, "if it had been the Minomoto attacking—"

"You ran without engaging the Minomoto even once!"

"My lord," said Munemori, "they had heard that the Minomoto outnumbered them more than two to one. It was a sensible retreat."

Kiyomori swiveled his bald head and glared at Munemori. "Do you know what is being said about the Taira in every post station between here and the East? That our warriors fled naked on unsaddled horses, leaving all of their armor and weapons behind. That our warriors are so terrified of battle they will use any excuse to flee. That all the Minomoto have to do is come into the capital bearing ducks and frogs, and the Taira will leap into the trees in panic." Kiyomori returned his cold gaze to Koremori. "You have made of our house a laughingstock."

Shaking, Koremori took his short sword from his sheath and placed it lengthwise on the floor before him. He said, "My lord, if I may have your permission, I will go into the courtyard and take my own life, for the shame I have brought upon the Taira."

Kiyomori stomped his high-sandaled foot upon the sword. "That is a warrior's honor, Koremori. You have proved that you are no warrior, not worthy of *seppuku*. No, I have decided you will be exiled to Kikaigashima, where you may spend a long life contemplating what your father in the Pure Land must think of you and your cowardice."

Koremori burst into tears. "Forgive me, Grandfather."

But Kiyomori had already turned away to Tadakiyo. "You, however, I will take pleasure in executing myself. I trusted you to advise my grandson. Now I must think of some suitably shameful place to hang your severed head."

"Forgive me, my lord!" cried Tadakiyo, flinging himself forward to lie prostrate on the floor.

Then Kiyomori turned to Munemori. "To you," Kiyomori said, in a tone coldest of all, "I have nothing to say."

Munemori summoned what pride and courage he could. *What would the Shin-In advise me to do?* he wondered. When he dared to speak again, Munemori said, "I beg you to reconsider, Father. If you enact these punishments, the people will know we are ashamed, and the slanders will continue. But if you reward Koremori and Tadakiyo, and let it be thought that they accomplished their mission—to learn the strength of the Minomoto forces, and to show the Minomoto the size of force that the Taira can gather—then it will be harder for anyone to speak against us. It is easier to strike a whimpering beggar than a proud nobleman. Let the people hear that the Taira are still confident, and then those who speak slander will be the ones who look foolish."

Kiyomori blinked in astonished silence for a moment. Then strange laughter burbled from his lips. "You . . . you would have us invent triumph out of this shame? You would have us make rice cakes out of mud?"

"I can see no other way, Father. Reinforcing the tarnish on the Taira would only give the Minomoto another unearned victory. Claiming that it is we, in fact, who have won, will give them pause. And, look, we yet have our seventy thousand men, whereas if there had been a battle at Fuji River, many might have been lost and the capital left undefended."

"Munemori-sama is right," said Tadakiyo, who was gazing upon Munemori with incredulous awe. "We still have all our men while the Minomoto have the ducks of Fuji River."

Heartened, Munemori went on, "Be merciful and sensible, Father. Tadakiyo has a reputation for courage, having defeated bandits single-handedly in his past. One could not possibly think his advice was from cowardice. Perhaps the flight of waterfowl was a warning from the gods, trying to protect the Taira from a terrible mistake. As for Koremori, he is young, and this was his first command. Surely he has learned from this. Keep him with you, and he may yet earn you victories in years to come. I beg you think on my suggestion and let us put this trifling event, which has truly cost us nothing, behind us."

Kiyomori paused, chin in hand, staring at Munemori. "A warning from the gods," he said at last.

"How could it be otherwise?" said Munemori. "Are the Taira not favored by fortune above all other clans?"

With a heavy sigh, Kiyomori said, "I am glad to see my son's wits have returned from wherever they had been sleeping. If only they had been present sooner. Let it be so, then. Since we did not outface the Minomoto with deeds at Fuji River, we will outface them with words here in Fukuhara. Koremori, mad as it may seem, I am going to promote you. You will henceforth be Middle Captain in the Bodyguards of the Right. As for you," Ki-yomori said to Tadakiyo, "you will get to keep your life."

"Thank you, Kiyomori-sama!" said both Koremori and Tadakiyo, press-ing themselves as flat to the floor as they could.

Munemori coughed gently, and said, "One more thing, Father."

"You dare to try my patience further?"

"I merely wish to offer a suggestion. There is something you can do that will greatly enhance the morale of the Taira, as well as all of the nobles of government, as well as distract them from the foolishness of Fuji River."

"And what is this miracle I may perform?"

Munemori explained.

The Return

Nii no Ama did not know what had changed her husband's mind and caused him to declare that the capital would return to Heian Kyō, but she thought it was the most sensible thing he had ever done. Riding back in the oxcart, on the Second Day of the Twelfth Month with her daughter and several serving ladies was a joyous occasion. Despite the cold winter outside, everyone sang and laughed and talked about what they would like best about returning to the Imperial Compound.

"I will sleep in a room with no drafts!" said one girl.

"I will never have to hear a seagull cry again!" said another.

"I will not have visions of men with black wings and long beaks," said Kenreimon'in.

Nii no Ama reached over and squeezed her daughter's arm reassuringly. It had been a difficult time at the New Imperial Palace at Fukuhara. When the Taira warriors had left to ride to Fuji River, Fukuhara had been left undefended. The *tengu* then had returned to bedevil what few palace guards remained, tearing down roof tiles, chattering and snickering and occasionally peering in to startle the residents. The ladies of the palace had gotten little sleep.

"What will you like best, Mother?" asked Kenreimon'in.

"The gardens, I think," said Nii no Ama. "Proper gardens would have been impossible in Fukuhara, on those dreadful sloping hillsides. I am glad to return to a place where there can be flowers and winding streams."

"It still seems a shame," said one of the ladies, "that all those houses we finally built must be left behind."

"Houses cannot float upriver," said Nii no Ama. "They cannot return the way they left. Perhaps it is only fair. The people who first lived in

Fukuhara were driven away so that we might have their houses. Now they may have ours."

"You mean filthy fisherman will be living in the New Imperial Palace?"

"If the *tengu* do not tear it down first," said Kenreimon'in.

It was on the second day of travel, late in the afternoon, when the Imperial ox-carriage finally came to the Rashō Mon. The ladies were pressed by the two windows in the carriage, holding open the curtain despite all modesty and winter winds, trying to catch a first glimpse of the beloved capital once more. Even Nii no Ama was caught up in the excitement, peeking out of the open carriage window, much to the amusement of the armed men who rode as escort beside them.

The hollow rumble of the carriage wheels beneath the great southern gateway subsided, and the ladies squealed to each other, "Oh, here we are! Here is Suzaku Avenue! Oh, here. . . . oh . . ." They lapsed into shocked silence.

The great willow trees that had lined the main avenue of the city had all been chopped down, presumably for firewood. The paving stones of the avenue had been torn out and stolen, presumably for the new, high walls that surrounded those houses that remained. The street was littered with filth and discarded things. Starving beggars, their ribs showing, wandered the street and had the audacity to approach the Imperial procession until the escort drove them off.

"Where can we be?" moaned one of the ladies. "This is not our home. What has happened?"

Nii no Ama gently closed both curtains and turned the ladies faces back to within the carriage. "It is but a temporary dream," she said. "Heian Kyō has clearly been sorely neglected with the Taira gone. But now we are back, and all will be well again. We will feel at home once we reach the Imperial Compound. It was guarded in our absence, and the gods will have preserved it for us."

The ladies returned to the game of what they most looked forward to seeing at the palace, and it seemed to raise their spirits a little. Still, the ride up Suzaku Avenue seemed longer than it should.

At last, the carriage stopped.

"Ah, we are there," said Nii no Ama, putting on a smile.

Shouting was heard outside the carriage. "They must not go in! You must take them elsewhere! Take them to Kuramadera."

"What!" cried all the ladies at once. "What do they mean we cannot go in? What is happening?" The ladies jumped up and flung aside the window curtains, pounding on the walls of the carriage with their fists. "Tell us what is happening! Why can't we go in? Please let us into the palace!"

After some minutes of shouting, at last the back door of the carriage was flung open. Munemori stood there, his face drawn and haggard. "Ladies, Majesty, please calm yourselves. I am afraid you cannot enter the Compound now."

"Why?" both Nii no Ama and Kenreimon'in demanded.

He swallowed hard. Softly, he said, "It is my fault. I was so concerned with the defense of Rokuhara that I paid little attention to the Imperial Compound. I did not know the guards had deserted it. I did not know brigands and common folk had broken down the gates and moved in. Everything in the palace is ruined. Most of the furnishings stolen or broken. All the gardens are trampled. It will take days for our men to drive all the interlopers out. It will take years to purify and rebuild. You must go on to Kuramadera, where at least you will be comfortable and safe. Forgive me. I have much to do." Munemori slammed the carriage door shut.

The ladies all sat down again in silence, mouths open. The carriage jolted forward, turning toward the north. Kenreimon'in began to chant the Lotus Sutra. The other ladies tried to join in but could not, as weeping overtook them. Nii no Ama put her arms around them and tried to console them, but soon her tears flowed down with theirs as well.

Kiyomori's Head

They call it *what*?" growled Kiyomori.

"It is just a wooden ball," explained the pilgrim who had returned from Nara. "The monks of Kokufuji use it for sport and recreation. I am sure they mean nothing by it. A joke, really."

"The Taira do not tolerate such . . . jokes," said Kiyomori. He was beginning to have had enough of monks. Kuramadera had been surprised with so many important winter visitors arriving and the monks had been slow in providing sufficient rooms and food for the Imperial family and the Taira. Kiyomori had a grudge, as well, against the abbot for allowing a certain exile to escape. Kiyomori had been glad to learn that the Taira stronghold of Rokuhara had been sufficiently well guarded that it was undamaged from neglect and he would be moving back there soon.

"I would be patient, Father," said Munemori, who looked haggard from having to travel between the ruined palace and Kuramadera each day. "Kōfukuji is the most venerable temple in Nara, and the family temple of the Fujiwara. You would lose all the goodwill you have gained if you overreact."

"These are the same monks who harbored Prince Mochihito."

"You have already punished them for that."

"Hah. Very well, send an unarmed expeditionary force to look into matters. I will wait on any further decisions until they return."

"Yes, Father. Very wise, Father."

As Munemori dismissed the pilgrim from Nara and sent an aide to gather the men to go to Nara, Kiyomori stood and stretched and walked out onto the verandah. A light snow was falling on the pines and a chill, dry wind blew down from the mountains. He missed Fukuhara and the smell of the sea.

"It is done," said Munemori, coming up behind him.

"Hm. Already I am regretting my decision to return the capital to Heian Kyō."

"You mustn't think so, Father. It was a very sensible decision under the circumstances."

"That is what you said about Koremori fleeing the ducks."

"Well, so it was, at the time."

"City of Peace," Kiyomori grumbled. "Heian Kyō to me has always been the City of Battles, in politics as well as war. I have never felt I belonged here. Fukuhara was home. We never should have left."

"You have told me that the Dragon King is now the enemy of the Taira. How long do you think he would have let us keep our capital at the edge of his domain?"

"All the better, that it annoyed Ryujin-sama. All the better to stick like a burr in his nose. Think what Fukuhara would have become in the years ahead. What a grand harbor! Trading ships bringing goods and scholars from Chang'an. Warrior ships leaving to subdue barbarians in the southern islands. It would have been glorious! I think leaving Fukuhara will be the greatest regret of my life."

"But the Dragon King—"

"Yes, that and marrying the Dragon King's daughter. What a mistake that was."

"But, Father—"

"I would never have made that foolish bargain about Kusanagi. I would never have had a son like Shigemori to betray all I believe in. So many regrets. I wonder if I have enough life left to number them all."

"But, Father," Munemori said with an embarrassed laugh, "if you had not married my mother, you would not have had a son like me, neh?"

Kiyomori did not reply.

A Winged Prince

Ten nights later, Nii no Ama rushed toward the sound of the women screaming. She nearly tripped several times over the monks sleeping in the hallways of Kuramadera before reaching the room in which her daughter the Empress and her ladies were lodged.

Nii no Ama flung the *shōji* open and rushed to her distraught daughter, embracing her. "What is the matter? What has happened?"

"Don't you hear them?" Kenreimon'in wailed. "The *tengu*! They have followed us here!"

Nii no Ama shushed her and the ladies-in-waiting and listened. She could hear distant, cawing laughter and voices chattering. She could not quite discern what they were saying.

"They are laughing at us," said Kenreimon'in. "They say Takakura is going to die. They say Kiyomori is going to die. They say my son is going to die. They say we all are going to die, horribly."

Nii no Ama hugged Kenreimon'in close. "Do not fear. Be calm. This is holy ground, and the *tengu* cannot enter here. It would burn their feet. That is why they shout at us from a distance. And they did not follow us. The monks say these are *tengu* native to these mountains."

"It is Father's fault," whispered Kenreimon'in.

"It is more complicated than that," said Nii no Ama.

The unarmed expeditionary force that Munemori sent to Nara did not return. The monks of Kōfukuji, fearing it was a Taira attack, attacked first and decapitated all of the expedition, sending their severed topknots back to Heian Kyō as an act of defiance. This enraged Kiyomori, who then sent a retaliatory force of several thousand Taira warriors to Nara. They burned down the venerable temple of Kōfukuji, and all the ancient images and scrolls within it, and slaughtered every monk who served the temple. The heads of the monks had been brought back to the capital, but rather than shamefully hang the heads from the Traitor's Tree, the Imperial jailers threw the monk's heads into the gutters of the city streets, to be buried under cold, wet snow. As Munemori had predicted, the destruction of Kfukuji only earned the Taira more enmity. Even among the *tengu*.

"How can we make them go away?" asked Kenreimon'in. "Our guards and bowmen are down in Heian Kyō."

Nii no Ama narrowed her eyes and said, "I will deal with it. I will speak to the *tengu* myself."

The ladies all gasped. "No, Mother," said Kenreimon'in. "You mustn't. Think what they would do to you?"

"What will they do to me? I am an old woman, and a Buddhist nun, and a daughter of the Dragon King, who is now their ally. I can chant a sutra fast enough to keep them at bay. I do not fear *tengu*. Rest now. I will return when I have finished."

Nii no Ama stood and left her daughter's lodgings. Draping a gray scarf over her close-cropped head, she strode out of the Kuramadera monastery compound. The monks and acolytes did not try to stop her. After the burning of Kōfukuji, they did not care what the Taira did, and had been hinting they hoped their Taira guests would leave as soon as possible.

Nii no Ama took a torch from its iron holder by the monastery gate and walked out into the forest. There was a sharp smell of pine where she walked on the needle-carpeted path. She followed the sound of the chattering *tengu* until suddenly there was silence. Nii no Ama stopped and waited.

Suddenly there was a crashing in the pine boughs around her, and a great flock of black birds, wearing colorful hats, flapped and clattered down, encircling her on the ground. Nii no Ama gasped and staggered a little, but did not drop the torch.

Another winged creature, the size of a man, dropped down from the trees and landed right in front of her. He wore the wings and beak of a raven, but the body of a human being, as well as a bright red silk jacket. "Greetings, Tokiko," he said. "Well met, daughter of Ryujin. My, how you have changed since you and your sister Benzaiten would play the *biwa* and sing on your little boats."

"I have lived the life of a mortal," said Nii no Ama, "and the years change mortal women in ways both cruel and kind. Who, may I ask, are you?"

The *tengu* bowed. "I am Sōjō-bō, prince of the *tengu* of these mountains."

"Then it is you I wish to speak to. I demand that you and your Leaflet Tengu stop harassing the Imperial family. Have you no respect for the blood of Amaterasu?"

Cawing laughter erupted around her.

"You do not know *tengu* well, do you?" asked Sōjō-bō. "We do not respect anyone. And I regret to tell you we respect the Taira least of all."

"If you have matters to settle with Kiyomori-sama then deal with him, not with his innocent family."

The Leaflet Tengu laughed again.

"We *tengu* have a saying," said Sōjō-bō, "There is no such thing as an innocent mortal. Particularly not a Taira. Your daughter is not wholly blameless, you know. As for Kiyomori, it is out of our hands now. Kiyomori has sinned so outrageously that the Kasuga *kami* will be taking matters into its own hands. Kiyomori does not have much time left in this world. Do you think he will repent and spare his miserable soul? I doubt it. A pity . . . I had set up a glorious death for him. A special assassin whom I trained myself. A son of Minomoto Yoshitomo, no less. How poetic it would have been!" Sōjō-bō sighed.

"Mortals have a saying," countered Nii no Ama, "that there is no such thing as a truthful *tengu*. Particularly not to a monk or nun. I have no idea whether what you tell me will occur."

Sōjō-bō shrugged. "It does not matter. You will see for yourself."

"And what do you mean, my daughter is not wholly blameless?"

"Do we not earn our future lives? Is it not karma that she was born a Taira? And there is something else she did that she should not have. Ask her, and she might tell you. But, now, go back to what little is left of your sordid mortal life. If I were you, I'd return to Ryujin's kingdom as soon as possible. You really don't want to see what's going to happen."

"It is the *mappo*, then?" asked Nii no Ama.

"Well, such things are relative, neh? One clan's *mappo* is another clan's rebirth. Let us say it is the Taira *mappo*."

"You delight in being cruel."

"I am a *tengu*, neh? But we will give up our nightly singing at Kuramadera. The good monks there deserve some sleep after all that you Taira have put them through."

"It must be the *mappo*, when a *tengu* has pity for monks," said Nii no Ama.

"Go, Tokiko-san," said Sōjō-bō. "Take heed of my advice and leave this world while you can." Sōjō-bō lifted his great black wings and jumped into the air. The Leaflet Tengu took flight as well, rising like a black cloud around Nii no Ama until they vanished amid the pine boughs. Her torch was nearly blown out by the wind from their wings, but a small, flickering flame managed to remain alight.

Nii no Ama turned and headed back down the forest path toward the monastery. She considered whether to take Sōjō-bō's advice. *How can I?* she asked herself sadly, *My daughter needs me. And my grandson, who happens to be the Emperor. And perhaps I may yet speak some sense to Munemori. No, I cannot go now, no matter what I might see.*

A ship tied to shore
With thick ropes no sword can cut
I await what comes

A Cold New Year

In recognition of the destruction of Kofukuji, there were no New Year's celebrations at the Imperial palace to mark the turning of the year, the fifth year of the era of Jishō. The Imperial family moved back into those quarters of the Imperial Compound that could be made suitable and avoided those buildings that remained burned out, decrepit, or defiled. Perhaps it was sorrow at seeing the once-magnificent Imperial palace reduced to a fraction of its former glory, or perhaps it was the upset of so many moves after so long an illness, or perhaps because he was a guest at the Taira Rokuhara stronghold; but on the Fourteenth Day of the First Month, New Retired Emperor Takakura breathed his last.

Priestly Retired Emperor Go-Shirakawa, standing on the verandah, once more confined at the Toba mansion, imagined that he could see the smoke from the pyre at Seiganji across the valley drifting up to join the overhanging clouds. Naturally, he had not been permitted to attend his son's funeral. "How have I lived so long," he whispered to the evening air, "to see so many die?" Favored wives and concubines, two sons, Nijō and Takakura, who had been Emperor, one grandson, Rokujō, who had been Emperor, and one son, Prince Mochihito, who should have been Emperor. "What sins did I commit in a former life," Go-Shirakawa wondered, "that I should suffer so in this one?"

He had become almost content in the Prison Palace at Fukuhara, as the little *tengu* brought him news of the new Minomoto uprising in the east, as well as their demonic pranks at the new palace. Go-Shirakawa had rejoiced when the announcement was made to return to Heian Kyō, and he regarded the Toba mansion as near Paradise after the close, dreary confinement at Fukuhara. But the gods, it seemed, would never allow him to be happy for long. There was always some new sorrow awaiting him.

"You are the fortunate one, my son," he said to the smoke in the distance. "Your life has been faultless, you observed the Ten Laws, and acted with the Five Constant Virtues. You will find a place in the Pure Land, surely. Pity, instead, those of us who must remain here, in this declining world. I owe you my life, yet now I wish you had not begged the Dragon King to protect me. Instead, I wish you had saved yourself."

Along with the announcement of Takakura's death, Kiyomori had sent a peculiar message. It had read:

I regret that such great sorrows should beset men of our advancing age. I have a daughter, just eighteen, whom I wish to offer to you as consort, to console you in your mourning. She is the child of an Itsukushima Shrine attendant, so surely the sea *kami* will look upon such a union with favor. If you will accept her, I will deliver her to you, with proper attendants and furnishings, in fourteen days.

A gift or an admission of guilt? Go-Shirakawa had wondered. He still marveled at the heartless audacity of the man. Go-Shirakawa knew he would have to accept the girl. He did not yet dare openly offend Kiyomori. But he doubted he would be able to offer the poor creature much companionship. Hers would be another life made miserable by Kiyomori.

Go-Shirakawa tilted his face up toward the Heavens, where heavy clouds gathered in the evening sky. "Great *Kami*, if you favor me," he intoned, "give me justice in this life. Give me vengeance. Let me see the Taira fallen and the world restored. If you have spared me for any reason, let it be for this."

Go-Shirakawa felt wetness on his cheek, but did not know if it was a tear or cold winter rain.

Boiling Water

That year, the fifth year of the era of Jishō, was unusual in that it had an intercalary month, a second Second Month, in order to reset the calendar of man in accord with the seasons. Perhaps because it was a month of setting-things-right, the event so many had longed and prayed for at last occurred.

On the second day of that second Second Month, Munemori was visiting Rokuhara, recounting to his father Kiyomori a list of the many uprisings in the Kantō and Eastern Provinces over the last twenty-eight days.

"Barbarians in all the Four Earthly Directions have taken advantage of the situation," Munemori said. "It is all our allies can do to keep them at bay while holding off the Minomoto as well. And Minomoto Yoritomo gathers more men by the hundreds daily."

"Huh," grunted Kiyomori, staring at the floor. He had not been well the past few days, Munemori had learned, not eating much. Munemori wondered if he had his father's full attention.

"The Council of Senior Nobles has asked me to take the post of Commander in Chief," Munemori went on, "and to lead new forces eastward. I have accepted, thinking it would be best. Our men are wary of following

Koremori after, well, after previous events. Naturally, I would not do so without your approval and support."

Kiyomori raised his shaved head and stared at the far wall. "Go away."

"What?"

Kiyomori staggered to his feet. "Go away, I tell you!"

"Father, who are you speaking to?"

"It is not time! I will not go!"

"Father!"

"Do you not see them, Munemori?" Kiyomori grasped his shoulder. His hand felt as hot as melted wax through Munemori's robe.

"Who, Father?"

"There!" Kiyomori pointed at the far wall. "It is Akugenda Yoshihira! It is the Shin-In! It is my uncle and Yoshitomo's father! They say they have come for me, that my luck has run out. But I will not go! Tell them, Munemori. I will not go!" Kiyomori shoved on Munemori's shoulder, sending him sprawling on the floor. "I defy you!" Kiyomori screamed. "I defy all of you!"

Munemori scrambled to his feet and took Kiyomori's arm. To his shock, it was hot, so hot Munemori could barely hold it. "Father, you are burning up. It must be fever. That is what is causing you to see these things."

Servants appeared at the *shōji*, concerned at all the shouting. Munemori ordered them, "Fill a bath, quickly! Cold water. Lord Kiyomori has a fever and must be cooled down."

They hurried off to do his bidding, and Munemori led Kiyomori out to the corridor toward the courtyard of the baths.

"Hot," said Kiyomori. "Hot. Hot."

"Peace, Father. We will have you cooled down soon. Be strong, as you always have been."

Finally, they reached the courtyard and Munemori led Kiyomori to one of the large, square stone cisterns. Already servants were pouring buckets of water into it. Munemori and another servant took off Kiyomori's robes and eased him into the chill water. Steam gushed into the air as Kiyomori's hot skin touched the water's surface. As he sank in deeper, the water began to boil.

"This cannot be happening," Munemori murmured.

The servants around him began to whimper and moan to one another, "It is the end. Surely it is the end."

"You," snapped Munemori at two of them, "stop whining and do something useful. This is clearly no ordinary ailment. Go to Mount Hiei at once and bring back water from the Thousand-Armed Well. That should drive away the demons that beset him."

The servants bowed and swiftly left, undoubtedly grateful to have a reason to go away.

Munemori looked around and noticed that the eave from an adjoining building sloped close to the bath. "You," he said to another two servants, "place a bamboo pipe there, along the eave, so it reaches over the bath. Place a barrel atop the roof, filled with cold water, and attach the pipe to it so that cold water may fall on him continually."

These servants also hurried off to comply.

Munemori knelt by the stone bath. "Father, do not leave us. I am not yet ready to take full command of the Taira. I do not know what will happen if you go."

But Kiyomori seemed not to hear him. His face was stretched into a wide, snarling grimace. Now and then he would grunt the word, "Hot. Hot."

Munemori looked up and through the mist of the steam, he saw someone standing at the edge of the courtyard. "Mother."

"So. It is true," Nii no Ama said, shock and resignation in her round, lined face.

Munemori stood and went to her. "How did you hear so soon?"

"Last night I had a dream. I dreamed I was here at Rokuhara, and an ox-carriage, surrounded by flame and drawn by *oni* demons, arrived at the gate. A voice called out for Kiyomori, saying Lord Emma-O, the Judge of the Dead, summons the Chancellor-Novice of the Taira to his tribunal. It said Kiyomori has been sentenced to the Hell of Torment Without End. I awoke from that dream and have not slept since."

"Mother, do not speak of such things. He might hear you."

"From the look of things, he hears nothing but the demons shouting in his ear."

Munemori glanced back over his shoulder. In the swirling steam rising off the bathwater he discerned a familiar face with sunken eyes and hollow cheeks. The Shin-In was smiling.

Munemori was distracted by a clattering from the rooftop. Servants there were hurrying to attach a long length of hollowed bamboo to a barrel, with little concern for their own safety. The pipe was tied down to the roof tiles and cold water began to flow down over the bath. When Munemori looked back at the steam, the Shin-In was gone.

But the piped water proved to be no solution. The water spattered in the air just above Kiyomori's skin, as if Kiyomori's chest were hot as iron in a forge.

"He is fighting them," Nii no Ama said. "He will not let the demons take him, and so his body burns as if it were already in the Nether Realm, though it remains in our world."

"What can we do?" whispered Munemori.

"I am going to pray," said Nii no Ama, "though it will do little good.

You may do as you wish." She began to murmur the Thousand-Armed Sutra, which had saved his sister two years before.

Some time passed, and the servants returned from Mount Hiei. "It would have been impossible to bring barrels of water back quickly," they said. "So we have brought boards soaked in the water of the holy well. The monks said he should lie upon these and that will ease his tormented spirit."

So the waterlogged boards were set down in Kiyomori's sleeping chamber and the servants carried Kiyomori out of the bath. It was difficult to do because he was so hot—the servants had to wind cloth as padding around their hands and arms. Kiyomori was laid out upon the boards, and serving girls knelt nearby waving fans over him frantically, but it did not reduce his temperature. If anything, the warmth became worse, and soon the girls had to move away from him, nearly fainting from the heat.

Munemori and Nii no Ama knelt as close to Kiyomori as they dared. "My husband, I feel the end is nigh," said Nii no Ama, "and although we have not been close in recent years, still it is my duty as your wife to see that your last wishes are carried out. What sort of memorial or stupa would you wish? What donations shall we make to temples in your name? What posts do you want disposed on your children and relatives?"

"Tell us, Father, if you can," agreed Munemori.

Kiyomori turned his face to them. "No . . . memorial," he growled. "No . . . stupa. No . . . donations. No . . . posts."

"What, then?" asked Nii no Ama.

"Want . . . Yoritomo's . . . *head*!" said Kiyomori, his shoulders rising off the pallet. "Hang it . . . over my grave. That . . . is my last wish."

"Father," said Munemori, "that is an unworthy last request. You should be thinking of the life to come—"

"It is . . . a warrior's . . . wish," Kiyomori snarled. "I . . . choose to die . . . as a warrior." He subsided back onto the soaked boards and closed his eyes.

Kiyomori fought the demons for two days more. Then, on the Fourth Day of the second Second Month, in a spasm of convulsions, Kiyomori died. Heian Kyō was shocked into stunned silence as horsemen rode everywhere, spreading the news. Matters hung undecided, like a knife thrown into the air, spinning. The future seemed unknowable.

Kiyomori's body was cremated three days later. His bones and ashes were taken to Settsu Province, and buried on Kyonoshima, the island he had built off Fukuhara. Even in death, Kiyomori defied the Dragon King.

A Great Disappointment

"No!" cried Minomoto Yoshitsune when the news of Kiyomori's death reached Izu. "No!" He flung down the rack that held his armor and tore at his jacket sleeves. He threw himself to the floor and beat the mats with his fists.

"Young master," rumbled Benkei as he ran into the room, "what is the matter? Kiyomori was your bitterest enemy and here you weep for his death?"

"I was supposed to kill him!" wailed Yoshitsune. "Sōjō-bō promised me! It is what I have trained my whole life for! And now the gods have taken my destiny from me. Why? Why? Why?"

"Peace, young master," said Benkei. "Surely this is what comes of believing the promises of *tengu*."

"What is there left for me?" asked Yoshitsune through his tears. "I feel again like a homeless child, adrift on a river with no rope to cling to. My destiny has been stolen from me, Benkei! What shall I do now?"

"Is it not clear, young master? Your brother needs you. Although Kiyomori is gone, there are plenty of other Taira left to kill. Why, the Chancellor-Novice wasn't even head of the clan anymore. Taira Munemori should be your quarry now."

"Taira Munemori," sneered Yoshitsune, "is an unworthy rabbit of a man. Everyone says so. I would take no more honor in killing him than in slaying a rat that had crawled into my granary."

"But there are many beneath him who are not so unworthy, young master. What of Koremori, Shigemori's son?"

"He ran from *ducks*. Need I say more?"

"But surely—"

"No, Benkei. Were it not for my brother, I would see no need to continue my useless life. I suppose I must do what I can to maintain my honor. I will make up in quantity what I cannot have in quality. There are no Taira warriors to match me, and, therefore, I will simply have to kill as many of them as possible. I must make a vow such as you did, to kill a thousand warriors before my life ends."

"I gave up that vow, young master."

"I take it up, then. My sword will drink Taira blood until the Inland Sea flows red. Only that will appease my honor. Tell my brother I have made this vow."

"But young master—"

"Tell him! So he will know with what fervor and strength I will serve him."

Reluctantly, Benkei bowed and replied, "Yes, young master. As you wish."

Yoritomo was bemused, at first, by his brother's "vow" when he learned of it. And then he became concerned. *Such a one, cut adrift from his perceived destiny, might do anything in battle. Foolish things. I cannot have a hothead leading forces against the Taira. I must be careful not to give him command of a large force. He will have to prove himself to me before I allow him that.*

Yoritomo scarcely thought upon Kiyomori's death, other than it might be beneficial to the rebellion. He had his hands full with pacifying relatives in the widespread Minomoto clan: the Satake, the Shige, the Ashikaga. These families were all descended from prominent Minomoto ancestry and each had generals to rival Yoritomo. With the exception of his cousin Yoshinaka, Yoritomo had been able to negotiate with some satisfactorily. Some he had had to kill. With the advice of the Shin-In, Yoritomo grew ever closer to consolidating his power in the East.

The Great Gift

Retired Emperor Go-Shirakawa was astonished at the visitor who was guided into his private chambers. "Taira Munemori. This is an . . . unexpected honor."

The Chief of the Taira clan knelt before him and bowed low, pressing his forehead to the floor. Go-Shirakawa noted that Munemori had grown thin in recent years, and now looked older than his age of thirty-six. "Most great and noble former liege, I have come seeking guidance, and to right a great wrong."

"Seeking guidance . . . from *me*? Your prisoner?"

"Prisoner no longer. Your confinement was an unfortunate notion of my father's, and I had been unable to dissuade him. Now that he is gone, I see no reason to continue his folly. You are free to choose whatever residence you wish."

Go-Shirakawa blinked and let his mouth hang open in surprise. *Is Munemori truly so foolish, as everyone says he is, or is this some new trick of the Taira?* "Any residence?"

"I understand," Munemori went on, "that you were in the process of building a fine mansion at Hōjūji when . . . the unfortunate matters occurred. If you like, I will see that construction there is completed in preparation for you to move in."

Hōjūji! They will let me live in Hōjūji! He truly is that foolish! thought Go-Shirakawa. He was filled with almost as much surprise and joy as when he had received word of Kiyomori's death. "Please do not go to such expense on my humble account. Allow me to move into Hōjūji as it is, and I will oversee the construction myself." *Particularly the secret meeting rooms, and passages so that visitors may come and go unseen.*

"If that is your preference," said Munemori.

"You understand," said Go-Shirakawa, "that I have been confined with so little to do in such dreary places. Naturally I am eager to apply myself to creating a pleasant new residence as soon as possible."

"Of course, Majesty. Be assured that the Taira are now pleased to be at your service and seek comity with you in all things. In these troubled days, the land has become like a boat with no wind in its sails. The people need a wise leader such as you to look to, the way flowers seek the sun."

Ah. So that is it, thought Go-Shirakawa. *You need the weight of legitimate authority behind you. Your own clan doubts you. You haven't the dominating presence of your father, nor the moral authority of your late brother Shigemori. Your little nephew Emperor is still a child. The Regent has fled. You need me. You poor fool. I have committed intrigue for longer than you have lived. You are no match for me.* "I am pleased to once again be of service to my people," Go-Shirakawa said, mildly.

"You understand," said Munemori, "that we may require an edict from you, permitting us Imperial permission to crush the Minomoto insurrection."

Go-Shirakawa tried very hard not to smile. "I will be happy to do whatever is necessary to punish those who threaten the legitimate government."

Munemori sighed, and his shoulders eased as if a great weight had been taken from his shoulders. "I am most heartened to hear this, Majesty. I must confess, I have been terribly adrift since my father's death. As you know, it was my brother who was supposed to lead the Taira in years to come. I was quite unprepared when the burden fell to me. And Kiyomori had been unwilling to let go the reins of power, so I had little chance to become the leader I must be. With your help and guidance, I am sure we can restore peace to this unhappy land."

Go-Shirakawa wondered if he were truly seeing a tear in the Taira's eye. "Rest assured, Munemori-san, to use my powers to unite all the country in peace has been all I have ever wished for."

Munemori bowed again. "Truly, Majesty, you are worthy of the throne you once occupied. It is a travesty of fate that you are no longer there. Rest assured that from now on, I will seek your advice in all matters of importance. Now I will go and see that proper escort is arranged for you to go to Hōjūji."

Go-Shirakawa nodded to him. "I thank you, Munemori-san, and I am very glad to see you are of different heart than your father. I look forward to all our future encounters, and you will be the first invited to Hōjūji when it is finished, and I am ready for entertaining again."

As soon as Munemori departed, Go-Shirakawa leapt to his feet and did a little dance of joy, fluttering his gray sleeves, not minding the aches in his old bones. He ran out to the verandah, ignoring the chill of early spring, and bowed toward the south, toward the sea. "Thank you, o Great *Kami*. Thank you, Ryujin-sama! Sweet is the justice you have given me. You have allowed me one more great game in my last years. No greater gift could there be for a man such as me."

Second Thoughts

Munemori pulled his black robes tightly around him as he entered his ox-carriage. He wiped the tears, which were not entirely false, from his eyes and sat on the carriage bench with a heavy sigh.

"How did it go, Uncle?" asked young Koremori, sitting on the bench opposite him.

"That old weasel," grumbled Munemori. "I am sure he meant nothing he said." The ox-carriage started moving with a jerk, and Munemori was jolted against the woven bamboo wall.

"The *kami* chastise you, Uncle. You should not speak so about the Imperial family. My father often spoke of how they must be treated with the utmost respect at all times."

"Respect, certainly," said Munemori, "but trust? Not one such as Go-Shirakawa. He has hungered to return to the throne ever since he left it. I hope he at least believed my suggestion that we Taira might see that he reigns again."

Koremori's eyes went wide. "A Retired Emperor retaking the throne? There is no precedent for such a thing!"

Munemori waggled his hand. "We have had many years now of unprecedented events."

"Are you actually going to arrange it?"

"Allow a schemer like Go-Shirakawa back on the throne? Never. The Taira would be done for. I merely want him to believe we may, so that he will not throw his support to the Minomoto. A would-be Emperor needs warriors, and the Taira are still the mightiest force in the land. I just hope he remembers that."

"Did he accept the offer to move back to Hōjūji?"

"He did. And I hope it keeps him too busy to meddle in our affairs, but I fear that may be a false hope."

Koremori sighed and stared down at his hands. "All this nastiness and disrespect . . . it is most disillusioning. I fear you are becoming like Grand-father."

"If I am to lead the Taira," said Munemori with genuine regret, "I fear I must."

The Wisteria Garden

Kenreimon'in sat in the Imperial Gardens within the Dairi beside her mother Nii no Ama. Both wore dark gray kimonos of mourning. In this garden, if one sat just so, one would not see the burned shell of the Great Hall of State or the broken roof tiles of the Bureau of the Wardrobe. For a little while, one could sit here and see the Imperial palace as it had been, the glorious beauty of days gone by. For a little while, one could forget that, beyond the Valley of Crystal Streams, the world was falling into chaos.

By some miracle, the wisteria trees in this garden had survived during the Imperial absence and had put forth plumes of white and purple blossoms which had lasted now into late spring.

"I had to show you these," said Nii no Ama. "A small sign of hope in such a sad year."

Kenreimon'in was not encouraged. "They are lovely, Mother. But the wisteria is a flower of transitoriness. I would feel more hopeful had you found a stand of *yuzuri-ha*, the flower of continuity."

"Alas, I have found none of those," said Nii no Ama.

"Here we are, two old widows." Kenreimon'in sighed. "Why should we find any constancy in life?"

"Old?" asked Nii no Ama, raising one eyebrow. "I am old. But you?"

"Mother, I am nearly thirty!"

Nii no Ama chuckled. "I scarcely remember being thirty."

"Is is not strange," said Kenreimon'in, "that a woman is young for so brief a time but is old so very long?"

"I have observed there are many strange things about the mortal world," replied Nii no Ama.

After a pause, Kenreimon'in asked, "What will I do, Mother? I wish I could become a nun such as you, and leave this world of trouble. But Munemori insists I stay to look after Antoku."

"He is right," said Nii no Ama. "Now that Kiyomori is gone, the Taira need all the morale and authority they can assert. You must remain in the palace."

Staring down at her hands, Kenreimon'in said, "I am not a worthy vessel for the hopes of my clan."

After a pause, Nii-no-Ama said, "When I was speaking to the prince of the *tengu*, he mentioned something odd. He said you were not entirely blameless and that I should ask you about it. Have you any thoughts on what he might have meant?"

Kenreimon'in felt the guilt swell within her, and she pressed her wide sleeves to her face. "Ai! I had hoped that I would die with my shame."

Nii no Ama moved closer and placed her hands on her arm. "Please, tell me. Surely it cannot be so great a sin as you think. The *tengu* are cruel and make more of our mortal follies than is deserved."

Kenreimon'in rested her head on her mother's shoulder. "It was the night of the great fire," she began softly. "I awoke from a dream in which I was troubled. It was so hot, and I wanted just a little breeze. We were at the Emperor's mother's mansion. I wandered to where the Sacred Regalia were being kept. I had heard stories about the magic in the sword—"

"Kusanagi," Nii no Ama breathed. "You touched it?"

Kenreimon'in grasped her mother's shoulder tightly. "I had no understanding of what would happen. It was as though some other spirit moved my arms. I waved the sword and commanded it and a wind came up. A wind that drove the fire into the palace." She lasped into sobs for a while as her mother held her and stroked her hair.

"My dear, you should not blame yourself. You did not know a fire was raging elsewhere in the city."

"There must be some stain in my soul," said Kenreimon'in when she could speak again, "that allowed such a horrible spirit to possess me. He tried again, when I was giving birth to Antoku. It was the same one, I am sure."

"The Shin-In," murmured Nii no Ama.

"What?"

"The Retired Emperor believed it was the spirit of his brother, the Shin-In, who tried to possess you at Rokuhara. If it was he, then it is because you are his blood relative that the Shin-In could more easily possess you, not because of any spiritual impurity of yours. Did you ever wield Kusanagi again?"

"No, no, never!" cried Kenreimon'in. "I vowed never to touch the sword again. Not even on the night of the earthquake."

"What happened on the night of the earthquake?"

"It is hard to remember clearly. But after the earthquake, I rushed out through the room in which the regalia were kept. The girls who were guarding it claimed there were two swords."

"*Two* swords?"

"Identical Kusanagis. The girls could not tell one from the other. I had the thought at the time that I could know the real one by grasping it, yet I dared not do so because of my vow. I rushed out of the room and on the verandah I ran into Munemori. I believe he had been . . . visiting the girls."

"Munemori. I see," said Nii no Ama. "It was Munemori who insisted you give birth at Rokuhara, as I recall."

"Was it? Yes, I suppose it was," said Kenreimon'in, now somewhat confused at her mother's words.

"And it was Munemori who left the palace unexpectedly early on the day of the whirlwind, due to some mysterious ailment."

"Munemori was often ill in those days, after losing his wife and child."

"Hmmm. There was something hidden between Shigemori and Munemori before Shigemori died. Some plan that went arwy, that Shigemori would not reveal to me. Do you know what it was?"

Kenreimon'in shook her head. "I am a younger sister. Why would they tell me anything? I do not know."

Nii no Ama hugged her more tightly. "Do not blame yourself any further. It is clear we have both been caught up in greater schemes than we knew. I believe it is time I paid a long-overdue visit to the now-illustrious Munemori."

Kenreimon'in sighed and rested her head in her mother's lap like she used to do as a child. "I hope he can give you answers. Our whole world depends upon him now."

A Mother Talks with Her Son

It took some time for Nii no Ama to catch up with Munemori, for he was forever at meetings at Rokuhara, at the Council of Senior Nobles, at Hōjūji Mansion. Finally, early in the Fifth Month, Munemori was at the Imperial palace, meeting with the Military Guards of the Left and Right. Nii no Ama stationed herself outside his palace office chamber and refused to leave until she was permitted a chance to speak with him. As Grandmother of the Emperor, and having the Rights of Three Empresses, she had some considerable influence. It was not long before she was ushered into Munemori's presence.

As she knelt before her black-robed son, Nii no Ama smiled sweetly at the green-robed, Sixth Rank secretaries and attendants. "If you please, I should like to speak with my son in private for a while."

With nervous glances at Munemori, not sure whom they wished to risk offending more, the green-robed young men swiftly bowed and departed.

Munemori sighed, clearly annoyed and impatient. "Mother, while it is always a joy to see you, I fear you have chosen an unfortunate time for a visit."

"Very true, my son," said Nii no Ama, in a cold, firm voice. "I should have had such a meeting with you long before now."

Munemori's head rose a little, and he weighed her with his gaze. "I regret that I have not been the most filial of sons. But surely you understand that matters of state have been quite pressing of late. Particularly since Father passed away."

Nii no Ama clicked her tongue. "You have grown thin," she said, noting his now more hollow cheeks and more sunken eyes. "Year by year you become more like a wraith. You really should take another wife. Clearly your concubines are not feeding you enough."

Munemori closed his eyes. "Mother, this is not the time—"

"Oh, I fear it is the time," Nii no Ama said coldly. "It is long past time. I have been a fool not to see it." She crept closer to him and affixed him with the dragon stare she used to use on Kiyomori to show him that she disapproved. "What is your relation to the Shin-In? What have you done with Kusanagi?"

His eyes snapped open, and his face paled. "I do not know what you are talking about."

"Ah, but you do. Your blood does, or it would not flee from your face so. What was your arrangement with Shigemori, the one that failed?"

Munemori looked away. "It is of no consequence now."

"How can you say such a thing? How dare you lie to me like this!" demanded Nii no Ama. "No consequence? Here you are, the most powerful man in all Nihon—and believe me, that thought terrifies me more than I can say—and you claim there is no consequence to consorting with evil spirits and magical swords?"

Munemori's hands tightened on his baton of office. "Mother, I pray you, keep your voice down. These are perilous times for the Taira, and we must provide no fodder for the gossip mill."

"The *mappo* is upon us, and you are worried about gossip?"

Munemori rolled his eyes. "You should hear them, Mother. The messengers who come from the east. Our forces have been having victory after victory against the supporters of the Minomoto. But is that what the people speak of? No, they speak of our one general who was struck down by lightning, and they claim it is the justice of the gods. There is drought in the countryside, and *we* are blamed. I now have an edict from Go-Shirakawa to destroy the Minomoto, but we cannot supply our armies because no one believes the Cloistered Emperor is sincere in his command. Father was right that the tongues of the people should not be allowed to wag freely."

"But while your tongue wags freely, you evade my questions."

Munemori sighed again. Softly, he said, "Shigemori knew of a copy of Kusanagi that hung at the Shrine of Ise. He was hoping we could switch the swords, and thereby see that the Dragon King's sword was returned to the sea. But the day I brought it to the palace, I became ill. And then the whirlwind happened. And then the earthquake. Clearly the gods intended that our plan was not to be. That is all there is to know."

"I find it a curious coincidence that you were handling Kusanagi on the day of the whirlwind."

"It was not coincidence. Have I not said the whirlwind was a sign of the *kami*'s disapproval?"

"What happened to the copy?"

"After the earthquake, I sent it back to Ise at once."

"Are you certain it was the copy and not the actual Sacred Sword that you returned?"

Munemori paused, the lines around his eyes deepening and his lips tightening thinner. "What does it matter?" he exploded at last. "It is just a sword, a symbol. As long as one remains with the Emperor, all is well. And if the real one lands at Ise, where is the harm? That is the safest place of all."

"Safe from whom?"

Munemori glanced away. "From whoever might misuse it."

"And who might that be?"

Munemori did not answer.

"Safe from me? Or safe from the Shin-In?"

"The Shin-In," growled Munemori through gritted teeth, "is a legend, a folk tale told by condemned men who wished not to take the blame for their crimes."

"Curiouser still," said Nii no Ama. "Your sister says this same spirit was the one that tried to possess her child as she was giving birth at Rokuhara. At your recommendation. I hardly think giving birth to an Emperor was a crime for which Kenreimon'in needed someone to blame. I felt that spirit's power, and it was formidable indeed."

Munemori very carefully set his baton of office on the cushion beside him. "Mother. These are matters of the past. I fear that matters of the present have become far more pressing—"

"Do you serve the Shin-In?" Nii no Ama asked.

He fixed his gaze on her. "I do not serve the Shin-In. There are those who say, however, that the Shin-In serves our enemies. Now please, Mother, I have nothing more to tell you."

Nii no Ama stood. "I do not understand the men of this family. None of you have trusted me, when I might have been of great assistance. Your father did not listen to me, and the children he pardoned now arm themselves to destroy us. Shigemori would not deal with Kusanagi soon enough, and now he is dead. And now you do not listen. What will be the price of your stubbornness? I fear I know."

"Good afternoon. Mother."

Nii no Ama stared at her third son for a long moment. Then she said, "So be it," and she bowed. She walked out as gracefully as her old legs would let her, without a look back.

A Year of Famine and Pestilence

As the year proceeded, matters worsened in the countryside. The clouds brought little rain and therefore the fields brought forth little rice. There were no provisions for warriors in the far counties, and so the rebellion slowed.

In hopes of changing the land's fortunes, the era name had been changed to Yowa in the middle of the Seventh Month. Munemori declared an amnesty for those nobles who had fled two years before, and so the Regent and the Chancellor returned and paid homage to Retired Emperor Go-Shirakawa.

There were rumors throughout the year that the temples and shrines secretly prayed for the destruction of the Heike in revenge for the burning of the temples at Nara.

Winter deepened and New Year of the second year of Yowa arrived with only a worsening of the capital's fortunes. There had not been enough rice to store for winter, and so there were beggars starving on the streets in great numbers. The Imperial Police could not clear the corpses fast enough, so sickness spread as well. People, even nobles, were afraid to leave their homes, in fear that the spirits of the dead would infect them with illness. Toward the end of the Fourth Month, the Imperial government sent lavish offerings to The Twenty-Two Shrines surrounding the capital in order to appease the gods.

A month later, seeing that the previous change of era name had been ineffective, the era name was changed again to Juei. But it did not help matters. Through the long, hot summer, the people of Heian Kyō suffered, and those who could fled the city for the surrounding mountains. Those who remained sold off their valuable possessions to buy rice. Those who had no valuable possessions begged and starved. Houses were cut down to be sold as firewood, and temples in the hills were broken into and robbed. Parents died, giving what food they had to their children. Lovers died, giving what food they had to their beloved.

The streets became carpeted with the dead. Those monks who felt pity would wander the city, tracing the *aji* symbol on the foreheads of the fallen, giving them a last rite.

Only one battle of any significance was fought that year. In the Ninth Month, a force of several thousand Taira marched east to attack Shinano Province. There they were met by Yoritomo's cousin Yoshinaka, who easily defeated them with a ruse: they approached the Taira carrying red banners, and only when close enough to attack raised the white banners of the Minomoto.

In the East, in Kamakura, conditions were not so dire, but there were still not enough provisions to mount a massive campaign. Minomoto Yoritomo spent his time offering gifts to the major shrines, securing their loyalty. He also heard complaints from shrines whose lands were being plundered by the gathering warriors, and did what he could to stop such depredations. His wife, Masako, gave birth to a son . . . and discovered that Yoritomo had had all the while a favorite concubine hidden nearby. This caused many upheavals in the Hōjō household, and two men who had helped the concubine stay hidden were murdered at Masako's orders.

And thus the first year of Juei passed, with sorrows in every household.

An Empty Banquet

Taira Munemori sat beside the ladies' *kichō* curtain beneath which a corner of dark gray sleeve protruded. "A New Year full of blessings to you, sister," he said. Munemori was the Minister of State in charge of the New Year's celebrations, and he was careful to hold them within the Shomenon Gate, in the Dairi, the Inner Palace Compound, where damage had been the least and repairs made first. A light snow was falling, but the outdoor celebration was still festive enough, the sake and plum wine flowing freely, allowing the assembled nobility to forget briefly the troubles of the world.

"Surely we cannot be cursed any worse," murmured Kenreimon'in from the other side of the curtain. "I cannot look at this meal without thinking of the poor souls outside our walls, who have nothing."

"The rice is not of the best quality," Munemori said. "And the onion and daikon are from gardens here in the Imperial Compound. Neither is fit for the lowly folk outside. Besides, in these perilous times, it is important for those in government to stay reasonably fed, neh? Or all will fall to chaos."

"What will it matter," replied Kenreimon'in, "if there is no one left to govern?"

"The gods will never let that happen," said Munemori. "People are one crop our land has no lack of. Perhaps it was time for a weeding."

"You have become callous," said Kenreimon'in.

"As a leader of a warrior clan must be," he reminded her. "You are compassionate, as a woman must be."

He heard his sister sigh explosively and knock over her rice bowl.

"Do not waste any, Majesty, if you are concerned for the starving."

"It was already empty. How many of us," she went on, "look on the snow falling on the plum blossoms just starting to bloom on those trees and think not of poems but of the fruit those trees will bear later?"

"The plum blossom is a symbol of hope. Such thoughts are entirely appropriate, I would say."

"What is there to hope for? I hear rumors that the Minomoto are amassing in Ōmi Province, not far from the city. They could sweep down on us at any time."

"Do not listen to rumors, Majesty. It is a small matter that Koremori will deal with once the mountain passes are clear."

"Our nephew Koremori? The one who ran from ducks?"

"Hush," Munemori said softly. "He has learned his lesson and is a much more seasoned warrior now."

"Hmmm." Kenreimon'in paused before saying, "I have also heard a rumor that you will be elevated to Junior First Rank next month. Congratulations."

"I have every assurance that it will be so. It has been long overdue. It is difficult, you know, to issue directives to the Fujiwara when one is merely Fourth Rank. They do not take one seriously. How fares His Young Majesty?"

Kenreimon'in paused again before replying. "Well enough, considering. He does not seem to thrive and takes little interest in what happens around him. Some are saying he sickens because the land itself is unwell."

"That is foolish nonsense. If the land is unwell, it is only because it is infected by the Minomoto. As soon as they are defeated, all will be well once more." But Munemori gazed out over the Dairi and the snow falling gently on its gardens, trying to commit the sight to memory. He had heard the estimates of how many troops the Minomoto were gathering, some to the able Yoshinaka, some to a young upstart named Yoshitsune. Munemori had heard how the famine and sickness was considered yet another sign that the Taira must fall.

Munemori knew that many places in the walls of the Imperial Compound had been undermined and damaged beyond repair. The Compound could not be held long against a siege. He remembered from the Hōgen and Heiji that fighting in the capital tended to favor the attacker—houses burned so easily, they were never defensible for long. Even the mighty Rokuhara could be felled with a few well-aimed torch arrows. Munemori knew at some point, perhaps sooner, perhaps later, the Taira and its little Emperor were going to have to leave Heian Kyō.

Kurikara

On the Seventeenth Day of the Fourth Month in the second year of Juei, Taira Koremori set forth from Heian Kyō up to the Northern Land Road to do battle with Yoshinaka. The forces he took with him were not nearly so grand as the procession that followed him to the Fujiwara, but still impressive in numbers. Many young men hungered for the opportunity to prove themselves in battle and make their name. Tens of thousands of warriors had flocked to the butterfly banner of the Taira, eager to do battle again after a year of dull peace. All except Uncle Munemori, who had remained behind in the capital, again, to "oversee matters."

An army of such size needed provision, of course, but with the two-year famine there had been no provisions available in the capital. So the Taira forces received an Imperial edict to seize whatever they needed from the countryside in order to feed the troops. The already hard-pressed commoners and landowners of the provinces north of Heian Kyō saw what little they had left looted by the oncoming Taira. Koremori watched from his horse as such depredations took place, watching the peasants flee for the surrounding mountains with only what they could carry on their backs. *These people will not remember the Taira kindly*, he realized. *Let us hope we are victorious, so that such people will not flock to the ranks of the Minomoto.*

By the end of the Fourth Month, Koremori's men had made it into

Echizen Province, and found themselves at the shore of a large lake. Across
the lake, surrounded by high mountains and tall cliffs, was Hiuchi Stronghold, manned with six thousand Minomoto warriors.

"We brought no boats," Koremori said to his great-uncle Tadanori.
"Nor did we bring boat-builders. How will we cross?"

"Surely our opponents must have boats for their own use," said old
Tadanori. "Let us wait for them to come to us. Our archers will cut the
Minomoto down as they cross the water."

This sounded wise to Koremori, and so he ordered his forces to encamp
and wait. For days, they waited, but no boats came out of Hiuchi Stronghold. As last, Taira sentries spotted an archer on the opposite shore. The
archer fired an arrow into the Taira camp, but it was not a humming arrow
to announce the beginning of hostilities. Wrapped around the shaft was a
message, which was delivered to Koremori. It read:

> The lake is not natural. It is formed by a dam of logs to the south.
> Destroy the dam by night and by daylight you will only have to
> cross a mountain stream. Your horses will find good footing and
> you may cross swiftly.

> The Heizenji Abbot-Master of Deportment
Samei

"What excellent news!" said Koremori. "We have a partisan in their
ranks." Without waiting for nightfall, men were sent to cut away the log
dam, and very quickly the lake dwindled until it was shallow enough for the
Taira horses to gallop across. The six thousand Minomoto defenders gave
good account of themselves, but they were vastly outnumbered by the Taira.
The Minomoto were driven from Hiuchi, and tried to reestablish themselves
in other strongholds in Kaga Province, to the north. But Koremori's forces
chased them and defeated the Minomoto in those strongholds as well.

Emboldened by his victories, Koremori encamped his forces in the
mountains near Tonamiyama, preparing to do battle on the coastal plain
below.

But his spies reported that Yoritomo's cousin Yoshinaka was hurrying
northward with a mighty force. Indeed, scouts were already reporting riders with white banners on the coastal plain and white banners fluttering on
nearby Kurosaka Hill. So Koremori ordered his men to dismount on the
slopes of Tonamiyama, let the horses forage and rest, and pondered his
next move.

That night, a spy was shown into Koremori's tent, bearing disquieting
news. "There is a shrine to Hachiman, the Minomoto's guiding *kami*,

nearby. I spoke with one of the attendants there. He said Yoshinaka had already been by to petition the god. The attendant said that upon receipt of the petition and prayers, three white doves flew up from the shrine's roof. This was interpreted by all as a sign of the god's favor to the Minomoto."

Koremori sighed. "My grandfather told me tales of white doves appearing to the great general Yoshitomo as well. While Hachiman is doubtless a powerful deity, he did not seem to do Yoshitomo much good during the Heiji. Very likely, these doves will mean little to Yoshinaka as well."

The following morning, the Taira awoke from their tents to find the Minomoto forces arrayed on the pine-forested hillside only three hundred yards away.

"They must have come silently in the night," Koremori murmured in wonder. "How did they manage that?"

"They know these lands," said old Tadanori. "And they may have wrapped their horses' hooves in cloth to muffle the sound."

Koremori could not determine their numbers, so hidden were the Minomoto among the trees. "Why did they not attack?"

"Perhaps they are few in number and await reinforcements from the plain. Perhaps they came upon us by accident and merely choose to observe."

"Fortunate for us. Have the sentries in the valley send word immediately if more Minomoto forces are coming up their way."

"Of course, Commander."

Koremori watched the Minomoto forces watching them as his own men hastily put on armor. The Taira bowmen readied their bows, horsemen saddled and untethered their mounts, foot soldiers held naginata and shields at the ready. But the Minomoto forces, other than creating a shield wall just in front of their stand of pine, did not move.

Not until midday, when suddenly a group of fifteen armored, mounted riders came out from behind the Minomoto shield wall. They rode forward a few yards and fired humming arrows into the Taira line.

"Ah. It begins." Koremori heard grunts from men struck by the blunt arrows but no one suffered serious injury. He gave orders for fifteen Taira riders to fire humming arrows into the Minomoto lines. Then he mounted his horse and waited the personal challenges that would surely come next. *I wonder if Yoshinaka will call challenge to me. What a great enhancement to my reputation it would be if I could take his head. No one would call me "the general who flees from ducks" anymore.*

But personal challenges did not come. Instead, the Minomoto sent out a group of thirty archers to fire humming bulb-arrows.

"What foolishness is this?" cried Koremori. "They have already announced their intention to give battle. Why do they not begin?"

"It is a delaying tactic," said old Tadanori. "They wish to keep us unnerved while awaiting reinforcements."

"But the sentries have reported there are no Minomoto approaching from the sea."

"Perhaps Yoshinaka wishes us to believe otherwise."

Koremori could see that the Minomoto warriors were eager to give battle. He could see arguments between the mounted warriors and their officers and retainers holding on to their lords' reins, restraining them. Koremori sent out thirty warriors to fire humming bulb-arrows as well.

Then the Minomoto sent out a group of fifty archers to fire the blunt humming arrows.

Ah, thought Koremori, *I understand. This is but a small army we face. They were sent to provoke us and hope that we will attack and chase them into the mountains. By scattering and spreading our forces thin, they hope to be able to pick us off more easily. That is the only way a small force has a chance against an army the size as ours. But that tactic did not work for Yoritomo at Ishibashiyama. It will not work for Yoshinaka now.*

So Koremori rested and enjoyed the game. As the Minomoto sent out more archers, the Taira did likewise in number to match them. He forbade any of his warriors to issue personal challenges and, apparently, so did the Minomoto. In this manner, the afternoon passed into evening, as if the encounter with the enemy were nothing more than an Imperial archery contest.

As evening fell, the Minomoto pulled back into the trees and set up cooking fires. *Hah,* thought Koremori, *they have given up. They have seen we will not fall into their trap.* The Taira forces did the same, taking down the shield wall and retiring to their tents. Koremori admired the silhouettes of deer moving along the ridges of the surrounding hillsides and the sound of the mountain wind in the pine branches.

But just as Koremori was bringing a rice cake to his lips, the vale resounded with war cries and the clashing of gongs. The surrounding ridges now were lined with men, not deer, each bearing a white banner that glowed in the late twilight. The gathered enemy lit torches until the valley seemed ringed with fire.

War cries then came from Yoshinaka's forces, and they rode pell-mell out of the woods toward the Taira camp. There were more of them, many more, than Koremori had estimated.

"Their reinforcements have arrived!" cried Tadanori, "only they came from the mountains, not from the sea!"

In panic, the Taira leapt to their horses, but some had removed armor for the night and were ill prepared to fight. Koremori's aides brought him his horse, and he just had time to mount before he had to draw his sword to fend off a Minomoto warrior. He stabbed the man in the neck and felt the welcome spray of hot blood across his face.

But he could not see the layout of his forces. His orders could not be heard over the roar of the oncoming Minomoto. They were pouring down the hillsides, momentum on their side, into the Taira camp. Koremori had no choice but to call retreat.

He scarcely had any need to. As his horse joined the rout, already every Taira warrior who could ride had leapt onto a horse and galloped down the valley, the only escape route the Minomoto had left open to them.

But it proved to be no escape. The Kurikara Valley was more like a canyon, so narrow and steep in places that horsemen would have to ride carefully, in single file. At full gallop, in full panic, in the dark, this was not possible.

It was not long before Koremori heard the screams of horses and men ahead of him. In the dark, with the roar and thunder of the Minomoto behind him, with pine branches slapping his face and armor, it was terrifying.

Someone rode alongside him, grabbed the bridle of his horse, and pulled him to a stop. "My lord, you must not go that way! Already the valley is three deep in corpses! More men will die of broken necks than of arrow wounds tonight. You must come this way, up the hillside."

Numb with fear and shock, Koremori let his horse be led into the forest, away from the terrible slaughter below.

A Midnight Pilgrimage

When the news of Koremori's rout, as well as other Taira defeats in the region, reached Heian Kyō, it was like a hammerblow to the morale of the Taira. Kenreimon'in and the little Emperor Antoku were moved from the Imperial palace to Rokuhara, where it was believed there might be a chance of repelling an attack, should one come.

By the Sixth Month, the few thousand survivors of the Taira forces, Koremori among them, straggled back into Heian Kyō. The cost of the northern battles had been terrible. The dead included Kiyomori's sixth son Tomonori. Munemori readily pardoned Koremori for his retreat. What else could he do, for he surely would have done no better himself.

An uneasy month passed, as Munemori petitioned the monks rebuilding the great Enryakuji to pray for the Taira and pledge loyalty to the Taira cause. Perhaps because Munemori had been partly responsible for the destruction of the monastery on Mount Hiei, the monks politely informed him that they had already thrown in their lot with the Minomoto.

*I*t was near midnight, on the Twenty-fourth Day of the Seventh Month that Kenreimon'in was awakened by the sound of running feet in the wooden corridors and the neighs of nervous horses out in the courtyards. She crawled to the *shōji* and flung it aside. "What is it? What is happening?" she shouted at the armored men running past, but only one stopped to answer her. "The Minomoto are outside the city!" was all he said before running on.

Kenreimon'in threw on two layers of kimono and hurried to the apartments of the Emperor and his nurse. She rushed over to embrace Antoku, four and a half years old now, still wearing his long hair in side-loops. The boy sleepily awoke in her arms. "Mama-chan? What is it?"

"I fear it may be the end."

The *shōji* slid farther open, and Munemori entered the room. "Ah, here you are. I am glad you are awake."

"What is the news?" asked Kenreimon'in, the breath stealing from her lungs in fear.

"It is the worst. Minomoto forces are situated to the north, east, and south of the city and will doubtless enter soon. Some of our generals wish to stay and make a last stand, but I cannot imagine the distressing things that might happen to you, His Majesty, and our mother if we remain. For your sakes, I am going to implement a plan I have had for a while. We are going to abandon Heian Kyō for the western provinces."

Kenreimon'in gasped and held Antoku tighter.

Munemori held up a hand to forestall her protest. "We have many more allies in the west than we do here, and it will be much easier to replenish our depleted forces in Aki and Settsu. This is not defeat but . . . a tactical retreat. Although, alas, this time we do not retreat from ducks. It may be a while before we can return."

"Naturally, we will go if you think it is best," said Kenreimon'in, shocked and bewildered. "When will we depart?"

"Before dawn, if possible," Munemori said. "If we are gone before the Minomoto enter the city, they will have little cause to chase and harass us. I have ordered men to gather the Imperial Regalia and other treasured objects. I will send men to secure the Retired Emperor so that we may bring him, too. The Minomoto may gain the city, but we will still have the legitimacy of rule."

A frantic knocking on the *shōji* frame caught their attention. A sweat-dripping man knelt there wide-eyed and bowed.

"What is it? Who are you?" Munemori asked him.

"I am called Sueyasu, lord, and I have the honor to serve as a guard at Hōjūji Mansion. Tonight I was on duty and I overheard a commotion in the Retired Emperor's ladies' quarters. I went to investigate and learned a thing most distressing for the Taira."

"Well, what is it?" Munemori demanded impatiently.

"My lord, the Retired Cloistered Emperor has vanished!"

R etired Cloistered Emperor Go-Shirakawa had not been idle that second year of Juei, though he had made every effort to appear so to the Taira. For many months now, Go-Shirakawa had been in correspondence with Minomoto Yoritomo, encouraging his revolt, and claiming that the Imperial edicts on behalf of the Taira meant nothing. Go-Shirakawa had known that Munemori was so useless a general, so hapless a leader of the Taira, that it was only a matter of time until the Minomoto prevailed.

That Twenty-fourth Night of the Seventh Month, a messenger had arrived from Yoritomo through one of the many secret passages in Hōjūji. The message he bore read:

Our forces are arrayed in readiness. Now would be a good time for the crane to fly to a higher perch.

Munemori had made the mistake of revealing to Go-Shirakawa his plan of fleeing the capital, should invasion ever be imminent. Go-Shirakawa knew that, should he leave with the Taira, it would only mean confinement again for him. So when Yoritomo's message arrived, Go-Shirakawa already had a plan of his own. A plan he told no one else, not even his closest ladies-in-waiting.

Just as he had escaped from the Imperial palace so many years ago, Go-Shirakawa dressed in commoner's clothes. Then he stole out through one of the secret passages, one that opened out to the north. He took with him only one servant, and under cover of darkness they headed into the hills toward the monastery of Kuramadera.

But one thing troubled Go-Shirakawa on his walk up the dark mountain paths. In a correspondence of a few days before, Yoritomo had mentioned a thing most troubling. His note, among other things, had said:

Victory is nearly ours. Daily we give thanks to Hachiman for his preservation of our clan's fortunes. Also I must give thanks to the advisor who nightly whispers in my ear—one whom you know well and once called brother. With such divine and Imperial guidance, how can we not prevail?

It can only be the Shin-In who advises him, Go-Shirakawa thought, his blood turning cold. *And my dear deceased brother wishes only chaos, not victory. I must do something about this, in time. But in time soon.*

The Flight from the Capital

The discovery that Go-Shirakawa had disappeared, most likely to defect to the Minomoto faction, made preparations for departure at Rokuhara all the more urgent. No one slept that night, as boxes and chests were packed up with the most valuable possessions, although much would have to be left behind.

At the Hour of the Hare, just before dawn, the Imperial Travel Palanquin was brought to Rokuhara. Kenreimon'in helped little Emperor Antoku step into the palanquin. She went through the curtains after him and seated herself on the soft cushions. Two boxes were put in the palanquin with them; a small box that contained the Sacred Jade Jewel, and a larger box that contained the Sacred Bronze Mirror. Last of all, the guards placed in the palanquin the Sacred Sword, Kusanagi.

Instinctually, Kenreimon'in moved away from it. But little Antoku reached forward and grasped the elaborate gold-and-sharkskin scabbard and pulled it onto his lap. Kenreimon'in watched in anxious dread as the little boy turned the sword in its scabbard over and over with curiosity.

It was not her place, even as his mother, to chastise the Emperor. Nonetheless, Kenreimon'in said, "An-chan, you must be very careful with that. It is very sacred."

"I know," he replied calmly. "Obaa-san has told me stories about it."

"Of course," said Kenreimon'in, wondering with what stories her mother had filled the Emperor's ears.

"I had a dream last night," Antoku went on. "About the sword. I dreamed I swung it, like the guards do, hyeah! hyeah!" He smote the air with his little fists. "And in my dream, I cut down all the Minomoto like they were blades of grass. And I used Kusanagi to call up a great wind to blow them all away. But then they all turned into hornets and came flying back at me. I had to jump in the water to get away from them."

"I see," said Kenreimon'in. "That was ... an impressive dream, An-chan." *Could he do it?* she wondered, her heart filled with a strange hope. *The sword may be properly wielded by the Emperor, after all. Could my little son save us?*

"But Obaa-san says I mustn't use it," Antoku went on. "She says it belongs to my great-grandfather, the Dragon King. People have kept it for too long. Now if it's used, it will only turn out evil. That's what she says."

Kenreimon'in let out her breath in disappointment, but also some relief. She wondered if Antoku was accurately remembering what Nii no Ama had told him. If so, then Nii no Ama had not been entirely truthful when Kenreimon'in had told her the secret. *In these troubled times, we can truly trust no one, not even those closest to us.*

Men approached the palanquin and took positions at the poles, three men on each. With a combined shout of *"Hei-ya!"* they lifted the poles to their shoulders. Kenreimon'in and Antoku were only jostled a little as the palanquin rose, and soon they moved forward, the palanquin bouncing gently to the gait of the marching bearers.

The interior of the palanquin darkened as they moved away from the torches and lanterns of the house. Antoku slumped onto the cushions, drifting off to sleep again with Kusanagi on his lap. Kenreimon'in peeked out through the center slit of the gauzy curtains. The sky was just beginning to lighten with the dawn, but one could still dimly see the River of Heaven sparkling overhead. Below it hung the cold, setting moon. In the distance, she could hear cocks crowing to welcome the sun. Nearby, on the streets of Heian Kyō, she could hear the weeping of the common folk who watched the sorry Imperial procession pass.

This is not a day on which the sun should be welcomed, thought Kenreimon'in. *It should remain dark from now on. Amaterasu should return into her cave until Antoku is permitted to coax her out again with the Sacred Mirror.*

The scent of burning wood stung her nose, and Kenreimon'in sat up suddenly, disturbing Antoku.

"What is it, Mama-chan?"

Kenreimon'in thrust her head out through the curtains and looked behind them. Flames were licking the rooftops of the mansion they had just left. "They are burning Rokuhara," said Kenreimon'in sadly. "They are burning all the Taira mansions; Nishihachijō, Ike, Komatsu, so that the Minomoto will find nothing to steal or despoil when they come into the city." She watched for a few moments more as the place where she had spent happy childhood years, the gardens where she had played, the rooms in which she had learned writing and music, the room in which she had been born, the room in which she had given birth, all were wreathed in smoke, vanishing into the cold autumn dawn.

A stream flows onward
Nothing remains as it was
All is illusion

Tears blinded her sight, and Kenreimon'in withdrew her head back into the palanquin.

"Why are you crying, Mama-chan?" Antoku slid over to her and put his short arms around her neck.

But Kenreimon'in could not answer him. She pressed the hems of her sleeves to her face and wept for a very long time.

The Old Capital

o you think we can begin again here?" asked Koremori. His eyes were still red from weeping for the family he had had to leave behind in Heian Kyō.

"I think not," said Munemori, looking over what remained of the former capital of Fukuhara. They had arrived in late afternoon of the Twenty-fifth Day of the Seventh Month. But, if anything, Fukuhara had become even more dreary now than when it had been abandoned almost three years before. The Bubbling Spring Hall, the Snow Viewing Palace, the Reed Thatched Palace—all were overgrown with weeds and ivies and had clearly been looted by the local fishermen. The New Imperial Palace was in even worse condition, clearly having been vandalized by the *tengu*.

"The Taira no longer have the resources to finance the rebuilding that would be necessary here," Munemori said, "and we are still too close to the capital. The Minomoto could reach us here in two days, not enough time to gather enough men to hold them off." Only an estimated seven thousand warriors had ridden with them from the capital. And there had been sad defections—Yorimori, one of Kiyomori's younger brothers, had chosen to stay in the capital and fight for the Minomoto. The Fujiwara Regent, Mo-tomichi, had disappeared from the Imperial procession and fled.

Munemori did not doubt that there would be more.

"Then what will we do?" asked Koremori.

"Gather all the boats you can. Search up and down the coast tonight and beg, buy, or seize every vessel of any size. The sea has always been home to the Taira. It will shelter us in these direst days. Tomorrow we will set sail for Kyūshū, to be as far from the Minomoto as possible."

Koremori's eyes widened. "That is far exile indeed."

"But one from which Fortune, I hope, will soon pardon us. Go."

Koremori bowed and rushed off. Munemori turned and walked up the broken stone pavement, up the hillside to where the New Imperial Palace stood. What was left of it.

For the moment alone, Munemori wandered the weed-choked grounds, noting the fallen roof tiles, which had been cast in the form of mandarin ducks. *Ducks were not a good omen for the Taira, it would seem*, he thought. Toward the south, from the prominent hillside, he could see Kyonoshima, the artificial island where the ashes and bones of Kiyomori lay.

"Forgive me, Father," Munemori murmured. "Things did not turn out as well as you had hoped. But I hope you understand that I have done the best I could."

He heard cawing laughter behind him. Munemori whipped around, drawing his short sword.

"Hah, hah!" said the *tengu* crouched among the weeds. He was nearly as tall as Munemori, with large black wings and a big yellow beak. "You'd better put that away, son of the sinful Kiyomori. Even the smallest Leaflet Tengu could best you in a fight, and you know it."

Warily, Munemori sheathed his sword. "What do you want?"

"I come to give, not take. I come to give you advice."

"We don't need advice from a demon."

"Ah, but you do. I offer a last chance, Munemori of the Taira. Kiyomori is dead, and the Dragon King has no particular quarrel with you. Therefore, he offers this to you: sail to the Shrine of Itsukushima. Have the little Emperor throw Kusanagi into the sea. Do this and the lives of the remaining Taira will be spared. If you do not do this, Ryujin will do nothing to aid you. In fact, he may aid your enemies."

"What madness is this?" cried Munemori. "The Imperial Regalia are our symbols of the legitimate right to rule. Now that the Retired Emperor is no longer with us, we need them to show that Antoku is the true heir of the Imperial line. Without them, we are nothing. If we throw the Sacred Sword into the sea, we will lose what little goodwill we have left among the people. All would be lost."

"You foolish man," said the *tengu*. "Don't you see? *All is already lost!* If you take the Dragon King's advice, your line will not completely vanish from the Earth, and some Taira will remain to sing songs about their days of glory. Refuse Ruyjin's offer and your fate is in the hands of the gods, which, I must tell you, are not at all well-disposed to the Taira."

"I will not listen to these threats," growled Munemori. "There are many precedents in history where great adversity was overcome by those of brave heart."

"Among the Taira," sneered the *tengu*, "there is no such person left."

"Enough! Begone, before I call for my archers!"

"I will go, but consider well what I have said, unfortunate Munemori. You have no other avenue of hope. All other roads lead the Taira to their doom." With a mighty clap of his wings, the *tengu* leapt into the air and flew up into the darkening sky.

Munemori returned his gaze to the ruins of the New Imperial Palace. "I must have this set afire before we depart," he muttered.

Messages from the Capital

Cheers were still echoing through the Great Hall at Kamakura, as Min-omoto Yoritomo read the missive from Yoshinaka, describing his se-curing of Heian Kyō:

> With no opposition from any Taira forces, I have today taken the city. We have escorted his exalted Former Majesty Go-Shirakawa to the Imperial palace, and he has done me the honor of granting to me those mansions still standing that formerly belonged to the treacherous Taira. I have been given an Imperial mandate to chase and destroy the traitors to the Jeweled Throne, and it is very possible that I will soon be given the title of *shōgun* by Imperial command. At this time, I have received the titles of pro-tector of the city, Governor of Iyo, and Director of the Left Horse Bureau. I hope this good news of the rising of Minomoto fortunes pleases you . . .

But it had only somewhat pleased Yoritomo. For he had in his sleeve another message, received in secret on that very same day from Go-Shirakawa's emissary.

> To The Lord of Kamakura—
> Now that Heian Kyō has been made peaceful once more, I wish to invite you to come with your forces to the capital. There is much work to be done that would be helped by someone with your ca-pablilities. While your esteemed cousin is an able commander, I fear there are some qualities he lacks that are necessary in a military lord . . .

Reading between the lines, Yoritomo understood that Go-Shirakawa feared Yoshinaka and did not trust him. Excusing himself from the drinking and dancing festivities in the Great Hall, Yoritomo retired to his prayer room, where he kept a small shrine to Hachiman. He washed his hands and rinsed his mouth and offered five prayers of thanksgiving to the *kami*. And then he burned a stick of incense in a brazier and summoned his other guardian spirit.

"All hail, great lord of the Minomoto," said the Shin-In, materializing in the incense smoke. "Today is a day of glory for you, is it not?"

Yoritomo bowed before the late former Emperor. "It is so, Noncorporeal Majesty, and my thanks must be given to you as well as to our clan *kami* at this happy turn of events. And yet, I am still troubled in my mind and yet again I seek advice from you."

"Unburden to me your thoughts, Yoritomo-san, and I will advise as always." The Shin-In's smile was almost benign.

"Your brother, the Retired Cloistered Emperor, has requested that I go to Heian Kyō with a force of warriors. I expect he intends that I will do battle and subdue Yoshinaka, or at least prevent Yoshinaka from untoward action. And yet, I fear leaving Kamakura at this time. There are still generals who see themselves as lords of Kantō and wish to usurp my place. I am truly torn. Yoshinaka has possession of the Retired Emperor, whom he may convince to side with him against me. Can you advise me in this?"

"Hmmm. Do not concern yourself with too many matters, Yoritomo-san. Keep your mind clearly on your goal. All is sorting itself out as it should. The time of Heian Kyō is past, the future lies here in Kamakura. You are wise to wish to remain and consolidate your power. If Yoshinaka becomes a problem, I suggest you send that braggart of a younger brother of yours, Yoshitsune, to deal with him. If you are fortunate, they will destroy each other and you will have two problems solved at once."

"Ah," said Yoritomo. "That is indeed very wise, Majesty. Very wise. I shall keep this possibility in mind."

As he left the prayer chamber, Yoritomo stopped to admire the maples in his garden. The leaves were just starting to turn to orange and gold.

An autumn wind blows,
Leaves change their hue, fortunes change
with the new season.

Yashima

Taira Munemori stood on the beach of Yashima in Sanuki Province, off the island of Shikoku, staring to the north. A chill autumn wind off the sea rippled the sleeves of his red brocade jacket and leggings. The tang of the salt air filled his nose and mouth, a scent that he had become used to, and had even learned to savor, over the past couple of months. While to many Taira, especially the ladies, it was a scent of exile and despair, to him it brought a feeling of wild freedom and endless possibility.

"Do you think, on a clear day," he asked the old man attendant beside him, "that one can see the far shore?"

"So I am told, my lord. You know, it is a curious thing, my lord, but I am told it was on this very beach that the late former Emperor Sutoku, called by many the Shin-In, used to walk during his exile. And he would ask that very question. It is said that it was right out there"—he pointed toward the rolling gray water—"that the Shin-In threw his sutra scrolls into the sea. That was over twenty years ago. Some fishermen still remember that dark day and they will not seek fish from that spot for fear they will catch some demon creature instead."

Munemori bristled at again being compared with the treacherous spirit. "My purpose here is entirely different," he grumbled at the attendant. "While the Shin-In no doubt bewailed his fate in self-pity, I am planning our return to the capital."

In the months after leaving Heian Kyō, the Taira had sailed ever southward to the island of Kyūshū. They had gathered more warriors and support there, but Yoritomo had managed, through messages and edicts, to frighten enough landowners there to ruin the Taira's welcome. And so the Taira had fled again, now to Shikoku Island across the Inland Sea from Honshū. It was a better location, Munemori reflected, even than Fukuhara. It was close to the mainland, but the strait between was often beset with winds and tides, giving effective protection from attack. And the Minomoto had never been good fighters upon the sea.

It was also a good location in which to receive messages and intelligence from the capital. There had been a message from the Retired Emperor, requesting that Munemori return Emperor Antoku and the Sacred Regalia to Heian Kyō, in return for peace. Munemori had refused. Without the Emperor and his symbols, the entire country could rise up and slaughter all the Taira.

There had been word from partisans in the capital that the Minomoto commander, Yoshinaka, was wearing out his welcome quickly. That his troops were seizing land and mansions, committing robbery upon the citizens, destroying what they could not steal. Now some in the capital were saying that, for all their dislike of the Taira, the Minomoto were proving to be worse.

That suited Munemori very well. "Let the ungrateful people suffer for a time," he muttered. "When we return, they will beg our forgiveness and never speak ill of us again."

"My lord? Did you say something?"

"Ah. Have you word from the earthworks at Ichinotani?"

"The last I had heard, they were progressing well, my lord."

Across the strait, to the west of Fukuhara, was a spit of land where the cliffs came nearly down to the sea. At that place, Munemori had sent engineers to put up a fort and earthworks. From there, the Taira could control the Western Sea Road, cutting off the western provinces from the capital and east. From there, even a small number of Taira forces could hold back the Minomoto onslaught until the tide had turned again in their favor.

Hōjūji Mansion

In early morning, on the Ninth Day of the Eleventh Month, Retired Emperor Go-Shirakawa sat in the reception hall of Hōjūji mansion, gazing approvingly at the assemblage of black-robed First Rank nobles. They were discussing possible promotions for the New Year, how best to redistribute duties among the remaining noble families. At last, thought Go-Shirakawa, matters were proceeding as they should, and Go-Shirakawa felt like the Emperor he always should have been.

In the past couple of months, the Taira had won a few small battles along the Western Sea Road and had been building forts and earthworks from which to control the western provinces. At last, Go-Shirakawa had been able to make the boorish Yoshinaka and his warriors leave the capital in order to do battle with the Taira. Yoshinaka was having mixed success, and Go-Shirakawa rather hoped some fortunate Taira arrow would find Yoshinaka and solve that problem for him.

In the meantime, his four-year-old grandson Go-Toba, a child from one of Takakura's many liaisons, had had his Accession Audience and was ready to ascend the throne as soon as the Taira could be convinced that Antoku was no longer the rightful ruler. Strictly speaking, Nihon was now ruled by two Emperors, but Go-Shirakawa did not expect that this strange circumstance would last for long.

A chill winter breeze slipped under the bamboo blinds, rippling Go-Shirakawa's gray sleeve. He paid it no heed. For a moment, he thought he heard cruel laughter, but none of the noblemen were even smiling.

Then, quite clearly, there came the sound of a Buddhist thunderbolt-bell being rung wildly out by the main gate of the compound. Someone was trying to keep out evil forces or dispel a spirit. The noblemen looked toward Go-Shirakawa in confusion. "What is going on?"

To a servant, Go-Shirakawa said, "Go and see what is happening at the gate."

They heard shouting then, followed by a battle roar of a thousand voices. A flight of humming arrows was heard passing over the roof from the rear of the mansion. These landed overhead with loud thunks. Soon thereafter came the smell of burning wood.

The *shōji* was flung open. "We are under attack!" shouted the servant who slumped there, an arrow protruding from his shoulder. "Yoshinaka has returned and chosen to rebel. You must flee!"

The noblemen jumped to their feet, bumping into one another in their confusion and fear.

"See to the young Emperor!" shouted Go-Shirakawa to anyone and everyone as he made his way to the nearest secret passage. He brought two servants with him and hurried underneath the main structure of the mansion until he came to a single-rider wicker palanquin waiting in an alcove near the rear gate of Hojuji. Go-Shirakawa crawled in and curled up inside the palanquin as the two servants picked up the poles.

There was a portion of the wooden wall of Hōjūji that secretly slid open, but as the servants bore the palanquin out onto the street, they were confronted by a small band of armored horsemen wearing the white badge of the Minomoto. These pulled back the strings of their bows, aiming arrows directly at the palanquin. "What despicable noble is this?" growled one of the horsemen.

The servant in front dropped his poles and held up his arms. "This is the *In*, the Retired Cloistered Emperor himself! Do not fire. Do not be rebels! Surely your souls will never find the Pure Land if you spill Imperial blood."

Go-Shirakawa opened the wicker door of the palanquin and looked out at the warriors.

The horsemen stared at him a moment, then slowly lowered their bows. They glanced at one another uncertainly.

"What is your name?" Go-Shirakawa asked one of them, who appeared to be the leader.

"Shiro Yukitsuna, of Shinano Province," he replied.

"Well, then, Shiro Yukitsuna, know that all true Minomoto serve the Imperial will, under the ultimate command of your *shōgun*, Yoritomo. Yoshinaka has turned rebel and given you false commands, choosing to disobey his Imperial edict. Do not stain your good names by obeying him in this sinful act."

The horsemen again looked at one another. "It is true," said Yukitsuna. "I heard myself Yoshinaka bragging that he might set himself up as Emperor."

"He has gone mad," agreed another warrior. "He has lost all sense of honor and propriety."

As one, the horsemen dismounted and bowed down on one knee before the Imperial palanquin. "Minomoto have always served the Imperial will, Majesty. Let us be your escort to safety."

Go-Shirakawa was thereby escorted to Gojō mansion, where Shiro Yu-kitsuna and his men formed a guard around the former Emperor. But it was no guarantee of safety. By late afternoon, messengers arrived from Yoshinaka:

> Your Hōjūji mansion is no more. I have taken over five hundred heads of the warriors and noblemen we have captured, including Archbishop Meiun. These will be displayed on the Traitor's Tree to-morrow, to show our displeasure with your rule. Do not trouble me further or we will come and burn down Gojō as well. I have seized the records for nextyear's promotions and destroyed it. I will choose who will have which post from now on. I choose Director of the Imperial Stables and governorship of Tamba Province for myself. You must declare me Seii Tai-Shōgun, and elevate me to Fourth Rank, so that I may outrank my traitorous cousin Minomoto no Yoritomo. I demand that you now write for me anedict declaring Minomoto no Yoritomo a rebel so that I may honorably send my forces against him. . . .

There were more demands, and Go-Shirakawa sighed with a heavy heart. "How the gods do make us mock ourselves. This morning I was filled with pride at my power. And now I have had yet another mansion burned out from under me, more of my supporters slaughtered, and I am again confined in one place."

Many faces in the stark hall of Gojō mansion wore tears as Go-Shirakawa wrote out the edict against Yoritomo. He wished he could send another messenger in secret to the Kamakura *shōgun*, to assure him that this edict was written only under duress. But anyone leaving Gojō would be searched by Yoshinaka's men, and there were no secret passages in Gojō.

The messenger departed with the new edict, and Go-Shirakawa se-cluded himself to await what fate would bring him.

A New Year at Yashima

Another month passed and another year arrived, the third year of the era of Juei. The Taira, encamped on Yashima, could not celebrate in any of the accustomed, appropriate ways for an Imperial Court. There could be no banquets, no Obeisances to the Four Directions. Musicians from the nearby villages did not come to entertain the Taira camp, for it was whispered the Taira were bad luck.

So it was a lonely celebration indeed in the Imperial residence—a rude fisherman's hut that had been expanded with tents and hastily built additional rooms.

Nii no Ama pulled her gray robe tighter around her as chill breezes from the sea blew in under the blinds. The sighing of the surf and the rattling of the reeds seemed to speak to her, "Come back, Tokiko, come back."

Loud laughter from across the room disrupted her thoughts. Munemori, who had had quite a bit of celebratory sake, was regaling all who would listen with the few happy bits of news from the capital he had.

"... so the Retired Emperor is cloistered yet again! So much for his scheming. And Yoshinaka, that barbarian Yoshinaka, had the nerve to write to me and say 'Let us join forces against Yoritomo.' As if we Taira would have anything to do with such a dishonorable turncoat!"

You almost took him up on the offer, thought Nii no Ama, with an ironic smile. *It was your generals who insisted that Yoshinaka must come to us and swear fealty to Antoku. Which, of course, Yoshinaka would not do.*

"And those battles at Muroyama and Mizushima! How we drove the Minomoto back to Heian Kyō. We killed hundreds of their warriors, did we not?"

And lost several of our own, thought Nii no Ama, *which we can less afford to lose than they can. And neither you nor Koremori would lead the battles, which has caused tongues to wag again about your lagging courage.*

"Our forts at Ichinotani and Ikuta no mori are nearly completed. Soon we will sail for Fukuhara once more and be within striking distance of the capital. And the Minomoto continue to fight among themselves. All is hopeful for the Taira in this New Year."

Our world is split into three, mused Nii no Ama. *We may have the West, but Yoshinaka has the capital, and Yoritomo has the East.* She knew, from her long years in the mortal realm, that too much pride and confidence could bring disaster. And in these Latter Days of the Law, when their luck had clearly run out, it was unseemly of the Taira, she thought, to cling to dreams of glory. But Munemori would not even speak with her any longer. She did not wish to waste her breath.

She gazed at Kenreimon'in, who had grown thinner and older with the sorrows of travel. The Empress sat in a corner with His Exiled Majesty, trying to teach Antoku how to pluck the *koto*. She was putting his fingers on the strings and showing him each note. As Kenreimon'in tried to sing along, a *saibara* about the beauty of Heian Kyō, she dissolved into weeping and could not continue.

Antoku put his arms around his mother's neck. "Everything will be all right, Mama-chan. Uncle Munemori says so."

Nii no Ama leaned against the flimsy bamboo screen that held the wintry ocean wind at bay. "Come back, Tokiko," whispered the reeds. "Come back to the sea."

"Not yet," she whispered in return. "Not yet."

White Banners

Retired Emperor Go-Shirakawa had had a dismal New Year as well. The little Emperor Go-Toba was safe, he had learned, but held as captive somewhere across the city. Go-Shirakawa had been moved again, to the Rokujō Mansion, where Yoshinaka's men could keep a better eye on him. There were no Imperial New Year ceremonials, no Seven Herb gruel for health, no spiced wine prepared by the virgins of the Palace Medicinal Office, no parade of "blue" horses, no archery contests, no poetry dances, no celebration of the Feast Day of The Rat. So far as Go-Shirakawa could determine, the world had already come to an end. It was only a matter of time until the Shin-In and his host of demons would rise from the Thousand Nether-Hells to claim it.

It was on the afternoon of the Twentieth Day of the First Month, when messengers hurried into Go-Shirakawa's writing chamber, where he was copying the Lotus Sutra for the tenth time.

"Majesty! Yoshinaka has arrived in the courtyard! He wishes to speak with you at once!"

Go-Shirakawa's brush hand began to shake. "What does he want now?"

"I do not know, Majesty, but he is very distraught. I cannot tell if he is angry or frightened."

"Well. Seeing that I have little choice . . ." Go-Shirakawa put down his writing brush and went out to the main hall, indicating to servants that he would allow Yoshinaka to speak to him from the verandah. Although Yoshinaka had risen in rank, he had still not been granted the right of entering the Imperial Presence, and Go-Shirakawa secretly enjoyed making a point of that. Sitting behind a bamboo blind, Go-Shirakawa waited until he could smell iron, sweat, and horse and heard someone kneel heavily on the other side. "Yoshinaka-san. What brings you to our presence in such consternation?"

"Majesty," panted Yoshinaka gruffly, "I bring sad news. Yoritomo has finally sent his troops. My own forces tried mightily to hold them at Uji Bridge and Seta Bridge, but they were driven back. I suppose I must flee to the mountains now. I expect this is the end for me. Probably the end for you, too, since you declared Yoritomo a rebel. What a sorry day this is."

Go-Shirakawa was very glad for the bamboo screen, so that Yoshinaka could not see the smile that was spreading across his face. "Indeed, this is a time of trial, the Latter Days of the Law," Go-Shirakawa said, cautiously, for he could not be certain if Yoshinaka was telling the truth or merely testing him. "The capital will not feel the same without you, Yoshinaka-san. The absence of your . . . powerful presence will be noted for a long time to come, should the gods permit us long lives after this day. But it would seem this turn of events leaves all our lives uncertain."

"So it does," said Yoshinaka, with what sounded like a sob in his voice. "I will leave you now, Majesty. Please accept my humble gratitude for all the kindnesses you have shown me. This lowly one never expected to rise so high in his lifetime. May the gods and the Buddha bless you. I must go. There is a lady I must visit before I die."

Go-Shirakawa heard the warrior rise and stomp away. *What a bizarre man*, he thought.

The Minister of the Right, who was also being held in the Rokujō Mansion, walked over, bowed, and knelt. "Majesty, I could not help overhearing. Is this joyous news true? Is Heian Kyō at last free of that barbarian, Yoshinaka?"

"Whether it is joyous, I cannot say. If it is true that Yoritomo's forces have entered the city, then we are indeed rid of Yoshinaka. But Yoritomo may have no love of our government after my last edict. Or it might all be a ruse on Yoshinaka's part to brand us all traitors. It is impossible to say. If you wish, now might be a good time to flee to one of the mountain temples."

"Should you not flee then, Majesty?"

Go-Shirakawa sighed. "I have had enough of running, only to be confined again. It is winter and my bones do not take the chill as they once did. I do not know if I still have the protection of the Dragon King of the Sea. But I will stay, this time. If flames consume Rokujō, then they may take me as well. I have seen enough of these fallen days, and if matters are to worsen even further, I wish to see no more."

"Then I will stay with you, Majesty. There would be no greater honor for me than perishing by your side."

It was not long, only an hour, before again there came shouting from the main courtyard of Rokujō. "White banners!" the guard at the gate shouted. "Six riders with white banners are approaching, riding like the wind!"

"What are your orders, Majesty?" asked a servant. "Shall our few troops fight to the end?"

"No," said Go-Shirakawa. "Let them not waste their lives. Open the gates and let the riders in. Let Fate take its course."

"As you wish, Majesty."

Go-Shirakawa moved to the blinds at the north side of the Reception Hall of Rokujō, from which he could observe the main courtyard. Peering out between the slats, he saw the gates open wide and the six riders come galloping in. Their *sode* hung tattered and askew from their arms, and their helmets sat far back on their heads. But he noticed that they were not wearing the pine-needle crest of Yoshinaka on their helmets. They wore the crest of Yoritomo.

The six young men dismounted in good order and knelt in the courtyard. The one in front wore a *hitatare* of red brocade silk beneath his armor, which was laced with purple cords.

"Who is their commander, there?" Go-Shirakawa asked. "What is his name?"

"That is Yoshitsune, Majesty. Yoritomo's own younger brother."

"Ah. Have him come to the verandah and speak to me."

The young warrior was escorted to a cushion on the verandah just on the other side of the blind from Go-Shirakawa. "Most Honored Majesty," said the young man, dropping to one knee and bowing low, "I am glad to have found you well and safe."

"I am told you are Yoritomo's brother," Go-Shirakawa said.

"I have that honor, Majesty."

"Tell me everything about the battle and what has occurred."

"Of course, Majesty. Yoritomo was greatly disturbed by Yoshinaka's revolt. He sent me and our brother Noriyori with sixty thousand warriors to deal with Yoshinaka. Yoshinaka's forces had pulled up the bridges at Seta and Uji, but our Eastern dragon horses are the finest in the land, and they easily swam the Kamo River. We charged across with little opposition and easily slaughtered the enemy."

"Excellent!" breathed Go-Shirakawa. "What excellent news! What of Yoshinaka himself?"

"He fled north, along the riverbank. I have sent men after him, and I am sure they will shortly capture and kill him."

"Ah." Go-Shirakawa sighed. "You do not know how much this news pleases me. But until all of his forces are accounted for, we may still be in danger. His men were such boors, the stragglers might return to burn down this mansion in spite. I would appreciate it if you could stay, if only through the evening and night, to help guard my gates."

"It would be my privilege to do so, Majesty." Yoshitsune stood, bowed again, and immediately set off, shouting orders to his men.

"What a splendid young man," Go-Shirakawa said. "If all of Yoritomo's forces are so well disciplined, I may rest easy."

Trusted Advice

When Minomoto Yoritomo received word in Kamakura of Yoshitsune's victory, and the death of Yoshinaka, he did not rest easy. "It is a curious thing," he said to the Shin-In. "I should feel overjoyed, and I do, and yet . . ."

"And yet you still have Yoshitsune to contend with."

"And he may be harder to deal with than Yoshinaka," said Yoritomo. "The latest message from the Retired Emperor describes how impressed with Yoshitsune he is, how ably Yoshitsune has reorganized defense of the city, how decorous and obedient Yoshitsune is. Yoshinaka was such a boor, I had no fears that the Imperial Throne would come to love him. But the *In* has nothing but praise for my brother. What if Go-Shirakawa prefers Yoshitsune over me? Yoshitsune might be chosen as Great Commander and I might be left with governorship of Izu Province."

"A danger to be sure," said the Shin-In. "But do not lose heart. You must insist that Yoshitsune move against the Taira at once. They have built nearly impregnable forts along the Western Sea Road. Yoshitsune is bound to fail heroically trying to take them. Your brother will die with honor, thereby adding glory to your clan's reputation, and you will be rid of a nuisance."

Yoritomo smiled at the hollow-cheeked apparition. "Truly, I regret that I have ever mistrusted you. What would I do without your guidance?"

The Shin-In smiled as well. "Truly, matters would be worse. I am glad to have been able to remain in this world, to give to Nihon the sort of blessings that were given to me in life. I hope to remain as your advisor, Yoritomo-san, for a very, very, long time."

I am sorry to see you go," Go-Shirakawa said, through the bamboo blinds, to Yoshitsune. "These past few days, I have felt more secure and hopeful than I ever did when Yoshinaka was here." It was the Twenty-eighth Day of the First Month, and swift messengers from Kamakura had brought Yoritomo's orders to Heian Kyō.

"My brother is quite correct, of course," said Yoshitsune. "We must move against the Taira as soon as possible. He receives excellent intelligence from unbelievable sources, which is why we have been so successful in the Kantō. I even hear rumors that he speaks to the shade of your brother, the former Emperor, at night. Surely it is this supernatural influence that has allowed us to prevail."

Go-Shirakawa watched Yoshitsune depart the Rokujō Mansion. He was impressed that, unlike Yoshinaka, Yoshitsune was willing to set out against the Taira immediately. But Go-Shirakawa had his spies as well. And he had learned that Ichinotani was becoming more strongly fortified every day. All of the Taira had now moved from Yashima back to Fukuhara and the Western Sea Road.

"Ah, my demonic brother," Go-Shirakawa lamented, "what are you up to now? Are you setting brother against brother so that even the Minomoto will destroy themselves, leading Nihon into anarchy and chaos? I remember your sinister influence long ago. I know how you whisper lies in men's ears. I cannot let you do this. There must be some way. I stopped you from possessing my grandson. I cannot go chant at Kamakura every hour of every day. But there must be some way . . . some way you can be stopped."

Go-Shirakawa sequestered himself in his writing chamber and began to write letters to every temple, every shrine that remained in the hills above Heian Kyō. Asking them for advice.

Ichinotani

A light snow was beginning to fall as Taira Munemori walked along the earthworks at Ichinotani, satisfied with what he saw. To the south, the walls were within a few yards of the sea. Any enemy riders would have to pass along that narrow strand, easily within bowshot of the walls and archer's towers. To the east, there was another force of Taira dug in at Ikuta, just beyond Fukuhara. Offshore, Munemori could see the glimmer of lanterns on the flotilla of boats where the Imperial family was staying. That way, should attack come, there was a route of escape for the nobility.

To the north, behind the fort, rose an enormous, precipitous cliff, preventing any approach from that direction. And to the west, of course, was all land that the Taira controlled.

He wrapped his *hitatare* more tightly around him. Munemori wore no armor here, certain that he had no need of any. The fort and his men were his armor, and he had never been comfortable wearing a heavy iron helmet or the woven iron *sode* over his arms. Munemori returned to the central wooden tower of the fortress, where reports had been arriving from outposts nearby on the movements of the Minomoto. Munemori wished to hear the latest.

A samurai in sand-spattered leggings spread out a map on a low table in front of the commander in chief, Tadanori, Munemori's uncle and Kiyomori's youngest brother. Tadanori was wearing armor, with cording of black silk over a blue brocade *hitatare*. To Munemori's eyes, he looked a fine warrior and Munemori was glad he had chosen Tadanori over Koremori, who was still suffering from loss of face from his defeat at Kurikara.

"My lord, our last messenger reports that the Minomoto have divided their forces. One section of three thousand warriors remains here." He pointed to a place on the map in the hills above Fukuhara. "The other three thousand have wandered this way, through the mountains. They have defeated a couple of our smaller outposts and set fires to some mountain villages, but that is all."

Munemori smiled. "Good. Let them get lost in the mountains. There is no path from there to Ichinotani, and from the look of the clouds, the snow is worse at higher elevations."

Munemori glanced at Tadanori a moment before asking the samurai, "Who leads them?"

"My lord, they say it is Yoshitsune who leads his army through the mountains. Although he is a fine swordsman, he is known to be an impetuous braggart. He only took back Heian Kyō because Yoshinaka's men were such cowards."

"Good," said Munemori again. "Half of the Minomoto forces are led into canyons by a fool, and the other half sit idly above Fukuhara."

"Yes," agreed Tadanori, "it appears the Minomoto are being too optimistic. They would have needed all their forces to have any hope of breaking the defenses at Ikuta."

"Then our fortunes have not entirely fallen," said Munemori. "Once the Minomoto break against us and fall back, like waves against the rocky shore, then we may move on to Heian Kyō. We will then recapture the Retired Emperor, depose his illegitimately enthroned false Emperor, and return the Taira to their rightful place in power."

Tadanori nodded once respectfully. "With the will of the gods, so it shall be." A tired cheer rose up from the warriors standing around him.

Munemori left the fortress by the gate near the beach and was rowed back to the flotilla, secure in the knowledge that the Taira had gained the upper hand.

· · ·

*T*ell me why we are doing this again, Benkei."

"Attacking the Taira, Master?"

"No," said Yoshitsune. "Why are we following the rump of that old roan?"

"Ah. As I have said, in folk wisdom one may find the best remedies. And it is said that, if one is lost in territory one does not know, take an old horse, throw its reins across its back, and follow it. The horse will surely lead you to a path."

"Ah. Even in the mountains in a snowstorm?"

"Most especially then, master."

Following Benkei's advice, they had found the oldest horse among them, an eleven-year-old pack pony, and put it at the head of the line, riderless, with a young page walking behind it with a switch to keep the horse moving.

Yoshitsune looked back over his shoulder at the warriors following behind, barely able to see the closest ones through the driving, heavy, wet snow. Those he could see made gestures of encouragement at him. "At least my men remain in good spirits."

"They think you know where you are going, master."

"I *do* know where I'm going. I just don't know how I'm getting there."

"Perhaps we will find help up ahead, master."

Barely visible through the pines and the snow was a small cluster of rude, thatched huts. "Ah. At least our horse-guide has led us somewhere. Go into that village, if it is large enough that I may call it that, and see if you can learn where we are."

Benkei dismounted and wandered off among the huts. Soon, however, he returned with an old man and a boy. "I have found a hunter, master, who knows this region well."

"Good. How near are we to Ichinotani?"

"Apparently quite close, master. The cliff may be found just over that rise."

"Excellent." Yoshitsune asked the old hunter, "Is there any path down the cliff to the fort below?"

The old man shook his head and waved his hands. "Oh, no, most noble and glorious lord, that is not possible. Too steep, too steep!"

"Nothing can negotiate it then, not even a rabbit?"

The old man began to shake his head again, but the boy beside him piped up, "Papa, we have seen deer go down that cliff." To Yoshitsune, he added, "We hunt them down where the streams widen just before they reach the sea. For thirsty deer, the cliff is sometimes the fastest way."

"Hah!" cried Yoshitsune. "If a deer can do it, a horse can do it. Clever lad, come join our force and be our guide. Lead us to the top of the cliff and let us have a look about."

So the boy's hair was done up in a warrior's topknot and he was given a short sword.

A short time later, Yoshitsune, Benkei, and their boy guide lay on the snowy ground, peering over the edge of the cliff of Ichinotani. The snow had stopped falling, and so they could see clearly to the huge fortress below.

"Look at that!" Yoshitsune said in a loud whisper. "They have almost no sentries posted on this side of the fort."

"Clearly, they believe they do not need them there," rumbled Benkei.

"We will show them for the fools they are. Bring up the horse!"

From behind them, a warrior brought up the small brown horse they had selected to be the "deer." They had cropped its mane and tail short so that any sentries below would not become suspicious. Though it seemed now that it had been an unnecessary precaution.

"Go on," Yoshitsune ordered. "Drive him off."

The warrior delivered a couple of hard switch blows to the horse's backside and the beast bolted forward, over the edge of the cliff.

Yoshitsune and Benkei watched in fascination as the horse landed on the scree and slid, its hindquarters sinking nearly up to its tail in the loose dirt and rock. But the poor horse managed to keep its balance and find some footing on more solid rock farther down. From there, it picked its way carefully, clambering, sliding, clambering, sliding, until it made its way safely down to the fort. So steep was the cliff that the horse jumped onto the roof of one of the fort's outbuildings and stood there, shivering in fear.

"Done!" said Yoshitsune. "Now we must wait until some of our forces pass Ikuta. While they attack from the front as a diversion, we will attack from behind. What a surprise we will bring to the Taira, neh?"

"Master, your eyes are nearly glowing."

"And why should they not? This will be glorious!"

What's that up there?" said one of the sentries on the north wall of Ichinotani.

"I can't tell in the twilight," said the other sentry. "Is it a horse or a deer?"

"What is a horse or a deer doing on the roof of Moritoshi's quarters?"

"I don't know. It seems to be just standing there."

"I meant, how did it get there?"

"I have no idea. Perhaps it is a magical horse or deer. Perhaps it is an omen."

"A good omen or bad omen?"

"I am not a Yin-Yang wizard. I do not know. Perhaps it is a *kirin*. They are said to be messengers from the gods."

"*Kirin* have flames sprouting from their knees. I do not think it's a *kirin*."

"There, did you hear it? It just whinnied. It is a horse."

"Oh, now that is simply unnatural. There should not be a horse on the roof. I will bring it down." The sentry fired two arrows into the horse's neck. It screamed and fell over, sliding down the roof beams to fall dead at the sentries' feet.

"What have you done? You have killed our omen!"

"If it was a demon in disguise, I have done us a favor."

"Look, it bleeds. It was an ordinary horse."

"No ordinary horse appears standing on a roof!"

"You have wasted arrows, killing a harmless creature. This sin will bring us bad fortune for certain."

"Shut up and help me throw the carcass over the wall before someone else discovers it."

But as the rest of the Taira were watching elsewhere, or sleeping, or playing music on flutes, or playing at games of chance, no one noticed the dead horse plummeting onto the beach.

*M*unemori was shaken awake the next morning at dawn by one of his retainers. "My lord, you should come see this. You might find it most amusing."

Rubbing his eyes, Munemori rose from his pallet and stepped out of the tent that had been raised on the boat's deck. He had become used to sleeping on the sea now, and the rocking of the water was as gentle of the rocking of a nursemaid to a child. It had meant sleeping fully clothed, and baths had been out of the question for a while, but it was no longer so uncomfortable as it had been at first. "What is it?"

"There, on the beach, near the shield wall. Do you see them?"

Squinting, Munemori could make out two riders bearing white banners, shouting and firing arrows at the shield wall near the gate of Ichinotani. "Hm. They must have slipped past Ikuta somehow. Why haven't our warriors dealt with them?"

"I assume it is because they are unworthy opponents, my lord. And it would be foolish for archers to waste their arrows to bring down two men."

"Hm."

"Oh, look. Here come a few more."

Six more riders with white banners rode up along the beach. Now Munemori could hear their shouts across the water, as they announced their names and residences, and called for worthy fighters to do one-on-one battles with them. "You are right. This could prove to be most amusing."

Munemori sat on a barrel on the deck as he was brought a bowl of rice and some fish for his breakfast. He ate, watching the horsemen rush the shield wall and then retreat. Finally, a few Taira warriors came out of the fort and did halfhearted battle with the Minomoto stragglers, easily holding them off.

And then Munemori choked on his rice as, roaring down the beach from the east, came a thousand riders bearing the white banner. "What is this?"

"Ikuta must have fallen," said the retainer, softly.

Munemori stood. "Well. That was our lesser position. Now we will see the worthiness of Ichinotani. The Minomoto will not get past us."

Squalls of arrows flew from the walls and towers of Ichinotani, holding back the newly arrived Minomoto. Mounted warriors rode out of the main gate of the fort and positioned themselves behind the shield wall.

"My lord," said the retainer. "Look. Up there."

Munemori glanced up at the cliff behind the fort, and froze. "By the sacred . . . Amida . . . Buddha . . ." He dropped his rice bowl.

*I*t is time!" shouted Yoshitsune, snapping his battle fan forward. "Let us fly as though we were hunting birds! Let us fall down upon the Taira like rain! Follow me!" With a mighty kick to his horse's flanks, Yoshitsune rode off the edge of the cliff.

For a few moments he and his horse were airborne, hovering over the cliff, his *sode* flared out like a gull catching the breeze, the bracing sea wind cooling his face. He let out a yell of exuberance, joy, and sheer bloodlust. Then he and his horse landed and sank into the scree. The horse shrieked, but Yoshitsune pulled the reins tight to keep the horse's head up and leaned back to keep the balance on its hind haunches. Other horses flew by, some fell hard upon rock, breaking their legs, some tumbled, riderless, down the cliff. But most stayed upright, as did their riders, and three thousand warriors made the rocks shake with their battle cries as they descended upon the fortress of Ichinotani.

*T*his cannot be happening," murmured Munemori. "It is not possible." He watched as the cliff seemed to come alive with a great waterfall of men and horses, flowing inexorably toward the nearly defenseless rear wall of the fort. He wished he could call out to Commander Tadanori, to the other Taira warriors. At last, the Taira samurai on the beach noticed the commotion at the north end of the fort, but too late, too late. Already the Minomoto were pouring off the cliff onto the upper platforms and roofs of the rear of the fort, firing their arrows. The Taira forces were caught between two waves of Minomoto and could not defeat them both. As soon as the Taira on the walls were distracted by the warriors on the cliff, the Minomoto on the beach charged over the shield wall.

Munemori watched in paralyzed horror as the walls of the fort ran red with the blood of the slain. Archers fell from the towers, transfixed with arrows themselves. Headless bodies draped across the earthworks, their heads held up joyfully by the victors. The gates of the fort opened wide, and men poured out on foot, running for the boats.

The Minomoto archers on the beach began to fire flaming arrows at the flotilla.

"Pull away!" Munemori shouted, heedless of the men flinging themselves into the sea, swimming out desperately toward him. "Pull away swiftly!"

Some of the boats nearer the shore caught fire and quickly sank beneath the waves. The refugees continued to swim out to those boats that were left.

"There won't be room for them all," someone cried.

"Then only allow those of noble family aboard," Munemori ordered. "No commoners!"

And so the warriors aboard the boats had the sad task of asking everyone who reached the side of the ship their name and noble rank. Only those of highborn family were pulled on deck, the rest forced to let go. Those who would not release their hold had their hands or arms chopped off. Thus the fleeing Taira ships left a trail of corpses in their bloodstained wake, stretching all the way back to the beach and the burning fort of Ichinotani.

A Shrine for the Shin-In

Retired Emperor Go-Shirakawa did not go to see the parade of Taira heads as it proceded down Suzaku Avenue. He had no wish to see the faces of noble Taira he once knew riding atop pikes and *naginata*. Instead, Go-Shirakawa sent a look-alike dressed in his finest monks's robes to sit in a carriage and pretend to be him, while Go-Shirakawa went to another part of the city for a far more private and important ritual, the result of the advice he had asked for recently.

On a side street in a quiet quarter near the Imperial palace, Go-Shirakawa had ordered a band of carpenters to swiftly build a tiny Shintō shrine. Its roof was thatched with cypress bark and had swooping eaves and little gilt silk hangings from the corners. The shrine was no taller than a man, and had only one small chamber inside.

Go-Shirakawa, dressed in a commoner-monk robe of black cotton, was met at the shrine by one Shintō priest and one Buddhist monk, both of

whom understood the seriousness of what they needed to do. But any pas-
serby not watching the grisly parade some blocks away would merely think
that the holy men were dedicating a neighborhood shrine in thanks for the
victory at Ichinotani.

The Shintō priest slid aside the front wall panel. Inside the chamber,
the carpenters had built a tiny dais, supported by four little porcelain Fu
Lions, surrounded by a little vermilion gauze curtain. Go-Shirakawa took
from his wide sleeve a small, narrow book between wooden covers.

It had been necessary to find a personal thing of the Shin-In, a difficult
task after so many years. But an elderly low-ranked secretary at the Imperial
palace happened to think of a book of not very good poetry written in the
Shin-In's own hand. The former Late Emperor had instructed him to place
the book in safekeeping just before the Shin-In's departure for exile. The
book had sat, undisturbed, on a shelf of the Single-Copy Library, of all
places, all these years. The ancient secretary had happily delivered the book
to Go-Shirakawa.

The Retired Emperor parted the little curtain with one hand and placed
the book of poems on the dais. Then he brought forth from his other sleeve
a slender stick of incense that one of his spies had stolen from Kamakura
at great risk. Go-Shirakawa handed this to the Shintō priest, who blessed
it, then handed it to the Buddihist monk, who set it alight in a lantern filled
with coals lit from the dharma lamp at Kuramadera. The lit incense stick
was placed inside the shrine chamber atop the book.

As the smoke filled the inner chamber, a face appeared behind the
vermilion curtain. A face with sunken cheeks and hollow eyes. "Who is it,
who—"

The Buddhist monk slammed the front sliding panel shut and slapped
a page of the Thousand-Armed Sutra across the opening, affixing it with
glue applied with a thick horsehair brush. Go-Shirakawa chanted the words
of the sutra as the Shintō priest waved a sakaki branch over the shrine. The
little shrine bucked and rocked back and forth as if a dog were trapped
inside. The sliding panel rattled but did not open.

The Shintō priest wrapped a hemp rope around the shrine and tied it
with a sacred knot. The shrine stopped rocking and went still.

When his chant was finished, Go-Shirakawa turned to the monk from
Kuramadera. "You know what to do?"

The monk bowed low. "Most assuredly, Majesty. I will travel to Shikoku
and find the grave of the Shin-In. There I will utter the prayers and perform
the rituals that will release your brother's soul from this world so that he
will travel on to whatever fate he has earned."

"Be careful. The remnant of the Taira are encamped in Sanuki Province.
And I have heard that my brother's grave was unmarked."

"I trust that the Enlightened One will guide and protect me," said the monk.

"I will chant prayers for your safe journey," said Go-Shirakawa. He placed his hands on the roof of the shrine. "Well, brother, enjoy your new palace. I hope you like being confined in unfamiliar residences as much as I did. But be of good cheer. If the gods, the *bosatsu*, and Fortune are with us, you need not stay in this one long."

A Summons Unanswered

Two days later, on the Fifteeth Day of the Second Month of the third year of the era of Juei, the news of the victory at Ichinotani reached Kamakura. *Can any man be so of two minds*, thought Minomoto Yoritomo as he listened to the messengers, *as I am at this news?*

The list of the Taira whose heads had been taken was stunning. At least nine of the major leaders: one son of Kiyomori, Kiyosada, five grandsons, and six nephews of the late Taira leader had been slain. Munemori, however, had escaped, along with the rebel-Emperor Antoku. Some two thousand supporters and allies of the Taira had also been killed. Munemori's young brother Shigehira had been captured and would be brought to Kamakura for interrogation.

Yoritomo thanked the messengers and gave them gifts of horses and bolts of silk. But as the celebratory plum wine was passed among the assembled nobles and samurai, Yoritomo found it difficult to join in the revelry.

"That Yoshitsune!" said one of the warrior generals. "What daring! He did what everyone said could not be done. Charging right down the cliff! First he drives Yoshinaka out of the capital, and now he has driven the Heike out of Ichinotani and Fukuhara. If any name is remembered for the defeat of the Taira, it will be Yoshitsune!"

"Perhaps now that Yoshinaka is dead, the title of *shōgun* will fall upon Yoshitsune," said another.

This will not do, thought Yoritomo. *Our land needs stability and discipline if it is not to fall further into chaos. My impetuous little brother knows nothing of administration. If he should be elevated over me, Nihon will know no peace. I must seek further guidance on what to do.*

Excusing himself from the gathering, Yoritomo walked down the long wooden corridor to his prayer room. He shut himself in to the darkened little closet, made obeisance to the image of Hachiman, then took a stick of incense from a wooden box. He noted there were fewer incense sticks than he had remembered. *Well,* Yoritomo thought, *if anyone has used this for some unintended purpose, they will receive a dreadful surprise and, no doubt, well-deserved punishment. I will ask the Shin-In for more when he appears.* Yoritomo lit the incense, sat back on his heels, and waited.

And waited.

And waited.

Yoritomo picked up the stick of incense, wondering if it had lost its efficacy somehow. He set it aside and lit another. Again he waited, with the same result. His hand shaking, Yoritomo picked up the box and closely examined the incense sticks. *Have these been tampered with? Has someone replaced them with false ones?* Yoritomo glanced around the tiny chamber, as if he might see a guilty servant hiding in a corner. But he was alone. Very much alone, with no one to guide him.

A Choice is Made

Nii no Ama listened in horror as the messenger from the capital spoke to her and Munemori.

"It is simply this, my lord, Holy One," said the messenger. "His Imperial Retired Majesty says that if you will return the Taira Emperor and the Sacred Regalia to Heian Kyō, Antoku will be reinstated, peace will be declared with the Taira, and Lord Shigehira will be released from captivity. Naturally, if this Imperial request is not complied with, the *In* will assume that you wish to continue to be rebels and you will be dealt with accordingly."

Nii no Ama pressed her sleeves to her face and watched the flickering flames in the firepot that provided the only warmth in the large tent. The cloth tent walls rippled and fluttered in the cold breeze from the sea. She knew the messenger and Munemori were awaiting some word from her, but she could not speak.

"Leave us," Munemori said, at last, to the messenger. "We must consider the matter."

"Very well. But be aware, my lord, that His Imperial Retired Majesty wishes a reply soon."

"I understand," Munemori said, coldly.

The messenger departed and Nii no Ama felt Munemori's hand on her arm. "Mother, this is an offer we must consider."

Nii no Ama gasped out, "Do you think I am not aware of this?" She tried to recall Shigehira's face. With so many children, taken from her care often at a young age to nursemaids and other relatives, their name changed

at adulthood, or marriage or receipt of a prestigious position, it was sometimes difficult to remember them. It was the strange way of mortals in this
land to use children as political *go* stones, moving them wherever it was
advantageous. Very few sons of noble or warrior houses, if they were not
Ason or heir, grew up in the same house as they were born. Shigehira had
been her fifth son, and Nii no Ama seemed to recall a bright-eyed little boy
who loved to catch crickets. And now she had to choose whether he should
live or die.

"We have lost so many already," Nii no Ama whispered, feeling a tear
run down her cheek.

"This is so," said Munemori. "And yet, can we trust Go-Shirakawa to
keep his word? I did not return the regalia before because without them,
the Taira cause was lost. If I return them now, what will we have gained?
I am certain Antoku would not be allowed to stay on the throne long—he
will be retired almost as soon as he reenters the capital."

"Go-Shirakawa would not harm his grandson," said Nii no Ama.

"No, but that does not mean he would let the boy rule when another
grandson has been chosen. As soon as he has the regalia, the *In* may do
whatever he wishes. He might arrest us, and execute me for treason. He
might yet kill Shigehira."

And we would lose the chance, thought Nii no Ama, *to return Kusanagi
to my father, The Dragon King. And the land will sink deeper into war, never
knowing peace.*

"I had a dream last night," Munemori went on. "Father appeared to
me, surrounded by the burning flames of the Nether Regions. He told me
that the torments of Hell were terrible, but worse yet was the torment of
knowing the fate of the Taira. He . . . cursed me, and said he was ashamed
of ever making me the Chief of the Taira clan."

"I regret that Kiyomori's soul did not achieve the Pure Land," said Nii
no Ama, "but it could not have been expected, given how he lived. I have
prayed for him, at times, yet I knew there was little hope for him. He is
hardly one to judge you."

"But he is right," said Munemori, sounding on the verge of tears himself.
"If I surrender the Emperor and the regalia, then the Taira will be remem-
bered as nothing but a clan of rebels who knew a few moments of glory.
The warriors who remain with us wish to fight to the last. They say the
Minomoto have risen from near extinction to great power. Surely we Taira
can do the same. At this point, I do not see how it is possible to achieve
any victory. But if we bow down to Go-Shirakawa, then any hope for the
Taira is lost for certain."

"Then it would seem," said Nii no Ama, "that your choice is made."

"I wish to have your agreement, Mother."

Nii no Ama clutched her hands into fists and held them tight against her stomach. "Tell His Majesty no. We will not return the regalia."

"Shigehira is a warrior, Mother. He has always been aware that he might give his life for his clan. I am sure he will understand." Munemori departed to summon the messenger again.

Nii no Ama burst into tears. In her heart, she said good-bye to the little bright-eyed boy who liked to catch crickets.

The Traveling Monk

The following day Taira Munemori walked the sands of Yashima, deep in thought. It was warm for a day late in the Second Month, but the clouds on the horizon promised rain or snow to come. Sunlight sparkled on the sea like false gold.

By now, all those Taira ships that could reach Yashima had returned, and they were far too few. *So many lost*, thought Munemori, *brothers, cousins, nephews. Some of them boys no older than fourteen, who had shown great promise as warriors and died valiantly*. Munemori had hardly been able to sleep at night for the weeping of the women in their tents.

He wondered if the decision to continue to defy Go-Shirakawa had been wise. Certainly it was what Kiyomori would have done, and so long as Kiyomori had lived, the Taira fortunes had risen.

A couple of his samurai came running up. "Lord Munemori. We have found a monk wandering past our camp. He says he has come from the capital. He may be a spy. Shall we execute him?"

Munemori was about to give assent, when he paused. "What temple is he from?"

"He says he is from Kuramadera, my lord."

"Hm. If we ever hope to return to the capital, we cannot risk insulting so powerful a temple. Bring him to me."

"Yes, my lord."

Munemori waited and soon a small, shaved-headed monk wearing the white robes of a pilgrim was brought before him. "Who are you?" Munemori demanded.

"No one of importance, O Lord of the Taira" said the monk, bowing.

"Why have you come to Sanuki Province, O Person of No Importance?"

If the monk felt any insult at the comment, he did not show it. "I have come seeking the grave of the former Emperor known as Sutoku, also called the Shin-In."

Munemori blinked, surprised. Warily, he asked, "Why would anyone come seeking the resting place of the Emperor who became a demon?"

"That is precisely the reason, Lord Munemori," said the monk. "It has been said for many years now that the troubles in our land are due to the unquiet spirit of Sutoku. But I have been charged to perform a rite over his bones that will cause his ravaging soul to leave this world and move on to his next turn of the Wheel. Perhaps it will bring peace to Heian Kyō at last."

And perhaps keep the Shin-In from helping the Minomoto any further, realized Munemori. He still harbored anger that the demon Emperor had deserted him. Here was a small chance for vengeance. To his samurai, Munemori said, "This monk is on a holy and appropriate mission. Let him continue his pilgrimage. In fact, I order you to assist him. Go to all the villages in Sanuki and ask where the bones of the Shin-In lie. See that this monk is able to perform his rite without interference. Treat him well and escort him safely off the island when he is finished. Bring me a report when he has gone."

"*Hai*, my lord," said the samurai, slightly bewildered.

The monk smiled. "Surely you are inspired by Fudō himself, Lord Munemori. I and my temple thank you."

"Offer prayers for the Taira," said Munemori, "and I am thanked enough."

Three days later, Munemori received word that the grave of Sutoku had been found. It had been easy to find, in fact, as no living thing had grown upon the mound in all the years since the Shin-In had been buried there. The common folk of the village where the Shin-In had spent his last days all knew the spot and gladly helped the monk with his ritual. As soon as the monk was finished, it was said, the unwholesome smell that had always hovered over the grave vanished, and a golden light was seen ascending into the sky.

At the Tsuruga Shrine

What do you mean, he is gone?"

"I am most humbly sorry, Lord Yoritomo. But I have prayed and fasted and spoken to the *kami*. And I was told the soul of the Shin-In has departed from this world."

"Have I not sent you enough horses? Have I not sent gold and silver for every festival day? Why do you jest with me?"

"Please calm yourself, Lord Yoritomo. It is no jest. Great Hachiman himself appeared to me seated upon a white horse standing on a lotus. He said the Shin-In is gone, and you are well off without such an advisor."

"You must be mistaken in what you have heard."

"I remember it very clearly, my lord."

"But the Shin-In told me nothing, no hint that he would be departing, no words of farewell."

"The *kami* intimated that the Shin-In's departure was not . . . voluntary."

"Who could have done such a thing? Who has such power?"

"It is not power, but knowledge and will that would accomplish it. Any of the major shrines or temples of Heian Kyō could have done so, once they thought of it."

"And I dare not chastise any of them, for I need their goodwill. What will I do now? Yoshitsune grows more popular with the nobles and the Retired Emperor every day."

"I am sure, with all your excellent wisdom, you will think of something, Lord Yoritomo."

An Imperial Audience

Retired Emperor Go-Shirakawa watched from the verandah of Rokujō Mansion with great pleasure as the oxcart adorned with the crest of eight lotus leaves was pulled through the main gate. Twenty samurai on horseback, their armor gleaming, accompanied the carriage. One of the riders was a huge fellow with an unruly beard who carried an ax on his back. The oxen, all well matched with black hides, were unhitched from the carriage, and the front door of the carriage opened.

Yoshitsune stepped out of the carriage, wearing a red brocade *hitatare* that matched the color of the autumn maple leaves that lined the courtyard. The riders dismounted—three of them removing drums from the saddles of their horses. As these warriors began to beat upon the drums, Yoshitsune began a ceremonial dance, celebrating his receipt of the honor of entering an Imperial residence. With quick, sure grace, Yoshitsune waved his sword and baton. With amazing agility, he leapt and postured as if battling imaginary foes. Then, his dance completed, Yoshitsune continued to twirl the sword and baton as he stepped smartly up the stairs of the main entrance to Rokujō, followed by the drummers and the other warriors in a jaunty parade.

At the top of the stairs, the sword was politely taken from him and Yoshitsune was escorted into Go-Shirakawa's presence. Yoshitsune went to one knee and bowed low.

"That was magnificent!" said Go-Shirakawa. "I am glad the Amida has allowed me to live so long as to see such performances again."

"I wished only to demonstrate, Majesty, what a great honor it is you give me to allow me to come into your home, and to greet you in this fashion."

"I am glad that I may permit you this honor, Yoshitsune-san, after all you have done for the throne."

"I only wish my illustrious brother would permit me to do more, Majesty."

"I am sure he will, in time," said Go-Shirakawa. "Please sit and be comfortable."

Yoshitsune sat down on a silk cushion as gracefully as a cat. Go-Shirakawa envied the young man's supple joints and sinews. "I must confess," Go-Shirakawa went on, "that I am grateful to your brother for allowing you to stay on in the capital. I had feared losing your refreshing company and your skills in defending the city. Many are the bands of *ronin* wandering the hills above Heian Kyō, ready to swoop down upon us should the capital be left undefended."

"This is well understood, Majesty," said Yoshitsune, "and no matter what should occur, I assure you that I will do everything in my power to see that you and His Imperial Majesty Go-Toba remain well guarded."

"That is reassuring, Yoshitsune-san. Have you any further news from your brother Noriyori in his attempts to engage the Taira?"

Yoshitsune hesitated. "Majesty, matters are not as smooth as we hoped they would be."

"But he was given the mandate months ago. I watched him depart myself this summer with thousands of men. Yet I have heard of no victories, other than little skirmishes. What has happened?"

Yoshitsune stared at the floorboards of the verandah. A red maple leaf, blown by an errant autumn breeze, slapped against his face and stuck there, as if a blush of shame. Yoshitsune reached up slowly and took the leaf from his cheek and turned it over and over in his hands. "Majesty, the countryside has not yet fully recovered from the famines of the past two years. The rice fields are now producing, but the farmers are keeping whatever they can. Many horses have died from hunger, leaving our warriors without proper mounts. And along the Western Sea Road, many still support the Taira and do not wish to give aid to our clan. Noriyori is waiting in Suo Province, in the far west of Honshu, hoping that he will someday have enough men and provisions to take Kyūshū. But so far, that day has not come. He has begged my brother to send horses and supplies. But because those supplies would have to travel down the Western Sea Road, and the Taira are still encamped at Yashima just a few *li* across the water from that road, a supply caravan could be attacked and robbed of such provisions long before they could reach Noriyori."

"And meanwhile," said Go-Shirakawa, "the Taira have the chance to regroup their forces. This delay is unconscionable."

Yoshitsune closed his eyes. "Your pardon, Majesty. If I had been sent, I would have routed the Taira forces by now."

"Hm. Perhaps I will send word to your brother that the mandate should be given to you."

"I would be most gratified if you would do so, Majesty. I promise I would not fail you."

Kamikaze

Kenreimon'in rocked back and forth, sitting on her sleeping pallet. She had awoken yet again from fitful dreams. She could hear other ladies and servants snoring or weeping in the rough, rapidly built structure that had become the Yashima Imperial Palace. The night was still and moonlight shone in through a hole in the roof near a central support beam. The moonlight gently bathed the face of the sleeping Antoku in a white glow, as though he were a *bosatsu* come to Earth from the Pure Land. Just beside the sleeping Emperor were the boxes containing the Jewel and the Mirror and the rack on which hung Kusanagi.

Spring had passed into summer which had passed into autumn and winter on Yashima. Each month brought more sorrows. In early summer, the Taira had learned that Koremori, despondent at the loss at Ichinotani, had taken monk's vows and thrown himself into the sea. The court of Heian Kyō had chosen again to change the era name to Genreki, to show the change of the tide of fortunes. In late summer, the Minomoto had positioned themselves between Yashima and Kyūshū, making reinforcement from the far island difficult. Through autumn, the Taira learned of traitors to their clan who were being elevated in rank and given the lands and properties the Taira had abandoned. And as the year turned, they had learned that Minomoto Yoshitsune, the bane of Ichinotani, was amassing forces across the strait from Yashima, at Watanabe.

Kenreimon'in did not fear for herself. She had lost interest in her own life after fleeing the capital. But she did fear for her son. Antoku was the only reason she wished to remain living. Wrapping her thick winter kimonos tighter around her, she watched the cold winter moonlight travel across his peaceful face.

Her dreams had not been peaceful. She had seen, over and over, a mass of Minomoto warriors riding across the sea, their horses able to gallop across the water as if it were dry land. A draft blew in under the bamboo blinds, setting the sword rack to rocking. Kenreimon'in reached out to steady it, lest it fall on the sleeping Emperor. Her hand fell on the hilt of Kusanagi.

A bright golden light flashed before her eyes, and then a sudden vision: she saw boats amassing on a shore, servants loading them with arms and provisions. *The Minomoto are sailing tonight*, she realized. *And we are unprepared to stop them.*

She sat back, and the sword came off the rack and fell into her lap. *I have sworn never to hold Kusanagi again. And yet, what does my life matter, what does my soul matter, if I must watch my son die?* She gripped the scabbard tightly, the sharkskin rough against the flesh of her palms. *I was wrong to think my son should save us through using the sword. His soul should remain untouched by sin. But I have already committed this sin, I am already doomed. Did my father not say that he would willingly commit more sins for the sake of his clan? How can I be such a coward to do no less?*

As quietly as possible, Kenreimon'in stood. She slipped Kusanagi within her kimonos and walked out of the central chamber, out through the eaves chamber, and outside.

The samurai guards were startled when she emerged into the cold, still night. "Please pardon me," she said demurely, covering her lower face with part of her sleeve, "but I must do a necessary thing."

Torn between embarrassment and duty, one of the guards offered to escort her to the latrines. There she raised her kimonos and pretended to squat. But when he had turned his back so that she might have privacy, Kenreimon'in took off running toward the beach. At the water's edge, she drew the scabbard from her kimonos and drew the sword from the scabbard, raising it straight up toward the starry sky. "Kusanagi, by my Imperial lineage, I command you! Bring us wind! Save us! Destroy the Minomoto boats across the water! Save us!" She felt a jolt through her entire body and a flash like lightning traveled from her hands into the sword blade and from there into the heavens.

A low moan echoed across the sky, and the stars vanished as black clouds rolled over them. Thunder rumbled in the distance and the sea swells began to rise into great, white-flecked crests. Cold, wet wind smote Kenreimon'in in the face, and she dropped the point of the sword into the sand.

Voices and the sound of running feet came toward her. "Majesty! Kenreimon'in! What have you done?"

The sand at her feet swirled around her, stinging the skin of her arms and face, whipping the hems and sleeves of her kimonos. Thunder rumbled louder overhead and wind roared in her ears.

"Daughter, what have you done?" It was Nii no Ama, grasping her arms, touching her face.

"I have saved us," Kenreimon'in whispered, before fainting into her mother's arms.

Watanabe

*I*t is a great storm wind, my lord!" cried one of the Minomoto samurai on the beach at Watanabe. "A kamikaze! We cannot set sail!"

The north wind howled down the steep slopes of the nearby hills, whipping up sand to obscure all vision. One by one, the pole torches were blown out and blown down, bringing darkness to the beach. The wind roared through the masts of the assembled ships, and its fury whipped up the waves beneath them. Horses on the ships screamed as they lost their footing. Boats were flung onto the shore, crashing onto the rocks, their hulls shattered and broken.

"We *must* set sail!" shouted Yoshitsune. "I swore to His Majesty, the *In*, that I would fulfill his mandate. We must set sail tonight!"

"This is madness!" cried one of his generals over the roar of the wind. "We are losing our boats! If we sail now, we will all be killed!"

"The wind is in our favor!" said Yoshitsune. "Let us run before the gale and take advantage of it. The Taira will gain advantage if we wait until fair weather. The boats will be safer if we take them out to sea. Benkei! Draw your bow and shoot anyone who disobeys me!"

The giant drew his enormous bow, and many servants and sailors ran to the boats to make them ready. Others simply ran to the hills. Yoshitsune swam out to a boat and cut its anchor rope with his sword. "Raise the sail!" he cried. His was the first boat to leap forward on the wind, and other warriors dared not seem less courageous than their commander in chief.

At last, five boats set sail from Watanabe, carrying eighty warriors in all. They sped before the wind across the roaring sea, leaving in the middle of the night and arriving in Awa Province on Shikoku by dawn. A journey that would normally take three days was accomplished in mere hours, because of the power of the unnatural wind, and the boldness of General Yoshitsune.

Severed Heads

Two days later, in early morning, Taira Munemori was inspecting 156 severed heads laid out in rows on the floor of his residence. His generals had brought the heads from a recent excursion to punish a traitorous landowner in Iyo Province.

"This is excellent work," Munemori told his general Noriyoshi. "This will serve as an example to those who choose to support rebels instead of the legitimate rulers of the land."

Shouting came from the front of the residence. "Fire! There is fire in the village of Takamatsu!"

Munemori, followed by all the other warriors and noblemen present, hurried out to the front gate of the residence. A mist was rising out of the narrow lagoon that separated Yashima from the main island of Shikoku. It was difficult to discern what was happening through the fog, but smoke was smeared across the southern horizon, indicating a great conflagration. Here and there, one could see a tall white banner fluttering behind a rider.

"We are being attacked!" said Munemori.

"It must be an enormous force of Minomoto!" cried Noriyoshi. "That is the only reason they would dare attack us in broad daylight, and announce their attack by setting the village on fire."

"To the boats!" shouted Munemori. "Save the Emperor!"

The rude log structure that was the Yashima Imperial Palace was only a few yards from Munemori's residence, so it was no difficulty to run to it and alert the Imperial family.

"What is happening?" asked Kenreimon'in, as Munemori ran into her quarters. Servants were rushing about in a panic, grabbing the Imperial Regalia and whatever clothing and valuables they could salvage.

"The Minomoto are attacking," Munemori said. "Who knows where they have come from, but we must leave at once."

"But . . . but . . . this was what I was trying to prevent!" cried Kenreimon'in. She rushed out to the verandah, and Munemori followed her. "Majesty! Sister! You must hurry to the boats."

From the verandah one could see out to the narrow strip of sea that lay between Yashima and Sanuki. Mounted warriors splashed through the mist across the shallow water, for the tide was at its lowest ebb and the water was no deeper than their horses' bellies. Tall white banners fluttered behind them. "My dream," gasped Kenreimon'in. "This is what I saw in my dream!"

Munemori tugged on his sister's sleeve. "Come away! You must go to the boats, at once!" He managed to pull her into the running throng down the long wooden corridor, out the north gate, and onto the beach. Nii no Ama, carrying the young Emperor, met them there. Warriors carried the noble ladies out over the water and placed them on the boats, as the anchors were hauled onto the decks. Oarsmen pulled on the oars with all their strength, and the boats leapt northward into the strait.

Munemori boarded a different ship from the Imperial ladies. He watched as most of the Taira warriors led their horses up ramps onto the remaining boats, and these, too, weighed anchor and put to sea. Only a small remnant of the Taira forces remained on Yashima to give token resistance to the Minomoto.

As Munemori's boat bobbed gently on the waves, he watched the Yashima Imperial Palace go up in flames. The Taira samurai left behind fought valiantly, but one by one they fell to arrows or sword blows. There would soon be more heads to join the 156 arrayed in his residence, but the new ones would be Taira.

"Where shall we go, Lord Munemori?" asked the steersman.

For a moment, Munemori could not answer him, could think of no place that would be safe. "Head for Kyūshū. There are still some Taira loyalists there, and Minomoto troops have so far not landed on its shores. If they will not welcome us, perhaps we'll sail to Korea or Chang'an. But Kyūshū, for now." *If nothing else*, Munemori thought, *it will give me time to consider if there is anywhere else worth going to.*

And thus it happened that the remnant of the once-mighty Taira were driven from their last refuge by a force of merely eighty Minomoto, under the command of Minomoto Yoshitsune.

Dan-No-Ura

A month passed, and the Taira sailed a hundred *li* west, gathering what few supporters they could for a last stand upon the sea. The Minomoto were still poor sailors and still poorly provisioned. If there was any chance of a major victory, it would have to be on the water, in the Straits of Shimonoseki, in the province of the Dragon King, who no longer supported them.

"It is a matter of the tides," said Tomomori, Kiyomori's fourth son, and chosen commander in chief for the coming battle. Despite the fresh spring breeze blowing from the mountains of Shimonoseki, and the rolling of the

boat beneath them, the sailors managed to keep the map on the table unrolled for the general's perusal. "Here at Dan-no-ura, the water travels
swiftly eastward in the morning. The tide would carry us faster than any
men could row into the ranks of the Minomoto. If they are not prepared
for this, they would be overwhelmed by our forces. It will give us a great
advantage."

"Begging your pardon, my lords," said one of the steersmen, "but the
riptides are treacherous in this part of the strait. The current might just as
easily pull us onto the rocks of Kyūshū or Nagato. Timing would have to
be precise. If we stay in the straits too long, the tide will turn against us."

"We must match boldness with boldness," said Tomomori. "And they
will be sending their most audacious commander against us. There should
be no need to stay in the straits long, in any case. The Minomoto have fewer
boats, and we will be able to overwhelm them swiftly."

"But what of the Minomoto land forces in Suo, on the Western Sea
Road?" ask Munemori.

"When they see their fellows routed on the sea," said Tomomori, "they
will not wish to interefere, given how their men and horses have been starving for months."

"But they might still prevent our escape should we need to seek land."

Tomomori scowled darkly at Munemori. "Should we need to flee and
seek land, it will not matter if there are forces there to meet us. It will be
our end."

*I*n the month after driving the Taira off Yashima, Yoshitsune had not
been idle. He sent messenger after messenger back to Kamakura, describing his victories and asking for reinforcement and supplies to finish off
the Taira. But he received surprisingly little support and encouragement
from Yoritomo.

"I do not understand it," said Yoshitsune to Benkei, as they stood on
the beach at Suo. "I have done all I can to contact all those who support
the Minomoto in this region, yet we are still short of boats. Yet my brother
gives me no assistance, except to say 'be patient.' "

"You should forgive him, Master," rumbled Benkei, leaning on his great
ax. "I am sure Yoritomo-sama has much to think about there in the East.
We are not the only arrows in his quiver."

"That is true," said Yoshitsune. "But I am his best arrow. Every warrior
knows that when the time comes to loose one's best arrow, one should not
save it on one's back out of caution."

"A good point, master."

"It is those cocommanders of mine. Kagetoki and his sons. They complained because they wanted to be the ones giving orders. Haven't they seen

how successful I've been? But I suppose my brother has listened to their complaints and now is suspicious of me."

"That is possible, master. Ah, here comes the man who I said wished to speak with you."

A stout, bearded fellow wearing a patched *hitatare* with mismatched leggings came striding up the beach, accompanied by two of Yoshitsune's samurai. He stopped a short distance away and gave Yoshitsune a measuring glance before bowing. "Do I have the honor of addressing the Minomoto commander?"

"You do. I am none other than Minomoto Yoshitsune."

"Ah. The bold one. I have heard of you. I am sent from Shiro Michinobu, of Iyo. We have no love of the Taira. They have harassed our seagoing folk for generations. Last month, they attacked some of our men who were defending our land and they took over a 150 heads."

"Yes, we saw them," said Yoshitsune, "at Yashima. We buried them with honors."

"That was gracious of you. But now we wish to offer you our assistance. I am pleased to say I know of over four hundred ships and boats I can offer to Your Lordship. They are of differing quality and size, but every vessel can help, neh? I will also provide the men to steer them, as I know you Easterners are strangers to the sea."

Yoshitsune felt his heart swell up with joy. "This is wonderful news! A great offering Michinobu gives us."

"Master," Benkei said in his ear, "I'll wager this man is a pirate, and so are the men who will sail the boats for us."

"What does it matter?" said Yoshitsune. "So long as they now serve the right side?"

"The other night," the pirate went on, "my people held a cockfight. Six white birds against six red. Three times they fought, and you know what? The white birds aways won. The red birds ran away."

"Undoubtedly, this is a sign," said Yoshitsune.

"Or someone has fed his white cocks better," mumbled Benkei.

"Hush."

"Not only that," the pirate went on, "our priests at the Iyo Shrine have had a vision from the Dragon King. According to the vision, the Taira have misused the Sacred Sword, and therefore he will give his blessing to the Minomoto. Where have the Taira said they will fight you?"

"Their heralds say they will meet us in the Straits of Shimonoseki, at Dan-no-ura," replied Benkei.

"Mmmm, Dan-no-ura. Tricky. It is fortunate for you, Yoshitsune-sama, that my men will serve you, for they know those straits well. Without us, you might have had great difficulty."

"Then I am all the more gratified," said Yoshitsune, "that you have joined us. May our banners fly together to great victory."

*I*t was morning, the Hour of the Hare, on the Twenty-fifth Day of the Third Month, as the Taira ships sailed out into Straits of Shimonoseki. The war drums boomed as the oarsmen pulled the hundreds of boats through the water. There were more boats than needed to carry those Taira warriors who were left, but by artfully draping bits of armor, shields, weaponry around the unoccupied ships, they hoped to fool the Minomoto into believing their force was far greater. The sea was calm, and the Taira warriors were in good spirit. Commander in Chief Tomomori spoke to those in the largest ship at the forefront of the armada, shouting loud enough to be heard on the nearby boats as well.

"This day's battle is very likely the last one for the Taira. Think no thoughts of retreat or escape, for if a man's luck runs out, it does not matter where he goes. Even the greatest warrior is helpless against Fate. Honor is all that matters. Show no weakness before the men of the Kantō. Fight well, and your name will resound throughout history. Die well, and show the Minomoto that they have done battle with the finest warriors who ever lived!"

A cheer resounded from every boat within earshot, resounding up to the skies, and surely resounding in the deep below, in the halls of the Dragon King.

Nii no Ama sat huddled in the Imperial boat, at the rear of the armada, along with Kenreimon'in and the little Emperor Antoku. Kenreimon'in had barely eaten since the flight from Yashima, and she had become a wraith of herself. Antoku sat playing with little wooden toy boats, making a sea of his voluminous olive-gray robes. His actions seemed carefree, but Nii no Ama noted a solemnity to his features. She had told him the stories again last night, in preparation for what might come.

They heard the roar of the cheering warriors up ahead.

"What is it?" cried Kenreimon'in, startled.

"It is only the samurai saluting their commander, Majesty," said an oarsman at the side of the boat.

Kenreimon'in subsided, burying her face in her sleeves. "This is my fault," she moaned softly. "It is my fault this is happening."

Nii no Ama reached out and grasped her daughter's arm. "You were only trying to help. You could not have known. Truly the *kami* must have been with the bold commander of the Minomoto, that he could take advantage of the wind. It only shows that when one's luck has run out even magic cannot help you."

Then Antoku piped up. "The guards say . . . that to fight well even when luck runs out . . . the *kami* like that. It brings more honor. And then your next life is better."

"There, you see?" said Nii no Ama to Kenreimon'in. "An Emperor speaks heavenly wisdom to console you. Surely he can be saying no less than the truth."

Kenreimon'in did not answer.

Nii no Ama squeezed her hand and held it as their ship sailed into the rising sun.

Yoshitsune stood at the prow of the foremost ship of the ragtag but large Minomoto fleet, peering toward the west. He was wearing a gray-yellow *hitatare* and armor laced with red silk cords, having changed out of his red *hitatare* and armor with white cords. This in case spies should have reported his appearance to the Taira.

The Taira ships were visible now, perhaps two *li* away, bearing down on them swiftly. The Taira had the incoming tide to their advantage, but they were facing east—their archers would be staring into the sun. Advantage to the Minomoto. Long, thin white clouds hung high in the sky, like white banners.

"Steady," he called back to the men at the steering oars. "Angle to the south, so that the Taira will be forced northward. It is better if we can beach them where my brother's forces can make quick work of them." Yoshitsune had noted that Kagetoki and his sons had taken a few boats along the coast, hoping to catch any unfortunate Taira ship sent spinning toward the land by eddying currents.

As the Taira neared, his oarsman called out, "The tide is upon us! We will have difficulty making headway."

"Bring forward the archers," Yoshitsune ordered. His best archers, Benkei, Yoshimori, Yoichi came to the prow of the boat. "Let the exchange of arrows begin!" said Yoshitsune. "Aim for their steersmen, if you can."

Benkei drew his bow of black rattan that was nearly twice the height of a normal man. He let fly with a simple lacquered bamboo arrow fletched with white crane feathers. The arrow arced high and then vanished in the distance. But from the movement of the men in the oncoming ship, it had clearly hit a target.

"Excellent, Benkei!" cried Yoshitsune. "Signal them and see if they can do as well."

Benkei held up a gold battle fan with a red circle painted in the middle and waved it. He was answered, within moments, as a low droning was followed by a loud thunk. An arrow shaft protruded from the rattan wall behind them.

"Whose is it? Whose is it?" the archers wanted to know.

Benkei pulled it out, a bamboo shaft fletched with pheasant feathers. "It reads Nii no Kishiro Chikakiyo of Iyo Province."

"Look, they are signaling for us to fire it back at them."

Benkei flexed the arrow shaft. "It is too weak for my bow. Let me send another of my own." He again put an arrow to the string of his enormous bow and let fly. It struck a Taira in the chest, and the man went tumbling overboard.

The cheers of the Minomoto archers were quickly dashed as a hail of arrows was returned from the Taira. Yoichi screamed as an arrow struck him in the arm. Blood running from his fingers, he withdrew to pull it out. Yoshitsune ran back along to boat to the steersman. "Faster! You must get us closer."

The steersman shook his head. "It cannot be done, my lord. Look, we are already moving backwards, under the pressure of the tide."

"Then steer to bring us alongside them," said Yoshitsune, "and we will do with swords what we cannot do with oars."

*I*t is taking too long," said the captain of the foremost Taira ship through gritted teeth to Munemori and Commander Tomomori. "We should have rowed faster, to be at the crest of the tide. It is slipping out from under us."

"What does that matter?" asked Munemori. "It has already given us the advantage. See, we have borne down on them, and the enemy has been helpless to steer." He pointed ahead to where the first ships had grappled and the Taira ships were pressing the Minomoto boats toward Kyūshū. Sunlight glinted off of sword blades and spears, and now and then Munemori could see a gout of red and a warrior falling overboard. Something else caught his eye, and he stared at the open water between the closing lines of boats. Gray bodies were arcing out of the water, flashing in the sun. "What are those?"

"Dolphins," said the captain of his ship with furrowed brow. "They are said to be the playthings of the Dragon King. They ride these tides like a child will slide down a snowy hillside."

"Are they a good omen?" asked Munemori.

"Perhaps. Watch their movement. If they turn to run alongside us, it is a good omen. If they dive when they reach us and continue swimming west, then it is a bad omen."

The three men watched as the leaping dolphins swam up to their ship . . . and then dived below, swimming beneath the Taira fleet.

"It is too late," said the captain softly. "We have lost. We—" He would have spoken more, but an arrow caught him in the throat, and he fell, choking, at Tomomori's feet. Tomomori swiftly drew his sword and cut off the man's head to ease his suffering.

Others had apparently seen the dolphins as well. To the north, a cluster of ships struck their scarlet banners and put up white cloth. "What is this?" whispered Munemori.

"I had feared this," said Tomomori. "It is Shigeyoshi. I thought he had looked fearful and despondent this morning. Now, at the first bad omen, he is turning his colors. I should have cut off his head then."

"You cannot kill a man simply for being anxious," said Munemori, "or we might have lost half our men long ago."

"He will tell the Minomoto which of our boats contain the warriors and which do not. Our ruse will be discovered. The enemy will know where to concentrate their forces. It is the end."

Another cluster of Taira ships began to collide with one another, their steersmen and oarsmen draped over the sides of their boats, Minomoto arrows protruding from their backs and chests. Unable to steer, the boats were prisoner to every swirling eddy that could catch them.

The ship Munemori and Tomomori were on heeled to the side for a moment, then rose as if a giant hand were lifting it. The boat began to move backward.

"The tide is turning," said Tomomori.

"If you will excuse me," said Munemori, "I think I will find a safer ship to board. It would not do to lose the clan chief so soon, neh? It might demoralize our men."

"Of course," said Tomomori, sardonically. "Go as far as you like, it will not matter. I think it is time I headed to the Imperial barque to apprise them of the situation."

"Do so," said Munemori. "That is the wisest thing." Munemori boarded a small rowboat and commanded the oarsman to take him to the ship farthest back in the armada. But as the oarsman struggled to row against the tide, those ships seemed very far away indeed.

Yoshitsune, on the other hand, was having one of the best days of his life. Leaving his protective entourage behind, he leapt from deck to deck, now onto railings, now atop roofs, sometimes with *naginata* and sometimes with *wakizashi*, he used every art and skill the *tengu* had taught him. Twirling his spear, he struck down archers before they could loose their arrows. Slashing with his sword blade, he cut off the hands of Taira swordsmen before taking their heads. No Minomoto warrior who saw him could fail to be inspired by his brave example.

It was not long before Yoshitsune saw the Imperial barque of the Taira not far ahead of him.

Nii no Ama was startled as a ship bumped up against the Imperial barque. Heavy feet hit the deck and soon the swarthy face of Commander Tomomori appeared in the doorway.

"What is the news? What is happening?" all the ladies clamored again.

Tomomori smiled sardonically. "You had best tidy yourselves up, ladies. You are about to meet some remarkable Kantō warriors." He then stomped away, leaving stunned silence behind him.

As the attention of the ladies in waiting was directed toward Tomomori, Nii no Ama quietly lifted Kusanagi off its rack and slipped it within her kimonos. She gently took Antoku by the hand and led him to the back of the boat, away from the others. "It is time. Are you ready?"

Antoku nodded solemnly. "Yes, Obaa-san."

"Then make your obeisances. Be quick."

Antoku knelt and, joining his small hands together, he bowed to the east, to the Great Shrine of Ise, to say good-bye. Then he turned and bowed to the west, whispering the name of Amida Buddha. Then he stood. "I am ready, Obaa-san."

"Then let us go, and you will meet your great-grandfather in his palace beneath the sea." Nii no Ama reached down and picked up Antoku in her arms.

By this time, a few of the ladies in waiting had seen them. "Great Lady! Majesty! What are you doing?"

Nii no Ama turned to them. "I have no wish to remain in this world to be captured. All you who are loyal to our Emperor, follow me." Pulling up the divided skirts of her underrobe, Nii no Ama ran with all her strength up over the low railing and into the sea.

The cold water was a shock at first against her face, but she managed to hold tightly on to Antoku. She felt her skin begin to stretch and tighten as her hands became webbed talons, as her kimonos, billowing out behind her, became a long tail. Her jaws elongated, and her teeth grew into fangs. With powerful strokes of her back legs, she dived down and down.

As the water darkened around her, she took a last look at Antoku's already dying face. The little boy looked as peaceful as if he were sleeping. But his soul would be traveling on ahead.

Other dragons swam up beside her, welcoming her with slaps of their tails. Far ahead, far down below, the dragon that had been Taira no Tokiko saw the lights of her father's palace beckoning her home.

·   ·   ·

*K*enreimon'in watched in horror as her mother and son jumped into the sea. Another lady snatched up the box with the Sacred Mirror within it and headed for the railing as well. Arrows from the nearing Minomoto ship struck the woman's kimonos, causing her to trip and fall forward, dropping the box.

Kenreimon'in stepped toward the mirror box, but another hail of arrows fell around it. Realizing she had little time, Kenreimon'in turned and ran off the end of the boat as well.

Perhaps it was because she leapt high into the air before falling into the water. Perhaps it was because she had grown thin and light. But the sea refused to take her. Air was caught in her voluminous sleeves and the folds of her gowns, and the tightly woven silk would not let it free. She floated on the surface like a lotus blossom.

"No!" cried Kenreimon'in, beating at the air bubbles. "Take me! Take me!"

Something jammed in her hair and pulled hard. Kenreimon'in screamed and reached up, grabbing the handle of a sea rake. She tried to disentangle herself, but it was no use. She was pulled through the water until she bumped hard against the side of the boat. Men's arms reached down and hauled her out of the water.

"No!" she screamed again, kicking and beating at the arms with her fists. "Let me die! Let me die, let me die, let me die!" But it was no use. She was pulled onto the deck like a fish.

A fair-skinned, mustachioed young man peered down at her. "Who is this?"

Another voice said, "That is the Imperial Lady. That is the Empress, Antoku's mother."

"Ah!" The young man's brows raised, and he gave a slight bow. "I am honored, Majesty. I am Minomoto Yoshitsune." He turned to someone beside him, and said, "Take her below and treat her well."

Ashamed by her utter failure even to die with honor, Kenreimon'in covered her face with her sleeves and wailed in sorrow as she was carried away.

*T*aira Munemori watched in shocked fascination from a nearby boat as one by one the Taira ladies and warriors leapt into the sea. Commander Tomomori slung an anchor around his neck and dived in, determined to have no chance of survival. His sister, his mother, the Emperor, others. On his own boat, the warriors stared at him in disgust and contempt as they prepared to fling themselves into the water. The railing of the boat was knocked out to make it easier.

Munemori stared down at the blue water. It looked cold. He could not move. His mind was churning. *What would the Shin-In advise? What should I do?* But the Shin-In's spirit was gone, and Munemori suspected his own was gone long ago as well.

"Oops," said someone behind him, and Munemori was bumped, pushed into the sea, arms flailing.

But Lord Kiyomori, having been a man of the sea, had taught all his sons to swim. So Munemori, quite unable to help himself, trod water until the Minomoto ship drew up beside him and hauled him out.

"Well, what have we here?" said the small, mustachioed young man. "Looks like the biggest fish of all. I had hoped to catch your father this way, but I suppose you'll have to do."

As the Minomoto warriors around him laughed, Munemori was taken below in shame.

By Carriage Window

A month later, at midafternoon, on the Twenty-sixth Day of the Fourth Month of the second year of Genreki, Retired Emperor Go-Shirakawa ordered his carriage to stop at the side of the street in front of the Rōkujō Palace, now Yoshitsune's residence in Heian Kyō. He had to know if the reports were true. Secretly, he watched from his carriage window as a particular procession of horsemen surrounding an oxcart drew up before the palace gate.

The oxen were detached, and a man was led down from the cart. His face was sunken-cheeked and hollow-eyed, but nonetheless Go-Shirakawa recognized him.

"Ah, Munemori-san. How like my brother, the Shin-In, you have become. But you did not have even the courage that he did, to become a demon. You are only the shadow of one, only the shadow of your former self, only a shadow of the greatness of the Taira."

Munemori was led into the gate without ceremony. Go-Shirakawa signaled to his driver to move on. He reflected, as the carriage rolled back toward the Imperial palace, that he had had to see the former Minister of State, the way a mourner needs to view the body of a loved one before it is cremated. To know that the person is truly dead. To know that the war was truly over. To know that the Taira were truly finished, and peace would come to the land again, at last.

Kamakura

On the Seventh Day of the Sixth Month, Minomoto Yoritomo sat behind a bamboo screen awaiting the prisoner. It had been suggested by his noble advisors that, now that Munemori had been stripped of rank, he was no longer worthy to be in the presence of the Lord of Kamakura, and therefore should be adressed by lesser men while Yoritomo observed discreetly.

It had been a strange, otherworldly three months since he had received the news of Dan-no-ura. So many Taira dead, others captured. The little Emperor drowned. The Sacred Sword lost. He had been told the best pearl divers in the land had been hired to search for Kusanagi, but to no avail. *What a strange, new time we have entered*, he thought. *If one of the Sacred Regalia has left us, it is a new world indeed.*

And then, there was Yoshitsune. Yoshitsune, Yoshitsune, Yoshitsune. Yoritomo could not pass a day, an hour, without hearing his brother's name praised. Already the Retired Emperor had given Yoshitsune new rank, new posts, a new palace, without consulting Yoritomo.

But not all loved the younger Minomoto. General Kagetoki had sent Yoritomo word of Yoshitsune's boasting and demand to be the sole commander. And hints that Yoshitsune intended to supplant Yoritomo himself as *shōgun. He must be stopped*, thought Yoritomo. He had deliberately forbidden Yoshitsune from entering Kamakura when he brought the Taira prisoners up from the capital. *But it is not enough*, thought Yoritomo. *My displeasure must be made more clear.*

The Lord of Kamakura was startled out of his thoughts by the announcement of the arrival of the prisoner. He peered out between the slats of the bamboo blind and saw the *shōji* slide open.

"Traitor to the throne, Taira no Munemori," an official announced, and the prisoner was led in.

Yoritomo nearly gasped. Munemori was dressed in a simple white ceremonial robe with a black, unfolded cap. But his face . . . his face was nearly that of the Shin-In. Munemori's eyes, however, seemed unfocused, his expression vague, as if there was no one there behind the face at all.

A lowly minister named Hiki no Yoshikazu sat before Munemori and delivered Yoritomo's message to him:

"I bear to you and your clan no personal animosity. It was your father's mercy, after all, that spared me from death and instead sent me into exile in Izu. But I was given an Imperial edict, and therefore was required to attack and defeat your clan. Nonetheless, I honor you as a fellow warrior, and I am pleased that I have this chance to meet you."

Yoshizaku bowed and waited for Munemori's reply.

But the Taira lord's reaction seemed bizarre. At first he sat bolt upright, as if a *bunraku* puppet. Then he fell forward in an obsequious bow, as if Yoshizaku were a greater noble than he was, nearly groveling. When Munemori sat back up, he began to mutter, not words of greeting warrior to warrior, but words of pleading. "I should like to become a monk. . . . send me far away. Sanuki, perhaps, to write sutras. And pray. If you please."

The display was unsettling. *If he has his wits*, thought Yoritomo, *then he is being contemptuous. If he does not, then this meeting is unseemly.* Without responding, Yoritomo signaled that Munemori should be escorted out of his presence.

When the former Minister of State had been removed, Yoritomo wrote out the order for Munemori's execution. And decided that Yoshitsune should be be in charge of it. The image would not leave Yoritomo's mind of how Munemori looked like the Shin-In. *What would the Shin-In advise, regarding Yoshitsune?* wondered Yoritomo.

The answer came to him as easily as thought itself. He wrote out another order, stripping Yoshitsune of his lands and promotions and posts. And then another, secret, decree . . . ordering Yoshitsune's death.

A Final Prayer

Yoshitsune knelt on the floor near Taira Munemori at a roadside inn along the Tōkkaidō. Together they admired the leaves of the maples in the gardens beside the inn, the leaves turning blood red with autumn.

Munemori had been an ideal prisoner, if a strange one. He had offered no resistance or contemptuous remarks. Only his strange pleading to become a monk, to copy sutras. Yoshitsune had been tempted to treat Munemori with contempt at first, but found he could not. Now he was only moved to a strange pity, and an even stranger commiseration.

"It is odd, is it not, Munemori-san, how things turn out. You, doubtless, did your best to protect your clan. Yet here you are, a prisoner, your worldly life over. Although where you shall go from here I cannot say."

"True," murmured Munemori. "Very strange."

"I have done my very best to serve my brother," Yoshitsune went on, "and yet he now seems to despise me."

"Despise, yes," said Munemori. "I tried to serve my father, but he despised me."

"So you understand. I had meant to kill your father, you know. It is what I had trained nearly my whole life for. But Fate denied me that satisfaction. Just as you were trained to be a great lord of the mighty capital of Heian Kyō. But Fate has denied you that satisfaction."

"Denied," agreed Munemori.

"But what can set brother against brother? Should I not be as close to him as father to son? And, surely, our father Yoshitomo knew and loved him for many more years than I. What cause does my brother have to be jealous of me?"

"Cause," echoed Munemori. "I was jealous of my brother. He died. Was I the cause?"

"So you understand, I suppose," said Yoshitsune, uncertainly. "And now allies of mine in Kamakura have warned me that perhaps I will die as well, from my brother's jealousy."

"Perhaps." Munemori sighed softly. In a more lucid tone, he went on, "The Shin-In once said that he had no power save that which men's hatreds permit him. Perhaps it is only that."

"Truly," said Yoshitsune. "The evils that men conjure in their hearts are as great as any demons that we conjure in our dreams."

"Truly," agreed Munemori. Then his voice became dreamy again. "A tonsure . . . a barren place to pray. Please let me become a monk. To copy sutras. To pray."

Yoshitsune knew the former Taira lord was lost to the world again. Gently, he said, "Show me how you would pray, Munemori-san. Recite for me a sutra."

As Munemori bowed his head and began to murmur the Lotus Sutra, Yoshitsune gestured to a swordsman waiting in the shadows. Silently, Yoshitsune stood and backed away. The swordsman waited until Munemori had uttered the sacred name of the Amida Buddha, and with a swift stroke removed the former Taira lord's head from his body.

The blood flowed across the matted floor, the last red banner of the Taira.

A Final Meeting

The nun, now simply called the Imperial Lady, formerly known as Kenreimon'in, walked along the forest path, holding a basket full of rock azaleas. It was late in the Fourth Month in the second year of the era of Bunji. A full year had passed since the tragedy of Dan-no-ura. And yet her mind was full of prayers for the fallen, never able to forget.

The forest was beginning to blossom with the arrival of spring. Cuckoos and *uguisu* sang in the pine boughs overhead. Deer pranced at a cautious distance. The brooks gurgled with fresh water from melting snows. The crisp, cool mountain air sang with a purity unknown in Heian Kyō.

But the Imperial Lady felt an alien in this land, though it was not terribly far from the old capital. It seemed a world apart. It was a place that had never known elegant *kichō* curtains, poetry readings to the summer moon, *koto* and flute concerts, no dragon boats on Imperial ponds, no wisteria gardens, no readings of *monogatari* by candlelight. It was a wilderness and, as such, it suited the Imperial Lady's heart very well.

She came around a bend in the forest path, nearing the hermitage known as the Jakkoin, when she stopped. There were people, men, gathered on the verandah of her hermitage.

Her handmaiden, who had been walking with her, stopped, too.

Another nun came running up the path to her. "My Lady, you will never guess who has come to visit!"

The Imperial Lady tried to cover up her face with her drab black sleeves and turn away. "Please, send them away. Whoever they are, they must not see me like this."

"You are in perfectly proper garb for one who has left the world. There is no shame in it. Besides, your visitor is none other than the Retired Cloistered Emperor Go-Shirakawa, come all this way from Heian Kyō. It would be utter rudeness to send him away without a word from you. Come, come."

Reluctantly, the Imperial Lady let herself be led down the path to the hermitage. She was suddenly ashamed of the overgrown weeds, the poorly patched roof, the worn wooden planks, the tiny flooded rice paddy, even though these things had suited her when she moved in. To her shock, the Retired Emperor sat right out in the open, surrounded by only a few retainers, and she could see him, face-to-face. He was older than she imagined, in his late sixties perhaps, and tired-looking, though still impressive in his gray monk's robes.

The Imperial Lady bowed to him and sat on a rock nearby, not daring to speak.

"Ah, Kenreimon'in," said Go-Shirakawa, his eyes wet with withheld tears. "How strange it is to see you like this, a former Imperial jewel, but out of her setting. Though I will add your holy garb has not diminished your legendary beauty."

The Imperial Lady blushed and hid farther behind her sleeves. "Your Majesty is too kind. Though each day I expect to see a vision of the Buddha at my window, summoning me to the world beyond, never did I expect this visit. As for me, I have found my way to this desolate place because of the sins of my family, and my own. It is only right that this should be my setting now."

Go-Shirakawa nodded. "It is best, yes. The world is no longer a place for such tender hearts as yours. It has changed. We had hoped that the loss of the little Emperor would bring the world to its senses and bring peace. But I fear what peace we have will not last long. The Lord of Kamakura is a powerful man, but a spiteful one. He has targeted his brothers one by one and seeks their death. He plans to move the capital to Kamakura, a most inelegant place, I understand. He puts greater and greater restraints upon the Imperial Throne. His samurai swagger with greater and greater power. I must tell you, in truth, the world has truly ended, for the world we knew is gone and shall never return."

"Then I am even more glad I have devoted my life to prayer," said the Imperial Lady. "For I do not think my heart can bear more sorrows."

"Come, then. Sit beside me a while. Let us listen to the birds sing, and remember all the beauty that has passed."

Epilogue

*T*he bell of Gion Temple sings. . . .

And so the Taira fortunes passed away, like fallen leaves hidden beneath the snow, remembered but not to be seen in their glory again. Perhaps the Dragon King was regretful at his part in their downfall, for he left a curious gift. Ever after, in the Inland Sea, fishermen have found a kind of crab they called the Heike or Taira crab. For on the back of every crab is the scowling face of a samurai, etched for eternity. Fishermen are careful to throw these crab back into the sea, rather than incur bad fortune.

As for Kusanagi, it is still not known whether the sword that was taken to the bottom of the sea was the true Sacred Sword or the copy, or whether it is the true sword that now hangs in the Shrine at Ise. It could be said that because the centuries that followed Dan-no-ura brought only more war, setting province against province, lord against lord, that it was not Kusanagi returned to the sea, and the Dragon King was not appeased. Or perhaps it was, but it did not matter. Perhaps it is as the Shin-In said, that the hearts of men hold the key to Fate, with greater power than any magic, prayer, or curse.